Much Ado
about
Prom Night

Much Ado about Prom Night

WILLIAM D. McCANTS

Browndeer Press
Harcourt Brace & Company
San Diego   New York   London

Browndeer Press is a registered trademark of
Harcourt Brace & Company.

Library of Congress Cataloging-in-Publication Data
McCants, William D., 1961–
Much ado about prom night/written by
William D. McCants.—1st ed.
p.   cm.
"Browndeer press."
Summary: Political uproar about a peer counseling program
in a southern California high school keeps two star-crossed
antagonists at odds before the upcoming prom.
ISBN 0-15-200083-6—ISBN 0-15-200081-X (pbk.)
[1. California—Fiction.   2. High schools—Fiction.
3. Schools—Fiction.   4. Dating (Social customs)—
Fiction.   5. Peer counseling—Fiction.]   I. Title.
PZ7.M47836Mu   1995
[Fic]—dc20   94-43349

The text was set in Simoncini Garamond.
Designed by Trina Stahl
First edition
A B C D E

Printed in Hong Kong

*For my family
and L*

Chapter 1

I T WAS A FRIDAY in mid-April and rays of golden morning sunshine streamed into my cubicle in the peely, creaky white trailer that served as the office for the Peer Counseling Network (PCN) at Luna Point High. My first counselee was Eddie Ballard, a longtime acquaintance and distressingly frequent visitor. He launched our session by asking: "So, Becca, have you got a date to the junior prom yet?"

No big surprise here. With only three weeks to go until the big event, this was fast becoming *the* hot question on campus. I didn't always answer such personal queries from counselees, but I'd served with Eddie on the Luna Point High *Beacon,* our school newspaper, for over two years before I quit at the end of last term, so I smiled and said, "I'll be going with Peter, natch. What's up with you today?"

Eddie flashed me the lopsided grin, which'd lured more than a few girls (mostly unwary ninth and tenth graders) into his octopuslike embrace, as he combed through his thick black hair with his fingers. His gray-blue eyes twinkled. "I just like seeing your face before school starts," he said with a wink.

"That's a really sweet thing to say," I told him. I was shifting into peer counselor mode now, where it's important to always be polite, no matter how heinously you're provoked. Eddie was small for his age and thin as a blade of dune grass. He was the only child of two greenback-cranking, chronically busy parents. My theory was that he was lonely and painfully insecure and tried to compensate for these problems by acting for all the world as if he had *the* hot inside tip on life. The results were predictably disastrous: he came off as a total dork. Whatever the proper diagnosis, his case was clearly way out of my league.

"Didn't you tell me the last time you came in that you've got access to a private therapist?" I asked him. "I think you're really lucky that way, Eddie, and I want to encourage you to take advantage—"

"But my therapist isn't nice like you are," he protested with a sudden—and seemingly genuine—burst of little boy charm and vulnerability. "Besides, he thinks I hate my mother. . . . Do you think I hate my mother, Becca?"

"You're coming off the wall again," I replied impatiently. Eddie liked to try to string out our sessions by messing with my head, but I usually caught him at it.

"Okay, I'll cut to the chase. I had a dream last night that I pushed Jeff Gardiner off Luna Point and he fell a hundred and fifty feet to his death on the foaming rocks below. His skull cracked open like a poached egg. What d'you suppose it means?"

Ouch! How very *Lord of the Flies!* Jeff was the domineering, hard-to-figure, sock-meltingly gorgeous, supertalented editor in chief of the *Beacon,* who seemed to take fiendish delight in writing editorial attacks against the peer counseling program.

"Dream analysis isn't an exact science, not by a long shot," I told Eddie in my professional voice. "Lots of therapists think that dreams reflect a current emotional hang-up; maybe you've been feeling, or repressing, some heavy-duty hostility toward Jeff lately. Or your dream might be construed as a straightforward wish fulfillment, although I'm sure in your conscious state there's no way you'd actually want to send someone sailing over a cliff. . . ."

Eddie seemed undecided on this issue.

"Well," I quickly went on, "*other* experts blow off dreams completely, saying they're just your basic random images awkwardly pieced together by a muddled brain shut off from sensory input. The important thing is, what do *you* think pushing Jeff off a cliff means?"

"An insanity plea, I suppose, unless my lawyers can convince the jury it was an accident," Eddie said solemnly, and then we both laughed.

"Is Jeff still running the paper like a medieval fiefdom?"

"Oh sure, but I don't mind that. He turns out a good product. In fact, I think you'll find this month's issue a real grabber; it should be out by lunchtime."

"It'll be the highlight of my day," I said dryly.

"What bothers me," Eddie went on, getting back to the core of the matter, "is that when I asked Darla Swanson to the prom earlier this week, she turned me down and used Jeff as an excuse." Eddie twisted the band of his Gucci timepiece.

"But why wouldn't she? Jeff *is* Darla's boyfriend!" I steamed, forgetting for a sec about professional detachment. Darla, the features editor of the *Beacon,* had the kind of looks that turn most guys into Play-Doh. She'd had to work on Jeff Gardiner for almost a year, though, before he finally looked up from his computer terminal and clued in to the fact that she was more than just a lively source of ideas for human-interest stories. (Maybe his obliviousness was part of what attracted her to him in the first place.)

"But I can't understand it!" Eddie exclaimed, putting one hand to his chest as he gestured with the other (what a total ham bone!). "Darla's a seven-course dinner at the Ritz-Carlton, a first-run show at the Center for the Performing Arts, a leisurely stroll on Balboa Island at sunset, a vacation condo on Catalina Island! Jeff, on the other hand, is so . . . so—"

"Middle class?"

"Exactly!"

And Eddie was such an outrageous snob, I just had to smile. "It's a burden that many of us shoulder, Sir Edward, but somehow we struggle along. Since you came in for my advice, I've gotta tell you flat out that your flagrant disrespect for a romantic bond, especially such a long-term one (Jeff and Darla'd been a couple for almost six months), bites in the extreme. Besides, I thought Jeff was your bud."

Eddie picked an imaginary piece of lint off his white Ralph Lauren Polo shirt and actually looked a bit sheepish. "I suppose he is. I mean, he always remembers my birthday, even when nobody else does, and he never, ever jokes about my height . . . but it's not as if we hang at lunch together every day. And besides, you haven't seen the way Darla's been sniping at him lately. I hoped she might be looking for an out." There was a sudden clicking sound, and Eddie fished a recorder out of his pocket, popped out the microcassette, and then put a fresh one in.

"Have you been taping this session without letting me know?" I asked, majorly appalled.

"I tape everything. Why, does that bother you?"

I stood up abruptly and said coolly, "Eddie, this meeting is history. If your hostility toward Jeff persists, I recommend you talk it over with a school guidance counselor or your own private therapist. You're really far too complex a case for my modest talents."

He stood up and leaned way over the desk to gaze into my eyes. "Don't sell yourself short, Rebecca darling," he said. "Fact is, except for that little zit on the right side of your nose, you're not a bad-looking girl." He winked at me again. "And once that unfortunate blemish clears up, maybe we could get together socially and—"

What a total slimewad! I removed myself from the cubicle at that point, for safety reasons. *His* safety. (I have this slight tendency to get physical when I'm pushed, and this retreat-and-regroup strategy'd been recommended by my guidance counselor, Mr. Gordon.) Eddie finally got the hint, and once he was good and gone, I excused myself from the waiting students on the threadbare green couch in the reception area and rushed to the nearest bathroom to see about that zit.

Adriana Fernandez, my next visitor, tugged at her gold necklace as if it were a noose and told me about the massive crush that she'd developed on her guy friend Omri. "For a long time he was just a bud, you know, until this one afternoon a few weeks ago when we were hanging out in his room listening to a Pearl Jam CD. Omri was doing that stupid air guitar bit that guys are so hooked on, but suddenly the routine seemed kind of clever to me, and later I noticed his fine chin and the cute way he licked the orange Chee-tos dust off his fingers. I felt all tingly and started perspiring, even though it wasn't hot in his room at all."

Adriana nervously gathered her long black hair up into a ponytail and then let it drop down to her shoulders again. "I'm thinking maybe this is all a temporary thing that will pass quickly, you know, like a cold? But then a few days later when I read over the rough draft of his latest English essay, I had the distinct impression it was about me and not Jane Austen."

"You're officially obsessed," I said, smiling.

Adriana made a pained attempt to smile back. "But Omri is totally oblivious! He thinks nothing about us has changed! *I* want to ask him to the prom, but I also don't want our friendship to be ruined if he says no. What can I do?"

We were getting this type of question a lot at the PCN lately, from both girls and guys. (We also talked to quite a few students who were getting unwanted attention from guy friends or girl friends.) "First of all, Adriana, there's nothing strange going on here. Tons of romantic relationships start out as friendships. In fact, my boyfriend Peter and I sang in chorus together for over two and a half years before things finally clicked."

Adriana looked relieved. The people who came to see me almost always seemed to think their problems were unique and therefore something to be ashamed of. It made me feel especially good when I could draw on my own personal experience to help out a counselee, instead of just relying on the secondhand insights I'd snagged from psych class, PCN training sessions, and a humongous stack of adolescent counseling manuals.

"But you've got to play your hand cautiously," I went on, "and even then there are no guarantees. If you don't want to ask Omri straight-out about his feelings for you, then maybe you could try a few pseudodates—you know, long drives together, walks at the beach, some carefully chosen flicks. Keep the conversation light and unthreatening. And whatever you do, don't stalk him at school!"

Adriana nodded firmly.

"If you feel like taking a bigger risk, get a friend of yours to tell a bud of his about your feelings and see what comes back to you. If Omri turns chilly, slack off, and the damage to your friendship should be minimal."

"But isn't there a quicker way to find out if he feels the same way I do?" she asked desperately.

I had to think for a moment. No ready answer to that one. "Maybe. Body language can sometimes speak volumes. The next time you're deep in conversation with Omri, touch him on the arm, the shoulder, or if you're feeling super brave, the face. If he flinches and draws back, the feeling is almost definitely not mutual, but if he smiles at you, or better yet, reciprocates—"

"I've got him!" she said excitedly as she smacked her fist into her open palm. Adriana was hunched forward now, her eyes alive with schemes and strategies. Then she bit her thumbnail. "But what about the prom?"

"You mean what if the feedback you've gotten from Omri is still nebulous and the big dance looms . . . ? I'd ask him to go as a friend. Stress that the prom is no big deal, but you think it could be fun anyway. That'll take the pressure off both of you, and then when you're all decked out in traffic-stopping formal wear and carving up that ballroom dance floor together, who knows?"

Adriana was smiling now. "You got a date?"

I smiled back.

As she got up to leave, though, she began frowning again and said, "What if I do all this stuff you suggest, and then when he eventually finds out how I really feel about him, he still freaks on me?"

"You can sue me for every penny I've got," I said, and she laughed.

"Seriously, Adriana," I went on, "this isn't

an exact science I'm practicing here. I'm just around to hear you out and try to give you a few informed tips on how to tackle your vexing probs." I pointed to a poster hanging on the back wall of the cubicle, a killer work of art I'd coaxed out of Lance Hughes, the *Beacon* cartoonist (the concept and the cautionary slogan were my two contributions). On it was a tennis player who'd tossed his racket into the air and was about to take a swing at it with his ball. "WE AIM TO SERVE," the caption read, "BUT WE DON'T ALWAYS GET IT RIGHT."

Chip Windeman was wearing a rainbow-colored knitted cap, a red-plaid flannel shirt, faded blue jeans with holes in the knees, and a deep scowl. "That Zoner guy, his schedule is full up," Chip grumbled.

"I know and I'm sorry." Zoner was one of our most popular counselors. "But maybe I can help you," I said.

Chip whipped out a Swiss army knife, extracted the scissors, and began clipping his fingernails. "You're a girl," he said accusingly as he worked on his thumbnail.

"That's a good start," I said, nodding with encouragement. "So far we're in complete agreement."

The clipping stopped for a moment, and Chip gave me a hard look. I held his gaze until he finally turned away. He closed up the knife, slapped it down on the desktop, and said, "Do you *personally* talk to many guys here?"

I nodded. "Not as many as Zoner and the other boy counselors, but I get my share."

Chip pulled off the cap and began to work it between his hands. His dark brown hair was matted to his scalp; grunge all the way. "This girl Flora wants me to ask her to the prom, and I really like her a lot, but I just don't have the bucks." He looked up at me sharply, as if daring me to make fun of him. When I didn't, his features softened, along with his voice. "Flora's got smoky eyes, and she smells like wild raspberries," he explained. "She writes song lyrics and wants to be an oceanographer." He gazed at me warily again.

"She sounds real special."

He grinned and nodded. "I bag groceries at this market down by the marina. The pay's fair, but most of it goes to rent and my car. I live with my grandma, see, and she's on Social

Security. Anyway, I've been checking out what the prom costs, and it's mind-blowing! Tickets, tux, dinner, limo, corsage—we're talking three hundred dollars and up! I wanna do right by Flora. Like you said, she's real special. But three hundred dollars is way beyond my reach. And you wanna know what? I've heard about some couples around here who're planning to shell out a thousand bucks or more! How's that possible?"

I shook my head. If I got into social class comparisons, I'd be worthless as a peer counselor at Luna High. "Let's focus on your problem, Chip. Can you see any solutions?"

"Well, no. . . . That's why I'm here!" he said irritably.

I held my hand up in a calming gesture. "My point is, the way you've got this figured, there *is* no solution. So you've gotta *rethink* the problem. D'you know, for instance, that a lot of girls are more than happy to pay their own way these days, and some even fork out for the guy, too? It depends in part on who's got the loot."

Chip had to ponder that a bit. It was obviously a new concept for him. "Flora's not rich, if that's what you mean—," he began.

"Neither of you has to be wealthy to make the prom happen. You just have to be realistic and resourceful. Is a limo out of your price range? Okay, then why not just wax up your own car and take Flora in that—"

"My wheels are in prime condition already," Chip said defensively. I looked at the desktop and noticed that his nail clippings were black. Grease.

"Then you're halfway there," I said with a smile. "And you can skip the fancy restaurant, too, if you want. Go for quality over price. It may take some extra time, but if you search long and hard enough, you're bound to find bargain rental rates on a tux. Or you could get creative, go to a secondhand clothing store and let your imagination run wild."

Chip looked down at his clothes and grinned. "Now you're talking," he said. Soon he was spouting out ideas of his own, and by the time the bell rang for first period, he'd decided to ask Flora to the prom right away.

"She's a lucky girl," I told him.

I went off to chem class, confident that Peter would make me feel just as lucky.

Chapter 2

KAYLA, ZONER, and I were eating lunch at our favorite table, the one on the grassy knoll that overlooks Luna High in all its pre-fab California mission-style glory. It'd turned into a "palm-tree day"—sunny, breezy, and dee-lish. Peter said he'd join us after his debate club meeting, but it must've been running super late.

"How can you be obsessing about the prom, Kayla," Zoner said after wolfing down his second peanut butter and banana sandwich, "when we've got tons of waste floating in orbit, just waiting to bail?"

Kayla turned to me, smiled, and said, "Can

you believe how blatantly this guy changes the subject?"

Zoner had a real talent for coming up with bizarre questions. Last week it was: "If you were going to die exactly one year from now, would you still apply to college in the fall?" And the week before that: "If the black box flight recorder survives even the gnarliest plane crashes, then how come the whole airplane isn't built like the black box?"

"Can you be more specific about this rubbish-in-reentry deal, Professor Zoner?" I asked him.

"Why, of course," he said as he pulled some of his long, straggly bleached-out hair away from his deeply tanned face and straightened out his faded burgundy LIFE'S A BEACH tank top. "The U.S. Space Command is currently tracking over seven thousand pieces of space junk that are the size of a baseball or larger. Seven percent of these objects are satellites and fifteen percent of them are spent rocket bodies—"

"Spent rocket bodies?" Kayla asked with a giggle.

"That's right, young lady," Zoner affirmed with NASA spokesmanlike formality. "And while I'd hate to fill that pretty strawberry blond head of yours full of worry, we can't dismiss the statistical possibility that there's a satellite up there with your name on it."

We all laughed together, and I noticed that Kayla's lagoon-blue eyes lingered on Zoner a little longer than usual. The three of us'd been friends since Zoner had helped Kayla and me learn to surf at a beach day camp the summer after junior high. (He'd also introduced us to surfspeak, a sort of second language that Kayla and I could now lapse into whenever the spirit moved.) His real name was Terry Kingman; the nickname came from his general off-the-wallness, as well as his uncanny knack for finding a surfable zone in waves that others thought unridable.

"I still don't see why you're so down on the prom, Zoner," Kayla said, going doggedly back to the previous discussion.

"I have nothing against the prom," he said good-naturedly. "I just think that if God meant guys to dress up like penguins, He'd've given us webbed feet and a craving for squid."

When I laughed and Kayla didn't, Zoner turned to me and said, "Help me out here,

Becca. You don't think the prom is the be-all and end-all, do you?"

"You're asking the wrong person," I told him. "I *want* the fairy-tale thing, the whole Cinderella transformation. I've had my dress picked out for ages; it's a Sylvia Casimiro design in pink lace, and I've been saving up for it for almost six months. I want the limo, the flowers, the dinner; I want to feel like a princess. You can dis the prom all you want, big guy, but some of us still believe in magic, and we're not gonna apologize for it."

"Outstanding defense, Becca!" Kayla said gleefully as we exchanged a high five.

"This session is a bust," Zoner conceded, throwing up his hands.

As a goodwill gesture, I offered Zoner the avocado and garbanzo bean pita-pocket sandwich my mom had foisted off on me that morning, but he turned it down. ("This could be the hot ticket to finally improving your skin tone," Mom'd said cheerfully, as if I'd *known* there was a problem with my skin tone.)

"Yo, Becca!" Peter called out as he trudged up the knoll. My boyfriend was tall, a little husky, and had short, shiny gold-streaked brown hair with bangs that never behaved. He looked like a big teddy bear. As a debater, he specialized in health-care issues, and he was a terrific booster for the PCN, even though he didn't have either the time or the inclination to be a counselor himself. He'd captured my heart not because of his tenor singing voice, which was only so-so, but because of his zesty, go-for-it personality. Two months ago he'd invited me to the Valentine's dance by handing me a bouquet of red roses, and I'd been hooked on him ever since.

Of course, Peter wasn't without his flaws; none of us are. What bugged me most was his tendency to flirt flagrantly with pretty girls. Lately he'd been spending an inordinate amount of time with a perky ninth-grade debater named Cindy Silber. Peter insisted that Cindy was just eager to "learn the ropes" from him, and that sounded plausible enough to me, even though it was getting to the point where she probably saw more of him on a daily basis than I did. I tried not to make too much of an issue out of it, though, because I figured if you can't trust your own boyfriend, you've got major problems.

"Sorry I'm so late," Peter said as we

hugged each other. He pulled away more quickly than usual. *Body language?* "We got caught up in discussing the legal issues surrounding terminal illness and then the *Beacon* was delivered," he explained as he caught his breath. (Peter wasn't into physical exertion, unless you counted making out, and so, much to Zoner's and Kayla's outspoken annoyance, I'd had to let my surfing slide over the past few months.) "You're not gonna like it, Becca."

I seized the copy of the paper that Peter offered me, and while he gabbed with Zoner and Kayla, I turned directly to the editorial page, to Jeff's column. This month it was entitled:

THE PEER DELUSION NETWORK: WHO NEEDS IT?

In December the so-called Peer Counseling Network opened its doors to the students of Luna Point High School. In a column written at that time, I questioned the need for such a service, as well as the qualifications of the student volunteers staffing it. But after a modest start, the PCN, started by former *Beacon* staffer Rebecca Singleton, soared in popularity.

In February I reexamined the network in

terms of issues of trust and confidentiality, wondering if your secrets would really be safe in the hands of a group of teen non-professionals who were subject on a daily basis to the same fierce social pressures that dog us all. I was intrigued to see some decline in patronage after that column appeared, but the PCN gradually recovered and now seems more vital than ever.

And, of course, why wouldn't it be, in this age of talk-show journalism and injustice collecting? Aren't we Americans taught now that we are all victims? If we face a crisis in our lives, especially one of our own making, aren't we encouraged to see a lawyer or a shrink (or a peer counselor) so that they can quickly assign the blame elsewhere?

Can the time really be far off when a student, unsuccessful in his or her quest for a prom date, will be able to sue a high school for "pain and suffering"? . . .

I read this attack piece to its bitter end and then threw the paper down in disgust. "Once again, that reptile Jeff Gardiner is totally misrepresenting what we're trying to do! And just like last time, he gave me no advance notice, so I had no chance to write a counterpoint column! I can't believe he had the gall to run this right in the middle of prom season, when so many people are feeling vulnerable!"

Peter, Kayla, and Zoner tried to calm me down and reassure me that almost nobody took Jeff's column very seriously, but I knew better and so did they (especially Zoner, who used to write the occasional surf story for the *Beacon*). Jeff's first attack had nearly smothered the network in its infancy, and after the second one we'd been mobbed by panicked counselees who were worried that their secret life crises were being illegally traded on the Luna High gossip exchange.

He knew full well I'd gotten the idea to start the PCN last spring when three guidance counseling positions fell under the budget ax. Those cuts happened in spite of a four-part series I'd just written on teen problems at Luna High— problems like suicidal depression, coping with divorce, and facing unplanned pregnancies. I'd thought about how much family therapy helped me after my parents' recent divorce, so with the full-on support of Mr. Gordon (and major assists from Kayla and Zoner), I'd worked through the summer and fall to scrounge together a peer therapy program.

Actually, as far as I was concerned, if even a single troubled teen was kept away from the PCN by Jeff's misleading editorials, that was one too many. It was clearly high time to meet the weenie on his home turf and kick some butt!

Ⴍ

I anxiously watched the clock all through my AP U.S. history class, and then rushed out of the room when the bell rang and ran over to the language building to get excused from British lit. We were studying Shakespeare's play *Much Ado about Nothing.* I'd seen the movie, and Kayla promised she'd share her notes with me later.

I waited outside the open door of the journalism classroom for about five minutes while Jeff got the monthly critique session under way. You might wonder how a junior got to be editor in chief of a high school newspaper. In the spring of last year, when Jeff was still just the opinion page editor, he published a pro-con piece on the merits of making condoms available to the students of Luna High. Then, in the following month, he wrote, with my assistance, a blistering editorial denouncing the planned layoffs of not just guidance counselors but a sizable number of teachers and support staff as well. Bernard Crampton, a school board member, blasted the *Beacon* editorials and called the paper a "one-sided mouthpiece for a liberal political agenda." Citing the board censorship powers granted to school officials over students in the U.S. Supreme Court's 1988 *Hazelwood School District v. Kuhlmeier* decision, Mr. Crampton insisted on the right to review future issues of the *Beacon* for "inappropriate" editorial content.

Jeff was fabulous; he went totally ballistic. He appeared before the board and pointed out that since the *Beacon* had long operated as a pro-con "open forum" for student opinion, the reasoning in *Hazelwood* didn't apply here. He also reminded Mr. Crampton that California law granted students free press rights that were more generous than the post-*Hazelwood* federal standards.

Several staffers, including myself, also helped Jeff to organize a rally against censorship. It featured a speaker from the American Civil Liberties Union and was covered by members of the local media, who of course ate this freedom of expression story right up.

We figured Mr. Crampton either hadn't done his legal homework or he was counting on our ignorance. Big mistake! He finally backed down (but only after a condom distribution proposal for the high school was dropped from the board agenda) and had to settle for speaking his piece in a special all-editorial edition of the *Beacon*.

So scarcely a year ago, when it served a cause *he* was into, Jeff'd manipulated the "talk-show journalists" and "injustice collectors" with the best of 'em.

What a hypocrite!

I walked into the classroom as he was in the midst of holding forth about "journalistic objectivity." The *Beacon*'s faculty advisor, Ms. Sullivan, was sitting at a desk behind Jeff. She favored me with a slight nod and a smile.

I positioned myself at the far end of the enormous meeting table (which was really just a bunch of smaller tables pushed together), directly across from where Jeff was seated, and said, "I'm sorry to interrupt a sermon, Your Worship, but I've come to lodge a complaint."

Jeff froze midsentence and regarded me with startled blue eyes. The twenty or so staff members present turned away from him to look at me, and I was flooded with enthusiastic greetings. (Darla Swanson, though, gave me only a halfhearted wave.)

Jeff recovered quickly. "You see, Becca," he said, "everybody here misses you. You were an awesome journalist. You never should've left."

"Having you as a peer, Jeff, was at times barely tolerable; suffering you as a boss was simply more than I could take," I responded. I picked up a copy of the *Beacon* from the table and tossed it in his direction. "Why another hatchet job on the Peer Counseling Network? Are you really that starved for story ideas? Can't you just go chasing after UFOs like all the other tabloid journalists?"

"I love you, too," Jeff replied, smiling as he clasped his hands behind his head and thrust his chest out. How pathetically transparent! I knew from my exhaustive summer psych reading that this was a classic gesture used by human males in an attempt to assert their dominance; it was right down there on the evolutionary scale with chest-pounding by gorillas. "Face it, Becca," he went on, "our last two shoot-outs in the *Beacon* generated a ton of reader interest, and that's what juicy journalism is all about. I can hardly wait for your next devastating rebuttal."

"Is that supposed to be a compliment?"

"Why—are you in need of one?" he said, as he dropped his pose and stood up to face me. "Has it been too long between award ceremonies? Has the Ivy League stopped calling with scholarship offers?"

"God, I miss this!" Lance Hughes said, and several staffers murmured in agreement.

"The people who come to my trailer don't give a damn about your 'reader interest,' Jeff. They come because they're confused or lonely or somebody hurt them or they hurt somebody and didn't mean to. They come because they know that for fifteen minutes they'll have the undivided attention of another human being. Not everyone has a captive audience like you do."

People laughed again, and Randy Strother, the staff photographer, snapped my picture.

"Wait 'til she throws the first punch, Randy," Eddie Ballard joked.

" '*My* trailer,' " Jeff repeated, ignoring the others. "That's kind of revealing, isn't it?"

My face felt very hot suddenly. "Not nearly

so revealing as your vanity editorials!" I replied angrily. Heads at the table were turning to and fro, as if this were a match at Wimbledon. "You keep blindsiding me, Jeff, and that's a wussy ploy. You make sure you have the stage all to yourself for a month at a time 'cause you're scared your flimsy argument won't stand up to an informed challenge. You don't believe in free speech these days any more than your old buddy Bernard Crampton does!"

"Ooooh!" said the staff.

"If you think I'm just posing here, Becca, you're dead wrong!" he said heatedly. "I honestly believe that therapy's used just to assign blame arbitrarily and to turn people against each other."

"Yes, I know; I read your piece, and it was a great hook! But I need to see your *research,* Mr. Editor in Chief. 'Opinions are easy; facts are hard.' Isn't that what you used to say? And how dare you take a cheap shot at people who don't have prom dates. That totally sucks! How insensitive can you be?"

Jeff glanced briefly at Darla, and she looked away. "Damn it, Becca," he said, pounding his fist on the table, "all I'm saying is that people need to take responsibility for their own actions and learn how to handle their own problems! What's so wrong with that idea?"

"Nothing," I said. "Except that most of us weren't born thinking we know all the answers."

Some staff members actually broke into applause this time, but before Jeff could return the volley, the classroom door opened. Mr. Grambeau, the assistant principal in charge of discipline, was looking for me. "It's Roger again," he whispered. "He's in the main office."

"Is this about your little brother?" Jeff asked gleefully as a smile returned to his face. "What's the tiny terror done this time? Set the science building on fire? Started another food fight in the ninth grade caf?"

"Your smugness'll come back to haunt you, Jeff Gardiner," I said.

"HEAD PEER COUNSELOR PLAGUED BY DE- LINQUENT SIBLING," Jeff announced, using his hands to frame the imaginary headline. "Now *there's* a tabloid story if I ever heard one."

I left quickly with Mr. Grambeau, totally steamed that in spite of my go-for-the-jugular attack on his journalistic ethics, Jeff'd still managed to get in the last jab.

⌐

"Where'd you get the idea to cut Mr. Limbrick's hair in the first place?" I asked Roger as I drove him home in my ancient, sputtering bronze Olds Cutlass.

Roger ignored me and looked out the window to focus on the street action of Pacific Coast Highway. He'd just recently turned fifteen and smelled of Reese's Pieces and dirty athletic socks. He was wearing, as always, his black leather Hard Rock Cafe jacket, a Christmas gift from our father, who'd moved to New York about a year-and-a-half ago. (Roger'd played a hot keyboard for the school jazz ensemble back in junior high but'd since given it up.) My brother's hair, which up until the end of eighth grade had been a quasi-medium brown with the occasional gold streak like mine, was now shaved on the sides and dyed jet black on top.

"I know Mr. Limbrick is not the best algebra teacher on the planet," I went on. "And even the principal admitted that it was out of line for a faculty member to fall asleep in class.

But that doesn't give you the right to pick up a pair of scissors and—"

"Can I turn on the radio, sis?" Roger turned to me to ask in his usual bored monotone. He had hazel eyes, also like mine, although he was no doubt in the market for a pair of jet black contact lenses.

"No, you can't. Roger, do you realize that you've been *suspended?* When Mom comes home tomorrow from her conference in Sacramento and hears about this, she's going to freak!" (Mom kept a roof over our heads as a public relations exec, but her true love was sculpting, and I think the fact that she had so little time to pursue her art these days worked her nerves in a major way. Roger's constant delinquency only made things worse.)

Roger shrugged at my mention of Mom, but his eyes betrayed some anxiety. "She'll deal with it. She always does. And if not, I'll just go live with Dad."

I gripped the steering wheel a little more tightly and tried to ignore the sudden flutter in my stomach. "Did Dad say you could?"

Roger nodded uncertainly.

I felt helpless. The family therapist that Roger, Mom, and I had gone to after the divorce warned that the transition to high school could be super rough for an adolescent boy with an absent father. "Just be patient with Roger and love him," she advised us. "Allow him his space and as much quality time with his dad as possible."

But Dad, also a public relations exec, was on the road more than ever these days, and Roger had this unfortunate tendency to corrupt or destroy whatever "space" we gave him.

"Can I switch on the radio now. Pretty puhlease?" Roger asked again as he moved the tuning dial to a different station and turned the volume way up.

"No way!" On impulse, I got off the highway and pulled into the parking lot of a 7-Eleven. I parked under a palm tree, shut off the engine, and said, "I know we agreed I'm never supposed to do the peer counseling thing with you. But can't we just *talk* for once, like a brother and sister are supposed to?"

This idea seemed to amuse him. "You mean like the happy, well-adjusted sibs on cable TV reruns? Brenda and Brandon, Alex and Mallory, Marcia and Greg?"

"Exactly," I said.

"Okay," he said gamely as he began scratching various body parts (ahhh, the ravages of testosterone). "I'll go first: Gee, Becca, how come you didn't tell me you broke up with Peter?"

"What?!"

"My friend Tony Zimmerman saw him kissing a girl in the balcony of the auditorium at lunch today, so I figured you two must be couple-toast," Roger said mildly.

"You— I'm sure you— It must've been somebody else," I sputtered.

"No, it wasn't," Roger said confidently. "Tony told me his eyes had adjusted to the darkness, 'cause he was on the other side of the balcony making out with Marcie Scott. It was Peter all right, and he was locking lips with this totally luscious babe from my class— Cindy Silver, I think her name is."

"Silber," I said dully.

Roger studied my face. "This is all news to you, isn't it?" he said, amazed. Then he clapped his hands together and started to laugh uproariously. "That's classic!"

Great. After over a year of trying, I'd finally managed to put Roger in a good mood.

Chapter 3

A̲s a peer counselor I'd seen more than a few relationships trashed by false second- and thirdhand rumors. So as I dropped Roger off at home and motored back to the high school at ambulance speed, I resolved to stay calm, to report the rumor to Peter in a good-humored, matter-of-fact kind of way, and then let him assure me of his innocence so I wouldn't have to kill him.

I found him in the almost-empty debate classroom (school'd let out a while ago). He and Cindy were sitting shoulder-to-shoulder, yukking it up over some item in a magazine they were reading together. I scraped a nearby desk across the floor to announce my presence.

"Hi, Becca!" Peter said when he looked up. "I heard you had to take Roger home. Is everything okay?"

"I sure hope so. Look, Peter, I need to talk to you about something for a minute. Preferably in private."

Cindy looked up and acknowledged me with a brief, tight little smile before going straight back to the mag.

"Sure thing," Peter said cheerfully as he stood up. "Where'd you like to go?"

"How about the balcony in the auditorium?"

Peter blanched and Cindy took on the aspect of a maraschino cherry.

I felt a sudden urge to cry but quickly smothered it. I grabbed my stunned and uncharacteristically silent debate chump by the arm and led him out into the hallway in search of a vacant room. Ms. Attanucci's bio lab was the first available.

"Oh, Peter," I wailed after shutting the door, "how *could you?!*"

"It was Cindy's idea," he blurted out as he backed up against a poster of a dissected frog.

"She came on to me, and I guess I just got caught up in the moment."

I shook my head. "Cliché central. Try again."

It took him forever to come up with something else. "You know," he said as he stepped away from the wall, "it occurs to me that we never actually agreed, at least in a formal way, that we were in an exclusive relationship here. The terms of allowable conduct, therefore, were rather ambiguous. Ergo—"

"Are you *kidding?*" I asked in disbelief, poking his chest with my finger and causing him to back away from me, toward the rear of the classroom this time. "Do you think this is a formal debate or something? (*poke*) I was really falling hard for you, you insensitive clod! (*poke*) I thought you were a guy I could *trust!*" (*poke, poke*) Peter suddenly stumbled and fell to the floor.

"God, I'm really sorry," I said sincerely as I got down on the floor to make sure he was okay.

"Jeez, Becca, why do you have to get so physical when you're mad?"

"I told you before. The family therapist said it was probably displaced aggression left over from my parents' divorce. Mr. Gordon is giving me tips on how to deal. . . . And look who's lecturing *me* about getting physical!" I said, getting mad all over again.

We sat on the dirty tiled floor in silence for a few more minutes.

"If you took our relationship so lightly, Peter, then why'd you have to go and tell me you loved me?" I asked.

He looked puzzled. "When did I say that?"

"In the parking lot at Jack in the Box, just two Saturdays ago! You remember—we went there for dessert after seeing that great Tom Hanks movie. I had an order of cinnamon churritos and you had two slices of chocolate chip cookie-dough cheesecake."

When this still didn't register, I said flatly, "The temp was in the low sixties. There were two other cars in the lot. I think one was a Honda Prelude, and the other was a—"

"Okay! Okay. I remember," he said. "But when a guy says 'I love you,' Becca, especially so early in a relationship, it doesn't necessarily mean what a girl thinks it does."

I was wasting my time. I stood up and slapped the dust off my pants. "Don't generalize about guys with me, Peter. A lot of them know exactly what 'I love you' means, and they're true to it. I suppose I should be grateful, though, that I found all this out *before* prom night."

Peter suddenly looked totally distressed. "You mean you're breaking up with me?" he asked in disbelief. "But I was planning to ask you to the prom this weekend, Becca. I swear I was! Don't you think you're overreacting just a little here? Cindy's only fifteen. A kid, practically. If you really want me to keep things platonic with her from now on, then that's exactly what I'll do."

I thought about Cindy for a moment and the flagrant disregard she'd shown for my romantic bond with Peter. "Don't bother," I said. "I'm sure she deserves what you have to offer way more than I do."

On the long drive home, as I kept mopping my tear-soaked face with Kleenex, I tried to remember strategies for handling breakups. It was a no-go. I finally switched on the radio for comfort and got blasted instead:

"Broken families and remote-controlled lives!
Buzzing nowhere in no-exit beehives!
No way to make it in this world on your own!
So give me cable and just leave me alone!"

I'd completely forgotten about Roger changing the station. No wonder the kid was so
twisted.

Not wanting to go back to one of my favorite stations, which all put a major stress on
upbeat love songs, I raced across the FM band
until I crashed into a country-and-western
tune:

"My dog was run over by a truck headed
    west;
My farm done gone under, the bank
    repossessed;
But that ain't enough to give me the blues,
Long as I've got my woman and a good pair
    of shoes."

I laughed out loud and cheered up just a bit.
No farm, no dog, no guy, but I did have several pairs of great shoes. Maybe I could walk
my way through this.

When I felt the reassuring embrace of home, I began to remember some of those elusive steps for coping with heartbreak that I'd studied up on as a peer counselor-in-training.

Step One: Talk to people who care. Roger was KO'd from this category the second he took his microwaved TV dinner lasagna into his room and slammed the door. I called Kayla, but she was apparently out with her family. I called Zoner, but he must've been out with his board. So I left a simple message on each of their answering machines: "Peter cheated on me; please send chocolate."

Step Two: Do something constructive to take your mind off your troubles. After dinner, once the dishwasher was running, I set about cleaning my bedroom. I started by taking down the small photo collage of Peter pictures that hung on the wall just opposite my pillow. I toyed with the idea of shredding every last one of them but found I didn't have the heart for it quite yet. (Couldn't he still surprise me? Show up at my door on his knees, with a bouquet of flowers in his hand, and . . . and more lame rationalizations for his slimy misdeed!) I dusted the furniture and fluffed my quilted bedspread.

As I began to straighten out my awards shelf, I remembered the "award ceremonies" crack that Jeff Gardiner'd made earlier in the day. Which brought me to . . .

Step Three: Do something that makes you feel good. I pulled out last year's high school annual and found Jeff's large photo on page 147. (Jeff'd won an *Orange County Times* citation for excellence in high school journalism, editorial division.) "To Becca," he'd scribbled under the picture in a bold, black hand, "a fearsome foe, a first-class collaborator, and a cherished friend. Love, Jeff." I'd gotten the chills when I first read that, last June. It was evidence for my private theory, long since tossed, that the "real" Jeff Gardiner was a warm, sensitive, caring human being who just needed the love of the right girl to draw him out.

Darla Swanson, though, was not the girl I'd had in mind.

I cut out Jeff's picture, removed the small garbage bag that lined my red-white-and-blue "Great Seal of the President of the United States" trash can (a gift from a relative who had high hopes for my future—and a twisted sense of humor), and then using some transparent tape, carefully affixed Jeff's image to the shiny metal bottom inside the receptacle. I got an amazing amount of pleasure from this petty little act, and it didn't even occur to me to wonder why I was using Jeff's picture instead of Peter's.

"That's really twisted," Roger said over my shoulder.

I hadn't heard him come in my bedroom, and I was so shocked that I literally jumped up from the chair and dropped the can. "Don't you believe in knocking?" I asked, my heart pounding.

"Your door was open," he said calmly. As I picked the can back up, he examined the mutilated yearbook and actually grinned a little. "Finally getting some of those repressed feelings for Jeff Gardiner out of your system, huh? You know, sis, there may be hope for you yet."

I sometimes forgot that Roger and I had gone through four months of family therapy *together*.

"You won't tell anyone?" I said, suddenly feeling very foolish and vulnerable.

"As if," he said, rolling his eyes.

"Thanks," I said, super relieved. "So what's up? You want to talk?"

He shook his head. "I want to invite Chris Bowen over."

"Chris Bowen?" A sophomore. Shaved head. Eats peanuts without removing the shells. "Isn't he in jail?"

"Not anymore. And besides, how was he supposed to know it was against the law to throw live explosives off a public pier?"

I laughed. "Yeah, that's an innocent mistake practically anyone could've made. But he can't come over tonight, armed or unarmed," I said firmly. "You've been suspended."

"You're just ticked at me for passing along the bad news about Peter," Roger said, and then he sulked out of my room.

Was he right? Was I acting out of sisterly concern, or was this just displaced aggression on my part? How could I be sure? I needed a second opinion. An objective judge. A parent, even! But I didn't dare call Mom in Sacramento; she'd take a red-eye flight home and be cranky for weeks. And Dad lived totally out of the loop, a whole continent away.

I put these thoughts aside and went back

to cleaning, which worked like a charm once again until I accidentally came across a snapshot of Peter and me at the Valentine's dance. We looked so happy together. And he seemed so gentlemanly! So trustworthy! I thought about our splendiferous March trip to Catalina Island, when we'd kissed at dusk at Casino Point; the late night yakfests in the Jacuzzi at Carolyn Preimsberger's house; the pork-out sessions at Baskin-Robbins after school on Friday afternoons.

I was in the midst of a second crying jag when the doorbell rang. It was Kayla and Zoner bearing chocolate, plus other decadent goodies. And God bless 'em, they aimed to kidnap me. "I'd come willingly, but I can't leave Roger here alone," I said, explaining about the suspension.

"No worries. I'll just hip the dude to the direness of the situation," Zoner said confidently as he shuffled off in the direction of Roger's room.

Zoner reemerged five minutes later with a smile on his face, as if he'd just snaked his way through a monster barrel, and he gave me a thumbs-up. "There was some resistance at first, but the grom finally decided to flow with it. He'll stay put," Zoner said. "When's he gonna take up surfing, anyway? It could cure what ails him."

"Probably when I give it up," I said grimly.

~

"Primo conditions for a Twinkie roast," Zoner said as we sat around a fire pit at the beach. Before we met Zoner, it'd never occurred to either Kayla or me that a Twinkie *could* be roasted. But they were surprisingly tasty in their blackened state—chewy on the outside, soft and hot and bubbly on the inside. For an extra kick we sometimes dipped them in an open can of Hershey's chocolate syrup.

Going to the beach that night gave my soul a major revamp. The night air was rich with the smell of the black sage and lemonade berry blanketing the nearby hillsides, and you could hear the waves playing their soothing riff as they crumbled into oblivion on the nearby shoreline. Happy surfing memories came to mind as mainland hassles receded. On the eastern horizon, a grinning three-quarter moon peered over the bold, black profile of the Santa Ana Mountains, and I could almost hear the lunar dude telling me, "Cheer up, babe."

"Make sure you pull down and stash everything that reminds you of Peter," Kayla told me.

"Already done," I said.

"Focus on new projects and goals and exercise daily to free up those mood-boosting endorphins," Zoner added.

"I worked up a sweat cleaning my room."

"Be nice to his new girlfriend when you cross paths at school. It'll show how classy you are and confuse the hell out of both of them," Kayla said.

"Spend more time with your buds and remember that you don't need a dude to be a whole and complete person," Zoner said.

"Smile big-time even when you're down. It'll trigger the brain chemicals that bring on happy feelings," Kayla said.

"Go back to surfing at least once a week instead of practically never," Zoner concluded. "Ancient Surf Sage says: ' 'Tis better to charge a peak than date a geek.' "

"Ancient Surf Sage? Puhlease," Kayla said with a laugh.

I laughed, too, and then applauded them

both. "One thing's for certain," I said. "If you're going to get dumped on by life, make sure your best friends are peer counselors."

"Wait! There's one more piece of advice you need to hear," Kayla said, reaching into her backpack and pulling out a paperbound copy of *Much Ado about Nothing*. She turned to the page she wanted, moved closer to the firelight, sat up straight, and read:

> *"Sigh no more, ladies, sigh no more,*
> *Men were deceivers ever,*
> *One foot in sea, and one on shore,*
> *To one thing constant never.*
> *Then sigh not so, but let them go,*
> *And be you blithe and bonny,*
> *Converting all your sounds of woe*
> *Into hey nonny nonny."*

"Thanks, Kayla," I said gratefully when she was finished. "I think the Bard pretty much captured where my heart's at tonight."

Zoner stuck a Twinkie into the center of the pit, and we all watched it catch fire. After about ten seconds he withdrew the charred remains and blew on them. Then he stuffed the entire smoking hot confection into his mouth, cried out in muffled pain, frantically reached over to the top of the cooler for the can of chocolate syrup, and quickly alleviated his suffering with one massive swig. "Don't try that at home," he told us after he'd swallowed.

We assured him we wouldn't.

He warmed his hands over the fire and then, rubbing them together with a sidelong glance at Kayla, announced, "Looked up the term *prom* in the old unabridged dictionary this afternoon."

"And what'd you find, professor?" I asked him with a smile.

"A prom is a ball or dance," he intoned, "often given by high school students, see also *anxious,* as a form of self-torture. It's a contraction of the term *promenade,* which means to walk about in a leisurely manner for amusement or show; see also *cruising, posing, hot-dogging,* and *avenue-riding.* But to get a real feel for the term, I believe you have to go all the way back to the Latin verb *prominare,* which means to drive a herd of animals forward—see also *high school students.*"

"That's awesome!" I enthused.

Zoner grinned appreciatively. "Etymology rules."

Kayla tossed her copy of Shakespeare over

her shoulder with an exasperated sigh and said to me, "I should just give it up and admit that we're destined to attend the big dance without the benefit of male companionship."

"Hey, don't panic. I might still go, *if* I can find the perfect date," Zoner said.

"Oh *really?* And just what would she be like, pray tell?" Kayla asked.

"Smart, good-humored, easy on the eyes, athletic, and always there for me," he said.

"Oh, terrific," I said, rolling my eyes at Kayla. "Zoner wants to date a Labrador retriever."

We all started laughing and throwing sand at each other.

⟳

Kayla spent the night in my guest bed, and per our usual custom, we had a gab session well into the wee hours. Late in the proceedings, she finally confessed the obvious: she'd fallen hard for Zoner. She obviously wanted my support in snagging him, but I found to my surprise that I just couldn't give it to her the way I had to others—Adriana Fernandez, for instance. "You, me, and Zoner make a supremo trio," I said. "And you know as well as I do that if you go after him and it backfires, all three of us could lose out. . . . Besides, I just couldn't risk playing matchmaker here. I'm way too enmeshed as a friend."

"Yeah, I've already thought through all the complications. In fact, I've been obsessing on this subject for weeks. But no matter what I tell myself, Becky, I still love him," Kayla said, using my grade school nickname. "So much that it hurts." Her stressed-out voice resonated in my darkened bedroom.

I'd never loved any guy so much that it *hurt*. In fact, the only guy who'd ever gotten under my skin to that extreme was currently my worst enemy!

It suddenly occurred to me that I might be psychologically bent in some way. I shared my fears with Kayla and told her all about my dynamic duel with Jeff in the *Beacon* classroom, as well as my way dorky trash can impulse.

"Don't stress. If anyone's disturbed, it's Jeff," she said groggily. "He's going out with the queen of the junior class, yet every other column he writes is 'bout you . . . but we're s'posed to be talking 'bout me and Zoner. How d'you s'pose I can get more athletic?"

"Take up skydiving!" I said, suddenly

wide awake. "Are you saying you don't think Jeff is really in love with Darla?" I asked, remembering Eddie's observation that Darla was on Jeff's case a lot these days.

Kayla mumbled something incoherent and then nodded off, apparently for good.

Some people pick the darnedest times to fall asleep.

Chapter 4

PETER CALLED ME about four times an hour on Saturday morning, but he never got any closer to admitting that what he'd done with Cindy was wrong, so I told him he was just tying up the line for nothing and rewarded myself with an Oreo each time I held my ground and hung up on him. When I got a stomachache, I had to stop answering the phone altogether.

Mom went off on Roger when she got home Saturday night and threatened to ground him for a week. I pulled her aside to reason in private. I clued her into the time-tested psychological principle of minimal sufficiency, which holds that mild or moderate punishment is far more likely than extreme measures to reform a delinquent kid. Mom said that it was super unnerving to get parenting tips from a seventeen-year-old, but then she agreed to pare the grounding down to four days, including time already served. After that she tossed back a few aspirin and faded off to slumberland. (She was so stressed that I decided not to keep her up to tell her about Peter and how he'd left me stranded without a prom date.)

Zoner talked Kayla and me into a dawn patrol session on Sunday, but the skies were slate gray and conditions sucked hard, with early onshores and one-to-two-foot slop. It was just as well, though, since I spent most of my time relearning how to paddle and get vertical on my board. Zoner tweaked out a few good rides, and Kayla did her best to match his pace. She bailed more often than not, though, and when Zoner finally razzed her by saying, "You once-a-week surfers don't have a prayer in crumblers like these," Kayla looked totally crushed.

On Monday morning, my arm and leg muscles in agony, I staggered into the PCN trailer to drown myself in other people's woes. As I feared, there was a notable scarcity of boys seeking help, and this was true throughout the day. Jeff's column was basically just a call for a return to "good ol' American self-reliance," after all, and that sort of thing really worked on the male ego. It made me steaming mad, thinking of all those unfortunate guys walking around campus with their problems tightly bottled up inside, just because of Jeff Gardiner's retro-macho attitude.

There were girls in abundance, though. Apparently word of Peter's unfaithfulness had gotten around, and this seemed to boost my popularity with my own gender. (There had to be an easier way!) A lot of the girls who came in just needed to hear the kind of advice I'd recently gotten from Kayla and Zoner, but one case really stood out:

"Walt asked me to the prom three weeks ago," Elaine Stillwell said as she pulled a fresh wad of Kleenex out of the ceramic dispenser (one of my mom's artistic creations; a glossy, cheesy, sunflowery thing that declared: LOVE BEGINS WITH YOU) I kept atop my desk. Elaine's green eyes were bloodshot, her black hair was a tangly mess, and her clothes hung on her like leaves on a dead tree. The poor soul looked as if she'd crawled straight out of bed and into my cubicle. "I was stoked beyond words because I'd been liking him for ages and dropping hints about the prom to him all spring long."

She paused to blow her nose and wipe her eyes again. "We both run cross-country and have the same pre-calc class. He seemed like the nicest guy, and he's *such* a babe—"

"What'd Walt do to get you so upset?" I prompted her. Watching her cry reminded me of how raw I still felt inside, and I was afraid if I didn't keep things moving I might start breaking down myself.

Elaine gave me a sheepish look. "We went out together like six or seven times over the next few months and hung out at school together whenever we could, and things got real intense really fast—the chemistry was just amazing. Even our friends said so. Walt was so gentle and caring, not your typical macho jock at all. He really seemed interested in me as a *person,* you know? Like when I told him about how I want to go into sports medicine someday, he was real enthused for me. He didn't ask me what my GPA was or hammer me with the long odds I faced. And God, I just turned to liquid when he held me in his arms and kissed me. . . ."

Suddenly my lips felt chapped, my throat dry and scratchy. Listening to this sort of thing was a whole lot harder after you'd just suffered a breakup yourself. I decided to follow my counseling instincts and cut to the chase. "So you had sex with him?"

Elaine closed her eyes tightly and nodded. "Last Wednesday, after midnight. In a sleeping bag under that big sycamore tree in Luna Point Park. I was a virgin, so it hurt real bad at first. . . ."

I let her go on describing "it" for a while because she seemed to need to, although by the time she finished I found myself chewing anxiously on a piece of Kleenex as I scribbled notes into my counseling journal. Maybe I should've taken the day off.

"And then within the next few days, Walt dumped you," I heard myself telling Elaine. I'd gone on autopilot, as I once again suffered steamy visions of Peter and Cindy going at it full-throttle in the auditorium balcony. . . .

Elaine's eyes opened wide with surprise. "You mean you *know* already? Has Walt been telling people? I'll *die* of embarrassment!"

I snapped out of my semicomatose state to reach over and take her hand in mine. "Easy, hon. Nobody told me anything. I guessed right only because I've talked to so many girls who've suffered through this same ordeal. And a few guys, too, believe it or not."

We went through the particulars of the breakup, and then Elaine said bitterly, "I feel so stupid and so used! I gave him my virginity, and I'll never get that back."

The Luna Point High School District required sex ed classes in the sixth and ninth grades, in which we were exposed to scads of mind-blowing stats on unwanted teen pregnancies, sexually transmitted diseases, various methods of birth control and their failure rates, and so on. By the time we were sophomores, we were all pretty well-versed. So when students came to *me* to talk sex, the last thing they usually wanted was yet another lecture on "the risks faced by sexually active adolescents." I gave them a pamphlet on the subject instead (the district required it) and then tried to deal one-on-one with the particulars of each case.

"Technically, no, you'll never get your virginity back," I agreed. "You're still master of your own bod, though. Not Walt or anyone else. Elaine Stillwell is in the driver's seat here. And you can decide to have a *second* virginity—"

"But why would Walt do this?" she wailed. "I can't believe he'd use the prom as bait just to score with me!"

Score. Screw. Get laid. Do the dirty deed. Hit a homer. . . . God, I needed some aspirin. "Maybe he did and maybe he didn't. But you'll never get an answer to that question unless you ask him face-to-face, Elaine."

She shook her head. "No *way* I could do that right now!"

"Hear me out first," I urged. I totally understood her feelings, but it was my job to goad her on anyway. "Walt could be lots of things. Maybe he's a creep who'd say anything to get a girl to put out. Or maybe he suffers from a bizarre madonna complex, meaning he loses respect for any female who seems to enjoy sex as much as he does."

Elaine looked totally dragged by these possibilities.

"But on the other hand, what if Walt is a decent guy who really *is* attracted to you as a person and just got so freaked when you connected that he's running scared? If that's the case, who'd you rather talked sense to Walt? His 'typical macho jock' buddies or the girl who loves him?"

"Do you really think I could get him to come back to me?" Elaine asked doubtfully.

"Yo, I didn't say that! First of all, don't think of it as 'getting him to come back.' Among other things, it makes it sound as if you lost him through some fault of your own. Walt's the one who has the explaining to do here, and it's up to you to coax it out of him, gently but *firmly*."

As Elaine thought that over, I took a breather and read through my notes. This was no connect-the-dots sort of case; it was more like a nail-biting nightmare. A girl in her frazzled frame of mind was capable of all kinds of self-destructive behavior, like, for instance, hopping right back into the sack. I could've used a few hours to think this whole thing through, but I'd learned the hard way that the more dire the crisis, the more impatient the counselee. They wanted advice *right now,* or forget it!

"It sounds like you spent your limited time together gabbing about way more than just sex, and I think that's grounds for hope. You don't need me to tell you that lechy boys out for a quick score are almost always zeros on the conversation front."

"You're basically saying this cut-and-run tactic is a universal guy thing?" Elaine wondered miserably.

I shook my head. "On my honor as a peer counselor, generalizations like that are bogus. Think it over. Can you honestly say, for example, that you don't know of any girls who enjoy sex simply for its own sake or of any guys who show loyal, long-term devotion to just one girl?"

"Yeah, I guess I see what you mean," Elaine said. She looked down at the desktop and asked shyly, "Are you still a virgin, Becca?"

Elaine was a junior, and we'd had a few classes together over the years, including, currently, British lit. I liked her well enough, but up 'til now she'd been more or less just a casual acquaintance. So I assumed the sphinx-like expression I practiced in my bathroom mirror for fielding questions like this and said, "Sorry, but that's one I can't answer. It might seem like I was taking sides, and if that impression got around, it might scare even more people away from peer counseling than Jeff Gardiner's managed to."

"You and Gardiner are always nailing each other in the *Beacon*. You totally remind me of Beatrice and Benedick in *Much Ado about Nothing*," Elaine said with a smile.

I let that literary allusion sail by, glad at this point for anything that brought a smile to her face. "I can't answer your personal question, Elaine, but I'd still like to offer you my personal opinion. Three weeks seem like an awfully short prelude to lovemaking, even *with* the prospect of the prom dangling before your eager eyes. I mean, when you think of the risks you're taking—"

"But I told you we were careful!" Elaine interrupted defensively.

"Yeah, *relatively*. But remember Life Skills in ninth grade when Mr. Gerwin showed us all the ways a condom could fail?"

" 'Only abstinence is foolproof, boys and

girls,' " Elaine said, imitating his nasal baritone. We smiled at each other, but then her face fell again. "You think I'm a total sleaze, don't you?" she asked forlornly.

"Not even!" I said, taking both her hands in mine. "All I'm trying to do here is get you thinking *for the future* about protecting your bod from harm . . . starting with your heart. Believe me, Elaine, I know that urge to merge. Virgin or not, I'm just as human as the next girl—"

She finally looked up at me and smiled again. "Yeah, and it's about time! I heard through the grapevine what Peter Karona did to you. Actually, that's sort of why I felt I could come in today. Last week you still seemed like the golden girl who always had her act together, but now that you've actually been screwed over, you seem a little bit more like the rest of us."

I was shocked. "You seriously think I've always got my act together?"

Elaine shrugged. "Practically *everyone* thinks so, Becca. In fact, I'll bet Peter is the first boy who ever got the best of you."

"That's a hoot! Holy smokes, could I tell you stories—," I began, but then I checked myself as I realized I was losing my grip on the session.

"Just tell me one," Elaine pleaded. "Lord knows you can trust me now."

The girl had a point. And we didn't call it *peer* counseling for nothing. "Okay, just one." I rummaged, took a deep breath, and launched in: "The summer I turned thirteen, my family took a vacation in Kauai, and at the hotel I met this sunburned, brown-eyed boy named Lionel from Grand Island, Nebraska. He was the first guy besides my dad to tell me I was pretty, and he made a big deal about my vocab and my swim technique and even the dorky way I ate my meals one course at a time, no matter what."

I hesitated about going on, but Elaine seemed truly enthralled.

"Lionel just generally made me feel so excellent," I continued, "that I was totally willing to overlook his bizarro habits, like the way he wore his T-shirt in the pool and blew bubbles—big bubbles—with his saliva, even in the hotel dining room where the whole world could see. We kissed on Lumahai Beach, where a movie called *South Pacific* had been filmed, and it was so incredibly romantic that I still get the chills whenever I think about it. . . . I even let Lionel put his hand up my top a few times, which felt pretty nice."

Elaine sighed and nodded.

"He got all pouty and quiet, though, whenever I made him stop."

"God, that's so typical!" Elaine said.

"Isn't it, though?"

I was really getting off on the hopelessly naive romance of the tale by this point and actually started to tear up a little. "Lionel and I had this solemn ceremony where we swapped addresses in the moonlight on our last enchanted evening together and vowed eternal devotion to one another. . . . I really *believed* in him—and in us—you know?"

Elaine assured me she knew.

"So like a goof I wrote him a whole slew of letters after I got back to southern California—"

"—and he never wrote back," Elaine concluded sympathetically as she handed me a tissue.

"Not even once." I dabbed at my eyes.

Elaine smiled at me as if she'd just discovered an old friend. "I'll bet you've had your prom dress picked out for months."

"Six," I said, nodding. "You?"

"A year."

We shared a laugh and then talked eagerly about prom stuff for a while, until my next counselee knocked at the door and reminded me of where I was. Embarrassed, I apologized and said, "We'll have this wrapped in just a few."

Elaine got all panicky then and said, "Shoot, Becca, I still have a ton of stuff to ask you! Like what do I say when I talk to Walt?"

I smiled inside. Their meeting was now a given. "First off, let Walt know you're still interested. In him, I mean, not sex." I pondered for a bit and then started to run down a list of his possible motives for bailing on her: "He may've been insecure about his performance; he may've dumped you as a preemptive strike against rejection; he may've decided after the fact that things went too far too fast; or he may think you hate him for 'taking' your virginity, since some guys are still brainwashed to think that way. Whatever the deal is, let Walt know there aren't any hard feelings. And assure him you aren't picking out china patterns—or even trying to find a college you can attend together."

Elaine grinned.

"If he's receptive, ease back into things. Do safe, casual, fun stuff like going out to the movies with a big group of buds. By all means, if he's willing, go to the prom and have a total blast, but pass on the hotel-room scene afterward. And for sure steer clear of those seductive sycamores."

Elaine giggled and then blushed a little. "But what if he isn't receptive?"

"Then you've probably been had, babe, and you'd best cut your losses and move on. Whatever happens, don't let the dude talk you into having sex again as a way of 'making up.' If he takes that line, he's a wolf and good riddance to him. You deserve better. Every girl does."

"Damn, you don't play softball around here, do you?" Elaine said wryly as she slung her backpack over her shoulder and stood up to leave.

I shook my head. "After you've talked to a pregnant sixteen-year-old girl who thought for sure a virgin couldn't make a baby, or you've tried to comfort a seventeen-year-old guy who's in tears over his new STD, 'softball' kind of loses its appeal."

Elaine nodded soberly and then surprised me with a good-bye hug. The gesture left me glowing.

I wished that Becca Singleton, the peer counselor, had been around late last summer at Catalina Island before Becca Singleton, the idiot, decided—after tossing back one too many wine coolers on a moonlit, grassy hillside near a clump of Saint Catherine's lace—to give up her virginity to a slow-handed, sweet-talking eighteen-year-old lifeguard she knew she'd never see again.

Fortunately, I didn't go in for Russian roulette anymore.

Chapter 5

THOUGH HE WASN'T physically there, Jeff Gardiner was very much a presence at the PCN's regular Wednesday afternoon staff meeting.

"Can't anyone force him to stop these attacks? Like the principal?" Ward Yip, a ninth-grade counselor, asked. Ward, who loved number-crunching, had calculated that over the past three days, male patronage of the network was down by about twenty-five percent from the previous week. Female patronage, by contrast, had only declined by about five percent, which was "just on the margin of statistical significance."

"You mean run crying to the administration and play right into the hands of Mr. First Amendment? No way, Ward-o," said Kenyatta Howland, a sophomore counselor. "Let's just go on about our business and pay the paper tiger no mind. The boys'll come back to us eventually, just like before."

"Yeah, but by the time Becca writes her rebuttal and we're back up to speed again, the prom will've passed and the school year will be practically over," Eric Taschner, a senior counselor, pointed out.

"That's exactly what I'm afraid of," I said. "And as you all well know, guys carry just as much baggage about the prom as girls do. The problem is, the *Beacon* only comes out once a month, and I can't see any way around that—"

"Drop in on the J-man," Zoner interrupted.

Everyone looked confused except for Kayla, who nodded and said, "Shoulder hop 'im." Kayla had been standoffish around Zoner since Monday, but at the moment they seemed fully tuned.

"There they go with that surf jive again—," Kenyatta began.

"Translation for the rest of us, please?" Vickie Coolidge, another senior counselor, asked Zoner.

"In most cases," Zoner explained, "it sucks in the extreme to cut in on another surfer when he's already caught a wave. The only exception is—"

"Kooks," Kayla interrupted. "Wave swine."

"Barrel hogs," I said with a smile as I gradually caught on. "But what move do I employ here? A carve? An aerial? A floater?"

"It doesn't matter, just so long as you *show no fear,* Becca," Zoner said, sounding very much like my surfing tutor of three summers ago. "The bottom line is, you don't need Jeff's say-so to get your message across."

"*Now* I'm with you!" Kenyatta said, her caramel-brown face lighting up in a smile. "Let's get the rebuttal out using a different forum. Hell, Zoner, why couldn't you just say that straight-out?"

"Life isn't linear, Kenyatta; it's a *wave* phenomenon," Zoner explained with a grin that only surfers know.

Kenyatta laughed and shook her head.

"How 'bout we do it by posting flyers?" Kayla suggested. "After all, that's how we drummed up business for the network in the first place."

"Of course," I said, getting all excited. "And we plaster the campus with 'em. Especially the hallway near the journalism classroom!"

"Why didn't we think of this before?" Ward wondered.

"I know why," Kayla said, looking directly at Zoner. "Sometimes people get stuck in a trough so deep, *they can't even see what's right in front of their faces.*"

Zoner turned to me. "Kayla's right. You still think too much like a *Beacon* reporter."

Kayla slumped down in her chair. I was kinda worried about her. As if school, counseling, and (above all) the Zoner thing weren't enough, Kayla's mom needed extra help at the family bakery over the next few weeks to replace a vacationing worker. Starting Monday, then, Kayla'd been getting up at five in the morning. When I offered to give her a break a morning or two a week, like I had during the Christmas season, she turned me down cold. Very un-Kaylalike. As I feared, her crush had put our gleesome threesome under siege, and I hadn't a clue what to do about it.

After the group talked over a few hard cases, Zoner, as PCN secretary, took note of referrals made to the regular counseling office during the previous week. "A pregnancy, two suicidals, and a severe drug-abuse case," he reported grimly.

"Those referrals are more important than ever, people," Mr. Gordon, our faculty advisor, said. He wore a crumpled gray derby, a pewter vest over a white Lakers T-shirt, baggy wool dress pants, and a pair of high-top sneakers. This was typical apparel for him; he was a genuine individual. In addition to being a guidance counselor, he taught two psychology classes each term. He liked to joke that "teaching abnormal psych to high school students is like teaching sex to rabbits."

Mr. Gordon always kept a low profile at PCN meetings, so when he spoke up, everybody paid close attention. "Mr. Crampton has been raising a stink at board meetings again about how peer counseling could put the district at risk for liability lawsuits if something went wrong and a parent or student decided to blame one of you. Much as I hate to say it, he does have a point. You've got to be cautious in there. On the other hand, he's also concerned that you may be dispensing advice which encourages, as he puts it, 'rampant sexual promiscuity.' "

Everyone laughed, and then I said, "Mr. Crampton doesn't get it. A lot of our counselees won't talk sex to adults *at all*. Are we supposed to just turn them away?"

"Look on the bright side, Becca. If they take sex off our agenda, you can totally do away with guy counselors," Zoner joked, and everyone laughed again.

Mr. Gordon smiled and said, "You know I fully sympathize here, folks. And as far as I'm concerned, except for abortion-related issues, you can talk sex until the trailer windows steam up, if that's what your counselees need. But be aware that Crampton has started a group called Parents for Total Teen Abstinence, and it's garnering a surprising amount of support in this supposedly laid-back community."

"Parents for Total Teen Abstinence? I don't like the sound of that at all," said Eric Taschner.

"I don't object to the name, per se," I said with a shrug. "After all, if we students have the right to form advocacy groups, it seems only fair to let parents in on the action." Several counselors laughed, but not Eric.

"Only abstinence is foolproof," Herlinda Duarte, a sophomore counselor, shyly but dutifully reminded him.

"And only dweebs quote sex ed teachers," Eric shot back. "I'm not gonna let you or anyone else shove their moral and religious baggage through *my* bedroom door—"

"Hey, *hey!*" I interjected. "Cool your jets, Eric. We're all on the same side here. Sex is a hot topic, for sure, but we've got to try to keep our perspectives, especially with each other."

Eric made a visible effort to calm himself, and then he grudgingly apologized to Herlinda.

Mr. Gordon watched this exchange with obvious discomfort and then gave me a See-what-I-mean? look. "I know many of you are getting questions about sex on prom night," he went on, "and the administration has asked me to remind you of your duty, which you all accepted at the get-go, to warn of the considerable risks and responsibilities involved." He looked directly at Eric. "No matter what, you've got to remember that when you're in that trailer, you're a peer counselor and not an individual advocate for *any* given political or social agenda. If you harbor contempt for the pamphlets you're supposed to hand out when sex comes up, your counselees are going to sense it. We can't afford to be sending mixed messages here. The stakes are way too high." He eased up a bit then and smiled. "But this is just a return to basic training for all you grizzly vets. We all see eye to eye on this, don't we?"

Most of the counselors nodded, but Eric didn't, and he refused to meet Mr. Gordon's conciliatory gaze.

"Are you okay with that, too, Eric?" I gently prompted him. Eric had a short fuse, but he was also an effective counselor, and as a varsity basketball player, he made the PCN "cool" for a lot of other athletes.

"Do you have any idea how many students at this school are sexually active?" Eric asked irritably as he finally looked up at Mr. Gordon.

Mr. Gordon glared back at him, folded his arms across his chest, and looked like he was shifting into heavy-duty lecture mode again.

But then Kenyatta arched an eyebrow and asked Eric, "Taken a bedroom-to-bedroom scientific survey, have you?"

An awkward silence followed, and then after we'd had a few secs to draw a mental picture of that survey-taking process, everyone started to laugh, including Eric and Mr. Gordon. I gave Kenyatta a thumbs-up for finessing away the tension and she beamed.

The meeting was running long by this point, so after rushing through a few remaining procedurals, I wrapped up with the usual reminder to "stay upbeat, listen hard, and don't be afraid to fail." After adjourning I made a point of giving both Eric and Herlinda a reassuring hug and telling each of them how much they meant to the PCN.

Later that night, though, as I was sitting at my computer sweating through the fourth draft of my rebuttal to Jeff's column, Eric phoned in his resignation.

"Having me argue for no sex on prom night," he said, "would be a total, hypocritical sham. There's no way *I'm* abstaining."

I tried for nearly an hour to change his mind about resigning, to persuade him that he had this pegged all wrong. "This isn't a simple case of 'practice what you preach,' Eric," I reassured him in about ten different ways. "If a counselee *brings up* the subject of sex on prom night, Mr. Gordon just wants you to convey that abstinence is the only totally safe option. That's the straight scoop, so no big deal, right?"

There was a long, staticky pause.

"Look, Becca, you've talked my ear off enough for one night," Eric finally said, his voice openly hostile now. "I turned eighteen last month. I'm an adult now. I'm going to *college* in the fall. Do you really expect me to keep pretending that sex is some big deal?"

That's when I had to give in and accept his resignation.

∽

I went to an all-night copy place to print out the flyers and then got Zoner and a few other counselors to come in super early the next morning to help tape and staple 'em up. In the intro to my rebuttal, I hit on a lot of the same points I'd covered with Jeff in our "tennis match" last Friday, as well as some new stuff:

The PCN doesn't exist to assign blame to third parties, as some would have you think. And we know we can't change the fact that this is a messed-up, unfair, and ever-changing world. In reality our main goal is a simple one: to arm you with better coping skills.

What about the stigma of "therapy"? All too often when a person faces a brutal emotional crisis, he is trashed and told scornfully, "Just deal with it; it's all in your head." To show how bogus this kind of reasoning is, imagine for a sec that the same person has just broken his wrist. What would you think of the bystander who approached the agonized victim with the glib advice, "Just deal with it; it's all in your arm?"

So please remember: talking to us in times of need doesn't mean you're "weak." On the contrary, it just means you're *human.* And happily, so are your peer counselors!

"This rebuttal cranks, Becca," Zoner told me as we posted a few copies on the bulletin board near the entrance to the junior/senior cafeteria. It was just after 6:30 A.M.; the air was cool, the campus was quiet except for the singing of the birds in a nearby oak tree, and the sky was a sort of misty blue. I loved this time of day.

"Thanks, bud," I said gratefully. "You and Kayla really inspired me. And I appreciate your giving up a dawn patrol session to be here for the network."

He shrugged off my thanks with a grin. But after we finished with the board, he turned to me with a look of concern and said, "Becca, are you getting weird vibes from Kayla these days? 'Cause I know I am."

Here it was. The question I'd been dreading. I put on my poker face and said casually, "It's probably just the prom workin' her nerves, you know?"

But Zoner's aquamarine eyes pierced right through my flimsy mask, and he said, "You were verging on a closeout there, Becca, but then you flinched. C'mon, this is the Zoneman you're talking to. Clue me in."

The surfer in me knew that I was riding the lip here, and the slightest mistake could get me pitched over the falls headfirst. I couldn't lie to Zoner, and part of me wanted super badly to help Kayla, but if I told him the flat-out truth and he freaked, our trio could be toast. So I finally said, "She's gone sweet on a guy and wants to go to the prom with him. But he doesn't know it yet, and she's hoping that he'll figure it out on his own." The truth, abridged. The best possible call, I figured, given the dicey circumstances.

"Who's the dude?" Zoner asked.

I tried to read his eyes and thought they betrayed either dread or disappointment. Either way, I was sure he'd caught on, and he wasn't happy about it. (So why was he trying to make me spell it out?!)

"Wait, don't answer that!" he said suddenly, letting me off the hook like the gentledude he was. "When Kayla wants me to know details, she'll hip me to them herself."

Killer-smooth roundhouse cutback, Zoner!

We shared a look of relief and then powershifted to other safer topics as we walked over to the English building in the direction of the journalism classroom. Still, I had to wonder about my next move. Would it be wise to tell Kayla about this nebulous exchange with Zoner or not? I didn't relish the prospect of being the bearer of bad tidings, for sure, but I also didn't want her to go on clinging to what were clearly false hopes.

I felt like I was caught in a riptide off a deserted beach, with no help in sight.

Chapter 6

JEFF GARDINER was already at work in the journalism classroom when we arrived. The room was deserted except for him, and for me it brought back happy memories of early mornings last year, when every so often he and I would pull up news stories on the Internet and play at solving the world's problems.

I was always amazed at how well we got along when there was no one else watching.

"Damn," he said with a half-smile as he smoothed back his platinum blond hair, "when am I gonna learn to keep that door locked? Yesterday morning it was two masked kindergartners with water pistols, demanding my lunch money." He stood up to greet Zoner with an enthusiastic high five. "Can't I wring another surf story out of you, Zoneman? The reading public cries for more! Who can ever forget phrases like 'premium quality shore-pound' or your epic narrative of 'Squirmin' Herman' O'Brien's ride to glory in that 'freak southern hemi tube' that carried him halfway to Laguna Beach?"

"Ease up on the hype, J-man. You embarrass me," Zoner said with a shy grin. He was actually blushing through his tan.

All Jeff's faults aside, when he hosed you with his charm, you felt like a million. He eyed the flyer in my hand a bit uneasily and then asked Zoner, "Whatever happened to Herman, anyway?"

"It turns out that somebody actually caught his miracle carve on video, and the redoubtable Squirmer is now endorsing boards and wowing hoards from Australia to Zuma. And don't josh me, dude. You know why I had to bail on the journalism scene."

"Yeah, yeah, no free time left after peer counseling," Jeff said, his smile waning. "Such a waste."

"Why not do two of your favorite

ex-scribes a little favor," I said, handing Jeff the flyer, "and try reading this piece with an open mind?"

He seized it and read it through with his usual thoroughness and intensity. When he was finished, he gestured at me with the flyer and said, "Not bad. I especially like the broken wrist analogy. But are you implying here that I'm inhuman just because I won't patronize the PCN?"

"Why?" I asked, cheerfully following his logic. "Are you currently in need of help with a personal problem?"

To my surprise his eyes flashed with pain, but he shook his head. "Get real."

Alarmed, I took a step toward him and put my hand on his arm. "Jeff?" I half-whispered, "Is something really wrong?"

He stared at me for a sec, but when he glanced down at my hand, I remembered myself and quickly withdrew it. He abruptly turned away from me and shoved the flyer into the IN box at his computer station. "I'll print this," he said, his voice sounding a bit husky.

"You misread us, J-man," Zoner told him. "We've already put up a hundred copies schoolwide, in places where they'll get max exposure."

Jeff turned back around and said to me, "That's gonna seem a little desperate, don't you think?"

I hadn't thought of it in quite that way and doing so took some of the wind out of my sails, but only for a moment. "That's a risk we're more than willing to take," I said, "considering the high stakes involved."

Jeff grunted. "Yes, God forbid there should be any self-reliant teenagers running loose on this campus." He sounded all too much like his usual contrary self again, and I didn't like it one bit.

"Don't you get it even now?! We want to help people to *become* more self-reliant!" I said, getting angry even though I'd promised myself I wouldn't. "Where'd this idiotic attitude come from? Did you watch too many westerns and action-adventure flicks as a kid and buy into that stupid, megamacho, strong-and-silent-type myth? That's Hollywood, Jeff, not real life!"

"Don't lecture to *me* about reality, Rebecca!" he thundered as he pulled the flyer back out of the IN box, wadded it up, and angrily tossed it into a trash can nearby. He then moved up so close to me that we were practically nose to nose and said, "You don't know a damn thing about my life outside of this school. You haven't a clue!"

My heart was pounding fast now, and it wasn't just from anger. His breath smelled pleasantly of mint toothpaste and his eyes were dazzlingly, intoxicatingly blue, like the ocean on a bright, cloudless day. I had this insane urge to kiss him, but then I remembered Darla. "I don't pretend to know what makes you wig out over the PCN," I said as I took a firm step backward. "And it's true that in all the time I've known you, you've practically never opened up to me about your personal life. But I'm ready to listen now." I'd reclaimed my space; I had the upper hand on the situation again. Now if my heart would just get wise—

"You want me to spill my guts, do you?" Jeff said with a scornful laugh. He turned to Zoner and said, "C'mon, bud, 'fess up. Aren't Becca and most of your fellow counselors just glorified busybodies?"

Zoner tugged thoughtfully on his outrigger canoe earring. "I've never actually seen you two go at each other before," he said. "Kayla's right. There's a definite buzz here."

Jeff and I both started jumping on his case for saying such an outrageous thing, but Zoner just grinned and said, "Methinks you dudes protest too much."

The door flew open wide, Eddie Ballard breezed in, and we all clammed up.

"Back already, Becca?" Eddie asked with a smile. "I thought you drew enough blood last Friday to fatten you up for a month." This was vintage Ballard; he managed to insult you even with his compliments. His gold T-shirt read: IF YOU HAVE TO ASK, YOU CAN'T AFFORD ME. He eyed Zoner uncertainly and then raised his hand in a peace sign and said, "Cowabunga."

Zoner turned to me and asked, "What's he saying? Is that French?"

I laughed and shook my head. Between the obnoxious T-shirt and the way he treated me last Friday, Eddie was fair game for garden-variety teasing. "It's a corruption of *cowadunga*," I explained, "from the Latin *cowadungus horribilis*. In other words, he's telling you you're full of—"

"That's not what I meant!" Eddie protested.

"Etymology—," Zoner began.

"Rules!" I said as we exchanged a high five.

"What's up, Eddie?" Jeff asked as he bit back a smile. "I know you didn't show up this early just to get dumped on."

Zoner and I laughed with surprise, and then Zoner gave Jeff a high five, too.

"It's about the school board meeting you asked me to cover last night," Eddie said, watching us all a bit warily. "It was rather more exciting than usual."

"How so?" Jeff said, sitting down on a desktop and giving Eddie his full attention now.

"Bernard Crampton got hold of the *Party Hearty but Wisely* pamphlet that the prom committee approved for distribution on prom night, and he got quite worked up about it."

"That sounds most alarming," Zoner said, and I elbowed him in the ribs to make him behave. I needed to hear this.

"Crampton thinks the whole Don't Drink and Drive campaign is seen by a lot of teens as an implied *endorsement* of alcohol consumption," Eddie went on. "He didn't get too far with that argument, though, because Cathy Irwin is a member of Mothers Against Drunk Driving, and she buried him in statistics. So then he blasted away at the—and I'm quoting here—'reckless promotion of contraceptives in support of the false and deadly notion of safe sex.' "

"That blows!" I said. "The prom pamphlet was adapted from the one we use at the PCN. Abstinence gets top billing."

Eddie shook his head. "Some reps from PTTA, that's Parents for Total Teen Abstinence, got up to speak, and they said that the pamphlet made it seem as if, quote, 'our kids are *expected* to have sex on prom night.' "

"That logic is hurtin' for certain," Zoner said with disgust. "Are we supposed to believe that if we stop talking about teen sex, it'll die of loneliness? *Not!*"

"How'd things turn out?" Jeff asked. He was furiously scribbling down notes on a yellow legal pad.

Eddie checked his own notes and said, "Crampton's motion to kill the pamphlet failed to carry at first, but the board later reversed itself and, quote, 'agreed to study the matter further' after a lawyer-member of

PTTA got all huffy and insisted, quote, 'abstinence was not given its proper due.' "

"Meaning what?" Jeff wondered.

"There's a district-wide ordinance based on state law," I explained, remembering my PCN training, "requiring all schools to inform students: 'in any forum in which sex-related issues are discussed, that, where intercourse is concerned, abstinence is the *only* entirely safe option.' But the pamphlet does that already, so I still don't see what the big deal is—"

"There's a hidden agenda," Eddie said, one eyebrow arched. "I got the scoop in an interview with Crampton after the meeting."

"Outstanding," Jeff said, slapping his hand down on the desktop. I was impressed, too. Crampton was quite the formidable presence and not easily approached, even by the adult media.

"I was bred to excellence," Eddie exulted, proving once again to be his own worst enemy.

Zoner neighed softly, like a horse. I didn't elbow him this time.

"Crampton's game plan," Eddie went on after a chilly glance at Zoner, "is to get the board to take a strict constructionist stand on the ordinance—that is, to delete references to all options *except* abstinence."

"No way! They'll never go for it," I said confidently. "That'd be a total curb on free speech, and Crampton's already lost that battle once."

"That's just what I was thinking," Jeff said.

"I'm glad," I told him. "I just wish you'd apply the principle more broadly yourself."

Jeff, who never could seem to admit he was wrong or sorry, turned back to Eddie and said, "Good work. This could be very big. I'll go with you to the next board meeting and—"

"Making more plans without telling me, are you, Jeff?" Darla Swanson said testily as she came in the door. I instantly moved several feet farther away from her boyfriend. We all exchanged good mornings and then Darla said, "I just read your flyer and liked it a lot, Becca." She was looking more at Jeff than me, though. "Maybe I'll make an appointment sometime. I'm just loaded with issues these days."

Jeff said to Darla, in an almost pleading way, "You never called me last night."

"Waiting by the phone for a call that never

comes is not a pleasant way to spend your evening, is it, darlin'?" Darla asked sharply as she
whipped her long, shimmering dark brown
hair over her shoulder.

Wow, I thought, *what goes on here?*

"Time to bail; duty calls," Zoner said, taking me by the arm and guiding my reluctant
self out of the classroom.

Eddie followed us out into the hallway and
took me aside for a moment. "Do you think
Jeff is really proud of me?" he asked with
touching eagerness.

"Yes," I said, "and I am too, Eddie. You
showed a lot of initiative."

"Thanks," he said, ambushing me with a
hug and resting his head on my chest. (He
really was short.) I gingerly patted his back
and then gently but firmly pulled away. "I
didn't want to say this around Jeff," he went
on quietly, glancing around as if for spies,
"but I think Crampton really has it out for
your Peer Counseling Network. He calls it the
blind leading the blind, and he's just waiting
for one of your counselors to screw up so he
can shut you down."

"You can't please everyone," I said distract-
edly as I took a quick glance back at the open

classroom door. You could hear Darla and Jeff yelling at each other now. She was going off about *his parents getting divorced.* I hadn't a clue! That would sure explain the pained look in his eyes. I started to move back toward the classroom, hoping to learn more, when suddenly Zoner appeared in my line of sight, gave me a scowl, and quietly shut the door.

"I think they're on the ropes this time," Eddie told me with undisguised glee. "Darla's turned me down twice for the prom, but the third time might really be the charm in this case."

"I don't want to get involved in gossip," I said, grateful that Zoner was around to keep me on the straight and narrow. Left to my own devices, I'm sure I would've given into my worst instincts and pumped Eddie for more info on Jeff's personal woes.

"Yeah, I can't blame you for being down on gossip these days," Eddie said. "There's probably not a soul left at Luna High who doesn't know about Peter Karona ditching you for a babe-a-licious ninth grader."

I went slack-jawed.

"But don't give up hope," Eddie quickly reassured me. "Santa may have a prom date for you in his stocking yet. Did you wash your hair this morning, by the way? It looks kind of flat . . . unlike the rest of you."

I again removed myself for safety reasons.

As Zoner and I crossed the main quad on our way to the PCN trailer, he went off about Eddie. "I don't see why you even talk to that barracuda. He gives me bad vibes galore. He drops names, makes claims, and plays games. He's as transparent as a jellyfish and every bit as irritating. And he slams you constantly!"

"I know," I said as I fluffed out my hair. "I know. . . . It's just I see these occasional flashes of promise, and I can't help thinking that somewhere deep inside Eddie there's this decent person struggling to get out."

I was starting to feel that way about Jeff Gardiner again, too. . . . In fact, Jeff was practically all I could think about for the rest of the day.

Chapter 7

IT'D BEEN a long week, and late Friday afternoon I left school feeling pretty well whipped. I went home, had a quick dinner, filled the tub with peach-scented bath foam, lit a few candles, and settled in for a good, long soak. I thought about my prom dress, which, after I worked one more shift at the public library tomorrow and picked up my paycheck next Friday, would be mine to wear at last. This led, for no good reason that I could see, directly into yet more thoughts about Jeff Gardiner. Alarmed, I turned quickly to mundane matters and plotted out Sunday, when I planned to catch up on my

French, chem, AP U.S. history, and Brit lit homework. Then I propped my head up on my inflatable bath pillow and decided to clear my mind completely by meditating. I closed my eyes and imagined a seagull flying slowly across a calm, sparkling sea . . . coasting up and down, arcing to and fro, gently, gently. Next, starting with my toes and working up, I imagined that I was relaxing each and every muscle in my bod. . . . Soon I felt a delicious sense of peace and contentment.

My mind drifted. . . . I was at Casino Point on Catalina Island. The lights of the Los Angeles basin were winking at me from across the twenty-five-mile-wide San Pedro Channel. I was wearing my excellent prom dress. Mariah Carey was singing about love. I was in the arms of a handsome stranger in a tuxedo. It wasn't Peter or the lifeguard.

Suddenly the clock tower on the hill above us began to strike twelve. "Kiss me! I have to go back to the mainland!" I said urgently. The stranger took me in his arms and did just that. It was the kind of kiss that was so perfect, so incredibly passionate and heartfelt, it made you want to cry. It tasted pleasantly of mint toothpaste.

"No!" I shouted as I sat bolt upright in the tub. My head was all numb and cottony, and I only gradually realized that I'd overdone the relaxation thing and actually fallen asleep. As I got unsteadily out of the tub, toweled off, and then rubbed on some body lotion, I tried without much success to shake off the weak-kneed feeling of longing the dream had left me with. "Get a grip, girl," I told myself. "It's just a reaction formation." (That's a hostile feeling turned into its exact opposite.) No way it could be a wish fulfillment!

As it turned out, I didn't have much time to obsess over my dream interpretation. A new family crisis flared up later that evening when Mom came home in an extremely cranky mood from a five-hour Ripsnortin' Western Hoedown theme banquet for retired utility execs and opened Roger's third-quarter grade report.

"Roger was never Mr. Honor Roll, but Cs and Ds? Will somebody please tell me how I'm supposed to exorcise the demon that has possessed my child?" she asked with exasperation as she tossed her Stetson aside and began to yank off her gun belt.

I calmed her down with some herbal tea, a

shoulder massage, a few choice tracks from her *Mellow Hits of the '60s* CD, and a plateful of granola bars. I even managed to distract her from waking Roger up for a midnight grill by telling her, finally, about what'd happened with Peter.

"Men are always looking for someone younger!" Mom complained sympathetically. She tended to generalize a lot about men these days. "Do you know your father is dating a thirty-one-year-old now? That cradle-robbing son of a—"

"Mom," I interrupted, taking her hand and putting it against my cheek, "you promised you wouldn't slam Daddy around us."

"Did I, sweetie? I'm sorry," she said as she looked forlornly at her prizewinning coffee table, which she'd fashioned from chain-link fencing and beach trash. She turned and examined my face. "Are you eating your garbanzo beans, honey? If you want to get a prom date on such short notice, you should start by working harder on your skin tone."

"Mother!"

"You're right," she said, throwing up her hands. "Who am I to talk about skin care at the ripe old age of forty-two?" She changed the subject by asking about the PCN and brightened considerably as I brought her up to date. (Mom'd been a psych minor in college and was supportive of the idea from the start.) "That's my girl," she said, putting her arm around me and giving my shoulder a squeeze. "Never step aside for anybody."

But then she smiled in a mysterious way and added, "Of course, in my business we know that free negative advertising can be almost as good in the long run as the expensive positive kind."

"What do you mean?"

"Just think, my little psychologist, about how much attention that 'stubborn and obnoxious' Jeff Gardiner has drawn to your fledgling cause."

This insight made me super uneasy, and I decided it'd be less than wise to tell Mom about my dream.

Early the next morning I slunk furtively into my little brother's lair to try to prep him for the coming onslaught. I hadn't been allowed to venture into his room for some time, and I was temporarily paralyzed with shock at the scene that confronted me. Convoys of dirty tennis shoes navigated uneasily past islands of unwashed clothes, by way of dingy carpeted straits littered with drifting computer game cartridges and treacherous banks of balled-up Reese's Pieces wrappers. On the walls, toothy, busty, half-naked women leered at me as they posed in positions rarely seen in nature.

Yuck! Was this normal fifteen-year-old guy stuff or did it betray a deeper problem? My instincts tended toward the latter conclusion, even though Mr. Gordon had warned us peer counselors lots of times about "the perils of psychoanalyzing your own family." But how could I help it? Roger was my only sib, and naturally I wanted him to be happy and well adjusted.

I did a quick survey of the titles on his CD rack and concluded that they could be neatly arranged into precisely three categories:

1. Death
2. Sex
3. Death after Sex

There was even a teetering pile of dirty dishes on top of his desk, a molding monu-ment to countless meals eaten in sullen solitude. I was amazed (but also relieved) to find no bugs in evidence. This was apparently the rare sort of environment that even cockroaches shied away from: "No, stay out of *that* room. It could ruin your health."

Saddest of all to me, though, was the fact that his long-neglected electronic keyboard now served only as a dust storage unit.

It seemed to take forever to rouse Roger, and once awake, he was anything but grateful. "So what's the big deal? It's not like I failed anything," he pointed out as he sat up, stretched, and began the scratching thing. I moved to the corner of his bed.

"You got a D in Life Skills, Rog. That's like getting a D in *breathing*."

"I'm enrolled in Life Skills?" he asked with mild surprise as he slipped his Hard Rock Cafe jacket on. At least, I thought with some relief, he didn't actually sleep in the thing.

I continued to stare at him.

"Cut me some slack here, sis," he said. "Isn't one grade grubber in the family enough?"

"I don't grub for my grades!" I protested. "I earn them."

"*Pardonnez-moi,* Saint Rebecca. Of course you do."

I tried to picture the well-groomed, budding musician Roger'd been only two years ago, when Dad was still here in the flesh (to play occasional backup on guitar) and not in the current form of a glossy black leather jacket. "Don't you see how much this hurts Mom?" I asked, trying a different tack.

Something like remorse passed briefly across the apathetic landscape that was my brother's face. But then he jerked a pair of headphones off the nightstand, slipped them over his ears, and used a remote to switch on his stereo system. "Don't you realize how much I don't want to be a little Becca clone?" he shouted, wincing as the sound waves began to assault his eardrums.

Forgetting to grant him any of the patience and courtesy I regularly showed my counselees, I yanked the remote out of his hands, shut off the stereo, pulled off the headphones, grabbed him by the shoulders, looked him straight in the eyes, and said, "That's not what I want, Roger. Look, I *know* it's lousy that Mom has to work all the time, and I *know* it sucks not having Dad around, but I can help you deal, if you'll just *let* me!"

Once again I sensed in him a slight stirring of constructive emotion, a nascent urge to drop the "misunderstood youth" thing and get real at last. But then he drew back and said contemptuously, "My guardian angel. The great peer counselor. Everyone at Luna High thinks you're so bitchin'. But why is it, sis, if you've really got your act so together, that you'll be going to the prom without a date?"

"The *prom?!*" I automatically crossed my arms over my chest, as if all my clothes had quite suddenly fallen off. "My God, Roger, I could care less about the stupid prom right now! I only came into this dump because I'm concerned about *you,* you little—"

I put the brakes on the expletive just in time, pulled out of the skid, and took a moment to try to compose myself. "One of the main reasons you can't play the role of peer counselor with your siblings," I *now* remembered Mr. Gordon saying, "besides the obvious lack of objectivity on your part, is that they often know exactly which of your buttons to push to keep you at bay."

"I apologize for coming into your room un-invited," I said in a quivering voice as I scooted back away from him and stood up, "and I'm sorry for taking such a keen interest in your welfare. Of course you don't need me to run interference for you anymore. You're fifteen now, and you can face Mom—and any other challenge, for that matter—totally on your own."

Roger eyed me uncertainly.

I staggered back up the stairs to my own bedroom and cried buckets over that brutal crack about the prom.

I'd barely regained my emotional balance when Peter and Cindy came by the Luna Point Public Library, where I was doing my thing as a reference aide and book stacker. They pretended to browse at mags and even looked up a few titles on the computer, but I wasn't fooled. I was sure that Cindy, at least, had come by for one purpose and one purpose only: to stick the knife called rejection into my back and twist, twist, *twist*.

I was on to their game, though, and refused

to be a victim. I remembered Kayla and Zoner's advice and smiled brightly whenever either of them happened to look my way. It actually seemed to make them squirm a bit, *especially* Cindy, which was great (although it didn't seem to be triggering any of those "happy" brain chemicals for me). I kept myself busy reshelving books in the how-to section (which just by coincidence afforded an excellent view of virtually the entire library). I paid absolutely no attention whatsoever to Cindy's tan, slender legs. *How to Get Rid of Unwanted Cellulite.* Or to the too-tight rose pink short-shorts that hugged her perfect little butt. *How to Get a Divorce in California—for Less.* Or to the way Cindy spoke in phony dulcet tones and giggled oh-so-softly at practically everything Peter said. *How to Learn Karate at Home.*

In fact, I eventually lost myself totally in the hypnotic monotony of my brain-numbing work, until—

"Hey, Becca, how are things?"

(Peter's voice. He's right behind me!)

(Betray no emotion. Be strong.)

"Just dandy," I said with elaborate politeness as I turned around to face him. "After all, nobody's betrayed my trust for an entire week."

(Damn. Forgot to play it cool.)

Peter's roly-poly face lost a bit of its color, and he said, "I was hoping we could still be friends."

That one was right up there with "I just got caught up in the moment." I'd given two months of my life to a guy who spouted more clichés than a politician on a campaign trail. "Why not. We're still in chorus together," I said agreeably.

"But you've moved all the way to the front of the soprano section," he complained, "which means I can't talk to you anymore. And the other girls aren't nearly as interesting—"

"Don't dis my choirmates, bud," I said, losing the smile completely.

"Okay, sorry," he said, putting his hands up in a gesture of appeasement. "I'm actually here with some good news. Eddie Ballard's thinking of asking you to the prom!"

"This you call good news?"

"Well, yeah," he said, looking a bit flustered by my less-than-ecstatic response. "I know Eddie can be a little abrasive at times, but he speaks *very* highly of you, and I couldn't stand the thought of you going to the prom alone on account of our little misunderstanding—"

"You mean our misunderstanding who stands about five feet two inches and weighs around a hundred pounds?" I said dryly. "How do you know about Eddie's prom plans, anyway? I don't recall that you two were exactly big-time buds."

Peter nodded. "True enough. But Sergio Hernandez threw one of his famous fiestas down at the beach last night. Eddie got kinda wasted, as usual, and before Serge finally gave him the ol' boot, Eddie got to bragging about his prom list."

"Prom list?" (ALL HANDS ON DECK! INSENSITIVE MALE SIGHTED OFF THE STARBOARD QUARTER!)

"Yeah," Peter said with a big smile, "a list of his top ten choices for prom dates. I'll tell ya, that guy has guts, carrying on the way he does. Anyway, the first seven girls turned him down 'cause they'd already committed. That's what they told him, anyway. And so after he hits up number one for the third and last time, he . . ."

(ALL HANDS TO BATTLE STATIONS! THIS IS NOT A DRILL!)

Peter paused for a moment. "Is there something wrong? Why are the corners of your mouth twitching that way?"

"If you have to ask," I said through clenched teeth as I pulled an appropriate title off the shelf, "I can't explain it."

Peter shrugged and went blithely onward. "So the way I figure it, Eddie'll be approaching you soon," he said with an encouraging smile, "because you're number—"

(FIRE ONE!)

As I began to take a swing at Peter with the hardcover book *What Men Should Know about Women,* he took a step backward, tripped on his own shoelace, and fell to the floor.

The next few minutes were sort of a blur. Cindy, who'd heard Peter fall, came running over from another part of the library, screamed, showered him with kisses, and then, with my shamefaced assistance, helped him to a chair.

Ms. Lopez, the reference librarian, rushed over and asked if Peter needed medical attention.

"No, no, I'll be okay," he insisted.

"Rebecca," Ms. Lopez said sternly, "what happened here?"

I opened my mouth to speak, but no words came forth. After all, what could I say? I knew perfectly well it was totally against library policy to try to club a patron with a book. (And I also knew that I'd watched *way* too many navy war movies as a kid, although doing so'd allowed me to spend major quality time with my dad.)

"I, uh, tripped—and fell," Peter finally said as he carefully avoided looking at me.

I know it's irrational, but I hated him even more for being so gracious about it.

Cindy leaped into his lap and got all cooey and clingy.

The sleaze.

"Tripped over *what,* young man?!" Ms. Lopez asked, more alarmed than ever. Her eyes quickly scanned the area where Peter'd fallen and apparently detected no obstructions. Then she turned around for just an instant to glance at the library entrance, no doubt expecting an army of attorneys to come streaming in at any moment.

"My shoelace," he said sheepishly as Ms. Lopez turned back to face him.

Ms. Lopez's features relaxed at once, and she expertly shifted gears into a quick, informative minilecture about shoelace safety. Before she could take questions, though, she was called back to her desk. It was just as well, because as far as I could tell, Peter and Cindy'd tuned Ms. Lopez out long ago as they lapsed into the notorious teen-couple-oblivious-to-the-existence-of-all-other-life-on-earth mode.

"Is my Pedew Wabbit all beddew?" Cindy asked in a singsongy, childlike voice as she continued to plant kisses on his head.

"Yeth, Thumperkins," he replied in a similar sort of voice. Then they twitched their noses at each other and shared a kiss on the lips.

Deliver me, Lord! I'd been planning to apologize to Peter, really I had, but witnessing this depressingly intimate and unself-conscious exchange had totally robbed me of the impulse.

Peter'd never called *me* by a pet name.

Peter'd never kissed *me* in a public place.

"I'm glad you're okay, Peter," I finally forced myself to mutter.

He turned reluctantly away from "Thumperkins," gave me a sharp, mistrustful look, and said, "Yeah, it's a good thing you're always around when I fall."

"C'mon, let's ditch this place," Cindy said as she glared at me and put a possessive arm around her boyfriend. "It's just full of creepy hazards today."

"Out of the frying pan, Cindy dear," I said as I looked directly at Peter, "and into the fire."

Cindy didn't seem to get it, but I knew she eventually would, one way or another.

Chapter 8

KAYLA SURPRISED ME when she came by near the end of my shift at the library and asked me if I wanted to go surfing. I actually preferred to carve in the early morning, before the afternoon onshore breeze began to howl, but after my sorry showing last Sunday, I figured I needed all the water time I could snag. Besides, we'd gone all week without a single good talk, and I was missing her intensely.

I had only two boards in my quiver, and I picked the longer, heavier one (seven feet four inches), dubbed Moby Dick for its girth and off-white color, because I was still feeling rusty and unsure of myself. When I caught up with Kayla at her house, though, she surprised me again by introducing her brand-new neon rainbow-colored stick, a six-foot ultralight missile that was ready to soar. Kayla stands just over five feet herself (not counting the inches added by her Pebbles Flintstone 'do), and she has powerful legs, but I still thought this was a bold investment.

"What goes on?" I asked after we had the boards secured to her roof rack and were motoring to the beach. "Won't this bust your prom budget?"

"I've decided to make my own dress," Kayla said with a mysterious smile. "I think it's great you're going the expensive lace/puffed sleeves/brocade route, Becca, but for me, this board is a better investment over the long haul."

As we shed our street clothes and waxed up our sticks on the beach, I complimented Kayla on her new black bikini and then told her about Peter's visit to the library and why I ended up trying to deck him. "Imagine what my counselees'd think if they found out how I handled *that* particular confrontation," I said guiltily.

"Give yourself a break. Once we start

expecting perfection of ourselves just because we're peer counselors, it's time to throw in the towel," she said. While we were both bending over to strap on our ankle leashes, she added, "Besides, your counselees think you're pretty hot. Just yesterday in my Spanish class, Adriana Fernandez was singing your praises for advising her on how to find out if her guy friend Omri might be ready for a more serious relationship. Seems he's rather keen on the idea. Could be a prom date in their future."

"Hey, Kayla, I'm really sorry—," I began as I stood back up and straightened out my gold-colored one-piece (I'd found out the hard way that when I'm in the surf, a bikini top and I are soon parted).

"Don't sweat it," she said as she picked up her board and flashed me a reassuring smile. "You hipped me to your stance on the Zoner issue already, and I totally respect it. Besides, I'm beginning to think I've got this wired all on my own."

As we started down for the water, I heard a familiar voice yell out teasingly, "Hey, I didn't know chicks could surf! I thought they only sat on the beach and watched!"

It was the Zoneman himself, already out in

the lineup. "Did you know he was down here?" I asked Kayla. It wasn't a trivial question, 'cause he frequented a whole range of breaks between Trestles and Seal Beach, especially on weekends.

"Can chicks surf?" she replied in an aggro tone as she charged the white water, slipped onto her new board, and began to paddle out.

The waves were breaking two to four with decent shape, and while the westerly was a presence, it was certainly no blowout. The ocean sparkled; the crowd was casual. I was still shaky in the clutch, but I wasn't wiping out nearly as much as last weekend. I was remembering how to ride the waves, instead of letting them ride me. And as luck would have it, I got one four-footer all to myself. I caught the slot, crouched low, and let my instincts take over. For the first time in months my mind was truly freed of static, and I remembered why I got into surfing in the first place. It wasn't just because it was the sport of choice for Nobel Prize winners like Donald Cram and Kary Mullis—surfing had *soul*. Totally pumped up with confidence, I carved my way up to the lip, slammed it, did my one tail slide of the day, and cut back down to the trough again. I could hear other surfers, especially Zoner and Kayla, hooting their encouragement. And then I lost control of the wave and ate it. It was a routine wipeout, though; I took some water up the nose, went with the flow, and came up laughing and happy. Wipeouts, like long waits between ridable sets, come with the territory for everyone who surfs, be they grommet or world champ. The sport is nicely humbling and democratic that way.

Kayla, though, was doing an impressive job of keeping her wipeouts to a relative minimum. She'd always been what Zoner called a natural talent, but I'd never seen her go for broke like this before. She ripped, she shredded, she slashed. She did tail slides, she did aerials, she slammed into overdrive and paaaartied! It was quite the riveting spectacle.

"You were awesome out there today, Kayla!" Zoner enthused when we all returned to the beach more than an hour later. He examined her board and said, "This is a fine design, but there's more to the rad moves you pulled off this afternoon than any new stick can account for. What gives?"

Kayla gave him the same mysterious smile

she'd flashed at me earlier and said, " 'Natural talent,' remember?" He watched her with more than casual interest as she toweled off, and he laughed like a little boy when she shook her wet reddish blond mop at him. He swallowed hard, though, when he noticed I was watching him. Did he feel put on the spot by her flirting, or was he enjoying it? I couldn't totally tell, but I figured if he *did* have the hots for her, he'd've told me on Thursday morning.

"Word's out there's a storm off Baja, which means we could have a killer swell coming in early next week," Zoner said. "You girls interested?"

We both were.

"You'll want to play it cautious in the big waves, though, Kayla," he said with concern. "The risks are way higher."

"No fear," she said playfully as she cast her towel aside, thrust her chest out, put her hands on her hips, and struck a defiant pose.

Zoner swallowed hard again. Twice.

Just then Barney "Barn Burner" Manaba came thundering up the beach from the water, hefting his surfboard under one of his enormous arms as if it were nothing more than an oversize clipboard. After greeting us girls and congratulating Kayla on her "epic session," he said to Zoner, "Look, brah, Sabrina needs to know pronto if you're gonna take her cousin Brandi to the prom or not. Brandi's losing her patience; it's not like she's hard up for a date."

Zoner grinned sheepishly at us, punched Barney on the shoulder, and said, "This is neither the time nor the place, dude. I'll buzz ya later."

"You better," Barney said. Then he winked at me and thundered up the beach toward the parking lot. What was the wink for?

"I was only hipped to Brandi's interest in me last week," Zoner explained without our needing to ask, "and I was too embarrassed to tell you guys about it. Truth be told, I've had yet another prom invite since then. With all the good vibes coming my way, I'm starting to think that spending Saturday night in the grand ballroom of the Luna Point Sheraton wouldn't be such a gruesome ordeal after all."

So he was already considering not one but *two* prom invites! Poor Kayla would just have to face facts. The dude was obviously not interested in her as anything more than a—

"Good for you," Kayla said, walking over to Zoner and giving him a hug. "But don't let yourself get pressured into making a choice you'll regret later. Most dances you'll forget, but word is, prom memories can last a lifetime. C'mon, Becca," she said, turning back to me. "Let's go, get changed, and have dinner at the mall. My treat. I'd invite Zoner along, too, but he has to speed home and make an important phone call."

As I picked up my backpack and my board, Zoner gave me a questioning look. I shrugged and gave him a tentative thumbs-up. Who'd've thought Kayla would take this so well?

∼

The Luna Point Mall had your basic food court: shiny tile floor, two illuminated fountains, a sea of white wrought-iron tables with matching chairs, a glass ceiling highlighted around the edges by swirling red, green, blue, and yellow neon tubes. It featured about a dozen fast-food outlets, offering the fresh, the fried, the filleted, and the floundering. Lots of dessert options, too, but for me there was only the frozen yogurt stand. I was especially partial to the nonfat Alpine white chocolate with—

"Becca, I know something's bothering you," Kayla said.

—with carob sprinkles, or, when they were out of that, the passion peach with fresh strawberry slices was a reasonably orgasmic substitute.

"Why do you keep saying that?" I asked irritably.

"Because you're jabbing your egg roll with a fork and stirring your chicken chow mein around. When you're upset you always tease your food instead of eating it. It's like you're testing it for character flaws."

I dropped my fork as if it'd betrayed my confidence. "Okay, Kayla, you're right. I can't for the life of me figure out how your surfing improved so much between last Sunday and today."

Kayla averted her eyes and took a humongous bite out of her tuna-pineapple-walnut-and-alfalfa-sprout sandwich from Flaky Frank's Bagel Blitz. I knew she was buying herself time to think. Once she'd swallowed, she took a long drag of her mango smoothie and then said, "I told you a little white lie because you said you didn't want to be involved."

"Involved in what?" I asked as I picked up my fork and began poking at my food again.

"Zoner, of course! I told you I had to work at the bakery for the next couple of weeks, but in fact, with my mom's okay, I've been heading up to Westport Beach every morning at five to practice my surfing. I happen to know Zoner avoids that break 'cause he got hassled badly there as a grommet. But as you saw, it's been doing wonders for me."

I was aghast. "How could you lie to me, Kayla?! I just told Peter this morning that I'd gone a whole week without someone betraying my trust, and now I find out—"

"Hey, I'm really sorry," she said, getting up from the chair across from me and moving into the one next to me. "I hadn't thought of this in terms of the Peter thing at all. But of course you can trust me, Becky. I'm your best bud." She patted my arm reassuringly and waited patiently for me to make eye contact so I could see for myself that she was being sincere.

Her manner was so caring and classically PCN that, in spite of my disappointment, I had to fight an urge to smile. "Promise me you won't do that again," I asked her. "Tell me a lie, I mean. White or not."

"Are you sure?" she asked skeptically.

I nodded.

"Okay," she said, "here goes. Your surfing stance needs major work; you stress too much over Roger; I never understood what you saw in Peter—you should've gone for Jeff Gardiner last year when you still had both the inclination *and* the opportunity—"

"Stop!" I said with a laugh, putting my hands up. "I think I get the point. . . . But you see mine, too, right?"

Kayla nodded, we exchanged a high five, and she pulled her bagel over to continue munching. I started to eat at last myself and discovered that doing so quickly chased away the dizzy headachy feeling I'd had for the last hour or so.

"Are you sorry you bought the board now, since things didn't work out the way you hoped?" I ventured to ask her a few minutes later.

"What do you mean? Things are going

great!" Kayla said brightly. "I've shown a deepening interest in something Zoner cares loads about, but I've also managed to pull back from him a bit as a friend—you know, to create some mystery."

"But what about the potential prom dates he mentioned?" I asked, amazed that she could still be so optimistic.

Kayla gave a dismissive wave. "No commitments have been made. And didn't you see the signs this afternoon? Zoner was swallowing like mad, and his pupils were dilating. He's clearly dealing with some heavy-duty emotions when I'm around."

"But what if they're not the emotions you think—," I began to say, when suddenly we were interrupted by a loud SMASH!

It came from a table over near the McDonald's. We turned and saw Chris Bowen and some other kid laughing like Beavis and Butt-head as they crushed Happy Meal toys with their fists.

"I thought Chris Bowen was in jail," Kayla said.

I froze suddenly as I realized that Chris's companion, whose back was to me, was wearing a black leather jacket with the Hard Rock

Cafe emblem on the back. His hair was shaved on the sides and black at the top.

I counted to ten. Three times. I did my deep-breathing exercises. I thought through the confrontation *before* it happened. "That's Roger with him, isn't it?" Kayla asked with a sympathetic look as she watched me do the breathing thing.

I nodded. I'd told her earlier about what happened—or rather, didn't happen—that morning.

I stood up and calmly walked over to their table. I came up behind Roger, and Mitch's eyes went wide as he announced, "It's your sister!" in much the same way he might've said, "It's a T rex!"

Roger's arm froze in midstrike, just inches above a soon-to-be-smashed plastic movie promotion cup. ("A limited time offer, available only at participating locations. Collect all four while supplies last!") I pulled up a chair beside his, put my arm around him, and said calmly, "Roger, it may've slipped your mind, but you're supposed to be at home right now, catching up on your schoolwork."

The mention of the word *schoolwork* caused Chris to flinch. He slipped on a pair of aviator sunglasses and began to knead his fully shaved head like bread dough.

"Nobody on the planet would be caught dead doing homework on a Saturday night, not even you," Roger said without looking at me.

Chris grinned. (I would reflect later that the absolute worst thing you can do to a fifteen-year-old boy is humiliate him in front of some older guy he is trying desperately to impress.)

"All the same, I'm taking you home," I said, still calm.

"In your dreams, Sister Do-Right."

Chris was smiling now.

"You're cruisin' for trouble, mister!" I said, starting to lose it.

"I'm paralyzed with fear," he said, shaking my arm off his back. "Look, Becca, do us *both* a favor and drop the mommy act. If I needed a parent, I'd have one at home."

The outburst of laughter from Chris shot through me like a flaming arrow. "We'll discuss this further in the car," I said as I stood up and took him by the hand.

"That's no *car*. That's a dumpster with windows!" he said as he stood up and yanked his hand away from mine.

Chris laughed even louder this time, and Roger beamed triumphantly.

"You don't want to make a scene here, Becca," Kayla gently advised me from the sidelines. "Let it be."

I couldn't. At that particular moment I was convinced I was the only remaining boundary in Roger's life, and I knew from my study of psych that we all *need* boundaries to feel loved. So I came up behind his back, laced my arms around him, clutched a hand on each side of the open front of his jacket, and vowed to hold on no matter what. "Please come home with me," I said.

"Have you flipped?" he said, beginning to squirm. "Let go of me!"

"Why've you become so determined to trash your life?" I said as I struggled to hang on (he was a whole lot stronger now than when we used to roughhouse as kids). "Don't you care about anything anymore?"

"Noooooo!" Roger declared in a loud, primal yell that choked back a sob. Then he elbowed me square in the ribs, tore himself loose, and bolted.

Chapter 9

I STAGGERED IN through the back door of my apartment with Kayla's aid and plotzed into a chair at the kitchen table. There was a note stuck to the chartreuse ceramic napkin holder; Mom had gone to an art film entitled *Winter in Helsinki* with someone named Ulrich, and before leaving, she'd given Roger "permission to watch TV after three hours of studying." At the bottom of the note she'd scrawled, "P.S. *Please* don't wait up for me!"

Mom always freaked when I burned the midnight oil for her. "Becca, you're seventeen going on fifty," she'd say. But who else was going to wait up and make sure the woman got home safely?

I unbuttoned my blouse and felt around my rib cage. No breaks, but there was certain to be a major bruise by tomorrow.

Kayla opened the freezer, located the ice tray, and pulled out a handful of cubes; she put them into a Ziploc bag, wrapped the bag in a hand towel, and then handed me the first-aid package.

"You're a saint," I said thankfully as I gently pressed the pack against the point of impact. Oh my *God* that hurt!

"Where do you suppose Roger is now?" Kayla asked after closing the freezer.

I shook my head. "I haven't the foggiest, although I suppose he might be casing out a Catholic church somewhere, hoping to take down a few nuns while the night is still young."

Kayla laughed. "C'mon, Becca, you were riding the poor kid. Literally."

"I know," I said with a sigh. "Mr. Gordon thinks I'm in danger of developing a savior complex. It's a hazard that all counselors face, he says. But I don't see how I can stand idly by while Roger makes a mess of his whole life—"

"It could just be a stage," Kayla said. "He may grow out of it."

"Then how come most of the ninth-grade boys at Luna High aren't getting into such dire straits?"

"You've got a point," she admitted. "So let's look at another possibility. The really bad stuff—the vandalism, the talking back to teachers and giving them unsolicited haircuts, the plummeting grades; that all didn't start until about midyear, did it?"

I had to think about it. "No, I guess not, now that you mention it. It was definitely after we'd gotten the PCN started." I suddenly caught on to what Kayla was driving at and didn't like it one bit. "You don't think he's acting out because of jealousy, do you?"

Kayla shrugged and said, "I've been amazed at the harsh feelings some of my counselees have for their star sibs. After all, it's a drag to go through high school in someone else's shadow."

Roger's question—"Don't you realize how much I don't want to be a little Becca clone?"—suddenly echoed in my mind, right along with "Everyone at Luna High thinks you're so bitchin'."

"Am I supposed to shift into low gear just so my kid brother won't feel like a failure?"

Kayla shook her head. "I'm not saying Roger's resentment of you is *rational*, Becca. I'm just trying to help you get a sense of where his mind is at."

Just then the phone rang, and I shook my head when Kayla motioned whether to pick it up. "Let's see first if it's important," I said. I was half-afraid it'd be Peter (one of his virtues was that he never stayed mad at anyone for long) with a hot new lead on a prom date, and I just couldn't deal right now. After four rings the answering machine came on:

"Hi, you have reached the Singleton residence," Roger's voice said. *"Roger is out charming the babes; Heidi is either at work or on a date with yet another loser; and Becca is out minding other people's business. Please leave a message, and one of us will get back to you when we damn well feel like it. Thank you."*

"I can't believe that little creep hijacked the answering machine *again!*"

Kayla nodded sympathetically and bit down on a smile.

"Uh, right-o," the message began. "This is for Becca, from Eddie. I hope you're sitting down when you hear this! After weeks of excruciating deliberation, I've decided to make *you* my prom queen!"

Long, dramatic pause.

"No, it's *not* too good to be true! I'm on the up-and-up here. Darla's loss is your gain! I know you've been hard up for a prom date ever since Peter was caught learning ninth-grade geography the hands-on way but despair no more. He should've recognized that a girl with your intelligence and integrity would not tolerate such a lustful indiscretion! Rest assured that when my limo pulls up at your humble doorstep on May fourteenth, you'll be entering the rarefied company of a guy who has only the highest esteem for your many breasttaking qualities. So call back ASAP to confirm, and I'll take care of the rest. (He left his phone number.) Bye for now, Rebecca darling."

Beep.

"Did he really say *breast*taking?" I asked.

We replayed the message just to make sure.

"Methinks that's what they call a Freudian slip, 'Rebecca darling,'" Kayla said as we both began to howl with laughter.

"And to think I told Zoner just the other day that I still had hope for this guy," I said, shaking my head in disbelief.

Kayla stuck her hand up into my face and said, in Eddie's faux aristocratic drawl, "Kissss my rrrring, peasant!"

"Uh, right-o," I said, giving Kayla's hand a doggie lick. Then I cupped my hand to my ear and said, "But forsooth, methinks my most esteemed gentleman beckons even now!"

"You'd breast be off, then!"

The two of us laughed until we both had tears in our eyes.

Later, after I'd tossed my blouse into the hamper and changed into a comfy terry cloth bathrobe, we brewed a pot of apple-cinnamon tea and used it to chase down some Oreo cookies as we brainstormed for a fitting response to Eddie's odious overture. The idea came to me in the middle of my third Oreo. . . .

"So it's yes, then," Eddie crooned with supreme confidence after we'd exchanged greetings.

"Well, not exactly," I said apologetically. "You see I . . . It's just that . . . Oh, this is *ever* so awkward!"

Kayla, listening on a phone that she'd brought in from the living room, gave me an encouraging thumbs-up.

"You're not playing hard to get, are you?" Eddie asked with obvious disbelief.

I almost went off on him right then, but Kayla shook her head and held up her free hand in a calming gesture.

"Heavens no," I managed to say with alarm. "In fact, I was so overcome with emotion when I first heard your message that I actually felt *faint*."

"Ah, well, that's understandable—"

"And rest assured that if it wasn't for this wretched list, I'd accept your gracious invitation on the spot!"

There was a very long pause, during which Kayla and I exchanged triumphant smiles.

"What kind of, er . . . 'list' would that be, exactly?" Eddie asked.

"Well, it's— God, Eddie, I'm so embarrassed to admit this; you're going to think I'm an absolute slug or something—it's a *prom* list. A rank-order roster of the ten guys I was considering as potential prom dates. And you see, the *really* awkward thing here is, I haven't gotten all the way down to your name just yet. I feel rotten about it, but there you are."

There was an even longer pause this time.

I drew a line across my neck with my index finger, and then Kayla pantomimed an elaborate, blue-blooded swoon to my silent but enthusiastic applause.

"Becca," Eddie said, his voice all crackly and indistinct now, like the dying signal from a distant radio station, "I don't know exactly what you've heard, but I'm sure if you'll just let me explain—"

"WRITE IT ON A CARD AND SELL IT TO HALLMARK, YOU JERK!" I raged, dropping the act completely. "I'd rather walk naked into a biker bar to talk sexual harassment than go to the prom with the likes of you! Good night and good riddance, you human oil slick!"

As I slammed the phone down, Kayla

crowed, "He's toast!" and we exchanged a triumphant high five.

An hour or so later, as I struggled to keep my worries about Roger in check and tried to calm my nerves with a generous serving of nonfat chunky peach sorbet, Kayla asked me why I was so pessimistic about her prospects for getting to the prom with Zoner. I finally told her about Thursday morning, when I'd indirectly hipped Zoner to her intent and he had seemed less than jazzed by the prospect of Kayla-as-girlfriend.

"But your reading of his reaction—that's pure speculation on your part," Kayla said after downing a spoonful of nonfat raspberry frozen yogurt. "Why make it sound conclusive?"

Frustrated, I laid out all the evidence for her one more time and said, "Maybe I'm wrong, but I just can't shake the feeling that you're setting yourself up for a big disappointment."

Kayla looked doubtful for the first time. She scooped out another bite of frozen yogurt and took her time about swallowing it. Finally she said, "Do you remember a few years ago at summer surf camp when Zoner told us not to dread wipeouts 'because if you're not wiping out, it means you're not going for broke and testing your limits'?"

I nodded, not sure what she was getting at.

"Well, maybe I am kidding myself and Zoner *doesn't* see me as anything more than a bud, and maybe my going after him in such an aggro way *will* screw up things for the three of us, although I don't really see how my friendship with you or your friendship with him will be hurt. The bottom line is, though, I'm fully willing to risk 'wiping out' here, if that's where things are headed. So be a friend and let me, okay?"

"If that's what you really want," I said reluctantly. "But I hope you'll take what Zoner said this afternoon seriously. You gotta be careful not to get in over your head if it really pumps next week."

"No worries, girl," Kayla said with a reassuring smile. "I have a Zoner wish, not a death wish."

I started to get *really* anxious about Roger when eleven o'clock came and went, but Kayla suggested I wait a 'little while longer' before firing up the Olds and embarking on a search-

and-rescue mission. To burn off some nervous energy (and Oreos), we closed the shades in the living room, stripped down to our underwear, popped a dance video into the VCR, and began to jam. Kayla did, anyway. I mainly held a fresh ice pack against my rib cage and paced like a lioness in a third-rate zoo.

"Kayla, what makes you think I wanted to go for Jeff Gardiner last year?" I asked after about sixteen passes around the coffee table.

Kayla blew a sweaty strand of hair out of her eyes and, without looking away from the TV or slowing her amazin' pace, said, "It was totally obvious. You never admitted to a crush, but you talked about him constantly. Not that *that's* changed. And anyone with half a brain can see you and Jeff make a natural pair . . . like salsa and chips, Goobers and Raisinets, or even Fred and Wilma."

I finally tossed my ice pack onto the table, kicked back on the couch, and said, "You lie. We've got practically nothing in common."

"I tell the truth," Kayla countered as she continued to make like Janet Jackson at a dance contest. "You and Jeff are both fiercely proud, superstubborn, megadriven—"

There was a sound of a key entering the

lock in the front door, and Kayla broke stride, whipped her clothes off the rocking chair, and disappeared from the room at lightning speed. I switched off the TV and had my bathrobe barely half on when the door opened and Roger came in.

His eyes went straight to my torso, and he winced when he saw the forming bruise.

I looked him over, too, and saw a scraped forehead, a swollen lip, and no Hard Rock Cafe jacket.

"My God, Roger, what happened?!" I asked as I finished putting on my robe.

"I'm sorry I hit you, Becky," he said, his eyes glistening. "I really am."

"Don't worry about that," I said, though I was extremely grateful and not a little surprised to hear those words come out of his mouth. "Please tell me what happened!"

"I was screwing around. I found some buds to hang with after I left the mall, and just for the hell of it, we went hopping fences down at the marina. I got snagged on that really high one around the storage area at the Luna Point Yacht Club and ended up tearing the jacket practically in half. Then I fell about eight feet and landed wrong."

He made minimal eye contact with me, especially when he was talking about the jacket, and the story came out sounding way too smooth and well rehearsed. He was almost for sure lying, at least in part.

"Why didn't you bring the jacket home?"

"I wasn't going to stay at the mall for very long," he said, totally shifting gears as he looked directly at me now. "You didn't have to make a federal case out of it!" A renegade tear escaped from his right eye, and he immediately wiped it away with the back of his hand.

"I'm sorry for going overboard," I said, feeling rotten.

"Prove it," he said. "Don't say a word about this to Mom or anybody else. She'll just figure I stopped wearing the jacket and jump for joy. It was from Dad, after all."

Unfortunately, Roger had Mom pegged perfectly on this one. "Okay," I agreed, "but first please tell me what *really* happened to you after you left the mall."

"Good night, my loving, ever-trusting sister," he said disgustedly as he turned away and started to walk toward his room. "It's been real, as always."

At a total loss for words, I sat back down on the couch, closed my eyes, and imagined I was surfing.

Kayla popped back into the living room a few minutes later, fully clothed and with a freshly washed face. "I heard Roger's voice," she said in an excited half-whisper. "Is he okay? Did you guys work things out already?"

"He's one hundred percent himself. And yeah, we swapped apologies," I said as cheerfully as I could.

"That's awesome," Kayla enthused, clapping her hands together. "Like they say, the darkest hour is just before dawn."

But I couldn't shake this terrible feeling that the "darkest hour" was yet to come.

Chapter 10

BY MONDAY AFTERNOON when two guys in a row came in to see me for counseling, I knew for sure that my rebuttal to Jeff's column was having some major impact on its target audience.

"No crisis too small, right?" Denny Chan asked. He was staring at me intensely over the round, silver, wire rims of his glasses. He had an open notebook in his lap and a pen at the ready.

"You bet," I said.

"Okay, here's the deal," he said, pointing the pen at me. "I've asked Kristen Stern to the prom and it's a go, but I'm a little worried about . . ."

There was a long pause here, as Denny worked his jaw muscles and pulled at the sleeves of his black wool blazer, which he was wearing over a faded football jersey.

From experience I knew that these long guy pauses meant I was supposed to guess at the problem, so after a minute or two'd passed, I started ticking off possibilities on my fingertips. "You're a little worried about: the cost, looking like a dork in a cummer-bund, gabbing with her friends, dancing, kissing—"

"*That's* it!" he said, snapping his fingers and looking relieved. "Thing is, Kristen and I haven't actually . . ."

". . . kissed yet," I ventured.

He nodded again. "And to tell you the truth, I've had some problems in that area. This one girl I went out with said I French-kissed like a Saint Bernard, although I've wondered ever since how she would know that. So I changed my technique, and the next girl I kissed said if she wanted her mouth exam-ined, she'd go to a dentist. Help me out here, Becca. What am I doing wrong?"

I'd gotten this kind of question lots of times, from both guys and girls, so I felt reasonably confident about handling it. I assured him first off that kissing was a mystery for *everyone* and that tastes (so to speak) varied a lot from person to person. "It sounds like in the first case you might've gone a little overboard on the saliva thing, and in the second, there was maybe too much tongue action on your part . . . although I think the way your kissing partners slammed you was totally uncool."

Denny looked up from his notepad and smiled appreciatively.

I'd had my share of loser kissing experiences, so I knew how dragged he must've been feeling about himself. "Next time," I went on, "depressurize by taking a follow-the-leader approach, at least until you and your partner've gotten to know each other better. In other words, let her show you what works for her first, and then gradually phase in what works for you. If the vibe is right in the rest of your relationship, you'll eventually reach a good space in your kissing, too. Don't be shy about asking her for make-out tips, either— most people love to play teacher, and besides, modesty is sexy."

Denny checked over his notes carefully. "This looks real. I can handle this," he said confidently. "And I assume from what you've said that this business of people being kiss-compatible from the start is just one of your basic myths, right?"

"I wouldn't go that far," I said, remembering the faceless "stranger" in my dream. "After all, kissing is an expression of emotion more than anything else, and the stronger the passion you're feeling—"

"—the better the kiss'll seem," Denny said, looking a bit crestfallen.

"But hey, by the same token, a great make-out session can boost a relationship to a whole new level," I quickly pointed out. "No matter what, Denny, the fact you cared enough to come in and ask about this at all can only mean good things for you and Kristen on prom night."

He brightened up again and said, "I hadn't thought of it that way."

~

"Marissa and I have gotten really tight over the past few months, and we're thinking that maybe on prom night we'll, you know, go the distance," Travis Meehan said. Travis was junior class vice president, a member of the varsity track team, and a fellow student in my French class. He was famously clean-cut, favoring striped button-down Oxford shirts and fleur-de-lis socks. I was surprised by his visit, and more than a little pleased, coming as it did after the now widely discussed resignation of star jock Eric Taschner from the PCN over the abstinence thing.

Travis and I had the usual talk about the risks and responsibilities that went with "going the distance," and he was so amazingly well versed on the subject that he could've written our sex pamphlet himself. "So what brings you here?" I finally asked.

"Even with all this stellar info, I still can't seem to make up my mind," he said. "I mean, I know my friends are all doing it, so I'm definitely trailing the pack. . . ."

Since I'd become a counselor, I'd discovered that an amazing number of my peers hung out with incredibly fearless "friends."

"Hold it," I said, making the T gesture for a time-out. "What your buds do with their bodies should have *zilch* effect on what you do with yours, 'cause if something goes wrong, only *you,* and probably your partner, will have to face the fallout."

Travis moved to the edge of his chair and looked as if he was poised to bail on me.

This was a dicey job because you had to shoot straight but without blowing away the customer.

"If I came on too strong, I'm sorry," I said with a reassuring smile. "But you wouldn't believe the number of students I've talked to in the last five months who've gotten into major jams because of this frantic, self-defeating, I'd-better-do-it-soon-or-I'll-be-the-last-virgin-on-the-planet attitude. It makes me crazy."

Travis nodded, eased back into his chair, and took some time to think.

After a while I said, "Your command of sex ed stats amazes. You thinking of going after Gerwin's job?"

"Not even!" Travis said, and we laughed. "No, my mom and dad are charter members of that new group Parents for Total Teen Abstinence. They give me lots of nutritious reading material, and I pretty much devour it."

"They must really care about you," I said.

"Yeah, I guess so. But sometimes I feel like

they're going to smother me with all of their love and concern, you know?"

I nodded.

"They'd totally freak, for instance, if they knew I was having this conversation with you."

"That's why it's confidential," I said. "But let's get back to your problem. If having sex would go against your values, then I'd definitely put it off. Based on what I've seen around here, I'd have to guess you'd just feel guilty and gross about yourself afterward."

"But it's not *my* values that are causing the problem here!" he said, giving me a deeply pained look. "*I* want to have sex with Marissa, and I think it's cool to 'cause I love her. A *lot*. I'm only in here right now because my folks have messed up my head so badly that I can't see straight, and I was sort of hoping you'd . . ." His voice trailed off.

"Hoping I'd what?"

He shrugged and gazed out the window.

Sometimes in this job you get mad at a counselee, and as the silence dragged on, I got plenty ticked at Travis. Sure, he was in a bad space, and I sympathized, but I was getting the distinct impression that he wanted me to make some kind of decision for him here, and I hated being put in that position.

Finally I said, "You've got a lot of baggage to sort through here, Travis. Maybe you'd like me to tell you that your mom and dad's values stink like yesterday's fish sticks, but that's not what I'm about here. Besides, we *all* carry our parents around in our heads, for better or worse, and you're not gonna get around that."

He still wasn't looking at me, but he seemed to be listening, so I chugged right on: "Why not just kick back on the sex thing for a while? Don't set the prom up as some kind of lame do-or-die deadline for 'losing' your virginity. . . . Maybe it would help you at this point to talk to a regular guidance counselor, someone who could give you professional insights—"

"No!" Travis said, pounding his fist on the desk. "No more adult advice!"

So he *was* listening.

"I'm sorry," he said, rubbing the desktop as if he'd injured it. "Look, Becca, even if I agree with you now that I'm not ready to make it with Marissa, what if I change my mind on prom night?"

"That's a killer-good question, Travis," I said, relieved to have him conversing again. "Fortunately, it takes two to tango. Have you talked over your worries with Marissa?"

He nodded. "And she's real understanding, too, up to a point. . . . I know this might sound crazy, but I think she wants to have sex at least as much as I do!"

"You thought guys had a total monopoly on these kinds of longings, did ya?" I asked with a smile.

Travis smiled back sheepishly.

"I know this might sound clichéd," I told him, "but it's as true for girls as it is for guys: if Marissa *really* loves you, she won't pressure you into making love before you're ready."

Travis nodded. "Oh yeah, she's aces. It's *me* I'm worried about."

"Let's sum up what we know about you, then. You're as well tuned to the risks involved as any counselee I've ever talked to. And you know there's a horbugulous pile of unsettled issues standing between you and a clear-headed decision. If, knowing all this, you still think you might end up wanting to go the distance on prom night, then I have one more reality check for you. Get thee to a drugstore and buy some condoms."

Travis blanched, looked away from me, and slowly shook his head. "Uh-uh. No way! I just can't see myself doing that."

I figured as much. "You've found your answer then, Travis," I told him. "You can't possibly be ready."

He thought that over and then nodded despondently.

⁓

I was feeling spent after Travis left—all the other peer counselors'd long since called it a day—and I was busy getting ready to lock up the trailer and head home when there was a loud knock on the door. I looked through the window at the tear-streaked face of Darla Swanson.

"I just broke up with Jeff," she said as I welcomed her inside.

"I'm sorry, Darla," I said, totally shocked that she'd actually come to see me.

"Don't be." She sniffled as she pulled a mirror out of her Saks Fifth Avenue handbag and studied her face. Even with tear tracks, it was a stunner: gorgeous, almond-shaped brown eyes; a straight, delicate nose; full lips; high cheekbones; and a fine, rounded chin. "I've already got a new guy," she said without much pride or joy. "He's captain of the tennis team at Primavera High School. We've been running into each other for years at league tournaments, and I started seeing him more seriously over the last few weeks." She wiped her tears away with her own tissue, snapped the hand mirror shut, and returned it to the bag.

"I know that sounds awful," she continued, "especially after what Peter Karona did to you, but you should hear me out first before you pass judgment."

"I'm not here to get judgmental," I assured her, struggling to stay ahead of this dizzying flood of info, "but you can't expect me to be an objective listener, especially considering my relationship with Jeff—"

"But that's exactly why I came here," she said. "I figured you of all people could see why I finally had to give up on him."

I gave in after about two seconds. "Okay. But I can only listen to you as a—"

"—friend," Darla said, graciously completing the sentence for me.

"Right. Not as a peer counselor."

She rolled her eyes. "You sound just like Jeff: 'I'm talking to you as an editor now, Darla. That feature about eating disorders on the cheerleading squad has potential, but you need to nail down at least two more interviews to make it credible.'"

It was a primo impression of Jeff at his most obnoxious.

"That's exactly the kind of thing that drove me nuts!" she went on. "The *Beacon* is just a high school newspaper, but he treats it as if it were the real thing."

"Maybe to him it is," I said.

"Right, which makes him an A-one editor in chief and a bargain-basement boyfriend. Jeff was always so damn busy and preoccupied. He had time for practically everybody's problems and needs except mine. Honest to God, the week before the *Beacon* went to press, I could've walked naked around his computer station playing love songs on an accordion and I seriously doubt he'd've noticed. Do you know he hadn't the slightest clue I'd started seeing another guy? You figure most people would pick up the signals and figure out that something's wrong, but not Jeff! All he cares about are his precious deadlines."

I thought about Peter suddenly and felt super uneasy. Had the Cindy thing happened because I was so preoccupied with the PCN? "But maybe Jeff figured he could trust you. And if you had all these issues workin' your nerves, Darla, why didn't you bring them out in the open?"

She gave me a guilty look and then an angry one. "That only works if a guy is willing to listen. I had give-and-take with Jeff up until about February, when his mom moved out. Now his parents are going through a divorce that makes my mom and dad's breakup look like a schoolyard scrape, and Jeff's reaction has been to just shut down emotionally, at least where *personal* feelings are concerned."

"I've seen that pattern before."

"You mean your little brother," Darla said sympathetically. "It's funny. I'll bet you're one of the few people around who could actually help Jeff talk through some of this stuff, but since he blames therapy for his parents' divorce—"

"What?!"

"Oh yeah—I forget you wouldn't know any of this. Jeff thinks his parents' marriage started its downhill slide after his mom started seeing a therapist last spring. She picked all kinds of fights with his dad, he says. But, of course, he also told me on other occasions that his parents'd been clawing at each other like wildcats ever since he was a little kid. The guy can be maddeningly inconsistent!"

"Yet you sound as if you still care about him," I pointed out, trying hard to maintain some objectivity.

Darla nodded. "I think I just got tired, Becca. I hung on for as long as I could because there's a lot of things about Jeff that are really awesome. He's smart, he's passionate, he makes things happen. And God, the way he kisses—I just can't describe it."

I was hoping she wouldn't try, either, but then her eyes started to gleam and I braced myself.

"I remember last Christmas at the Luna Point boat parade. My dad's yacht was sparkling, and JOY TO THE WORLD was spelled out in red-and-green lights on a giant net hanging down from the Ballard estate on the Luna Bluffs."

I closed my eyes and found myself at Casino Point again. The clock tower on the hillside was just beginning to strike twelve.

"I had on this tight-fitting red Santa's helper dress with white fuzzy trim. Jeff was decked out in this adorable red-and-green felt Santa's elf costume—I had to beg him to wear it, of course—and I pulled him into the master stateroom, where we yanked off our caps and kissed for what seemed like hours, until I completely melted in his arms and said, 'You're the best Christmas present I've ever had.' "

"But that feeling is gone now," I said hoarsely as I opened my eyes, shifted around in my chair, and tried once more to shake off that overpowering sense of longing.

" 'Fraid so," she said glumly. "The only things he seems to feel passionate about these days are the *Beacon* . . . and you."

"Me?"

"Sure. You know, the editorial give-and-take over the PCN, the fireworks show at the *Beacon* staff meeting two weeks ago, et cetera.

After that it got to the point where Jeff'd mention you on an almost daily basis—nearly always to slam you, of course, except when he was carrying on about what a great writer you are—but it still wore on me after a while."

"Hey, there's never been *anything* between us—," I began.

She laughed. "Don't you think I know that! You two were born on the straight and narrow." Then she said more seriously, "Blowing off a person you care about in favor of your work can be just as bad as cheating on them, though."

"Did you ever tell Jeff that?"

"Yes, lots of times! And he always promised to 'do better.' He could never actually bring himself to *apologize,* though. . . ."

"How well I remember that," I said, and we smiled at each other.

Darla checked her watch. "I'm keeping you way too late. Thanks loads for hearing me out . . . and maybe I can return the favor in a small way. That pest Eddie Ballard has drawn up a prom list, with me at the top. He actually saw fit, for some reason, to show it to me after I turned him down for the third consecutive time—this is all while I'm still going out with Jeff, mind you!—and I'm afraid I saw your name on it—"

"I know all about the list," I said quickly. "And I've already told him I'm not interested."

"That's good," Darla said, nodding, "because he thought of you as his 'safety date,' which means he's exhausted the list now, and we might all be spared his obnoxious presence at the prom."

"I was *number ten?!* I could throttle that little weasel!"

"You think being number *one* on his list was some kind of honor, do you?" Darla asked dryly, and then we both laughed.

As we walked to the parking lot together she said, while flipping her shiny, curly, high-maintenance, dark brown locks back over the shoulders of her white, short-sleeved pointelle cardigan, "Have you given any more thought to coloring your hair?"

My hair has a slight natural wave to it, which I've always been happy with, and I usually let it grow to about six inches beyond shoulder length. I was never too concerned, one way or another, about my quasimedium brown, blond-streaked hair color until last fall at a *Beacon* party held in Darla's palatial home. One of her many toys was a computer imaging machine that let you see how you'd look in a wide range of different hair colors and styles. We really had a blast with it, putting dreadlocks on Jeff, a red punker cut on Darla, an orange clown wig on Eddie, and so on. We tried traditional styles, too, and everybody seemed to be really taken by how I looked in an even medium brown shade, with golden summer highlights around my face. I never took the idea of recoloring my hair all that seriously, though. It hadn't done a thing for Roger.

"I have no plans to dye," I told her. "I guess I just don't feel 'passionate' enough about it."

She laughed and said, "I was only asking because I remembered how much Jeff liked your computer makeover."

Hey—what was she getting at here?

"Well," I said dismissively, "then maybe he can ask my computer image to the prom. They'd make a terrific couple. Both are rigid, two-dimensional, and totally uncommunicative."

Darla laughed, gave me five, and split off toward her car.

I stopped by a drugstore on the way home and took a casual, noncommittal tour of the hair-care section.

Chapter 11

THE CALL CAME in at around 4:45 A.M. on Wednesday.

"They're firing!" rasped the voice on the phone.

"I think you have the wrong number," I said groggily.

"*No comprende,* dudettamente! We're talkin' double overhead out of the southwest here! Perfect, peeling tubes and not a kook in sight."

My surfer self suddenly roared to life, like a fuel-flooded camp stove when the match finally takes. This was Zoner on the line, and he was talking *monster waves!* "High on the hoot meter?" I asked as I sat up at attention.

"Off the scale, Becca my girl. One hundred and ten percent *pure stoke!*"

"Should I call Kayla?"

"Already done. Shall we wing by your dwelling in about fifteen?"

"Let there be surf!"

I splashed some water on my face, swished the sleep out of my mouth, brushed out my hair and pulled it back into a ponytail, yanked on a wet suit, downed some orange juice, left a note for Mom, grabbed my board out of the garage, and caught the Zoner express in just the nick of time.

Our conveyance was an old sunflower yellow rust-pocked 1961 Sahara Vista wagon. It featured whitewall tires and a Sphinx-shaped hood ornament and seemed to be held together in key spots by stickers for various types of surf products (CREATURES OF LEISURE BOARD COVERS), destinations (SURF COSTA RICA), and environmental causes (JOIN THE SURFRIDER FOUNDATION). The front bench seat was basically upholstered in silver duct tape, and the back of the vehicle was hollowed out to accommodate a max number of boards.

Kayla and Zoner looked so highly torqued you'd've thought they'd been awake and alert for hours. It wasn't just the prospect of epic surf that had them on edge, though; they were sitting as far apart from each other in the front seat as space would allow. Once I got situated between them, they both seemed to relax.

"In this dream last night, I had one of those near-death experiences," Zoner said as we sputtered down the nearly empty predawn streets of Luna Point. "But instead of seeing that comforting white light I'd been led to expect by all those TV specials, I beheld this mammoth bowl of Cocoa Pebbles and heard a voice thunder, 'PART OF YOUR COMPLETE BREAKFAST!' What do you girls think it means?"

Kayla and I burst out laughing.

"I also had this dream that I showed up at school wearing nothing but a pair of Velcro briefs," he went on in a perfect deadpan, "and the gnarly thing was, I really had to pee."

We laughed even harder this time and almost upset the plastic palm tree Zoner kept situated on the dashboard for good surf karma.

"What kind of peer counselors are you, anyway?" he asked, taking mock offense. "That second dream ended up causing me a lot of pain!"

He went on like this for a while, until we were so winded from laughter we had to beg him to stop.

When we got to the lot at the beach, though, our mouths clammed and our ears perked for that unmistakable pulsing thud. We got out of the car in our bare feet and felt the vibrations of the shorepound rippling through the asphalt. We ran up to the first rise in the sand and beheld the cool, blue-gray, mirror-smooth, six-to-eight-foot walls roaring shoreward under dawn's early light. Only a handful of surfers were out at this point, which would leave us plenty of room for thrills *and* spills with no fear of hassling drop-ins. "This is as core as it gets," Zoner said excitedly as we went back to fetch our sticks. "Be careful out there, girls, and don't hesitate to bail shoreward if you're getting hammered."

"We got it wired," Kayla said confidently. In spite of Zoner's objections that it was inappropriate for these conditions, she'd brought her new lighter board. I, on the other hand, had Moby with me.

Zoner paddled out first, caught one early, and went pedal-to-the-metal down a barreling groove, sliced up to the lip, pulled a floater down the falls, cut back up into the groove again, and finally threw his fist into the air and howled in triumph as he bailed out at the end.

Kayla would also manage several fine rides over the next hour or so—her aerials, especially, continued to amaze—but I, much to my chagrin, was eating it on virtually every wave I challenged. I dumped the takeoff on the first really good one and bailed in the trough on the second before I realized I was just too preoccupied to focus. So I paddled outside for a while and settled for floating over the humps.

My problem was yesterday'd been quite the raw experience. Eddie Ballard came by the trailer in the A.M. and took me to task for "being cruel and insensitive" to him on the phone Saturday night. "That's no way for a therapist to act," he said.

I wasted no time in straightening him out. "Don't think for even a second you can use my role as a peer counselor as a means to abuse me as a person, Eddie," I told him. "Now that you've exhausted that horrendously ill-conceived prom list of yours, I suggest you take some time out to examine why a person with all your resources and potential has managed to alienate so many people at this high school."

When he then became verbally abusive and vowed to take some sort of vague 'revenge' on me, I angrily insisted that he leave (while keeping my hands entirely to myself). He broke at that point and got all morose and apologetic before finally sulking out the door.

Later Elaine Stillwell came in to see me. "I met with Walt, like you suggested, and it went really well at first. I think having sex so soon really *did* freak him out, and he was totally relieved that I didn't hold it against him. We agreed to 'downshift,' as he put it. We went to a movie with friends last Friday night, and all we did was hold hands—it was totally great! We remade our prom plans, too. But then last night, we were doing math homework at his house and there was no one else home . . . and he tried to talk me into having sex with him again. When I started to explain why that'd be a bad idea, he got all hyper and basically threw me out!"

I felt bad for Elaine, who was crying by this point, but not nearly so awful as I would've felt if she'd given *in* to his pressure. She was way bummed about the prom again, of course, but I told her that if she still wanted to go, she was welcome to hang with me.

"What if you get a date?" she wondered.

"That's not gonna happen," I said with a laugh. "And even if it does, my invitation to you still stands." That seemed to cheer her up a lot.

Now, as *el sol* slowly rose up into the sky behind Saddleback Mountain and the Luna Bluffs turned the color of gold foil, I got the uneasy feeling that the humps beneath me were getting larger. Time to catch a relatively small but juicy one, I decided, and ride it into the beach.

I successfully paddled my way onto one of the few remaining user-friendly six-footers, crouched into a trim stretch, and began what looked to be my one and only decent ride of the morning. I brushed my fingers on the glassy face and watched the lip glisten and sparkle with transparent splendor in the early morning sunlight.

And then for no good reason at all, my mind arced back to yesterday again. Jeff Gardiner had confronted me as I left my lunch table. His breakup with Darla was by then public knowledge, and I felt bad for him, but the question he directed at me and the tone he used were still way out of line:

"Did Darla come to you for counseling yesterday afternoon?" he demanded.

"That's confidential info, Jeff. You of all people should know that—"

"Did she talk to you about my parents?" he persisted. I thought I saw some real anxiety in his eyes now. The great and powerful Wizard of Oz was obviously terrified that Dorothy'd gotten a peek behind the curtain and discovered he was just as frail and human as the rest of us. "I can't have this conversation with you, Jeff. I'm sorry," I said coolly as I turned away from him and started off toward class.

"And people call *me* a power-tripper!" he shouted at my back.

I spent the rest of the day and most of the

evening worrying about whether or not I had in fact abused my position by talking to Darla. But the bottom line was she'd sought *me* out, not vice versa. And we'd talked *expressly* as friends.

The wave I'd carelessly lost track of suddenly picked me up and dipped me, fondue-style, into the shallows. Conditions were a lot more turbulent than last Saturday, and for about ten seconds I twirled like an Olympic figure skater in the award round. I angrily clawed my way back up to the light, cursing myself for wasting such a beautiful wave on Jeff Gardiner. When I broke the surface, I took in a few huge gulps of air, reeled in Moby, and with a feeling of defeat, headed for the high ground. When I got there, I was startled to see two surfers contemplating their broken boards. One of them was Zoner!

"Where's Kayla?!" I asked him anxiously.

He shook his head, pointed out at the lineup, and said in a very worried voice, "I told her she'd better come in, that conditions were getting way too intense, but she just blew me off. The growler I rode in on chewed me up and spit me out, as you can plainly see."

He gestured at his ruined board. "I don't know what *she's* thinking. . . ."

But I did.

I ran down to the shoreline. Kayla was relatively easy to spot because there were now more surfers on the beach than there were in the water. This, in and of itself, was a major danger sign. "KAYLA!" I screamed over the roar of the surf. "COME IN NOW!"

Kayla heard me and held up her index finger, apparently to indicate "just one more."

Zoner arrived at my side, holding one-half of his board up above his head as the ultimate warning sign. Kayla didn't see it, though, because she was already in the process of lining herself up for the next wave, a fat, hissing monster that was *easily* double-overhead for her. "She's gonna get creamed," Zoner said unhappily as he tossed the useless chunk of fiberglass aside.

Kayla actually made such a clean, controlled launch, though, that it looked to me like she might pull it off after all.

But gradually I came to realize what Zoner obviously knew already: Kayla just flat out lacked the strength and skill needed to tackle a barrel of this magnitude. It finally buried her with the cruel, cold inevitability of a mountain avalanche. I screamed once as she disappeared under the thundering white wall of Pacific spume and then again moments later as her board rocketed skyward and the leash broke.

"It's a blitz!" Zoner cried out (this was a call to arms meaning "Surfer in trouble!"), and there was an impressive rush of bodies toward the section of froth where Kayla'd gone down. Precious seconds ticked by with no sign of her, as a battalion of equally powerful waves continued their inevitable assault on the beach. We rushed around frantically, sloshing our arms through the water in search of a solid floating object.

It was Zoner who spotted her hand flailing around in the foam, and he shouted out triumphantly, "I found her!" He hauled her limp form out of the water and carried her as fast as he could to the beach, nearly falling over at one point under the impact of yet another wave.

Zoner laid her out in dry sand and immediately cupped his ear over her mouth to listen for breathing. He nodded. We found no sign of broken bones. "Kayla," he said gently as he held and patted one hand and I did the same with the other. "Wake up, girl."

She opened her lagoon-blue eyes slowly, looked directly at Zoner, and suddenly burst out crying. She sluggishly rolled away from him toward me and said miserably, "Don't let 'im see me like this, Becky." Then she began to cough up seawater.

"Why'd she say that? What goes on?!" Zoner asked me.

I figured things couldn't possibly sink any lower than this, so I said, "She's in love with you, Zoner, okay? She wants to go to the prom with you." Kayla squeezed my hand tightly as I told him.

"Well, sure, I love her, too," he said, as if this were the most obvious thing in the world. Several of the surfers gathered around us began to murmur to each other; your typical major wipeout wasn't usually followed by declarations of this sort.

Kayla let go of my hand and rolled back over to face the Zoneman. "What are"— *huah*—"you talking a"—*cough*—"bout?" she wheezed.

"I've been hot on you for ages, babe," he said, "but I was afraid if I bared these feelings and you found them hurlworthy, our budship would be pushin' up ice plant. And then Becca here told me you were in love with some guy—"

"That would be you," I said with a fast-growing sense of irony.

"What about"—*cough, cough*—"Sabrina's" —*huuuaaahhh*—"cousin Brandi?" Kayla asked him.

"She's for real but not in my plans. I had Barney hip you to her existence and intentions only so you'd know I'd become prom-willing."

Which would explain why Barney'd winked at me on Saturday.

"You know, I'll bet a peer counselor would've advised us to handle this whole thing in a much more straightforward manner," I said, and the two of us who could breathe had a good, long laugh.

"Becca, please help me up now," Kayla asked me a few minutes later. I did so and getting vertical prompted another coughing fit. After it passed, she gestured for Zoner to come closer.

"Kiss me, you surf bum, before I"—*cough, cough*—"fully regain my consciousness and change my mind about you," she whispered with a big ol' grin. And so he did, with considerable gusto, to the hoots and high fives of a greatly enthused assembly.

Shortly thereafter, a surfer came running up from the shoreline with the two halves of Kayla's board in hand. He gave them to me, and I placed them directly beside Zoner's. I then gestured at the four fiberglass-'n'-foam fragments and said to their embracing owners, "Can I ask you guys a prom-related question?"

They nodded.

"Do you dance any better than you surf?"

For some reason, they started throwing sand at me.

Chapter 12

ZONER AND KAYLA dropped me off at home and said they'd probably come into school a period or two late, depending on how fast Kayla rebounded. I rushed into the garage, propped up Moby, and then charged into the apartment to shower, consume, and head for school. There was no possible way I'd make it to the trailer by seven, but Vickie Coolidge was scheduled to counsel that morning and she had a key of her own, so I figured, no problem.

Wrong!

Mom'd already left for work, but she'd written me a note saying there were several messages waiting for me on the answering machine:

"Becca, this is Jeff, calling from the *Beacon*. You're probably on your way to school by now, but I thought you should know that there's something really weird going down in front of your trailer. I'm walking over to investigate. . . ." *Beep.*

"Hey, Becca, this is Vickie. For all I know you're getting to campus right this second, but I decided to call you at home anyway, just in case you were running late. A district police officer is putting special security locks on our trailer doorknobs! I asked him why, and he was super vague about the reason. He thinks one of our counselors violated a district code or something. He slapped this big orange sign on the side of the trailer that says: CLOSED UNTIL FURTHER NOTICE BY ORDER OF THE BOARD OF EDUCATION, LUNA POINT UNIFIED SCHOOL DISTRICT. It's all too Orwellian for me. . . ." *Beep.*

" *'Violated a district code'?!"* My heart was racing now and I was filled with a gargantuan sense of dread as I moved on to the last message:

"Hi, Becca, this is Mr. Gordon. . . . Doctor

Cayuso [the principal] just called me to say that Bernard Crampton has chosen the PCN for his latest political stunt. Crampton claims you instructed a seventeen-year-old boy to go out and buy a condom so that he could 'indulge in sex on prom night.' [Travis!] I'm sure that's not true, but I'm calling you now because I have a feeling you'll be required to make a full accounting of your actions at tonight's emergency school board meeting, which Crampton is in the process of arranging even as I speak. Come by to see me in my office ASAP, and we'll talk strategy. . . ." *Beep.*

My head was whirling. They'd actually put locks on the trailer, as if we'd been selling drugs in there or something! It didn't seem possible!

I anxiously retrieved my counseling journal and ran through the notes I'd taken at the session with Travis and then reviewed them over and over in my head as I showered, dressed, and downed a tall glass of milk. I was sure I'd stayed within the legal bounds. But would that even *matter?*

(And why on earth had Jeff Gardiner cared enough to call me?)

When I got to campus at about 7:20, Dr.

Cayuso was already ordering the district police officer to remove the padlocks from the trailer, and the officer was raising a stink about authorization. "Someone has already alerted the news media to this unfortunate turn of events, Officer Roberts, and the phones are ringing off the hook in my main office," Dr. Cayuso told him. "Now do you think I want my school to look like some sort of prison camp when it appears on the six o'clock news?" Our principal had piercing dark brown eyes; an attractive, no-nonsense face; and, when she chose to employ it, a formidable scowl.

Officer Roberts looked at her uncertainly for a moment, then said, "Why no, ma'am, I don't think you'd want that at all" as he promptly got to work on removing the locks.

Dr. Cayuso greeted me with a warm, friendly smile and a firm handshake. "The locks are coming off, Becca," she said, taking me aside from the large group of curious students and bewildered counselors who'd gathered to check out the action. "But I don't have the authority to actually let you in there until this is all straightened out. You know I support the PCN—you've helped a lot of kids when they needed it most—but this," she said, gesturing at Officer Roberts, "is unfortunately about a lot more than peer counseling."

"I understand, Dr. Cayuso," I said. "But how can Mr. Crampton resort to these kinds of strong-arm tactics, especially after he got so badly burned on the freedom of expression thing last year?!"

"He's an elected official," she said in a carefully measured tone. "Mr. Crampton will do whatever he sees fit to serve the vital interests of his particular constituency. . . . I'm sure you've learned by now that democracy is not always a savory business." Two boys having a scuffle over by the industrial arts building suddenly knocked over a trash can. "And neither is being a principal," Dr. Cayuso added resignedly as she went over to intervene.

I eased back into the crowd to calm my fellow counselors and hipped them to the fact that the trailer was still off-limits to us, at least for today. "I'm going to see Mr. Gordon right now, though, and he seems pretty optimistic that we'll pull through this okay. In the meantime, go ahead and take advantage of this lockout by meeting with your counselees in less cramped quarters. Like maybe a phone booth." A few counselors laughed, but most of them still looked majorly stressed, and I found myself wishing that Kayla and Zoner were here to help me cope. I apologized to the handful of counselees who'd come to see me specifically, made other arrangements with them, and then took off toward the guidance counseling office.

As I passed under the large stucco-and-adobe arch that had LUNA POINT HIGH SCHOOL—HOME OF THE SEA HAWKS emblazoned on it in the school colors of red and white, I nearly collided with Jeff Gardiner. He said he'd been looking for me.

"I assume you know the full scoop now?" he asked with obvious excitement.

"Yeah, unfortunately, I do." I told him briefly about who I'd heard from and talked to, so far, and thanked him for his message.

"I've made anonymous calls to a bunch of local and regional media outlets for you," he said. "There seems to be a lot of interest in this story. And why not? It's a real grabber. You've got the prom, sex, teen therapy, sex, freedom-of-speech issues, sex. . . ."

I laughed, though I felt a bit let down. While I was glad to be rid of the creepy Jeff Gardiner who'd accosted me after lunch yesterday, I still had the distinct impression that he was only taking an interest in my crisis because it would make good copy. So I decided to call him on it. "Don't think I'm not grateful here, Jeff, but what gives? *They've shut down the PCN.* Isn't that exactly what you've been hoping for the last five months?"

Jeff shook his head and gazed down at his Nikes. "Not like this," he said. "If the PCN failed, I wanted it to be for lack of *student* support." He looked back up at me, his blue eyes focused and intense now. "But that sure hasn't happened, has it, Becca? To be honest, the mail from my last column is currently running three to one in your favor."

"Really?!" I said excitedly. "How many letters have there been so far?"

"Four," he said with a smirk, and we both laughed.

"So are you actually admitting that you were wrong about the PCN?" I asked hopefully. There was a stray lock of platinum blond hair hanging down the middle of his forehead. It was really cute.

"Get real," he said, rolling his eyes. "This issue goes a lot deeper for me than you think."

I nodded with understanding and almost offered my sympathy over his parents' divorce. I caught myself just in the nick of time. "So . . . are you going to help me fight off Crampton?"

Jeff grinned. "We'll go straight for his Achilles' heel, which is still the free-speech issue."

I grinned back and told him I'd been thinking along those same lines already.

"I'll get an all-day pass from Ms. Sullivan, you get one from Mr. Gordon, and we'll meet in the library second period to start brainstorming," he said.

"Just like the old days." I hugged the notebook I was carrying super tightly and my toes scrunched up in my shoes.

"If you say so," Jeff replied casually.

⌒

When I got to Mr. Gordon's office I was surprised—and more than a little relieved—to find that he was already talking to Travis Meehan. Travis told us what happened. "I had a long talk with Marissa on Monday night, and then I decided to try that 'reality check' you suggested. I went out yesterday after school and actually bought a box of condoms. You should've seen me; my hands were shaking the whole time at the register. But I did it. And I *still* wasn't sure if I was ready for sex. Anyway, I brought 'em home and then sped back to school for a nighttime class council meeting. I guess my mom must've noticed something weird in how I was acting because she searched my bedroom right after I left and found the condoms.

"I won't go into the gruesome details, but suffice to say I came home to a wicked awful scene. Marissa's never allowed to step foot in my parents' house again, and I've been forbidden to attend the prom. . . . (Travis faltered here.) Anyway, my parents wanted to know all about how I got the idea to buy the condoms in the first place. As if the things aren't advertised all over the place, right? I was pretty played out by that point, and I did what turned out to be a stupid thing. I told them about our counseling session.

He shook his head. "Instead of helping them to see how sane and sensible buying condoms was, like I'd hoped, I just ended up giving them someone else to blame. My folks called their school board buddy Mr. Crampton, and now, as you know, he's planning to shut your whole network down.... (Travis faltered again.) You've got to believe I didn't mean for this to happen, Becca! I'm so sorry!"

I gave him a long, reassuring hug and told him not to sweat it. Then we ran through his counseling session together and found that we'd interpreted it in basically the same way.

"I don't think Crampton really expected to use Travis as some kind of witness against the PCN," Mr. Gordon said as he hooked his thumbs through his rainbow-colored suspenders and tugged at them thoughtfully. "I talked to Cathy Irwin, the school board president, about a half hour ago. She's a real fan of the PCN—probably without knowing it, you helped her best friend's daughter through a very tough Christmas last year. Anyway, Irwin says Crampton is really just maneuvering to force a board referendum on the hot-button topic of sex ed before the June elections. Here's how the political math breaks down: Cathy Irwin and Jason Woods are firmly behind us, while Ofelia Roberts and Crampton are both PTTA members. Which leaves Winslow Taggert as the swing vote."

"And Mr. Taggert is up for reelection," Travis said.

"Which means we're toast," I said forlornly.

Mr. Gordon shook his head. "Taggert's nobody's toady. But if you're going to sell him on peer counseling, Becca, you'll have to be good and sharp and avoid getting sidetracked into a debate about things like 'condom distribution on high school campuses and its contribution to the decline of all things American.' "

I laughed, but Travis said in a serious voice, "It'll be impossible to avoid that line of argument completely."

"I know that only too well," Mr. Gordon said ruefully. "I've suffered through several recent board meetings."

"I think we should focus on the issue of free speech," I said. "Jeff Gardiner has already offered to help me out with that angle, and if you can give me a day pass, I'll get to work on it with him starting next period."

Mr. Gordon smiled. "I think that approach could really work with Taggert. . . . But how exactly did you manage to enlist the aid of our greatest student critic?"

I guess I blushed, because Mr. Gordon started to laugh. "Never mind," he said. "Here's what I think you can expect tonight: Crampton and Robbins will come at you like gangbusters, and you're gonna have to stand firm all on your own. Much as we'd like to, Doctor Cayuso and I can't really go to bat for you in this situation. The board wants to hear from a living, breathing teen peer counselor and not a well-intentioned faculty member or administrator acting as a proxy. You've been put on the spot, Becca, and you've gotta show the board just how wrong the PTTA is about your intents and purposes."

My stomach felt sort of queasy now, and I was starting to actually feel nostalgic about that morning's monster surf.

"If you want to run role plays, I can fill the part of Crampton for you," Travis offered. "I know all his arguments."

"That'd be great!" I told him.

"I figure it's the least I can do," he said with a deep sigh.

⌒

Jeff, Travis, and I—and by fourth period, Zoner and Kayla—worked almost nonstop on fact-gathering, argument-structuring, and simulated verbal warfare. As word got out that we'd hunkered down in the library, Elaine Stillwell and several other counselees came by and offered to speak before the board on our behalf. Kayla, Zoner, and I thanked them all and eagerly encouraged them to show up that night, but we also made it clear we didn't want anyone to compromise themselves by describing, in a public forum, the very personal problems and issues that'd brought so many of them to the PCN in the first place. Besides, we'd already heard through Mr. Gordon that so many parents were phoning the board office to demand the right to speak at tonight's meeting, it was doubtful there'd even be time for student testimonials.

At lunch the four of us (Travis, for obvious reasons, was keeping a low profile) were interviewed under the photogenic main arch by the local press and TV media, and we thought the whole thing went pretty well. I defended the need for teen peer counseling and tried to lighten up the proceedings a bit by concluding with the observation: "We teenagers don't pretend to fully understand you adults. You seem kind of standoffish at times and prone to severe mood swings. Your popular tastes are worlds apart from our own and your value judgments occasionally strike us as both arbitrary and ill-considered. But we want you to know that we love you anyway and trust that, over the long haul, you'll give us reason to be proud."

Jeff did the Patrick Henry thing: "You can't teach us about the proud American tradition of free discourse for eleven-plus years and then expect us to sit idly by when it is taken away arbitrarily, without any pretense of due process!"

Kayla posed this puzzler: "If God meant for teenagers to totally ignore the subject of sex"—*cough*—"then why'd he see fit to juice us up with all these extra hormones?"

And finally Zoner warned ominously that if the discussion of condoms was banned on campus, "talk of dancing would almost certainly go next."

Chapter 13

THE SIX HUNDRED-SEAT auditorium at Luna High was packed. The five board members sat behind a table on stage, under a big array of superbright lights. I'd felt primed for this challenge earlier in the evening when I put on my mom's green power suit, but now, looking up at this awesome jury of powerful adults, I felt like a poser, a mere tyke playing at dress-up.

Thousands of words and legions of agitated parents preceded my turn at the podium, and at times it seemed like the whole scene might just erupt and go totally out of control. When a motion was passed to link the fate of the prom pamphlet with that of the PCN, the pressure on yours truly became all-time.

As I made my way up to the podium, I got that panicky get-me-the-hell-out-of-here-before-I-croak feeling that'd dogged me as a novice surfer. But I couldn't bail now. Way too many people were counting on me! I launched my presentation with the customary greetings and was so freaked at first by the sound of my own amplified voice that, like a total dork, I actually looked around the auditorium to see who else was speaking.

But then I chilled by remembering that Kayla, Zoner, Jeff, Mr. Gordon, the PCN staff, and five months' worth of counselees were all literally right behind me, sending positive vibes my way. This gave me the confidence I needed to charge: "Not one of the many parents who've spoken up for the PCN tonight—and we're super grateful to all of you—has said that they're in favor of teens having sex on prom night. (pause) I'm not here to take that line, either. Truth be told, I've been called up tonight for one reason only: to defend the fact that I subscribe to the notion—which some in this auditorium have openly declared to be a bogus one—that we teens share in common with you adults certain basic, inalienable rights, among them the right to freedom of expression."

There was loud applause from the students in the audience, and Ms. Irwin quickly gaveled them into silence. She was wearing an impressive dark red suit with shiny gold buttons. I wondered if she was ticked at me for getting a rise out of the crowd, but since her emotions were currently hidden behind a world-class poker face, there was no way for me to tell.

I went on to talk about constitutional law as it related to teens (this was Jeff's contribution). Since in his earlier remarks Mr. Crampton had already invoked the U.S. Supreme Court's 1988 *Hazelwood* ruling to justify censoring (i.e., shutting down) the PCN, I cited the high court's 1969 *Tinker v. Des Moines* decision, which had established that students do not "shed their constitutional rights to freedom of speech or expression at the schoolhouse gate." Mention of this landmark ruling, which was not explicitly overturned by *Hazelwood,* set off a buzz in the audience.

I talked about how the PCN got started, ran through its brief history, and read excerpts from my recent flyer. I thanked Mr. Crampton for his long, emotional speech on the dangers of STDs, the fallibility of condoms and various other forms of birth control, and the epidemic of unwanted teen pregnancies. (Listening to Crampton I'd gotten the distinct impression that he genuinely *cared* about teens at risk; this clearly wasn't just political posing on his part, as I had assumed. Still, he was no champion of free speech, and that really rankled.)

Finally, feeling weak in the knees and hoarse in the throat, I cut to the chase: "We at the PCN have always emphasized, and will continue to stress, the indisputable fact that abstinence is the only one hundred percent safe-sex option. . . . But the use of police state tactics in a totally misguided attempt to make this the *only* option that can be freely discussed at Luna High—*that* we object to in the strongest possible terms!"

There was an uproar from the crowd, a lively mix of cheers, jeers, applause, and cries of protest. Ms. Irwin gaveled the audience into silence again, while Mr. Crampton whispered something into Ms. Robbins's ear. Mr. Taggert seemed to be taking copious notes and occasionally chewed thoughtfully on the tip of his pen. Mr. Woods favored me with a wink and a smile, which lowered my jackhammering heart rate just a bit.

The first question came from Ms. Robbins: "I realize this is an unusual query, Rebecca, but I think it's important that the board know something of your personal background so we can put your eloquent presentation into a proper perspective. Are you, yourself, sexually active?"

And some counselees thought *I* played hardball! Fortunately, I'd gotten hit with this question once in practice, so I wasn't totally unprepared for it. "N-no, Ms. Robbins," I stammered, "I-I myself am not ... if you wanna know the truth, I don't even have a date to the prom."

That last part was a total ad-lib, but the crowd roared with laughter.

"She means," Mr. Crampton said in his deep bass voice as he struggled to be heard over the raucous yukfest, "are you still a *virgin?*"

His angry brown eyes seemed to drill right into me, and I was temporarily paralyzed into speechlessness.

"That's an outrageous question, Bernard!" Ms. Irwin snapped. "She doesn't have to answer that!"

Ms. Irwin's anger rallied my spirits. I leaned into the mike and said unsteadily, "With, um, all due respect, sir, my, uh, sexual history is . . . (I had to scramble for just the right words, and it took a few painful seconds) is no more a matter for public scrutiny than your own." *So there, you bully!*

The crowd went totally hyper, Crampton gave me the stink eye, Mr. Wood and Ms. Irwin laughed and applauded, and Mr. Taggert looked up from his notes and gazed at me directly for the first time. Somehow, miraculously, I seemed to actually be stumbling through this ordeal.

"Do you not agree, Rebecca, as well informed as you are," Ms. Robbins said in a distinctly less friendly tone than before, "that the only rational way for teens to protect themselves against sexually transmitted diseases is to practice abstinence?"

"That's a values question, ma'am, and I'm only really here to tackle the issue of free speech," I replied simply.

(Earlier that day Jeff'd advised me: "If they

throw a curveball at you, Becca, just swing at it with the First Amendment. That way you can't miss.")

"The two cannot be separated in this case," Mr. Crampton insisted.

I thought he was flat-out mad-dogging me now; it was really starting to piss me off. (And oddly enough, getting steamed seemed to calm my nerves a bit more.) "I beg to differ, sir. According to the best current stats available on this issue, well over two-thirds of unmarried women and men will have had sexual intercourse by the time they reach the age of twenty. That's why I feel you've asked a 'values' question." (Kayla got credit for chasing down these stats.)

"Shall we follow the herd, then, as it stampedes off a cliff?" Mr. Crampton asked.

God, this guy was relentless! He had a point about peer pressure, of course, and Zoner'd used this same herd metaphor in his slammin' prom definition, but I thought in this case the idea was being taken (literally) too far. "Shall we compare teenagers to cattle, so that we can lead them around by the nose?" I responded.

The teens in the audience cheered and the whole crowd got riled again, but I quickly plowed on: "Strained metaphors and stunning stats aside, I think we've all seen, in the parent speeches made here tonight, ample evidence that a superwide range of values exists here in Luna Point itself. A peer counselor, to be of any use at all, *has* to be wise to this fact."

"To the point that you would knowingly put your fellow students at risk for contracting potentially deadly diseases?" Ms. Robbins asked with alarm.

"You've got us peer counselors pegged all wrong," I protested. "We try to help our counselees make informed choices, *but there's no way we'd ever actually make those choices for them.*"

The grilling continued like this for almost another half-hour, until at last Ms. Irwin signaled that there was time for just one more question.

I was super relieved to hear that, 'cause by then I was pretty much played out.

The final query was a two-parter, and it came from Mr. Taggert: "Do you know, Ms. Singleton, approximately how many condoms are sold in the United States every year?"

I rummaged through my weary brain in search of the stat. Everything was coming more slowly now. "Over half a billion, sir," I finally said. (Zoner'd found that one.)

"Thank you," Mr. Taggert responded. Then he leaned back in his chair, folded his arms across his chest, and said to me, "Earlier this evening, my fellow board members Ms. Robbins and Mr. Crampton savaged the federal Centers for Disease Control and Prevention for their promotion of condom use. But they also freely cited the alarming statistics on STDs produced by that very same agency. Now I don't know whether I should trust the federal government or not! (The audience laughed.) Can you provide me, Rebecca, with an alternative, but equally authoritative voice, on this extremely vexing issue?"

Mr. Taggert was *helping* me, I realized with a growing sense of relief and excitement. My brain kicked back into high gear, and I quickly realized that, at around four-thirty that afternoon, I'd found just the thing he was now asking for: "The World Health Organization identifies condom use, along with education about sexual transmission of disease, to be the cornerstone of effective AIDS prevention programs around the globe, sir," I reported.

" 'Around the globe,' " Mr. Taggert repeated as he smiled broadly, put down his pen, and leaned forward to address the audience. "I can't speak for my fellow board members, but I for one feel fortunate to live in a land where a capable young woman like Ms. Singleton is free to marshall such an impressive array of information in the service of informed debate—"

Made bold by a growing sense that victory was at hand, I interrupted him at that point to draw attention to my "research staff" (except, of course, for Travis, who I'd have to thank later in private). The audience applauded the grinning trio, and Jeff looked surprisingly touched by my gesture.

"We're proud of you all," Mr. Taggert said. "And let me assure this assembly that I plan to cast my vote most enthusiastically in favor of continuing the Peer Counseling Network, with full confidence that it will continue to dispense its advice to our teenagers with the kind of thoroughness and even-handedness we've witnessed here tonight."

The audience went totally nuts, and I let loose with a megamongo sigh of relief. *The PCN was saved!*

Chapter 14

WHEN ALL THE heady post-board meeting interviews, handshakes, and hugs were finally history, Kayla, Zoner, Jeff, and I motored to a minimart to snag some Dove Bars before returning to my place (where we'd all rendezvoused shortly before going to the meeting in Jeff's car). Kayla and Zoner went inside to make the purchase, while Jeff and I stayed in the dimly lit front seat and talked through the events of the day.

"You were really awesome up there," he said for about the fifth time since we'd left the auditorium. "You seemed so sure of yourself."

"It was a total illusion, but thanks. And you

know I couldn't've done it without you," I once again reminded him. It was the absolute truth, too. Jeff'd worked with me on every angle of the presentation; in fact, he hadn't really left my side since second period that morning!

And so I wondered: were his *true* feelings for me coming out now because Darla was gone from the picture, or was he just caught up in the temporary thrill of a battle well fought? And now that his hand was resting on the car seat only about an inch away from mine, should I take a chance on gauging his affection for me by reaching over and boldly taking hold of it, or would that be too much too soon? (Jeff's pupils were dilated, yes, but it was, after all, dark out. And he hadn't swallowed hard yet, at least not when I was watching.) Finally I scooted my hand about a quarter-inch closer to his, figuring if he then moved his hand, it would almost certainly mean—

"Got the treats, kiddies!" Zoner said as he opened the back door and got into the car.

Damn.

"I think he bought four bars just for himself," Kayla said with good-natured disgust as she also got in.

Jeff looked at my hand and then at me and smiled knowingly before reaching for the ignition and starting the car. So we *had* been on the same wavelength! Totally encouraged, I started sending major prom vibes his way and began to agonize over who should ask whom.

Zoner was already plotting out quite the unconventional preprom festivities, including a chauffeured hearse, a fast-food dining experience, and a predance trek to a bowling alley. (He and Kayla were totally cool about including Elaine Stillwell in the fun, too, once I explained how she was a stranded counselee and a kindred spirit.)

When we got to my place, Mom raved about having watched an excerpt of the board meeting on the tube and totally hosed us with praise before heading off to bed (she had an early A.M. meeting with a group of nuclear engineers). Roger made a point of congratulating each of us, with awkward formality, on a "job well done." (The swelling in his lip was gone and the scrape on his forehead had scabbed over; Mom'd readily accepted his "bike accident" story and, as predicted, didn't once inquire about the missing jacket.) Zoner offered Roger a Dove Bar, and he not only accepted it but actually sat down to hang with us for a few. He didn't say much, though, and mainly just stared at Jeff and me with this really bizarro smile. Truth be told, I was pretty much relieved when he finally bailed back to his room.

"Why don't you give Jeff a tour of your humble abode?" Kayla suggested. She'd been glowing nonstop since this morning, a phenomenon that'd led me to conclude that it was actually requited love and *not* the vitamin B-15 in garbanzo beans that improves your skin tone.

"I don't think Jeff is really interested—," I began.

"How 'bout we just cut to the chase and you show me your bedroom," Jeff said playfully as he licked the last remaining bit of ice cream off the stick. "That's where these tours always end up anyway."

"Oh my, we've got a man of the world here," I said with a laugh as I secretly thrilled at his suggestion.

"Well, awright, but don't stay up there

any too long," Zoner said in a nagging voice as he shook his (third consecutive) Dove Bar at us. "I wasn't born yesterday. I know you youngsters've got only one thing on your mind!"

"Yeah," I said as we got up, "unfinished homework."

As it turned out, Jeff laid not a finger on me and instead explored my room with all the thoroughness of an investigative reporter prepping a major bio piece. He asked tons of probing questions as he examined the inflatable holstein cow's head hanging near the door; the quilted bedspread that depicted the San Francisco waterfront in breathtaking detail; the posters of the L.A. Philharmonic, Tom Hanks, Daniel Day-Lewis, and Avalon on Catalina Island; and my awards shelf. He rummaged through my bookcases, too, and eventually came across last year's annual. He smiled in a nostalgic way, pulled it out, and began to flip through it. . . .

Oh my God!

"You don't want to waste your time on that!" I said with way too much urgency as I rushed over to relieve him of the yearbook.

Jeff thought I was just playing, though, and

held it up out of my reach. "I only want to look up what I wrote to you last year," he said with a wry, suggestive smile.

He actually remembered! It'd meant something special to him, too! I wanted to die.

"You won't find it in there," Roger said mildly as he appeared suddenly in my doorway.

On second thought, maybe I wanted to *kill*.

Kayla soon appeared right behind Roger and gave me an anxious look that said, "I knew he was up to no good, but I couldn't stop him." And then Zoner showed behind Kayla. Where there's a serious accident, there's always a traffic jam. . . .

"What's your brother talking about?" Jeff asked with concern as he brought the annual down to eye level and flipped straight to page 147. There he saw the ragged blank square where his picture used to be, and the sparkle in his eyes died out.

Now I suppose this much *might've* happened even if Roger hadn't appeared in the doorway when he did; I'd've tried to explain the missing picture to Jeff with some sort of convoluted but hopefully plausible story (a white lie—the deluxe version). But since

Roger *was* there now, I figured the only way to salvage this situation was to plead guilty right up front and hope that Jeff was better at accepting apologies than he was at offering them.

"Jeff," I began contritely, "I did a really lame and pathetic thing last week. Your last column got me really steamed, and . . ." I gave all the petty details and then sheepishly handed him the trash can. "Needless to say," I concluded as he stared dumbly into the receptacle, "I don't feel that way about you at all now, and I hope you'll accept my deepest apology." I took a split second to glare at Roger; he had the dazed and confused look of a hunter who'd just watched his quarry commit suicide.

Jeff suddenly started to laugh, and he put the can down. I yukked right along with him at first, totally stoked that he was taking this in such good spirits, but then I saw his face and realized he wasn't laughing *that* way at all.

"Too pathetic for words," he said, gesturing at the can. "Imagine what the people you won over tonight would think now, if they could only see this."

"They'd think: 'I've done stupid things like

that when I've been mad, too,' " I said as my heart sank.

"Oh, really?" Jeff said disgustedly. "Well shucks, I forgot for a sec that you can always see *exactly* what's going on in other people's heads."

"And just what is that supposed to mean?" I said, gearing up for battle. "I never made any such claim!"

"*Please* don't do this, you guys," Kayla said anxiously.

"Didn't you gain any insight into what I'm about tonight, Jeff?" I went on. "Or has it now become impossible to penetrate that thick wall of insecurity you call 'self-reliance'?"

"You counseling types live in constant fear of not being needed, don't you?" Jeff asked contemptuously.

"You're veering toward the boil here, kids," Zoner warned.

"*All* human beings are terrified by the thought of not being needed, Jeff! My God, you've lost Darla, your parents are divorcing, and yet you still strut around pretending like you're some kind of superman—"

"So you *did* talk to Darla! I should've known! Did you encourage her to blame me for everything that went wrong in our relationship? Did you drool as she gave a third-hand account of my family misfortunes? You gossip-mongering phony! And to think I actually aided your cause today—"

"Darla spoke with me as a bud, not as a counselee! She didn't gloat over your family problems, either—anything but! She said she wanted to help you when you were hurting, Jeff, but you just shut her out. *She came to me because she was starved for someone to share her feelings with!*" I paused for a moment and realized to my horror that Jeff'd just said he regretted our whole day together. Wounded deeply, I struck right back. "Of course, after enduring all those months with *you* as a boyfriend, I'll bet even an ATM would've seemed like warm company to Darla!"

"Becca!" Kayla gasped, while Jeff's face turned crimson.

"OH IS THAT SO, YOU DATELESS, PSYCHO-BABBLING HYPOCRITE?!" he shouted at me.

"Hey, dude, that's south of the border—," Zoner protested.

"YES, IT'S SO, YOU SELF-DELUDED, MUD-SLINGING MEGALOMANIAC!" I screamed right back as tears began to blur my vision.

"Is there any way to stop 'em once they get going?" Zoner shouted at Kayla.

"NO NEED—I'M OUTTA HERE!" Jeff roared as he wheeled around and charged down the stairs.

Zoner went after Jeff. Kayla went after Zoner. And that left just Roger and me.

My brother went for the door, but I blocked his way and then slammed it shut.

"First you make fun of me for not having a prom date," I seethed as I angrily wiped the wetness from my eyes with the back of my forearm, *"and then you come up here to try to sabotage my last, best chance at one! Well, damn you, we're going to have that little brother-sister chat now, whether you like it or not. Sit down!"*

Roger's eyes flashed with anger and defiance at first, but the more he studied my face, the more the bravado seem to drain out of him, until finally he seemed to despair of escape and instead slumped down on the edge of my bed.

"What have I done to you to make you hate me so much? Why do you want to ruin me?" I asked in a voice hoarse from yelling as I sat down at my desk.

Roger didn't answer for a long time, and when he finally did I had to strain to hear him: "Life totally sucks when everyone thinks your big sister is Ms. Perfecto."

"Everyone? You mean like Jeff Gardiner?"

My brother went on as if he hadn't heard me. " 'Oh, you're so lucky,' people say. 'You can get great advice anytime you want.' But all I get are questions: 'Roger, why are you so moody today? What's with these loser clothes you wear? Can't you find any *decent* friends to hang with? What the hell happened to your hair? Why don't you play the keyboard any-more? Why don't you apply yourself more at school?' *Yak yak yak. Blah blah blah.*"

The world according to Roger Singleton. My first clear look into the murky depths. I took my time absorbing what I was seeing and hearing here, because I really had to get a handle on it this time. I didn't want what'd happened tonight to *ever* happen again.

After many minutes of intense reflection I said, "I can see your point about the clothes, the hair, and to some extent even the friends, Rog. Mom and I are definitely going to have to work harder on giving you your space in those areas. But your moodiness and your laziness are a totally different story. And what *about* school, anyway? Your grades, the vandalism—?"

"You tell me!" he exploded. "You're the expert! God, now that you've been on TV, Luna High'll be *unbearable* for me! 'So, Rog,' they'll ask, 'what's it like to live with a genuine celebrity?' As it is I get crap like: 'Are you *really* Becca's brother, or was there a mix-up at the hospital?'"

I shook my head. "I'm not gonna let you guilt-trip me, bro, so just forget about it. And sure, I'll 'tell you' what I think, only I'm talking as your sister here and not as some sort of 'expert'! I think you basically checked out of life when Dad left, and you've been pissed off at me ever since because *I didn't!* Maybe you've been thinking if you screw up badly enough at Luna High, Mom'll be forced to send you to live with Dad. But that's just not gonna happen. Dad's a great guy, and you know I love him loads, but he simply doesn't have what it takes to go the distance as a full-time parent. He admitted as much at Christmas. *In front of both of us.*"

Roger sat stock-still for a long time.

Eventually his eyes began to well up with tears.

And when I went over to his side and put my arm around him, he didn't pull away.

Instead he told me, in almost a whisper, "After I elbowed you at the mall, I hitched a ride down to the marina with these guys from out of town. We were just screwing around— you know, hopping fences—when two of them jumped me from behind and stole my jacket."

I tensed up, thinking about what *else* could've happened. But Roger didn't need me to spell that out for him. "That must've been awful," I said, holding him a little tighter.

"They knew I wouldn't rat on them to the police, because I was already breaking the law myself. *I am such an idiot! Dad spent a fortune on that jacket, all for me, and now it's gone!*" He started to bawl, and I held him tightly while he cried it out.

"There's no way I can compete with you, Becky," Roger said much later when his eyes were dry again.

"Stop thinking that way," I said. "You're just finishing up the ninth grade. I didn't even get the *idea* for the PCN until the spring of my sophomore year. . . . You'll eventually find your gig, Rog, but you're probably gonna have to bust your butt to make it happen."

He thought about that for a while, and then he sorta grinned at me and said, "My gig, huh? D'you remember when you paid me fifteen bucks to play the keyboard at your thirteenth birthday party? I thought that was a fortune!"

"So did I. But God knows you earned it. What other sixth grader in Luna Point could play the Beach Boys' 'California Girls' and the title song from *Grease* on the same bill?"

We laughed together and started full-on reminiscing about his keyboarding days, until I realized how obscenely late it'd gotten. "I'm majorly sorry for what happened tonight," Roger said contritely as he finally got up to leave. "I hope I haven't totally trashed your prom plans."

"Thanks for the a-a-a-apology, bro." I yawned appreciatively as I retrieved the trash can and carefully peeled Jeff's picture off the bottom. "And don't sweat the prom, 'cause I'm still going, no matter what."

After Roger left I fetched some tape and

made motions to return the photo to the yearbook, but then sleep overcame me and I
crashed on my bed fully clothed.

I woke up in the morning to find I was
clutching Jeff Gardiner's image firmly against
my chest.

Chapter 15

I DID SOME CAREFUL bargain-hunting in the week before the prom and finally settled for a pretty white-and-silver dress with a tulle skirt, a genuine steal at just under one hundred dollars. I also bought matching high-heeled shoes and kept the accessorizing simple: a tiny rhinestone choker, bracelets, and earrings. It would've been great to go the more expensive Sylvia Casimiro lace/puffed sleeves/brocade route, but I figured driving into downtown L.A. and forking out 225 bucks for a black leather Hard Rock Cafe jacket was a better investment over the long haul.

Roger sure thought so. When I surprised him with the gift, his eyes opened up like beach umbrellas and he hugged me killer-tight, like he used to when he was a little kid. He even played me a very rusty version of "California Girls" on his newly resuscitated keyboard.

I was now in the process of adjusting my hair color. I knew it was risky, waiting until the morning of prom Saturday to dye my hair, but I figured since I was going to the big dance without a date, it was up to me to generate the magic I'd been counting on. And besides, I desperately wanted to convey to Jeff (who, according to Zoner, was also going to the prom solo) that I was doing just fine without him. Absolutely great, in fact.

I sat on a stool in the bathroom in front of the sink and mirror. I had my hair clipped back on the left side, except for a one-inch-wide strand that I was using to preview the dye. In just a few more minutes, when the egg timer went off, I'd be able to wipe the strand clean and check the results.

Kayla and Zoner'd done their awesome best to bring about a reconciliation between Jeff and me, and it'd almost worked. As a result of gnarly negotiations in which I played only a peripheral role, Jeff met me at the public library after I picked up my paycheck on Friday afternoon. With a preagreement to make no mention (at least at first) of our Wednesday night brawl, we exchanged friendly smiles and walked down to the marina together and out onto the jetty.

The wind was blowing briskly out of the west, and billowing clouds sailed majestically across the azure blue sky, like Yankee clippers bound for Boston. Just off Luna Point a rust red navigation buoy rocked to and fro, clanging out in protest against its heavy burden of dozing harbor seals, which were stacked up like sausages at a Lion's Club charity breakfast.

We watched the waves crash at the jetty's end and marveled at how the spray shimmered in the rays of the setting sun. We could see the surfers taking waves on the beach south of the marina, and Jeff said, only half-teasingly, "I'll bet you'd rather be over there right now."

"You'd lose that bet," I said with a grin as I watched his platinum blond hair whip around in the breeze. He smiled and wordlessly took my hand in his. Holding his hand felt amazingly like falling into bed at the end of a long, exhausting day.

His intense blue eyes gazed into mine, and he said, "I want to tell you about my parents' divorce. Would that be okay?"

Would that be okay? Trying hard to contain my excitement at what this could mean for him—and for us—I nodded. We found a huge granite boulder to perch on, and he proceeded to talk. And gesture. And rage! After a while the pent-up anger, guilt, confusion, and resentment were just geysering on out, like spent coolant from an overheated radiator. I'd never felt more close to Jeff than I did that Friday afternoon.

⌒

The egg timer went off.

I wiped the strand clean and examined the color. Perfect! A pure, true medium brown, almost exactly as it'd looked on Darla's computer screen. Wasting not a moment, I excitedly mixed the color and developer together in the applicator bottle, put on the plastic gloves, placed my right index finger over the applicator tip, shook the bottle vigorously, and then began applying it evenly onto my dry hair. When I'd worked it up into a thick, rich lather, I set the egg timer again.

∽

When Jeff was done talking, I shared with him how I'd tried to cope with my own parents' divorce. He seemed fascinated by what I had to say and grateful for my reciprocal show of trust. Feeling more confident than ever now about our future prospects, I asked him, "Why blame the therapist for your mom and dad's split when it sounds as if they'd been miserably unhappy with each other for years?"

"Because he made things worse. Along with the blaming business, he put it into my mother's head that she and my father should start *apologizing* to each other. But that was a game my dad wouldn't play."

"It's not a *game*, Jeff," I said, taken aback. "It's as important to be able to say 'I'm sorry' to someone you care about as it is to say 'I love you.'"

"You sound just like my mom! I guess this must be a female thing."

"It is not! C'mon, don't you feel awful about some of the things you said last Wednesday night? I sure do."

"I thought we weren't going to bring that up," he said defensively as he yanked his hand away from mine.

"Not at first, yeah, but *surely* we can talk about it now—"

"There's no point," Jeff said. "Let's leave it in the past where it belongs and move on, okay?"

"But I can't just pretend it didn't happen! I'm *sorry* for the terrible things I said to you, Jeff, and it's important to me that you know that!" I said as I stood up.

"Okay, so I know it now," he said reassuringly as he also stood up. "You want to go to the Jolly Roger for dinner? My treat."

"Don't you have something to say to me first?" I asked with a growing sense of hopelessness.

"Oh, boy," he said, rolling his eyes. "I'm supposed to say 'I'm sorry' now, too, right? But wouldn't my apology seem just a wee bit artificial, seeing as how you had to badger me for it?" Then he smiled as if that'd settled the matter and said, "Hey, I've been thinking a lot about what you said in your presentation, about not having a prom date—"

"You just don't get it, do you?!" I asked in disbelief. "When people apologize, they're showing mutual respect for each other; they're meeting at a halfway point. Don't you respect me?"

"I'm here, aren't I?"

"But that's not enough! I'm here too, *and I also apologized!*"

That was apparently too much for him, and he finally went off on me: "Well then maybe your halfway point is further than I want to go!"

I was devastated.

I turned away from him, choked back a sob, and ran all the way back to my car.

⟋

Ding!

I put some warm water in my hair and worked the dye into a lather again. Then I rinsed over and over until the water ran clear. With hardly a pause I picked up the pump spray bottle of highlighter, applied it "generously," per the instructions, to my "clean, damp hair," and then combed it out. After that I picked up my blow-dryer, turned away from the mirror with an ear-to-ear grin (I wanted to surprise myself with the final outcome), and began to blast away. The amazingly swift and simple process of Becca transformation had almost run its course!

∝

What made Jeff's terrible stubbornness all the more ironic in the meantime was the fact that Eddie Ballard had come into my cubicle just two days ago and "surrendered" his tapes of our counseling sessions together. "These belong to you," he said contritely, with almost none of his usual bravado. "I was planning to selectively edit them into a single devastatingly incriminating recording, which I would have then given to Mr. Crampton to use against you, but my heart just wasn't in it. . . . I'm sorry I offended your sensibilities with my prom invitation, by the by."

"Thank you, Eddie," I said uncertainly. I was totally surprised and delighted by his apology and utterly appalled by his plan of revenge.

"Can we still be friends?" he asked in

that anxious, heartbreaking little-boy-lost way of his.

I looked down at the tiny pile of tapes and suddenly saw in it one of those "flashes of promise" I'd told Zoner about. "As a peer counselor I'm big on second chances," I told Eddie with a smile.

"Right-o," he said, smiling back. "By the way, have you been getting enough sleep lately? Your eyes look—"

"I don't want to know," I said firmly.

He nodded and proceeded instead to tell me about a dream involving a fast-moving train, a dark tunnel, and a beautiful conductor named Jennifer, who was actually his lab partner in chemistry. . . .

～

My hair was dry now, so I shut off the blowdryer and whirled around to get a first look at my new self. But what I saw made me shriek in horror and grab instantly for the bottle of hair lightener. I reread the label at lightning speed. I'd followed the instructions! Every last one of them! But then I read the fine print, which I'd skipped earlier, and found the warning: *"Not recommended for use on color-*

treated hair. Undesirable hues may result." I looked back in the mirror and screamed and then screamed some more at the top of my lungs, until finally my mother and brother burst frantically into the bathroom and demanded to know what was the matter.

I instantly tore a towel off the nearby rack and covered my head with it, but it was too late.

They'd already seen the perfect medium brown hair with the pumpkin orange highlights around the face.

Chapter 16

MOM WOULDN'T let me recolor it. "You'll have to wait at least a few days, honey; otherwise, you'll irritate your scalp and ruin your hair."

Ruin my hair?!

It was too late to get a wig. And a scarf would only draw more attention to the problem (if such a thing were possible). So that was that.

All was lost.

I couldn't possibly go to the dance now.

Becca Singleton, Prom Night No-Show. Peer Hypocrite.

What would Jeff Gardiner say?!

Still wearing the bath towel ghost-style, I moaned and lay my head down on the counter.

"I think it looks great, Becca," Roger said sincerely. "And original, too—there's only like three other people in the whole school with orange hair."

"That's not the sort of statement your sister was looking to make, honey," Mom told him.

I wondered dully if it was possible to smother yourself with a bath towel, even when your family was watching.

No doubt some medium brown-haired girl with *natural* blond highlights around the face would come up to Jeff at the prom and ask him to dance. They'd hit it off in a major way. No insults, no misunderstandings, no "history." People would watch them with jealous awe and whisper, "Wow, can't you just sense the chemistry? The trust? The mutual respect? And I hear he exchanges apologies with her all the time. . . ."

"I'm calling your friend Kayla right now," Mom said as she gently patted my back. "And please take that towel off your head before you smother."

⌁

The last of Kayla's many well-meaning suggestions was to put my hair up in a French twist and camouflage it with a strategically assembled crown of California poppies. "Thanks," I said gratefully, "but I think I'd prefer to just leave it the way it is, looking like a shower curtain from the late nineteen sixties."

"But you can't just give up on the prom after all you've been through!" Kayla insisted. "Besides, the dance'll be a total drag without you there. A *total* drag."

"Kayla, you're really sweet, but get serious. I look like a walking ad for Minute Maid orange juice. Like I told Zoner not ten minutes ago: I'll do the hearse, I'll do McDonald's, and I'll even bowl a few games, if you insist, but the prom is *absolutely out of the question!*"

A call came in from the Zoneman himself as we continued to argue while doing our nails and makeup. Kayla surprised me by insisting on taking it downstairs, "in private." Since when did we keep secrets from each other?!

Even worse, when Kayla came back she not only wouldn't talk about the prom anymore but she didn't drop a single hint about what she and Zoner'd discussed. "He just had some last minute questions about wardrobe issues," she said with a smile.

I was already beginning to get that dreaded "third wheel" feeling.

Kayla wore a blue tie-dyed slip dress, black pumps, a black beaded necklace, and sterling silver cresting-wave earrings. Zoner wore black leather flip-flops, white canvas "dress" trunks, a magenta Zog's Sex Wax T-shirt, a tie that was shaped and colored like a surfboard (right down to the sponsor decals) and sported three tiny plastic fins jutting out at the tail, a white Casablanca dinner jacket, a pair of varnished wood-framed sunglasses, and a neon palm tree earring.

Elaine wore a gorgeous blue sequined dress, and Kayla and Zoner promised to stick by her at the dance even if I "flaked out."

The hearse was rather cozier than anyone expected, with its plush purple velvet bench seats and coffin-shaped mahogany table.

Zoner surprised me and Elaine with corsages and then popped the soundtrack from the movie *Grease* into his portable CD player. We all sang along to the title tune (and I thought happily about Roger); Elaine and Kayla howled "Hopelessly Devoted to You" in the manner of two love-struck coyotes; and then Zoner serenaded me with "Beauty School Dropout," with the girls doing background vocals. I was totally mortified at first, but gradually the corny lyrics got to me, and by the end I was singing along, relieved to figure out that this song must've been the innocuous subject of Kayla and Zoner's secretive phone call.

All three of us girls lip-synched "You're the One That I Want" to a cute window attendant at McDonald's, and he rewarded us by doubling up on the fries and tossing in three free hot apple turnovers. "Nice wheels," he said as he handed me the last bag. He must've thought my hair was part of some gimmick, 'cause it didn't seem to faze him in the least.

"To die for," I said in a sultry voice.

The attendant laughed so hard, his headset nearly fell off, and everyone teased me all through dinner about my new Drive-thru Don

Juan, the Fast-Food Figaro, Prince of Packaged Pulp, Connoisseur of Cholesterol.

"Jealousy," I said disdainfully as I waved off their taunts with a Chicken McNugget, "pure jealousy."

Jimmy Buffet, R.E.M., the Trashmen ("Surfin' Bird"), Aerosmith, and the Rivingtons ("Papa-Oom-Mow-Mow") accompanied us on the long haul to the bowling alley in Fountain Valley.

Our formal attire created quite the stir when we arrived and seemed to have a distracting effect on the bowlers in adjacent lanes, especially in one memorable frame when Elaine got her fingers stuck in a ball and it literally tried to score with her.

Overall, though, we girls did pretty well. Poor Zoner, on the other hand, was teased and distracted so relentlessly by his female companions that most of his efforts went into polishing the gutters.

"I hope he dances better than he bowls," Elaine whispered to Kayla and me after the last frame, and then she watched in amazement as we both doubled over with hysterical laughter.

The mood in the hearse had gloomed up

considerably by the time we got back on the San Diego Freeway, southbound. Elaine stared out the window at the passing cars and blurring buildings, her expression now as blue as her dress. Kayla kept giving me sad, sweet, I-can't-believe-this-is-happening-to-my-best-friend looks, while Zoner patted her hand and whispered reassuringly, "Don't stress. It'll be cool, it'll be cool."

"Zoner's right, Kayla—I'll be fine," I finally said out loud. "I had a great time tonight, thanks to you guys. *I really did.*"

She nodded doubtfully.

⌁

Kayla, Zoner, and Elaine made one last desperate plea to me as the hearse pulled up in front of the shimmering lobby doors of the Luna Point Sheraton, promising to guard me from hecklers as conscientiously as Secret Service agents on a presidential detail. By then, though, I was already crouched way down in my seat, begging them to leave as quickly as possible before I was spotted by someone I knew (name: Jeff Gardiner).

Elaine squeezed my hand as she left, and Kayla kissed me on the cheek. Zoner patted me on the shoulder and told me that "orange hair is way more of a turn-on than you realize."

After he shut the door I found myself alone at last, idling in a hearse in front of the junior prom I had so pointlessly fantasized about for months on end. "Take me home, quickly!" I yelped at the driver as the tears began to flow like party punch.

The hearse lurched forward but then screeched to a sudden halt. "What the—!"

Outside, I heard several loud hoots from Zoner, followed by unmistakable shrieks of delight from Kayla and Elaine.

And then the car door opened!

I sat up and shrank back defensively as a big, tuxedo-clad male entered my lair of sorrows.

Jeff Gardiner!

The bane of my existence and the sole object of my thoughts for the past eleven days. Here. In the very same hearse. "I've decided I want to meet you halfway, after all," he said as he sidled up next to me.

Thrilled by his words I turned to take a good, long look at him. I gasped in amazement and then melted like an Eskimo Pie on a summer dashboard. I probably would've fallen hopelessly in love with the guy even if he *hadn't* dyed his hair orange, but that definitely sealed it.

Jeff took me in his arms and kissed me. It was the kind of kiss that was so perfect, so incredibly passionate and heartfelt, it made you want to cry . . . and it tasted like nothing I had ever known before.

"Any sign of th

Bethany didn't answe
direction. She was as
herself as close as pos

He laughed. He couldn't help himself. The look on her face was just too comical to ignore. "Are you okay?"

She shook her head. "No. You're wild!" The tone of her voice made it perfectly clear what she thought of his driving.

"What?" He raised an eyebrow, giving her his best innocent look.

"Remind me to never let you drive anywhere ever again," she said under her breath. "I think I'm going to throw up all over your nice floor mats."

"Come on. I'm a good driver," he said with a smile.

She narrowed her eyes. "At least tell me you lost our tail."

"Yep."

"Then it was worth it." She moaned. "I guess," she qualified.

Daniel pulled up behind the storefront and killed the engine, then turned to Bethany. "Okay. Are you ready for this?"

Bethany grimaced. "Ready as I'll ever be."

Kathleen Tailer is a senior attorney II who works for the Supreme Court of Florida in the office of the state courts administrator. She graduated from Florida State University College of Law after earning her BA from the University of New Mexico. She and her husband have eight children, five of whom they adopted from the state of Florida. She enjoys photography and playing drums on the worship team at Calvary Chapel, Thomasville, Georgia.

Books by Kathleen Tailer

Love Inspired Suspense

Under the Marshal's Protection
The Reluctant Witness
Perilous Refuge
Quest for Justice
Undercover Jeopardy

UNDERCOVER JEOPARDY

KATHLEEN TAILER

⟨H⟩ HARLEQUIN® LOVE INSPIRED® SUSPENSE

Recycling programs for this product may not exist in your area.

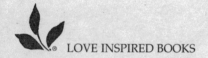

® LOVE INSPIRED BOOKS

ISBN-13: 978-1-335-67891-1

Undercover Jeopardy

Copyright © 2019 by Kathleen Tailer

www.Harlequin.com

Printed in U.S.A.

And we know that all things work together for good to them that love God, to them who are the called according to his purpose.... If God be for us, who can be against us?
—*Romans* 8:28-31

For all the missionaries around the world who have dedicated their lives to sharing the love of Jesus Christ, including Beverly and Greg Wootton, Isaac and Clea Wootton and their wonderful children, and Connie Rose. May God continue to bless you as you do His work across the African continent and beyond.

ONE

Detective Daniel Morley wrote the date on his deposit slip, then double-checked it against the large calendar the bank had posted on one of the columns near the customer service desk among the green pine trim and the red-and-white candy cane decorations. December 14. It had been one year since Bethany Walker had disappeared from his life. An entire year of searching and coming up empty. He was a detective—one of the best in the business, but he'd utterly failed to find her, despite his herculean efforts. She had been his fiancée but now, instead of celebrating their wedding anniversary, he was solemnly remembering the last time he'd seen her and the hurtful words he'd spoken during their argument right before she'd driven away. He should have gone after her. Now, he didn't know if he'd ever even see her again, and the calendar before him was just one more reminder of how long she had been missing from his life.

People didn't just disappear, and yet, Bethany seemed to have done just that. Her apartment lease had been paid in advance, but despite several evenings of surveillance, he had not seen a single person enter or leave. He'd even used his law enforcement credentials to complete a welfare check. Daniel and the landlord walked through the rooms together, but there was no sign of Bethany, or any clues as to her whereabouts. Her refrigerator was bare, and there were only a few staples left in the pantry. It was obvious that she wasn't living there. But then where was she staying? And if she'd moved and left the Chattanooga area completely, why had she kept the lease? It was a mystery.

"Excuse me, can I please have one of those?" An older lady smiled at him as her voice brought him out of his reverie. She motioned toward the stack of deposit slips sitting in front of him, and he smiled back at her as he pushed them in her direction so they were within her reach.

"Of course. Here you go."

The bullets from a semi-automatic machine gun slammed into the ceiling, quickly covering Daniel with dust and debris from the tiles overhead as the noise shattered the peaceful Friday morning. He instinctively crouched, taking the older woman with him and pushing her under the desk for safety. He pulled out his service 9 mm pistol, his eyes darting around the room as he assessed the situation.

"Everyone get down on the floor!" The voice was masculine and accentuated by more gunfire. Several of the customers screamed, and the fear in the room was palpable and made the air feel heavy and thick. A man in a black hoodie and jeans jumped up on the counter and started waving his rifle around. He let loose with another stream of bullets into the ceiling.

"Quiet, now! The next person who makes a noise dies!" he yelled.

The room was instantly silent, and all eyes were on the robber, awaiting his next command. The man's face was covered by a mask that distorted his features, and he paced back and forth like a caged tiger. The mask gave away the fact that he was Caucasian and little else, and there was a grotesque smile on it that made his expression seem malevolent and evil.

The robber swung his gun toward a woman teller in a gray suit who already had tears streaming down her cheeks. She was trembling and seemed almost frozen in place. The color seemed to drain from her face once she realized the robber had focused his attention on her. "Get your hand away from the counter!" he yelled, as he fired a barrage of bullets over her head. "If you touch that silent alarm button, you're dead." She ducked and dropped to the floor, her body still shaking uncontrollably.

He turned back to the crowd in the lobby and immediately fired a burst toward the ceiling again. "Okay, everyone. You have five seconds to get down on the floor. Anybody still standing after five seconds will be shot. Understand? One, two…"

Daniel scanned the room. From his vantage point where he was still partially concealed by the table, he could see three other robbers. They were all wearing the same black hoodies and jeans. They even had the same masks with identical evil smiles, just like the one worn by their leader. One large muscular robber had positioned himself near the bank's front door and had put a metal cable around the handles, effectively locking the doors and everyone inside the building while also keeping others out. This man was taller than the others and looked like he either worked out on a regular basis or, at a minimum, played a sport that kept him in excellent shape. He had disarmed the guard who had been stationed by the front door, and was motioning to him and two other men to join the rest of the hostages in the lobby of the bank.

The other two robbers were both skinnier than the man by the front door and younger, if Daniel was any judge of the way they held themselves. Maybe they were in their twenties? Their movements seemed reckless and exceedingly hyper, or they could have just been high on the adrenaline rush that came from shooting up a bank and scaring innocent people. Either way, it was obvious that they were extremely dangerous and volatile. One of the robbers approached the customers who were slower to obey, and he tossed his gun back and forth between his hands, yelling at them and forcing them into compliance. He seemed to have some sort of facial hair under his mask, and Daniel nicknamed him Hairy in his mind. The other robber followed closely behind Hairy at first, but then finally moved away and started spraying paint over the security cameras that were set in three corners of the room. Once the cameras were disabled, he tossed the spray can aside and stationed himself near a doorway that appeared to lead back to the public bathrooms. Daniel noticed he had a small limp and tended to drag his right foot a bit.

"We're not here for you," the leader yelled over the confusion, still pacing from his perch on the countertop. "We just want to make a small withdrawal." He made a point of making eye contact with any of the hostages who dared to look in his direction. "No one will get hurt as long as you do everything we say."

Daniel looked to the left and saw two men, both crawling away from the front counter area and heading toward the back of the bank where the desks and offices were found. One was wearing a suit and appeared to be a bank employee. The other was wearing shorts and a button-down shirt and seemed to be following the other one. It was apparent that both were looking for a safe place to hide. They didn't escape the notice of the lead robber, however, who jumped down, ran so that he was directly in front of them and pointed his gun straight at their heads. "Put your faces on the floor. Both of you. Now!"

Daniel moved so he could get a better look at the leader but still be shielded by the counter. So far, he had escaped the robbers' notice, but he knew it couldn't last much longer. He raised his gun, taking aim at the man's chest. One quick shot was all it would take to stop the leader in his tracks and foil this robbery attempt here and now. He might even save the two men on the floor in the process. His finger flexed on the trigger.

"Freeze." The cold metal of the barrel pushed against his skull. He tried to turn a bit to see who was behind him, but the pressure increased against his head and he stopped. He hadn't realized there was a fifth robber. He mentally kicked himself for missing that important fact. His inconceivable mistake might just have cost him his life.

"Hands up. Now."

The voice sounded familiar to him, but he couldn't place it. He guessed that the robber was a woman by the tone of her voice, even though she was obviously trying to disguise the sound by making it gritty and deeper. He slowly raised his hands as she leaned forward and grabbed his pistol, then pushed him from behind. "Get over there by the wall, hero."

He chanced a look behind him but only got a quick glance before she pushed him again. It was enough of a look to get a basic impression of the robber, but little else. All he could tell was that she was definitely a woman. Her stature was lean but still feminine, despite the baggy jeans and hoodie she was wearing, and she was quite a bit shorter than the other robbers. Even with the mask that disguised her features, he'd also gotten a good enough look to tell that the eyes and lips were quite ladylike.

"Against the wall, everyone," the leader yelled. The robbers continued motioning with their guns and herding the customers and bank staff toward the far wall until the whole group was lined up against it. Daniel watched the process as the woman robber marched him over to join the rest of the hostages. So far, he counted eighteen of them, including both customers and bank employees. He saw the old lady that had been near him when the robbers had entered the bank, and her eyes were large and wet beneath her glasses. Her skin had paled, and her weathered hands desperately gripped her large black pocketbook that she held close to her chest. She was obviously terrified. He glanced at the others. There were seven other women and ten men, including himself. He kept his hands up as he walked to the group of frightened people, but when he took his place at the end of the line, he didn't sit like the others. Instead, he turned and kept his hands raised in mock surrender and took a step toward the woman robber. When he spoke, he kept his tone low and calm.

"You don't have to do this. Nobody's been hurt. You can turn around and walk away now before this goes any further."

"Just shut up and do as you're told," she responded, her voice cold.

"Think about what you're doing," Daniel implored softly, still trying to sound as non-threatening as possible.

"I can assure you that we've given this a great deal of thought. Now have a seat." She gestured with her gun and Daniel acknowledged her but didn't sit. He could see the bulge of the weapon that she had taken from him and stuffed into the waistband of her jeans. No cop wanted his service pistol to end up in the hands of a criminal, and Daniel was no exception.

He made a vow to recover that gun before this episode was over. Funny—she hadn't asked why he had been carrying a gun. Tennessee did have very liberal concealed weapon permit laws, but still...

He pushed that thought aside and decided to try talking to her one more time. "The laws have gotten tougher," he said quietly. "Bank robbery is federal. You could get a life sentence. The minimum is twenty-five years when guns are involved. If you give up now—"

"Not happening," she said roughly, aiming her gun directly at his midriff. "Don't be a hero. Sit down with the others." Her voice was low but threatening.

"Is this guy giving you a problem?" Daniel turned and saw one of the younger robbers coming toward him. He thought it was Hairy, the one who had been tossing the gun around, but he couldn't be sure. The criminal's stance was aggressive as he approached, and Daniel braced for the battle that was heading his way.

"It's under control," she snarled.

"Doesn't look like it's under control to me." He lifted his rifle as if to hit Daniel in the face, but before he could do anything further, the woman stepped in front of Daniel, her stance protective.

"Back off," the woman exclaimed angrily. "I said I have it under control."

The young man paused a moment, his body moving from foot to foot as if he was filled with energy and was about to explode. "Sure you do."

She took a step closer to the other robber, her voice tight. "The deal was nobody gets hurt. Now stay out of my way, J.P.," she growled.

He leaned closer and his whisper was a low hiss. "No names, remember?"

She motioned around her. "Who's gonna hear me? I'm serious. Stay out of my way."

"You stay out of *my* way, girl. I didn't want you here in the first place." He spun around and angrily threatened one of the other customers with his rifle. "Get back, did you hear me?" He raised the weapon up as if he was going to hit someone else, then abruptly stalked off.

Bethany blew out a breath of relief as the man moved away. Her heart was beating so strongly she was sure J.P. could hear it. What in the world was Daniel doing here, of all places? Thankfully, she had been able to dis-

tract J.P. before any further violence had happened. She had once seen J.P. beat a man into
unconsciousness for borrowing his truck without asking. He was vengeful and a loose can-
non, and there was no telling how far he would
go if he continued unchecked. She said a small
prayer of thanks under her breath, then motioned to Daniel with her gun.

"Sit with the others. Now."

Daniel put his hands up in a motion of mock
surrender, then nodded and sat. She didn't like
the way he was studying her, but it couldn't
be helped.

She glanced over at J.P., who was stalking
the floor, threatening anyone who dared to
look up. The kid was a hothead, and she had
been trying to avoid him ever since she'd infiltrated this band for the FBI a year ago. He
was always challenging her, and if anyone was
going to blow her cover, it would probably be
him.

She looked down at Daniel and her heart
continued to pound. She didn't think he had
recognized her, and she wondered how long
she could keep her identity a secret from him
if this robbery took longer than expected. Her
feelings were in a jumbled mess where Dan-

iel was concerned. She had loved him once, or thought she had, but that seemed like a lifetime ago. Their last words had been said in anger, and she had taken this undercover assignment only a few days later. It had been an excellent escape and helped her refocus her energy after their breakup. Now that a year had passed, she had no desire to bring those feelings to the surface and sort through them all over again. The past was better left in the past.

"Okay, I want everyone's cell phones. Now!" She turned to see their leader, Jackson, swinging his gun around and carrying a trash can. He walked down the line of hostages and waited impatiently as they each deposited their cell phones in the metal can. The captives were all in different stages between panic and disbelief. A couple of the women were crying, and a few of the men were pale and withdrawn, but they all complied with Jackson's orders. When he came to Daniel, he stopped and Bethany held her breath, hoping that neither Jackson nor Daniel would start an altercation. Being undercover meant sometimes walking a thin line between the legal and illegal. Her participation in this bank robbery had been authorized by her handler at the FBI, so they could trace the stolen money and make bigger arrests, but it was hard to see anyone get hurt. Still, she would blow her cover in a heartbeat if any of the robbers tried to kill an innocent victim. The problem was that she knew Daniel was a fellow officer who would do everything within his power to foil this robbery. She held her breath, not sure what to expect, her body tense and ready to react.

"Was this man giving you trouble?" Jackson asked, looking between Daniel and the other robbers.

A cold sweat ran down her back. Should she tell their leader that Daniel was a cop? Her mind focused on the heaviness of Daniel's weapon resting in the waistband of her jeans. If he saw Daniel's police badge or somehow discovered that she'd known he was law enforcement and hadn't said anything, it could blow her cover. But if she did tell, Jackson might lose his temper and try to hurt Daniel, and she would be forced to intervene. There was no telling what he would do if he found out one of the hostages was a detective with the local police department. This entire assignment could blow up in the next few moments if she didn't quickly think of a solution.

Her mind was spinning when surprisingly J.P. solved her problem for her.

"He was mouthing off. I had to show him who was in charge," J.P. offered with a sardonic grin.

Bethany blew out a breath of relief, her dilemma temporarily fixed. She watched Jackson carefully, waiting for his reaction.

Jackson finally nodded, apparently accepting the response, and pointed his gun at Daniel's head. "Give me your cell phone."

Daniel's pulled out his cell phone that was clipped to his belt and in the same motion, surreptitiously pushed his detective shield into his pocket, hiding it from view. Bethany noticed and quickly looked down so it seemed like she wasn't paying attention. He dropped the phone in the trash can with the others and Jackson continued down the line, none the wiser.

Suddenly a shot rang out, and J.P. shrieked and grabbed his side. A dark circle of blood appeared on the hoodie near J.P.'s abdomen, and J.P. slowly sank to the floor, his face contorted with pain. Bethany crouched, her weapon ready, searching the room for the source of the shot. Would the next bullet take her out?

TWO

Bethany turned just in time to see a security guard slip back behind a corner in the hallway leading to the back of the building. She fired back, but made sure her shots were high. Good grief! Hadn't Jackson cleared the building? She noticed Jackson motioning to Terrell, the big, well-built robber who had locked the front doors and was closer to the guard's hiding place than any of the other robbers. They had all studied the floor plans of the bank before the theft, and they all knew that if Terrell was careful, he could sneak up on the guard from behind and disarm him by going through a second hallway that was accessible from behind the tellers' counter. Terrell nodded to Jackson and silently disappeared through the door. Bethany hoped Terrell would be reasonable and not hurt the guard. He was a true believer in the cause, but he wasn't by nature a violent person. A few minutes later, they heard some shouting from the hallway, and Terrell led the security guard out with his hands up and forced him to join the line of hostages. He had been disarmed and had a recalcitrant expression on his face, but he didn't look injured. Bethany was instantly relieved. Her biggest dread in participating in this crime was that someone innocent would get hurt or killed. It was bad enough that J.P. got shot. She surely didn't want any other casualties.

"Trying to be a hero?" Jackson sneered when the guard and Terrell reached the group. The guard didn't answer, and Bethany glanced at her watch. Things were going downhill, fast. They needed to get into the vault, get what they came for and get out of here. This whole robbery was taking way too long. A wave of anxiety washed over her as she watched Jackson motion to the guard with his gun. "Sit down with the others." The guard complied, warily eyeing J.P., who was still laying on the floor, bleeding and moaning loudly and intermittently. He was right to be worried. If J.P. weren't hurt so badly, he surely would have been so angry about being shot that he would have killed the guard outright just for revenge. J.P. had always been the one wild card in the whole operation. It was almost a blessing that he was out of the mix and wouldn't be able to hurt anybody. Still, she didn't want him to die.

As Jackson gave orders for Terrell to sweep the place and make sure no one else was hiding in the back, Bethany went over to J.P.'s side. She put her rifle down and pulled up J.P.'s shirt so she could examine his wound. The fabric was already soaked with blood. He grabbed her arm and squeezed her hard. "I can't believe he shot me. Help me, Hailey. He wasn't supposed to shoot me."

Bethany nodded and met his eye, trying to reassure him. "Sure thing, J.P. Just let me take a look." Hailey was her undercover name, yet it still sounded odd to her ears. She thought she'd eventually get used to it, especially since she'd been undercover for a year with this group.

She examined the wound carefully, then gingerly rolled him to his side so she could see if the bullet had gone out his back. Thankfully, she found an exit wound. Even though it was bleeding profusely, she thought it was merely a flesh wound. If she could just stop the blood flow, he should be back to his normal nasty self in only a few weeks. She carefully pulled off her hoodie, found some scissors in a drawer in a nearby worker's desk and cut the sweat-shirt into strips, thankful for the latex gloves that the robbers were all wearing that kept her hands free of the blood. She kept her mask in place and still had on the black T-shirt she had been wearing underneath the hoodie, but now it was clear to everyone that she was a woman. There was no way to hide her body shape or her dark blond hair that was pulled back in a slick ponytail. She made a bandage out of the fabric and applied pressure for a few minutes before wrapping the rest of the strips around him to securely hold the bandage in place. Once she finished dressing his wound, she tied a knot and leaned over him.

"Alright, J.P.," she whispered for his ears only. "You lie still, okay?" She put his hands on top of the knot. "Hold that bandage right there as tightly as you can to stop the bleeding. Got it?" She squeezed his arm. *God, please save his life and change his heart.*

She grabbed her rifle again and stood. At least now J.P. had a fighting chance. She glanced nonchalantly in Daniel's direction, but a sliver of fear slid down her spine when she saw the look on his face. His eyes were burning into her like hot coals. It was obvious that he had recognized her, and anger and frustration radiated from his head to his toes. Now that he knew who she was, would he blow her cover? She met his eyes, which were following her every movement. Maybe it wasn't anger she saw there but confusion and hurt instead. She looked away, not ready to confront Daniel or the emotions that caused a tightening in her chest.

Bethany Walker, his ex-fiancée, stood not twenty feet from him. Daniel still couldn't believe it. But what was she doing robbing banks? He sat up a little straighter and watched her carefully as she tended to the other robber. He wanted to march right over to her and demand an explanation, but something inside of him urged caution. Bethany was a top special agent for the FBI. She had to be on assignment. Still, law enforcement was in the business of preventing crime, not creating crime, so why was she involved in an illegal activity like bank robbery? In Daniel's book, Bethany's actions violated the oath of a law enforcement officer.

How could she protect and serve if she was the one wielding the rifle?

Daniel's attention was quickly diverted as the leader abruptly shot another stream of bullets into the ceiling. "Alright, who is the manager here?" He paced in front of the terrified group of hostages. All of the other robbers besides Hairy, wait, what had Bethany called him? Oh, yeah, J.P. All of the robbers besides J.P. stood behind the leader, keeping a wary eye on the situation, their guns at the ready. J.P. lay moaning on the floor right where he had fallen. The leader moved closer to one of the men who obviously worked at the bank. "Are you the manager?"

The man put his hands up in mock surrender and shook his head. "No, no, it's that guy." He pointed to an older man in a dark suit who gave him a withering look.

The leader smiled and sauntered over to the manager. He motioned with his gun. "Get up, mister manager. I'd like to see the inside of your vault."

"It's time locked," the man sputtered.

"You're quite right," the leader said with a smile as he checked his watch. "Isn't it wonderful that we're here at precisely the correct time? Now, if you'll just come punch your code into the keypad, we'll be in business."

Daniel could tell the man was terrified but was also trying his best to stall and protect the bank. His hesitance wasn't lost on the leader either, who grabbed the manager's tie and brought him to his feet. Then he pushed him toward the back of the bank where the vault was located. The man stumbled but righted himself and started walking. The leader, the robber with the limp and the bodybuilder robber all followed him, each carrying a large black duffel bag they had brought in with them when they'd first entered the bank. Daniel noticed there were two other bags of supplies the robbers had carried in, and he wondered briefly what was inside of them. He remembered that bank robberies usually averaged six minutes from start to finish, and he wondered fleetingly when this team was planning to make their escape. They had already been in the bank quite a long time by robbery standards and had gone way past the average.

Bethany was the only robber left to watch the hostages, although J.P. was still lying on the floor, suffering from his injuries. She took over the pacing in front of the line of people, and Daniel watched her carefully, wondering if there was any way he could find an opportunity to talk to her in private so he could figure out what was going on.

The phone suddenly rang, the shrill sound startling the group. Bethany ignored it, but after the tenth ring or so, Daniel spoke up. "Want me to answer that for you?"

"Stay where you are," she said flatly, pointing her gun at him. Now that he knew her identity, Daniel knew he wasn't in danger and she wouldn't fire, but he didn't want to push her too far and ruin her cover either. Still, he had big questions for her. How could he get her alone to talk? Was it even possible in the confines of this insane robbery situation?

The ringing continued.

"Look, you must know this is taking too long. The police are probably already outside surrounding the place. They're undoubtedly controlling the phones, and that's a negotiator calling to talk you through this mess. You need to listen to him." A couple of the other hostages groaned when he spoke, apparently frustrated with his goading.

"Shut up," Bethany said roughly, taking a

step in his direction. "It's too early for the police to be here."

The ringing continued.

Daniel couldn't help himself. All of the hurt and frustration he'd felt at losing Bethany suddenly came to a head, and now that he had found her, he had to push forward, regardless of the circumstances. "It's got to be them," he said, not knowing if it really was or not, but trying hard to sell the bluff. He started to stand and confront her, but she moved in closer and actually pointed the gun directly at his head. When she spoke, her voice was low and cold like ice. "I said, stay where you are. Don't move again unless you want a new hole in your head."

He looked up into her eyes, those gray-blue eyes that reminded him of polished steel, and backed off. There was strength there, and memories flooded back at him. He remembered her laughing during a funny part of a movie and accepting his comfort when her cat died. They had shared a lot during their relationship, but the woman standing in front of him brandishing the gun as part of a robbery gang seemed like a total stranger. Yet, the love remained. He couldn't erase it, no matter how much he had tried to forget her during the last year. He eyed her critically, noticing small details about her. She was thinner now, and her hair was a bit longer, but now that he knew her identity, it was hard to figure out why he hadn't identified her sooner, even with the mask distorting her facial features.

Why? Why had she left him without an explanation? Had she never loved him in the first place? Why had she never followed through and walked down the aisle with him? Where had she been for the last year? Pain slashed across his chest, but he tried his best to push those questions out of his mind. As much as he wanted to confront her and demand answers, they would have to wait. This wasn't the time or place. In fact, he might never get a chance to talk to Bethany privately during this bank robbery. Right now, he needed to focus on stopping this crime, if it was possible, and make sure nobody got hurt, including the woman he loved.

Suddenly, another man from the middle of the group started to stand, as well. Bethany swung her rifle in his direction and let fly a short burst of bullets. She must have aimed high on purpose, because each shot missed and hit the wood paneling about two feet above his head. Still, the shots had the desired effect, and the man quickly sat back down again, his eyes wide with fear. She took a few steps back, apparently making sure she had a good view of all the hostages.

When she spoke, her voice was tough as nails, and her body language said she was more than just angry. "I said, stay where you are, all of you. Make no mistake, I am in control of this room and I missed on purpose. The next person that moves will be dead. Got it? I don't have to miss. I'm an excellent shot. We'll be out of here in just a few more minutes, and then you can all go back to your lives. Until then, you stay quiet and out of our way."

Daniel couldn't keep silent despite her orders. He changed his tactic, knowing Bethany would always want to make sure a life wasn't lost during an operation but also ensuring he didn't make her appear vulnerable in front of the other hostages. The last thing he needed was for the hostages to feel empowered and attempt to rush her or try to take away her weapon. "We get it. You're in charge. But please, let someone take your man outside. He's injured and needs medical attention."

Daniel paused, waiting to see how Bethany would respond to his argument. Seeing no change in her expression, he tried a different approach. "If he dies, it will go worse for you in the long run." Daniel knew she had a better chance of keeping her cover intact if no one died during this operation, and if law enforcement could interrogate the robber lying on the floor, all the better.

She laughed. She actually laughed at his suggestion. "So the police can arrest him on sight? No, thank you."

Was she being sincere, or acting the part? He honestly couldn't tell. Maybe he didn't know her anymore after all. A lot could change in a year. "He'll die if he doesn't get help. He'll also slow down your escape." He pointed to one of the stronger looking men. "Let him do it. He can carry the guy out and make sure he gets the help he needs."

He waited as the seconds slowly ticked by, stretching into minutes. The air felt thick.

THREE

As if on cue, the phone started ringing again, slicing into the silence. Bethany eyed her watch, then the doorway that led to the vault. Something must have gone wrong; they were taking way too long to get the money and emerge from the back room where the vault was located. She knew that Jackson had already knocked out the video feeds and alarm system, but she wondered fleetingly if there was an issue with the bank manager's code. Jackson swore he could bypass the electronic lock on the vault by doing some fancy wiring if he had to, but she wasn't as confident in his abilities as he was. If he wasn't going to be able to open it after all, her undercover mission was going to last even longer than she'd thought. The group she had infiltrated needed money to operate, and if they didn't get it here and now, they would have to commit more crimes in the future to fund their operation. It was better all-around if they were successful here today. Then she could focus on building her case and making her arrests as the robbers put their more devious plans into motion.

She eyed the group of hostages in front of her and tried to look tough and demanding. So far, she was confident that they wouldn't do anything foolish—except for Daniel, that is. She could tell he was testing her. Maybe if their relationship hadn't ended so badly he wouldn't be challenging her, but now he knew her true identity, and she wasn't sure what to expect. No matter what, she couldn't blow her cover. Not here and now when she had come so far and given this operation a year of her life.

"Let me get that phone for you," Daniel suggested again. She swung back and stalked toward him. She doubted that the ringing phone was the police. This was a place of business after all, and phones probably rang constantly throughout the day. Still, the sound was eerily annoying, but not as annoying as the look of hurt in Daniel's eyes that he was apparently unable to hide. His expression surprised her. Hadn't they both said angry words to each other on that fateful day when they had ended their relationship? Pride made her push past the feelings that were starting to bubble in her chest.

Maybe she had hurt him by not giving him an opportunity to explain after the big blowup. He never apologized, but she had basically vanished and never given him a chance to do so. She paused, reliving some of the argument in her mind. She was mature enough to realize that the fault had been hers, as well. Her disappearance had been swift after their relationship had collapsed, but her superiors had required an immediate response when they had offered her this assignment, and there had been no time to contact anyone. She had jumped at the opportunity to go undercover and further her career, but it had also been an excellent way to avoid the hurt and anger she had felt and evade any further confrontation. She had never thought of herself as a coward, but she had definitely wanted to avoid ever running into Daniel again. She glanced at him now and another wave of emotion swept over her. Why did he have to be here today? He was already pushing her buttons. Why wouldn't he just sit down and stay out of her way?

Terrell suddenly emerged from the back room, which instantly stopped her woolgathering and made her alert. His hands were empty except for the rifle, and he approached Bethany and leaned forward so only she could hear. "Jackson is having trouble with the safe. The manager couldn't get his code to work, so Jackson is working on the wiring. He's trying to override the system."

"We don't have time for this," she hissed. "The cops will be here in no time."

"Jackson wants to wait. He's convinced he can open it if he's just given a few more minutes."

"J.P. might die."

Terrell laughed. "I never liked him anyway, and I sure never thought you'd care with the way he treats you."

"I've never liked him either," she whispered back. "But that doesn't mean I want him to die." She glanced around at the people lined against the counter, then at her watch. "We really need to get out of here. Forget the vault. Let's get the cash out of the registers and bounce." Fear swept down her spine. She wasn't afraid of getting caught. Her FBI handler would deal with that if she were arrested.

But the longer this robbery stretched out, the more probable it became that someone would get hurt.

As if to accent the point, the phone started ringing again.

Terrell motioned toward the phone. "Go ahead and answer it. I'll keep an eye on these folks. If it's the cops, we need to start the dialogue so they don't raid the place."

She hesitated but finally slung her rifle over her back and walked over to where the phone was ringing on the desk. She picked it up. "What?"

"This is Sergeant Michaels with the police department. Who am I talking to?"

"You can call me Bonnie." Bethany smiled, thinking of Bonnie and Clyde. "By the way, you get an A+ for response time. I must say, you got here quicker than we expected."

"We aim to serve," he responded dryly. "Am I speaking to the one in charge?"

"Not likely."

"Well, who would that be?"

"He's a bit busy right now. We'll have to hold introductions later."

Sergeant Michaels paused, obviously taking notes. "Alright, Bonnie. Is anybody hurt in there?"

"We've had a few mishaps."

"Do you want to let me send in some emergency techs to take care of them?"

"No, Sergeant, I don't think that would be a good idea. In case you haven't noticed, we've strapped some C-4 on the doors. It would get a bit exciting if you tried to get in here."

There was another pause. "We don't want anyone to get hurt here."

Bethany nodded, switching the phone from one ear to the other so she could keep a better eye on Terrell and the hostages. "We share that goal." She lowered her voice. "My boss, however, isn't as concerned about that as we are. I urge you not to try to breech the front or the back of the bank." There. She'd warned them. Her handler should have already notified the local authorities of her role in the heist and of what they were facing, but there were no guarantees. She had notified her handler of the details and he, in turn, had passed on the details, such as the explosives at the doors, to the local teams. Still, she knew she was in a risky position, and there was always a possibility that things could go terribly wrong. Since

banks were federally insured, the FBI always
got called in when a robbery occurred, but that
didn't mean the communication between the
various law enforcement agencies was decent
or accurate.

Sergeant Michaels cleared his throat. "Can
you give your boss a message for me?"

"Sure thing, Sergeant."

"Well, Bonnie, first let him know we've
got control of the landlines coming out of the
bank, so you can reach us by picking up any
of the phones in the building. Anytime you or
your boss want to talk, I'll be available."

"Aren't you the Southern gentleman?" She
let a tad of sarcasm touch her voice. She was
supposed to be a bank robber after all. Sergeant Michaels didn't take the bait though, and
when he spoke again, his voice was calm and
controlled.

"You should also know that we have this
bank surrounded. You're not going to be able
to get out of there without my help." He paused.
"You believe that, don't you, Bonnie? That I'm
here to help you?"

She laughed. "Sure. You'll help me all the
way to a prison cell."

Again, he didn't react to her taunting. "I'm

here to help make sure you don't get killed. I don't want any more bloodshed. Let's end this peacefully. I want you to be able to see tomorrow."

"Sergeant, let me remind you that we have eighteen hostages in here. If you want them all to walk out of here, you'll keep your distance. Otherwise, you'll be picking up the pieces."

"Well, Bonnie, like I said, my goal today is to make sure no one gets hurt. What can I do for you to make sure we resolve this quickly and quietly?"

"I'll get back to you on that." She hung up, not willing to drag out the conversation. She was sure they were recording her voice and doing a voice recognition test. Hopefully that would remind them that she was law enforcement and the snipers that would inevitably be put in place wouldn't put a target on her.

She glanced at her watch and noted the time. Jackson was taking way too long to get into that safe. They'd had a plan in place if the police showed up before they could escape, but it was dangerous. Now they had no choice but to start following it. She thought about J.P. lying on the floor and stole a glance in his direction. He was still grimacing and holding his side where he'd been shot, but he was moving around less. His face was also much paler, and she wondered if he was going into shock. She decided to check on him and went back over to his side. She bent and took a look under his bandages while Terrell checked in with Jackson at the vault. She kept a close eye on the hostages while she did so, but none of them seemed anxious to challenge her authority this time, even though she had to lay down her rifle to check J.P.'s wounds.

"How's it look?" J.P. asked, his voice laced with pain.

"Not so good," she said softly. She kept the panic out of her voice, but she was deeply concerned about the amount of blood on the bandages. Daniel was right. J.P. needed a doctor, and he needed one now. If he didn't get one, he might end up bleeding out right there on the floor. She adjusted the bandages and tied them a bit tighter. "Don't worry, J.P. I'm going to get you some help."

He grabbed her arm and held it way too tightly. "Don't turn me over to the cops," he hissed.

"I don't have a choice. If I don't, you'll die right here and right now. Is that what you want?"

"Don't do it, Hailey. I'm warning you."

"Warning me?" she laughed, even though there was no mirth in her voice. "What do you plan to do to me if you're six feet under, pushing up daisies?"

He tried to pull himself up but groaned and fell back against the floor. He grabbed for her arm again, but she stayed just out of reach. "I'd rather die than get caught. If you turn me over to the cops, I'll end up in prison, and it will be all your fault. If that happens, I'll make you pay. I swear I will."

"Maybe," she said with a frown. "But at least you'll be alive." She knew J.P. was a true believer in the cause, and the chances of him ratting them out were next to nil once he was arrested, but she took his threat against her seriously. J.P. was a dangerous enemy to have. Still, she couldn't just let him die.

"How is he?" Terrell asked as he reappeared and sauntered over to her side. He must have noticed her worried expression because some of the confidence went out of his step as he looked between her and J.P.

"Not good." She stood and motioned toward the vault. "How's the progress back there?"

Terrell shrugged. "The same. Slow but steady."

She motioned to J.P. "He's going to die if we don't get him some help. He's bleeding way too much."

Terrell shook his head. "Then he dies. The boss won't like it if we let anybody in here or if we let them take him to a hospital. You know the rules."

J.P. called out to Terrell. "Hey, man. Don't let her turn me over to the cops."

Bethany moved so she was blocking Terrell's view of J.P. and caught the bigger man's eye. "Did you hear what I said? He'll die if we don't get him to a hospital."

"Then let him die," Terrell suddenly yelled, his voice filling with anger. "Aren't you listening? There's a bigger picture here, woman. You can't take a chance that he'll talk." He stalked up to Bethany and leaned over her, his stance threatening. "The cause is the only thing that matters."

She didn't back down. "I won't let him die."

"It's not up to you. Listen to what he's saying. He doesn't even want your help."

"Do you want his death on your conscience?" she spat. She knew Terrell was twice her size and strength, but she had to stand up to him. This was important. This was life and death. She looked into his eyes and wondered how far he would go. He looked angry enough to shoot her just for daring to challenge him. Or would he shoot J.P. himself and make the whole argument moot? Despite his glare, she couldn't back down. "I don't want him on my conscience when I know I could have saved him."

"The boss will not be happy about it. Let him die."

Bethany looked from J.P. to Terrell, both of whom were glowering. Her insides were fighting a raging battle. Was this the end of her undercover assignment right here and now? Even if it meant she had wasted a year of her life on this mission, life was too precious to just throw it away.

"I'm sorry, boys. I can't just stand here and do nothing. I won't."

Terrell nodded. "Okay. You've made your choice."

He raised his weapon.

FOUR

Daniel watched the confrontation and felt his adrenaline surge as his protective instincts kicked in. Even if it cost him his life, he would not stand by and watch Bethany get hurt. He didn't know if the bodybuilder robber would actually shoot her or not, but he couldn't wait and find out. Daniel didn't like the way the man was holding his rifle. He stood and moved toward them. "Hey now."

In one fleeting second, all of the bigger man's anger focused on Daniel. He took several steps toward him and raised the butt of his weapon as if preparing to hit Daniel across the face. "You stay back, do you hear me?"

Daniel put his hands up and retreated a few steps. He had accomplished his objective—he had distracted him and gotten him to move away from Bethany. "Yeah, I hear you."

The bodybuilder loomed threateningly over him, and Daniel could see the red in his eyes and smell garlic on his breath even through the mask. "Sit back down! Now! Or I'll make sure you never stand up again!"

Daniel obeyed, his hands still up in front of him. He didn't know what to expect and wouldn't have been surprised if the robber had bashed him with the rifle just for good measure. The man was so angry his hands were shaking. It had to be the stress. This heist was taking longer than any of them had probably expected, and the threat of capture had to be looming in all of their minds. Daniel wondered if they were criminals by trade or if this was a one-time deal.

The phone broke the silence once again with a steady ring.

Bethany held back and didn't move. She simply looked at the big man, apparently waiting for permission before answering the phone or doing anything else. Daniel didn't blame her. The robber was an incredibly large man with heavily developed muscles and a threatening presence. He would be a dangerous foe in any situation, and in his current stance of agitation, it wasn't worth challenging him without a very good reason.

The phone stopped ringing, then started again after about thirty seconds or so. No one else said a word. The air felt heavy. Even the other hostages were smart enough to stay quiet and subdued.

Finally, the bodybuilder relented. He motioned with his weapon toward the phone, then started pacing in front of the hostages, glaring at them as he did so. "Fine, answer the stupid phone and do whatever you want to do with J.P., but I'm not taking the blame. When the boss finds out, it'll be you who answers to him. Not me."

Bethany nodded and swung her rifle behind her, then walked over and quickly picked up the receiver. "Yeah?"

She was silent as she listened, then turned and looked into the other robber's eyes as she spoke. "Look, we've got a man down. He's been shot, and he needs a doctor. I want you to send in someone to get him. One man and a stretcher. That's it."

She listened again and then stood straighter as her eyes narrowed. "No, I'm not letting a hostage take him outside. You're going to send in one EMT with a stretcher on wheels and he's going to come in and get the guy, and then he's going to turn around and leave. If he's armed, I'll kill him. If he does anything foolish, I'll kill him. Got it?"

She listened some more and then slammed down the phone and turned to the body-builder. "Okay, they're sending in a guy with a stretcher. Can you let him in the front door?"

The big robber blew out a breath, then nodded. "Yeah, I guess. The boss is going to blow a gasket over this. Cover me while I work."

J.P. groaned loudly. "Don't hand me over to them." He tried to sit up again but failed miserably. "I'll get you back, Hailey. I promise you that."

Daniel was surprised that the wounded man said Bethany's undercover name out loud. Hailey must be what Bethany was calling herself these days. He could tell it was a major breach of etiquette for the robbers to mention names because even the bodybuilder balked at his words.

"Shut up, man. Just close your mouth and keep it closed."

Daniel watched as the bodybuilder slung his rifle behind him and went to the front door

and undid some wires, apparently disarming
the bomb temporarily so the doors could be
opened. Then he released the cables that were
holding the door shut and opened one of them.
A man dressed as an emergency tech pushed
in a yellow stretcher on wheels, noticed the
man lying on the floor and rushed to his side,
but Bethany frisked him before she let him get
close to the wounded man, and she searched
the bags he brought in, presumably for any
weapons or other suspicious devices. Meanwhile, the bodybuilder robber stayed near the
front door and pulled his gun back around to
the front and held it ready, his eyes following
the EMT's every movement.

When the EMT approached him, J.P. started
thrashing his arms around, trying to keep the
EMT away from him. Bethany pointed her
weapon at Daniel and motioned toward the
fallen man. "Hey, hero. Help him get that man
on the stretcher. Now."

Daniel nodded and moved quickly to help
the EMT, glad that Bethany had allowed him
to help. He glanced at the rest of the hostages
as he did so, but although a few were watching the scene unfold, most were turned away
and trying to stay as uninvolved as possible.

It was probably wise of them not to challenge the robbers like he had, but doing nothing went against his basic ideals, and he knew Bethany was a cop, which gave him the advantage. He was also driven to help resolve this problem and was grateful to play even a small part in the resolution. He grabbed and secured the injured man's hands and helped lift him to the stretcher, being careful of the man's wound as he did so. Then he continued holding the man steady as the EMT strapped him to the gurney. Once the injured man couldn't pull away or fight any longer, the EMT checked his wound and re-bandaged it, then started an IV.

"Is he going to live?" Bethany asked.

"Looks like it," the EMT answered. "You called us just in time. He's lost a lot of blood and is in shock, but the hospital is close. I think he'll make it."

Bethany nodded, but kept her gun trained on the tech even as he spoke to her. She even kept it on him as he turned and pushed the gurney back out through the front door. Once he was gone, the bodybuilder lost no time in rewiring the door and securing the door handles with the cables.

"Why don't you let the women go?" Daniel asked quietly. "You'll still have plenty of hostages…"

Bethany swung around and pointed her weapon right at Daniel's chest. "Shut up." She motioned toward the line of hostages. "Sit back down and keep quiet."

He put up his hands again but didn't obey. "Look, you just did something decent. Don't stop now. Let the women go. You'll still have all of the men…"

The bodybuilder advanced quicker than Daniel had expected and loomed above him, his weapon once again pulled back like a club. "She told you to sit down and shut up. I've had enough of you and your mouth. Do you hear me? Do as she says, buddy, or I'll make you comply. Got it?"

Daniel backed down and sat on the floor again, but he kept his eyes on Bethany. She had done the right thing by getting the injured man to safety, but how far was she going to take this robbery? She could put an end to it right now if she wanted to, and with his help, they could arrest the bodybuilder and catch the robbers in the vault unprepared and un-aware. What was holding her back? Was she actually going to see this robbery through to the end? A chill went through him as he considered the possibilities. What was their endgame? What was the bigger picture that the bodybuilder had alluded to earlier? He didn't want to blow her cover, but he didn't want anyone else to get hurt either. As long as the robbers were in the bank, more violence could erupt at any moment.

Bethany's teeth chattered and she realized they had turned off the heat in the building and the temperature was slowly dropping. She'd given up her hoodie to make bandages for J.P., and the T-shirt she was wearing did little to stave off the cold. They were going straight down the law enforcement playbook. Step one was make them uncomfortable by cutting off the heat. Step two was keep the communication lines open while SWAT got into place in case a tactical operation was required. She was sure they already had snipers in place, looking for a clear shot if the negotiator couldn't talk them out of the building.

She glanced around the bank's interior and noticed all of the Christmas decorations for the first time. Wreaths were placed under each teller station, and candles with pine cones and ribbon decorated some of the counters. She had been so wrapped up in this robbery that she hadn't given much thought to the season. Christmas had always been her favorite holiday—that is, until she and Daniel had broken up last year just a few days before the special day had arrived. She stole a look in his direction. He was still as attractive as ever, with dark hair in a short military cut and piercing blue eyes. His features were clearly defined, and he had a strong jaw and firm chin. He took good care of himself, and his athletic build showed it. She wondered if he still ran five miles every morning the way he had back when they were together. He had been on a serious health kick back then and played basketball with his squad on a regular basis. If she had to guess, she'd bet he had probably thrown himself into his exercise routines with gusto after their breakup. That had always been his way of dealing with stress or problems in his life as long as she'd known him.

She turned, trying to push the memories away. Their relationship was over and had been for over a year. She didn't need to be wallowing in the past; she needed to be looking forward. She wished he wasn't here now, forcing these memories to come flooding back in the middle of this operation. Once this undercover assignment was over, she would have her pick of assignments. Maybe it would be better if she moved out of state and started over someplace where there was no possibility of ever running into him again. Yes, that was a good plan. She'd heard Florida was nice this time of year. Or maybe South Carolina near the beach…

The phone rang again, bringing her out of her reverie. Terrell nodded at her, tacitly giving her permission to answer it. She slung her rifle to her back and walked over to the phone, then picked up the receiver.

"Hello," she answered.

"Your man is doing well," Sergeant Michaels stated.

"Good to know," Bethany answered.

"Can your boss come to the phone now?"

Bethany looked toward the back of the bank, but there had been no news from the vault. She assumed the rest of the robbers were still working on opening it. "Nope."

"Well, I need to get the rest of those hostages out of there before someone else gets hurt. What can I do to help move this along?"

"Sit tight and wait," she replied caustically. "We'll be out of your hair soon enough."

Sergeant Michaels seemed undaunted. "You have eighteen hostages. What would it take to get you to release ten of them?" Bethany's gut tightened. She wanted the people out of danger, but she worried about moving forward with the negotiations without Jackson's approval. He was already going to be upset that J.P. was gone. He might get even angrier if she went in the back to talk to him and interrupted his work while he was trying to open the vault. Jackson was usually a benevolent leader, but he was sometimes hard to read, and she never knew what was going to set him off. When he did get angry, his actions were often unexpected and violent. This robbery had already gone down a road they hadn't expected. She suddenly found herself in an uncomfortable position but didn't know quite how to get out of it.

Lost in thought, Bethany didn't answer, so Sergeant Michaels pushed forward. "Look, Bonnie. You probably realize we have an entry team ready to roll. We also have snipers in place, but we don't want to use force. We want this to end peacefully. Tell me what I need to do to make that happen."

Bethany was stuck. She knew that if she didn't give Sergeant Michaels something, it was going to push law enforcement into acting sooner than they wanted them to, and Jackson apparently needed more time to work on the vault. Michaels was also right about one thing. If the robbers and the police did have a confrontation, more violence was going to erupt. "Alright. We got in here before we ate lunch, and now you've got us freezing because you turned off the heat. Turn the heat back on and send in some pizzas, and I'll give you five hostages. That's the deal, and it's not negotiable." She hung up, trying to stay in character. Terrell was watching her every move, and the last thing she wanted was to make him suspicious. Too late, she realized Terrell's eyes had narrowed and his back had stiffened. He was angry once again.

"You're giving away hostages? Who put you in charge?" He stood and walked toward her, his stance threatening. Had she blown her cover, or was he just angry about her involving the hostages? A sliver of fear went down her spine as she replayed the words she'd spoken in her mind. Little details mattered in undercover work. One slip and it could mean her life. She knew that a single misstep or, even in some circles, mispronunciation could set off alarm bells, and she couldn't afford to have even little finger cymbals going off. She needed to be constantly without any suspicion whatsoever.

"First you give them J.P., and now you're giving them five more? Why? What's wrong with you?"

"Hey," she answered defensively, staying in character. "You're the one who told me to answer the phone. I'm just following your instructions and keeping the cops busy while we get into that vault, and I don't want to go back to the vault and interrupt them in the middle of their work either. If you want to talk to the guy on the phone instead of me, be my guest. They're threatening to bust in here with an assault team, not to mention taking potshots at us with snipers. Feel free to start negotiating with them instead of me any time you want. I'm just trying to buy the boss enough time to get the job done."

Terrell stopped a few steps away from her, his weapon held tightly in his hands. "No one put you in charge," he said, his tone deceptively soft and threatening. "You shouldn't be giving those cops anything. Jackson said our job was just to keep the hostages quiet. That's it. Now, because of you, J.P. has been arrested and you've got someone coming in here delivering pizza. Did you order extra cheese?" Now his voice was dripping with sarcasm.

"The boss didn't know the police were going to threaten to burst in, or that J.P. was going to get shot. Now he's alive because of me. Don't forget that," she said, straightening and meeting his eye.

"Yeah, well, I would have just let him die. For all we know, he's out there singing like a bird, giving them a complete list of our members including birth dates and shoe sizes. You've put this job in jeopardy." He took a step closer. "You put the organization in jeopardy."

FIVE

Bethany's heart started beating faster as Terrell's anger consumed him. The pressure had to be getting to him, and the way he was griping the rifle was starting to make her nervous. It wasn't unheard of for robbers to turn on each other during the middle of a job, and for the second time in only a matter of minutes, she felt like she was in real danger. Terrell had always seemed levelheaded to her in the past, but stress and fear could change that like the flip of a switch. She was walking a thin line on this assignment by participating in a crime of this magnitude. The stakes were already high, and they were getting higher by the minute.

"Hey, which five are you going to release?" Daniel asked, drawing Terrell's attention as he stood up and took a few steps toward Terrell. "You should let the women go—"

"You should shut up," Terrell said roughly as he once again turned his anger on Daniel. "I'm getting really tired of telling you to keep your mouth shut."

Bethany glanced at Daniel's eyes and understood that he was giving her the perfect opportunity to look tough and convince Terrell that her persona was real. She was instantly both grateful to him and angry with him. She could take care of herself. She didn't want him to put himself in danger for her sake. Before Terrell could act, she stepped in between them and pushed Daniel back. "Hey, hero, haven't we told you about a hundred times to sit down and shut up?" She pulled her rifle back and hit him in the gut, then as he bent over, she hit him over the back. Her blows looked good but actually had very little force behind them, so she did little to no damage. Thankfully, Daniel seemed to instantly understand what she was doing and did a good job of acting and responding to her actions. He ended up on the floor, clutching his stomach and rolling as if the force of her blows had severely injured him. When he landed, he hit his nose awkwardly, which caused it to start bleeding. The sight of the blood made the entire scene seem more real, and Terrell bought it all, hook, line and sinker. He reached for Bethany as if to stop her, but she pulled her foot back and gave Daniel several vicious kicks in the abdomen before Terrell actually succeeded in grabbing her shoulders and pulling her back from the victim on the ground.

"Are you trying to kill him? Good grief, girl. We agreed we weren't going to kill anyone. Didn't you just give me a speech about how important it was to save someone's life? Leave that guy alone!"

Bethany didn't want to point out to Terrell that two short minutes ago he had been threatening both her and Daniel with violence. Daniel moaned loudly, and Bethany put her foot on his pelvis and pushed him over on his chest to lessen the noise.

"You said I was putting the operation in jeopardy," she spat. "But I'm just as committed to the cause as you are, and if I need to kill this guy to prove it to you, then that's what I'm going to do." She tried to pull away from Terrell, but he held her fast and turned her to face him so their eyes met.

"Back off. I was out of line. Look, why don't you take this guy back to the bathroom and clean him up. We don't want to leave anyone in that condition when we clear out of here."

"You clean him up," she said severely as she slung her rifle on to her back. "What do I care what he looks like?"

Terrell released her and straightened. Apparently, he wasn't willing to go that far, or he didn't like her saucy mouth. Either way, he wanted his command obeyed. "I told you to do it, and I meant it. I'll stay out here and keep an eye on things. You don't know how to operate the charges on the front door. I do. If something happens, I need to be here."

"What about them?" She swung her rifle toward the hostages and a few of them whimpered at her implied threat.

"I'll shoot any of them who move a muscle."

"Fine." She shrugged as if the time with Daniel didn't matter, but she was secretly pleased. She had been trying to figure out a way to talk to him in private anyway, to explain to him what was going on, and this situation had worked out perfectly. She nudged Daniel with her shoe and he moaned in response. "Let's go, hero."

He cringed as if he was afraid of her touch, and Bethany silently thanked him for putting on such a realistic performance. She nudged him again. "I said, let's go, hero." She handed Terrell her rifle and then reached down to help Daniel up. He looked at her suspiciously when she offered her arm but eventually reached out and grabbed her right wrist, and she pulled him to his feet. As soon as he was vertical, she put his arm around her shoulders and wedged herself under his arm so she could support him as he walked. They made slow progress without saying a word until they had entered the family bathroom and flipped on the light. Bethany pulled the door closed and let him ease against the sink. Then she pulled her mask up and left it sitting above her head. It felt good to finally get out of the sweaty thing. She leaned against the door frame and watched as Daniel turned on the water and started rinsing the blood from his face.

"I'm sorry if I hurt you, Daniel."

He continued washing his face but eventually grabbed the paper towel she offered and dried his face. "When?"

She raised her eyebrows. "What do you mean *when*?"

"You're sorry you hurt me just now, or when you disappeared without a trace a year ago?"

He tossed the paper towel away, straightened and gave her a small smile.

Bethany narrowed her eyes. Good grief! He wanted to have this conversation now? "Hey now. The way I remember it, we both decided it was over last year. It was a mutual decision."

"No," he said softly, "we had an argument. We both said things we regretted, and you didn't give us an opportunity to fix it. Instead, you disappeared." He paused. "I've missed you, you know."

Bethany tapped the lid down on her emotions. There was an element of truth to what he said, but she didn't want to examine it. She didn't even want to have this discussion—not now, and not ever. The scars had already healed over. She didn't want to reopen the wounds. "Maybe I didn't want to fix it," she said back, her tone derisive. "We were over, Daniel. You just didn't want to accept it."

He looked up quickly. "That's not how I remember it."

His eyes met hers and contained a pain that she hadn't expected. She looked away first, unable to bear the look in his eyes. "I am sorry, Daniel, both for today and for a year ago. I didn't want to hurt you. I never meant to do that."

He gently grasped her arm, then touched her chin and turned her head to look at him again. His touch sent a shiver down her spine. "I looked for you for months. I watched your apartment. I searched high and low. Why do you say we were over? We were just beginning."

He leaned forward as if to kiss her, but she pulled her head away. She did not want to continue this conversation. He was forcing her to feel things she didn't want to feel. It was safer all around if they left the past in the past. "We can't talk about this now. Terrell is waiting for us."

A wave of frustration swept through Daniel, and he realized he wasn't going to get the answers he was seeking. At least not today. Bethany's heart may have closed over, but he had never stopped loving her. How could he help her see that? He had seen fear in her eyes that long ago day, and the fear was back today. What was she afraid of? Had they gotten too serious, too soon? Is that why she had run away? He remembered the day she had driven off and disappeared from his life, the angry words still on both of their tongues. He should have gone after her, but he'd always thought they'd have another opportunity to talk and sort things out, and he thought waiting for them both to cool down was the wiser course. Apparently, he had been very, very wrong. But even so, it wasn't in him to give up. He might not be able to convince her to return to him, but before he let her go, he at least wanted to understand what had happened and why. He leaned back against the sink. "Then when can we talk? You're obviously undercover. When does this assignment end? Will you disappear again once they've brought you home?"

He saw the answer in her eyes. She would leave as soon as it was over, and she wasn't going to contact him. Exasperation and the fear of losing her once again caused a tightening in his chest. "Bethany, please. At least give me an opportunity to talk to you before you take another assignment."

"I don't know when this will end…"

"But it will, at some point. Please promise me we'll talk."

She said nothing in response, and it was obvious she wasn't going to say another word on the subject. His face was throbbing and he touched his nose gingerly. "I think I broke my nose."

A look of worry crossed her face, and she tore off another paper towel, wet it and handed it to him. "I'm sorry. Here. You're still bleeding."

He took the paper towel from her and put his head back, hoping to staunch the flow. "Can I have my gun back?"

"Sorry, no, at least not yet. Someone might have seen me take it, and I don't want to blow my cover. You have my word though that I'll get it back to you as soon as I can."

"So your handler approved a bank robbery?"

"Yeah, there's a bigger picture here that we've been investigating for about a year."

He brought his head back down. "Care to share?"

She gave him a small laugh. "You know the rules. I can't do that."

"How can you stand to be a part of this? I've never done undercover work—I'll admit it. And I respect those of you that do. I just don't think I could get past the crimes going on all around me. I mean, a man got shot out there. That's got to be tough."

She leaned back against the door frame, giving him an expression that showed she was pleased with his interest. Her work had always been very important to her. Sometimes he thought she liked being an FBI agent more than any other aspect of her life. "I look for the gray and stay away from the black and white. There's usually something good about a person, even if they are a criminal, so I focus on that aspect of their personality. Criminals can tell if I'm scared, and they know if I'm being judgmental about their lifestyle. I have to show them that I see them as a person, not just as someone doing bad things. Take Terrell." She nodded toward the door.

"You mean that big bodybuilder guy?"

"Yeah, that's the one. He loves dogs. Can you believe it? He saw a stray the other day that almost got hit by a car, and he made us stop, right there in the middle of the road, so he could grab the dog off the street. Then we had to change all of our plans, turn around and head in the opposite direction, just so he could drop the dog off at his sister's so she could find a good home for it. How crazy is that?"

Daniel smiled. He was glad she was talking to him, even if she wasn't willing to discuss their relationship. Something was better than nothing. "I can't imagine that big guy caring that much."

"Neither could I, but since I love dogs myself, it makes it much easier to be around him now that I've seen that side of his personality. We've found some common ground." She sighed. "This is a really important assignment. I've been thrown into the deep end of one of the region's most dangerous criminal organizations, and I really want a win so I can put an end to their activities. By the time I'm through with this, I hope to bring down some of the most powerful people in the state. This investigation reaches all the way up to the senator's office."

Daniel could hear the passion in her voice, yet the fact that they were committing a crime here today still didn't sit right with him. "I understand, but is it ethically okay to rob a bank to reach that objective? I know you're in deep, but isn't this going too far?"

"This isn't just an adrenaline-filled journey I'm on, Daniel. I'll be able to trace the money we steal today and get the final pieces to the puzzle. They've been building a war chest for a reason, and we need to know why. They're planning something big, something that's going to do a lot more damage than a bank robbery and will hurt a lot more people in the long run. I know it's dangerous, but my handler and I both thought it was worth the risk."

Daniel could see that he would never win this argument. And he had to admit, undercover cops were some of the bravest people he had ever worked with. Bethany wasn't short on guts or determination. She was a dedicated, hardworking FBI agent who got the job done. "Well I just don't want to see you go native and get caught up in this lifestyle. I would hate to visit you behind bars."

She smiled, a smile that always made his gut tighten. She was so beautiful, and her beauty was so much more than skin-deep. "No worries. I'm still a cop when I go to bed at night. I'm not switching sides." She motioned toward the door. "We'd better get back out there before Terrell comes in here looking for us." She pulled the mask back down to cover her face.

"Do you guys have an exit strategy?"

"You bet. And no one will get hurt. I promise."

He let her wedge herself under his arm again, and he took a wounded stance so they could return to the bank lobby. He was fine with acting the injured party as long as it helped keep her safe. He just hoped she could keep her promise.

SIX

Jackson was pacing in front of the group of hostages when Bethany and Daniel returned to the lobby. She noticed that he and the other robbers had several bags at their feet—hopefully full of cash that they had taken from the vault. She led Daniel over to the line of hostages, dropped him unceremoniously on the floor, then retrieved her weapon from Terrell and joined the group of robbers. She tried to act nonchalant and not attract attention to herself as she took her place with the other robbers.

"Where have you been?" Jackson asked when he got her attention. He had a suspicious look on his face, and she hurried to reassure him.

"Cleaning up a mess," she responded tightly,

but in a voice that was still low enough for only the group of robbers to hear.

There was still an apprehensive look in Jackson's eyes. "Where is J.P.? Did I understand correctly that you let the cops in here while I was in the back working on the vault?"

A sliver of fear washed over her when she saw Jackson's eyes narrow and darken as he spoke. He was pacing nervously, and his hands were fisting and releasing over and over again. Had she blown it? The last thing she needed was for Jackson to get suspicious of her and find out she was really an FBI agent at this late date in the game. Still, she stiffened her spine and pushed forward. He had always respected strength during their relationship. That's what she would show him now at this critical juncture. "He was going to die without help," she said roughly, her tone matter-of-fact. "His wound was serious, and he'd lost too much blood. He was going into shock."

"And being a doctor, you'd know what shock looks like, right?" His voice was derisive.

She deliberately softened her speech but still spoke with authority. "I may not be a doctor, but I'm also not an idiot. Shock isn't too hard to identify, and neither is a large pool of blood on the floor. I happen to value life. J.P. is a true believer. He's a valuable asset to the cause. I wanted to save him."

Jackson took a threatening step toward her, but she still didn't back down. "That was my call, not yours. I wasn't in China. All you had to do was come back and ask."

His words made her heart beat even faster. It had taken months to gain Jackson's trust. She'd had an informant introduce them, and from there, she'd become a provider for Jackson, bringing him electronics and other "stolen" items that she claimed she'd gotten from other jobs she'd pulled around town. They were actually items provided by the FBI, but they had been good enough to please Jackson. She had quickly gained the reputation as someone who could lay her hands on whatever the group needed. She had even given him the latest and greatest cell phone, which, unknown to Jackson, included a bugging device that allowed the FBI to track Jackson and listen in on his conversations. Despite this track record of success, her elevated status could disappear in an instant if Jackson began to suspect her. She decided a strategic retreat was in order.

"You're right, Jackson. I should have asked.

I'm sorry. I don't want to do anything that would jeopardize the mission."

"Did you consider that now the cops might be able to get him to talk? He could blow our entire operation."

She shook her head. "I was just trying to save his life. I didn't think. I really am sorry." Her heart continued its pounding for another very long moment as she watched Jackson consider her words. Even the rest of the team were all silent and completely still as they watched and waited for a cue from Jackson. Terrell's face had a look that said *I told you so* written all over it, but to his credit, he said nothing.

Finally, Jackson shrugged, and the rest of the group followed his lead and relaxed, as well. She let out a breath in relief as he spoke. "Next time, ask me. I'm in charge. Got it? There's a lot riding on this. Our friends are counting on us."

"Yes, I get it. Definitely." She tried to change the subject and hoped he wouldn't notice. "Were you successful with the vault?"

"Of course," he answered with a sly smile. "Did you doubt me?"

She shook her head. "Not even for a minute."

"Did the cops call back since they took J.P.?"

"Yeah," Bethany answered. "They think we're trading five hostages for pizzas and having them turn the heat back on. I had to give them something to work on. They were getting antsy and threatening to send in a strike team if I didn't agree to something."

Jackson raised an eyebrow but didn't comment, which made Bethany nervous again. Finally, he shrugged once, then took a step back and addressed the group, apparently putting her negotiations with the police behind them. She was glad to see that he was ready to move on. The last few minutes had been extremely uncomfortable for her, and she was ready to get out of this bank. "Let's go, folks. We're ready for phase three."

Bethany knew that phase three meant they were putting their escape plan into action. She glanced over at Daniel, glad that this robbery was finally coming to an end. Soon they would be gone, and the pain this encounter had caused him to relive would end. She hoped he could move on and find some measure of peace once she disappeared again. There was no reason for them to see each other once her team of robbers escaped, and she wished him well on whatever path he chose to follow.

She turned back to Jackson, who was talking to Terrell. "Get those hostages in the back room and lock the door. The rest of you, come with me."

Terrell nodded, turned to the hostages and started barking out orders. "Okay, everyone stand up!"

He started pacing in front of the group, waving his weapon up and down to encourage them to move faster. The faces of the hostages showed their trepidation, but they quickly obeyed and stood up against the wall.

Daniel stood with the rest of them, glad that this episode would soon be over but still fighting the host of sensations that seeing Bethany had evoked. Once the robbers escaped, would he see her again? Bethany hadn't committed to any future conversations with him, and he had no idea when her current assignment would end. When it did, for all he knew, she would accept a post in a city on the other side of the United States. How had things gone so badly between them? One moment, they were in love and planning their wedding and the next, she was gone. A sense of emptiness swept over him and he sighed inwardly, knowing there wasn't anything he could do to change the status quo. At this point, it looked like he would probably never even get an opportunity to try.

Suddenly a shot rang out and one of the female hostages pointed at Terrell and screamed. Daniel's eyes followed the woman's pointing finger and saw Terrell's body crumple to the floor. Within seconds, more shots rang out, and Jackson's body also hit the floor, as well as the robber's with the limp. Daniel didn't think. He was only a few feet away from Bethany, and he took a running dive toward her and hit her hard, taking her to the ground. She wasn't wearing the black hoodie like the other robbers and in a perfect world, the snipers all knew that she was law enforcement. But on the off chance that no one knew the truth, he wanted her out of the line of fire just in case.

He heard a bullet whiz by only inches from where their heads had just been. They hit the floor hard and once they landed, they slid for several inches on the slick tile before coming to a stop near a small table. Bethany lost her grip on her rifle when they hit the floor and it landed a few feet away, out of reach. Daniel felt the air whoosh out of both of their bodies due to the force of the fall. Total chaos ensued all around them.

Oh, dear God. Please don't let Bethany be dead. His prayer was short but intense. He moved closer and tried to feel her pulse. "Are you okay?" He crouched above her protectively, trying to shield her from any other flying bullets or danger.

Bethany didn't answer, and he wasn't even sure she'd heard him. Women were screaming, and several policemen had come in the bank through the ceiling, rappelling in full battle gear and wielding weapons just seconds after the first shot had been fired.

"Bethany?" Daniel couldn't find a pulse, but his hands were shaking. He shook her gently but still got no response. In fact, she wasn't even moving. Fear gripped his heart. Had he been too late? He shifted, trying to get in a position where he could remove her mask and check her vitals and repeated his prayer.

"Freeze!" A SWAT officer was suddenly standing over them, his weapon pointed at Bethany only inches from her head. He had steel gray eyes and a two-inch scar on his chin. A few seconds later, another officer joined him, this one pointing his weapon at Daniel.

"I'm a detective," Daniel responded. "My name is Daniel Morley. My shield is in my left front pocket. Can I get it out and show you?"

The more recently arrived SWAT officer motioned with his rifle. "Slowly."

Daniel carefully moved to Bethany's side and gradually pulled his shield out of his pocket and offered it up for inspection. The officer Daniel had now nicknamed Scar took it and looked at it cautiously while the other kept his weapon trained on Bethany, who was still lying motionless on the floor. Satisfied, he handed it back.

"Okay, Detective. Move away from the suspect."

Daniel slowly did so, but he was getting more and more worried about Bethany by the second. She still hadn't moved since he'd tackled her. Had she been hit by the sniper? Had her head hit the ground when they'd landed? Why wasn't she moving? There was a lot of noise and general confusion in the bank, but he tuned it all out and was entirely focused on her.

Was she even breathing? He couldn't tell. His heart seemed to stop beating. Had she been killed like the others? He didn't see any blood, but he couldn't see all of her, and her mask still covered her face. Had he been too late?

Scar leaned over and pulled off Bethany's mask while the other SWAT officer kept his rifle trained on her prone body. It came off easily, and Daniel breathed a sigh of relief when it didn't reveal any injury on her face or head.

She must have been unconscious, but then abruptly she moaned and moved slightly, causing both officers to stiffen and move closer with their weapons. "Freeze!" they both ordered in unison.

She opened her eyes and took a moment to focus as she slowly recuperated and returned to the here and now.

"Hands out to your sides," Scar ordered. She slowly complied, and once her arms were parallel to her body, they kicked her feet apart until she was spread eagle on the ground. She glanced at Daniel but said nothing.

Daniel wanted to protest their rough treatment of her, but he still couldn't blow her cover. That was for her to do at the correct moment when she felt like she was out of danger, or for her handler to do once she was arrested. Whatever the case, there were protocols to be followed, and now was not the time or place to notify them of her FBI status.

While Scar pointed his rifle at her, the other officer frisked her for other weapons, then roughly flipped her over on her stomach. They found his service revolver that was still in the waistband of her pants and pulled another small revolver out of her right boot. They also pulled a small knife out of her left boot.

"Got any other hardware we should know about?"

She still said nothing, but shook her head. As Daniel watched, the officer pulled her hands roughly behind her back, handcuffed her and yanked her to her feet.

"You have the right to remain silent…"

As soon as they finished going through her Miranda rights, the two men led her out of the bank.

Daniel watched her go, surprised at how much things had changed in the last fifteen minutes. He felt like he was on a wild roller coaster ride that was both terrifying and exhilarating at the same time.

He had lost her again. But a lot of his questions had been answered. And for the next few hours, he knew where he could find her.

And there was a possibility, ever so small, that he might be able to see her again.

SEVEN

"I can't believe you killed them all. Good grief! One entire year of investigation ruined!" Bethany's handler, Justin Harper, banged his hand on the conference room table, and three of the individuals in the room jumped in response to the noise. "What is wrong with you people!" He had a handful of folders in his arms, and he called off the names as he slammed each folder down on the table in front of him.

"Terrell Mason, shot dead. Jackson Smith, shot dead. John Hoss, shot dead. And let's not forget, if not for the quick thinking of Detective Morley here, you would have also shot my special agent through the head, as well!"

"Hold on now," Captain Dennis Murphy intoned, leaning back in his chair. "The communication failures weren't all on our end.

We didn't even hear about this operation until we were on our way in. You should have let us know you had an operation in the works months ago, and that you had an agent in the field committing armed robbery. How did you expect us to react? Roll out a red carpet for the robbers and let them reel the money out in golden wheelbarrows? We followed standard operating procedure. SOP. Sir." He banged the table himself as he said each letter. "Do not lay your gross failures at our feet."

Bethany flicked her nails, incredibly tired of the blame game going on in front of her. They had already been sitting here for over an hour, and they still hadn't gotten anywhere. She was just as angry as her handler, but she was not convinced that a show of rage and frustration was going to further this meeting. The bottom line was that people in both agencies had screwed up, and the mistakes had almost been at the cost of her life. It had also cost her all the progress she'd made in the investigation, and she wasn't sure it was salvageable. She had spent an entire year infiltrating that group, and for what? The leader, Jackson Smith, was dead, and he was the one who had trusted her and had been the source of information that she had been using to build her case against the entire criminal organization.

She glanced around the room at the various faces. It had been quite a few months since she had seen the inside of a police station, not to mention a conference room. Many of these people she'd never seen before. Both the local and federal law enforcement agencies had a contingency at the table, and both the state district attorney's office and the federal attorney general's office had sent a team, as well. Captain Murphy had brought Daniel and his assistant, a petite African-American lady who was furiously scribbling notes on a legal pad and trying to look unobtrusive. So far, she hadn't said a single word and if Bethany had to guess, she doubted the woman would speak a single syllable during the entire meeting. Sergeant Michaels, the hostage negotiator she had talked to on the phone during the robbery, was present as well, but he had also said very little. Apparently, he was content to have his captain do the talking. He seemed more like a man of action rather than a verbose member of the team, and he kept watching the clock as if he had someplace else to be.

Her eyes roamed over to Justin Harper, her

handler. She hadn't known him very well before they were assigned to work together on this detail, but he had been reliable to date and good about providing the products and intelligence she needed to worm her way into Jackson's cell within the criminal organization. She glanced over at his assistant, a young man with shortly cropped blond hair and stunning green eyes named Max Westfield. Westfield was the newest member of the team and had only been there for a couple of months. He was also taking notes, but he was typing on a tablet computer, and occasionally looking around the room at the various occupants as if he were taking the measure of each of them. Despite the intriguing color of his eyes, Bethany was a bit repelled by the man. It wasn't so much anything Westfield had said or done; in fact, he had been very courteous. He just seemed to be watching her constantly and was almost flirtatious in his looks and actions. She may be single, but she certainly wasn't looking for a relationship. She wondered if he would get the message through her body language, or if she would actually have to say something to him to make him move on to somebody else. She hoped it was the former. She didn't relish a confrontation with him.

"How did you even plan on getting out of that bank alive?" Captain Murphy asked, finally addressing Bethany for the first time during the meeting. She looked up, surprised, and put an end to her woolgathering. "Explosives, sir. I'm sure you found the C-4 in some of the duffel bags that were still in the bank. That building was built over a crawl space, which easily accessed the laundry room of the apartment building to the north, which led to the parking garage directly northwest of that location. We had a van ready and waiting to go on the bottom level of the parking deck. I'm sure it's been moved by now by others from the group, but we figured it would take us approximately twelve minutes to get from the bank to the van through access tunnels that we'd completed over the last few weeks. It was going to be a bit tricky to ferry the money over there because of the weight, but the operation was certainly doable for a group of motivated bank robbers."

"What about the hostages?"

"What about them?" she asked, raising an eyebrow.

"What were your plans for them?" he asked, leaning forward. His stance was aggressive, but instead of taking offense at his behavior, she decided to lean back and speak softer, hoping not to engage the man and make matters even worse. She had already listened to the yelling for an hour. Her ears hurt. All of the bravado and posturing was giving her a headache. With each new argument, she was beginning to appreciate her undercover assignment more and more. It had been good to be away from the politics and office maneuvering that was apparently required in order to succeed.

"We never wanted anyone to get injured, sir. That was the plan from the beginning and, of course, the FBI would never have signed off on the robbery if the hostages had been at risk. Once the vault was breeched, our plan was to lock the hostages in the back of the bank in the conference room and leave them there during the explosion and the escape. They wouldn't have been impacted by the detonation."

Captain Murphy stood quickly, put up his hands and took a couple of steps in her direction. "Now hold on just a minute. You don't call firing high-powered weapons near innocent people putting them at risk?" he yelled.

"No, sir," she responded calmly. "I was constantly with the hostages, and I had a high-powered weapon myself so I could stop any trouble before it started. I kept them where I could see them at all times for exactly that reason."

Captain Murphy pointed toward Daniel. "What about my detective's nose?"

She'd had enough. What did the man expect? A perfect operation? A golden guarantee? If he wanted to find fault, he needed to point that finger back at himself and his own operation. After all, she was the one who had almost been killed. "What about it, Captain? I am sorry about Detective Morley's nose, I truly am, but he's alive, isn't he? That's more than I could have said if he hadn't been there when your team came storming into that bank. They would have killed me if he hadn't knocked me to the ground in the nick of time. Detective Morley saved my life. That's something I won't soon forget, but it sure would be nice if you remembered that it was your men who killed the rest of the suspects and tried to take me out, as well."

Captain Murphy's face turned red. "I've never heard such insolence! You just hold it right there, Special Agent—"

Daniel stood and held up his hands. "Captain, please. I know I'm outranked by most of the people at this table, and until now I've been quietly sitting here listening to everyone's point of view, but I was there, in the bank, and I can tell you what happened from my firsthand experience. Since we've finally gotten around to my injury and my role in the operation, I think I've earned a chance to speak." His voice was soft yet in control, and Bethany admired the way he showed a quiet strength. He didn't need the bluster that the captain showed to get his point across or the threats and anger that her handler kept throwing around. His tone was matter-of-fact and to the point. "We seem to keep talking about this in the past tense, but to my way of thinking, this operation isn't over, not by a long shot. I don't know all of the details or the background information, but I do know Special Agent Walker. I know her level of commitment and I know this is an important undercover operation that has high stakes. We may have lost a golden opportunity by killing Jackson Smith and his cohorts, and I don't know the ins and outs of the organization that Agent Walker is infiltrating, but I do know that we aren't out of options, at least not yet. I suggest we move forward as a team. We can't forget that J.P., the robber that got shot, is still in the hospital. As far as he knows, three of the robbers were shot and killed. He doesn't know that Bethany survived, or why. We can use that fact to our advantage."

Bethany nodded, her excitement starting to grow as she began to understand the idea that Daniel seemed to be suggesting. "You're right. We can tell him that when the police stormed in, I was in the bathroom cleaning you up. I pulled off my mask and blended in with the other hostages…"

Captain Murphy snapped his fingers, apparently also grasping Daniel's train of thought. "And that's why you weren't arrested," he finished. "You were able to escape detection because you hid your mask and rifle and got lost in the general confusion that occurred when the bank got raided."

"But what about you?" Justin asked, motioning toward Daniel, his tone skeptical. "J.P. knows that you know she was a robber. He knows that you would have identified her to law enforcement when they came in. She couldn't have changed her clothes…"

"No," Daniel agreed, "but she could have let her hair down out of the ponytail, and without

the mask she would have looked quite different. She also removed the hoodie when she
was tending J.P.'s wounds. When people are
stressed and in a difficult situation, they have
trouble remembering details and might not
have remembered what she was wearing underneath. The robbers were identified by their
hoodies and masks."

"Are you willing to bet her life on that?"
Justin said, his tone sharp. "I'm not. And I'm
not sending her back into a dangerous situation without more. We need a stronger story.
I know J.P. I helped compile the background
on him. He's a hothead, but he's not an idiot.
He'll see holes in any story that isn't a really
good one, and that will put my agent in jeopardy. We can't give him some half-baked tale
and hope he'll swallow it."

Daniel sat back down. Instead of looking
discouraged, he seemed thoughtful. Didn't
this guy ever give up? At least he was trying to help her make lemonade from a bowl
of lemons. She had to appreciate his efforts.
"I'm definitely not suggesting we put Special
Agent Walker in danger either," he said. "If
we need to come up with a better story, then
we come up with a better story. We're an in-

telligent group of professionals here, ladies and gentlemen. I'm sure if we put our heads together, we can solve this problem. All I'm suggesting is that we move forward with the operation. We suffered a setback, yes, but we still can make this right."

"I have the solution."

All heads turned toward Captain Murphy, some with skeptical looks on their faces. His tone was more moderate, which Bethany appreciated, but when he spoke, his words shocked her. "The answer is simple. We send in Detective Morley undercover with her."

"What?" This time she stood. "Are you nuts?"

His head snapped toward her, and she instantly regretted her impetuous words. He was a captain after all, even if his idea was completely ludicrous.

"No, Agent, I'm not. Detective Morley is one of my best. He can be brought up to speed on your case, and we can say he decided to join your group of robbers. Anti-government, aren't they?"

Daniel turned and looked at Bethany's expression. She was obviously not pleased that

Captain Murphy had been so flippant with his comment about the group she had infiltrated. His captain was a good man, even if he was a little unpolished at times. He got the job done, and his superiors rewarded him for it, but he had never been known for his tact.

Bethany slowly retook her seat. "I meant no disrespect, sir. I agree that Detective Morley is outstanding at his job. My surprise was based upon your suggestion that he join my undercover operation. It took me over a year to gain their trust, and they are much more than an anti-government organization. It's a complicated belief system that goes back several generations and stretches into the members' livelihoods, even into how they raise their children. You don't just join the group. You live it."

"Believe it or not, agent, my people know a thing or two about police work. We may not have your FBI funding, but we do have the grit and determination it takes to do the job correctly."

"Sir…" she started to protest again and Daniel smiled inwardly. She wasn't going to be able to dig herself out of this hole, no matter how hard she tried. The captain had been offended, and there would be no soothing his pride, at least not today after all of the yelling and blame that had already been passed around.

"It makes a good legend, Agent," he said gruffly. He had enough rank that he could interrupt her with impunity. "He helped you escape because he believes in the cause. If both of you go in, you'll be less vulnerable because you can watch each other's backs."

Daniel shook his head. "That may not fly after what J.P. witnessed at the bank between us, sir, but we can figure something out. Give us some time to come up with some background scenarios, and we'll create a story that works." He glanced at Bethany. He could tell by her expression that she wasn't happy, but he was looking for any opportunity he could find to spend time with her, and if it took accepting an undercover operation to do it, then so be it. He had never wanted to do this type of job in the past, but he would do it now if it meant working with Bethany and getting a second chance to figure out what had gone wrong between them.

The group hashed out a few more details about the joint mission and then slowly started to break up and separate.

Max Westfield stopped Bethany as she was leaving the room and blocked her by the door. "I really admire you and the work you are doing. It's incredibly dangerous, but very worthwhile."

"Thank you, Mr. Westfield." She forced a smile at him but tried to push by. Daniel noticed this from across the conference room but was waylaid by the deputy attorney general, and although he could hear their conversation, he couldn't intervene.

She gave Max Westfield a tentative smile. "I appreciate your comments, Mr. Westfield, and your support. It is dangerous but if we are successful, it will all be worth it. Please excuse me." He moved a little closer and made it impossible for her to get by him. She actually took a step back and looked slightly uncomfortable.

"Please, call me Max. I might have some ideas for your backstory, if you want some help—"

She cut him off. "Thank you so much, but we have a team for that. I do appreciate the offer." She tried a second time to walk past him, but once again he blocked her path.

"I have a background in undercover work.

I know I'm just an assistant right now, but I came from the New York field office where I did that kind of work, and I'm up for promotion."

She nodded. "I'm sure you did, but that's not the way we do things here. Like I said, I do appreciate the offer. Special Agent Harper is the boss, and we do things his way. You'll have to take this up with him."

Daniel finally excused himself from the attorney general and moved over to Westfield's side. "Agent Walker, I have a few things I'd like to discuss with you before you leave, if you have time," he said softly. "We need to get some details straight about this undercover operation."

"That would be fine. We can talk on my way out." She nodded at Westfield. "Thanks again." Westfield looked disappointed, but he finally stepped aside, glaring at Daniel as he did so.

"You know he was flirting with you," Daniel said for her ears only once they were well away from the group.

"Of course," Bethany said, frowning a bit. "But he's not my type at all. He looks like he just graduated high school, and honestly, I think he's a bit too pushy." She smiled, but this time it was genuine. "Thankfully, I rarely have to deal with that guy."

Daniel didn't like that someone was flirting with her, but he did like the way that Bethany smiled. It lit up her entire face and brought out a small dimple on her cheek that was simply adorable. It was the first time he had seen her smile in quite some time. He wished she smiled more. "So what do you think about this undercover idea?"

Suddenly, the smile disappeared completely. She was obviously not pleased. "I think it's a mistake, just like I said during the meeting. It puts you in unnecessary danger, and me too if I have to babysit you."

Babysit? She felt like she had to babysit him? "Now hold on—"

"Look, don't let your male pride take a hit. That's not what I meant. You're a good cop. All I'm trying to say is that being undercover is hard enough when I have to watch out for myself. Everything I say and do is constantly being scrutinized. If you're there too, it's double the work and double the danger. You've also never done an assignment like this before. That makes it even more risky."

"Is the mission important?"

She frowned. "You know it is. I wouldn't have gone so far as participating in a bank robbery otherwise."

"Then let's do it. Together. Bring me up to speed, and let me do my job."

She paused as if considering his words, but it wasn't as if they had a choice. Their orders had already been decided. Still, he wanted her buy-in. "Look, I know I haven't done undercover before, but I'm not a rookie, Bethany. I won't let you down."

"I know you're good, Daniel. I've never doubted that. I'm just used to working alone."

He wanted to ask her if she had personal reasons for hesitating too, but now wasn't the time or place for that discussion. She hadn't wanted to talk about their past at the bank, and he knew intuitively that it was going to take time and effort to pry the answers out of her. One thing he did know though—she was worth the effort.

She met his eye. "Thanks for saving my life at the bank. I owe you one."

It was his turn to smile. "You're welcome. It was my pleasure."

She winked at him, then turned. "See you at the rendezvous location tomorrow at 9:00 a.m," she said with a wave.

He watched her leave, then left the building separately through a different side door.

Unfortunately, neither one of them noticed the people tailing them.

EIGHT

"You're going to have to pretend to be a dirty cop." Bethany sat back, running her hands through her hair and pulling it back from her face. "I just don't see another way around it." They were at a small diner in St. Elmo, a small neighborhood at the foot of Lookout Mountain, seated near the back where they had a good view of everyone in the restaurant, as well as everyone coming and going in the parking lot through the large picture window at the front. They had just spent the last two hours going over every detail, no matter how small, of the bank robbery and what the other hostages had witnessed during the various exchanges. They had also discussed what they thought J.P. had seen and heard, and how they could use him as the key to moving forward. He was the only real link left to the organization that Bethany still had, so she would have to use her relationship with J.P. to get back into the group. They were all hoping that bond was strong enough to allow her not only to get reconnected but also to bring Daniel into the fold.

"Being labeled as *dirty* really stinks, but I don't see any other option," Daniel agreed. "Too many of the other hostages know I was a cop or could find out by asking a few simple questions. They would all start to wonder how you escaped without me looking the other way."

Justin Harper, the third party at the table, nodded. "We just don't have time to put another cover story in place in time. You'll also have to use your own name. We can't come up with a believable legend for you after what happened at the bank." He took a drink of coffee. "Don't worry though. We'll be sure to restore your name and reputation once this mission is completed. For the time being, you've been temporarily assigned to the FBI task force. Captain Murphy knows, but no one else. Everyone else at the Chattanooga Police Department has been told that you've been assigned to a special detail and that's it. Keep the FBI connection to yourself."

"Bringing you on board might be easier than I originally thought," Bethany said as she took a sip of her hot chocolate. "We'll be offering them something—someone in law enforcement with an excellent reputation that they think they can manipulate. That's a big carrot. It also took them a year to trust me, but in their eyes, I'm Hailey Weber, a criminal with a spotty past. I had to prove myself. You, on, the other hand, already proved yourself by saving me at the bank."

"Do you think J.P. can get you the introductions you need?" Justin asked.

"That's the crux of the entire problem." She looked to Daniel, who was hearing most of this information for the first time. "The organization is set up in cells. Jackson Smith was the head of our cell, but he was really the only one who had contact with the other cells. I was just getting to the point where I was trusted enough to know a couple of the other players, but I don't know many, and I don't know how to get in touch with them. With Jackson dead, I'll have to try to make contact with a man named Bishop Jacobs. He was the man Jackson reported to. If J.P. will vouch for me and for you, Daniel, it will go a long way with

Bishop and might just ease our transition into a new cell. If he doesn't, well, that could spell the end of this undercover assignment." She took another drink of her hot chocolate. "Let me start at the beginning. The group I've infiltrated is called the Heritage Guard. It started back in the 1980s up in Virginia and was basically formed as an anti-government group that created its own regional militia and recruited local families. The members thrive on conspiracy theories, and believe they are fighting to save America from a government that is too big, mismanaged and destroying the freedom of the common citizen. They're violent extremists, and they set out a plan to gradually gain strength and money so they could pursue political power and take their ideals to a larger audience. Members have to take an oath of allegiance, and there are different levels of membership."

"What are the different levels?" Daniel asked.

"I still don't know all the ins and outs," Bethany admitted. "But new recruits are at level one. If I'm still accepted, I'll be moved up to level two now that I participated in the bank robbery. There are six levels, six being the top of the pack. Jackson was a three. Bishop is a four."

"What do you have to do to get moved up to the next level?" Daniel asked.

"The threes have planned and executed jobs like the bank robbery. The fours have committed assassinations of enemies of the Heritage Guard. I have no idea what the fives have done. You can bet it's horrific."

Justin leaned forward. "I can tell you about one of their projects that failed. They had a scheme to devalue the American dollar and cripple the economy back in the 1990s by counterfeiting money. The scheme was detected and several of the key players were arrested before the counterfeit bills were actually introduced into the major market streams. Twelve members of the Heritage Guard were tried and convicted under the Racketeer Influenced and Corrupt Organizations Act. The trial dealt a heavy blow to the Guard, but they slowly grew again. Now, they are a lot more secretive and a lot more careful, hence the new organization and the cells that have developed to safeguard their internal structure."

Bethany put down her cup. "They planned to use the cash they were going to steal from the bank to support their political candidates in upcoming elections. They're convinced that placing Guard members in the government is the only way they can get their ideas accepted across mainstream America, and they only want true believers in office. They will do whatever it takes to advance their agenda, including robbing banks to fund their efforts, causing social upheavals, even murdering the opponents. To them, the ends justify the means, no matter the cost, and they have a lot of true believers in their group who will stop at nothing to get their goals accomplished. They have a big project in the works right now called Operation Battlefield. I know it exists, but I don't know what it is or what it entails, although I do think it has something to do with the elections. I don't even know the dates for when it's planned, but there was a sense of urgency around the discussions the last few times it was mentioned, and that's what I'm trying to stop it from happening. From the little I have been able to discover, I know that a lot of people will get hurt if I can't stop it. I'm trying to figure out the details now."

Daniel rubbed his hands through his hair. "So what's our next move?"

Justin handed him a folder and gave one to Bethany, as well. "We created a background for you that melds with the usual type the Heritage Guard tries to recruit, and we've already changed your personnel file and other documents to match this profile. Memorize it. Bethany's background is also in there so you can become familiar with it. Her undercover name is Hailey Weber. Your story is that you knew each other at the University of Tennessee and even dated a bit but didn't want to give that away during the robbery. Now that a few days have passed, we want J.P. and the rest of the Guard to think that you've rekindled your relationship. They already believe Bethany is a true believer, so it won't be that much of stretch for them to think that she dated one in college. Since they didn't score any cash at the bank, they're going to have to plan something fast to find the money they require somewhere else. You need to find out what they're planning and get them to accept you as a member as soon as possible. We also want to know who the other Heritage Guard members are and any details at all about Operation Battlefield."

Bethany widened her eyes. Slow down. Rewind. They wanted her to pretend that she was dating Daniel? She looked over at Daniel and swallowed. He didn't seem bothered by the idea in the least. In fact, if she had to guess, she'd say the look on his face was somewhere between pleasantly surprised and smug. How in the world was she going to do this and keep her emotional distance from him as she'd planned? It was clear that Justin had no idea what he was asking her to do. She felt like going outside and hyperventilating in private. This was not what she had signed up for! She pinched herself hard on the leg. *Okay. Keep it together.* This wasn't the time or place for a meltdown. She tried to focus on the immediate problem. She needed to help get Daniel accepted into the Heritage Guard. "With J.P. arrested and in the hospital, should Daniel escort me there so we can have a visit?"

"That's what I was thinking. He'll obviously realize something is up because he'll recognize Daniel from the robbery. That will be the perfect opportunity for you to feed him the story about Daniel being dirty and wanting to join the cause." Justin stood, his hands on his hips, his voice serious. "I don't have to tell you how dangerous this mission is. The problem at the bank wasn't just a communication failure.

There's more. I think there might be a mole in law enforcement. Someone is dirty somewhere, and the communication breakdown was deliberate."

Bethany leaned back abruptly. "Are you kidding me?" She tossed the folder down on the table. "How can I go back in there if I don't know you have my back?"

"I do have your back," Justin said fervently. "And I'm going to find out who the mole is. But this operation is too important to stop right in the middle. We have to push forward. While you're investigating the Heritage Guard, I'll be investigating at the bureau, and I have contacts at the local level that will be looking into the Chattanooga Police Department. We're going to find the mole. I guarantee it."

"Yeah? Well it wasn't you they were targeting at that bank, was it now?" she said vehemently. She knew he outranked her and she was being insubordinate, but good grief, she had almost lost her life, and now he was telling her that her life was at risk both due to her undercover work and from her own team in law enforcement! This day was going from bad to worse. What other great news did he have to share with her?

"I'm not going to let you down, Bethany, or you either, Daniel." He handed them both cell phones. "Talk to me and each other only. No one else. Got it? These phones are clean and untraceable." He handed them each a set of keys. "Because of the bank job and the risk of a leak, I want you to stay at a different apartment. The address is in your folders. I just set this up this morning. Nobody knows about this place but me at this point. It was a last-minute decision."

She smacked her leg with her hands. "Wait a minute. You want us to stay in the same apartment?"

"Sure. It's got two bedrooms."

"But, sir…"

He straightened and furrowed his brow. It was obvious that he was not enjoying her reaction to his edicts. "Do you have a problem with any of this, Agent Walker?"

She glanced over at Daniel again. He seemed to be intensely studying a rather crooked picture of Ruby Falls that was hanging on the wall, trying to stay out of the fray. She felt a sudden urge to kick him under the table. Hard. But she refrained.

"No, sir."

"That's what I thought. To be on the safe side, don't go back to your old apartments, either one of you. I brought you both bags with cash and a few essentials. Let's start this operation fresh from this point forward and see where it leads us."

"Yes, sir," Bethany responded.

Justin shook both their hands. "I think we're close to the end here. Once you two infiltrate the organization again, I think you'll be able to bring this case to a successful conclusion. Operation Battlefield is close. I can feel it. Keep me informed." He gave them a smile and headed out of the restaurant.

Daniel watched him go, secretly pleased that the situation had created an opportunity for him to spend quality time with Bethany. If nothing else, he would have time to figure out what had gone wrong in their relationship. He might not be able to fix whatever problems had arisen, but at least he would understand what had happened.

He opened his folder, pulled out the sheets inside and started scanning the information about his new persona. They hadn't changed much—just added a few new details and altered a couple of things that made his résumé perfect for a Heritage Guard recruit. He found living a lie much easier than living the truth, and he had been doing just that most of his life anyway. His early days had not been pleasant, and he never revealed that part of himself to anyone. He was pleased to see that according to his new dossier, his childhood and teenage years had actually been improved. Maybe this undercover work would be easier for him than he'd thought. It would be like acting in a play. He folded the sheets and put them in his pocket, then turned to Bethany, who had also been reading the file. She raised her eyebrows a couple of times as she took in the information but otherwise didn't react.

"So are you ready to talk?"

She put down the folder. "About what?"

"About us?"

She raised her eyebrows. "I don't think so, Daniel. Now is really not the right time or the place."

"Really? Then when is the right time? Where is the right place?"

She crossed her arms, making him wonder if he would ever be able to pry the answers out of her. Her body language made it clear that she wasn't interested in having him try, at least not right now.

Suddenly a large explosion shook the building, shattering the glass windows and sending bits of debris throughout the restaurant, covering everything and everyone within. Daniel and Bethany immediately hit the floor, but then stood with their weapons ready once they realized there were no further explosions or any bullets flying. Realization hit them both at the same time.

"Oh, no! Justin!" Bethany cried as they caught sight of his SUV that had exploded in the parking lot.

They secured their weapons and rushed outside. Flames were still licking the metal roof of the vehicle and surrounding area, but it was clear that Justin Harper had been killed. The inside of the car was completely black with soot and melting fabric and damaged material, and the bitter smell of burnt rubber and plastic met Daniel's nostrils. He grabbed his police cell phone and called in the explosion, his eyes surveying the scene as he did so. There were no suspicious people milling about, and there had only been a few customers in the diner, none of which had raised his concern. If he had to guess, the bomb had probably been set to go off when Justin turned the ignition of the vehicle. The bomber was probably long gone.

He looked behind him and noticed Bethany had returned to the restaurant and was helping the customers. It didn't look like anyone was seriously injured. A young married couple who had been closer to the windows both had some cuts on their faces and hands from the flying glass. An older man also had a cut on his left cheek, but the restaurant staff seemed unharmed. The waitress had brought out a first aid kit and Bethany was already cleaning and applying salve and Band-Aids to the worst of the cuts. The Christmas decorations that had brightened the diner only a few minutes ago now seemed to be a haunting and macabre sight among the damage and debris.

A few minutes later, Bethany was back by his side. Her features were grim. "I've called Max Westfield at the FBI and let him know what happened."

Daniel wanted to wipe the fear from her eyes, but he knew it was impossible. "Do you trust him?"

She shook her head. "No, but to be honest, I've been gone for so long that after what Justin told us about the mole, I'm not sure who I can trust at the FBI and who I can't. I've been working on my own for a long time, and Max is my only other real contact. Justin was my lifeline. Now I don't know what to do."

"Who's Justin's boss?"

"A woman named Sandra Duval. I've only met her once. I assume she'll replace Justin at some point now that he's gone."

"Well, we have three options. We can contact her, or we can go straight to the US attorney who prosecuted the Heritage Guard under the RICO statute. Maybe they can help us."

"And option number three?"

"We can contact Captain Murphy, my boss, and bring in the local team."

Bethany paced a few steps back and forth, her arms tightly wrapped around her stomach. "I have to think about this. *We* have to think about this before we contact anyone. If whoever killed Justin killed him because of this case, they probably also know about me and maybe even you and our connection to the Heritage Guard. We could be next."

Daniel rubbed his hands through his hair. "Or maybe the killer doesn't know about us. Perhaps the mole knew he was being investigated, and he killed Justin to stop the investigation. He might know Justin had someone trying to infiltrate the Guard, but the mole might not know that anyone was successful, or that you are the one who actually became a member of the Guard. There's no telling what the mole knows or doesn't know at this point. There are a hundred possibilities. We need more information before we talk to anyone else."

He heard a siren approaching from the distance and he gently grasped Bethany's shoulders. "You need to disappear. I'm the cop that called this in, so they'll expect me to be here, but I don't want you anywhere near this place. I'll tell them Justin had some questions about the robbery, we talked and then the SUV exploded when he left. We'll meet up in a couple of hours at the hospital and see J.P., okay?"

"Okay. Call me on the new cell if there are any developments."

He leaned forward and gave her a quick kiss on the forehead, and he was surprised when she didn't protest before she turned and disappeared into the gathering crowd.

Their handler was dead. He had declared that there was a mole and that he was in the process of investigating that mole, and then he had subsequently been murdered. The implications of what had happened were just starting to sink into Daniel's thoughts.

The Heritage Guard had to have infiltrated law enforcement, but was the mole in the FBI, or was he in the local police office where Daniel worked? Who did they report to now? Who could they trust? There were too many questions, and not nearly enough answers.

NINE

"Hailey!" The smile that greeted her instantly disappeared when J.P. saw that Daniel accompanied her. "What's he doing here?" He pulled against the cuffs that had him shackled to the hospital bed as if he could somehow get farther away from the dreaded man by doing so, his expression hostile as he watched Daniel enter his room.

Bethany nodded at Daniel, hoping he would get the message and stay near the door. He would still be able to hear from that position, but it would give J.P. the illusion of privacy. Daniel got the silent message and leaned against the door frame as she went up to J.P.'s side.

"He's with me, J.P."

"Why? And why are you here? You betrayed me. And I've been hearing rumors.

Bad rumors about what happened to the rest of the team."

Bethany pulled up a chair. "Look, I know you're not happy about being arrested, but you're alive. You would have died from your wounds if I hadn't acted. That's a fact that was confirmed by the EMT at the scene. Surely, they've told you that here at the hospital, as well. You were going into shock because you had lost so much blood." She looked him directly in the eye. "You're too important to the cause, J.P. We can't afford to lose you."

The man was nothing if not prideful. He looked like he still wanted to argue with her, but at the same time, he seemed pleased with her compliment. He stole a look at Daniel, then lowered his voice. "Tell me what happened after I got pulled out of there. I need details. Nobody is telling me much."

"It's bad, J.P."

"I know Jackson is dead."

Bethany nodded soberly. "Yes. They killed Terrell and John too. It was awful. So you see, if you had stayed, you would probably have died regardless."

J.P. shook his head, his expression somewhere between sorrow and anger. His brow was knit together, and his frown put deep creases in his face. "Tell me what happened. Don't leave out a thing."

She glanced up at Daniel, and could tell he was listening, but to his credit, he was looking into the hallway as if he still couldn't hear their conversation. She turned her attention back to J.P. "Well, Daniel Morley, the guy I'm with, he's actually a cop. But he's not just any cop. Turns out, I know him. He and I used to date when we were in college."

J.P. turned and quickly looked over at Daniel, who was still appearing to ignore them. "Yeah? I thought you seemed to be protecting him a bit too much."

She ignored that. "I didn't know he was a cop at the time. We hadn't seen each other in a few years and we hadn't kept in touch. I didn't know what he ended up doing for a living. Anyway, after you left, I, ah, well, I had to rough him up a little to keep him quiet and afterward, Terrell made me take him into the bathroom to clean him up. While we were back there, local law enforcement decided to raid the bank. They came in through the ceiling in full riot gear and shot and killed the rest of the team in a matter of seconds. It turns out

Daniel still has feelings for me, and he didn't want me to get killed like the others, or even arrested. He helped me hide the gun and mask, and I walked out with the rest of the hostages."

J.P. narrowed his eyes. "Why would he do that? You just said he's a cop, right? Why didn't he just arrest you and turn you over?"

She leaned in closer, her voice quiet. "While we were back in the bathroom, I was able to talk to him again, you know, really talk. He's a true believer too, J.P. He agrees with the Guard's manifesto. When I explained to him why we were at the bank and what we were trying to do, he said he wanted to help."

"Was he a true believer back when you were dating before?"

She shrugged. "Not as much as he is now. I mean, we wouldn't have dated if we hadn't shared some of the same beliefs, but now, well, he's had some setbacks."

J.P. raised his eyebrow. "Setbacks?"

Bethany smiled inwardly. The FBI had created a good backstory for Daniel. Now they only had to sell it. "Turns out his father lost his construction business due to the government unfairly giving out contracts. It had been in the family for three generations. His father lost everything. I'm telling you, he used to be a straight arrow, but he's not anymore. He's ready to fight for the cause."

Bethany watched J.P. carefully, trying to gauge if he was believing her story. He seemed to be mulling it over in his mind, but he had always been a hothead and difficult for her to read. Why couldn't it have been Terrell who had survived? At least she had always had a laidback camaraderie with Terrell that made it easy to talk to him. J.P. was a young, impetuous firebrand. Working with him made her nervous, but she didn't have any choice. J.P. had survived, and J.P. was the one she had to deal with.

"Do you trust him?"

"I don't know," she said softly, trying to make it seem like she was hiding the answers from Daniel's listening ears. She didn't think J.P. would buy it if she joined forces with a cop in a matter of a couple of days, so she wanted to introduce the idea to him gradually. Without Justin to guide her, she was making this all up as she went along. "I haven't been around him in a very long time. I know he's passionate about what he believes. He always has been, and now he's even more so. We've started dating again, so we'll see what happens. I do know I'm not in jail. That's a pretty good start. He helped me out at the bank, and that's a fact. Sometimes actions speak louder than words."

J.P. nodded and took another look at Daniel as if he were considering Bethany's opinion. "Yeah, talk to him a lot and see if you can see if he really is a true believer. If he is, we could use a cop on the inside."

"That's exactly what I was thinking." She leaned close again. "Look, J.P., I don't know what to do next. Jackson was my leader, and I don't know anybody else but you from the Guard. I mean, I've seen some faces here and there, and I know a few names, like that guy Bishop Jacobs, but I really don't know how to contact anyone now that Jackson's gone. How do I get reconnected? I'm feeling a little lost right now and I need your help."

He raised his eyebrows as if considering her words. He studied her face for a moment as if judging her veracity, then finally seemed to make a decision. "Go to the dry cleaners on Fifth and Stadium downtown. Tell them you want to sign up for the monthly special. Tell them J.P. sent you. Then leave your name and cell phone number. Someone will contact you."

"That's it?"

"That's it."

"How long will it take?"

J.P. frowned. "Are you in some sort of hurry?"

She blew out a breath. "Of course not. But I want them to pay for what they did to Jackson and the rest of the team. That was my family. They killed *our* family. I want to make them pay. Don't you?"

J.P. seemed satisfied. He grinned at her. "Don't worry. We've got something bigger coming down the pike. They'll pay for what they did at that bank alright."

She grabbed his arm and gave it a squeeze, thinking it was prudent not to push him for more right now. She didn't want him to get suspicious in any way. "Thanks, J.P. You're the best." She leaned back. "So are you going to be okay?"

"I've been arraigned and have a public defender. They want to do a deal but I won't rat on our friends. And I've got plenty of friends on the inside. I'll be safe enough."

"How's your health? Did that bullet do any serious damage?"

"No worries there. In a month or two, I'll be playing basketball in the jail yard, reading about you and the glory of the Guard."

"You can count on it." She patted his hand and stood. Then she joined Daniel who nodded at J.P. before they left the hospital. J.P. would be reading about the Guard in the news alright, but if she had anything to say about it, it would be because the whole lot of them had been arrested and thrown in prison.

Daniel and Bethany rode in silence to a nearby grocery store, and even said very little as they purchased a few items. Bethany called Max Westfield on her burner phone and they discussed Justin's death in more detail. She told him about their visit with J.P. Max was very supportive and promised he would contact her again once a new supervising agent was assigned. For now, he told her that she and Daniel should lay low until Justin's murderer was found. Bethany listened, but Daniel doubted she had any plans to lay low.

After navigating to their new apartment, they made it up the stairs and entered the living room of the second-story unit. Daniel could tell that the loss of Justin Harper and dealing with J.P. at the hospital were all weighing heavily on Bethany, and he wished she weren't quite so independent and would let him ease some of her burden. She had always wanted to handle everything by herself, which at times had been a source of contention between the two of them. Since they were no longer a couple, he hoped she would at least allow him to offer some friendship and support, but so far, her silence seemed to be sending him only one message: *Stay away, I don't need you.* How did he bridge that gap? He wasn't sure, but he wasn't going to give up either. He still had feelings for her. Strong feelings. She was worth fighting for, and he was going to do whatever it took to show her that she could love him and maintain her independence at the same time. He had made a mess of it the first time, but God had granted him a second chance, and this time, he was going to get it right. Finding Bethany and getting to spend quality time with her was an answer to his prayers.

Daniel threw his duffel bag carelessly on the couch and made his way to the kitchen with the groceries while Bethany did a sweep of the bedrooms.

"See any problems?" he asked as he put the cold groceries into the refrigerator.

"No. It's your basic apartment layout. The bedrooms are almost identical. You can have your pick. Each has a bath and balcony."

She had never been one of those females that fussed over fluff and nonsense. She had never wanted jewelry or flowers as presents either. Her idea of the perfect gift was always something practical that she would use on a regular basis. He liked that about her, but it also made it hard to shop for her for Christmas and birthdays. Funny, but he had forgotten that detail about her until just this moment. He offered her a smile and a bottled water. "Want something to drink?"

"Not really." She yawned and stretched. "Thanks anyway."

He could see the weariness in her face and the haggard expression in her eyes. He wanted to just hold her and lend her some of his strength, but he could tell from the standoffish way she held herself that she wouldn't accept his overture, and wouldn't appreciate the offer either. She was in her independent mode again, and if he were correct in his guess, she was about to call it a day and disappear into her room and lock the door.

He tried something else, hoping it would keep her in his presence and communicating with him for little bit longer. "I got you a surprise."

She raised an eyebrow. "Oh, really?" She tried to look into the brown grocery bag he was protectively guarding but he folded down the top and pulled it out of her reach. "No, ma'am. Make yourself comfortable on the couch and I'll bring it over in a minute or two."

She playfully narrowed her eyes. "You know I have a gun, right, and that I'm trained in how to use it?" she said, her voice full of mirth.

He smiled, relieved that she was willing to play along. "Don't forget, missy, I've got a gun myself. And I've logged a few hours at the firing range too. Trust me. Have a seat and you won't regret it."

She watched him for a moment or two before finally heading to the couch. He moved out of her line of vision, prepared the surprise and called out to her before he headed back into the living room. "Close your eyes."

"Really?"

"Really! Come on now. Play fair."

"Okay, fine," she said in mock exasperation. She closed her eyes.

He joined her on the couch and held a bowl up a few inches under her nose. "Okay, you can open them," he said softly.

She opened her eyes, and smiled in delight when she saw the bowl with triple-chocolate ice cream that was swimming in chocolate syrup. Underneath the ice cream was a warm brownie with nuts that Daniel had heated in the microwave. It was a chocolate lover's dream, and he knew it had been her favorite dessert since middle school. He was even wearing a red Santa's hat to help celebrate the season.

She sighed. "You remembered." She grabbed the bowl from him and eagerly took a bite.

"Of course, I remembered," Daniel laughed. "There aren't many people who can eat that much chocolate in one sitting without overdosing and being rushed to the hospital. It's kinda hard to forget." He took a bite of his own ice cream, which had half the amount of chocolate syrup on it and no brownie, and leaned back on the couch. Even though the day had been difficult and demanding, he was enjoying the camaraderie they had shared through the sorrow, pain and even exhilaration at getting what they needed from J.P. at the hospital. He enjoyed working with her, but more than that—he enjoyed having her back in his life.

"So how is your family?"

The question she asked seemed innocent enough, yet it caused a tightening in his stomach that he hadn't expected. He rarely talked about his family with anyone. He shifted. Okay, he never talked about his family. Still, he couldn't expect her not to ask. He shrugged as if the question didn't bother him. "Mom is still living out west. Not much has changed. My brother is in Miami."

"Have you heard from either of them lately?"

"No." He didn't elaborate, and he changed the subject. "What about you? How are your parents?"

She looked him in the eyes and he was aware that *she* knew there was more to the story, but she didn't challenge him on his answer. Instead, she sighed and took another bite, just watching him. Her look told him she was disappointed in him, but there was no surprise in her features. Finally, she shrugged and answered his question, allowing him to change the subject. "They're living the retired life down in Tallahassee. They're happy between their church family and their Florida State Seminoles women's basketball games. There's always something to keep them hopping. They even started going to the theater at FSU, although Dad still doesn't love the musicals, even though he tolerates them for Mom's sake. They'll be Seminole fans till they drop I suspect."

"Have they seen any good plays?"

"They mentioned *Arsenic and Old Lace* and *The Music Man,* and they were pretty excited to see *The Phantom of the Opera* on the playbill for next year's opener. That's Mom's favorite show ever. She can't get enough of the music."

He smiled, remembering Bethany's mom was a theater buff and drummer in her own right. "Didn't she see *Phantom* on Broadway?"

Bethany laughed. "Yeah, twice, and she saw it in Las Vegas too. She says the music still gives her goosebumps when she hears it live. She just loves it." She smiled, reminiscing. "You know, the lady rarely spends a dollar on herself, but when it comes to a good theater production, she'll actually splurge and buy front row tickets just to enjoy the experience. She took a few of the kids to New York recently and got front row seats to *Les Misérables*. They all said it was amazing. They could actually make eye contact with the actors." She finished her dessert and took the bowl to the kitchen and rinsed it, then passed him again on her way to her bedroom.

"I'm done in. See you in the morning?"

He nodded, glad the dessert had given them an opportunity to talk about something besides work and the Heritage Guard. "Sure. 8:00 a.m.?"

"Sounds good."

He was glad that she was willing to share about her family, but why did she seem so disappointed that he didn't want to talk about his? That was all the past, and he didn't understand her need or desire to dig through the remnants of where he had come from. It was over and done with, yet she still asked those same questions. He wanted to focus on the here and now. He didn't want to live in the past. He certainly didn't want to dredge up old memories or talk about people who no longer had a place in his life.

His new cell phone vibrated and he pulled it out and looked at the screen. It was the phone

Justin had given him right before he was murdered and so far, he hadn't received a single call on the line. Justin had told them to trust no one. Should he answer? He didn't recognize the number. He was tempted to ignore the call. It vibrated again and again in his hand. He had meant to turn it off and take the battery out once Justin had been killed, or at a minimum discuss it with Bethany before he acted, but it had simply slipped his mind. Could someone locate them now that his phone had been called? Had he just jeopardized their mission? After all, it was a clean phone from the FBI, and as far as he knew, only Justin, Bethany and he knew the number. It was probably a wrong number, but even so, he was incredibly curious about who was on the other end of the line. The phone vibrated again, but he didn't answer. Instead, he wrote down the number that was calling on a slip of paper, then made a mental note to call it in tomorrow to his contact at the office to run a trace on the number. Could it be Justin's killer? Or someone from the Guard? Time would tell. He turned off the phone and removed the battery just in case.

TEN

Bethany looked to the left and right, then crossed Stadium Street and entered the dry cleaners on the corner. It was a busy store and there were three customers in line ahead of her. She pulled out a brochure from a display on the counter and perused it as she waited, looking up from time to time. There was nothing out of the ordinary about the store to suggest it was anything but a dry cleaners. Racks of clothing in dry-cleaning bags were behind the counter and the shop smelled of cleaning fluids and bleach. Posters on the walls advertised a variety of prices and deals available to special customers, as well as special ticket discounts for tourists that wanted to visit Ruby Falls or the Tennessee Aquarium. A small Christmas tree was also standing in the corner, decorated tastefully in red-and-green glass balls of various shapes and designs. Underneath the tree were several wrapped packages that added to the festive air.

A holiday tune played on the sound system and Bethany sang along to the Christmas carol. When it was her turn, she approached the young man at the register. He was blond with blue eyes and a ready smile. "May I help you?"

She smiled back. "Yes, I'd like to sign up for the monthly special."

The man looked a bit confused. "Monthly special?"

Bethany nodded. "Ah, yes. My friend J.P. gets all of his clothes dry-cleaned here. He told me about the monthly special for your best customers, but said I needed to sign up to get the discount. He recommended that I come in here."

The man pushed a pad across the counter. "I'll have to ask the manager if we're still offering that deal. Please write down your name and cell phone number, and he'll call you back as soon as he gets a chance to check on the latest specials. Will that work?"

She shrugged. "Sounds perfect to me. I'm

not in a rush. I'm more interested in quality than speed."

"Well, we just might be able to help you then." He pulled the pad back over to himself after she had finished writing, removed the top sheet with her information and pocketed the paper. "We'll be in touch."

"Thanks."

She left and returned to Daniel, who was waiting across the street for her. It was a bit chilly and she pulled her jacket closer as she approached. "See anything?"

Daniel shook his head. "Nobody followed you, and I didn't see any suspicious people milling about, but my money is on surveillance cameras. I see three things that could be cameras, and they're making surveillance equipment so small these days, there could be even more. There's no telling for sure." Bethany noticed a spark in his eye, but when he took her in his arms and leaned forward to kiss her, she pulled back, unsure. "What are you doing?"

He gave her a smile and touched her nose affectionately. "We're supposed to be dating, remember? We've rekindled a lost love and are sharing an apartment? If anyone from the Guard is watching us, you can bet they have someone stationed near this dry-cleaning place, and I'm sure they've got their eyes on us right now."

He made a valid point. She laughed, hoping to cover up her gaff in case he was right. She had to sell this romance between them, whether she felt it or not. "You're right. I'm sorry." She drew her hand down his face in a gesture of intimacy, then pulled him into an embrace. She found herself enjoying the contact more than she thought she would, yet still she felt herself awkwardly tighten up in his embrace. Daniel was warm and his strength made her feel safe and secure, but letting Daniel go and moving on with her life had been two of the hardest things she'd ever done. She didn't want to open herself up to that kind of hurt again. Letting him be a part of this mission and pretending they were a couple were both going to be harder than she'd ever imagined.

"Is it really that difficult to let me help you?"

She pulled back, surprised at his question and also frustrated that he had hit the nail on the head. Instead of admitting her own issues, she went on the offensive. "I can't believe you're asking me that. I should be asking you that question."

He took her hand and they started walking down the street as if they were carefree lovers but inside, her stomach was in knots. She had been avoiding this conversation with Daniel ever since she had first seen him at the bank, but maybe it was time they hashed it out. If they weren't going to be able to work together, they needed to know it now before the Guard drew her into the new cell and Daniel became even more deeply entrenched in his role in this undercover assignment.

"Do you know why I never set the date to walk down the aisle with you?" she asked quietly.

His grip tightened on her fingers, but that was the only sign that he was affected by her question. He was apparently quite aware that they needed to maintain appearances in case their performance was being watched by the Guard, even as they got farther and farther away from the dry cleaners.

"No, I still don't understand. I thought we were in love."

She smiled at him. "There are so many things I love about you, Daniel. I love that you remembered my favorite dessert. I love the way you are considerate and kind to others. I love your giving heart." She gave him a playful nudge as they walked and he laughed. "And I think you are the most handsome man I have ever met in my entire life. You have the most amazing shoulders…and you look absolutely fantastic in a Santa's hat."

He laughed with her but stopped when he noticed the look on her face. "Why do I sense a big *but* coming my way?"

She shrugged. "Do you remember last night when I shared a few details about my family?"

"Sure. I enjoy hearing about them."

"Well, last night was a perfect example. When we talk, Daniel, it's always me sharing, never you. I can't marry you because I don't even think I know who the real Daniel is. You rarely share details about yourself. You don't tell me about your past, and I'm left guessing about who you really are inside."

He stopped and looked her in the eye. "That's not true. I've shared more of myself with you than with anyone."

She met his eye, but then dropped his hand and kept walking. He paused a moment, but then followed her, taking her hand again. "That might be true, but I still don't really know you, Daniel. Even after we dated for a year. Even after you asked me to marry you."

"We talked all the time. I remember having long conversations."

"I talked. I told you about myself and my family. And don't get me wrong, you were a good listener. But when you talked, it was about your job or maybe current events. We'd talk about anything and everything *but* you. There was never anything personal in the conversation. You never told me about your past and where you came from. I don't really know you. I don't even know what you feel or what you think. I never have."

"Yes, you do. You know me better than anyone. The rest are just details. They don't matter. What you see here and now, that's who I am today. I don't want to live in the past. I didn't have a great childhood, and there's no reason to relive it by bringing it up."

They turned down a different street, and she was glad for the diversion of walking so they could discuss this difficult topic. She couldn't imagine sitting on a couch and having this conversation. She was sure he would have shut her down after the first sentence if they'd been in the apartment trying to sort this out. There was something good about walking and talking that helped get the words out. She took a deep breath and pushed on. It was time to broach the subject that had been eating at her the longest. "You told me your mother lives out west."

Once again, she felt his hand tighten on her own. She could tell this conversation was difficult for him, yet, they still needed to talk about this elephant in the room if they were going to work together or ever have anything more. "That's a lie, Daniel, or at least a huge omission."

He raised an eyebrow, and for the first time, she saw a look of fear cross his face. "What do you mean?"

"I work in law enforcement, remember? I did some research and tracked her down. Your mom is in prison out in Texas for drug possession. She's been incarcerated for over ten years. You've never mentioned that. In fact, you've never told me anything about her. And apparently, you have an older brother. Don't you think you've left out a few of the important details?"

He didn't speak for a long time. When he

finally did, his voice was rough and there was anger in its depths. "What do you want to hear? That my dad abandoned us when I was five and my mom's drugs were more important to her than I ever was? It didn't take me long to figure out I needed to make myself scarce whenever she was using. I got pretty good at disappearing. Is that what you want to hear? Or maybe you want to know about how my older brother used to beat me up whenever he felt like it? Or about how I spent my evenings hiding outside under the car, or went for days without eating a decent meal? Is that what you want to know about?"

Bethany stopped and tried to pull him close, but this time, Daniel was the one that reeled back. "I don't want pity. That's a big reason why I don't talk about it. I'm not that scared little boy anymore. I grew up quickly and I learned how to take care of myself. But I did a lot of things that I'm not proud of too. I had to survive. And survival meant stealing sometimes so I could eat, and some things that were a lot worse. I had to do a lot of terrible things. Is that what you want to hear? Is this what you want to talk about?" His voice was angry and when she reached for him again, he put up his hands and walked away from her. She followed a short distance behind, and for almost two blocks, they walked in silence.

Finally, he stopped and ran his fingers through his hair. He turned to face her, but he wouldn't look at her directly. "I can't believe I just told you that," he said, his voice soft. "I've never told anybody that."

She touched his chin and raised his head so she could see his eyes. He had such beautiful eyes. "I'm really glad you did, because that's who you are. I want to know you, all of you, the good, the bad and the ugly. I am sorry that happened to you, Daniel, but I don't want to hear the stories so I can pity you. I want to hear so I can get to know you better. So I know that you trust me enough to tell me. So I can know the real you. You're an incredible person, Daniel. You must have overcome some amazing hurdles in your life to become so successful. I want to know how you did it. I want to get to know you in here." She touched his chest.

He studied her for a moment or two, then took her hand again and started walking. "And if I don't want to tell you?"

Bethany considered his words. Could they have a relationship without trust? Maybe for a while. But months from now, that lack of trust would eat at her, just as it had when she had found out the truth about his mother and her prison sentence. She had read that law enforcement file and it had been like someone had stuck a knife in her gut. She'd had a serious boyfriend before who cheated on her and ended up humiliating her in front of her friends and coworkers. She had trusted him and vowed to never make the same mistake again. Daniel was a different man, and she could never imagine him cheating on her, but trust was a vital part of any relationship. Without it, she would rather be alone and take her chances on her own.

"Then I guess friendship will have to be enough, Daniel. For both of us. I don't want to force you to do anything you don't want to do. That's not what I'm about, and it's obvious that you don't want to give more than you've already given. That's fair. It's your life and it's your choice. You don't have to give more. I know we're pretending to be more for this job, but I'm glad we were able to talk and clear the air. Now we know where we stand. We'll play this game for the Heritage Guard assignment, but once this is over, we'll go our separate ways, okay?" She stopped walking, and when he turned to face her, she reached up on tiptoe and gave him a quick kiss on the lips. "But now we'll part friends, okay?"

He looked like he was about to argue with her, but then her cell phone rang, and she answered it on the second ring. "Hello?"

"Did you make up with your boyfriend?"

She smiled and looked around, completely in her role for whomever was watching from the Guard. "Making up is always the best part. Where are you?"

"Nearby."

"Who am I talking to?" Bethany knew it had to be someone associated with the Guard, because the only person she had given this phone number to was the man at the dry cleaners.

"We've met before, but it was quite a while ago. My name is Bishop Jacobs. You were part of Jackson's team."

"That's right."

"I've heard you can get things."

"That's also right," she agreed.

"I have some friends I'd like for you to meet," Bishop stated, his tone friendly yet businesslike.

"I'm all for that. When and where?"

"Two hours. Coolidge Park. By the carousel."

"How will I recognize these new friends?"

"You don't need to worry. We'll recognize you," Bishop stated, matter-of-factly.

"Alright then. I'll be there," Bethany agreed.

"Don't bring your boyfriend."

"Why not? He wants to join up."

"We might let him. We might be able to use someone with his particular skill set. But we're still checking him out. Leave him at home, understand?"

She shrugged as if it didn't matter. "Whatever. It's your show."

"Yes, it is," Bishop agreed. "And it's going to be fabulous."

ELEVEN

The Dentzel carousel in Coolidge Park was a true work of art. Daniel admired the hand-carved animals and ornate decorations between the gold leaf benches through the binoculars as he kept an eye on Bethany waiting for the Guard contact to arrive. The park had also been decorated for Christmas, and bright red ribbons were on every post between hanging swaths of garland intertwined with strings of cranberries and popcorn. Hand-drawn pictures of traditional Christmas designs like reindeer, nativity scenes and snowflakes were posted on some of the walls, as well as a sign stating the art was donated by a local elementary school's fifth grade class. Daniel was tempted to put down a couple of dollars and take Bethany on a ride once this entire episode was over, but the seriousness of the job at hand kept his mind off of his surroundings and focused on the job at hand.

Their discussion this morning had been like pouring salt on open wounds, and he still couldn't believe that he had blurted out so much about himself. He and his older brother didn't talk. They didn't have a relationship worth mentioning.

He *never* talked about his mother.

It was a rule he had lived by since he had closed that chapter of his life when she was arrested. He had watched her being cuffed and led away on that fateful day, and in his mind, that was the end of their relationship. He hadn't wanted to think about her or even know what was happening in her life since the police took her away. He was done. He had moved on. If he never saw either one of them again for the rest of his life, that would be okay with him. Yet, he had shared bits and pieces of his past with Bethany this morning and it had been oddly cathartic. Still, he had no desire to go any further with the discussion, and he tried to put it from his mind.

Why was Bethany so set on knowing his past? The question ate at him as he used the binoculars to scan the area. He saw two other men surveilling the area around the carousel that were probably with the Guard. He texted Bethany about them, using a special code they had devised so no one would understand their messages if either of the phones were confiscated. She texted back and let him know that she had seen them too, and he leaned back against the fence, once again surveying the area through the binoculars. Both men were obviously not there for the carousel. He kept watching.

He thought back over the year that he and Bethany had dated, and sorted through as many of the conversations they'd had as he could remember. He grudgingly had to admit that she had a point. He *hadn't* told her much about himself. But why did it matter? She had seen that he was a caring and good person, right? They had spent a great deal of time together, and she had learned a lot about his personality. He knew her last boyfriend had been a real prince and had publicly cheated on her. Surely, she knew he wasn't cut from that cloth. Wasn't that enough? He grimaced. Apparently, it wasn't. Especially if her "parting as friends" comment was anything to go by. Now he was well and truly stuck in a quandary. He didn't want to talk about his past, and he didn't want to lose Bethany either.

"Freeze, buddy."

Daniel heard the words seconds before he felt the metal of the gun barrel against his side. He kicked himself mentally. He had been so engrossed in his thoughts that he hadn't even noticed that the two men had snuck up on him. He felt like an idiot. He did as he was told as one man wearing a Rays baseball cap took Daniel's gun out of his waistband, while a man on his left wearing a red flannel shirt took his binoculars and his cell phone, then patted him down. Both men were blond and looked to be in their thirties. They were well built and both gave off a self-assured and aggressive vibe. They could have been brothers, with similar features, including high cheekbones and deep-set hazel eyes.

"Look," the one Daniel nicknamed Flannel said lightly, nudging his partner as he found Daniel's badge and pulled it out of his pocket and examined it. "Our friend here is a cop."

"Is there a problem?" Daniel asked in a nonchalant voice. He hoped they were Guard members but didn't want to assume anything. He chose not to challenge them and thought a non-aggressive response was the best way to respond. It made sense that the Guard would want to have people on the perimeter of the meeting as well; he just thought that he had been far enough back that he wouldn't draw their attention. He had been wrong. If he were also wrong about who they were and he had just let common criminals get the jump on him and take his gun, he was in a great deal of trouble. In either case, he was on high alert and his muscles were tensed and ready for action at the slightest provocation.

"Are you on the job or off?" the Rays fan asked, pushing the gun a little harder against his ribs.

"I'm looking out for a friend."

The man got even closer and spoke in a low tone, yet the threat in his tone was obvious. "You didn't answer my question, *friend.* And I'm not fond of repeating myself."

Daniel gritted his teeth. "And I'm not fond of getting threatened. A cop is always on the job, but to answer your question more specifically, I'm not here representing the police department today. I'm here helping out a friend."

Flannel motioned with his hand. "Helping out how? I don't see anyone but you. Maybe you're some kind of criminal just casing the place. Maybe that isn't even a real badge."

"It's real alright."

Flannel laughed. "You really don't like answering questions directly, do you?"

The Rays fan took a step back and looked more carefully at Daniel's expression. When he finally spoke again, his voice was thoughtful. "I'm pretty sure you were told to stay home."

Daniel nodded, but inwardly relaxed a measure. The man's words reassured him that they were with the Guard and knew about Bethany's meeting. He was still on high alert however. He didn't know what to expect, but his undercover mission to infiltrate this group had officially begun. "You're right, but it's hard to stay back when you care about someone. I was out of the way if you wanted to meet with her in private. I'm not eavesdropping on any personal conversations. I just wanted to verify that she was safe."

"You didn't trust us?" Flannel scoffed. The Rays fan shot him a look that shut him up. It was clear that he was the one in charge and he didn't want any superfluous conversations.

Daniel shrugged. "I don't trust blindly. Do you? I don't even know you. Yet."

The Rays fan stepped closer again and this time there was something dark and threatening in his eyes. "We don't trust people who don't follow orders." He looked Daniel up and down as if taking his measure. "We also don't trust cops." He handed Daniel back his badge, binoculars and phone, but stowed Daniel's gun in his own waistband and covered it with his shirt. Then he pushed Daniel forward. "Head toward the carousel. Keep your hands where I can see them."

Daniel obeyed, but stayed on alert. "I'll need my gun back after this meeting."

"You'll get it back when I'm good and ready to give it back. Not before. Now keep walking."

They walked in silence for a few minutes, but then Daniel said, "Not all cops are the same you know. We don't all live by the same code."

"How do you figure?" Flannel asked.

"I believe a man should earn what he gets and get what he earns. There are no free rides in this world. But not everyone in law enforcement agrees with me." When he got no response, he pushed on, knowing he had to play a role, even though he didn't necessarily agree inside with everything he would be saying and doing while trying to infiltrate the Heritage Guard. "My point is, you might actually trust a cop if you knew the right cop. Some of us agree with what you're trying to accomplish." He could tell that they were thinking about his words, so he didn't push. The key to being accepted might also be to keep his mouth shut for the most part and just listen and learn. The FBI had created a very credible background story for him, and if he said a bit here and there that supported it and then just shut up and did what was asked of him, he might be accepted into the Heritage Guard without even a raised eyebrow.

Daniel said a prayer for Bethany's safety since he was no longer able to keep an eye on her. Yet, he was cognizant of the fact that she had already been undercover with this group for over a year, so she was probably safer than he was in his current situation. He followed Flannel into a building that was behind the carousel, quite aware that the Rays fan was still armed and following him from behind.

The room they entered was bare except for a long table and six folding chairs. There were no windows, and the room only had one door in or out. It was probably normally used for storage and was dusty and smelled like stale cleaning supplies and paper goods. The Rays fan motioned toward one of the chairs.

"Sit."

Daniel picked the chair farthest from the door so he could be the first to see anyone coming or going from the room. He eased himself down, keeping an eye on Flannel and the Rays fan as he did so. Both of the men stationed themselves by the door, almost like sentries. He wasn't sure why he had been brought here, and neither man seemed ready to volunteer any information. After about ten minutes of waiting, impatience finally got the best of him.

"We waiting for someone?" Daniel asked.

"Yeah. Just hang tight," Flannel answered.

Suddenly, the door opened and a bull of a man barreled in and tackled Daniel, even though he was still sitting in the chair. Both men ended up on the floor and the chair Daniel had been sitting in went flying. It was all Daniel could do to keep from getting his nose bashed against the floor again as both men landed hard on the concrete. Daniel struggled to free his arms and once he did, he hit the aggressor's head against the wall as they rolled and wrestled for supremacy. Daniel knocked the man hard in the chin with his elbow and the attacker loosened his grip just enough so Daniel was able to roll him over, gain the upper hand and end up on top. He straddled the larger man and hit him hard in the mouth, drawing blood with the blow. A second punch drew blood from the man's nose, but before he could throw a third, Flannel and the Rays fan joined the fray and pulled the two apart. The one Daniel had nicknamed "the Bull" spat blood on the floor and tried to pull away, his face contorted by the mess Daniel had made with his fists.

"Filthy cop!" the Bull roared. "Because of you, my cousin is dead!" He tried again to pull loose from the Rays fan but the bigger man held him fast.

"I don't know your cousin, and I don't know you," Daniel answered, also jerking against Flannel's grip. He'd had enough of these guys. Maybe they would respect him more if he showed them some fire, but either way, he was done getting attacked without provocation. He was going to defend himself. He felt blood trickling down his face and realized he hadn't successfully protected his nose after all. The rush of adrenaline kept him from feeling the pain for now, but he was sure his face would start throbbing again once this episode was over. The way his week was going, he figured his nose would never heal normally again.

"So tell me about your boyfriend," Bishop said as he leaned back and crossed his legs. His phone beeped and he looked at the screen, then silenced it and put it in his pocket. Bishop and Bethany were alone in the room, sitting across a rickety table from each other in a small building not far from the carousel. Another man had frisked her and taken her cell phone and sidearm when she was brought in. He gave both items to Bishop, then slipped outside and was probably guarding the door.

Bethany shrugged. "His name is Daniel Morley. We dated a bit in college, then went our own ways. I ran across him again during the bank robbery. He saved my life."

"He's a cop?" Bishop asked.

Bethany smiled. She was having trouble reading Bishop, but she could tell he already knew the answer to the question before he even asked. She had met him a couple of times before, but didn't really know him, or what role he played in the organization beyond the basics. Justin had started to dig into his background, but they still knew little besides the fact that he owned and operated a mid-size rental car company. She did know he was powerful within the Guard, and she needed him to trust her if her mission was going to be a success. He was a distinguished looking man in his early fifties, with weathered skin and dark intelligent eyes. He had shortly cropped dark hair that was just starting to gray and a silver mustache. She could tell by his demeanor that he was used to being in charge and not having his orders questioned. Now he seemed to be testing her, but she wasn't sure what he was looking for. The direct approach always seemed to work best for her. She tried it now. "Let's quit playing games, Mr. Jacobs. I'm sure you already know his full history and have done a thorough background check. Is there something specific you want to know?"

"Fair enough," Bishop answered. "Let's cut to the chase. I want to know why he came with you today when I specifically told you not to bring him."

She raised an eyebrow and tried to act calm

and collected, even though her heart was beating through her chest. If they had found Daniel in the park, then he was probably in danger. They'd thought if he stayed far enough back, he wouldn't be seen by any of the Guard. Obviously, they had been wrong. Was he hurt? Had their mistake jeopardized the mission? Questions fluttered across her mind, along with a healthy dose of fear. Still, she kept her emotions well below the surface and answered in a nonchalant voice. "He wasn't close enough to get in the way," she said quietly. "But since I almost got killed at the bank just a couple of days ago, Daniel was worried about my safety."

"We take care of our own. You should know that."

"I do," Bethany answered. "But I just lost my entire team, and I still don't know why. Something went terribly wrong at the bank, and until I know the reasons for their deaths, I'm being extra cautious, and so is he."

"Cautious is good," Bishop agreed. He steepled his fingers as he considered her words. "Defiance is not. I'm inclined to assign you to a new team, but I need to know that you are still loyal to the Guard. I need to know that you will follow orders in the future without question."

Bethany tightened her fists. "The Guard is my family. I lost everything and everyone I cared about in that bank job. I'm still loyal, but now I'm also on fire for the cause even more than before. The police killed my family! They have to pay for that. It's time for the Heritage Guard to take their rightful place in society and lead this nation. That's the only way our future will be secure."

Bishop's eyes lit up as he heard the enthusiasm in her voice. She pushed on, knowing she was on the right track and that her passionate words were fanning the flames of his zealousness. "I brought you Daniel as a new recruit, as well. He proved his loyalty at the bank by saving my life and getting me out of there without getting caught, even if he is law enforcement. He's a well-respected detective with the local police department, and can be very helpful to the Guard with our future projects, especially Operation Battlefield."

Bishop narrowed his eyes. "What do you know about that?"

"Not enough," she said forcefully. "Jackson only told me he needed me to get some C-4 explosives to help with the project. I'm working on that, but since he is dead, I need to know if you still want it and how much to get. He was only starting to share the plans with me before the bank job."

"Does your cop know?"

"No," she answered, her tone firm. "But he can help. Both of us can. Jackson said Operation Battlefield was going to bring more glory to the Heritage Guard than anything else we've ever done. I want to be a part of that, and I'm sure Daniel will too if you decide to bring him on board." She leaned forward. "Of course, that decision is totally up to you."

Bishop considered her plea and was silent for a few moments. Finally, he spoke. "I will consider your request, but you have to realize Daniel is untested. You've proven your loyalty by participating at the bank, but Daniel will have to show us his loyalty before he can be trusted. I'm willing to give him a chance, but he starts as a level one and has to earn his way up the ladder, just like everyone else."

Bethany was relieved by his words. "I understand, and I'm sure he will. Thank you." If Bishop was considering letting Daniel join the Guard, then even though they'd found him in the park, they wouldn't hurt him. He was probably with Guard members right now who were already sizing him up.

Bishop smiled. "I know you can get your hands on things, and we need a few items besides the C-4 for Operation Battlefield. Can you help us out?"

Bethany nodded. "Give me the list. I'll let you know what I can get and when."

"I was hoping you'd say that. Our immediate problem is funding. Since the bank robbery didn't yield any cash, we've had to come up with alternative methods to fund our operation. I'm going to put you with a new group, and your first assignment will be to help us obtain some of the money we need. After we get the money, we'll sit down and go over the Battlefield plans. Are you ready?"

Bethany nodded. "Absolutely."

"Good. Let's go meet your new family." He pushed her cell phone and gun back to her across the table and stood. She surreptitiously pushed a select number on her phone, then put it in her pocket. It only took a few short minutes to clone a phone, and then she would be able to access all of Bishop's contacts and listen in on his cell phone conversations. Things were looking up.

She said a short but heartfelt prayer of thanks. God had helped her get this mission back on track, and she was immensely grateful.

TWELVE

Bethany followed Bishop into a nearby room, and her eyes widened when she saw the scene. Daniel and Derek, a man she had only met a couple of times before, had obviously been fighting, and were being held apart by two large, bulky men who were strangers to her. Daniel's nose was bleeding again, and Derek was sporting an eye that was starting to swell and a fat lip. Furniture was strewn about and blood had been smeared on the floor and walls. It was a huge mess. Daniel's expression was angry and he pulled against the larger man's grip.

"What's going on?" she asked incredulously.

"This man is responsible for Terrell's death!" Derek cried, his eyes shooting fire. Again, he tried to free himself from a man wearing a Tampa Bay Rays hat, but the bigger man held fast.

Bethany couldn't believe what she was seeing. She'd thought that working with J.P. was difficult because he was such a hothead, but Derek was apparently just as much of a firebrand as the man they'd visited in the hospital the day before. This was her new cell? A wave of dread swept over her. Working with this man was going to be challenging to say the least. She marched up to Derek and got right in his face. "I was at that bank. I was with Terrell. He was like a brother to me. This man had nothing to do with Terrell's death. Yes, he's a cop, but he's on our side. He saved my life, and he would have saved Terrell's too if it would have been possible."

"You're just saying that because he's your man, Hailey," Derek spat.

She moved so quickly that Derek didn't have time to react. In seconds, her automatic weapon was pressed tightly against his forehead. When she spoke, her voice was low and lethal. "Are you calling me a liar, Derek?"

The entire room got quiet and everyone was still, waiting for the scene to play out. Bethany was one of the few women in this organization, and she knew strength was valued. It was a gamble to pull her weapon when she was meeting new members of the Guard, but she wouldn't get another opportunity to make a first impression. She rolled the dice.

The man restraining Derek looked over to Bishop for guidance, and for a moment, Bethany wondered what he would do. Then she inwardly breathed a sigh of relief when she saw the older man shake his head and hold up his hand, keeping the man in the Rays baseball cap from intervening.

"Well?" She increased the pressure of the barrel of the gun on Derek's forehead.

"Fine!" he finally said under his breath.

"Fine what, Derek?" she asked, her eyes still boring into him.

"I believe you, Hailey, okay? If you say he didn't kill Terrell, then I believe you. Come on, put the gun away. Like you said. We're all on the same side."

She slowly lowered her weapon, but her eyes were narrowed. "Don't ever question my loyalty again, Derek, or Daniel's either. I trust this man with my life."

"Sure, Hailey. Whatever you say." The guy in the Rays hat released Derek and the guy wearing a flannel shirt released Daniel and handed him a bandanna that he had in his pocket. Daniel used it to staunch the blood that was running out of his nose. Daniel's poor nose! He was going to be hurting tonight. She made a mental note to buy some pain reliever for him on the way home once they got out of this meeting. He still had bruising under both of his eyes and swelling around his nose from his initial injury, and this latest knock was only going to make it worse. Just like at the bank, she had to stop herself from going to his side and fussing over his injury. This wasn't the time or place; nor would he appreciate her interference. Here, she was Hailey Weber, a tough woman who lived on the fringes, knew how to get things and fought for the Heritage Guard.

"So if we're done posturing," Bishop said, "I'd like to get down to business." He righted one of the chairs that had been knocked over during the fray, took a seat and motioned for everyone else to sit except for the man in the Rays baseball cap, who stood guard by the door. "As most of you know, my name is Bishop Jacobs. We've suffered a major setback with the loss of Jackson and his team, but thankfully, Hailey survived and is still here to help us fight the cause. We also have some new help. You've all met Derek. As you now know, he's Terrell's cousin who just moved here from Alabama. Liam—" he nodded to the man wearing the flannel shirt "—and his brother, Ethan—" he motioned to the man wearing the Rays cap "—round out the rest of the team. We've been assigned a new project with a quick turnaround. It's going to take some planning and a lot of teamwork. We don't have time for fighting among ourselves. The timeline for Operation Battlefield has been moved up, so everything we're doing has to happen faster than we expected." He looked at Derek. "If you can't handle working with a cop, say so now and we'll find you another team."

Derek gave Daniel a look of derision but stopped when he noticed Bethany's glare. Finally, he looked back at Bishop. "If you vetted him, Bishop, that's good enough for me."

Bishop nodded. "Then the subject is closed. I don't want to hear about it again."

"So what's the job?" Liam asked, leaning forward.

Bishop pulled out some documents from a

pocket inside his jacket. "We've got a friend who works inside a bank." He glanced at Bethany as if to reassure her. "Don't worry, Hailey. It's not the same one we tried to rob last week. They receive half a million dollars by armored car every month that then gets distributed to their various ATMs around town. There won't be any tracking devices or dye packs because those don't get added until after the money gets distributed." He leaned back and smiled. "We need that money for Operation Battlefield. We're going to rob that armored car when it comes to the bank to make the delivery."

"Bethany, Daniel, I'm David Hooker, your new contact at the FBI. I'll be in charge of the Heritage Guard case going forward." Bethany had an eerie sense of déjà vu as she shook hands with the large, middle-aged man before taking a seat across from him at the small restaurant in Chattanooga. The mom-and-pop place was a local favorite and was amazingly similar to the diner they had been sitting in right before Justin Harper was killed in the parking lot. This time though, Max Westfield was with them, sitting next to Hooker with his laptop, taking notes as usual. Daniel also shook hands with Hooker, then nodded at Westfield before taking the seat next to Bethany.

Bethany surveilled the small diner, looking for anything suspicious or out of place. Nothing seemed overtly dangerous, so her eye strayed to a Christmas tree that was standing in the corner that was flashing with strands of red-and-green mini lights. Several homemade ornaments that looked like they had been made from a homemade clay recipe of flour, salt and water were in the size and shape of sugar cookies and decorated the tree. It was a charming piece of nostalgia that brought back happy memories. She'd made many of the same type of ornaments with her mom when she had been growing up.

She pulled herself back from her recollections and studied the new man before her. She had never seen Special Agent Hooker before, and she was not impressed with her new handler. She couldn't put her finger on the problem. He seemed normal enough. His suit was dark and appeared like the normal FBI style the agency was known for wearing, and he was fit and clean-cut. If anything, her gut was just telling her that David Hooker was too distracted to take her and the job she was doing seriously. And why was Max Westfield, a low man on the organizational ladder, even here at this meeting? Granted, she had been away from the FBI offices for quite a while, but something just seemed off.

"So you drew the short straw?" she asked Hooker, partially joking, but also partly hoping that he would contradict her and reassure her concerns.

"I wouldn't say that," Hooker said in a business tone, "but I admit I haven't been able to get completely up to speed on this case yet. It's only been temporarily assigned to me during the investigation into Justin's murder. Then the top brass will reevaluate the case in its entirety and determine the wisest course of action during the next few days."

Bethany's gut tightened, her fears confirmed. They were reevaluating her case? This was the first she'd heard of it, and she wondered if she'd even be consulted before the decision would be made to continue the investigation or pull the plug completely. That irked her. She needed to be a part of *any* conversation the FBI had about the Heritage Guard case, and she should certainly be consulted before anyone tried to shut it down. She was about to let the agent have a piece of her mind when she felt Daniel's hand squeeze her thigh under the table. He undoubtedly wanted to remind her to proceed cautiously. She ignored him.

"So let me get this straight. I'm putting my life on the line, and so is Detective Morley, by the way, and the FBI has given the case to someone who doesn't even have time to read the file?" She moved toward the edge of her seat as if to leave, but Hooker's no-nonsense voice stopped her.

"I'll have it read by the end of the day, Agent, and I promise you that I'll know every last detail. I take this job very seriously. I also recognize the gravity of your situation, and that of Detective Morley, I assure you."

She looked him in the eye. He seemed somber and his expression was resolute. Beside him, Westfield was smiling and his green eyes flashed, as if he had warned Hooker about her temper and had just been proven correct. She wondered if Westfield was on her side because he believed she was a good agent, or if it was only because he was interested in having a relationship with her. If she had to bet, she would guess it was the latter. Being around him still made her skin crawl. As if to accent the point, she felt Westfield's leg touch hers suggestively underneath the table. She kicked him and gave him a small smile of satisfaction when he winced.

"I'm glad to hear that," Daniel said, joining the conversation before she could dig herself any deeper into a hole she couldn't climb out of. "I'm sure Mr. Westfield has informed you that my boss, Captain Murphy, wants to be kept apprised of the details of this case since it is a joint operation between the FBI and the local authorities."

"Yes, I'm aware of that aspect of the operation," Hooker agreed. "So why don't you bring me up to speed so I can help you do your jobs."

Daniel squeezed Bethany's leg again and she gave him a look. Finally, she swallowed and gave Hooker a short overview of the Heritage Guard undercover assignment, and finished by telling him about how she had recently cloned Bishop's phone.

"I was able to download his list of contacts. If you can give me a secure site, I'll send you what I've found so far. I would imagine that many of the names from his phone are Guard members. Can you start checking them out?"

Hooker nodded. "Yes. We also need recordings of his conversations. I secured a warrant authorizing the recordings, so now they can be used in court to help our case if you hear anything useful."

"We've already worked out a way to do the recordings. Every number he dials and every word he utters is being saved. I'll start weeding through them tonight." Next, she told Hooker about their upcoming Guard assignment and every detail she knew about the armored car robbery. He was taking notes, and she was glad to see he was interested enough to do so.

"Okay, I'll get this approved and make sure there's no interference during the job. What else do you need?"

"He mentioned C-4. I don't know how much, or what else he'll want, but I imagine he'll need the detonators and timers. He said we'll talk again after the armored car heist."

Hooker raised an eyebrow. "Did he mention Operation Battlefield?"

She nodded. "Yes. I think the C-4 is going to be used for that mission. The bank job also seems like a test. If Daniel and I can help pull that off, I think he'll start trusting us with more. He seemed anxious to get the details straight. Last I heard, they had moved up the date, so whatever they're planning, they need to get their ducks in a row and fast."

Hooker wrote a few more notes, then closed his notebook. He leaned forward, his expression intense. "Okay, Agent Walker, let me tell you the bottom line. I've talked with the brass about this case. They're worried that it's been dragging out so long and they don't have anything to show for it except the fiasco at the bank. On top of that, they believe, and I agree, that Justin's murder is related. You've been given two more weeks to tie up all of the loose ends and bring this case to a close."

"Two weeks?" She pushed back from the table. "I don't think that's realistic. I can't get you what you need in that short amount of time. It's just not possible."

"Make it happen," Hooker intoned, apparently ignoring her flash of temper. "With Bishop's cell phone, you can record all sorts of conversations in the room, even if he's not using the phone. Get him to say what you need. Meanwhile, I'll be researching the list of names you send me from his contacts and cross-referencing them with what you've given us in the past from Jackson Smith's contacts.

Together with Detective Morley's help, I'm confident you can get the job done."

She fumed inwardly, but it was patently obvious that he wasn't going to budge. And why should he? He wasn't the one that had devoted a year of his life to this case. All he saw was the loss of Agent Harper and the deaths at the bank, which she had to admit were very large losses. Still, if they could figure out the plans for Operation Battlefield and head off whatever the Guard was planning, they could probably still save hundreds of lives. She just didn't think two weeks was a realistic time frame.

She glanced over at Westfield. Instead of offering her support, he seemed to be trying to flirt with her with his eyes. Good grief! She wanted to shake him and kick him again. He was such a letch! Why couldn't he take the hint and keep his mind on arresting the Guards?

Daniel looked at the computer screen, still not believing his eyes. He rubbed them and leaned back. It had been a very long day, and he had been very happy to finally get back to the apartment and put his feet up. He was sitting on the couch now with his legs resting on the coffee table, sipping a soda and reading through the information that had thus far been gleaned from Bishop's phone. The FBI had some amazing software that had already made transcripts of many of the calls he had made, as well as created lists of his contacts and call records. The man had been incredibly busy since his phone had been cloned, and the information they were gleaning was a gold mine.

"Is everything okay?" Bethany asked as she came from the kitchen and sat down in the chair that was sitting kitty-corner to the couch. She had a cranberry juice bottle in her hand and she took a drink, then propped her feet up on the table next to his. He liked that she was able to relax around him and be herself. He set the laptop aside and reached for her right foot, then gently started massaging it.

"That's wonderful." She smiled. "I'll give you an hour to stop."

He laughed at her joke, but would gladly keep rubbing if it would keep her smiling. She had such a lovely smile and it lit up her entire face. "I'm impressed by the software that is capturing all of this information about Bishop. If Hooker can research the backgrounds of his contacts, we might have a pretty good membership list for the Heritage Guard."

"Yeah, Bishop seems very connected. Once we do the armored car job tomorrow, I'm hoping he'll share more of the Operation Battlefield plans with us. If he drops a few names, I'll be ready. Now that we have to come up with our case in two weeks, we'll really have to push for information. Pushing hasn't worked in the past, but maybe once I see his list of items he needs, I can think of some way to weasel the information out of him."

Daniel switched to her left foot and she sighed. When she spoke, however, her voice held a note of concern. "So are you okay with what you have to do tomorrow? I mean, this will be the first time you've ever committed a felony. The first time I had to do it, I was sick to my stomach for hours."

Daniel was silent for a moment. He wondered how much it would change her opinion of him if she knew more about his history. He shook his head, more convinced than ever that he needed to keep his past in the past. "I'm not pleased, but I don't really have a choice. I've been praying that there isn't any collateral damage and that no innocent bystanders get hurt. Those are my main concerns."

"You're right," she agreed. "Thankfully, you're just the driver, so you won't have to pull your gun on anyone."

He put her foot down and sat back. "I keep trying to tell myself that what we're doing is for the greater good, but in my mind it's still hard to justify. Maybe once I understand the details of Operation Battlefield, my conscience will be clearer. Then it will all seem worth it. Right now, it's hard to see how it all fits together without knowing the bigger picture."

He told Bethany about how his cell phone had rung that first night they had been in the apartment, and how when he had tried to track down the phone's owner, the number had come up as untraceable. "Only you and Justin were supposed to have that number. So who could have been calling?"

"Maybe it was a wrong number?" she said hopefully.

Daniel raised an eyebrow. "Do you really believe that?"

She shook her head. "No. So if we assume the worst, that means the Guard knows where we are staying and is probably watching our every move."

"And how did they get that information? Those phones were supposed to be clean. Justin said so himself."

He pulled the laptop over and showed her the screen he had been looking at. "We also have another problem. See this chart? It's a list of everyone Bishop has called in the last month." He pointed to three of the entries. "See these? These are to Captain Murphy, my boss."

Bethany's eyes widened and the shock was visible in her eyes. "How do you think they know each other?"

"I don't know, but we're going to have to find out. Captain Murphy grew up in this area, but I don't know anything about Bishop Jacobs. I've been searching the internet but nothing has jumped out so far. Let's hope Hooker can find some connection. It makes me wonder if Captain Murphy is the mole we've been searching for." He didn't want to believe it was true. Captain Murphy had always seemed to be an honorable man. Yes, he was rough around the edges, but he always seemed to get the job done, and he was a good cop. Could he be the reason Bethany had almost been killed at the bank? And if so, why? If he was dirty and a member of the Guard himself, why would he sanction the killing of the rest of the Guard team? Had Captain Murphy been the one who had gotten Justin killed? None of this was adding up.

Justin Harper had been right about one thing: they couldn't trust anybody.

THIRTEEN

Daniel's hands were sweaty. He wiped them on his jeans, then looked over at Bethany, who was calmly reading more of the transcripts of conversations from Bishop's phone that were saved on the laptop. Today, he would commit a crime. He hadn't broken the law since he was a teenager and he was forced to steal to survive. He hadn't realized that this undercover assignment would bring up such old memories, but between the actions he would perform this afternoon and his conversation with Bethany when he had spilled the truth about his mother, a lot of unpleasant recollections were surfacing that he thought he had buried forever.

He remembered picking the pocket of a man who had been wearing a dark green woolen jacket one cold winter evening. Daniel had bumped into the man and netted over a hundred dollars from the man's wallet. The man had also carried a picture of a young girl in the leather folds, as well as some old newspaper clippings that Daniel had never even glanced at. He'd tossed the entire thing in the trash soon after the theft, but he'd always wondered how much damage his actions had caused. Had that been the only picture of the girl the man had owned? Had his victim treasured that photo and news stories that he'd carried? Had he caused the man hours or even days of angst because of his actions?

He wondered why God was allowing all of the pain from his past to resurface, especially now when he so desperately wanted to keep it buried. What good could come from it? Yet, he did know that God would never leave him or forsake him, no matter what was happening in his life or the difficulties he faced.

Daniel glanced at Bethany again and envied her calm demeanor. She had an amazing ability to stay focused, no matter what the circumstance. It was an admirable trait, and something that no doubt made her excellent at her job. She was the consummate professional, and he had always respected her dedication and work ethic.

A wave of longing swept over him that took his breath away. He ached to just hold her in his arms. She was so beautiful. Her hair was pulled back in a ponytail, which only accented her delicate cheekbones and classic lovely features. Her eyes had always been her best feature in his mind, and were like lakes of blue on a warm summer day. It wasn't just her outer beauty that captivated him, however. Her inner strength and fortitude were just as attractive. Yet, to share himself in the way that she required would be to lay open his heart completely and would make him totally vulnerable. He didn't think he was capable of doing what she was asking. It was too hard. But could he let her go? Was it worth the sacrifice?

Dear Lord, help me decide what to do about Bethany. If You want me to tell her about my past, please give me the strength to do so. I can't do it without You. If You don't want me to share, please help her understand. I need You. I need Your guidance. Please help me know what to do, and lead me with Your perfect will for my life.

"This is it!" Bethany exclaimed, bringing him back to the here and now. She picked up the laptop and brought it over to the table where he was sitting and positioned it so he could see the screen. "I've been sorting through hundreds of texts and phone transcripts, but finally found something. Bishop was talking to someone named Bradley, and they mention Operation Battlefield. Then they say *stadium* and *detonation*. That can only mean one thing." Their eyes met and they said the next words together.

"They're planning on blowing up a stadium!"

"But which one?" Daniel asked. "There are three I can think of right off the bat. AT&T Stadium where the Lookouts play, Engel Stadium and Finley Stadium."

Bethany opened another window on the browser and did some quick searching. "It has to be AT&T Stadium. They wouldn't want to do something unless it brought maximum notoriety to their cause. According to these schedules, there's nothing planned during the next two months at Engel or Finley. But look at this." She pointed to the screen. "There are two events coming up at AT&T, and look—all of the seating is basically along the first base side, so it would take a minimum amount of explosives to do a lot of damage."

"What are the two events?" Daniel asked, leaning closer.

"There's a marching band competition next week, and three weeks from now, there's a huge multi-state track meet." The worry was palpable in her eyes. "Good grief. It could be either one of those. Either one would be horrific."

He took her hand and squeezed it. "We need more information. Hopefully, after today's robbery they'll trust us enough to let us know more about their plans. Or if they don't, maybe Bishop will let more of the details slip."

The driver pulled the armored truck up to the bank door at exactly 3:15 p.m., right on schedule. As was the company policy, the driver stayed in his seat, surveilling the area, while the other guard got out and opened the back doors of the truck.

As soon as both of the doors were open, the robbers struck.

"Hands in the air, now!" Derek yelled. He grabbed the guard from behind, getting a good grip on the man's bulletproof vest and pulling him to the side of the truck with his left hand as he kept his gun pointed at him with his right. The guard complied and raised his hands.

"Okay, don't shoot. I'll do what you say. Please don't shoot."

Bethany appeared from the other side of the truck, her gun also pointed at the guard. All of the robbers were dressed in black pants and jackets, and they were also wearing ski masks that obscured their features. She moved to the front of the truck where the guard was standing so she had a clear view of both guards, as well as the inside of the truck. Ethan was on the other side of the armored truck, also wielding a weapon and keeping an eye on the surroundings.

"Get on your knees," she ordered.

The guard complied. His eyes were wild with fright. She was sorry for that. She didn't like this part of the job, but it was necessary. Hopefully, this would be the last crime she would be committing in the process of taking down the Heritage Guard.

"Take out your gun and put it on the concrete. Now," Derek yelled.

The guard did as he was told and Bethany kicked the gun away, just as Daniel, also dressed as the others, backed up the late model

SUV to the armored truck and opened up the back. Liam jumped out of the back of the SUV and got inside the armored truck. A few seconds later, he was throwing wrapped bundles of cash into the SUV.

"Lie down on the ground," Bethany ordered, her eyes still on the guard. She looked up and saw the other guard calling in the robbery.

"The driver is calling it in," she yelled to the others. "We have fifteen seconds. Go!"

Liam threw in the last few bundles and slammed the back trunk of the SUV. "That's it. We're done. Let's go!"

Suddenly a shot rang out. Bethany looked quickly at both of the guards, but neither one of them had fired the shot. Her eyes flew over to Derek, who was loosely holding a pistol in his hand that he had taken off one of the guards, then toward Daniel, who was still sitting in the driver's seat of the vehicle. The bullet had hit the frame of the SUV only inches from his head.

Daniel, wearing his mask, got out of the van and slammed the door, his eyes blazing. His weapon was pointed at Derek's head. "If you're going to try to kill me, you'd better not miss the next time!"

"The gun just went off. I wasn't aiming for you," Derek said, holding the pistol up, the barrel pointing to the sky. They couldn't see his face beneath the mask, but his voice held a smirk. Bethany felt a surge of relief that Daniel hadn't been hurt and took a step toward Derek, ready for some retribution, but Liam reached him first and grabbed his collar.

"You idiot! You'd jeopardize our plans here and now? For what?"

Derek tried to pull away, but Liam grabbed the pistol away from him, secured it in his own waistband, and pushed him to the ground. "Keep your eye on the ball."

"Don't you care about Terrell?" Derek yelled.

A siren sounded in the distance and Bethany motioned with her gun. "We've got to move. We'll hash this out later."

Bethany met Daniel's eyes and nodded. They both understood that they had to do something about Derek, but it had to be done later when the police weren't breathing down their necks. Derek was a hothead who wasn't going to roll over no matter what the Heritage Guard ordered him to do, and it was obvious that Daniel was in danger as long as Derek was in the picture. He could ruin all of their plans if something wasn't done to control him.

Daniel got back behind the wheel and Bethany joined him in the front seat. Liam got in the back, and a few seconds later, Derek and Ethan joined them and slammed the door closed. As soon as the door was closed, Daniel hit the gas and the SUV sped away. The entire robbery, including the stray shot, had been completed in under four minutes.

"Woo-hoo!" Derek yelled, when they were about five miles away and still not being followed. "We did it!" He drummed on the seat in front of him with his hands as if he was still trying to burn off some excess energy.

No one answered him and the entire group pulled their masks off and began to let the adrenaline that had come from the robbery slowly escape. Everyone except Daniel, that is. Bethany could tell that Daniel was still burning about the bullet that had hit only inches from his head. His lips were pulled into a thin line and his eyes were narrowed as he drove, focused on the road before him.

After a few turns, Daniel pulled the SUV into the parking lot of the car rental company, which was the prearranged site where they would all separate. Bishop was waiting and came out of the office and met the car when they arrived. He approached Ethan, who was the official leader of the group, but before a word could be said Daniel had pulled Derek out of the car, pushed him up against the side of the SUV and punched him hard in the face. Blood oozed from the wound as Daniel hit him a second time before Liam and Ethan were able to pull him off and separate the two. Derek swiped at the blood and then pulled his fist back as if he was going to hit Daniel, now that he was secured, but Bethany stepped between them.

"No way, Derek. You deserved that, and more."

"What's going on?" Bishop demanded. "Did you have trouble on the job?"

"The job went just fine," Liam answered, "until Derek took a shot at Daniel's head."

"It was a stray bullet," Derek whined as he wiped at the blood from his lip. "I wasn't aiming for him. The gun just went off."

Daniel pulled against Liam and Ethan's grip. "Liar. You were trying to kill me."

Bishop raised an eyebrow. "Ethan?" He looked to the leader, apparently wanting some clear direction from the one who had run the job and could give him an unbiased opinion.

Ethan met his eye. "We got the money and it's in the back. Derek was either very sloppy or intentionally took a shot at Daniel. Either way, I don't want him on my team again. He can't be trusted."

Derek suddenly turned all of his anger on Ethan. His face was flushed with rage and even more blood bubbled out of his nose. "What? How can you take his side? He's a cop, just like those cops who killed Terrell! He's the enemy."

"I'm not taking sides. I'm trying to do what's best for the Heritage Guard. That's the reason why we're out here doing what we're doing in the first place," Ethan said in a matter-of-fact tone. "When you make it personal, you make mistakes and people get hurt. That's not how I operate."

Bishop put his hands up in a motion of surrender. "Ethan is right. I'm sorry, Derek, but we can't use you anymore. You're out."

Derek looked like he was going to explode. "What?"

"You heard me," Bishop repeated. "Clear out of here."

Derek's face turned even redder, and he

looked around as if he was trying to find something to throw or kick. Seeing nothing, he charged toward Daniel, but Ethan released Daniel, crossed his arms and blocked Derek with a move that looked like it came from a football field. Derek ended up on the ground with gravel embedded into his hands and face, and he brushed it away angrily. He apparently realized that physically he wasn't going to get anywhere today, so the venom spewed from his mouth instead.

"You'll be sorry," he spat. "You'll fail without me. Just wait and see."

"I'd advise you to go quietly," Bishop said, his voice calm in the middle of a storm. "You don't need to make enemies of the Guard."

Derek fisted his palms and looked from one face to another. He finally knelt over and picked up his wool mask that he had lost during the scuffle, then turned and started walking away from the group, a scowl still on his face.

Once he had disappeared, Daniel turned back to Bishop and handed him the keys to the SUV. "The money is in the back. Unfortunately, there's also a bullet hole that will need to be repaired."

Bishop took the keys and pocketed them. "Congratulations on a job well done."

Daniel pulled Bethany against him and kissed her cheek. "Success, darling." Still holding her, he turned toward Ethan. "What's next?"

"Disappear," Ethan said, an enigmatic smile on his face. "We'll contact you shortly for the next job."

Bishop pointed to Bethany. "I need to speak to you. Without your boyfriend."

Bethany shrugged and kissed Daniel on the lips, then pulled away from him. "I'll catch up with you later."

Daniel watched her follow Bishop into the small building. His lips burned from her kiss. He knew it had been for show, but he still enjoyed it. He wanted to follow after her into the meeting to make sure she was safe, but it was obvious that he wasn't invited; he knew she could take care of herself and that the danger was minimal. He needed to do some research anyway on the stadium, and this was the perfect opportunity to do so. He pulled his keys out of his pocket and headed to his truck, saying a prayer for her safety as he did so, just in case.

* * *

Bethany took the chair that was offered to her and leaned back, keeping her back to the wall so she could see everyone in the small room, as well as the door. The room was furnished with only a small desk, a floor lamp and a few chairs. A car rental poster was plastered on the wall, advertising the latest specials. She glanced around the room and felt a measure of relief. She knew Bishop and also the large man standing by the door, but it paid to be cautious, so she kept a wary eye open, just in case she needed to act quickly. Her pistol was in her waistband, and she had another spare sidearm tucked in her boot, as an extra precaution.

Bishop took the seat across from her. "Good job today. Any problems?"

She shook her head. "Only that issue with Derek. The rest went off like clockwork. We emptied out the truck and no one was hurt, and all within the time frame allotted. It was a clean job."

"I'm glad to hear it. The money will be put to good use." He leaned forward. "We need fifteen to twenty blocks of C-4, as well as the ribbon charges to set them off, and timers for each of the blocks. Can you help us?"

She whistled between her teeth. "Wow. That's a big order. When do you need it?"

"Four days."

She leaned back. "You don't ask much."

"We've got the money to pay—now that today's job was successful."

"You'll have to pay a bit more than the going rate if you want it that quickly."

Bishop smiled, but there was a malevolent air to his attitude. "Make the deal. I'll get you the money."

"Will do," she said with a nod. "You have someone who knows how to set it up?"

"Don't you worry about that. You just get the explosives. We'll take care of the rest." He took his cap off and ran his hands through his hair.

"Do you need anything else?"

Bishop shook his head. "We'll let you know."

The tone of his voice said the meeting was over, so she stood, nodded to each of the men and left the room. She'd ridden with Daniel to the meeting site for the armored car heist, so now she started walking away from the car rental company toward the downtown area. She pulled out her cell phone and couldn't reach Hooker, even after several attempts, so she tried Westfield next. He answered on the first ring.

"Bethany. It's good to hear from you. Is everything okay?"

"Max, I can't get Hooker. Any idea why he's not answering?"

"I'm not sure, but I can tell you this. They've decided to pull you in and close the investigation."

Indignation rose in her throat. "They can't do that! He gave me two weeks!"

"Have you made any progress?" Westfield asked.

"Yes, we think we've identified their target, and they want me to buy the C-4 for them. Everything is coming to a head. We'll lose this opportunity if we pull out now. I really need you to talk to Hooker and change his mind. Can you do that?"

"I can try, but it won't be easy."

A wave of alarm spread over her. She couldn't let this investigation fail now. She had invested too much, and she needed Westfield on her side. "Please, Max, do what you can. I also need fifteen to twenty blocks of C-4 in four days, along with the ribbon charges and timers. This is the one, Max. It all comes down to this." In the past, Justin had always gotten her what she needed to maintain her cover. If Hooker couldn't help, she desperately needed Westfield to come through. If the Guard wanted the C-4 in four days and they were planning on blowing up AT&T Stadium, then the upcoming marching band competition was the likely target, and she had to do everything in her power to stop them before it was too late.

"Can you get me the C-4, Max?"

"I don't know, Bethany. That's a pretty tall order, especially with the brass wanting to shut down the investigation. Like I said, it won't be easy."

"It's the last thing I need. The Guard has been putting all of their efforts into Operation Battlefield. This C-4 has got to be for that mission. If I can provide the explosives, they'll include me in the planning, and I can learn all of the details. Once I know what's going on, we'll be able to stop them."

"We seized some C-4 from a case about three years ago that is still in the evidence locker. I may be able to get you a few blocks off the record, but I don't know about twenty."

"Off the record? What does that mean exactly? I don't want you to do anything that will jeopardize this case." His comment surprised her. Even though the brass were in a hurry to have this case concluded, there were still procedures in place that had to be followed when it came to using FBI supplies for a job—especially for munitions. Was Westfield going to steal the explosives?

"Nothing. That's not what I meant. Of course, I'll go through official channels. I'm just under a lot of pressure to finish this case, just like you are, Bethany. Can't you do it with less?"

His tone was filled with exasperation, so she pushed on, filing her concerns in the back of her mind to consider later. "I've got to have at least fifteen."

She heard Westfield sigh. "You're asking a lot from me, Bethany."

"Max, this is the culmination of my entire undercover operation. The arrests will be significant. I'll share the credit with you. I'll make sure everyone knows that you're the one that made the operation possible. If we're successful, it will mean a big boost for your career."

She heard him sigh again. "Bethany, I want to be promoted, sure, but I have feelings for you. Strong feelings. I must have been very clumsy with telling you about how I feel, but I'm telling you know. I think I'm in love with you."

Good grief! This is not what she had expected when she'd dialed Westfield's line. She didn't share his feelings, but she needed his help and didn't know how to get it and let him down gently at the same time. She opted for the truth, since she wasn't good at subterfuge when it came to relationships. "Look, Max, I appreciate you telling me how you feel, so I'll be honest with you right back. Daniel and I used to have a very committed relationship, and lately since we've been working together again, we've talked about getting back together. I don't know where it's all going to lead, but I'm really not ready to date anyone else until I know for sure if that relationship is going to go somewhere or not." She didn't know how to even describe her relationship with Daniel right now, but she did know that she didn't want to pursue anything with Westfield, regardless of what happened with Daniel. She didn't want to hurt him though, so this was her way of trying to let him down as easily as possible. She paused, but when he didn't comment, she continued, hoping that he understood. "Does that make any sense at all?"

"I guess," he admitted, finally breaking the silence. "I can't say I'm not disappointed. But I'll respect your decision. I'll check into the C-4 and let you know what I can do."

"Thanks, Max." She hung up, and stored her phone, still ruminating on what she had learned during the call.

Westfield's words seemed appropriate, but there was something in his voice that seemed sinister and sent a chill down her spine. She had always felt a bit strange around him, but he had never seemed dangerous to her until today. Could she trust Westfield? Someone had murdered Justin. She had no proof that his murder was directly related to her investigation, but she couldn't prove it wasn't related either.

She thought back through their conversation. Westfield had basically offered to steal C-4 from the evidence locker to help her, even though he backpedaled when she questioned him. Had it been just a slip of the tongue? She knew for a fact that Justin had always requisitioned what she needed to bolster her undercover operation. Her former boss had always followed the rules and left a paper trail a mile wide. Would Westfield actually steal the C-4 from the evidence room? He claimed her bosses were trying to shut her operation down immediately, but she hadn't heard that from Hooker, and even if it were true, Westfield should never have volunteered to steal the C-4. It was a crime.

Thoughts that she had never considered began to swarm in her mind. Was this the first time Westfield had considered stealing evidence, or had he done it before? Had he stolen C-4 in the past and used it to kill Justin?

But what possible motive could he have? Justin had hand-picked Westfield to be his assistant, and the two men had seemed to have a good working relationship. But if not Westfield, then who? Who else would want to take Justin's life?

There were too many questions. Westfield might be a bit creepy, but as far as she knew, he was a top-notch FBI agent who had an excellent reputation. Surely his comment today had just been a mistake. As Westfield himself had said, they were all under a lot of pressure to bring this case to a swift and successful conclusion. People under stress misspoke. It happened.

Bethany sighed and rubbed the muscles in

her neck. Even she was feeling a bit edgy. For the first time in a very long time, she found herself glad that she could share her burden with Daniel and bounce ideas off him. She found herself looking forward to seeing him tonight. She quickened her step toward the bus stop to grab a ride back to the apartment they were sharing. It was going to be a long night.

FOURTEEN

Bishop looked in the duffel bag that Bethany offered, then zipped it up and met her eye, disappointment heavy in his features. "Eight bricks? That's it?"

"It's a start, Bishop. I'm working on the rest." Bethany had met with Westfield early in the morning and gotten the eight bricks of C-4 from him, but it had been an awkward exchange. They had barely spoken during the few minutes it had taken to hand off the explosives. She still had not heard from Hooker, even though she had tried several times to contact him, and through several means. All she could guess was that her superiors had decided that her investigation was winding down or was canceled outright and had left Westfield in charge to tie up the loose ends. It was odd, but she had been left out of the loop for so long that she didn't know what else to think. After Justin's dire warning about the mole, she didn't know who she could trust at the FBI and dared not try to contact anyone else at the bureau—at least not until this case was well and truly over.

"You know this is time-sensitive, right?" Liam growled.

"Of course, I do," Bethany said defensively. "But C-4 isn't something you can buy at Walmart, and I wasn't given a large time frame in which to operate. I'm doing the best I can."

Liam made a derisory sound. "Maybe your boyfriend can do better. Let's bring him in here and find out. Maybe he has better connections than you do."

Bethany's stomach constricted. If they brought Daniel in, what would he say? She and Daniel were already working on getting the extra C-4 they needed from Daniel's boss, Captain Murphy, and the local Chattanooga Police Force, but so far they hadn't been able to get the delivery confirmed. They also had hoped that dealing with Captain Murphy would help them determine if he was the mole or not. However, they hadn't learned anything new. One thing they did realize—if Murphy couldn't get them the explosives they needed, they would have to start looking at alternatives, and fast. Either way, they hadn't planned on having this conversation in front of Liam, and she didn't know how Daniel would answer the interrogation.

Could she trust Daniel to say the right thing? As Daniel entered the room, their eyes met, and she wondered if he could see the fear mirrored in her own. This situation exemplified why she worked alone. When she worked undercover by herself, she didn't have to worry about anybody making a mistake and putting her life at risk. She didn't have to depend on anyone else but herself. It was lonely, but it was easier.

With Daniel, however, there was even more to it. With her boyfriend before Daniel, the man had cheated on her and then humiliated her in front of her friends. He had said terrible things that had made it hard for her to ever trust a man again on a personal level. Would Daniel humiliate her now? A year ago, when Daniel had gotten too close and started talking about marriage, it had been easier to push him away than it had been to trust him not to hurt her like her ex had done, especially since he wasn't willing to share his past with her. She preferred the loneliness to the pain. It was safer. Over the past few days, Daniel had slowly started breaking down her defenses again, and it scared her, both professionally and personally.

What would he do now? This was his first time undercover. Would he make a rookie mistake? Would he throw her under the bus to look good and score points with the Guard? Would he humiliate her for the sake of his male pride? Anything was possible, and she braced herself, not sure what to expect.

"Daniel, Hailey here says she's having some trouble getting the C-4 we need for our Operation Battlefield," Bishop said in a matter-of-fact tone. "Can you do any better?"

Daniel raised an eyebrow and Bethany's stomach clenched again, waiting for his response. He looked from Bishop to Liam, then at Bethany. "Has Hailey ever let you down in the past?"

Bishop thought about that for moment, then responded, "No. She's always proven herself to be very responsible." Even Liam shook his head once he considered Daniel's point.

Daniel shrugged. "Then I'd quit worrying.

I'm not going to be able to do any better than she can. She's the expert. You've trusted her in the past. I'd trust her now."

Bethany let out the breath she hadn't even known she was holding. Daniel had said the perfect thing, and diffused the situation with just a few simple words. She silently mouthed the words *thank you* to him and he winked in response, then turned and left the room.

"Somebody is following us," Daniel said quietly. He tried to keep the frustration out of his voice as he glanced at his rearview mirror, but he wasn't successful.

Bethany looked behind them, then quickly faced forward again. "The black sedan?"

"Yeah. I've changed lanes twice and he's staying with me."

"Can you tell who's driving?"

"A white male wearing a black watchman's cap and sunglasses. That's about all I can tell. He picked us up about ten minutes ago."

"Good grief. That could be anyone." Her voice held her own note of frustration.

Daniel didn't blame her. Another day had passed and they had still not been able to talk to Hooker, despite trying a new number that

Westfield had provided. They had been able to contact Captain Murphy about the C-4, and he had agreed to provide them with the additional seven bricks they needed, so they were on their way to meet him. So far he hadn't let anything slip that made him seem like the mole, but they were both on high alert while dealing with the man, just in case.

The captain had only one condition during their conversations to get the explosives—that the Chattanooga Police Department would share in the arrests at the stadium and in the credit for the joint operation's success once the indictments were handed down. Since that had always been part of the original agreement of this joint operation, it was easy to agree. But Captain Murphy wanted to be absolutely sure that CPD wouldn't be left on the sidelines, so Daniel had done his best to reassure him that CPD would be included.

Daniel and Bethany still had their doubts about Captain Murphy and his history with Bishop Jacobs, but to date they couldn't prove anything beyond the fact that they knew each other and had talked to each other on the phone. Bishop Jacobs owned a rental car company, and as far as they knew, the captain had rented a car from him—nothing more. Still, they both harbored suspicions of the man, and had agreed to be extra careful during the exchange. They needed the FBI's help to run background checks on their suspects and right now, they just weren't getting the help they needed to find the connections to build their case, or prove Murphy's guilt or innocence.

Daniel looked into the rearview mirror again and changed lanes, then grimaced as he watched the car tailing them do the same once again. He glanced over at Bethany and could tell that she was getting restless and nervous.

He thought through everything that had happened during the short time since he had gotten Bethany back in his life. Her entire Guard team were killed at the bank, someone killed her boss at the FBI and Derek tried to kill Daniel at the armored car robbery. Related or not, there were a lot of people dying all around them, and it felt like they were no closer to figuring out how everything was connected than they were when they'd started. And now, someone was following them. Was it someone from the FBI? Someone from the Guard? Or was Derek trying to get his revenge for Terrell's death?

He reached across and squeezed her hand, then released her and put both hands on the wheel. "Hold on." With a quick turn and squealing tires, he cut the truck in front of another vehicle and executed a U-turn, then maneuvered the truck into a large alley behind a warehouse that fronted an entire city block. Gravel spit from beneath his tires and water and debris spewed as he raced along, dodging obstacles along the way. He could hear car horns and traffic squawking in the wake of his driving, but he ignored it all as he sped to the end of the alley and made a quick left, then entered the street and flow of traffic. He changed lanes several more times, speeding around three more cars before he was finally stopped at a red light.

"Any sign of them?"

Bethany didn't answer and he glanced in her direction. She was as white as a sheet and had pressed herself as close as possible to the truck door. She was also clinging for dear life to the seat belt and the grab handle on the ceiling. Her knuckles had turned white where she gripped the plastic for all it was worth.

He laughed. He couldn't help himself. The look on her face was just too comical to ignore. "Are you okay?"

She shook her head. "No. You're crazy!" The tone of her voice made it perfectly clear what she thought of his driving.

"What?" he raised an eyebrow, giving her his best innocent look. He'd totally forgotten that she got motion sickness if he drove too fast and made too many quick turns in the vehicle. Bethany was tough as nails 99 percent of the time. It was almost refreshing to be reminded that she was human after all and had weaknesses like the rest of the people on the planet.

"Remind me to never let you drive anywhere ever again," she said under her breath. "I think I'm going to throw up all over your nice floor mats."

"Come on. I'm a good driver," he said with a smile.

She narrowed her eyes. "At least tell me you lost our tail."

"Yep."

"Then it was worth it." She moaned. "I guess," she qualified.

He drove in relative silence for another fifteen minutes or so until they arrived at a small brick building that was near the outskirts of town. Pine trees and rocky outcrops surrounded the area, and the other nearby buildings seemed to be abandoned, with no signs of life. It was about ten in the morning, so there was plenty of sunlight to help them see their surroundings, but it was strange that no other cars or people were anywhere nearby.

Daniel pulled up behind the storefront and killed the engine, then turned to Bethany. "Okay. Are you ready for this?"

Bethany shrugged. "Ready as I'll ever be. I'm feeling better now." They got out of their truck and closed the doors, looking warily around them. "Are you sure you have the right address? This is a strange meeting place."

"Yes, I double-checked it," Daniel answered. He glanced at his watch. "We're right on time. Captain Murphy said he'd meet us here, and he's usually a very punctual man. Let's give him a couple of minutes. Maybe he's just running late."

He noticed that Bethany still seemed a bit unsteady. "Are you sure you're feeling alright?" When she didn't answer, he reached over and took Bethany's hand, then pulled her closer as they locked eyes. His look was searching, asking for permission to go further.

When he saw no resistance, he pulled her into an embrace.

"I'm really sorry my driving made you sick." He gently took his thumb and ran it slowly down the side of her cheek. Her skin was soft like rose petals. "You're so beautiful." He moved his thumb and drew it across her bottom lip, then gently cupped her head with his hands and drew her even closer as his lips met hers. Electricity seemed to sizzle between them and his heart was beating like a bass drum so loudly it felt like it was coming out of his chest.

"I guess I forgive you," she murmured against him. She pulled back a bit and he could see a smile as it slowly crossed her face, yet there was hesitance in her eyes. Still, she had responded to his overtures even though nobody was around, so she was clearly not acting a role. The thought pleased him immensely.

Suddenly, they heard a car approach and the intimate mood instantly dissipated. They broke apart and she took a few steps back. She turned away from him, her eyes wide, and she covered her mouth with the back of her hand. She looked as if she was trying to compose herself as the car pulled up beside the truck and parked.

Daniel recovered first and met Captain Murphy as he got out of the car. He hoped to draw attention away from Bethany and any embarrassment she might be feeling. The police chief stood and nodded his hello, swinging a set of keys in his hand.

"Good to see you, son. I'm glad we were able to come to an understanding here. You're doing excellent work with the FBI."

"It is a joint operation, Captain. There's no reason why CPD and the FBI can't both get credit for any arrests that come from this undercover assignment. Our mutual goal is to stop the Guard before anyone else gets hurt."

Captain Murphy turned and went to the trunk of his car, opened it and pulled out a dark green duffel bag. He handed the bag to Bethany. She took it and unzipped it, then showed the contents to Daniel. He saw the bricks of C-4 inside, as well as the detonators.

"How many are in there?" he asked.

"Seven bricks, just like you asked," Captain Murphy answered.

Bethany zipped it closed and slung the bag on her back. "This has been a huge help for our mission," she said. "Thank you. You really came through for us." Despite her words, she narrowed her eyes and rested her free hand on the butt of her pistol. "Even so, we have some questions to ask you about your relationship with Bishop Jacobs."

Captain Murphy raised an eyebrow. "What do you want to know?"

Daniel stepped forward. "He is a member of the Heritage Guard. And we know you've had contact with him on several occasions lately. Can you explain that?"

Murphy straightened as his muscles tightened, but a moment later he relaxed again. "We were fraternity brothers back in college. I didn't really hang out with his crowd all that much, but we're having a reunion of sorts in a month or so and I was contacting all of the guys to invite them to the festivities. Somehow, I drew the short straw and had to make all of the phone calls." He paused, his face thoughtful. "Bishop was a little odd, but I can't see him as a terrorist. Are you sure he is part of the Guard?"

Before either of them had an opportunity to answer Murphy, a shot rang out, clipping a tree only a few feet behind them. They all heard the bullet whiz by their heads and instantly dropped to the ground, searching for cover. More bullets followed, several ricocheting off the rocks on the road and the boulders that were sporadically strewn around the landscaping. Other bullets hit the building, the vehicles or imbedded into the wood of the trees behind them. They crouched down behind the truck Bethany and Daniel had arrived in, using it for cover as they kept it between them and the gunman.

"Only one shooter?" Bethany asked as she turned and fired her 9 mm in the direction of the sniper.

"It appears so," Daniel answered as he checked his ammunition supply in his own sidearm. The bullets all seemed to be coming from the same direction and location, but since none of them had a rifle with them, they couldn't stop the sniper from firing at them. None of their handguns had anywhere near the range or accuracy of a rifle. The best they could do was lay down some cover fire while they tried to escape. The truck had taken some shots, but still seemed drivable. Since Captain Murphy had parked between the shooter and the truck, his vehicle had taken the brunt of the rounds.

"Were you followed?" Daniel asked as he snapped his clip back into his firearm.

"I didn't see anyone, but I guess anything is possible," the captain answered. "I wasn't expecting trouble. Were you?"

"Not like this," Daniel replied, sending even more rounds toward their aggressor.

"Let's get out of here," Bethany said as she threw the bag with the C-4 in the back of the truck. "Cover me," she said, meeting Daniel's eye.

She fired two more shots, then opened the passenger door and slid in, staying down and out of sight as she did so. Daniel fired at the sniper to keep him occupied, then followed her through the passenger door and into the truck as Captain Murphy fired at the shooter. He crawled over her to the driver's seat, then started the engine and rolled down the window so he could fire while Captain Murphy got into the truck. They all stayed as low as possible while Daniel backed up, spun the truck around and sped away from the building. Bullets followed them, and even though one hit the top metal door frame behind them and a few hit the side of the truck, they ended up escaping unharmed.

Daniel didn't know what to think. Was Murphy innocent? After all, he had almost been killed during the C-4 exchange. Or had that entire scene just been a clever ruse to make it look like his life was in danger to throw them off the trail? Had he and Bishop really been fraternity brothers? It was easy enough to prove or disprove with a small amount of research. Was Murphy a Guard member or not? Daniel was more unsure now than ever. After all, his phone clearly showed that Murphy had ties with Guard members who were knee-deep in suspicious activities. Were those ties innocent, as Murphy claimed? Or was he the one who had killed Justin?

Lord, please help me sort through all of the lies and get down to the truth. And thank You for protecting us today. Please help us stay safe, and figure this case out so the Heritage Guard is stopped completely before anyone else gets hurt.

FIFTEEN

Hooker shook his head, his hands on his hips. "I don't understand why you haven't been contacting me, Agent Walker. I also don't understand why I had to be contacted by Captain Murphy of the local police force to set up this meeting today. Captain Murphy reported to me that my agent was shot at and nearly killed by a sniper. That's information I should have been told by my agent, don't you think?"

Bethany raised her eyebrows, but to her credit, she held her tongue and gathered her thoughts before responding, even though Daniel could tell she was livid by his lack of insight. Daniel was also surprised by his questions. They had both followed FBI protocol to the letter, but they had been unable to get any response from Special Agent Hooker ever since he had taken over the investigation. Was the man totally out of the loop, or just incompetent?

"Sir, I've been calling you constantly without getting a reply," Bethany answered, her voice professional and controlled. "I've been leaving messages for you on a regular basis, and have sent texts and emails. In fact, Max Westfield told me that you were shutting down the operation, so I even doubled my efforts to get in touch with you. I *wanted* to communicate with you to convince you not to give up on this investigation. I still think it's worth the time and effort to keep pushing ahead, sir."

"Well, there's obviously been a communication breakdown here, Agent. Mr. Westfield claims you demanded that he provide you with fifteen blocks of C-4, and when he couldn't get the amount of explosives you demanded, you broke off communication with him and went rogue. For my part, I haven't heard from you since I was first introduced to you when I took over the case, and I'd like to know why. All I know about you is that you are involved in a highly dangerous mission, and we've already lost one agent for reasons unknown. I don't want to lose another."

Bethany was obviously struck speechless.

If Westfield had been there in the small room, she probably would have gone ballistic on him, but since only the three of them were at this meeting, all she could do was start pacing to get the anger and frustration out of her system. Daniel barely knew Max Westfield, but the pieces just didn't seem to fit together. Why was he torpedoing the mission? What was his game? Daniel didn't like the guy because of the way he flirted with Bethany, but until now, he hadn't understood the depths of his treachery. He watched Bethany carefully, knowing she was close to the boiling point. Her face was flushed and her jaw had tightened. He stepped forward, diverting Hooker's attention and giving Bethany a chance to cool down.

"Mr. Westfield is giving you bad information, sir," he said quietly. "We have both tried to contact you on several occasions, especially after the armored car heist. Here are the numbers we were given to reach you." He pulled out his cell phone and read off the numbers. "The first two seem to have been disconnected. The third allowed us to leave messages, which we did, with no response. We can also provide you with texts and emails. Both Agent

Walker and I left several for you, sir. We got no response."

Hooker took down the numbers and shook his head again. "Well, I don't have an explanation. Those are not my numbers. I don't even recognize those as FBI numbers. Where did you get them?"

Daniel stowed his phone. "Justin gave us each cell phones that were supposed be clean right before his death. Everything else was provided by Mr. Westfield."

"As long as we're putting our cards on the table, have you been able to discover who killed Justin?" Bethany asked.

Daniel was pleased that she had calmed down and was engaged again in the conversation.

Hooker shook his head. "We've discovered where the explosives came from and how they were detonated, but we haven't been able to tie them to any group or individual yet."

"Where did the explosives come from?" Bethany asked.

"They were stolen from the evidence locker. They were actually logged in as evidence on one of Justin's old cases."

Bethany raised an eyebrow. "Westfield told

me he was going to steal the C-4 I requested from the evidence locker too. When I called him on it, he said it was just a slip of the tongue and he was actually going through official channels, but now I'm thinking he really meant it. If you check how much is missing, I'll bet it lines up with what he gave me, and what was used to kill Justin." She leaned forward. "Do you know for sure if his death was related to my case, or one of his other cases?" she asked.

Hooker shrugged. "We honestly don't know, Agent Walker. It's still too early in the investigation to know for sure, but you've given me some good information to research when I get back to the office."

Daniel's and Bethany's eyes met. He asked her the silent question, and she agreed by nodding her head. He turned to Agent Hooker. "You should know that Justin told us there was a mole in law enforcement, sir, right before he was killed. He didn't know who, but he was just starting to investigate it before his death. He thought the mole was somehow connected with the Heritage Guard and Bethany's case. From what we know now, it looks like Westfield is that mole."

Hooker raked his hand through his hair and

grimaced. He leaned forward, his body rigid with anger. "You're telling me this now?"

"We didn't know if you were the mole or not," Bethany said, her tone matter-of-fact.

Hooker turned and looked her in the eye. "I'm going to forget you said that, Agent." His voice was low and fuming.

"Someone tried to kill us yesterday when we got the extra C-4 from Captain Murphy," Daniel said, pointedly. "A sniper was taking shots at us and we barely escaped. Bethany was also almost killed during the bank robbery, and Justin was killed right after talking to us. It might have been wrong of us to withhold that information, but you have to realize that right now, we're just not sure whom we can trust. When we couldn't get hold of you, well, we didn't know who else to contact within the FBI that we could trust either. Agent Walker has been out in the field for almost a year with Justin and Westfield as her only contacts. We're taking a big leap of faith by even talking to you now."

A moment passed, then another. The room was silent as the FBI boss pondered the situation, his eyes boring into Bethany. "Then I need to bring you in," Hooker finally replied, taking his eyes from the younger agent's. "If you're in that much danger, I can't continue putting your lives at risk."

"No!" Bethany said, her stance adamant. "We're too close. We've been called in this afternoon to help plan Operation Battlefield. This is the culmination of what we've been working for during this entire mission. If we stop now, then all of the risk, even Justin's death, will have been for nothing."

Hooker pondered the situation a few moments more, then pulled out a chair and motioned for them to sit, as well. "I admire your passion, but are you sure it's worth the risk? At this point, Westfield has to suspect that we're on to him. For all we know, he's already blown your cover with the Guard and you've both got targets on your backs."

Bethany and Daniel looked at each other, then answered together.

"Yes. It's worth it."

"In fact," Bethany added, "if Westfield did suspect anything, we'd be dead already. Our covers must still be intact."

Hooker let a few more minutes pass as he processed all of the information. Finally, he ran his hand through his hair again and sighed.

"Okay. Tell me where we are. And don't leave out a single detail. I'll be contacting the attorney general's office later today to make sure they are up to date, as well. I want them ready to issue indictments as soon as we start making arrests."

Daniel was relieved. Maybe this man was going to be an ally after all. The three sat, then brought Hooker up to speed on the entire investigation. The situation was coming to a head quickly and they needed him on their side. Daniel just hoped their trust wasn't misplaced.

Bethany stood, the anger seething inside of her. For the second time today, she was boiling with anger. "Him? You invited him to this meeting?"

Derek swaggered in and pulled up a chair next to Bethany, his smile more of a smirk. He winked at her and wiggled his shoulders cheekily. "Turns out I'm valuable to the Guard after all."

Bishop held up his hands, palms out, almost as if he were apologizing. "Some things are out of my control. I advise you to accept it and move on."

"You should be happy." Derek smirked, ignoring Bishop's comments. "They let your boyfriend come too."

Bethany glanced behind her and caught Daniel's eye. This was bad. But Derek had a point—it was a bit odd that Daniel had been invited to the meeting. But he had just proven himself at the armored car heist, so his presence wasn't altogether out of the ordinary. Derek's situation was a different story. Derek had clearly been thrown out of the Guard. There were only a handful of reasons they would have allowed him to come back, and none of them were good. Were they going to use him as a fall guy? Or had he found out Bethany or Daniel's true identity and traded that information for a seat at the table? Anxiety burned through her stomach. Derek was staring at her and smiling in a leering way that made her skin crawl. Was he a leech, or did he know she was FBI? Was she blown? She couldn't think of a single good reason why he had been invited back into the fold, and the situation was extra dangerous now that Westfield's treachery had been discovered.

Daniel gave an infinitesimal shrug and she looked away. It was too late now to turn back.

She was all in. This was the meeting to plan Operation Battlefield—the one she had been waiting for. When the call had come, she'd answered it with her eyes wide open, ready for the culmination of her last year's work to finally come to fruition.

Bishop pulled out some blueprints and unrolled them on the large table that they circled. "As some of you might have guessed, we're going to bomb AT&T Stadium this coming weekend. Hailey has brought us the C-4, detonators and timers. She'll be working with Derek, Daniel, Liam and Ethan. After they set all the charges, we'll have them rigged with timers so they'll blow at about 1:00 p.m." He pointed to several places on the blueprints. "We want the charges placed here…here… and here." He pointed to another section. "And here along this structural beam." He pulled out some brochures. "There's a high school band competition going on there this weekend, so unfortunately there will be some collateral damage."

Bethany's eyes widened. "Sounds like there will be quite a lot of lives lost if we blow it in the afternoon. Shouldn't we aim for a differ-

ent time when we won't hurt so many innocent people?"

Bishop gave her a cold stare as if she was a
heretic, and Bethany instantly knew that she
had said the wrong thing. "If you're not with
us, you're against us," he growled.

Bethany narrowed her eyes. A strong offense was always a good defense in her book.
"I'm with you, Bishop. You know that. I just
don't like hurting innocent children."

Bishop studied her for a moment, as if
weighing her answer, then nodded. "I understand, but every decision we make has a reason. Those who made this plan determined
that the sacrifice was necessary for the greater
good. I know you have a soft heart. I heard
what you did for J.P. at that bank job. But all
I can tell you is that this is phase one of the
project. All of the pieces have to fit together
like a jigsaw puzzle, or no one will be able to
see the bigger picture come together."

"Well, what is the greater good? If this is
phase one, what is phase two? I've proven my
loyalty to the Guard, and I'd like to know the
big picture. Can't you tell us why we're doing
this?"

Bishop tilted his head. "No, I'm sorry. I can't."

She weighed his answer. It wouldn't do any good to keep pushing, and it might even cause more problems. She decided a strategic retreat was in order. "Alright, Bishop. I trust you, and I trust the leadership," Bethany agreed. "Please continue."

"So what's my role?" Derek asked a bit too eagerly.

"You've worked with C-4 before, right?" Bishop asked, turning to him.

"Sure, back in my army days. We used it all the time."

Bishop turned to Bethany. "Hailey, show him what you brought."

Bethany nodded and pulled out her duffel bag. She had combined all of the supplies into one sack and she opened it now on top of the blueprints for all to see. "I have fifteen bricks, along with the detonators and timers. We should be good to go." She knew that even though the material was authentic, they would be arresting everyone before the material was actually detonated. Still, a tad of nervousness swept through her. C-4 was dangerous, and no plan, no matter how well thought out, was foolproof.

Although they had made her leave her phone

at the door before this planning session had started, she had a pen in her pocket with an imbedded recording device that was taking down every word. Daniel had a similar device imbedded in his sunglasses in his shirt pocket, just in case her pen device failed. Between the two of them, she knew they would have enough to arrest Liam, Ethan and Derek at a minimum, as well as Bishop. She hoped she could add even more to the count based on Bishop's cell phone contacts and the transcripts from his conversations, but they'd noticed that he'd been making very few calls lately, so they wondered if he'd somehow figured out his phone had been cloned.

For the next ten minutes, Liam went through the details of how to handle the C-4 safely and how to actually set the explosives in the various locations around the stadium. They were going to be breaking into teams of two and working in a grid pattern underneath the major support girders. Then they would set the timers and disappear without rendezvousing later so they wouldn't get caught. After Liam was finished going over the plan, Derek pulled out one of the bricks and acted like he was examining it. "Hey, where did you guys get these?

Are you sure it's good quality? This stuff looks pretty cheap to me."

"I have a connection inside the CPD evidence room," Daniel answered. "It's good quality, I'm sure of it. For a fee, the evidence clerk was willing to make sure the C-4 was liberated from the shelves."

Derek raised an eyebrow. "What about these detonators? These are a special type that are hard to find."

Bethany snatched them out of his hand and threw them back in the bag, then zipped it closed. "If you think I'm going to share my sources with the likes of you, you've got another think coming," she said derisively. "All you need to know is that I got them for a good price and they are high quality. I wouldn't cheat the Guard."

Derek obviously didn't like the insult and stepped closer to Bethany in a threatening stance, but Liam and Ethan both saved Daniel from having to step in once again.

"Good grief, Derek," Ethan said tightly. "Can't you meet once without causing a problem?"

"Leave her alone," Liam added.

Bishop went through the rest of the details, including where they would meet the next morning before heading over to the stadium. Once every detail was explained, Bishop handed each of them one of the packs of money they had taken from the armored car heist.

"What's this for?" Liam asked, surprise in his voice. "We don't expect to be paid for our efforts. We're doing this for the Guard."

"After the stadium is destroyed, you'll need to lie low for a while. This money should tide you over until you can show your face again."

"If we disappear, won't that make us look suspicious?" Daniel asked.

"You're complaining?" Derek sneered. "Take the money and be glad the Guard is taking care of you!"

"I'm not complaining," Daniel answered. "I'm just making sure I understand my orders."

"Consider it your lifeboat," Bishop answered. "It's there if you need it. Hopefully, no one will suspect you and you can go back to work the next day, business as usual. But if problems arise, and you do have a problem and need to disappear, you'll have this to fall back on. If you don't end up needing it, you can always donate it back to the Guard after things settle down. We haven't done anything of this magnitude in quite a long time. We just want to make sure all of our bases are covered."

"We're thankful that you've thought of every contingency in your planning, Bishop," Bethany replied. She put her packet of money in her tote bag. "Hopefully, we won't need this and we can give it back to the Guard, just like you said."

The small group broke up and started to leave.

"Look at that," Bethany whispered quietly in Daniel's ear as they collected their cell phones and guns at the door. Daniel surreptitiously glanced toward Bishop and she hoped he noticed what she had—Bishop had a new cell phone and was making a call from across the room. This one was larger than the old one he had been using and had a dark blue case. No wonder his calls had all but stopped on his old phone.

SIXTEEN

"We need to clone that new phone," she said under her breath as she received her handgun from the man at the door. She kissed Daniel flirtatiously near his ear to cover up what she was saying and gave him a smile and a wink.

He laughed and kissed her back. "Oh, darling, you're amazing," he said out loud. Then quietly for her ears only, he leaned in and said, "Got it, I'll make a diversion. You do the clone."

He stepped away from her and right in the way of Derek, who was swaggering by. "Derek, do you really know how to set a C-4 charge, or are you just filled with hot air?"

Derek puffed out his chest. "I was a specialist in the army. I served overseas in Operation Enduring Freedom," he said roughly. "I know more about setting charges than you've ever dreamed about."

"Can you prove that?" Daniel asked. "I doubt you were even part of that military operation over in Afghanistan." He took a step closer, getting right up into Derek's face. "Could you even recognize an Al-Qaeda soldier if you saw one? Do you know what the Taliban is or what they stand for? You're all about hate, pure and simple. I doubt you actually ever served at all."

Derek's face turned red and spittle spewed from his mouth. "I don't have to prove anything to you," he answered hatefully. "You're just some murdering police scum." His voice started to rise and Liam and Ethan were suddenly on the scene, trying to calm everyone down. Bethany took the opportunity to take a few steps back and pull out her own phone. A few clicks later, the cloning process had begun.

"You do if you expect me to be on the same team with you again," Daniel answered, his voice also rising. "I'm not giving you another opportunity to take a shot at me. I need to know there's really a good reason to have you on that team and that you really do know what you're doing. Were you even listening when Liam was going over the details of how to set the charges? I don't want this mission to fail because of your incompetence."

Derek took both hands and pushed Daniel hard. "There's your reason. Because I say so. Is that good enough for you?"

Daniel scrambled back and threw a punch, landing his fist hard against Derek's chin. He didn't have an opening to throw a second blow, because seconds later, Ethan and Liam had gotten between the two and were once again physically holding them apart.

Bishop was quickly on the scene, as well. His face was serious, and his brow furled. "Are you two going to be able to put aside your differences or not? We're counting on you two to make this happen. This mission is very important to Operation Battlefield. If we can't trust you to do your jobs, we'll have to give them to someone else that we can trust. This isn't a game for children with attitude that put themselves and their personal agenda before the Guard."

Daniel pulled against Liam's grip, but relaxed once he got the signal from Bethany that the cloning was complete. "It was my fault. I'm sorry. I let my anger get the best of me. It won't happen again." Liam released him and he took a step away from Derek, putting his hands up in a motion of surrender. "You can count on me. I'm all in."

He took Bethany's hand, gave her a kiss on the cheek and hugged her close.

"We're committed to the cause, Bishop. Both of us," Bethany reassured him. "And we'll be there tomorrow morning. You can count on us." She watched the worry lines slowly disappear from his face.

"Alright, Hailey. We're putting a lot of faith in you to get this job done."

The two left the building and quickly got into Daniel's truck and drove away from the warehouse where the meeting had been held.

Bethany immediately started reading through Bishop's cloned texts and data as Daniel drove. "Anything interesting on that phone?" Daniel asked.

She kept scrolling. "He refers to a phase one and phase two a couple of times. It makes me think that the stadium demolition is only part of Operation Battlefield, like he mentioned today, but what could phase two be? And really, what's the point of killing all of those people at the stadium? I don't understand the reasoning behind it. There has to be something else going on that we haven't figured out yet. It has to be a piece of a bigger plan."

Daniel glanced over at her. "Well, we'd better figure it out soon since this whole thing is supposed to go down tomorrow. Let's pull Captain Murphy and Agent Hooker in and see if they have any ideas. We need help with the research." He turned a corner. "Do you see anything about Derek in those texts? I still can't understand why they brought him back into the fold. That guy is a menace and a problem just waiting to happen."

"No, and their decision to do so makes me nervous. It's not a wise move on their part and they're usually smarter than that. They have to see that decision raises big red flags."

Bethany kept scrolling. "It makes me think they've got something planned for him, like making him a scapegoat for the stadium tomorrow." She looked over at Daniel, who kept checking his mirrors. "Anybody following us?"

"Nobody so far. I'm keeping an eye out though." He checked again, made several turns and lane changes but drove carefully, presumably so Bethany wouldn't get sick this time. She smiled at him, appreciating his efforts.

"Wow, your driving has really improved. I'm impressed."

He laughed and she saw the dimple appear on his left cheek. "Well, I was rewarded for my efforts with a kiss the last time. I'm hoping to be rewarded again."

Her own cheeks burned as she remembered the kiss they had shared right before Captain Murphy had arrived to give them the C-4 they needed for the operation. She had to admit, it had felt good to be held in Daniel's arms. They had been stealing kisses and touches frequently when they were around the Guard, but that had been for the benefit of the roles they were playing. Or had it been? At first, it had been hard for her to receive the small intimacies, but now she was slowly not only accepting them but actually looking forward to them. She liked holding hands and the gentle caresses he offered without being pushy or demanding. He seemed to know when to come close and when to give her some space. It was uncanny. Just knowing he was nearby had once made her nervous and jumpy, but was now giving her comfort and making her feel whole and complete.

She stole a look at him from the corner of

her eye. At first, she had dreaded this assignment. Daniel was untested in the field and had never done any undercover work, but she also had to admit that he was doing his job well. He had fit in with the others and so far had played his role without gaffs or rookie mistakes. But there was more to it than that. She could tell that he was looking out for her, and that he really cared about her. She felt…*cherished*.

But could she trust him? Her old boyfriend had cared about her too, or at least he had said he did. He had said and done all the right things at just the right times too. And then the next thing she knew, she found him in the arms of another woman and was utterly humiliated in front of all of her friends and coworkers. She had thought she knew him, but he had publicly shattered her trust. Could she ever trust again? Was it worth the pain if she was wrong?

She stole another look at Daniel as he kept his eyes on the road. She was attracted to more than just his good looks, but she also knew for a fact that he wasn't willing to share his past with her, and it hurt to know that he wasn't willing to open up to her about his family. She didn't think he would ever be so cruel as to make promises to her and then be unfaithful.

Daniel was too loyal, too considerate to treat anyone that way. He would never intentionally hurt her. But she didn't think he would voluntarily tell her about his private life either, and she didn't think it was right to try to force him to reveal his secrets. The problem was, if he was hiding his past, what else would he hide from her? What other parts of his life would he keep secret? She would always be wondering. There would be no trust. And the relationship would inevitably suffer.

Her stomach twisted in knots as the realization of the depth of her feelings overtook her. She loved him. That made it even harder. She hadn't wanted to admit it, but she could no longer push those feelings aside. But could she compromise? Even though she cared for Daniel, she didn't think she could. She didn't want to love him, especially when there didn't seem to be any future for their relationship, but she couldn't help herself. It was a good thing this mission was almost over. Tomorrow they would make the arrests at the stadium and then Operation Battlefield would be over, and they would go their separate ways. She would take her new FBI assignment and move to a new city, putting Chattanooga and Daniel far behind her.

She wondered fleetingly what her options would be. Miami? New York City? Or maybe a smaller city in a rural area? Why didn't the prospect of moving on fill her with excitement the way she would have expected?

She knew it was time to pray. God was always her strength in difficult times. If there were ever a time to seek His guidance, it was now. She poured out her heart in her prayer, as well as her fears about what the future would bring. She also prayed for protection for both herself and Daniel as they entered this most dangerous part of their undercover mission.

Her FBI phone suddenly rang, bringing her back to the present. She looked at the number and identified it as the new number that Hooker had supplied.

"Yes, sir? This is Hailey." These days, she always used her undercover name, just in case the phone was compromised in any way. It also made it easier to stay in character if she always answered with her undercover name.

She listened for a while, then answered. "Yes, sir. Thank you for the information." Then she told her FBI boss about what had happened during the meeting and the plans for the stadium. She also told him where he could pick up the pen and glasses that had recorded the meeting that morning, and their need to research and figure out the rest of Operation Battlefield. A few minutes later, the call ended and she stored her phone again.

"Everything okay?" Daniel asked.

"Not really," she answered. "The FBI has found incontrovertible proof that Max Westfield was intercepting all of the communication between us and Special Agent Hooker. That's why we weren't able to contact him. They've found evidence that Max was tampering with the Heritage Guard files, as well. He was definitely the mole and was probably also behind Justin's death. They're trying to tie him to it as we speak. And now, Max Westfield has disappeared."

SEVENTEEN

Daniel stood guard as Bethany pressed the C-4 into the crevice between the two girders at the stadium, his hand on the butt of his pistol. They were alone in the shadows and it was about noon, although people were scattered throughout the stadium, working and setting up for the afternoon festivities. Several bands had already arrived and were warming up in different areas around the field and out in the parking lot. Workers were manning the concession areas, as well as the ticket booths and the top deck where the officials who would be judging the event had congregated.

Although they were still playing a role, there was no way the stadium would actually explode—that is, if law enforcement had anything to say about it. Bethany and Daniel had met with a joint FBI and Chattanooga Police

Department task force yesterday after their Guard meeting and filled them in on all the details, so there were plenty of plain-clothed officers on the scene ready to make the arrests once they got the word to do so. The law enforcement teams were all connected by radio and were checking in on a regular basis. Until they knew the rest of the plans for Operation Battlefield, however, the FBI wanted to continue going through the motions as if the stadium explosion would still go on as planned. It was the hope that either the research team would discover a connection between some of Bishop's texts and some other bit of news, or that Bishop or one of the other Guard members would let something slip in the moments leading up to the explosion that would give the rest of the Guard's plans away.

Daniel hummed along to the loud speaker that was playing Christmas music from a local radio station. The tune just added to the cacophony of sounds echoing off the walls of concrete, but he could still hear the law enforcement announcements through the speaker in his ear, as well. Every once in a while, the DJ would come on and announce a current event that was planned for the upcoming weekend in Chattanooga, but there really didn't seem to be much going on besides the normal holiday and charity galas that happened every year. Bethany and Daniel had been sure to report what they had discovered on Bishop's phone about the phase one and phase two events and their theories, but it was hard to pinpoint anything that would have garnered the attention of the Guard as being worthy of a phase two event. Nothing scheduled in Chattanooga or the surrounding area over the next few weeks seemed to be noteworthy enough. However, agents and officers were still scrambling to come up with anything that might fit the Heritage Guard agenda.

What added to the frustration was the fact that there was no hard evidence against anyone in the Guard organization who ranked above Bishop Jacobs to prove the conspiracy. They had a few vague texts, and a few names, but nothing concrete. The Heritage Guard had also only used a small amount of the stolen money on the C-4 they had purchased. The Guard was still planning something bigger. They just didn't know what that bigger picture could be.

Daniel spoke into his microphone attached to his sleeve. "All clear at checkpoint delta."

He turned to Bethany, who was still listening in on Bishop's phone with a small earpiece. "How's it going?"

"I'm almost done," Bethany replied.

"That's good," Westfield answered, stepping out of the shadows. "I was afraid you wouldn't follow through on your task for the Guard."

Daniel was quick to unholster his weapon and point it at Westfield, but the rogue FBI man was quicker. He also had a silencer on the end of his weapon, so when he fired his shot at Daniel, nobody heard the bullet that hit Daniel in the arm above the wrist and tore the skin as it skirted toward his elbow. Daniel dropped his gun, unable to keep his grip or even hit the button on his microphone to notify the other law enforcement officers due to the pain.

"Max, no!" Bethany yelled. She went for him as if to tackle him, but he instantly swung the gun in her direction and she stopped short, apparently realizing that she couldn't stop him without getting shot herself.

"Keep your voice down, and no sudden moves, either of you. I will kill you, Bethany. I won't enjoy it, but I'll do it." He looked behind him to make sure no one had noticed their activities, but they were still alone in the shadows.

Daniel grabbed his wounded right arm, trying to staunch the flow of blood. His arm felt like it was on fire, and he pressed the fabric from his shirt and coat against the wound, hoping the pressure would help stop the bleeding. He gritted his teeth, angry that Westfield had been able to sneak up on them without his noticing.

"Put your guns on the floor, now," Westfield ordered, pointing his weapon at Bethany. "You too, Daniel. I know you carry a second piece. And pull out that microphone you have up your sleeve and your phones." Bethany complied, pulling her service pistol from her waistband as well as her small derringer from her boot. She slowly added her cell phone to the pile growing at her feet. Daniel also gave up his second gun, his phone, and the microphone. Westfield collected the weapons and secured them in the pockets of his coat, then crushed the rest with the heel of his boot. Then he forced them up against the concrete wall of the stadium and frisked them. When he came to Bethany, his hands were overly friendly and Bethany kicked him hard in response.

Westfield's face turned red and he grabbed Bethany's hair, hard, obviously hurting her and causing her to gasp. "It must have escaped your attention that I'm in charge now. Try that again and I'll shoot you right here and now." He pushed her against the concrete so roughly that her head hit the corner edge, causing a scrape and a line of blood to form on her temple.

Westfield smiled when he saw the wound and the blood start to trickle down her face. "Now you have a gift to remember me by." He finished frisking her, found Bethany's knife in her boot and confiscated that, as well.

"Any other hardware I should know about?"

She shook her head but didn't verbally respond. Her eyes were burning with fire. Daniel couldn't help thinking that Westfield was an idiot. If he thought his rough treatment of Bethany was going to subdue her, the result was actually the opposite. Bethany was now fighting mad.

"So you're a member of the Heritage Guard?" Daniel asked, his voice filled with derision.

Westfield laughed. "Look who just caught up."

"Which means you killed Justin," Bethany added.

He shrugged. "He was unfortunate collateral damage. I actually liked the man, but he couldn't be swayed."

"Collateral damage?" Bethany said coldly, trembling with anger. "He was a person, with a family and friends. You act as if his death meant nothing at all."

Westfield shrugged. "He got in our way." He took a few steps to the left and quickly looked behind himself, making sure they were still truly alone. Once satisfied, he returned his attention to his quarry in front of him. "The Guard has known about you for a couple of months now, Bethany, and has been using you and your abilities to advance our agenda. You've been able to provide us with quite a lot of valuable commodities—not to mention the fact that you make a very talented armed robber." He gave her a chilling smile. "I have to admit, it took us a while to figure out that you were the one who had infiltrated our group. We knew someone had because the FBI kept thwarting our plans, but we didn't know it was you until I joined the FBI myself and got access to the files."

"The FBI does thorough background checks before hiring anyone," Bethany said defiantly.

"How did you manage to hide your connection to the Heritage Guard?"

Westfield smiled. "I had references from powerful people in high places, not to mention computer specialists working for the Guard who smoothed over any questions about my qualifications. Not a single red flag appeared. The Guard is not without resources, Bethany. You should know that. We have friends everywhere." He leaned closer. "Instead of worrying about me though, you should really be worrying about yourself." He shifted, but kept his weapon trained on both of them. "We thought about killing you outright but figured the FBI would just send in another agent. That's why we decided to take out Justin instead. By taking out the head of the snake, we figured that would kill the investigation. We didn't realize you would keep pushing so hard to keep the mission going, or that the FBI would listen and let you stay involved with the Guard. We were able to make sure you didn't get too much intelligence, but now the time has come for you and your boyfriend here to be eliminated, as well." He smiled again, a smirk that made Daniel's blood boil. "Don't worry though. Once the stadium blows up, we'll be sure to verify that you and Daniel, along with the FBI and the Chattanooga Police Department, get all the credit for the explosion. They'll find your bodies here in the rubble, along with your fingerprints all over the materials. Plus, they'll be able to trace the materials back to the CPD evidence locker, which will further prove your involvement."

"You won't get away with it," Bethany said fervently under her breath. "You may think you've won, but even if we die today, others will stop you."

"*If* you die today?" Westfield laughed. "Darling, that's an *absolute certainty.*" He took a step closer and ran his hand suggestively down her cheek. "And won't it prove interesting when they find out that you were also in on the bank robbery and on that armored car heist. It will add even more fuel to the fire when they find money that was stolen from the armored car back in your apartment. Yes, the FBI will be kept quite busy defending you and its actions. We've thought of everything. Let me assure you—you'll be quite the news story. Now turn around and finish setting that explosive properly."

It was all Daniel could do not to pounce on

Westfield and shove the gun down his throat. He couldn't stand seeing him touch Bethany, especially in such a personal manner. But he could also see the message in her eyes. *Wait. Watch.* There would be a better opportunity to strike. Right now, Westfield held all the cards. He was too close to them with his loaded gun, and if either of them tried something, one or both of them could end up dead. No, the smart move was to wait, just as her wordless missive was suggesting.

Bethany turned and continued working on the explosive, but she kept the conversation going. "Well if you're so convinced, Westfield, there's no harm in telling us the rest of the Operation Battlefield plan. We've been trying to figure it out all morning. Phase one is blowing up the stadium. What is phase two?"

Westfield was silent for a moment, as if considering the situation, and Daniel wasn't sure if he was going to answer. Then the hubris got the better of him and the words spilled from his mouth. "Well, I guess there's no harm in telling you since you'll be dead soon anyway." He started to pace, yet kept the gun trained on their midriffs. It was almost as if he were dancing to the Christmas music that was playing in the background.

"The governor is hosting a Christmas party tonight, and has invited several dignitaries, including both senators from Tennessee and three of our nine federal representatives. Unfortunately, some of the food at the party is going to be tainted, and a lot of the people are going to get sick. Some of the people are even going to die—including the three congressmen and two senators. It will all look like a terrible accident, but no one will really care, because everyone will be talking about the horrible bomb that took out the stadium and all of those dear children at the marching band competition. The entire focus will be on the corruption within the FBI and the CPD and how they could allow a joint operation to go so terribly wrong. In the meantime, new senators and congressmen will need to be appointed to finish out the terms of the people who accidentally died at the party. While the nation hones in on the stadium tragedy, the Heritage Guard has people in place to make sure Guard members are selected to fill those empty spots in the federal government with little to no opposition."

Bethany stopped her work and glared at Westfield. "All of those people sick or murdered, just to advance the Guard's agenda. There are other ways to reach your objectives without all the killing."

"You make think so, my dear, but with five new members of congress pushing the Guard's agenda at the federal level, amazing things can happen, and we just don't have time to wait." He shifted. "And don't start believing that the Guard has a limited influence only in the tiny little state of Tennessee. We're growing every day. This is just the beginning. The Heritage Guard has a glorious future. We'll be moving mountains in no time."

He pulled some rope out of one of the pockets of his jacket and threw it on the ground in front of Bethany. "Tie him up. Tightly. And believe me, I'm going to check, so do a good job."

Bethany picked up the rope and turned to Daniel. She met his eye and he saw worry and love radiating back at him. *Love?* Wait, was that really love there? He was so excited to see the emotion there written on her face it almost made him forget that a madman was standing a few feet away, pointing a deadly weapon at them.

"How is your arm?" she asked softly.

"I think it's the least of our problems right now." He put his hands up, and she tied them together.

"Now, sit and tie his feet," Westfield ordered. "And add this gag," he said, throwing a bandanna on the ground.

They complied, and once Daniel was incapacitated, Westfield pocketed his gun and faced Bethany with a length of rope. "Put your hands together. Now."

Bethany complied, but then at the last minute, she struck out with her fist and caught Westfield in the chin. The traitor had been expecting defiance, however, and the blow didn't hit with the full force that Bethany had intended. Westfield countered with a hit to Bethany's gut that took her breath away. He was then able to grab her left arm and wrench it behind her, causing her to cry out in pain. She struggled against him and Daniel writhed against his bindings and bit against the gag, frustrated by his lack of ability to help.

Westfield pulled even harder against Bethany's arm, yanking it so roughly she cried out again. He pushed her against the wall, forcing her face against the cold gray concrete and pulling her arm up her back in an awkward angle so she could barely move without being in severe pain. "Keep fighting me, Bethany, and I'll break your arm, I swear I will."

She finally quit fighting and nodded. "Okay, Westfield. You win."

He released her arm and flipped her around so he was seeing her face-to-face. "I didn't want it to end this way between us. I really didn't. I wanted us to be on the same side. We could have been so good together, you and me. We could have made an excellent team."

"I would never join you," Bethany said, her voice full of derision. "You disgust me."

It was apparently the wrong thing to say. Westfield's eyes turned cold, and he brought his fist back and slammed it into Bethany's face. Her head bounced against the concrete behind her, and her body went limp and fell to the ground.

Daniel yelled, but the gag kept him from making any real sound. He tried to kick out at Westfield, but being trussed up like a Christmas turkey made it hard for him to do much, and Westfield ended up giving him two hard kicks in the gut in response and pushed him away. As Daniel tried to regain his breath,

Westfield tied Bethany up and left her in a heap in the corner.

Then he stood over both of them and laughed.

"Relax, Daniel. You're about to be famous. And don't forget, it's for a good cause."

With that, he checked the explosives to verify that they were set properly, then turned and left, sauntering down the stadium walkway, leaving them with the C-4 and the detonator set, the timer silently counting off the minutes before the explosion would rock the stadium and take out the entire south wall.

EIGHTEEN

Bethany's head was pounding. Was that a bass drum playing in her brain? Why wouldn't it stop? She tried to sit up, but the pounding got worse.

"Bethany? Lie still. You might have a concussion."

"Daniel?" Her mind was a bit foggy. She remembered... Suddenly, it all came rushing back to her and she opened her eyes at the same time that she tried to move her arms and legs.

"How long was I out?"

"Only a few minutes."

Her hands were tied behind her and her feet were bound together, both rather securely with lengths of white rope that Westfield had brought with him. She looked over at Daniel. He had apparently bitten through the thin bandanna that Westfield had used to gag him and was now working on trying to loosen the ropes on his own hands and feet. He actually looked like he was having a bit of success, and Bethany had to admit that she was impressed. Westfield had checked her knots when he had forced her to tie Daniel up. He was bound securely.

"I can't believe you're getting out of those ropes. How are you managing it?"

Daniel was silent for a moment as if contemplating his answer, then finally swallowed heavily. "Unfortunately, I've had some experience with escaping difficult situations like this. My brother used to tie me up for fun when I was younger. It was a game to him and his friends. They would tie me up in knots with rope or whatever they could find and then leave me that way for hours. I got pretty good at getting untied. I had lots of chances to hone my skills."

Bethany looked at him, sure that her wide eyes were reflecting the shock and disgust she was feeling. How could a brother do such a thing? Especially an older brother who should have been protecting a younger one from an abusive parent? Still, she made sure to keep her voice level and calm. She knew instinctively that pity was not what Daniel would want to hear—now or ever. "How long did they leave you like that?"

Daniel kept working on the ropes as he spoke and didn't meet her eyes. "At first, it was only for a few minutes at a time. I was six or so. Then it stretched into longer periods because they lost interest and forgot about me. A couple of times, I was stuck like that for almost twenty-four hours."

"Oh, Daniel," Bethany muttered. Still, she was pleased that he had shared part of his past with her, even if it was a series of horrific memories from his childhood. He had actually told her something about his family, and she could tell that even though it had been difficult for him, he was glad that he had done so.

"Yeah, well, like I said, I've had a little practice at getting out of tight situations, and that might actually come in handy right about now." He grimaced. "I apologize in advance. I'm about to do something and, well, this sound might bother you."

She heard a *pop* and he winced as his shoulder went out of joint, but that movement made the rope just slack enough around his wrists that he was able to pull at the bindings and release the rope from around his hands and free himself. He popped the joint back in place, then untied his feet, moving a little slowly because of his injured arm.

"Tell me you did not just pop your shoulder out of the joint so you could free yourself," she said softly, wincing as she imagined the pain that must be associated with such a maneuver.

"It hurt a lot worse the first time it happened, believe me."

She raised an eyebrow. "And now?"

"It makes my arm sore for a while, but I don't really notice it anymore."

There was quite a bit of blood on the rope near his wrists and on his coat and shirt where he had been bleeding from the bullet wound, but he seemed to be ignoring that as well, as he turned his focus to untying Bethany's bindings. Once he had her free, he gently cupped her head in his hands and kissed her on the lips.

"I love you, Bethany. I'm so sorry that Westfield hurt you."

It was a wonderful kiss, sweet and full of promise. "I'm sorry about your brother," she said softly. "Thank you for telling me."

"Yeah, well, you wanted the unvarnished truth. That's one reason why I don't send him Christmas cards every year. We've never been close. He's six years older than me, and he had a different father, so when my mom started losing it, she sent him to live with his old man. I haven't heard from him since."

"Did he know you were being abused growing up?"

"I don't know what he knew or didn't know. Frankly, once he was gone, it was just one less problem I had to deal with. If he did know, I don't think he cared." He gently wiped the blood off the cut on her temple where Westfield had bashed her against the concrete wall.

"We only have a few minutes until this C-4 is set to blow. Do you know how to disarm it?" Daniel asked.

"Sure. That's the easy part. Then we need to get through to the rest of the stadium and make sure all of the rest of the C-4 is disarmed, as well. Who knows how far Westfield has gotten or if law enforcement had any trouble making the arrests."

"He smashed both of our cell phones and the radio," Daniel said, his tone matter-of-fact, "but we'll get Westfield and a status report.

This place is loaded with law enforcement. I'm actually surprised no one has come up here to check on us." He stood and examined the charges. "Can you tell me how to do it? The timer says we have eight minutes left before this is set to blow."

Bethany shook her head, then regretted it when the pain got worse because of the movement. She gritted her teeth and started to stand, and Daniel grabbed her hand with his uninjured arm and helped pull her to her feet.

"I'll take care of it." She quickly disarmed the bomb and removed the C-4, detonator and timer from the girder. Once she was sure they were safe, she secured all of the material into different compartments of her coat. Then they left the secluded area and immediately headed for the lower area of the stadium where the concessions and more populated sections were located. All they needed to do was find someone in law enforcement before they ran into someone from the Heritage Guard.

Unfortunately, Derek was the next face they came across, and he was quick to whip out his gun and point it directly at Daniel and Bethany.

"Well, if it isn't the two traitors I was looking for," he said, a sneer in his voice.

"What are you talking about?" Daniel asked, immediately putting his hands up while at the same time moving in a protective stance in front of Bethany.

Bethany would have objected—she was usually able to take care of herself, thank you, but her head was still not right after Westfield had bounced it off the concrete. She did know this—it didn't make sense that Derek was still in the stadium and running around with a loaded weapon. He should have been arrested with the rest of the Guard members. Hopefully, law enforcement had already made sure that all of the other charges had been disarmed throughout the stadium, but if Derek was still free, then maybe the stadium was still in jeopardy and all the people were still in harm's way after all. A nervous knot tightened in her stomach as she glanced at her watch. "What are you doing here?" she asked. "You were supposed to set your charges and clear out like the rest of us."

"Bishop told us all that you two had betrayed the Guard. He sent me up here to deal with both of you."

* * *

Daniel took a step forward. "Really? Well, let's just think about this. The timers are set to go off in less than five minutes. If what you say is true, then it sounds to me like he sent you up here to die, don't you think?" As he spoke, he got closer and closer to Derek, until he suddenly reached with his good arm and grabbed for the gun, forcing it up so the barrel was pointed toward the ceiling. It fired, the noise echoing off the concrete walls as the two men struggled for supremacy of the loaded weapon. The bullet ricocheted away and zinged against walls as the two men wrestled.

Daniel tried to wrench the gun away, but Derek's grip was tighter than he'd thought and he only had one good arm to fight with. Without realizing it, Derek hit Daniel's bad arm where the bullet wound injury was fresh. Daniel grunted and quickly kicked Derek's knee in response and the man's leg collapsed. Derek shrieked in pain and when he fell to the left, Daniel hit him hard in the stomach with his good arm and then again with his knee. Derek coughed in response and released the gun, then fell to the ground and grabbed his injured knee with both hands, writhing. "I think you broke my leg!" he spat, as he rolled back and forth.

Daniel ignored him and kick him again, making sure he wasn't getting up again any time soon, and also ensuring that he wouldn't try anything while he was down. Bethany was quickly there, frisking him for weapons. She found his phone and immediately called their law enforcement contact to find out the status of the bombs in the stadium while Daniel kept the weapon trained on Derek's midriff. "Don't move a muscle, Derek."

"We're clear," Bethany said, visibly relieved. She blew out a breath, and closed her eyes for a moment, then opened them again. "The other thirteen bricks of C-4 have been accounted for. They've arrested Liam, Bishop, Ethan and two others from the Guard that Bishop must have called in to assist."

Two security guards suddenly appeared on the scene, their weapons drawn, apparently coming to check out the source of the gunshot.

"CPD," Daniel announced, as they approached. "This man is a perp and needs to be taken into custody." To his credit, Derek kept his mouth shut, even as the two guards arrested him and handcuffed him. Daniel was glad Derek was done fighting. He didn't have much strength left in his hand that was holding the gun, but he didn't have time to stop and get medical treatment either. They needed to stop Westfield and the Guard before they hurt the congressmen at the Christmas party.

Bethany came to his side and touched his arm gently. "Are you okay?"

He looked into her eyes, and could tell that she was asking about more than just his physical condition. He thought about what he had told her about his brother's abuse. He hadn't planned to share that with her—but he hadn't stopped himself either. He had never shared that story with anybody before and hadn't known exactly what kind of reaction to expect, but afterward he was glad that he had told her about his brother's behavior. She wanted to know the true story of his past, and it had actually felt good to tell her.

"I will be," he answered softly. He holstered his gun and took her hand. "Let's go stop the Guard from doing any more damage." He looked down at their entwined fingers and smiled.

The difference was the love, he realized. Although she hadn't said the words, he had seen it in her face and mirrored in her eyes. He knew her feelings for him were growing and were stronger than they ever had been. He was patient. Their relationship had strengthened over the last few days, and he had seen changes in Bethany that he hadn't seen even when they had been dating the year before.

There were changes in him too, he realized. Before, he hadn't wanted to tell her about his life growing up, but now he had taken the plunge and decided that it was worth the sacrifice. He wanted Bethany in his life. Period. If that meant he needed to tell her every detail of his past, then he would do it. He loved her. He would do whatever it took to make sure they could be together. He wasn't going to blurt it all out in one sitting, but little by little, he was finally willing to share that part of himself with her—only with her.

Thank you, Lord, for giving me the strength to share my past with Bethany. I've buried the pain inside for so long that I didn't think it was possible to talk about it out loud, but You've helped me see that it's not only possible, but necessary so I can move on and deal with my past. Thank You for bringing her back into my life and giving us a second chance.

NINETEEN

"Freeze, Westfield," Daniel said, his voice cold and clear. His weapon was unwavering as he pointed it at Westfield's head. The man was sitting in a chair in a small private airfield's lobby, waiting for the small jet he'd hired to whisk him away into obscurity. Thankfully, Daniel and Bethany had been able to track Westfield down through internet purchases a mere twenty minutes before the plane was set to take off, despite the man's attempts to stay hidden and escape.

"I wouldn't do that," Bethany said, as Max turned slightly as if he were going to either close his laptop or push some of the buttons on the computer. She also had her weapon drawn and was coming at him from the opposite doorway.

"Ah, Bethany. I'm so glad you came to see

me off." He smiled, but it was a sad smile, as if they shared some secret together.

"I'm sure you've heard by now that the stadium was saved," she said quietly. "None of the C-4 charges detonated and no one was hurt." She took a step closer. "The governor's Christmas party also got canceled. The food is being tested as we speak. Anything tainted will be destroyed before it can harm anyone, and whoever poisoned it will be prosecuted. Operation Battlefield has failed, Westfield. Both phase one and phase two were a complete wash."

Westfield shrugged. "You'll undoubtedly arrest a few, but the Heritage Guard operates in cells for a reason. You won't be able to get at the true leaders. They're too deeply hidden—too entrenched for you to find them. The Guard will live on and will rise again."

"That's what we thought too, until we found the hidden hard drives in the dry cleaners when we did a very thorough search of the place about an hour ago. Our search warrant pretty much let us tear the place apart, and you'd be surprised at the membership lists we found, not to mention the financial records, offshore accounts and other valuable information we discovered. The attorney general and local state attorney are going to be delivering a joint statement within a few hours, and will be issuing subpoenas and indictments on a national scale. This case is huge. The Heritage Guard is finished."

Bethany took another step closer. "What did you say to us when we were in the stadium all tied up? Oh, yeah, you're gonna be famous!" She pulled out her handcuffs. "Now set down that computer, stand up and put your hands behind your back."

He slowly set the computer aside and stood, but then he quickly put something in his mouth and then held his hands up and closed his eyes.

"No!" Both Daniel and Bethany yelled it in unison, holstered their weapons and tried to get the substance out of his mouth, but he clamped his jaws together and wouldn't open them. Within a few short moments, white foam started to ooze out between his lips and his body started to convulse. He fell to the ground, and Daniel kept trying to save him while Bethany pulled out her radio and called an ambulance for help. The faint smell of almonds hung in the air.

"I need an emergency bus for a suspected

cyanide poisoning," she said hurriedly, and rattled off the address.

"He's seizing," Daniel said. "He's already unconscious and his pulse is weak. They're not going to make it here in time."

Bethany felt in Westfield's pocket and found a small empty packet. "He must have had this on him just in case he was captured." She looked at his face that was already pale. "He chose the coward's way out." She stood, disgust and anger warring on her face. She kicked a chair, sending it flying across the room. "I didn't want him dead! I wanted him in prison, but not dead!"

"He made the choice," Daniel said, feeling for a pulse. "You didn't kill him. He did this to himself." He stood, pulled out a handkerchief from his pocket and wiped his hands. "He's gone."

EPILOGUE

Daniel paced back and forth outside of the entrance to Rock City on Lookout Mountain, Georgia, just on the outskirts of Chattanooga. It had been almost three weeks since the big arrests from the Heritage Guard had come down, yet the case was still making huge headlines and being discussed on the nightly news on a regular basis. Christmas had come and gone, but he had barely had a chance to celebrate or spend time with Bethany because she had been so busy at the FBI with follow-up work from the case. His reputation and personal records had all been restored, and he had returned to his normal work at the Chattanooga Police Department, but he really missed working with Bethany side by side as they had on the Heritage Guard case. Today, she had asked for him to meet her here, but he had a sinking feeling that she was meeting him today only to say goodbye. It was a bitter pill to swallow.

She had succeeded professionally beyond her wildest dreams, and he was sure that the FBI was going to offer her the assignment of her choice once things settled down at the bureau. Where would she go? California? New York City? The thought of losing her hung over his head like a huge storm cloud, ready to thunder and let loose a deluge of rain.

She had never told him she loved him. It weighed heavily upon him. He had blurted out bits and pieces of his past and told her his feelings, but it obviously hadn't convinced her to stay. He'd thought he'd done enough to get her trust him, but apparently, he hadn't. He'd failed, and now she was going to break his heart for good.

At least she was going to meet him and say goodbye. The last time, she had disappeared without a trace.

His heart felt like a stone in his chest and the pain seemed to radiate out and seep into every other part of his body.

He paced some more and watched in trepidation as he saw her pull her car into the parking lot, park and approach. She was wearing jeans, a red sweater and a blue coat that brought out the color in her cheeks and made her face look radiant. She smiled and gave him a quick kiss on the cheek.

"Sorry, I'm a tad late. There was a car accident at the bottom of the mountain and the police are rerouting folks around it."

He ran his hands through his hair. "I hope nobody was hurt."

She shook her head. "I don't think so. Looked like a fender bender." She reached over and gently touched his nose. "Hey, that's really healing up nicely."

He laughed nervously. "Yeah, although I think it will be crooked for life. It's a little souvenir of the Heritage Guard case that I'll get to keep with me forever." He took her hand and squeezed it, then tensely walked to the ticket booth. They bought tickets and together they entered the attraction. It was a beautiful day, and even though it was chilly, the sky was sunny and blue and they could see for miles from the bridges and overlook. Daniel was secretly glad that there weren't many other people around, and they basically had the beautiful location to themselves.

Daniel wanted to start a conversation, but

he was so worried that today was the last time that he was going to see her that he didn't even know how to begin.

Bethany must have sensed his nervousness. She squeezed his hand. "I'm really glad you were available to meet today. I'm sorry I've been so out of pocket. I've missed you."

Daniel stopped walking and looked her straight in the eye. He took his free hand and gently touched her cheek. "I've missed you too."

They started walking again, then Daniel suddenly stopped and took both her hands. "Okay, I can't take it anymore. Are you here to say goodbye? Just tell me now, okay? I mean, I'm glad you didn't just disappear without telling me, but—"

She stopped him with a kiss. He took a step back, surprised, but didn't break the kiss.

She took a step closer and twined her hands around his neck.

When the kiss finally ended, he pulled her close and whispered in her ear. "That was a wonderful goodbye kiss."

She pulled back. "Who said I'm saying goodbye?"

A small seed of hope was planted in his

chest. Maybe God truly was the God of second chances, and had granted him a second chance with Bethany. He looked into her eye and saw—dare he hope—love reflected back at him. But would she say the words? "With all of your success at the FBI, I thought they would probably give you your choice of assignments."

"They did."

"Well, what did you choose?"

She smiled. "They offered me a promotion right here in Chattanooga, so I took it."

He hugged her close. "I thought you would take New York, or something more exotic."

"Why would I do that?" she asked. She pulled back so she could see his face again and cupped his cheeks in her hands. "I love you, Daniel Morley. And I'm not going anywhere."

* * * * *

Don't miss Kathleen Tailer's
next thrilling novel,
Perilous Pursuit

Available June 2019 wherever
Love Inspired Suspense books
and ebooks are sold.

Get 4 FREE REWARDS!

We'll send you 2 FREE Books plus 2 FREE Mystery Gifts.

Love Inspired® books feature contemporary inspirational romances with Christian characters facing the challenges of life and love.

FREE Value Over **$20**

YES! Please send me 2 FREE Love Inspired® Romance novels and my 2 FREE mystery gifts (gifts are worth about $10 retail). After receiving them, if I don't wish to receive any more books, I can return the shipping statement marked "cancel." If I don't cancel, I will receive 6 brand-new novels every month and be billed just $5.24 for the regular-print edition or $5.74 each for the larger-print edition in the U.S., or $5.74 each for the regular-print edition or $6.24 each for the larger-print edition in Canada. That's a savings of at least 13% off the cover price. It's quite a bargain! Shipping and handling is just 50¢ per book in the U.S. and 75¢ per book in Canada.* I understand that accepting the 2 free books and gifts places me under no obligation to buy anything. I can always return a shipment and cancel at any time. The free books and gifts are mine to keep no matter what I decide.

Choose one: ☐ **Love Inspired® Romance**
Regular-Print
(105/305 IDN GMY4)

☐ **Love Inspired® Romance**
Larger-Print
(122/322 IDN GMY4)

Name (please print)

Address   Apt. #

City   State/Province   Zip/Postal Code

Mail to the **Reader Service:**
IN U.S.A.: P.O. Box 1341, Buffalo, NY 14240-8531
IN CANADA: P.O. Box 603, Fort Erie, Ontario L2A 5X3

Want to try 2 free books from another series? Call 1-800-873-8635 or visit www.ReaderService.com.

---

*Terms and prices subject to change without notice. Prices do not include sales taxes, which will be charged (if applicable) based on your state or country of residence. Canadian residents will be charged applicable taxes. Offer not valid in Quebec. This offer is limited to one order per household. Books received may not be as shown. Not valid for current subscribers to Love Inspired Romance books. All orders subject to approval. Credit or debit balances in a customer's account(s) may be offset by any other outstanding balance owed by or to the customer. Please allow 4 to 6 weeks for delivery. Offer available while quantities last.

Your Privacy—The Reader Service is committed to protecting your privacy. Our Privacy Policy is available online at www.ReaderService.com or upon request from the Reader Service. We make a portion of our mailing list available to reputable third parties that offer products we believe may interest you. If you prefer that we not exchange your name with third parties, or if you wish to clarify or modify your communication preferences, please visit us at www.ReaderService.com/consumerschoice or write to us at Reader Service Preference Service, P.O. Box 9062, Buffalo, NY 14240-9062. Include your complete name and address.

LI19R

Get 4 FREE REWARDS!

We'll send you 2 FREE Books <u>plus</u> 2 FREE Mystery Gifts.

Harlequin® Heartwarming™ Larger-Print books feature traditional values of home, family, community and—most of all—love.

FREE Value Over **$20**

THE FORTUNES OF TEXAS COLLECTION!

18 FREE BOOKS in all!

Treat yourself to the rich legacy of the Fortune and Mendoza clans in this remarkable 50-book collection. This collection is packed with cowboys, tycoons and Texas-sized romances!

YES! Please send me **The Fortunes of Texas Collection** in Larger Print. This collection begins with 3 FREE books and 2 FREE gifts in the first shipment. Along with my 3 free books, I'll also get the next 4 books from The Fortunes of Texas Collection, in LARGER PRINT, which I may either return and owe nothing, or keep for the low price of $5.24 U.S./$5.89 CDN each plus $2.99 for shipping and handling per shipment*. If I decide to continue, about once a month for 8 months I will get 6 or 7 more books but will only need to pay for 4. That means 2 or 3 books in every shipment will be FREE! If I decide to keep the entire collection, I'll have paid for only 32 books because 18 books are FREE! I understand that accepting the 3 free books and gifts places me under no obligation to buy anything. I can always return a shipment and cancel at any time. My free books and gifts are mine to keep no matter what I decide.

☐ 269 HCN 4622   ☐ 469 HCN 4622

Name (please print)

Address _____ Apt. #

City _____ State/Province _____ Zip/Postal Code

Mail to the **Reader Service:**
IN U.S.A.: P.O. Box 1341, Buffalo, N.Y. 14240-8531
IN CANADA: P.O. Box 603, Fort Erie, Ontario L2A 5X3

*Terms and prices subject to change without notice. Prices do not include sales taxes, which will be charged (if applicable) based on your state or country of residence. Canadian residents will be charged applicable taxes. Offer not valid in Quebec. All orders subject to approval. Credit or debit balances in a customer's account(s) may be offset by any other outstanding balance owed by or to the customer. Please allow three to four weeks for delivery. Offer available while quantities last. © 2018 Harlequin Enterprises Limited. ® and ™ are trademarks owned and used by the trademark owner and/or its licensee.

Your Privacy—The Reader Service is committed to protecting your privacy. Our Privacy Policy is available online at www.ReaderService.com or upon request from the Reader Service. We make a portion of our mailing list available to reputable third parties that offer products we believe may interest you. If you prefer that we not exchange your name with third parties, or if you wish to clarify or modify your communication preferences, please visit us at www.ReaderService.com/consumerschoice or write to us at Reader Service Preference Service, P.O. Box 9049, Buffalo, NY 14269-9049. Include your name and address.

50BFT19R

100 Years
A Journey to End a Vicious Cycle

By Mark Baynard

100 Years

ISBN 13: 978-0-9861380-0-3

ISBN 10: 0986138002

Library of Congress Control Number 2015902069

Editor: Sarah Lingley Williams for Lingley Editing Services, LLC, lingleyediting.com
Book Cover Design: Ida Jannson for Amygdala Designs, amagdaladesign.net

Contact Information: mark100years@yahoo.com

Website: www.journey100years.com

Social Networks:
Twitter @mark100years
Facebook Page: www.facebook.com/journey100years
Linked: www.linkedin.com/pub/mark-
baynard/a1/30/502/en
Goodreads @mark100years
Instagram @mark100years
Google+ @mark100years
Goodreads @mark100years
YouTube Channel Mark Baynard

In Pursuit of Freedom Publishing

"Freedom comes with a price while bondage takes hold without notice"
Mark L Baynard

"Freedom is a Must"

Table of Contents

100 Years

Acknowledgements

I am very thankful for the things that I've learned through my experiences. I am especially thankful for being allowed to wake up and see the devastation that I caused. I thank my grandmother in Delaware who passed on before I came home from prison. She did not have the opportunity to witness me get my life together. I learned a lot from her. I also thank my grandmother in Alabama who is 92 years old. She has always offered helpful advice and provided me with words of encouragement. I still remember the paragraphs that she wrote me while I was in prison. She continues to tell me the truth and offer wisdom. I remember those who I was in the struggle with, some of whom have helped me or given a word of encouragement. I would like to thank the Most High God for guiding me through some very dark times. I also thank Him for giving me the courage to stand when those times were very difficult. I am thankful for my wife and my daughters. I am thankful for my mother, my dad, and my step-mother. I am thankful for the many warnings even though I didn't take heed at the time. I am also thankful to all who visited me, wrote letters, or even prayed for me while in prison. I thank Dean Keith Ray at Alabama State University, who was my Professor at Faulkner University, for motivating me to excel beyond my limits. I thank Reverend Cokelia Dunn for her support in her role as liaison for the Project Aware Program. I thank all of my family and friends for their support. Much thanks and love to my brother and friend Timaiya "Nafear" Peak. I thank my barber and friend Maurice for the support that he's shown me. I thank Catherine Hamrick for her advice and guidance in answering my questions concerning this book. I also thank David Antrobus in Vancouver, Canada for his sincere advice and insight as an author. I thank my editor Sarah Lingley @ lingleyediting.com. I also thank my book cover designer Ida Jannson @ amygdaladesign.net. The book cover is exactly what I had in mind. I also want to thank Fred Fistzgiles @studeo22live.tv for conducting my first interview, even before my book was released.

Prologue

Life is a journey that we all take until the day we transcend into the hereafter. While here on earth, we each have an opportunity to make the very best of our lives. The ability to care for and better one's self is innate, and this makes sense when we consider the fact that we each have only one life to live. Without this ability, the value of life would be minimal. The truth of the matter, however, is that sometimes we choose not to make the best of our lives. Our lives can be whatever we decide; life is a valuable, yet delicate, gift, and a terrible thing to waste. At times, we may feel sabotaged by the fact that others appear to have more control over our lives than we do, and we may regret that there is no magic button that allows us to start over. Yes, birth is when our opportunities to value life begin, but we have until our lives stop to make and maintain positive changes.

Mark was one of the ones who took his life for granted. He did not always take the time to think before he acted, and it took many years for him to realize the many mistakes that he had made, and the magnitude of the consequences. A lot of his mistakes led him into some dangerous situations, but his decision to ultimately take full responsibility for his actions and change the direction in which he was headed was the catalyst for redeeming the value of his life. Though it was difficult for him to do, Mark knew that the foundational step in this process was for him is to be honest with himself about his life. First, Mark realized and accepted the fact that a vicious cycle existed in his family; vicious, because it affected many lives, and cyclical, because so many of his family members became habitually entrapped. For various reasons, many of Mark's family members found themselves in very difficult circumstances in life, and prison became a common denominator. Second, Mark noticed and acknowledged that numerous other families within his life were or had been in similar situations, and that he, in good conscience, could not sit back and allow this cycle to continue.

According to the Old Testaments of the Bible, "We are destroyed because of a lack of knowledge." Mark has knowledge, wisdom, and understanding concerning the consequences of poor decisions; by openly sharing the experiences that he has gone through, he hopes to help others who may be standing at the crossroads of life. These crossroads can be any point at which a life-changing decision is about to be made. Often, it is more appealing to take the easy path and run from life's problems; such action frequently leads to emotions of anger and frustration and ultimately causes transformation into a strangely different person. Mark, as well as several of his relatives, made many wrong decisions while standing at various crossroads of life, and the result was more wrong decisions and, ultimately, destruction. While there may be others nearby who are available to offer advice or assistance during these times, each individual ultimately faces their crossroads alone. The problem lies not in standing at these crossroads, but in each individual's response. Mark believes that the journey of his life happened to him for a reason. His honest evaluation of himself and his family has provided him with the unique opportunity to personally and actively work toward seeking productive solutions to the vicious cycle in which he was born and raised. He is a realist and understands that his efforts may not put an immediate end to this cycle; he does believe, however, that he can challenge the ills that lead to criminal behavior and make positive social change. Many communities are plagued with criminal activity, and Mark understands the need, and importance, of intervention. Without this intervention, statistics will continue to grow and the results will be catastrophic.

One hundred years is a very long time to do anything; an entire city can be built in less time, and an entire society can change. Things were very different during the 1800s compared to the 1900s, and during the 1900s compared to the 2000s. Mark's grandmother, on his father's side of the family, is ninety-two years old; life for her is very different now than it was when she was a young girl. She is a walking wealth of information, full of knowledge and wisdom. Mark is able to live vicariously through her memories, such as getting to know his strong-willed and hard-working grandfather. These generational differences exist for the benefit of those too young to have shared these experiences; passing along wisdom is vital to the value of life that the younger generation must learn. Mark's grandmother had a famous saying: "Thank God for the pain." Mark did not learn the true value of this saying until his mistakes caught up with him years later, but it will always hold deep meaning to him.

A kingdom or even a dynasty can be built within a hundred year time period. Within Mark's family alone, there has been one hundred years wasted within the prison system. This is his dynasty! This is his story! Some may ask: "How can one family invest over one hundred years within prison?" Some may even place judgment on the individuals described in this memoir, and Mark understands this reality. He believes that sharing his story may assist someone who is standing at the crossroads of life, or is emerging from a difficult situation that wrong choices caused. There are many individuals who have been affected by prison, and Mark is willingly offering himself as an example of what not to do, and who not to be. His hope is that his audience will be inspired to look at their own lives, their family's lives, and at the reality of so many of our communities. His goal in sharing his story is to address criminal behavior and the frequently entertained idea of settling for crime as a way of life. There are many positive alternatives to crime and the criminal lifestyle, and in this memoir

Mark shares his personal exploration of some of these alternatives. Above all, Mark wishes to point out that the realities of his journey to make better decisions within his own life are and can be the realities of anyone reading this book. He faced many challenges along the way, and there will be many challenges that each individual seeking positive change will have to face. He experienced the loss of many loved ones, and understands your losses; he has struggled with low self-love, and understands yours. His journey led him to an understanding that he can be a successful member of society, and he wants nothing less for you.

This memoir is a testimony of change, of taking the life we are born into and turning it in to something powerfully positive, of taking responsibility for our wrongs and choosing to do right. While some individuals can brag about their family's success and happiness, the reality of the matter is that Mark doesn't have that kind of story to tell. His story is centered on the realities of poor decisions, street life, prisons, drug sales, drug use and abuse. The book you hold in your hand is the passionate effort of a man who has traveled the wrong road, and is now reaching out to you as you stand at the crossroads of life. He hopes that his story will help you understand who *not* to be, what *not* to do; the decision you are about to make could change your life.

100 Years

Chapter I
One Hundred Years

It was a sunny day in Alabama, that hot summer day in 2012. Those summer months in Alabama can be hot, and the safest place is inside under an air conditioner! The minute that I stepped outside, I started sweating. I had just left the required monthly meeting with my probation officer, and was starting my day as usual. Going to see my probation officer each month always reminded me that my freedom could be taken away at any time. My probation could be violated by something as simple as getting a speeding ticket and not reporting it to my officer. Whenever I met with my probation officer, I did a lot of thinking afterwards about my life. After this one particular meeting, I reflected over my life and the many mistakes that I had made; I came to a very harsh reality as I considered the time I had spent in prison, and the actions that had led me there. I realized that prison would continue to be a part of my life unless I made significant changes. I realized that there were two options available to me: I could point fingers at others, and play the blame game, or I could take responsibility for my own actions and figure out what I could do that would keep me from repeating my negative choices and behavior. I chose the second option, and right then decided to take full responsibility for my actions. I knew that there was truly no one to blame for my current situation other than myself, and instead of blaming others, I chose to look at the man standing in the mirror.

As I looked at my reflection, I quickly began to see my own faults. I was not satisfied with the state of my life, and I believed that I had the power to make it better. I believed that making more responsible decisions would lead to a better outcome. During this process, I realized that it was necessary for me to take a very honest look at who I was, and why I did the things that I did. I began taking a closer look at myself, and identifying the mistakes that I had made. I had wasted a lot of time in prison, and I thought about my other family members who had also been, or currently were, in prison. When I looked at my situation as it related to my family, I immediately saw that there was a pattern. That day, as I stood looking at myself in the mirror, I made the decision to change the bad example I had been setting for others around me. I knew that I could have been a much better role model to my younger brother, as well as to my young cousins. Today was the day I would change.

I usually felt a lot of different emotions after leaving the probation office, and often chose to disregard them. This particular day, however, I could not ignore these feelings any longer, and I decided to use them as motivation to remain focused on being free, and leading life as a productive participant in society. I thought about all of my various family members who had been to, or were currently in, prison: my dad, my younger brother, and many of my cousins. Once home, I got a piece of paper and wrote my name, and everyone else's names, in a list; beside each name, I marked the time served in prison. I absentmindedly neglected to include several of my uncles, nephews, and other cousins in this list, but when I started tallying up the totals, the number quickly reached one hundred years.

For quite a while, I kept this finding to myself, shut away in my heart and mind; I knew the calculations were significant, but I really did not know what to do with this information. The more I thought about it, the more I knew that I had to share my findings with someone. One day while visiting my dad at his place of business, I mentioned the numbers. At first, he looked at me as if I was exaggerating, but when I grabbed a piece of paper and showed him the numbers, he agreed and kind of put his head down in disbelief. In that moment, we both understood that we can't cry over spilled milk, and we can't change the things that have happened in the past. We also understood, however, the importance of starting the process of necessary change within our family; if we did not initiate such change, this number would only continue to increase. Our conversation was the catalyst for my decision to use the information I had discovered to inform others of my own mistakes, and hopefully motivate my family, and other local individuals, to break the cycle. Initially, writing a book about my findings was not something I considered, but before long, I realized that doing so was very necessary.

My past is not something that I am proud of, at all, and looking back at my life can be a difficult thing for me to do. Once my eyes were finally opened to the curse of this vicious cycle, I had a number of different feelings. I consider myself to be a strong person, but I will admit that I felt very weak and helpless during this time; my feelings went from one end of the spectrum to the other, and my heart was full of questions of how and why this destructive cycle was allowed to happen. I felt a sense of disappointment and disgust, and a great deal of guilt for the heavy contributions that I made to this reality.

During this phase of self-examination, I began to see how and when my life had begun to take drastic changes for the worse. Looking back, I saw where and how I had started looking at my life differently, and when my dreams and desires had begun to change. I realized I had given up on wanting to be a doctor, lawyer, fire fighter, or a police officer very early in life. I recalled, however, that even though I gave up on certain childhood goals, I had always known, albeit subconsciously, that I did not want to live poor and struggle for the rest of my life. I was reminded of how my mother struggled to raise us, and I did not want to experience that in my own life. I reminisced over my struggle with making money, and of taking unnecessary risks with my own life. As I continued to evaluate the realities of my past, I clearly saw just how these struggles and risks had led me to prison. I wasted a lot of time in the prison system, and now, as I reflected over the events that had taken place in my life, I was able to see how and why I needed to help others realize the consequences of taking the wrong route in life.

I spent my teenage years walking around in complete darkness. I did what I wanted to do, without considering the thoughts or feelings of others. I did not take seriously the consequences of my actions, and this behavior eventually led me down a path of destruction. I was bound for a dreadful end, based on the decisions I was in the habit of making. The end result of drugs and street life are prisons, institutions and death, and, for better or worse, I know this more than most. I can remember telling myself, as a young teenage male, that "I could accept responsibility for my wrongs even if they led me to prison," or that "If I returned to prison, I will serve double digit numbers." But while I knew that I could handle prison and that I was willing to accept the consequences of my actions, I did not consider the ways in which my poor decisions would affect my family. When we go to prison, we ultimately take our loved ones with us; they will have to make adjustments in order to continue a relationship with us, such as taking the time to visit, or to write letters. As well, there were many younger individuals within the housing projects that I grew up in to whom my actions were regrettably poor examples and influences.

Taking time to evaluate the realities of our lives often brings us back to our childhood, that place where life as we know it began. As far back as I can remember, I lived with my dad and step-mother, and stayed with my grandmother, on my dad's side of the family, on frequent occasions. I have many good memories of staying with my grandmother in the state of Alabama; I remember being around my aunts and uncles and wanting to go to school with them, walking on dirt roads, and just being a kid. My grandmother had an outhouse outside her home; it was a dark and very scary place, and on top of that, it stank! Many years later, I was very happy when my grandmother had a regular bathroom built inside of her house; I knew that I did not want to use another outhouse ever again!

When I was five years old, I lived with my dad, my step-mother, my brother, and sister, in Spain. This was my family, and I did not know anything different; I was lucky and happy to be raised by such a nurturing family. Soon after, my dad took me to the state of Delaware on the pretense of visiting other family members. My dad was in the military, and we did a lot of traveling; it was normal for us to travel to different places and visit family and friends. I quickly found out, however, that this trip was not just another vacation, and I could not have anticipated the changes that this trip was going to have on my life.

From my earliest memory, I thought that my step-mother was my biological mother. (I am using the nouns of step-mother and biological mother in this memoir for the purpose of differentiation; I greatly appreciate the job they both did in acting as a mother figure in my life, and I hold them both in high esteem.) During the time that I lived with my step-mother, she raised me as her own son, and I have nothing but admiration for her. On this particular day, we arrived in Delaware at a house that I was not familiar with; later I learned that this house belonged to my grandmother on my mother's side of the family. Everyone was really nice to me, and I received the normal compliments of, "You got so big!" There were a lot of people there that I did not know, but I managed to find other children to play with while the adults conversed throughout the house.

My memory of everything that happened that particular day is a bit unclear, but I distinctly remember being called into the living room at some point. There was a lady I had never seen before, sitting quietly off to one side as I entered the room and sat down; there were several other women standing around the room, or sitting on various pieces of furniture. Then, one particular woman stood up, looked at me, and said, "This is not your mother," as she pointed at my step-mother. This visibly shocked me; life as I knew it had changed, I had believed that my step-mother was my mother, and now I was being told differently. The woman then pointed to the lady who was sitting quietly and said to me "This lady here is your real mother." At that point I was very surprised, and kind of confused; I did not know what to think or even how to feel. She then asked me, "Who do you want to live with?"

Don't ask me why, but I pointed to the quiet lady. I guess being told that she was my real mother is what made me want to go and live with her, to get to know her. I do not know why I made the decision I did, or even why I was asked; I was only five-years-old, and these were things that adults handled, not children. I do know, however, that I am very glad that I made the decision that I made. Later, I learned the rest of the story; according to my mother and other relatives, my dad wasn't happy about the whole situation because he felt that they had taken me from him. He fervently expressed his disagreement to them, but later gave in to my wish. My mother was such a nice lady and later that day we walked several blocks to where she lived.

I met my brother and sisters that day, and my mother showed me pictures of us being together before I went to live with my dad. I got along really well with my brother and sisters; I was accepted by them, and we had a lot of fun together. I came to know a very loving and caring woman who put her family before herself, a woman that is my biological mother. She taught me much about life; I learned a lot of good things, and useful information, from my mother, and I watched her exemplify what a good woman really is. She was not perfect, and she faced a number of challenges throughout her life, but throughout it all, she stood strong and worked hard. Many times she put her life on hold in order to take care of her five children. She was a very hard worker and came home tired almost every night, only to wake up the very next day ready to do it all again.

I had the same love and respect for my biological mother that I had for my step-mother, and years later, I still have a very good relationship with both of them. It felt good to re-connect with my mother, even though I did not remember her from birth. My brother was one year older than myself, and my mother told my brother to take me with him when he went places. Sometimes he would go to the park to play, sometimes we would go other places together where we would play and have fun. Sometimes, however, he did not want to be with bothered with me, and he would run away and leave me on my own. My older brother remembered when we used to live together previously, and he told me plenty of stories. I enjoyed hearing these stories, and was eager to make a connection with the life that I had before going to live with my dad. We began making new memories each day; my mother was very instrumental in encouraging us to do things together, and with her. I learned nursery school songs, word games (start with a word and continue until you run out of words that rhyme with it), and the name song, where you rhymed your name with other words. My mother was very active in our lives, and she spoke to us about a lot of different things, frequently checking to see that we were alright.

My mother was happy to have me back with her, and was hesitant to allow me to visit my dad; she feared that he would not send me back after my visit, and declared that she would not allow that to happen. Despite the fact that my dad was initially unhappy concerning the situations that led to me living in Delaware with my mother, he decided to reach out to her in an effort to convince her to allow me to visit him. He said that he would send me back, but my mother denied his requests with a simple "No." For a few years, he let the issue alone before asking if I could come and stay with him during the summer time, or during the Christmas holidays. My mother remained hesitant, but ultimately, my Uncle Mokeem was very instrumental in convincing my mother to allow me to visit my dad. He vowed to my mother that he would ensure my safe return to her if she would allow me to visit my dad; my uncle saw the importance of maintaining a relationship with both my parents. My Uncle Mokeem is my dad's brother, and he drove me down to Alabama to visit my dad and other family from the south. I enjoyed living with my mom, but I really did want to see my dad again; I had a lot of good memories of when I lived with my dad, even if he was a very strict disciplinarian. I always got in trouble whenever he got home from work; once he even punished me for having difficulty learning how to spell my last name. But I still wanted to see him.

My dad lived in Montgomery, Alabama, the capitol city. At the time, I did not realize or appreciate the rich history that existed there or the significant role Montgomery played in the Civil Rights Movement. During the 1960s, the famous year-long bus boycott took place, Martin Luther King, Jr., pastored one of the local churches, and it was the destination of the famous march from Selma. During the 1970s, there was a low key element of criminal activity. When we started our drive south, I attempted to stay awake as long as I could but soon fell asleep. It seemed to take forever; I must have asked my uncle countless times, "Are we there yet?" Every time he stopped for gas, I woke up thinking that we had gotten to Alabama.

When we finally arrived at my dad's house I was embraced and accepted by everyone, and I was just as excited to see them as they were to see me. My dad took me to visit a lot of other family members who lived nearby. Some of them I didn't remember, and often I would be asked the question, "Do you remember so-and-so?" I was reunited with my brother and sisters on my dad's side of my family, and we had a lot to talk about and many things to catch up on. My step-mother appeared to be very happy to see me also, and my dad gave her the money to take me shopping for clothes.

During this visit and the ones that followed, my dad took me to my grandmother's house out in the country. There were a lot of dirt roads near her house, and she had chickens and hogs, and grew vegetables. My grandmother, as well as my aunts and uncles, always maintained an old school approach to life and a belief in the implementation of "tough love." Any of the adults were responsible for, and could discipline, any of the children. I always learned a lot of good things from my grandmother, even though I was not able to internalize some of those lessons until later in life. Many years later, while sitting in prison, some of her lessons and messages would randomly come to mind, and the truth of her wisdom always hit home. My grandmother's words have inspired me to become a better individual. I learned to make do with the things I have. An example of how they made do is a "black and white" picture of me. The picture is of me standing in front of a sheet that was hanging on a clothes line and used for the purpose of a background. I was around four or five years old at the time, but the picture came out badly because of the funny look on my face; I am very glad that it is not shown in this book!

While I really enjoyed being able to visit my dad and the rest of my family in the south, the time to return home came pretty quickly and I left again with my uncle. It was sad to leave, and I may have shed a tear or two when it was time to go. After my safe return to Delaware, my mother was confident that my dad would send me back whenever I went to visit him, and it soon became normal for me to visit my dad each year. On one of my visits, I discovered the truth behind his lifestyle: my dad was involved in the drug trade. While I didn't know the extent to which he was involved, I chose to disregard the severity of this truth. My dad was probably my first real-life hero, and I held him in very high esteem.

In a way, I wanted to be like him and possess the strengths that I noticed he had. I was impressed with how strong he was as an individual, and by the fact that he did not take any mess from anyone. Despite the lifestyle that I now knew he lived, he didn't openly promote any of the negative behavior associated with such activities to his children. His method of teaching probably came from the idea, "Do what I say and not what I do." My dad did his best not to expose his children to the life which he lived, but seeing as I was a very inquisitive child, I quickly began to notice certain things.

My life started out pretty good, but eventually it began to take a gradual slide backward toward the dark side. As I entered my teenage years, I began making my own decisions, some of which were not good. I initially had a good perspective of life, and I was considered a smart child; soon, however, I began to decline in my academics and teachers started sending home notes about the fact that I was having difficulty paying attention in class. I became involved in delinquent behavior instead of working hard at a job or other productive project. I slowly began to transition from a smart young boy into a lazy, irresponsible young adult. It can sometimes take only a minute to get into trouble and a lifetime to get out of trouble and I fell into a habit of finding those crucial moments. Within a mere couple years, I unknowingly followed my dad down the wrong path. I developed a sense of low self-esteem, and I did not feel good about myself at all. I had no idea of who I was, as a person, or what I wanted to do in life. Despite the goodness around me, I felt very empty deep inside my heart. This emptiness begged me to find something, *anything*, to fill that void.

Chapter II
Whose Problem Is It?

I can't blame any one person for the vicious cycle that I was born into; while we all individually made poor decisions, I am the only one to blame for my participation in it and for the choices that I myself made. We all had a choice to do something other than the wrongs which we did. I made poor decisions; my dad made poor decisions, my younger brother made poor decisions, and a few of my cousins made poor decisions. I also have uncles who made poor decisions throughout their lives. Each of us faced a variety of challenges in our lives, but facing challenges was never, and will never, be the problem; everyone on this journey of life has a very high chance of facing challenges. The problem, then, lies in how we each respond to those challenges. The common denominator within my family, the common response to life's challenges, was making poor decisions. Some of our intentions may have been good, in a way; I can say that my intention was based merely on wanting to make things better for myself, to be able to buy new clothes, to take better care of myself and be able to help others. Regardless of what our intentions might have been, however, our individual actions eventually led us to a common place, and that common place was prison.

When I entered my teen years, I found myself overwhelmed with a variety of negative feelings which included low self-worth, lack of confidence, and a lack of faith in both whom I was and who I could become. I attempted to minimize these feelings by self-medicating. I did not like the person that I was or the financial situation that my mother was in. I knew that I didn't want to be poor for the rest of my life, but I did not realize that I was making matters worse by allowing the negative feelings to take control. Metaphorically, I guess that I was attempting to ease the pain by punching the sore. I had become very frustrated and angry about my own life, and I eventually decided to get involved with the drug trade as an avenue to earn money; my dad was a drug dealer, and he had plenty of money. As well, the thought that I was bucking against a system through which I seemingly did not have any opportunities to succeed gave me a sense of empowerment.

While I now realize that my perception was flawed, the reality was that my young heart was full of hurt and pain, and I did not like the person that I saw when I looked in the mirror. I chose to accept a number of lies about whom and what I could become, and I began medicating my problems with drugs, and sometimes alcohol. Very quickly I realized that once I was sober, the problems were still there, and that I then had to get high again in order to minimize the pain; I got sober again, and the problem reappeared. Each day, this process was repeated, but I soon found that getting high and living the life which I was living was not my only problem. There were other deeper issues also going on for me, my younger brother, my cousins, and some of the guys that I grew up with in the housing projects. We each had our own issues to deal with, and we each made our individual choices in response, many of which ultimately led us to prison. It was like there was a carrot dangling in front of our faces which distracted us from the big picture; the big picture shows us the destruction behind the glamour, and the damage which we were causing, or would cause, within our own communities.

The vicious cycle within my family was similar to the reality for many of those within the housing projects in which I was raised. Many of my close friends were sent to prison, as were their family members—dads, sons, grandsons, brothers, and cousins serving a variety of sentences—and this was considered normal. Sometimes families hated each other, and fought against each other as enemies; I never experienced this in my own family, but the ramifications of my actions on those around me were as damaging as if I'd chased them down with a loaded gun. We have all heard the statement, "One bad apple can spoil a bunch," and I am here to admit that I have been a bad apple on many occasions. My decision to get involved in the drug trade forced me to mislead others; many of my poor decisions affected both my own life, and the lives of those around me. My younger brother has been to prison on more than one occasion, and while I am not sure whether this was directly or indirectly related to my behavior, I do know that I could have done a better job as a big brother.

Some may argue that the dynamics within low income housing projects like those in which I lived, namely the economic status, social status, and limited educational opportunities, are the underlying causes of these realities. While I believe and understand that there are correlations between these factors, I also hold fast to the idea that individuals aren't born to behave in such ways. There are two questions you may want to ask those of us who grew up in the aforementioned communities, first: "How can a person throw away their own life for a place such as prison?" and, second: "How can a family throw away their own generation to a place such as prison?" Someone looking in from the outside might say, "The family should be able to wake up, and just stop doing wrong."

As someone who was raised in various housing projects, I can tell you that to simply "stop doing wrong" is often not that easy a thing for a family to do. It is crucial to understand that the vicious cycle was initiated by a particular act at a particular time in the past, and each additional act only contributes to that cycle. The ability of most parents to effectively guide their children and steer them around the many arrows that sit and wait for them is, the majority of the time, nearly impossible. Ninety-five percent of the families in our housing projects were headed by single mothers; many of these single women did a great job raising children in the absence of fathers and worked very hard. Some held two or three jobs in order to sufficiently provide. This meant that, while the mothers were out working, the children were left to hang out with friends, learning both good and bad habits and behaviors from one another. In many cases, the habits and behaviors learned were not conducive to becoming a productive human being.

In addition to such external influences as the absent dad epidemic, there are internal factors that also contribute to the vicious cycle. On many occasions, I found myself holding on to the hope that something good or better was just around the corner. When things didn't go how I expected them to, I often became discouraged. At an early age, my hope began to diminish. While there are a few who become lazy and expect others to give them what they want, I quickly decided to take what I wanted on my own, at any cost. I wanted money, and I would sell drugs to get it. Negative pressures from media and social networks often portray this mindset, and I, along with many of those around me, bought in to it.

The prospect of getting what I wanted correlated well with the sense of low self-esteem that plagued my community. I knew that many of the teenagers and young children in my neighborhood also experienced these feelings, and I would learn many years later that a lack of love for one's self is often closely connected with poor decision making. Selling drugs in the streets is actually putting one's life on the line, and this makes it very easy for us to hate one another, in addition to ourselves. The absence of good formal education further pushed us to doubt our ability to succeed outside of street life. Few educational opportunities resulted in a lack of a GED or high school diploma, pursuit of a vocational trade, and marketable employment skills necessary within the competitive job market; what remained was a ubiquitous sense of discouragement and worthlessness. I thought with such a mindset, and I did not believe in my potential to succeed via the "American way." While I respected others and did not bother anyone who did not bother me, I was angry and bitter, and had many thoughts of dissatisfaction running through my mind. I viewed drug dealing as the only way possible to get what I wanted; I envisioned myself becoming a successful drugs dealer who would retire rich; the reality, however, is that the odds of making it in the drug game are low.

After making the decision to become a drug dealer, things didn't change in the ways I expected. My dissatisfaction with life drove me to turn to drugs for my survival; my perceptions of myself, as well as of the world around me, were the determining factors in my decision-making process. I would learn later, however, that my perception of life at this time was wrong. I didn't realize that what I wanted and deserved in my life could not be found in drug dealing, and my decision began to add to the vicious cycle, or curse, within my family and community. I viewed being a drug dealer as a positive change to my life; I saw that my dad was successful, and there were many others in the game who lived attractive lives. I disregarded the realities of certain negative personal experiences, and was accepting of the truths of life on the streets. The reality is that everyone is not promised to come out alive, and many times those who did come out of bad situations were beat and banged up, both mentally and/or physically. I gained many permanent scars during this time, both emotional and physical, but I foolishly saw these things not as a sign that I was making poor choices, but merely as familiar components of being a drug dealer.

My family life was filled with many different dynamics. Though my family was blended, I had, and still maintain, a good relationship with both sides of my family, my mother's and my father's. As with any family unit, there were many situations that various members experienced that were good, bad, and ugly. While I understand that this is common, I think it is necessary to highlight the fact that we each responded to these types of situations differently. Within my family, there were many of us who did not do a good job when it came to dealing with bad, poor, and even some good, situations.

An average family may be able to outline a number of accomplishments within their unit, as well as failures they have experienced. From my earliest memories, there were a number of good things I enjoyed and celebrated about my family and I was thankful for the family that I was born into.

There are also components of my family that I am not necessarily proud of; I guess that these could be categorized as failures. During my teens, I stepped in stride with the cyclical mistakes of my family; I came of age by joining various family members on the streets. Yes, I made my own decisions and lived with my mistakes, but collectively, my family consistently found themselves in trouble with the law. If it wasn't one family member it was another, and I played a major role in contributing to this reality. I did not see my actions as negative, but merely an acceptable response to the realities around me.

While my mother spoke shamefully of street activity and participation, the majority of those around me seemed to ignore, or even disbelieve, the idea that practicing criminal behavior would continue to set us back and further contribute to an increase in incarceration, homicide, and other crime rates. This life in my community and neighborhood was simply accepted. As a young teenage boy, I was oblivious to the importance of "waking up" to the many traps that existed around me, namely, the means by which I chose to escape from the reality of life in low income housing projects.

Chapter III
My Single Parent Mother

Most of my very young years were spent between my mother's house and my dad's house, although I spent the majority of my time living with my mother. My mother was a single parent who worked hard for minimum pay to raise five children alone. While living with her, I attended school in the state of Delaware; I would visit my dad in Alabama once or twice a year. My dad was more financially stable than my mother, but my mother was a very hard worker; for most of her life, she held two jobs. At the time, I did not see the value in her hard work, but I now respect and appreciate all that she did and how hard she worked for us. There were times when we would have her bath water ready for her when she got home from her first job of the day so that she could get ready for her second job. She would get in the tub, clean up, and head right back out the door. My mother was a very loving and caring person and I learned a lot from her. Even in her absence, she did her best to keep us well cared for and safe; we were not allowed to let

anyone into the house while she was at work.
She prepared us for certain tricks that some
people may try, such as claiming to be our
relative so we would let them in the house.
One exception to this rule was Dexter; he was
my brother's friend and one of my mother's
favorites. There was also Terrell, a very good
and popular dancer, whom my mother
allowed to live with us for a while. My
mother treated him like a son, and we treated
him like a brother. I learned how to cook food
and wash dishes, to respect my elders, and
others.

Though my mother worked very hard to
sufficiently provide for our care, our
household constantly struggled. I did not
understand why we were financially poor; this
conflict began to brew in my heart, and I
started to blame my mother for our financial
state. I understood that she loved us, and we
were taught to appreciate the things which we
had, but I did not want to be poor, and I was
filled with embarrassment and shame. When I
visited my dad I noticed the very obvious
difference between my parents' finances
situations; at my dad's, there was minimal
tension and challenges while at my mother's,
and life was very difficult. Others would tease

us for the clothes that we wore; sometimes we didn't get new school clothes at the start of school, and I often had to share clothes with my older brother. Sometimes we shopped at the Goodwill Thrift Store, or discount department stores such as Gaylord's, but there were times when my mother could not afford to buy us school clothes. In these cases, we would get hand-me-downs or just wear the same clothes that we had from the previous year. I can remember the feelings of dread on the first day of school; everyone else would be in their new school clothes that their parents bought for them, and they would laugh at and tease us for wearing last year's clothes.

While my mother was very loving and caring, she disciplined us by spanking us when we misbehaved. I quickly learned to not cry in the midst of physical pain, even though my brother and sisters would encourage me to cry, saying, "Cry Mark, cry." I was more likely to cry over something emotional than physical. I once got my fingers closed in the door of my mother's old Nova car. The door of that car had a small gap in the door panel; it did hurt my fingers, but there was no real damage done to my hand. I chose not to cry or make a noise because I did not want to get into trouble for getting my hand closed in the door.

When I first arrived in Wilmington, Delaware, I was able to speak both English and Spanish; while living in Spain with my father, the school I attended taught both languages, and whenever I went to the store for my step-mother, I had to speak Spanish. One year while in Spain, I had to wear a clown costume to a school Halloween party, complete with a traumatizing wig and embarrassing red nose; to this day I strongly dislike clowns! I used to tell my mother the meaning of different things in Spanish, and she was always very excited that I was able to speak both languages. I would tell her what a television was in Spanish, and I also knew the word for a television that didn't work (we had a television that didn't work). At that time, I thought that I was fairly smart, and I did very well in my classes. I liked to help my teachers, and to learn new things. I frequently got notes on my report cards suggesting that I was the teacher's pet. At the end of that school year, however, a traumatic experience took place; I did not realize it at the time, but I now see how this change contributed to my descent into darkness. My good grades allowed me the opportunity to be skipped from the 1st to the 3rd grade and, while this seems like a positive thing, I had trouble learning to keep up with the older children, and to focus in class. I day dreamed a lot, and I struggled with paying attention to the teacher. My teachers soon realized that I still depended a great deal on them for assistance, and that I needed more attention than the other children. My teachers decided that I should be put back into my right grade, the 2nd grade, for the remainder of the year, but my confidence immediately started to decline at this point.

My mother was a very good mother in my opinion; she did not have any formal education but she worked hard at two very low-paying jobs from as far back as I can remember. She always put her children first. She was very stubborn, and would not accept any handouts simply because she was a single parent raising five children. When I was very young, she used to receive food stamps (back then food stamps came in the form of colored paper money, not a credit card), but this did not last long because my mother refused to accept assistance. When I used to go to the store with the food stamps, I would only go to the checkout line if it was empty; I was embarrassed by the food stamps, even though everyone in my neighborhood had them, too. There were times when I would head to the line and turn around if someone else was there. Shortly after is when my mother started working two jobs; one of her jobs was at a nursing home where she cleaned up after the elderly, and her second job was at a country club where she cleaned up after other people. My mother worked very hard for many years. She taught us many valuable lessons, though I didn't take many of them to heart until years later; she kept very few secrets from us in her efforts to prepare us for the harsh reality that awaited us out in the world, and was honest about life. She told us about the people who hung out on the street corners selling drugs, and I knew that I did not want to be that type of person when I grew up.

We ate Thanksgiving dinner at my grandmother's house each year. Thanksgiving was a very big holiday for us; everyone would come together and visit with one another. All of my cousins and I always had fun being around each other, and every Thanksgiving we watched two great football games. We would watch the Detroit Lions play during the first game, and we would watch the Dallas Cowboys play during the second game. I was (I still am) a very big Dallas Cowboy fan who enjoyed watching them play on television. I would celebrate when they won, and some of my cousins would tease me whenever they lost. After the games on television, we would play outside, sometimes racing up and down the street.

One year my mother was very upset with some of the family and she refused to take us to our grandmother's house. We were disappointed because we wanted to eat Thanksgiving dinner, and we did not want to miss out on the largest family gathering of the year. When news of my mother's refusal to attend Thanksgiving dinner got around, several family members stopped by the house in an effort to convince her to come to the dinner. My mother ignored the knocking, and refused to open the door. She also instructed us to not open the door. Eventually, however, my mother gave in and allowed us to have Thanksgiving with the rest of the family.

All the lessons my mother taught us were backed by her examples. My siblings and I watched her quit smoking cigarettes, and then return to smoking shortly after. She eventually found the strength to quit for good, but this is one example of how she taught us to not give up. My siblings and I watched her frequently put her life on hold in order to take care of us. On pay day my mother would sometimes buy each of us a famous Italian G and P $2.00 sub. Today, they are still in operation in Wilmington, Delaware, and I have many fond memories of the incomparable taste and size of a G and P sub. Despite the fact that we were economically poor, my mother somehow managed to provide us with many good times. If there wasn't enough food for all of us, she would do without so we could eat. I have seen a number of family photos in which my mother had spent her small wages to buy one of us a birthday cake. If there is a parenting award, then my mother would be a great candidate for it. We were taught the difference between right and wrong, how to take care of ourselves in the home, how to cook meals, and to treat everyone fairly and with respect. My mother preached adamantly against stealing and taking things that did not belong to us.

One year, my mother bought me and my brother a pair of metal skates. This was the first and only pair of skates that I owned. Whenever I rode those skates, they made a loud sound as the metal scraped against the concrete. While I never really learned how to skate properly, I liked and appreciated my skates very much. Many years later as an adult, we rented the skating rink for my daughter; I put on a pair of skates and realized that I still could not skate! I had to stay close to the wall and I could only go straight forward, no dancing, or turning, or anything else. Skating will never by my strong point, but I do thank my mother for those loud metal skates so many years ago.

During the holidays at my grandmother's house, most of my cousins and I used to walk to her house on the other side of town in order to stay over during the weekend. Whoever called her first was allowed to stay. We would help out around the house and she would give us a few dollars. At that time, penny candy was popular and I would buy between fifty and one hundred different candies. Even later in life when she needed to use a walker and was in and out of the hospital, I really enjoyed sharing time with my grandmother.

If I were to describe the type of child I was, I would probably use such adjectives as "good" or "average." Before any of the drugs or criminal activity, I was a fairly normal child; I spent a lot of time playing by myself, and had a collection of Hot Wheel cars that I used to have fun with. I would pretend that the cars were people, and I acted out things that I had seen or heard about. I would pretend that the cars attend parties, and sometimes make the cars get into fights; you could say I had an imagination typical for a young boy. Sometimes, out in the street, I played football games with myself. "How is it possible to play a football game with yourself?" you might ask. Well, I would throw the ball high in the air and run ahead to make the catch. I imagined I was a player on my favorite team, the Dallas Cowboys, and was playing against another team; most of the time my team would win, but once in a while I would allow the other team to win.

I also used to play football with my cousins and friends sometimes. They all liked to play "free for all" football, which is where someone throws the ball into the air and everyone plays for themselves. I never wanted to get the ball during these games because everyone would tackle the person who caught the ball. After a while, someone caught on to my dislike of the game, and they would throw the ball to me so that I would get tackled. I used to be afraid of heights, and I can also remember being afraid to walk across bridges, even flat ones. Throughout the city of Wilmington, there were a few bridges we had to cross whenever walking to the other side of town. Everyone else would walk straight across the bridge, and I would stop and hesitate. Despite the fact that I was afraid, my cousins and friends would keep walking and threaten to leave me. Eventually, I would get the courage to run across the bridge, but the process would be repeated on the way back and every following time.

One time, some of my cousins and I stayed the weekend over at my Aunt Shelly's house. This particular aunt had very clear, and sometimes stringent, rules in her house. We weren't allowed to play the radio, and with all of her rules, there wasn't much for us to do. While playing in the backyard, we got creative. We were all growing pre-teens and wanted to show our strength. Our aunt had an old garage in the backyard that had an old door, and we decided that we would take turns locking each other inside. The goal was to see which one of us was strong enough to fight our way out. Well, I am not quite sure how, but one of us managed to break the door to the garage; needless to say, our aunt found out about our misdeed, and was furious! Not only did we damage her property, we mindlessly destroyed something that wasn't ours. Inside, she told us to line up as she pulled out her belt; she placed one of my cousins in the chair face first and then sat on top of him. I knew that I had done something wrong, and I was terrified that my turn was coming soon. I knew that my aunt loved us and only wanted us to teach us a lesson, but after that I was hesitant to do a sleepover there ever again!

As I got older, my grades began to decline significantly. When I was once making A's and B's, I was now also making some C's and D's. Once in high school I began to make a few Fs. My mother refused to accept my low grades, and she never deviated from her expectations that we work hard and try our very best. I did not want to try my best, however, because I didn't think that I was smart; the incentive I once had to please my teachers had diminished, leaving me to merely go through the motions of life. Growing up in the ghetto had many challenges, but until my early teens, I blindly accepted the realities of being raised in a low income household. In school I received a free lunch card so I could order food, and in the summer, the city gave out free lunches in the park, compliments of the Parks and Recreation Department. They would serve things such as sandwiches, fruit, and milk; I enjoyed whatever they served, but especially loved it when they served chocolate milk. For me, my siblings, and friends, chocolate milk was considered a delicacy! The loss of incentive I felt only added to my discouragement and depression; I no longer wanted to blindly accept being poor, and the slope toward prison grew more and more slippery.

Parks were popular in the city for a couple of reasons. For one it was one of the main gathering places for teenagers; the Parks and Recreation Department offered a number of games out for us to play, such as checkers, chess, jumping rope, hula hoops, and basketball tournaments between different parks. When the free lunch truck arrived, those who volunteered to unload the food from the truck had first chance at any extras. There were some people who would follow the food truck from one park to another in order to get another lunch. During the day, local DJs would bring their music equipment and throw block parties, and everyone would stay for the movies that played at night.

There were a few main parks in the city that my friends and I would hang out at; Prices Park was a rather popular spot, perhaps because it had a free swimming pool that a lot of people would swim in. On the west side of town there was a park on 6th and Madison Street; many of the guys from that side of town hung out there. There was the 24th Street Park and the 30th Street Park, both of which were on the north side of town. The Brandywine Park was positioned more or less in the center of the city and while it was not the biggest park in Wilmington, its neutral location attracted those coming from each side of town. The Brandywine River runs through The Brandywine Park; often cars would park up and down the street and a steady flow of traffic would ride slowly through. Summer brought visitors from places like New Jersey, Pennsylvania, New York,

Baltimore, and D.C. While individuals from a variety of areas mingled at the park, each side of town would usually congregate in a certain area. Everyone would drink beer and smoke marijuana, or just sit and chill. My friends and I enjoyed these social weekend events. The crowd would probably start dying down around 6:00 pm and everyone would then head back to their own side of town.

Hanging out with my friends provided somewhat of a distraction, albeit temporary and periodic, from life at home. The blame I placed on my mother for our economic status created bitterness in my heart; this attitude led to me to disrespect her. It started very subtly and then grew overt. I began talking back to her under my breath and she would ask, "What did you say?" I feared my mother and the consequences that came with my actions, and I did not want to get hit in the mouth, on the head, or anywhere else within her reach. I would reply, "Nothing," but these interactions quickly escalated into cursing, and accusing her of loving my brother more than me. Spending time away from the house allowed me to ignore the feelings I felt toward my mother and subsequently minimize our interactions

Chapter IV
Street Exposure

Wilmington, Delaware, is a small city located in the heart of the northeastern coast of the United States. There are a lot of ghetto-type areas with row houses and one-way city blocks; though it is small, it has many of the elements of large cities, such as a high crime rate. A 2014 *Newsweek* article by journalist Abigail Jones named Wilmington, Delaware, "Murder Town USA," and highlighted the examples of Wilmington's reputation as being one of the most dangerous small cities for many years. Wilmington is surrounded by a number of other cities which, in many ways, makes matters worse. During my teens, I became very familiar with our bordering cities; around 20 miles to the north is Philadelphia. The Delaware Memorial Bridge leads drivers onto the New Jersey Turnpike who, within a short time, will then reach the cities of Camden, and Trenton, New Jersey. Also a straight shot up the New Jersey Turnpike are the cities of Newark, New Jersey, and Jersey City, New Jersey. New

York City is less than two hours away, and Baltimore, Washington, D.C., and the state of Virginia are an hour and a half south.

Due to the close proximity of these larger cities, a lot of out-of-state people pass through Wilmington; local drug dealers have a variety of choices when it comes to finding a supplier or connection, and the city is subsequently central to heavy drug traffic. Drug dealers either pass through, or otherwise find their way into the city, perhaps to run from crimes committed in other cities or to rob one of the many drug dealers who reside in Wilmington. According to statistics given in 2012 by the Delaware Health and Social Services, HIV rates in Wilmington are comparatively high, with African Americans making up 66% of all known HIV and AIDS cases. The combination of all these factors creates a sad reality for this small city.

I was exposed to drugs and the street life at a very young age. Even before becoming a teenager I experimented with a little beer; a few of my uncles, all of whom held good jobs and worked hard all week, would get together once in a while and drink beer. I think that this was their way of repaying themselves for their hard work, and sometimes they would share their celebratory beverages with me. There were a number of times when my uncles would tell me, "No" when I asked for the beer, but my persistence usually paid off and they would sneak it to me. My mother would not have approved at all, and they would tell me that I better keep it a secret. I was cool with that, and I enjoyed the opportunity to be around those uncles and listen to them talk; I gained a lot of knowledge from them as they spoke about life, and old times.

My mother moved us in with our Aunt Angie and Uncle Jay. My mother's family was close like that; she had previously allowed one of her brothers to move in with us, and we lived with our aunts and uncles on two separate occasions. When we moved in with this particular aunt and uncle, my Uncle Randall also came with us, which created an interesting experience. In that one household there was my mother, my uncle, my brother, my three sisters, my three cousins, and my aunt and uncle. My three cousins were: Edgar, Lil' Jay, and Makel. We all got along with one another fairly well and there was only minor tension in the house; mostly I remember good times that we had while staying there.

My mother wanted very much to get her own place for us to live in, but at this time my aunt and uncle were more financially stable than we were. My Aunt Angie and Uncle Jay had a nice home on the north side of town, and they both had good jobs. They were able to buy things for my cousins like name brand jeans and clothing. In their living room, they had a floor model television that they later used as a stand for another television. I can remember watching *Cornbread, Earl and Me* on that floor model television. Sometime later, my aunt and uncle decided to get separated and she moved out, although I was too young at the time to really know the reason for their separation. After my aunt moved out, my uncle's house became somewhat of a hangout for family; a few of my uncles would come over and drink beer and socialize with one another. My cousins started having more of their friends come over, and even after we moved out, I stayed the night there on several occasions when I wanted to spend time with my cousins.

There were a lot of good times, as well as bad times, in that house and I have many good memories of being with my cousins and friends. We had a few friends on that city block; there was Darnel, and he was really good friends with my cousins. There were the twins, Randy and Doelt, who lived at the other end of the block; next to them was Shaw. Even though Randy and Doelt were twins, they were very different from each other; Doelt was short and would later grow no more than five feet, while Randy was tall and would grow to be about six foot seven. Randy ended up going to college and earning a college degree, while Doelt chose to hang with the guys who sold drugs and ran the streets, and he eventually became a drug dealer, too. Everyone that I grew up with on that block, despite the various people they would become, was like family, and no one could mess with anyone.

When I was around eleven years old my mother eventually got approved to get a house; all of us were happy about getting a place of our own because we felt like we were moving on up, just like the Jefferson's. Our new residency was in a housing project unit known as Riverside; even though we were in the projects, it was my mother's own house and she was very excited to be able to provide a roof over our heads. My older brother and I had our own personal reservations about this move but we kept our thoughts to ourselves. While living there, I met a whole new group of friends. I met a guy named Marlon who was a little younger than I was, and I also got to know his sister, his mother, and some of his uncles. What began as a friendship between two normal teenagers who went out and played like everyone else would later transform into a woeful tale of two troubled young men.

Behind our housing project there was a hangout spot, and I started frequenting this area when I was eleven or twelve years old. Previously, the location was an old club and had since been turned into a social gathering spot. There was a juke box and a few arcade games inside, and my friends and I would buy things like soda or hot food and hang out. There was a corner store connected to the hangout spot which sold penny candy, chips, bread, milk, eggs, etc. During this time, our part of the projects was having conflicts with another part of the projects, yet few of us thought much of it; fighting was a normal part of living there. As well, no one thought much of the fact that even with all the fighting, those same "enemies" would stick together when warring against another community.

One particular day while at the hangout spot with friends, I decided to leave early. As I started heading home, I saw a group of five or six guys walking towards me, probably a block away at the time. There was a shortcut that I normally took, a path which cut through a section of the houses, and as I hurried along, I saw the group of guys cut through pretty fast, as if to cut me off. My instincts kicked in; I immediately realized they were chasing me, so I ran as fast as I could. I knew that if I allowed them to catch me, they would have all jumped on me. When I got near one of my brother's friend's house, I yelled out to him as I continued running.

Somehow I managed to lose them, and when I saw that the coast was clear, I walked back toward my house. As I approached, I saw a very large group of people congregating in front of my house; most of them were our friends from that area, but also in the group were the guys who had been chasing me. One of them said that he wanted to fight me and, while I really didn't want to fight him, I was not going to back down. So we fought and, to my surprise, I got the best of him; at one point, when I had him on the ground, one of my younger sisters tried to hit him with a belt. My mother heard the commotion and came outside and told us to come in the house. I made like I was going to follow her, but paused on the back step; I should have listened to my mother and gone inside the house because the guy said, "You got that," and reached and grabbed me and pulled me off the step. He hit me with his forearm and elbow, and my mother had to take me to the hospital that night because, while I was not that hurt, she was worried about all the swelling. Around a week later my brother and his friends went over to the other part of the projects, and my brother fought one of their toughest guys, and easily won the fight. After that it seemed that everyone got along well with one another.

By the age of twelve, I was very familiar with some of the things related to life on the street in the larger cities. I spent time hanging out with my cousins who lived on the north side of town, and I used to ride around with them and their friends. Despite the attention we drew to ourselves by overloading a car with a group of African American males, a bunch of us would pile in and drive all around. We would also chill out in one of the various parks throughout the city; most of them had basketball courts with the metal chains and metal backboards for us to use. Even as young as I was, it was normal to see holes cut or torn out in the fencing where people had attempted to make a quick getaway when being pursued by the police.

We did not have much money, but we always found a way to get high. I would ask a couple of my uncles for money and, collectively, I may get around $5.00 or so. We would all pitch in our money to get gas for the car, buy weed and alcohol, and maybe a slice of pizza. Several local pizza shops sold a slice of pizza for seventy-five cents or $1.00. My cousin would put $2.00 in the car for gas, and we would buy a bag or two of marijuana, and a bottle of alcohol. Often we drank Jack Daniels, Hennessey, or Jim Beam, and we would also sometimes buy cheap wine such as Boones Farms, or Wild Irish Rose. Two hours south of the city was a different kind of drug; in the Washington, D.C., and Baltimore area, there was a very potent form of marijuana called "love boat," which had to be rolled into small "pin joints" as a result. A person would take one pull of the joint and pass it, and I heard many stories of how people would hallucinate while high on this particular marijuana. I was too skeptical to ever use it. We eventually graduated to sniffing cocaine, although it quickly became something that we did only on occasion, since it was more expensive. We would usually share a $10.00 or a $20.00 piece, but once in a while we were able to buy a gram. We would ask each other about the numb feeling that we got after sniffing coke.

Our local radio stations didn't consistently play the music that I enjoyed listening to. The local DJs were the most convenient way to hear the music that I enjoyed listening to. Several of my cousins, as well as my Uncle Randall, were local DJs back then, and they did most of the parties in the area. My cousin Makel used to mix and scratch records really well and they would use pennies and nickels to hold down the needle. Once I went to the basement of one of my cousin Rock's house; he had a lot of DJ equipment, and always played the music really loudly. The song "Numbers," by Kraftwerk, was playing and that day is when I fell in love with both that song, and hip hop music. Kraftwerk's music was universal because, while they were a European group, they also appealed to the hip hop audience. The group Soul Sonic Force made the song "Planet Rock" around this same time, and this further expanded my love for hip hop music. The music made by Kurtis Blow, The Sugar Hill Gang, Spoonie Gee, The Treacherous three, Run DMC, and Whodini, among many others, were all major influences in this love which I had for hip hop music.

Rock, actually a friend of my cousin Makel, was like family even though he wasn't an actual relative; as far back as I can remember we referred to him as our cousin. He lived on the north side of town, and his grandmother lived next door to my grandmother on the west side of town in the Hilltop area. Sometimes I went to parties with them; I would sit on the stage, since I was too young to be there, and I would help the DJs by passing them records (I knew which records were in which of the crates). There was a very popular club in the north east section of the city called Studio East, and I became familiar with much of the local talent.

The very first and youngest rapper that I learned of was Rapping Bee, a talented rapper who used to rap at local teenage clubs. He was probably around eleven or twelve years old, and he eventually went on to locally produce a few records in the 1980s. Years later, I crossed paths with Rapping Bee at the prison work release center; he was in his thirties then, and he performed a short talent show. He was working on several new songs, and I was very surprised that he was still writing music and rapping.

There was also Dark Devo, a rapper from the south side of town who lived in the South Bridge Housing Projects. He made a very popular record, and represented the projects that he grew up in; in the late 1980s his record became the famous anthem for our local housing projects. I grew up in the Riverside Housing Projects, and this was my anthem, too. Had these two local talents gone national, Wilmington, Delaware, could have been put on the map! Despite the crime and drugs, Wilmington had it all; there were rappers, break dancers, and a number of other talented acts including very good poets, several female fashion groups, and the East Side Steppers, who performed in many local parades.

Mark Baynard

Both inside and outside of the artistic community, there was a lot of violence. When they weren't at the club or driving around, a lot of teenagers stood out on the street corners, and in the parks. City officials began to enforce no loitering laws and this resulted in more police presence. Teenagers were no longer allowed to stand in one place without officers telling them to keep moving. At this time, the term "bum rush" became popular; this term was used in one of Public Enemy's songs, and it meant to force your way into a place or situation, such as a large group of people who would bum rush the door of a party and get inside without paying. Even though there were some very large bouncers at the door of the local clubs, people would still manage to bum rush the door. The word was also used when a large group of people physically jumped on someone. More than once I saw large groups of people bum rush the local 7-Eleven store. They would heat up sandwiches, make Slurpee's, and take things without paying for them. The issue of bum rushing got so bad that the store eventually had to hire security. The officers would allow only two people inside at a time, and keep the

doors locked until they had paid for their
items and were ready to exit.

Another type of violence was what we
called "beat-down." While it was generally
understood that fights between neighborhoods
were not fair, there were times when people
would instigate a one-on-one fight. As soon as
anyone started to lose such a fight, others
from their neighborhood would jump in "with
the quickness." There was an odd sense of
unity within the community when it came to
things like this, and the old heads would not
allow outsiders to come into their hood and
cause problems. Beneath the overarching
cloud of badness, each community somehow
maintained a sense of togetherness. Neighbors
would borrow things like sugar, milk, bread,
and sometimes eggs, from one another.
Sometimes, in the absence of one household
head, another would correct and guide the
youngsters.

During the day, everyone would chill out
in the park and then go down to the strip on
the north side of town at night. Car loads of
females would come from the other sides of
town; everyone would park, and then just
walk up and down the strip. Talking about it

now, it doesn't sound very exciting but back then it was the place to be, and the thing to do. Very large groups of teenagers would hang in the streets until two or three in the morning. Sometimes a crazy teenager would throw bricks at cars as they were driving by, and things ultimately got out of hand. The increased violence required officials to implement a curfew for teenagers, and police officers began to post up on the corners of each block. If anyone attempted to stop and hang out, the officers instructed them to keep moving. Sometimes the paddy-wagon would pull up at a street corner and officers would jump out and grab anyone within reach.

My previous challenges with education notwithstanding, I eventually made it to high school. At that time, William Penn High School was the largest high school in the state of Delaware; three busses came to our housing projects, and the one I rode on was very crowded, with three people on most of the seats. Besides William Penn, students also had the option of attending one of the vocational schools, if they registered and were accepted. There were a number of trades that were offered to high school students; one of the schools even had a very good basketball team. There was a freshman who went to Howard High named Windful; he was from the same housing projects as I, but he went to Howard High in order to learn a trade, and to play ball. He played for the basketball team and, while he was not the only star on the team, he made stellar contributions. His team ran through the entire state that year, and won the state championship; the entire city supported this team and wanted them to win.

After their win, someone arranged for them to play against a team in Pennsylvania. Chester High School also had a good team, and welcomed the invitation to play against Howard High. The game was held in the Chester High School gymnasium; the game was sold out, and the gym was filled to capacity with Wilmington fans on one side, and Chester fans on the other. The game quickly shifted from a game to a battle between the two cities; even though Chester and Wilmington are two small cities, they are both very dangerous places. When the smoke finally cleared, Howard High came out the victor; the city of Wilmington had something to celebrate, and everyone said that it was a good and exciting game. One of the stars of the team later went to college and his name became popular in the city, taking his skills to the NBA for a few years. Windful, as well, was known throughout the entire city that year, though his life didn't continue down the path of professional basketball.

High school may have been much more difficult for me had I not been joined by good friends. There were a lot of different people that I hung out with at one time or another while living in the projects but Purcey, however, who lived around the corner from where I stayed, had been friends with me for many years. He was taller than I, but that didn't matter to either of us. During my teenage years we became close friends; he was a pretty cool guy to be around, and we had fun together every time we hung out. He would joke a lot, and we went all the way up through our high school years together. He later moved to the other side of town, and our relationship changed, but we continued to show love towards one another whenever we crossed paths. He later made some of the same decisions as I did concerning the streets and that lifestyle, and we didn't know it then, but we would both serve time in prison.

Harry moved to the same housing project, too, from somewhere around New York City or North Jersey, perhaps Brooklyn. When I met him we quickly became friends; we were around the same age, and he later attended William Penn with me, as well. He had a complete New York style about himself; he wore a kangol - style hat, made popular by a young rapper named L.L. Cool J. Everything Harry did seemed to yell "New York City," from his very particular walk to his selective choice in music. He had a lot of new music on cassette tapes, and he also had a boom box, the kind for which the batteries would quickly run out. He used to breakdance, and would sometimes sit his boom box down and perform, even spin on his head at times.

My friends and I were under the impression that getting high was cool. While were still very young, we were not naive; we knew that using drugs was wrong, and were aware of the many drug marches and slogans, such as "Just say no" or "This is your brain on drugs." In and around our projects, we saw the drug marches that sometimes took place within the housing projects, but we also didn't see much change come from all these efforts; after the marches were over, we watched as drugs were still sold and used within the community. There were a number of drug raids that took place, most of which would happen around election time; sometimes individuals on the drug task force would raid the projects and arrest a number of people, other times drug dealers and users would come right back out after some of the drug raids as if nothing took place.

By the time that I was fourteen years old, I was already involved in a lot of different things. Once I hung out with a friend of my cousin, Reague, who was from the north side of town. He was into the drug game, and he allowed me to hang out with him. On this particular day, we sniffed a little coke together before going to the William Penn Housing Projects, located in Chester, PA. Chester, like Wilmington, is a small city that has all of the elements of a large city. After sniffing the coke, we also smoked a few woolies together. Woolies are joints of marijuana in which you put a little bit of cooked coke. Most people would use brown weed to avoid experiencing an upper high and downer high at the same time. I had seen guys smoking coolies while standing on the corners, and I can remember the unique smell they emitted—it's a very terrible smell that is difficult to forget.

Once we got to the William Penn Housing Projects, there was a large crowd of people mingling in the courtyard, perhaps fifty individuals or more. They were all selling drugs, and several people had large zip-lock bags full of powder cocaine, measuring it out to their customers by using a Slurpee straw or by breaking off pieces of the rock of cocaine. They would serve each customer based on the amount of money that person had. They had several empty bags which were of different sizes, small bags for grams and sixteenths, larger sandwich bags for eight balls, quarters, halves, and ounces. I watched as Reague picked up a very large zip-lock bag of cocaine from someone within one of the buildings, and I noticed how much respect he received from the others. I found this to be very appealing, and was oblivious to the amount of danger we were actually in; I knew that there was a degree of danger to the situation, but I felt that I was safe with him, even though we both could have died that night. We were surrounded by a lot of dangerous people who would kill at the drop of a dime.

Another factor that caught my eye that day were the number of Cadillac Deville's that were parked around the project; I learned that hustlers would buy a Cadillac, and fix it up, adding a soft top to the vehicle to give the car a customized look. It was common to see a Corvette, Mercedes Benz, or another such clean vehicle parked around the projects. Later I would look back and realize that I learned a lot of what I knew about the drug game by hanging out with Reague. That evening, Reague dropped me off and went and got his hustle on. I was high and feeling good when I left him, and until now, I have never told anyone who I had been with that day, or what we had done.

For those who want to blame childhood drug use and delinquency on the environment within the low incoming housing projects should take a good look at my brother. We lived in the same house, in the same project; while I chose the streets, my brother chose to better himself. He started working as soon as he was legally able to do so, and each year he worked a summer job in order to help my mother. He worked at McDonald's, for an armored truck company, and a variety of other places. He was always very respectful to my mother, and during his senior year in high school he did half a day at the high school and the other half at a vocational training school. Upon graduating from high school, he went to the military, and later he got married to his high school love. During his time in the military, my brother's wife stayed with my mother; we had been raised in the very same housing project, and she was like family to us.

My brother and his wife soon had their first child together, a beautiful girl for whom my brother was very excited. He was a proud dad, and took good care of her; because he worked hard, my brother was able to buy things for his daughter and his wife. When my mother was able, she also helped him and his small family out a little. My first nephew was born a while later, and while my brother and his wife are no longer together, they have always maintained respect for one another. I love my beautiful niece and nephew, and my former sister-in-law will always be like a sister to me. My brother was always very independent, and focused on the dreams that he had set for himself; even when he was honorably discharged from the military he continued to maintain a consistent job. Had I been willing, I could have learned a lot from my brother about love, life, and dedication. But I wasn't.

While I chose a very different path than my brother, he was always trying to help me better myself. At one of his jobs, he informed the manager that he was soon leaving for the military, and was asked to recommend a good worker. My brother wanted to be able to trust me with such a big responsibility, and since he knew that I wanted a job that year, he recommended me and a friend. His former place of employment was a diner where customers could watch a play and eat dinner at the same time. During the play, coffee was served, followed by dinner, then desert. My friend and I were hired as bus boys and were responsible for setting the tables, bussing the tables, and washing the dishes.

The manager told us that we could eat when we got a chance, but the dishes would stack up too quickly, and too high, and we were always too busy to take a break. The manager constantly told us to hurry up and do this, or hurry up and do that, and while we were busy washing dishes, they would call us to bus the tables. When we started the job, we were specifically told not to touch the tip money; though we never did, the manager often asked us if we touched the tip money. Of course, I always told him no, that I was not into stealing. After the second or third day, my friend convinced me that we were being overworked, and we devised a plan to quit and walk out. Before we could do so, however, I heard my coworker arguing with the manager, and then I watched as he quit and walked out. The manager quickly came to me and very nicely asked if I could stay and do the work. Despite the fact that he offered me a raise right then, I respectfully told him that I could not do all that work by myself because the dishes were pilled too high in the kitchen. He begged and begged, but I walked out and quit my job. I went to a phone booth and called for a ride, not thinking about how foolish I was, or how bad we made my brother look. Without a job, I returned to hanging out on the street.

Life on the street wasn't all drugs and alcohol. I enjoyed the many festivals that were held throughout the year in Wilmington. Even today, the festivals are filled with large crowds, and there are new people to meet at each of these main festivals. I specifically remember the Italian Festival, the African

American Festival, and the Puerto Rican Festival. The Puerto Rican Festival was held on the Hilltop area on the west side of town, home to a very close-knit Puerto Rican community. The African American festival was originally held on the east side of town, and this festival will always be significant because it represents the majority of the city's population. Festivals are usually a time of peace in Wilmington, when everyone can come out and enjoy themselves. Often the theme is about peace and unity, and the vibe is always positive and friendly. The only difficulty within the African American community is that of preventing beefs from spilling over into the festival. The Italian Festival was held on the top of the hill on the west side, in the Little Italy section of the city, where there was a strong sense of Italian pride. Generally, this was a very quiet neighborhood in which the Italians lived, but it was not quiet during the week of the Italian Festival! There were venders who sold Italian food, musicians performing shows, and there were even carnival rides. Of all the festivals in Wilmington, the Italian Festival is the most multi-cultural; even though the majority of Wilmington's population is African

American, the Italian Festival is the biggest and the oldest.

When there were no shows or events to attend, my friends and I would listen to the radio. Wilmington had a local radio station that came on once in a while, and we would also listen to a station out of Philly, Power 99. We listened to Power 99 more than to our own local station or to the other New York hip hop or R&B radio stations. There was a radio personality on the Philadelphia radio station that I always loved to listen to; she was hot, and used to play the latest hip hop. Every Sunday she was on the air from 12:00 pm until 6:00 pm, and when she first came on, she would always say, "Start your tapes." My tape stayed in the cassette deck with the record button pushed down and the pause button engaged. I stayed ready to get the newest rap music from the radio, and I had a lot of cassette tapes with music and the radio personality's slogan on it. She would give all of the neighboring cities a shout out over the radio; I saw her once at the Spectrum in Philadelphia during one of the concerts. The spectrum is the old basketball stadium for the Philadelphia 76ers, and when I was young, it was host to a number of memorable events and performers, such as the Fresh Fest Tour, Run DMC, Whodini, Grand Master Flash, and others. I also saw L.L. Cool J burst out of a large radio at the Fresh Fest II.

There was a local party and concert promoter in Wilmington name Dane-Dane. His had a business with which he promoted most of the local parties. Some referred to him as the godfather of productions, and most of the parties and concerts in Wilmington during the 80s were produced by his production company. He was large in physical stature and weighed around 500 pounds, but his influence goes back into the 70s and he helped a lot of people during his career. He had his own faults, as we all do, but he provided an avenue for income to some who otherwise may not have had one. Some of my cousins were DJs at a number of events under his productions company, and my Uncle Randall did some work with him. Dane-Dane later passed on to his resting place of eternity, but his contribution to that era of hip hop made a memorable impact on me and my friends.

Chapter V
Seed Planted

My Uncle Jay was a very soft spoken and easy-going individual. He was father to my three cousins: Makel, Lil' Jay, and Edgar. They lived on the north side of town, and I hung out up there often. I especially enjoyed hanging out with my cousin Makel, who used to DJ at a lot of parties at that time; once he met a very talented rapper named Kevin Go. My cousin took him in, and allowed him to stay at their house. My Uncle Jay did not mind additional people in the house, just as long as no one got in his way. Whenever my uncle started drinking, however, he turned in to a totally different person; he would openly speak whatever he had on his mind, and sometimes he was harsh about it. One day, while drunk, my uncle came out of his room; he had a very serious look on his face and he said that he wanted everyone to get out of the house. I knew that he was not talking to his sons, and that he was most likely not talking to me either, because I was his nephew. This was clearly, albeit uncalled for, an attack on my cousin's friend, Kevin Go.

In addition to his natural musical talents, Kevin Go was also a natural-born hustler. He would go out and come back with new clothes and brand name glasses. He eventually became more popular as a rapper, and started doing shows for money. When my Uncle Jay put him out, I asked Kevin Go if he would like to stay with us at my mother's house; I told him that we could walk down to my mother's house right then and ask her if he could stay there. At the time, my mother did not know him, or anything about him. We walked several street blocks from my cousin's house on the north side of the city to my mother's house in the projects on the north east side. I can't remember if I asked her or if he asked her, but I do remember that she said, "Yes." Kevin and I became close, and soon considered one another brothers; he continued to do live rap performances at local parties, and we hung out for some of the summer until my dad sent for me. I left for Alabama, and Kevin Go stayed behind. He was a likeable person and established a few friends within the housing project and became well-known throughout the city.

Back in Alabama, things with my dad were good. Within his household lived my dad and his wife, my brother, and two sisters. I am the oldest of my dad's children, and my younger brother was excited to see me every time that I came to visit. I was always very happy to see him and my sisters. We had a very good relationship, my brother and I, and he knew that I had his back and I knew that he had my back. During each visit, he and I would always pick up where we left off from the previous year; at that time, music would come out in the north before it hit the south, and I would share some of the new music with him that I had heard. My brother and I truly enjoyed being together and we had all kinds of fun. We would exchange stories about life in our separate regions and I told him stories about the gang wars between different sides of towns up north.

On one occasion, we were traveling on vacation to visit family in the Washington D.C. area. My dad was driving one of his vans, and my younger brother and I sat in the back on one of the bench seats. We eventually got on the floor to play the card game UNO; we were gambling against one another, and having a blast. I initially won most of my brother's money, and at that point I told him that I was done playing. He wanted to keep playing, but I said, "No;" my brother threatened to tell on me if I did not continue playing, so I conceded. As I figured, my brother got the lucky hand all of a sudden and won most of his money back, then told me that *he* was done playing. I demanded the chance to win my money back, but he refused. Now it was my turn to threaten him, but he had the nerve to shrug me off! I lost my money that day, but we both knew we would never betray each other.

My dad was a real go-getter. He took good care of his children, and even though I did not live with him, he would sometimes send for me during the holidays or during the summer time. There were several occasions when he sent money, and came up north to visit. My dad left home at the very young age of sixteen to find work; when he was of age, he went into the military, and later settled down and got married. When he wanted something, he went out and got it for himself. During many of my visits to his house, I remember doing things with him that we could not afford to do with my mother. He tended to be very organized in everything that he did, and there were rules that he expected us to follow; even the way he dealt with his friends was structured. He dabbled in a few business ventures, but I do not think that he took those seriously. He owned all kinds of vehicles, from a Mercedes to a Cadillac, various boats, and even eighteen-wheelers. My dad lived in a nice house; it wasn't very big, but it was nice, and each time I visited, there were new home improvements which had been done. One year he re-did his kitchen and dining area, another year he cemented an area in the backyard for cookouts and family gatherings. My dad did a lot of traveling, so he put burglar bars on the windows and doors to provide protection for his family and for his own peace of mind during his absence. Over the years, he converted the driveway into a horseshoe style driveway, and edged it with lights and flowers, added a swimming pool in the backyard, and put an addition on to his house. He also built a wooden deck in the backyard, and converted his garage into a lounge area. My dad will probably never get back all the money that he put into his house, but his life was a lesson to all of us on the importance of family, something that I have never forgotten.

My dad was a very strict man, but he was fair. I didn't see it that way when I was younger, so I can only speak of his fairness in hindsight. Even though he did a lot of things for us when we were young, I saw him as a mean man. The reality, however, was that he understood the dangers associated with his lifestyle, and he wanted to protect us. As a result, there were a number of restrictions; my brother and sisters and I were not allowed to give our phone number to anyone, and we also had to get permission if we wanted to walk to the store. Life with my mother was very different, and I was not used to these kinds of boundaries. Earning an allowance was also new for me, as was having regular chores to do. My dad required us to rake the yard and put the leaves in garbage bags, vacuum the swimming pool and pick the leaves out of the water. After school, the chores came before our homework.

Even though I hated the work, I slowly began to develop a good work ethic; I learned a lot of good lessons from my dad, and he was very active in my life, even though I did not live with him all year round. In addition to teaching us how to work hard, he also wanted us to use our money wisely. I learned this lesson the difficult way, albeit quickly. The very first time I received my allowance, I started buying a lot of fast food; my dad would say, "You sure are spending a lot of money," but I still went out and bought food whenever I was hungry. Shortly after that, when I needed deodorant or other hygiene products, or a school book, I asked my dad to buy it for me. Up until that point, my mother always bought me things like deodorant, and would also wash our clothes for us. My dad told me that I would have the money to buy the things I needed if I had not been foolish with my spending. From then on, thanks to my dad's lessons, I began to understand the concept of being responsible.

That year, at the age of twelve, my younger brother got arrested for possessing a handgun. Even though he was released later that day, I was the one who got punished. My dad felt that I should have been more responsible as the older brother, and set a better example. At the time, I was in total disagreement with his logic, though years later I would see that there was a method to his madness. My dad was trying to instill in us that family is very important, and that we should look out for one another. I did not take seriously my chances to set a good example for my younger to follow. I had a lot to learn about life, but wasn't very interested in doing so.

Two of my cousins from Connecticut, Terry and Kelton, recently moved with us and, being around the same age, we attended Lanier together. Even though my dad had several vehicles at the house, I used to ride to school with my cousins. One of my punishments for not setting a good example to my brother was that I was no longer allowed to ride to school with them; I had to walk, which I hated. We decided that I would leave the house for school, and walk up to the store, where my cousins would pick me up and we would all head to school. On the way home from the school they would drop me off at the same store, and I would walk home. One day, I walked into the house after school and saw my step-mother and my aunt sitting in the front room with my cousins. As soon as I saw their faces, I knew that we were busted; somehow they had seen what we had been doing, and for the next few days all three of us had to walk to school.

One year while my dad was having concrete poured in the backyard, he let me help the guys who were working. They allowed me to push the wheelbarrow full of concrete, and my dad was bragging to the other workers about how strong I was. Just knowing that he believed in me made me feel strong and confident. I think that I weighed about one hundred fifty pounds at this time, and I did not see myself as being big or strong at all. My heart and will were a lot bigger than my physical stature. My job was to push the wheelbarrow from the cement truck to the place where they were pouring the cement. On one of the trips, I began to struggle; my arms were tired and they began to shake, causing me to lose control of the wheelbarrow. Suddenly, it became too heavy for me to keep balanced, and it tipped over. I always wanted to make my dad proud of me, and all I could think was that I had disappointed him and that he was going to be mad at me for spilling the concrete. Instead of getting angry and reprimanding me, my dad did something that really surprised me; he looked at me and said, "Go ahead son, just go get another load." He told one of the workers to pick up the cement off the ground that I had spilled. At that moment I felt really good on the inside, and this experience was very motivational to me.

When I was sixteen-years-old, my mother wanted me to go live with my dad; I left Wilmington and relocated to Montgomery, where I attended 11th grade at Sidney Lanier High School. While I had not gotten into any serious trouble up to that point, my mother was concerned and believed that my dad could help me get on the right path. The problem was not the city of Wilmington, however, and I took my troubles with me to Montgomery. No matter where I went, I found a way to get high, and people to get high with. I found ways to secretly smoke marijuana and sniff cocaine even while living with my dad. Whenever I do something, I tend to do it hard, and this applied to my drug use. Once when I was traveling on a Greyhound bus, I got high in the bathroom at a bus stop with complete strangers; I noticed a group of older guys getting high, and I pulled out product and joined them.

"You can take the boy out of the city, but you can't take the city out of the boy" is a true saying. I used to smoke weed on one of the main walkways to the school, and as other students would walk by, I would offer marijuana to them by reaching it out. Most of the time the other students would accept my invitation to get high, but sometimes they would "Just say no." I would go in the bathroom and sniff coke, and when others walked in I would offer them some. They would usually look at me with surprise, and either says "No" or just laughs and walks away. After a while, the reputation I was building for myself began to backlash; females who used to smile at me now just shook their heads as they walked by, and the ones that used to like me no longer did. I stayed high all day while at school and everyone seemed to know it, despite my efforts to hide it by putting Visine in my eyes and chewing gum to cover the smell. I eventually found the students who used drugs; I connected with a few guys, and it was a must for us to get high before school.

One particular day, my teacher was calling us up to his desk to show and discuss with us our scores from the previous day. When I went forward, he smelled marijuana on me; he asked me if I had been smoking and I quickly told him, "No, sir." He then asked me if I had been riding in a car with someone who was smoking marijuana, and I told him, "Yes, sir." Be it my proficiency at deception or the aura of innocence I projected, my teacher simply asked me to agree to not ride with those guys anymore. I agreed and, thankfully, I did not get sent to the principal's office; I would have most likely gotten suspended from school and my dad would have come down on me hard for being so reckless.

That year, Sidney Lanier High School had a pretty good basketball team. They had a very tall player, Michael, who stood around six foot ten inches; he was not a skinny tall person, he was a big tall person. When the team would break the huddle, they would throw up a towel in the air and Michael would stick his hand up and catch it. They made the playoffs that year, but didn't make it to the state championship. There was a lot of pride at the school, and a lot of support for the basketball team. I enjoyed attending Lanier, and met a lot of wonderful people there. One of my sisters went to one of the rival schools, Lee High School; her school's basketball team was not as good as ours but they did have the best football team in the state, ranked #2 or #3 in the nation. Michael played football, too, but his abilities on the court were better than those on the field. On my birthday that year, my sister's school's football team played against my school's football team, and they beat us pretty bad! Lee High School went undefeated the rest of the season, and won the state championship.

Though my dad had very strict rules for us to follow, he would occasionally allow me and my brother to go to the high school basketball games. Whenever I was given permission to go to a game, I was required to take my younger brother with me. I knew that basketball games usually last around two- or two-and-a-half-hours, and this gave me an opportunity to hang out with some of the guys, and also let me do what I wanted to do, namely, go out and chill while getting high. I would tell my younger brother to meet me back at a certain place, at a certain time; he never told on me because he also wanted to hang out with some of his own friends.

There was one specific time when I got permission to go to a basketball game. I wanted to go hang out with my friends, and so I convinced my younger brother not to go. Instead of going to the game, my friends and I smoked marijuana and drank alcohol. I still had plenty of marijuana and cocaine in my possession at this time. I also had a pistol on me, just in case my friends got crazy. For some reason, we decided to drive over to the other side of town, and on the way back their car broke down. One of my friends got out and went to a nearby phone booth to call someone to come and get them. When the person arrived, he told me to call someone to come pick me up. I knew that I could not call me dad to pick me up because I was supposed to be at the game, not hanging out with friends. I did not know what my dad would have done if he found out, but I didn't want to know; I was running out of options and it was getting close to the time that I needed to get home. The guys did not leave me there, but waited to see what I was going to do.

Right then, a police car pulled to stop at the red light with two officers in it. I approached the vehicle and asked if they could take me home; I probably looked like I was around thirteen or fourteen years old. To my surprise they told me to get in. I sobered up real quick when I got into the patrol car, and at that moment, I was one of the most respectful young men in the city. The officers asked my name, and I told them; I was more concerned about what my dad would do if I did not make it home on time than the fact that they were questioning me. They pulled in to the driveway of the house and I got out, but they didn't leave until my step-mother opened the door and let me inside. They backed out of the driveway and drove off, and I hoped that she just saw the headlights and not the fact that it was a cop car. Whenever I came home under the influence of drugs, I would always act like I was tired in an effort to disguise the "high" look on my face. Just like at school, I used Visine for my eyes, and had gum to cover the marijuana smell. My dad was not home at the time, and I managed to vaguely answer my step-mother's questions about how things went before I went off to my bedroom and passed out.

My dad did not allow many people to come over to his house. There were a few of his friends who would come over occasionally, though, most of which were hustlers to some degree. They were cool, and carried themselves in that manner; unlike some of the guys I saw standing on corners back in Wilmington, however, none of my dad's friends would give me anything because they knew that my dad would object. At times, he was known to be a bit extreme when it came to such circumstances so, when no one was looking, I simply helped myself to what I wanted. There was always a refrigerator full of Michelob beer—more beer than he could count or keep track of—and his friends would always additionally bring a couple six packs. My dad would sometimes ask me and my siblings to go get him a beer out of the refrigerator, and I started taking them and drinking them myself. I would hide them out back, or find a place in the house, and drink it really quickly. Sometimes I would take one to school with me. I was smoking marijuana, sniffing cocaine, and now drinking Michelob beer.

One of my dad's friends did allow me to hang out with him once. He was a local musician who dressed well and carried himself well. He knew that I had already been exposed to smoking marijuana. At the time, I thought that I was fast to the game and knew a lot; I was already an active user, and had been around people who sold drugs on the streets. We went to his house and I turned him on to smoking coolies. Coolies are when you put powder cocaine into the back of a cigarette. I really thought that I was showing him something, but I quickly learned that this guy was a lot faster than I was, and he showed me another way to get high; he started cooking the cocaine until it was like crack, and then he took out an empty soda can, and started smoking from it. I had never seen that before, but I kept the activities of that day to myself and did not tell anyone about what I learned. I didn't view my dad's friend differently after he enlightened me to other aspects of drug use, but I did, however, begin to understand why my dad was as strict as he was: he wanted to protect his family from the negative influences that existed outside of the house.

My family in Alabama has a very rich tradition of togetherness. Each year our family holds a reunion, and this tradition has continued for more than thirty years. This event is very important to the entire family, and each year a different family member is given the honor of opening their home, planning, arranging, and being the host or hostess. A few times the reunion was held at a community center. One particular year, my dad sponsored the reunion; his house was a good location, given the fact that he had recently done a number of renovations to his house. He had a swimming pool built in the backyard that had a diving board and slide;

the swimming pool stayed very clean, since
he used cleaning chemicals and a vacuum.
There was also a nice wooded deck that he
installed, which provided an additional social
area in the backyard, especially for the aunts
and uncles who enjoyed sitting in the shade. I
can remember having a lot of fun during the
reunions when I lived with my dad. All of my
cousins, aunts, and uncles from the south
would be there—some would travel one
thousand miles or more from Michigan,
Delaware, Connecticut, New York, and
Pennsylvania—as well as a few local friends,
and everyone swam, played cards, and
enjoyed themselves. Family reunions were not
only an opportunity for everyone to come
together, but also, for many of the elders, to
visit with their loved ones for what was often
the last time. Terry, Kelton, and I enjoyed
throwing others in the pool, and my older
cousin Tozy was always an enthusiastic
assistant. My brother's friend Vadero spent a
lot of time at my dad's house, and the day of
the reunion was no exception; one year,
though we were all under age, we discovered
that the punch was spiked. My younger
brother and I found what we believed to be
corn liquor in the cabinet, and drank quite a

bit of it. We did not tell anyone, of course, because we didn't want our dad finding out.

During this time the family was very close and supportive of one another; the entire family would attend the reunions, and anyone who didn't show up had better have a legitimate excuse. Everyone who lived in Alabama made sure that they attended the reunion. This was one of the last few times that, as a family unit, we were so close, strong, and healthy; young and old alike were laughing and joking and the video camera was running nonstop. Today, the number of attendants at our family reunions had decreased, due to both individual busyness and elders passing on; those remaining are trying hard to uphold the traditions and unity, but things are not the same. The video of this reunion still exists, and I watch it every chance that I get. The majority of the family was there that day; some of those present at the reunion are no longer with us today, and some of my cousins that were very young in this video later ended up in prison. Everyone in the video was living in the moment, and the camera captures well the joy, excitement, and beautiful simplicity of life as we knew it. If it were possible to return to any point in my life, this would be it; I would tell everyone what the future held, and offer a warning, to them and myself, against the curse that would soon come crashing down upon us.

My dad was known for speaking his mind; he said what he meant and he meant whatever he said. I now fully appreciate the directness with which he spoke to me, and the lessons he taught me, but at the time, I only saw him as being unnecessarily strict on me. In a way, I thought that the way he treated me was cruel. He would not allow me to go places alone, and I had to ask for permission to go to the store. I still managed to get high despite all the restrictions, and would smoke a joint of marijuana on my way to the store, or go out in the backyard where the dogs were and smoke marijuana. Eventually, I got to the point of not wanting to deal with it any longer. As a teenager back in Wilmington, I did not have to ask for permission to go anywhere, or to hang out with my friends; I enjoyed the freedom my mother gave me, and I made a personal decision that I was going to do something about my dad's ridiculous rules.

Near the end of the summer of 1986, I asked my dad if I could go back to Delaware.

He told me, "No," and said that he felt I would get into petty trouble. Looking back, he could not have been more right about me, because getting into trouble is exactly what I did. In response to him not allowing me to leave, I decided to make a great escape. One day my younger brother, Terry, Kelton, and I had a few friends over in the swimming pool. My dad had taken some women on a trip, and we were alone for a couple days. I had money in my pocket from the allowance I had earned, and I told Terry I was going to leave while my dad was gone. Terry attempted to persuade me to stay, and even actually begged me once he realized I was adamant, because he thought that life at my dad's was better for me than running away. He also knew that my dad would be very upset when he found out that I had left. We had a long conversation about the matter, and I finally told Terry that this was something that I had to do, and that was final. I assured him that I would not put him in the middle of the situation, and I came up with a plan that I was sure would work. Inside, I called the bus station to get the price and departure schedules, then went and loaded my luggage in the vehicle.

When it was time for me to leave, I made an announcement to everyone outside. I said, "I am going to the store." I wanted everyone to think that I had left alone, but my cousin sneaked out a little while later to pick me up from the store and drive me to the bus station. I needed a one-way ticket to Delaware, but I only had enough money to make it to Virginia or South Carolina, so I called my mother and she purchased the ticket I needed to make it the rest of the way. When I left my dad's house, I was hurt and sad because I wanted to say goodbye to everyone and tell my little brother, my sisters, Kelton, and the rest of my family, that I was going back to Delaware. I did not want to get anyone involved, however, in what I felt was something I had to do. I didn't know if going back to live with my mother was a bad decision, but I felt that it was necessary for me, and I was very stubborn. I do know, however, that this decision caused a number of hardships for me that I would not have experienced if I had only stayed in Alabama!

Chapter VI
Hustling

Life back in Delaware was a lot different than in Alabama. Yes, the weather is usually colder than in the south, and the demographics of Wilmington were rougher in many ways than those of Montgomery. But the aspects I am referring to went beyond these typical characteristics. At this time in my life, I enjoyed hanging out with my cousins and smoking marijuana; I did not have any real goals, and I pretty much did whatever I wanted to. I lived for the moment. In the housing projects, a lot of people sat on green electrical boxes that were scattered throughout the neighborhood. Those green boxes were metal and stood between three and four feet high. We referred to the guys that hung out on the street corners as "corner boys." The main corner boys were the ones who controlled things; they were popular among the local women, and they controlled neighborhood crime and offered protection against outside invaders. Daily life back in the projects meant fights, gun fire, and yelling. Some of the corner boys sold drugs, while others just used the drugs or were mere bystanders. There were also neighborhood "look-outs," or people who guarded against hostile individuals from the surrounding community. All of these, at the time, were roles that *appeared* to be cool.

Looking back, there can be no "cool points" given for this type of behavior. Some of these guys seemed to simply be hanging out for the sake of hanging out, and this did not make much sense to me. Hanging out is one thing, but hustling to make a living is another, and I knew from the beginning that I wanted to hustle, to be like the ones who had nice cars and seemed to make productive decisions. The reality is that these individuals were the neighborhood role models, and I was comforted by the fact that if anyone violated the projects, they had to answer to the corner boys, the look-outs, and the hustlers. I respected the guys who hustled hard in order to take care of their families, and who stood up for what they believed in. Though I was surrounded by very different figures in Alabama, this crowd was most influential to me while growing up. My mother frequently warned us to strive for better, and to not be like the "druggies," as she called them. She did a very good job of putting drug boys in an unpleasant and unappealing light and, because of that, I did not want to be like the druggies. It was many years before I discovered just how right my mother was about a lot of the things she told me when I was young, and I regret my neglect to heed her many warnings. Her warnings, after all, were an attempt to prevent me from hitting the proverbial "brick wall," and I freely, and regrettably, walked right into it.

The distasteful image of druggies that my mother drew was challenged by the very different picture I saw when I lived at my dad's. My dad and his friends made selling drugs look good. While I eventually came to realize that their glorification, and misrepresentation, of such behavior was illegitimate, I saw things differently at the time. My dad appeared to be doing very well for himself; he and his friends were all family men and all had nice houses, and plenty of cars. When I lived with my dad, we went on a lot of family trips, and had a lot of cookouts and family gatherings. Before long, my mother's lessons were thrown out the door and I began to change my thinking. *I wanted to become a hustler.* I felt that I had finally found something that I was confident I could succeed at. I was now seventeen years old and I was ready for the world.

My grades in school were mediocre and, with my prospects for graduating with a marketable GPA being as low as they were, I thoroughly believed that I would not be able to "make it" any other way besides hustling. I placed value on the saying, "It is not what you do, but how you do it." I had seen my dad's crew hustle with great purpose, and this made sense to me; I already knew what it was like to be poor, and I did not want to live like that for the rest of my life. I was familiar with some of the dangers associated with the hustle game, and I knew that getting arrested, robbed, and killed were high on the list. More than once I saw former hustlers become addicts. Despite this knowledge, the game greatly appealed to me and I was still willing to put my life on the line for the game.

Perhaps the biggest difference between living with my dad and living my mother was our financial situation. We also moved from place to place a lot. Each time that we moved, my siblings and I had to change schools and find new friends. At some point or another, we stayed with various aunts, uncles, and cousins in apartments all over town, and lived in the west side, hill top, north side, east side, and Riverside housing projects. I faced most of the trouble that I experienced with the law while we were living in the Riverside projects. I hated living in the projects at first, but it wasn't so bad once I started meeting new friends. I had a lot of personal experiences while there. For many years I have kept in touch with several of those friends, although a lot of them have since dispersed, either caught up in their own situations, passed on, or in prison. A few have moved on to bigger and better things.

When I moved back to Wilmington, both my attitude about life, and the city itself, were going through changes. Unlike when I was younger and more naïve, I realized that I deserved respect, and I vowed to myself that I would demand this from others. I did not go looking for trouble, but at the same time I was not going to allow anyone to disrespect me. Very quickly, I began to see the benefits of maintaining this outlook. One day I happened to attend a party on another side of town, and ran into a childhood friend, Salty. He was with about three or four other guys and I noticed he had a ring on each finger, and that he was dressed nicely. He showed love to those around him, and freely passed out cocaine to whoever wanted some. Salty and I swapped phone numbers, and he told me to get with him. I took him up on his invitation, and walked out to the neighborhood that he was both living in and working. I noticed that his neighborhood was in a racially mixed community, and that, as a result, Salty did business a little differently. He gave credit to a lot of his customers, and collected his money at the end of the week; to my surprise, his customers actually paid him on pay day. He allowed me to hang out with him and see how he did things; I did not have to sell anything, he just wanted an extra pair of eyes and ears. He trusted me inside of his house, too, and I met his mother and his girlfriend.

Salty was not a big-time hustler, but he was getting money. Once he showed me a number of shoe boxes filled with money, and in one of his rooms were rows upon rows of sneakers. He was among the main street hustlers in that neighborhood and he would jokingly say things like, "I turned out an entire community." He was paying me as he was showing me how he did things, although

I cannot speak for the other guys he was training. Salty bought food and we ate well each day; we had some very good conversations, and he would offer a few hints on making money. I didn't do much more than just be there with him, and listen. Surprisingly, Salty did something that most hustlers would not do; he turned me on to a lot of his connections, and took me to Philadelphia were he got his supply from. Additionally, he took me to the place where he bought his nice clothes, and to his jeweler. As shady as the entire situation was, Salty taught me a lot and I have a lot of respect for this brother. He was very fair in his dealings with others, and I know that he treated me good. That was, and still is, real to me. The gate to my new future had been opened.

I have never been the type of person that enjoyed depending on someone else and expecting them to do things for me, and I decided that I was going to save any money that he gave me to jump-start my hustle. I saved up $250.00 and told him that I wanted to buy my own quarter to sell in the projects. At the time, quarters were going for $150.00 to $300.00. I was willing to pay the $250.00 because of the high quality of the product. I also asked him if it was cool for me to start going to his connection, and this brother gave me the green light to go on my own. I refer to him as "brother" because he played the game fair. Actually, he played the game beyond fair, and did not mind seeing others prosper; despite the fact that he received a lot of hate from a few hustlers that he grew up with, Salty didn't hate on others who wanted to make money. Once, I was with Salty and his good friend Yancy at an Eric B and Rakim concert, and the aforementioned haters plotted to rob Salty. Yancy was well-respected in the hood, and the group of guys approached him and asked him to turn a blind eye while they robbed Salty. Yancy wasn't with that, and informed Salty of the plot; we quietly slipped out of the concert early, and went and did something else.

Now that I was on my own, I took the quarter I had purchased and went to the housing project I grew up in. Salty gave me his graces, and I was thrilled. The realities of doing business within this particular project, however, greatly differed from those in Salty's community. There was no such thing as credit in the projects, and the rules of the game were very different, and much more dangerous. The competition was quite steep, and there were a lot of people serving cocaine; the abundance of dealings, however, meant the traffic was heavier. Before becoming a hustler, I did not realize the amount of money that was generated throughout the projects from drugs. Some of the hustlers worked twelve hour shifts, and the drug trade was a twenty-four-hours-a-day market; customers could get served at midnight, or 5:00 am. In the projects, there was a great need for touters, or people who would tell customers who they thought had the best product and bring them to the dealers.

A few years prior, I had tried my hand at the drug game within the projects. I had fifty dollars and wanted to make more. I bought a 16th with my fifty dollars and wanted to make one hundred dollars. I had an older guy with me at that time, and I had to pay him for assisting in selling the drugs. His share might have been most of the profit and I made a mere eighty dollars for my troubles. This time was different, however, since I was more committed to making it happen, and I used a different strategy to get customers. Within the projects, the strong will survive and the weak will be swallowed up by the many elements of the game. I saw no other options for earning a living, and I put my whole heart into making hustling a success. Faced with this reality, I set out for the streets in search of a dollar. Every so often, Salty would come through the projects and checked on me, then he would return to hustling in his community and I in mine. I always appreciated him checking on me, and enjoyed seeing him and sharing good conversation.

There were a number of older dealers who were out there on the "front line," and then a number of us teenagers who fell in behind them. A few of them were even younger than I. These others were not of much concern to me, since I knew I had good product and my clientele was constantly growing. Most hustlers at that time would buy cocaine and add cut to it in order to get a larger profit. This is how the drug game works in most areas. While I needed a speedy way to get in the game, I decided that I would not add any cut to my product and, just as I suspected, my strategy brought customers. Initially, I would break off the rock as I served it to my customers, which gave me an advantage, since my profit margin was not too large at the time and I was able to flip my product very quickly. Sometimes there would be a line of customers waiting, and I would sell my package in less than thirty minutes. The increase in customers was always welcome, but in these situations I had to be extra alert, since there were a lot of people around all at one time. The money started to come fast and I wanted more; my first true payout brought in $500.00, after taking care of my touters. It felt good because the money came quick and I realized that I could make more money by simply purchasing more drugs and staying out longer. I heard many other hustlers speak about how they stayed out through the entire night and made thousands; I was tempted to try this, but never did, and since I did not directly work for anyone, I was able to hustle however and whenever I wanted. There was no deadline to meet except for earning the money that I needed and wanted. I was not greedy, I just wanted to hit and miss and make enough for me. There were some people who did eight, ten, or twelve hour shifts, and would rotate individuals to ensure the greatest income. As I learned how things went, I started making more money, which caused anger and disappointment from my competitors; I did not care, however, and there were times when I would re-up several times in one day. Once my clientele grew, I would add a little cut—Mannitol or Isotol—in order to increase my profit. I felt that I was doing alright for myself, and thought that I was on my way to the top; I had always wanted to show my dad that I could make it on my own, and this was the time. It felt good not to have to ask anyone for anything, and I eventually got to where it wasn't a problem to come up with five or ten thousand dollars at a time. In hindsight, I realized that this wasn't real money, but at the time it was more than I had ever previously had; I was a teenager, and this sure felt like living to me. I thought I was doing something big, and that I had reached a point at which I did not need anyone to help me. My problem was that as quickly as I could make, say, $1,500, I would just as quickly spend it. I bought a lot of new clothes during this time, and different kinds of rings, a different one for each finger.

One day, after my mother had noticed all the clothes and jewelry I had recently bought; she sat me down in her living room and said that she wanted to talk to me. I was kind of nervous because I did not know what she needed to discuss. My mother asked me if I was hustling, and I told her the truth: "Yes."

She told me to be careful because she already knew that, at that point, I had my mind made up and there was no stopping me. That's not to say that she gave me her seal of approval; after speaking with me, she called my dad and told him the bad news. My dad contacted me and spoke to me about it; initially he wanted me to stop, and even asked me, "Son, what are you *doing*?" Just as my mother had, my dad knew that he could not change my mind about it; at the same time, I could hear the disappointment in his voice, and knew he didn't want me to follow in his footsteps. Shortly after that conversation, my dad came up north for a visit and to speak to me face to face. He knew that I was stubborn, but he didn't want me to be out there reckless on the streets without a purpose; he understood the game and the many dangers associated with it. All I wanted was to make a living by myself without having to depend on my mother or my father, and I felt that I was smart enough to do so; I just needed the chance to prove this to everyone else. As sad as it is to say, I think my dad would have preferred that I dealt with him rather than being alone on the streets; it would have been safer, and he also would have been a better plug than the one I had.

Drugs and women frequently go hand in hand, and I became involved with a particular older female name Angle. Some of the community members thought she wasn't good for me. In retrospect, they were right, but at the time I was just having fun. One day while out on the corner, a group of females approached my woman. Among them were Kellen and Lentel. There were two more of which I don't remember their names. They told Angel her that she wasn't right for me, and that she wasn't going to be with me any longer. They jumped on her and beat her down to the ground. I had previously interacted briefly with Kellen, and while there was mutual interest between she and I, nothing had been set in stone and I was still technically going with Angel. After the incident took place Kellen began to come around more often, and on several occasions we hung out on the street and had good conversations. She attempted to prove to me that she was different, and I ultimately chose her. She did seem to be better for me than the other one; she was about six years older than I was, and had graduated from high school a few years prior. She used to help me with my school work, and soon we became very close; when you saw me, she was not far behind. We sat out on the green boxes in the projects while I sold drugs, and when I went to the city of Philadelphia to buy clothes, she was right there with me. Kellen had my back while I hustled in those streets. She became an extra set of eyes for the backstabbers. She was also the one who initially turned me on to smoking woolies, and was the first person I actually smoked woolies with; previously, my main choice for getting high had been sniffing coke and smoking marijuana. Woolies marijuana joints with cooked up cocaine inside. When she introduced me to woolies, I figured that this would be another way that I could get high. I would smoke a few joints each day with her while counting money, but I still preferred sniffing cocaine because I thought that it made me stronger—it sounds crazy, but I really thought that I could fight better after sniffing coke. When we sniffed cocaine together, it always seemed that we had very good conversations while we were high. We shared a number of experiences in a short time. Our relationship didn't last long, or go as we expected, however; there was abuse from both parties, and I knew that I needed to get out of that situation. We were simply not good for one another.

My work on the street brought me into contact with a large amount of people. One day I ran into Kevin Go; it had been a while since I had seen him, and I was glad that he appeared to be doing well for himself. He drove by in a small car, and wanted to tell us about a connection he knew of that would make us money. We wished one another well, and a month later he came through driving a Mercedes Benz. Some people did not think that he owned the car, since he came back shortly after without the Mercedes. He informed everyone that his car was in the shop getting customized, which only increased people's doubt. Until, that is, he came back later with the Mercedes thoroughly customized with a complete body kit. Another day he came through with an Excalibur. Yes, being a hustler was attractive.

During my senior year in high school I continued getting high every chance I got; I would smoke weed and sniff coke on the back of the school bus, and before leaving the house to go to a party, I would always take a personal stash. I always made sure that I had a personal supply in order to pass some out; that was my way of showing love. Even though I started smoking woolies, I continued sniffing coke all the while. For some reason, I thought that this was cool. I would smoke a few joints while counting the money that I made during the day, and I viewed this as a personal treat or reward for a hard day's work out there in the streets. I did not realize that I was an addict until a few years later. During this time there were a number of teenagers that started using heroin, most of the time sniffing it in the powder form. The rationalization for the young men was that heroin stimulates them to sexually "stand tall" for greater periods of time. There is an old saying that refers to this process as putting the dope "D" on a female. Heroin is nicknamed "boy" and cocaine is nicknamed "girl;" I can see how they both got their nicknames. Many of my friends would swap stories of how long they were able to perform while under the influence of heroin. Not long after, I noticed that many of those using heroin became heavily addicted, and some of them even graduated to shooting it in their arms and other places with a needle. There is a fundamental difference between these two drugs; heroin causes a shift in biological chemicals, thereby creating physical, sickness-causing cravings, while cocaine is more of a physiological stimulant and creates merely a mental addiction.

One day I was on the block within our housing projects hustling, as was my morning routine. On one of the corners, an officer was walking the "beat," as it was referred to. Shortly after, one of my cousins drove past through the housing projects with his music playing loudly. The officer began to walk in the direction in which my cousin had driven, and because I knew that my cousin was most likely dirty—in possession of either drugs or a gun—and I figured I should go try to warn him. When I had almost caught up with him, however, I saw that the officer was talking to my cousin near my mother's house. I stopped and waited across the street, then watched as my cousin took off running around the buildings. I hollered at him to throw me his car keys, thinking that I should take his car and whatever was in it to safety while the officer chased my cousin. My cousin got away, but the officer returned to the car before I got the keys. Several other guys had joined me in my spot across the street and I suddenly heard a couple of them say, "Look out, Mark!" I looked back across the street just in time to see that the officer had started to chase me. He had too much of a head start on me, however, and I felt his blackjack hit my legs in an attempt to trip me as I ran. I tripped but I did not fall, and I kept running until someone saw the chase and hid me inside their house. They gave me a change of clothes and handed me a baby. While I managed to escape, I knew that when you run from the police, sometimes you get away and sometimes you don't.

Another time while hustling, the police were doing their routine drive-through of the projects during which they always drove slowly in order to thoroughly evaluate things in and around the neighborhood. The sight of them worried me, and I quickly changed direction by walking around a few houses as they drove by. But as I was coming around the other way, the officer slowly backed up in my direction; I turned and walked back in the opposite direction, and we went through this routine a couple of times. The last time that the officers drove by, one of them got out of his vehicle and walked in the other direction, hoping to trap me. At this point, I took off running and the officers started to pursue me. The camaraderie of those in the housing projects is always most evident when one is running from the police, and a lot of people came come out to encourage me to get away. I eventually ran into a house that I was directed to, and when I entered the house there was a young guy sitting in the living room watching television. I immediately sat down and joined him, just as if I belonged there. A large crowd had gathered in the courtyard between the houses, and before long the officers knocked on the door and entered the home. They asked, "Who just ran in here?" The young guy and I both looked at the officers with feigned confusion, but right then the mother of the house came down and asked, while pointing at me, "Who is that, and why is he in my house?" The officers arrested me, and gave me all kinds of charges, but at the time I did not comprehend just how serious things were getting. I didn't realize that my actions were heavily contributing to the curse that would haunt my family for many years to come; I had relatives who had served time in prison, but I was not able to connect the dots between that factor and my behavior. I posted bail and, once release, I returned to hustling because it was all that I knew.

One day I allowed a guy I knew to hang out with me in the housing project while I hustled. He did not touch any of the drugs at all, and the only thing he had to do was pay close attention to everything around us; I told him that when I was finished, I would give him a treat. Part of the treat was allowing him to hang out with a particular female that I knew, but he didn't clearly understand the game and grossly misinterpreted what I'd said. His time alone with this woman was thoroughly enjoyed, so much so that he wanted to go back after we had started to leave. I attempted to inform him that it was not a good idea, but he ignored me. He quickly returned, and said that she had refused to open the door. I explained to him that the drug game is very different from normal life; most of the associations and relationships within this lifestyle are artificial, since most people are in it only to get something. No one can be trusted, and there are mostly bad intentions, as well as a lot of leaches and vultures. Others will use you to the very last drop, and love will grow into hate at the drop of a dime. Betrayal and dishonestly are rampant character qualities within this game and this lifestyle is dangerous and unforgiving. "Self" is the name of the game, and anyone who expresses trust and loyalty immediately becomes suspect. Some people participate in this lifestyle ignorant of the realities of "the other side," namely all the people that don't make it; the money may look good from the outside, but the truth is that the game is very dangerous and no one can be trusted. As we used to say in the hood, "It's a dirty game."

At this time, while I knew the dangers of the game, I attributed my success with hustling to my own street smarts and to the guidance and instruction of more experienced dealers. Learning from them allowed me to not have to make my own mistakes, many of which would have been debilitating. When I was a bit younger I heard about a guy who took local pictures with a Polaroid camera, the kind that developed pictures immediately after he took them. He had an area in the back of a particular club with backgrounds set up and everything he needed to hustle pictures. He worked hard and carried himself well, and I developed deep respect for him; sometimes he would visit my hood, usually surrounded by a posse of women, and take pictures. Once he told me that in the early 1980s, the best time to make moves in the city of Philly was between the hours of 12:00 pm and 2:00 pm, since the police department had fewer hands available during this time. He told me that, according to the tale, organized criminals made their moves within this time bracket and that officers were encouraged to turn a blind eye to prevent unintentionally stopping some of their shipments. This tale was never proven, but I never had any problems with the law when I made moves or conducted business during those hours.

Chapter VII
Drug Use & Arrest

Self-image can be defined as the way that a person sees and feels about themselves, the motivational factor which encourages us to do certain things. A person who feels good about themselves is less likely to put themselves in dangerous situations, and vice versa. The reality of my situation was that I did not feel good about myself, and didn't have a good self-image. My self-esteem was very low, and I believed almost every negative thing that I ever heard someone say about me. While none of these factors sufficiently excuse the behavior I exhibited, I truly believed that I was going to be a drug dealer for the rest of my life simply because I was not good enough for anything else. I clearly understood a lot of the dangers associated with the hustle game, but I was still willing to take that chance; I knew that I could face prison time—not to mention robbery, turf wars, and even murder—as a result of using and selling drugs, but I continued to do these things. While I stuck with high school, and even attended all my required classes throughout my senior year, I didn't try very hard. There were times when I sniffed coke in the classroom while the teacher taught. I would place my head down on the desk and pull my coat over my head, and in one of my classes, I would pass some to another classmate who also had his head down. I put the minimal amount of effort toward my academics, just enough to get by; as a result, I ended up missing graduation by a half-credit in English. I am, and always will be, a part of the class of '88, but without a diploma and any marketable skills besides selling drugs, I wasn't prepared for the world.

During my senior year in high school, I used to wearing a lot of jewelry and carry a lot of money. I did not sell drugs in the school—I only ever sold drugs within the projects—but I would carry a wad of money in each of my pockets. While in class I would pull one of my wads, or knots, of money out of my pocket and I would tell one of my classmates that they could keep the money if they correctly guessed how much was there. They would often guess a number like $500 or $800 when, in reality, there was usually between $1,500 and $2,500 in my pocket at any given time. I used to think that it was cool to carry around a lot of money. During this time, I used to hang out with one of my Jamaican friends, Derrock. Though they lived in Delaware, he and his family were well connected with Jamaica, and they went home to visit once or twice a year. Derrock and I shared a lot of experiences together, and we each conducted our own hustle.

I was always considered to be a very quiet person, at least around people that I did not know. After realizing the ramifications of missing my graduation, I became even more reclusive and I got high more often to escape my dismal reality. I paid for a correspondence course through a program based in Illinois, and started working on my assignments so that I could graduate, since I really wanted to attain my high school diploma. My older brother had graduated the year before me with the class of '87, and I was so very close to being finished. My lifestyle, however, provided me with excuses to procrastinate, and I continuously put my correspondence work on hold until the next day. I then decided to apply for the GED class; the name of the program was "70,001" and the classes were held at Howard High School on the east side of town. The first day that I arrived in class, I noticed how overcrowded it was with students. There was not much room to move around, as several extra desks had been placed within the room. That day I ran into a local rapper, and we started hanging out during breaks and after class. He was from a middle class family and lived in a nice home. Before long, we both eventually stopped going to that class; it was summer time and we had better things to do, well, at least this is what we thought. He was cool with some of the other local rappers and there were times we all hung together and went to a hideout on the north side. The owner of the house was an older man. We smoked a few joints, and despite the older man preference to smoke coke from a glass, none of us was with that; we chose to smoke our coke in marijuana joints and for some reason we thought that we were better than him. I would pay the older guy, with cocaine, to stay in one room while we got high in another room, since we didn't want him looking at us as if he were crazy. Each time I gave the guy some coke, one of my friends would say, "Mark, you're giving him too much;" one of the rules of the game I learned early on, however, is that you always take good care of the house, i.e. the place where we did whatever it was we were doing there.

I didn't like getting high alone while in my addiction. There were several examples of the people that I entertained with a free "get high" session. The street term for the way that we got high was called "going in session." I guess that it was called going in session because of the time spent there. Die-Die was the younger brother of a guy that I knew from when I was growing up. They both typically hung out in the same park on 24th Street, and lived two blocks from the park. Their grandmother lived next door to where my cousins lived, and when my mother's family lived with one of our aunt and uncles for a short time, it was next door to his grandmother. Now that I was grown, Die-Die and I started hanging out together. During the time that I was smoking woolies, hustling, and trying my hardest to hide it all from most people. Die-Die's older brother did not approve of me selling or using drugs, and probably thought that I was a bad influence on his younger brother. He would never actually say anything to me, but he would look at me a certain way; I see now that he was just trying to be a good older brother, and that his concerns were very valid.

There was another guy, Wallo, who once lived around the corner from my mother's house. One particular time, I had two large bags of cocaine and I asked Wallo to hold one of them while we got high with the other. I paid the house to take their product to the other room; Wallo and I rolled many coolie joints, constantly lighting and smoking one after another. Before I realized it, the entire bag was empty and I told Wallo to give me the other bag so that we could continue getting high. Wallo told me, "No," that we were supposed to hustle the other bag. I then told him that we were going to smoke the other bag also. It should have been obvious to me that I was an addict but I guess that I was in denial. There is a thin line between an addict and a hustler! As we stepped out into the early-morning dawn, neither of us realized that prison was awaiting both of us right around the corner.

I did not see it as the time, but I was a drug addict. Once I got high with my cousins Lil' Jay and Edgar. When I went in session, I *really* went in session. This particular day, we cooked up some cocaine and smoked it in marijuana joints; we probably smoked five joints in that one sitting. For a period of time, we all fell asleep; when I awoke, I woke up Lil' Jay, and he woke up Edgar. We smoked four or five more joints, then went back to sleep. The next time that I woke up, as I walked to stairs of the house, I saw Lil' Jay waiting. He looked at me and said "let's get high once more." We then went to wake Edgar but he would not get back up. We knocked on his bedroom door, but he refused to come out; finally he yelled through the door and told us that he did not want to get high again. We continued knocking on the door, but finally gave up. Again, Lil' Jay and I smoked a few more joints together before going to sleep for the night. In the moment, I was frustrated that Edgar's cravings didn't match mine, but I later felt guilty for trying to convince him to keep getting high with us.

One particular day, I had my young friend, Tejam, with me; we had been hanging out and having a good time, and he had fun messing with some of the women and enjoying the other so-called pleasures of the game. As we were leaving the projects, I was pulled over and searched. The officers quickly found the cocaine, but I told them that Tejam didn't have anything to do with the drugs and they released him. As for me, I was arrested and was released on bond. I then hired an attorney who would represent me at trial. This would be a difficult case to defend, since the drugs were found in my possession. I later found out that someone had called the police on me and notified the authorities that I had drugs in my possession. Still, with two arrests looming over me, I continued to hustle on the street corners.

At my trial, I was offered a plea bargain and was advised by my attorney to accept it. I accepted, and was sentenced to two years in jail, and ten years of probation. Despite the fact that the prosecution wanted me to get arrested on that same day, I was allowed to remain free for an additional two weeks so that I could get things together before starting my sentence. The judged agreed with my attorney—the prison system was overcrowded already—and I remained free until I needed to turn myself in to the prison on a certain date. The next couple of days were challenging for me as I tried to decide whether or not I would report to the prison, or wait until I got caught. I spoke to a number of family members and friends and considered all of their perspectives; some said to go serve my time and get it over with, while others said, "Let the police catch you when they can." The day before I was scheduled to turn myself in I got high with my cousins, and smoked a few joints laced with cocaine; it felt like a celebration of some sort, even though there was nothing to celebrate and I really did not even want to get high. We counted the money that we both made during the night, and I had a nothing-to-lose attitude. We smoked anywhere from five to seven joints of woolies that night; I did not know it then, but this would be the last time that I would ever get high with any substance. The next morning I woke up early and made the necessary preparations; I was eighteen years old at the time, and I was headed to turn myself in to prison.

I remember that day as if it were yesterday; the weather was hot but for some reason it felt like a gloomy day. Upon my arrival at the institution, I was told to take off all of my clothes and stand in the shower area, where my entire body was sprayed with a solution. I was told to keep my eyes closed— they were going to spray me from head to toe—and to allow the solution to sit for ten minutes before taking a shower. The purpose of this solution was to prevent individuals from bringing crabs or lice into the prison; I remember very clearly that the solution was ice cold, and that it had a very distinct smell. Ten minutes later an officer informed me that I could get into the shower, and when I finished, I was given a bologna sandwich (one small slice of bologna and two slices of bread). I had asked for a phone call when I first arrived at the prison, but I did not receive one. The others and I just sat in the cell and waited, and no matter how many times we yelled for the officers, no one came. I found out later that we all had to see the nurse and get tested for tuberculosis before being placed in our respective housing units. We could hear a lot of noise coming from the units within the facility, and every so often there was a beeping noise over the intercom, followed by a code and the area of the incident. I later learned the codes were used to notify the authorities of certain behaviors or incidents; for example, Code 6 might refer to inmates who were refusing to lock inside their cells; Code 8 could mean there was a group fight, or riot; Code 4 was perhaps a call for medical attention. There was a quick response team

(QRT) which responded when these codes were called; they would come prepared for physical confrontation, and were equipped with helmets, shields, and other equipment.

When I got to the facility in the year of 1988, I saw a number of people that I had not seen in a while. I saw a few former addicts and touters, many of whom were now physically much bigger than when I last saw them. The father of my childhood friend, Marlon, was there and I learned that he was serving an extended prison sentence. My childhood friend, Reague, was here, and it was good to see a familiar face that I could trust. Besides the fact that Reague was the one to give me a glimpse of the drug game many years prior, I considered him a good friend. As was true on the streets, Reague appeared to be in good shape and was well-respected inside the prison. Somehow, he had a way of encouraging officers to take him to other units to see different people, and he frequently checked on me and asked if I needed anything.

Previously, a wide variety of new mandatory drug laws were put in place; as a result, large numbers of young people were sent to prison for drug charges. I was eighteen at the time, and many of the others were between the ages of eighteen and twenty-one; we had all been involved in some capacity with trafficking cocaine, possession with the intent to deliver, and simple possession. I knew many of them from the street, and I later got to know and become pretty cool with some of them. I can honestly say that I did not take that time seriously. The older guys said that we younger guys were messing the game up; while they wanted to smoke weed, drink wine, and do their time as comfortable as possible, we would go to the chow hall and cause a ruckus. More than once I threw my tray behind the counter because they wouldn't give me enough food on it. Of course, we didn't consider the fact that we were only making matters worse for ourselves, since causing problems beckoned unwanted attention. The most common punishment for this was having your building shaken down, which meant the officers came through and took away everything that we were not supposed to have. The prison washed our clothes in mass bundles, but our white tee shirts and underwear wouldn't really come clean. An alternative was to wash our own clothes in the shower or in the sink. Some prisoners paid other prisoners to wash their clothes, but I preferred to clean them myself.

I saw a lot of people that I grew up with come inside those walls. There was one particular guy named Marvin, and he used to spend a lot of time at his aunt's house, which was in my housing project. He was a very good basketball player and while I can't remember whether or not he ever won a state championship, I do recall that he had the purest shot around. He definitely had the potential to make it in the NBA. His parents were well-off and he actually lived in a nice neighborhood; he went to an academically well-respected high school, but he often hung out in the projects with several of his cousins. While I was serving my time, Marvin came in with a mandatory drug sentence; soon after, however, scouts came from a community college in the state of California and managed to get him out of prison so he could attend college. This was a very rare case because judges were not keen on reducing anyone's mandatory prison sentence. I later heard that he continued to struggle with drugs while in college, and had returned to prison on various charges. The last time that I saw him he appeared to be very fed up, and was too depressed to play basketball. All the inmates wanted to see him play, but his mind wasn't in it anymore.

I got into a lot of trouble and received a number of write-ups while in prison. I got into fights with other prisoners and into altercations with officers. My constant negative behavior kept me in lock-up for probably the last six months of my sentence. The very day that I was released was spent in lock-up, which was twenty-three hours in the cell and one hour out. Part of the reason I did not take this time seriously was because I had a foreseeable release date. I vowed to myself that I would never get high again, and that I would no longer sell drugs on the front line; I knew I could make a lot more money if I were to use different ways to sell drugs and I had all kinds of ideas for businesses that I could use as fronts for the illegal activities. I did not want to be the person who sold drugs hand to hand for the rest of my life.

Prison became a norm for me and I was able to adjust quickly to the routine of being there. I knew what I needed while I was there and understood the importance of metaphorically releasing ties to loves ones.

Though my family would sometimes write letters, I did not expect them to. I preferred to remain focused on serving my time, rather than allowing myself to become weak by reminiscing about life on the outside. Being in lock-up offered additional challenges; there was a lot of tension even though we only came out for one hour each day. In that hour we only had time to work-out and take a shower, and once a week or once every other week we were allowed to make a short phone call. Because of the ubiquitous hostility, it was advised that we be with another person at all times. While doing push-ups, for example, it was very beneficial to have someone with you to watch your back; he stood watch while I did my set of push-ups, and I would then do the same for him. This applied for the shower, too, and one person would look out for the other until both were finished. The buddy system did not always ward off attackers, but even then, it was helpful to have the additional assistance in that situation. While in lock-up I had a roommate who was from the same city and who used to hang out in the same neighborhood. We spoke about a lot of different things, mostly about what we wanted to do once we were released from prison. Many times I considered telling him how close my release date was, but I always decided against it.

Before my sentence was up, my grandmother on my mother's side of the family and Uncle Mokeem came to visit. I was very happy to see my grandmother, and made sure to let her know that I had plans on doing well for myself upon my release. When they were ready to leave, my uncle asked my grandmother to go on ahead. He then told me that my dad was locked up, and that he wanted me to come down and see him once I was released. When I first heard this information, I was shocked. I was also disappointed to some degree, and I did not know how long he had left to serve, or what things would be like without him. My dad played such a huge role in giving to others and organizing so many of our family functions. I was very confused at this time, and there were a lot of different thoughts that went on in my mind. I didn't understand why a good man like my dad would get caught; in many ways I thought that he was untouchable, and unable to ever get caught. My dad had always been my hero and role model, and I placed a lot of weight and value on the things he did and said. Above all, my dad was a

family man; he always made sure that his
family was taken care of, and he had a special
kind of love for the elderly family members.
At this time I still did not realize how the
curse of prison was forming within my
family, but my release date was not far away
and I wanted to help any way that I could.

Chapter VIII
A Master Plan

It was the year of 1990 and my roommate did not know I was being released until the officer called my name. I had woken up early that morning, ready to go. We embraced one another and wished each other well; we would see each other again soon, since he only had a few months left on his sentence. As I was transported by the court van to be released at the courthouse in Wilmington, I reminded myself of the vow I had made to never get high again. I knew that using drugs would only contribute to my continued downfall, and I was not willing to give control of my life over to the effects of drugs. I felt that the best way for me to control my life was to maintain a clear and drug-free mind; I even went a step further and decided not to drink any kind of alcohol or liquor. The problem was that I did not make the same commitments when it came to playing the drug game.

From the courthouse I walked to my cousins' house on the north side of town. My cousins were excited and surprised that I was home, and Edgar drove me down to my mother's house in the projects. I was excited about going to Alabama to help my dad, but I wanted to remain in Delaware for a few days first. While I was in prison, my mother had moved from one unit to another within the same project. She and my sisters were happy that I had made it home. Other hustlers that I grew up with waited out front of my mother's house to see me; some of them had new cars, and they appeared to be doing very well. Edgar drove me through town so I could visit my grandmother, aunts, and uncles. At one point, he decided to take me to the all famous Al's Sporting Goods, a local athletics store that has been around since I was a child. Back then they specialized in sneakers, but also sold accessories such as socks, shoe strings, shorts, and other athletic gear. Edgar bought me a pair of sneakers, and a couple short sets; he was a good cousin, and was always looking out for me. When I was a teenager, Al's had a very large sneaker on the shelf that was said to have been Doctor Jay's personal shoe, yes, Julius Irving, the professional basketball player for the Philadelphia 76ers in the early 80s. At some point during our travels around town that day, my cousin stopped to speak to a female. They spoke for a few minutes and exchanged hugs, and when we pulled off I asked him who she was. He told me that she was one of the twins who used to live in our old housing projects, my little sister's friends. I could not believe how much she had grown in two years and this was my first taste of how much prison steals from you.

I later went to one of the main hustling areas in the projects to hang out. There were a lot of guys and females there, and I just sat on the porch of one of the project houses. Suddenly the police drove through and everyone scattered. Everyone, that is, except me; I looked around and realized I was the only one still out in the open. For the first time in a long time, it felt good to not have anything illegal in my possession that would force me to run and hide. The officers drove by slowly as they looked in my direction; I looked at them and they looked at me. The officers continued on without stopping, and everyone finally returned to the courtyard. Business as usual was back. After a few days, I said my goodbyes and prepared for my trip to Alabama. I knew that my dad needed me and I wanted to help anyway that I could. When I got to my dad's house I noticed things were more structured and organized than I had expected them to be; even while in prison, he continued to do a very good job of taking care of his household. My step-mother, sisters, and my younger brother were as excited to see me as I was to see them. We embraced one another with a brotherly love, and I could see that my younger brother was quickly growing up and beginning to experience things on his own. We then went to visit my dad. Even though he was in the federal prison, he was allowed to leave and enjoy himself however he saw fit. He appeared to be doing well; he still had connections on the outside and was able to make things happen. By this time my dad, my younger brother, and I had all been in prison.

I eventually went back up north because I had to report for my probation. When I arrived in Delaware I quickly got back into the hustle game, since I knew that I would not be able to find a good enough job to take care of myself otherwise. My cousins and friends were happy to have me back in town, and I hustled with a renewed sense of purpose. I did not want to work the front line, but I wanted to make more money; I had million dollar dreams and I was motivated and determined to be successful in the game. My biggest problem was that I was too stubborn to use all of the resources that I had readily available to me. I could have chosen to stay in Alabama; even though my dad was in federal prison, he still had connections and could have plugged me in. My pride required me to do it on my own, however, and I was on a mission to make a lot of money. A few hustlers I knew in Delaware embraced me back into the game, and I was focused on succeeding. There were a few younger guys who had started hustling; my old friend, Marlon, was now active on the scene, and I let him know that I met his dad in prison.

Any fear of prison that I may have previously had was gone. I was on probation and knew that I could get sent back on a violation, but I wasn't afraid. I was required to report to my officer each month and take regular drugs tests, the latter of which I was not concerned about since I was no longer getting high. My probation officer told me that I needed a job, so I put in a few job applications but I did not get any phone calls. I then decided to open a business. I sold short sets, incense, oils, hats, and similar things from a stand; I set up two or three tables on the Boulevard and would sell these things. I could make a few hundred dollars in sales, but I didn't take the enterprise very seriously because it wasn't my main source of income. I just needed to get my PO off of my back.

When I was asked about my experience in prison, my story was usually that "it wasn't too bad." I explained how we would wrestle and challenge one another to see who was the strongest, and that I got into a lot of fights, which was normal there. I did not tell the stories that needed to be told to young people, the ones about the overwhelming feelings of hurt, loneliness, uncertainty, and of feeling less than human. Looking back, I could have described how it felt to be allowed outside the cell for only one hour a day. Instead, I chose to glamorize a bad and dangerous situation to the extent that such harsh realities were nothing worth fearing.

I did learn a few things after serving my first prison sentence. I knew that I wanted to make more money, and that I did not want to be the nickel and dime hustler forever. This time around I made a lot more money. The problem is that I spent a lot more money, too. I would spend money without thinking much about it, knowing that I could make it all back in a short period of time. I can think of several other hustlers within the projects that had more money than I did; I was a small-time hustler but could still come up with $50,000 or maybe $100,000 on a good run. I could make thousands quickly but I always saw thousands slip right out of my hands just as quickly. I had a lot of plans that I did not get a chance to fulfill because of these habits; I did not reach my goal of a million dollars, but I thought that I was on my way, and I was in the process of getting very close to my goal. I had contacts in Philly and New York City, and when I returned to Delaware there were people who were on top buying a quarter key at a time. I can remember selling those people that same quarter key once I got back on my feet.

One day while driving past a used dealership, I saw a car that caught my attention. I pulled in and bought it; the car was a stick shift, which I did not know how to drive, but I showed it to my mother and she got into the passenger seat. We drove through the projects with the car jerking back and forth as I accidentally kept shifting the wrong gears. I had an anger problem during this time, and I remember my mother trying to calm me down when others blew their horns at me for stalling or for being unable to find the right gear. I stuck with it, however, and I learned how to drive a stick shift that day. I enjoyed that car and ended up putting an expensive sound system inside—more expensive than my car. Yes, my priorities were in the wrong place, but money was starting to come in faster and I was well on my way to being a successful hustler.

There was a particular guy that I used to drop packages off to. He was pretty loyal in having the money on time and I considered him to be a trustworthy person. I would drive near his house, we would take care of business, and then I would leave. One day I went to drop off some product to him and we sat in the car for a few minutes, discussing something. My car was one of many on a one-way street; suddenly an unmarked car with four detectives pulled up next to my car and we swapped glances. The detectives sat there for about fifteen or thirty seconds and then pulled off. Those fifteen seconds seemed endless, and my heart nearly dropped to my toes. The only product I had in my possession was what I had just given to the guy, but if the cops would have gotten out, things could have gotten ugly very quickly for us. Still, I continued to hustle and flip packages. If I bought a quarter key of cocaine one time, I would buy a half of key the next time.

One day while driving down 30th and Market Street I noticed one of my childhood friends in a physical altercation right in front of the Chinese restaurant on the strip. I pulled over as quickly as possible and ran towards the situation; I helped as much as I could, but when it was over he was not happy with me. He told me not to get involved in his situations because he could handle himself, and that I should focus on my own goals. At one point, this particular friend was a very good-hearted person, and I still respected him even though he was angry. Years before, we used to hang out together at parties or get high; apparently, he was going through a very troublesome time, however, as he was found dead a few short months later. It was believed that he was killed in a vehicle and then dumped on the side of the road, but whatever the case, it hurt my heart when I heard this. He was from the projects across the highway from where I grew up, and we had nothing but positive encounters. His rage and untimely death were warning signs to me of the harm drugs and life on the streets can bring, but I chose not to pay attention. As the old saying goes, "You can learn the easy way, or the hard way."

Chapter IX
Making a Pickup

It was now the year 1991. One day I went to one of my connections in order to make a score. He lived in Philadelphia and I had a pretty good relationship with him. I would usually park my car several blocks away from his house and walk there; on some occasions he would drive me back to my car when we were finished. As I continued to increase the amount of product that I purchased from him, the more concerned he became for me. One day, I went to see him because I needed to make a few quick dollars but he told me he wasn't doing anything because the feds were hot. It may have been better for me to leave and come back the next day, as he suggested, but I was t too interested in making a quick flip. I attempted to convince him to serve me, but he wouldn't. Frustrated, I left his house and searched for someone else with good product.

I saw the guy who introduced me to my current supplier, and I thought that he might be able to turn me on to someone else that I could purchase from. He told me he knew someone, and proceeded to take me to his house. As we walked down the street, I noticed that a guy who had been crab-walking low to the ground in the crowd, suddenly stood up with a large gun pointed at me. I believe that it was a 357, but I was more concerned with the safety of my own life than determining what type of gun he had. He took the very large bag of money I had around my waist, and then told me to take off my shoes and run without looking back. As I ran, I kept visualizing getting shot in the back; that half a block felt more like a mile! Once I made it to the end of the block I turned the corner and ran down another block; I continued to run for several blocks in my socked feet. Finally I slowed down, and as I walked through the streets of Philly, I felt very thankful to be alive. When I made it back to the car, the female who had ridden with me was sleeping so I got in and drive off. Later, when she woke up, I informed her that I had gotten robbed; I was very upset because my loss had been a heavy one, but I was also embarrassed that this had happened to me. Yet again, I was being careless in a very dangerous game. I think that it was a good thing that I did not have my pistol on me that day, as the gunman may have been more inclined to shoot me as I ran away if I'd been armed.

Around this time, two of my younger cousins Mack-Mack and Manny were coming of age; they had both started working out and getting into good physical shape. They always knew about the lifestyle I led but I made sure that they never saw me do any of the actual hustling. On several occasions, Manny came to the projects and hung out with me, but I did not allow him to see or touch any of the drugs because I did not want him to follow in my footsteps. One day, I heard that Manny had been shot. This came as a surprise to me because he had never been a violent person. I don't know the details of what happened, but I do know that my cousin is no longer with us; he was young, with his whole life ahead of him, and this was very difficult for everyone in the family to bear.

One day a friend and I took a trip to New York City. Everything went well until we were on our way back, when soon after exiting the tunnel, I got pulled over on the New Jersey Turnpike by New Jersey State Troopers. We were told to sit on the side of the turnpike while one of the officers searched the vehicle. I watched as he opened the particular door in which the drugs were hidden in the door panel and continued to search, as if he didn't know the drugs were hidden in there. He walked around the car, as if to continue his search, and suddenly pulled his gun out and demanded that we get on the ground. We were both arrested and taken to Essex County Jail in Newark, New Jersey. The Essex County Jail is twelve stories high, and we traveled on a broken elevator to our cells. We were both given a bail which we needed to post in order to get released; I told my family to use my money to release my friend, but the bondmen would not allow me to pay the ten percent for my bail, since I was considered a flight risk. I eventually found an interstate bondsman in Baltimore, Maryland, who required twenty percent of the bail, and three signatures. After paying the percentage, I still needed two additional references. I got two of my uncles to drive to Baltimore, Maryland, and provide the necessary signatures. Later, the officers went back to our car and confiscated the product out of the door panel. This arrest was another big loss for me.

My friend Kandy, a female soldier I had known since I was young, was the first person I called when I got arrested. As kids we hung out a lot, and I knew her dad and mother, and her brother who hung out on the north side of town. When I called her, she said she was ready to get to work; she still had some of my product left from my last package, and she wanted to help me get back to the street any way she could. We agreed that she would sell what was left, and then go from there. I initially disagreed with her efforts to help me in this way, but I knew she was going to do it anyway. I reminded her to be careful, and she did a few flips and I had the money for the rest of my bail, and then some. She was familiar with one of my connections in Philly and she was the only one who knew the door that I went through. Initially she was met with resistance, but my connection finally agreed to work with her. I guess money does, in fact, talk.

I remained in the facility in New Jersey for a total of about ten or eleven days. While waiting to make bail, I was exposed to the harsh realities of the jail itself. There was a lot of pride in New Jersey at that time, with everyone hyped about the rap group Naughty by Nature, and thrilled that Latifah was the Queen. During this time the song "OPP" was very popular, and there were a number of standup guys at the facility during my stay. One day a situation broke out between an officer and an inmate in the day area; the officers came to the dorm and requested that the accused inmate come out, but a group of guys stepped up and said he was not coming out. It was already late in the evening, and they wanted to postpone the reprimand until the next day, when a sergeant or lieutenant was present. The officers told the guys that they would take the guy and work everything out in the morning, but the guys said that they were not giving the guy up. Several times the officers returned to renegotiate, each time with a higher ranking officer; the last time they came, they brought the warden. The guys still refused, and that's when I heard the officers say, "Strap up."

I knew it was time for action, and that something very serious was about to go down. It was around 11:00 pm or 12:00 am by now, and the group of guys woke everyone up and told them to put wet towels over their faces and their arms. The bunked beds were pushed to the entrance door and very hot water was poured on the floors. One of the guys told everyone that the officer would ask that "you to step out if you don't have anything to do with it," but would then say that "if anyone attempts to step out, that person will get the beat down." I heard a lot of noise, such as sticks and metal clicking together, which lasted for forty-five minutes to an hour. Finally, officers dressed in riot gear such as shields, helmets, and gas masks marched to the dorm; they did not enter through the door, however, but walked around the cat-walk, the area around the dorm which was fenced in. Once they completely surrounded the dorm, they stuck what appeared to be guns through the gates and started firing. After the first cans hit the floor, smoke immediately filled the dorm as the officers shot tear gas again and again. I could not breathe or see, even with the wet towel over my face, and my eyes and face were burning. Just as I was starting to choke, another guy and I made our way to two separate beds in an attempt to find relief from the tear gas. As you can guess, there was no relief for us at all. Suddenly, I heard a voice say, "Guys, I can't take it any longer; I'm going towards the gate." I could hear others also head towards the door and, while we could not see, the officers told everyone to follow their voices. Outside, the officers put plastic cuffs on us and took us to the elevator with our faces forward. My cuffs were pulled so tight that they tore the skin on my wrists. We were taken to a room on the lower level, and held there for a while. It was around 3:30 am when we were finally allowed to return to the dorm. Everyone was allowed to return to the dorm except for five to ten guys. I am not sure what happened to them, but I do respect their willingness to stand up for themselves. Once we returned to the dorm, all of our property and our mattresses were on the floor, and all of the water from the buckets had been poured on our mattresses and property.

Thankfully, I was released the very next day because I had gotten all of the necessary signatures and Kandy had raised my bail money. All of my cash was taken when I got arrested. I called home for someone to buy me a train ticket so I could travel the two hours back home. It felt good when I walked out of that place, but when I had walked the several blocks to the train station I found that the ticket booth was closed and I could not retrieve the prepaid ticket. I did not call anyone because I didn't want anyone to know exactly when I got out. I went outside in front of the station and attempted to convince a taxi driver to drive me home, and that I would take care of him when I got there. I even planned on paying him extra, if he agreed. He briefly considered it, but ultimately declined. Back inside, I attempted to find a comfortable place to sit down but each time I did so, the security guards would come banging their loud clubs against the metal and demand that I move. After a while, I decided to walk outside; I was surprised to see a park with a lot of homeless people, perhaps one hundred or more, sleeping on pieces of cardboard. I felt like joining the people who were sleeping across the street in the park, but I decided against it. Around five or six in the morning the ticket booth opened, and I was able to get my ticket. Once I got home, I returned immediately to the streets; I had no intentions to stop hustling and I knew it would take something very drastic to make me stop.

I found myself in a high speed chase in the city of Philadelphia, where I had gone to see some people that I knew and get some product. After being in the drug game for as long as I had, I knew what unmarked detective vehicles looked like. As we went up the ramp, I saw one sitting on the shoulder. It pulled out and got in the lane behind us, flashing his lights to signal us to pull over. I had already informed the other person who was driving to not pull over, and to look straight ahead. The officer sped up and pulled to the left side of our car in order to get my friend's attention, but we did not acknowledge him. The officer then pulled to the right side where I was the passenger, and our response was the same. This went on for quite a while, and we finally decided to throw the product out of the window. I watched the bag bounce several times on the road, and then saw the officer suddenly pull over and collect the evidence. This was yet another loss that I took, and yet another warning sign which I ignored.

One day in the projects near my mother's house, my little sister was hanging out. I had just gotten some product cooked up and it was ready for sale; I set the bag down so that I would not have it in my possession, and asked my sister to keep an eye on my lunch meat. I was planning on giving the product to a particular person as soon as they showed up. My sister left the spot where I put the product and evidently someone was watching the whole scenario because it went missing and I became very upset with my sister. When my mother heard me getting on her she asked us what was going on. I could not tell my mother the truth, so I simply said that that nothing was going on; I later apologized to my sister, since the whole thing was my fault. The drug game was beginning to get very ugly for me, but my stubbornness disallowed me to quit.

I was a small time hustler with big plans. I planned on hooking up with my dad, once he got out of prison, and with the many connections he had in Alabama. I did not want him to give me a handout, but my goal was to increase my money and then allow him to connect me with the right people. I wanted us to have a family business where we would trust one another. My dad still did not approve of my lifestyle, but he understood that it was my own choice. While waiting for that plan to work out, I had made arrangements to buy a few birds from my connection; this plan was about two weeks away, and it was so close that I could taste it. My plans, however, were interrupted by the many mistakes and my goals of being a successful hustler were slowly coming to an end. I quickly began to learn that our plans aren't set in stone, and what can go wrong, in some cases, will go wrong!

Chapter X
Return to Prison

My run as a newfound hustler lasted only a short year. When I got arrested this time, I knew that I would face a longer prison sentence since this was my second drug offense in the state of Delaware. By this time, I had a lot of anger built up inside, and I felt a sense of hopelessness; I could not see any light at the end of the tunnel, and at that point, the thought of getting locked up again made me feel that my life was over. I had a detainer hold on me from the state of New Jersey, since I got into a lot of fights while I was there. The day that I went to court for trial I was prepared for the worst case scenario, but still stuck with my story: "I am not guilty." I understood that I had a good chance of being found guilty of the charges against me, but for some reason I thought that I had a good chance to win an appeal. The reality of the matter is that I was young and had made a lot of very bad decisions in my life, and I was guilty of the charges. At this time, my entire life was full of uncertainty, and I wondered whether or not being in prison this time would be the conclusion of my life. My dad was still locked up in a federal prison, and my younger brother was in a state prison; on more than one occasion I heard people talking about my situation and saying, "He is done." In a way, I felt like I *was* done—the amount of time I was facing strongly suggested that—but even in the face of my reality, I planned to fight for my freedom.

The officers woke me up around 4:30 am in order to transport me to court. Before trial actually started, I was given one last chance to take a plea bargain. The prosecutor recommended a three- to five-year sentence but, being as stubborn as I was, I refused to accept the plea. For some reason I wanted to take my chances at trial. This would force the state to prove my guilt in a court of law. Little did I know, that is exactly what the state of Delaware planned on doing. The jury was made up of all white older males and females and I was a young African American male; within two hours, the jury came back with a guilty verdict. When the verdict was read, I stood there without emotion; I was found guilty on every count, and I was to return to court a month later for the sentencing phase. I was taken into a side room and asked to accept a plea bargain, since the prosecutor said that he did not want to give me the maximum sentence. This was very unusual since I had already been found guilty. Plea bargains are given before a trial is held in order to save the state money that would otherwise have to be spent on the trial. In my case, the money had already been spent on the trial; even today; this is still a mystery to me. The prosecutor offered me a ten-year sentence, which I refused. I was given the maximum amount of time that the charges carried, a twenty-year mandatory sentence; I stood there once again without expressing any emotion. I was also given an additional sentence for violating my probation. The preexisting anger stemming from unresolved issues in my life only increased as I was charged with my sentence.

During my trial, my childhood friend Marlon was also facing the fight of his life. He had gotten arrested a month prior, and was waiting for a trial date; soon after, he was convicted of murder and sentenced to the death penalty. I could not help but feel something when I heard this; we had been tight for many years, and I thought about his mother, sister, and brother now having to deal with his choices. Looking at my own life, however, I was not thinking about how my choices hurt my family, but rather, with a new sentence to fill, about how angry and hurt I was. I got into a number of fights while I was in prison, and I had to be moved to different housing units. At one point, I was in the same housing unit as Lil' Jay, who was also serving time for drugs. Lil' Jay introduced me to one of the correctional officers and told him that I was his cousin. Instead of saying, "What's up?" he said, "That's not something to be proud of," as if to say that it was not a good thing for us to be locked up together. One morning when we got up we heard a new individual making a lot of noise in the unit; he wasn't there the night before, and must have been moved to the unit during the night or very early in the morning. When we came out for breakfast the new guy was yelling something at the tier men about the food; Lil' Jay was one of the tier men that morning, one of the guys working the food cart, and no one responded to the new guy. After breakfast we went outside; the outside area was a very small pyramid shaped area with one basketball goal and three very high walls that had an opening at the top. The ground was painted green to give the illusion of grass. While standing around waiting for each person to shoot the basketball in order to pick team captains, Lil' Jay suddenly punched the new guy; I came to assist and a number of others started kicking on this individual. I heard the code being called over the intercom, and the QRT arrived within seconds to break up the fight and escort us to lock-up.

I tried my hand at hustling even while I was in prison. I maintained what is referred to as the "store," which is when the commissary is open to a particular housing unit on certain days. A store is simply meant to allow others to borrow items and then return the items with interest; popular items often consisted of deodorant, soap, toothpaste, cookies, chips, tuna fish, cigarettes, and other things. If a person borrowed a bag of chips or a pack of cigarettes, they would have to pay two items back on store day. If a person borrowed two items, they would have to pay three items back. Managing the store provided additional opportunities for me to get into trouble; whenever a person did not pay, regardless of their excuses, I made sure they suffered the consequences. Looking back, I will say that I was a selfish individual. Some of their excuses were valid: "My money did not come in the mail yet," or "The mailroom must be holding my money," or "Can I pay you next week?" I would attack them and, after the fights, would then add another item to the person's charge for not paying on time. This conduct was against the rules of the prison; I could have been charged with extortion or officers could have confiscated my excessive commissary but fortunately I grew out of this behavior before that happened.

I received news that a murder had been committed in Wilmington. The victim happened to be related to one of the women I dealt with while on the street. After my female friend informed me of what happened, she told me the shooter's name was Vine, and that he was being sent to the same facility I was at. When he arrived, a strange coincidence happened; he was moved to the exact same housing unit I was in and while I did not know him or the victim, my friend on the outside was sad and I decided I was going to make things kind of hard for this gentleman. I regret this now, since Vine and I got to know each other over the years and eventually became pretty cool.

While locked up in Delaware, I missed my court date in New Jersey. My mother informed me that the police had surrounded her house and were looking for me. She didn't understand this, since she knew I was currently locked up. After serving my time in Delaware, I was transferred back to the Essex County Jail in Newark, New Jersey. Newark, New Jersey, has various nicknames such as New Jerusalem, New Jerus, and Brick City. I was transferred to New Jersey in 1992 in order to answer for the pending drug charges. While at the Essex County Jail, I realized that it was around the time for the birth of my very first child. Whenever I called my mother on the phone I asked her whether she had heard anything concerning the child. I was named after my dad, and my dad was named after my grandfather; I badly wanted a son in order to continue this tradition. I also had a lot of plans to teach my son about responsibility and manhood, and could picture myself sharing with him all that I knew. When I received the news that a daughter had been born, I was excited and disappointed at the same time; I was glad to be a dad but was discouraged by the fact that I was not able to be there for her. I received a picture of my daughter, and she was beautiful; the reality of the matter, however, was that she was born while I was serving a long prison sentence.

After the experiences I had during my previous stay in New Jersey, I didn't know what I was going to run into this time. Fortunately, things were different, and I met a lot of good people there. There was an older guy named Mohammed. He was an old school guy from one of the local projects in the city of Newark, New Jersey; he was a former drug addict and had become well-respected within the facility. He practiced the faith of Islam, and it provided his mind with something positive to focus on.

When I first arrived in the dorm I had to find a bed to sleep in, since there were no assigned beds back then. At that time, the only bed I could find was in an area that mostly Muslims slept in. They referred to this area as the "back cage." Mohammed came out and told me that I could sleep in there for the night, but that I would have to move to another area in the morning. I guess that we somehow became cool overnight, since he didn't ask me to move the next day. That night they put down old newspapers in the kitchen and set out a lot of food; I started to walk out since I did not know anyone, but Mohammed said, "Brother, where are you

Mark Baynard   170

going?" I informed him that I was going to leave while they ate, but he told me that I was welcome to share the food with them. These brothers collected the food that the kitchen was throwing away and would feed the entire prison dorm with it. Mohammed and his friends had an organized process with which this whole thing was done; everyone got into line, and waited respectfully to be served a plate. It wasn't about where we were each from, or who we were, but about brotherhood and respecting one another; I thought to myself that this is how brothers should treat one another, with kindness.

I soon became friends with a few of those brothers in Jersey. I did a lot of physical exercises with Mohammed and Abdullah. We did push-ups, dips, and pull-ups on the bar across the shower; we took turns seeing who could do the most pull-ups on the bar without taking a break. When one of us came off the bar, another would get on it. We each usually managed to do about twenty pull-ups at a time. As I spent more time with these brothers, I began to gain a new perspective on life, and began to change the way I thought. Where I previously had a mindset of only dealing with people who were from my neighborhood, these brothers taught me that it is not about where a person is from but more about their character. It would be accurate to say that it was during my time in New Jersey that I started the process of growing spiritually; I attended a few religious services while there, and heard some good messages. There was a Cuban who was fifty-one at the time and even though he was more than twice my age, he did a lot of push-ups every day, about fifty in each set. He would say, "I am fifty-one and I do five hundred push-ups a day." This person was a motivation to me and, years later, I frequently remember both his words and his hard work throughout life in general, and during my own physical exercise sessions in particular. I later got a job in the kitchen, and after a while I started sending food to the second floor dorm, just as the brothers had previously done. Those in the dorm ate well every night, and I wanted to continue the tradition of goodwill.

When I went to court, there was a very large group of us piled in a bull pen, one of the large holding cells. There were probably one hundred people or more waiting to be seen by the judge, and a number of fights broke out during this time. When the fights broke out the officer did not come in, but rather made the problematic individual come out; to get out of the cells, a prisoner would first move into another caged area and the gate would close behind them. After that gate was secure, the officers would then open the other door that led to a hallway; these caged areas were rather large, and could accommodate up to fifteen or twenty prisoners at one time. In court, I pleaded guilty to the drug charge, then I stood in front of the judge and listened as he spoke; he informed me that, while he understood that I was serving an extended sentence in Delaware, the state of New Jersey needed justice also. He then handed me a sentence of five years, which could be served either concurrently or consecutively; a consecutive sentence is when one sentence is served at a time, and a concurrent sentence is when two sentences are served at the same time. The judge chose to give me the concurrent sentence, which meant that I could serve my five years to New Jersey while also serving my twenty-two years to Delaware and thus reach the cumulative twenty-seven-years. Shortly after receiving my sentence, I was transferred back to Delaware to spend the next two decades of my life.

Mark Baynard 173

Back at the prison in Delaware, I was housed in a recently expanded section of the facility. In the housing unit I was assigned to, I saw Kevin Go; we both had long prison sentences to serve, and were very happy to see one another. A few months later we were transferred to the State Prison and housed in the Pretrial Unit. This is the intake area before getting our initial classification, which can take anywhere from two weeks to a month. A prisoner's initial classification determines which security level, as well as which housing unit, they require. The next process is waiting for bed space in the general population area. I was housed on the same tier as Kevin Go and my Uncle Mantol. The last time that I had seen my uncle, an officer had him on the ground and was placing hand cuffs on him; it was good to see him doing so well and maintaining a clear mind. He did not have a long sentence, and was scheduled to go home within a year or so. Before he left, we got to enjoy a visit together with our family, when my mother visited me and one of his relatives came to visit him. I told my mother that Kevin Go was in the prison with me, and that we were looking after one another.

I did not worry my mother with the details of life in prison. Kevin Go had informed me that word was sent from the compound that he needed to pay $800 to one of the guys who had been in prison for more than twenty years. He asked what I thought he should do, and I asked him the same question in return; he said he was not going to pay the money and that he was not going to be intimidated. This was taken as a real situation, but somehow it was discussed and settled by a few key people, and there was no trouble. There was another guy back in the Pretrial Unit when I first arrived; he had been on the tier for a while, and claimed to have known Kevin Go from the street. Kevin Go did not know the individual at all, and while this particular guy was cool with a number of the other guys, I was in a position to make sure no one jumped on Kevin Go. One day as we left the chow hall and entered the tier, I noticed there was a large crowd on both sides of the hall. Kevin Go and I knew a situation had been brewing, but we were not looking for trouble and continued walking. One of the guys reached out and sucker punched Kevin Go, and the two started fighting; I encouraged Kevin Go to fight with all of his might, since

there was really no other option. I yelled,
"Fight him, Kevin Go!" and fight him, he did!
I was prepared to jump in and help if it was
necessary, but Kevin Go went hard and put up
a good one-on-one fight. After that, Kevin Go
earned himself quite a lot of respect,
particularly from the person who initially
claimed to have a problem with him. The
instigator and his guys had a meeting, and the
majority of the guys on the tier assured us that
there wouldn't be any more issues.

Kevin Go and I were transferred from the
Pretrial Unit to the compound on the same
day. Even after our relocation, Kevin Go had
fights with a few others; some were based on
jealousy and hate, some in response to a claim
that Kevin Go caused them this or that wrong
back on the street, or harmed a family
member in some way. After the first year or
so, he didn't have any more problems, at least
not any more than the average prisoner faced.
We continued to hang out together and look
after one another as best we could. One day
while we were standing in front of the
building and talking, an older guy came up
and handed Kevin Go a note. I recognized
him from my housing project; his name was
Steamy and I, and many others, had a lot of

respect for him. When Kevin Go read the note, he saw that it was a list of some sort and asked Steamy, "What is this?" Steamy said he wanted Kevin Go to purchase those things for him from the commissary, but when Kevin Go refused, Steamy wanted to fight. I quickly stepped in the middle of them, and despite Steamy's adamant request to punch it out, I managed to prevent an altercation.

The compound of the prison was the closest thing to the outside world as we were allowed to experience; in it was housed the general population of prisoners who were serving time for everything from burglary to murder. There were prisoners serving sentences ranging from a few years to life sentences. Circulating among the prisoners were drugs, alcohol, cash money, and other contraband. Once I was transferred to the compound, I found that I had another uncle and a couple cousins who were there serving time, as well as a host of people that I grew up with. It was almost like a reunion of sorts, and I was more focused on daily life than on how bad things really were, or that my family was being affected by a curse.

After arriving at one of the housing units in the compound, I was then assigned to a tier and given my own cell. Once, even before moving into my cell, I saw several more people that I knew, some from the streets and some from my previous imprisonments. Uncle Randall and Lil' Jay were both there, as well as Big Bob, a guy that I knew briefly during high school because he shared a class with one of my sisters. Big Bob was vaguely familiar with some of my dealings on the street, but we did not hang out together. Apparently he was doing well for himself, because the last time that I saw him he was riding good, had jewelry, and nice clothes. When I entered the tier we acknowledged one another, and later we communicated often. We got to know each other better, and there were times when he intervened in my situations to keep me out of trouble and I did the same for him. He was a pretty big guy, but he was a teddy bear at heart; not a pushover, but rather a person who showed genuine concern for others.

Most of the buildings on the compound are separated by fences for security purposes. It was summer time and all of the gates were opened and prisoners could move from building to building freely. This is referred to as "open compound." On the main compound, there would typically be more than one thousand prisoners at once, and it was very important to be on guard. Anything can happen at this time, and the potential for violence during open compound is heightened since prisoners can group up in larger numbers to take care of old beefs. This was the perfect time for Steamy to settle his differences with Kevin Go, and he waited until he found Kevin Go in a vulnerable position. Kevin Go had some real rapping talent, and was rapping on the compound with a crowd around him, hyping him up. Without warning, Steamy ran into the circle and hit Kevin Go; I can still hear the Riverside Project crew saying, "Don't anybody touch my boy, Steamy." Regardless of such instruction, Kevin Go fought back, just as he should have, and apparently made his point because he and Steamy appeared to get along better after the scuffle.

I did not realize it at the time but I was slowly growing in my spiritual walk with God. I had gotten into reading the bible quite regularly, and would read it in the morning when I first woke up, then again before and after chow, and during the afternoon and evening. I was hungry for knowledge, and I wanted to know more about God. At this time, I also started attending Christian services, and noticed that my faith was starting to grow; before long, my faith was so strong that I believed I was going to be release in a few years, rather than in twenty-seven. It was during this time when I truly started feeling remorse for all the wrong things that I had done before coming to prison. As I reflected on my behavior towards my mother and the other women in my life, I started repenting for the ways I had treated females. I wrote a lot of letters to my mother during this time, telling her of the changes that I was making and also asking her for forgiveness for the disrespect that I showed her. Even though I was growing spiritually, I could not let me guard down to those around me; I knew that I was constantly in a potentially dangerous place and that anything mundane could spark into something serious. I remained aware and very watchful, and I was always prepared to defend myself whenever the situation required. I used to work-out several times a week in order to keep my body conditioned; I lifted weights in the gym, did pull-ups and dips on the yard, and push-ups on the wall. At one point I went through a running phase, where I ran three to five miles around the yard each day. I did not realize that running could be so addictive, and before I knew it I had lost twenty or thirty pounds. I eventually went back to my regular routine of lifting weights and doing other physical exercises, but I was still committed to taking care of my mind, my body, and my soul.

I considered myself to be a first generation hip hop enthusiast. When I was younger I enjoyed listening to hip hop music, and can still go back to the late 1970s and early 1980s and tell you the different rap songs that were out at that time. In the late 70s, I was a huge fan of Kurtis Blow, and during the mid-80s I got more into conscious rap artists such as xklan, Public Enemy, Boogie Down Productions/ KRS-One, Eric B. and Rakim, Brand Nubian, Poor Righteous Teachers, Run DMC, Whodini, L.L. Cool J, and many others. In prison, however, I drifted away from listening to any music, and I wasn't even watching music videos at the time; I chose instead to study and learn from my bible. I would still hear the music being played by other prisoners, but I did not play any of my own. Looking back to my childhood, I would be inclined to say that I was a thinker ever since I was very young; I did not know how to use those abilities in the way that I should, though I did know that I wanted more than the things that I was experiencing. Even during my time on the street I wanted more.

One day Big Bob came to talk with me; he came and hung out on a regular basis, and we would have different discussions. This particular day he wanted me to hear a certain rap song; he knew that I wasn't really listening to much music, but he thought that I would like the song. I agreed to listen to the song, and he hollered for me the next time it came on the radio. Big Bob was right, I did like it, and it was like I was back in love with hip hop again! The song was "Juicy" by The Notorious B.I.G. and the words described some of the things that I had experienced in my own life, that of making a change, and going from being poor to living rich. Even though I knew I was still poor, I had not completely given up my dreams of doing better. Later on I would come to embrace The Roots, the Refugees, and others during the 90s.

Chapter XI
Life on the Compound

After I had been on the inside for about three years, my dad had filled his sentence and came home from the federal prison. One of the first things he did was start sending money to me, and later he came to visit. I finally managed to complete the classes to receive my high school diploma, and my dad came to my high school graduation within the prison. I was very excited to see him since we had not seen each other in a few years; he wore a nice suit and was dressed very appropriately. My mother also attended the ceremony. The time with family made me think about my daughter, who was now around the age of three; I felt a lot of guilt and shame for leaving my first and only child. Every day I spent a lot of time reflecting on all of the mistakes that I made throughout my life, and I realized that I did not use all of the resources that I had readily available to me when I was out on the streets hustling. On one occasion, my dad brought his friend Frost with him to visit me; Frost had previously been in prison, too, and he and my dad both told me that they could not wait for my release. The three of us had a number of good conversations about life and true success, and I was glad to see that my dad was working on getting his life together after being locked up for a few years. At the same time he was seeing what he could do in order to help my chances of getting out sooner rather than later.

This helped in my efforts to take a very serious look at myself. I knew that I wanted more for myself and I began reading a lot of books. I read books on black history, I read slave narratives, and I read books about Africa. And, as always, I read the Holy Bible many times from front to back. I was on a mission to learn more about God, as well as about my African American history. I participated in several drug and behavior treatment programs, and attended classes that taught topics ranging from parenting to self-esteem, as well as a few college courses. While attending these groups I was able to be honest about myself, and it was encouraging to hear others do the same. Often I spoke about how I viewed myself as well as how I felt about myself. This honesty was the beginning of my personal growth. I later became involved in two programs, Men with a Message and Project Aware. Men with a Message taught us how to transcribe textbooks into braille so that visually impaired students in public school had reading material; while in the program, I became certified in literary braille after going through a one-year program, which ended with my submission of a thirty-five-page manuscript to the library of congress. Project Aware is a program that allows prisoners to speak to young people about the realities and dangers of risky behavior such as drugs and street life. I was grateful for the opportunity to be able to address many of the issues that had been going on inside of me for so many years. I made an effort to hang around people who were doing positive things and I attempted to prevent certain negative situations by removing myself, although this not mean that I backed down if someone attacked me. I did not pick and choose who I would fight, but merely tried to maintain a balance between benefitting and protecting myself.

Taking these steps revealed to me the severity of my situation; though I was sorry for my past behavior, I had to pay the price by serving time. This realization made me feel that my life was going to pass me by, and the thought that my life would end as nothing more than that of someone who got high and spent a lot of time in prison frightened me. I knew that the quality of my future rested on the quality of the decisions I would make from that day on. At this time I viewed my situation as personal, rather than familial, and I used to tell myself many times that "I can handle whatever happens to me." I knew that I could have accepted it if I had gotten hurt on the streets, and I knew that I could serve my time for selling drugs. Not until later, however, would I consider how my actions affected others.

The norms of prison are a lot different than the norms of free society. There was another day they had open compound, and I ran into a guy, Stance, that grew up in the same housing project as mine. We were walking around the compound and sharing with one another about the changes we were trying to make in our lives, and about the power of having faith. I had purchased some kind of cake from one of the guys in the kitchen, and I can remember sitting the cake down and telling Stance that the cake would be there when I returned. We walked another lap around the compound, talking and sharing, and when we returned the cake was still in the same place I had left it. We were standing there, continuing to talk, when another person approached. This gentleman was very hostile, and he looked at Stance as he pointed at me and said, "Come on cousin, let's get this guy. This is one of the guys that jumped on me." Stance looked at him and said, "No, Mark is not like that any longer." I stepped forward and apologized to the guy, and reiterated to him that I had changed. I told him that if he still wanted to fight, it was up to him. The guy decided to decline and eventually left; as I remained there with Stance, I thought about what the guy had said, and felt bad in my heart for the things that I committed in the past. Yes, I was in the process of making a change, but I was still dealing with some of my own demons. Due to the frequent violence and the problems the officers had of dealing with the large groups of prisoners, the prison soon decided to stop allowing open compound.

I was committed to making a personal change in my life; I came to the realization that I was not satisfied with my life, and God was continuing to give me guidance and help me make better decisions. I knew that I wanted more for my life, but I also wanted to be a good dad to my daughter. I had started writing to her once a week; even though I knew she was too young to understand the letters. It was important to me to write to her, as I wanted to prove to her that she was in my thoughts and prayers. I did not blame anyone else for the situation that I was in because I knew that it was my fault; I took full responsibility for both my actions and for being in prison. In prison we were told what to do, and when to do it; we did not have any control over our own lives. Yes, we could go against the grain and break the rules, but then we would be put in lock-up; I did not want the prison to have any more control over my life than was absolutely necessary. I made a conscious decision to do certain things on my own, such as stop drinking the juice that they gave us, which later I found out was used to dye our white tee shirts. Prisoners named the juice after a person who used the beverage to kill others, and it was said to cause long-term health issues, such as cancer. While this rumor was not a proven fact, it was enough for me to stop. I was already inclined to think that the prison did not have our best interest at heart, and this added to that concern. In the end, though, I just wanted some of my freedom back. I even cut back on the amount of salt I used, and only used a portion of the entire packet that was placed on our tray during chow time. I also started my day well before the officers yelled down the tier to wake us up. I would get up probably thirty minutes earlier; if the officers were scheduled to wake us up at five o'clock, I would get up around 4:30 am. When I was a child, my grandmother used to tell me that she did not need an alarm clock in order to wake up. I thought that was amazing. For many years I did not believe that I could do it, but one day I thought prison would be a good time to see if I could do the same thing. I went to sleep knowing that I wanted to wake up before the officers were scheduled to wake us, and the next morning I did wake up early. Without an alarm clock! By the time the officers called to wake us up, I had already brushed my teeth and washed my face. From that day forward I have not used an alarm clock to wake up.

After several years of working hard on my attitude about life, there were others who began to notice my shift in demeanor; I started to think that my good efforts were beginning to pay off. By "pay off" I mean that good things started happening for me. Joseph, another prisoner who was very active in the prison community, began to notice me. He was well-respected throughout the entire prison—even the administration held him in high regard—and I started attending church services with him. Joseph was also active within the Protestant community, and one day he approached me with the idea of becoming the chaplain's assistant. My initial response was negative because, given the past I had, I did not consider myself a legitimate candidate. Joseph convinced me that the chaplain had approved his idea of hiring me, and I eventually agreed to become the assistant to Chaplain Penelton. For more than three years—the longest I had ever held a job—I typed memos and letters for the chaplain, and kept up with the filing and record keeping. The job gave me a sense of accomplishment, and I took pride in it; I showed up on time and did my work to the best of my ability. I started out using a regular type writer, but he eventually bought a word processor with a monitor. This was a major upgrade for us, and allowed me to make corrections before printing any of our documents. Chaplain Penelton was very well organized and disciplined, and I learned a lot while working in his office. His children were all home schooled, and his wife attended

Sunday services in the prison chapel with
their children each week. Chaplain Penelton
came from a Mennonite religious background,
and there was a time when they did not have
electricity or a television in their home. When
he got the job at the prison, he became a
Baptist minister.

Joseph was also the one who initially
invited me to the Project Aware program, one
of the most respected organizations inside the
prison. I was previously housed on the same
tier as the director of this program, Edville,
and was somewhat familiar with it. I was
welcomed as a visitor and later accepted as a
member. Several years prior I had
successfully completed a treatment program
that Edville facilitated, and I successfully
made it through the probation portion of the
program. Outside youth programs brought in
their students as a final effort to intervene,
and prisoners within the program did their
very best to reach those youth. Prisoners, i.e.
counselors, were paired with the youth; each
session included a brief presentation from one
of the inmates, followed by a question and
answer segment. I spoke on several occasions,
and while I stumbled over myself the first few
times, I learned how to remain confident

while speaking to the youth. I met a number of honorable individuals within this program and I was inspired by the ways they passionately shared their experiences with the youth. I became pretty close to the members of the Project Aware program and they became individuals whom I could talk to as well as learn things from. This program was run by the prisoners without assistance from any officers—some administrators did not entirely support the program—and none of us were promised an early release for participating in the program. The Project Aware program was somewhat of a controversy at this time; one local newspaper quoted our Treatment Administrator as saying that he did not believe in rehabilitation, though he never clarified his statement when prompted. Outside the prison, several local individuals not only offered support, but played active roles. Reverend Diane, a minister in the state of Pennsylvania, worked as a liaison between our efforts in the prison and the needs of the community. She assisted in reaching out to area youth programs and informing them of our program.

In addition to the youth programs, a few other guys asked the officers if we could go into the prison infirmary where the sick prisoners were housed to visit and encourage the inmates. The chaplain backed our request, and we were given permission to do so; I found this to be a very good experience because I felt that I was finally doing something good. We would go and offer encouragement to the sick prisoners, and play a few games if they wanted to. Some of these people did not have anyone else coming to see them, so this was a blessing to them. My friend Vine had gotten very sick and was transferred to the infirmary with a terminal illness; he began to lose weight and deteriorate very quickly, and I became close with him during the last few months of his life. Despite the poor condition that he was in, his spirit remained strong and I learned a lot from him. We had a lot of good conversations during this time, and he always had encouraging words to offer.

While serving time, I frequently heard about some of my younger cousins who had gotten arrested and charged with murder. My shock was primary based on the fact that I had always seen them as good children, and I suppose that I may have expected more out of them. While I knew that we each had to work out our own salvation, and while I did not know who was guilty or innocent, I did see that my family was falling into what appeared to be a curse. Already my dad, my younger brother, my cousins, my uncles, and I had been in prison, some of us at the same time and even in the same facility. Added to that number were now my younger cousins. At this point, one of my uncles and one of my cousins had been released, but another of my uncles was still there with me. My grandmother on my mother's side of the family passed away while we were in prison and this hit me hard because I knew I would never get the chance to show her that I could change my life. She had previously watched me get arrested, serve time, and eventually return right back to the same lifestyle. Uncle Randall was allowed to attend my grandmother's funeral, but I was not, since the prison policy which permitted a pass for immediate family members of the deceased had recently been changed to exclude grandchildren. Chaplain Penelton was very strict and followed and supported most of the restrictions set in place by the administration. I was upset by this fact, since my family was very close and I considered my grandmother to be my immediate family. My only consolation during this time was that during her last visit I assured her I was making changes. It is one thing to talk the talk and another to walk the walk, however, and I do regret both my refusal to change sooner and my subsequent inability to properly pay my final respects to her. There was a second chaplain, Chaplain Watkins, who was a little more lenient when it came to facility standards and he did allow phone calls to prisoners who had deaths in their families. He was also an advocate for the prison population and spoke about equal treatment for all. In addition to his contribution to the prison, Chaplain Watkins reached out to some of the African American Churches in Wilmington, Delaware, as well as some in Pennsylvania and New Jersey. He later died after serving the prison for a number of years and he was missed by all.

Soon after, Uncle Randall was released from prison after serving his entire three-year sentence. I was happy for his release, but came to miss his company; during my time on the streets I had many memories of Uncle Randall having my back. He was always there for me when I needed help; there were numerous times that I called him to assist me when I had problems in the housing projects and he would get there within a few minutes. During one of those situations he got shot in the hand while pursuing a person that was shooting at him.

One day I was watching the news and I saw a report of a shooting that had taken place at a night club in Philadelphia when someone shot the bouncer; this upset me, and I thought to myself, "Why would someone shoot a person who was just doing their job?" The next day Lil' Jay's picture flashed across the television as the suspect of the shooting and I had mixed feelings about this information; initially, I did not want my cousin to get caught but I was sad about what he had supposedly done. Lil' Jay went on the run for a while, but was eventually caught in another state. There was another report showing a person on the news claiming to have previously been shot by Lil' Jay, and that the shooting at the night club could have been prevented if Lil' Jay had been put in prison for shooting him. In the prior incident, my cousin Lil Jay was arrested, and later released due to lack of evidence but this case was different. The vicious cycle of street life and prison continued to grow without any of us noticing. My younger cousins who had gotten arrested for murder had all received long prison sentences. I could see that there was a problem within my family, but I did not fully realize the realities of the situation; where I come from, this is simply life.

Kandy came to visit me a few times to offer support. I always knew that we could team up together and make money if necessary, but I was happy that she had been able to move on and was now doing something different with her life. I had received a few letters from her after my transfer to the prison in Delaware, but it had been a while since I had seen her in person. Then one day I got the news that Kandy had been shot and killed in a senseless shooting between two groups in front of a club. This made me very sad as I thought of the many times that she had my back through the years, the time she wanted to hustle for me in order to get me out of jail, and of the many personal conversations that we had about life. I had always admired her as a person and as a young lady; she had goals and dreams just like the rest of us. I knew that she did not deserve such an ending to her life. Even today, the song "Gangsta B**ch" by Apache reminds me of her; she was not a b**ch, but the song speaks about a female who has your back. When Kandy was with a person, she had their back. She had been very popular in the city because of this, and always received love from the guys in the prison, many of whom knew her from the hood. After her murder, a number of attacks broke out in the prison as people fought anyone that they thought might have been affiliated in even the slightest ways with her shooter.

Life in prison eventually got to the point where all of my dreams consisted of prison; there were a few times that I dreamed about my family or other people from the free world but even these were set in the prison environment that I saw and experienced each and every day. In prison, no movement is allowed until count is cleared. According to the administration, count time is one of the most important things in prison; the purpose of the count is to make sure that everyone is there and that no one has escaped. Count usually takes around thirty minutes or so to clear. One day I noticed that the count of the prisoners did not clear. At that time I was housed in an open dormitory with the beds placed next to one another. As I waited, I looked out the window and saw prisoners pushing carts, the kind used when moving one unit to another. Shortly after, the door opened to our building and several officers entered; one of them walked directly to someone near my bunk and handed a piece of paper to him. He said, "This is what you can and cannot take." The same officer then made eye contact with me and walked in my direction. He gave me a piece of paper with the same list on it. The officer did not tell us where we were going but only said, "You have five minutes to pack." The state of Delaware had recently made an agreement with the state of Virginia to send three hundred of its prisoners; this new policy was an effort to better handle the problem of prison overcrowding and to save money. The reality is that it was a big inconvenience for our families; our choices had sent us to prison, however, and left our lives in the hands of another. There had been rumors circulating among the prisoners that some of us would be transferred, and I was among those selected. Some of those who had not been selected felt that we were unjustly taken, since they too could just as easily have been chosen. We were shipped by bus in two separate trips of one hundred fifty prisoners. The backs of our seats were against the walls of the bus with a cage separating the driver and the prisoners. We were handcuffed while on the buses and the security was heavy; several armed officers rode up front with the bus driver and a number of armed officers escorted us in vans. They all carried semi-automatic weapons. On the bus I rode on, we talked about entering the unknown territory of a prison in a different state, and the need to put any of our differences to the side and stick together. We each knew all too well the realities that anything can happen in prison. Back in Delaware, Edville got the names of everyone who was shipped to the state of Virginia and he designated those individuals as MIA whenever roll call was made.

Life at the prison in Virginia was different in a lot of ways. To our surprise the officers were kind of nice; they tried to treat us with respect and, after we got settled in, gave us jobs. Once again I got a job as the chaplain's assistant. The food was a lot better at this facility; we were allowed to go back for seconds during chow and that was something that we had not been allowed to do at the prison in Delaware. When it was time for count, the officer would blow a whistle as he entered each hallway; this alerted the prisoners to then stand for count. This was very different from count at the other prison, and I initially felt uncertain; the unfamiliarity of this and other aspects added to my worries about what I may possibly encounter in this new prison. Eventually I began to settle in, and was soon able to relax. I received a letter from my brother's ex-wife; she informed me that she now lived in Virginia and that she would be able to visit me whenever it could be arranged. While she had always been like a sister to me, it had been many years since we visited, and I was able to reestablish a relationship with my niece and nephew when she came to see me. She also helped make arrangements for my daughter, who was now six-years-old, to come visit me. My dad was able to travel to visit me more often, as was my younger brother.

I was in this facility during the whole "Y2K" buildup when it was believed that all computers were going to crash. Most prisoners wished that the computers would crash and that all of their prison records would be lost; perhaps then the prison system would be forced to release us since they wouldn't know when our actual release dates were. Yes, this was wishful thinking, but despite the fantasy aspects, everyone stayed awake that night to see what would happen. I went to sleep the usual time, and when I woke up I discovered that things had remained the same and I would have to serve the entirety of my sentence. At this time, the state of Virginia was rated second in the number of prisoners executed and we happened to be housed where the executions were conducted; a few of us used to gather and pray each time someone was executed, but then it started happening so frequently that we eventually stopped doing so.

I saw many prisoners get shipped in from a wide variety of other prisons, and I met a lot of people from Michigan, Connecticut, Vermont, and Washington D.C. We organized sporting events, such as softball, basketball, and baseball, and individuals from the various states competed against each other. I played in some of the football games. The high tension levels at this particular prison created increased potential for danger; the sporting events provided an alternative to fighting and killing by giving the prisoners a different outlet for their aggression We competed to the highest level, and despite their propensity for violence, the prisoners from different states maintained at least a level of peace during the three years I was there.

There was only one close call that happened during a basketball game between the Detroit, Michigan, and the Wilmington, Delaware, teams. The Wilmington team was difficult to beat; they had a great coach who was nicknamed Head Coach, and he only ever played seven or eight of his best players at a time. Head Coach was originally from the city of Detroit but had been arrested in Wilmington and was serving his time in a Delaware prison before being transferred to Virginia. The Detroit team was just as strong; they matched players at every position, and it was a very intense and exciting game. The gymnasium was packed with about five hundred prisoners and, while there was no security inside of the gym, a few security guards would occasionally look inside to make sure things did not get out of hand. Loud cheers from both sides of the audience made each play seem like a prime time highlight on ESPN. The referees were split equally between prisoners from each state to minimize the claims that another team was cheating. Near the end of the game the referee from Detroit either made a call, or didn't make a call, that allowed the Detroit team to win by a very small lead. While they celebrated, someone off the Wilmington team punched Snelle, a Detroit referee, in the face. The hint of a fight drew in a large group of Detroit fans. One of them asked Snelle, "What happened?" Snelle turned to his hometown friends and said, "Nothing happened." I see now that Snelle prevented a major incident from taking place; if Snelle had told the truth, there would have been a big fight between the Wilmington and Detroit guys. I knew Snelle from the church services I attended at the prison, and I have to say that his actions exemplified what it means to put one's self aside for the good of others. Maybe he knew that a lot of people would get hurt if a fight broke out, and as a result, chose to be the bigger person. At that particular time, I can say that I would not have had the strength to do that, and I admired the way he put his faith into action. Despite their loss, the Wilmington team later went on to win the championship that year.

After three years in Virginia, I was sent back to the state of Delaware. Upon my return, I became thoroughly focused on attaining an early release. My faith had gotten stronger and I believed that my release would come soon; for the first time in many years, I had a very strong desire to make it home. I knew that I still had a lot more time to serve, but I claimed my freedom through faith and I had a fresh motivation to make things happen instead of waiting for God to do them for me. I knew God had given me the inspiration to do what was necessary to earn my freedom, so I sat down and started the process of gaining my freedom. I wrote a list of reasons why I should be given an early release and then, since my handwriting is terrible and I wanted the package to be legible, I paid someone to transpose these points into a letter to the pardon board. I then approached the people who knew me best and asked if they would be willing to write a favorable recommendation. With my letter to the pardon board in the mail, I waited.

Chapter XII
My Last Honor Visit

On Tuesday, September 11, 2001, I was in the education building of the prison waiting to return to the braille room. When I initially heard the story of the attacks on the World Trade Center, I visualized a small prop plane stuck in one of the towers with the tail sticking out. After watching the news, however, I realized that the reality of the situation was more than my mind could grasp. Even for those of us in prison, the tragedies of all four airliners changed the way life was viewed. That day, and now, I pray for all of the victims.

I played a lot of chess when I was locked up. One particular day as I was returning from my work in the braille program, I entered the dorm and noticed a new guy playing; he was pretty good at chess, and he was very vocal about letting that fact be known. Before I had returned from work, others in the dorm had told this guy, Tomack, that I was also a good chess player. When they told me this, and after I listened to him tell me how good he was, I asked to play the winner of the game.

The new guy won, and I easily beat him; I did not know it then, but that game was the start of our brotherhood. We played a lot of games after that, and we each won our fair share. Whether he won or lost, Tomack always wanted to play again; I was okay with this, since I noticed that my skills were improving more with each game. His game was also improving, and we were both learning from one another. After having a few conversations with him, I realized that we shared similar ideas and value systems and we quickly became really good friends. He shared with me that we wanted to attend college after he was released; a few months after he had finished his sentence, I received an encouraging letter from Tomack. I was surprised to hear from him, since he had not promised to write or stay in touch; I had heard many empty promises from others who said that they would write me when they were released. Tomack shared with me all of the positive things that he was doing in his life; he had enrolled in college, just as he told me he would, and we continued to write letters to one another for quite some time. I had gotten used to seeing others come and go while serving my time, but knowing Tomack was doing so well was an encouragement to me as

I continued to serve my time and tried to stay out of trouble.

Decision making is a very important part of our lives, as the decisions we make today will affect our tomorrow. The ability to make decisions is a gift from God, but with this gift come the responsibility of living with our decisions. Many members of my family, myself included, made decisions that contributed to the cycle of prison. One of the main problems I noticed when reflecting over my life is that I constantly looked for validation from others. I now understand that true validation can only come from within; a thousand others can offer encouragement to you but if you don't feel those things about yourself, it won't help much. A person has to believe in the value that exists within them, otherwise feelings of low self-esteem and a lack of self-worth may develop and ultimately ruin a person. I realized that, in addition to making better decisions, I had to identify and embrace the value of myself.

Throughout my life, there have been many people who positively influenced me; I could fill a book with names of family and friends, and how they influenced me in different ways. There was one particular guy that I knew while growing up in a housing project during the 1980s. His name was Derrow, and he actually lived in the projects across the highway from me, but frequented the project that I stayed in. Derrow kept his appearance up and was respected by others. He was known for being something of a ladies man back then, and he eventually became a local hustler. Around the time that I started hustling, he began to use more than he was selling and his appearance quickly started to decline. I found out that Derrow was serving a long prison sentence during the time I was serving mine; I learned that he was back to his prominent status by then, taking good care of himself, keeping his clothes looking like they had been ironed, and staying clean cut. Derrow had always been very intelligent, and while in prison he joined the ranks of the Islamic community; he became a member of the Nation of Islam and spoke to the younger population in an effort to inspire them to do something positive upon their release. He wrote articles in the prison newsletter and his topics mostly addressed taking responsibility for our actions. I read a few of his articles and found them inspiring; I was always impressed with his wisdom. His insights were helpful to me in my process of growing and developing as a young man, changing the friends that I hung around, taking accountability for my actions, and re-evaluating my values. At this point I was a member of the Christian community within the prison and as I started establishing different values I felt the urge to share this information with others. I decided to start by writing articles for the prison newsletter. My goal was to reach out to the large African American population within the prison, and in my articles I reflected on my own behaviors and how we, as a community, were leaving our children out there to make it the best way they can. I was passionate about how I felt, and the things I wrote about were very personal for me because my daughter had been born six months after I got arrested.

There was an older correctional officer, close to retirement at the time, who approached me about one of my articles. He appreciated what I wrote in the prison newsletters, and could often relate to their content. One particular day, however, he wanted to know why I spoke primarily to African Americans, since white people share some of the same concerns. I explained to him that the community I came from primarily African American and were directly and significantly affected by the lack of fathers and father figures. While there are always good fathers out there somewhere, I wanted to focus on the ones who weren't. In retrospect, I probably wrote this article more for myself than for anyone else, but I did understand the officer's point of stepping outside of the box in order to reach a larger audience; this has helped me in my interactions in the years since.

There was a guy name Leonard who grew up in the same housing project as I did. He may have been the best example of the continual battle with addiction. He was a few years younger than I, but we had a number of things in common. As kids, we shared the world of drug addiction and street life; as men, we shared life in prison. The gravitational pull of the streets can be strong, but Leonard was stronger; he had a natural talent for writing, and later wrote several novels. In prison, while writing his first novel, he would write on sheets of copy paper and then pass out ten or twenty sheets at a time and let us read the stories. I was amazed at his skill level, and noticed that he knew how to create scenes and build up anticipation by breaking at the right parts. The streets continued to beg his return even during his years of success, but Leonard chose to pursue his heaven-sent gift. While experiencing years of successful writing, drug addiction continued knocking at his door.

The day I had been waiting for finally arrived. I received a response from the pardon board, and was given a court date. When I walked into the hearing, I saw that most of my family was there. I knew these kinds of hearings could be intimidating, but I believed that God was going to deliver me. Sitting high on the board were high-ranking members of the state, but I noticed that the attorney's seat was empty. The board asked me a number of questions: "Why do you think we should recommend you for a sentence commutation?" "Where will you live?" "How do you plan to stay away from the life of drugs and crime?" and "Where will you work if we recommend you for release?" After serving an extended prison sentence, it was necessary for me to have a solid plan; I was prepared to answer the questions that they asked me, and there were a number of people who spoke on my behalf. My mother, my dad, my cousin Jack Willie, Tomack, my daughter, sisters, brother, and family friend, Poetic, were all there. My dad came up from Alabama with Jack Willie and one of his friends named Cocoa. I did not know Cocoa at the time, but he was dressed in a clean all-white suit.

Jack Willie attempted to soften the hearts and minds of the board with a moving argument that my sentence for drug possession was the same as that of a murderer. Tomack shared his own story as an ex-felon who made significant changes once he was released. My mother and dad spoke of the support that they would give upon my release, and my sister spoke of how I was the missing link to the family and deserved an opportunity to return home. Finally, my daughter went forward; she became very emotional, and I can still hear her simple yet powerful statement to the board that she needed me home with her. There was silence in the room as everyone waited for the board to make their decision; finally they announced their unanimous agreement to recommend me for a sentence commutation. A very loud cheer erupted from the audience, so loudly, in fact, that the board had to ask everyone to quiet down. I was told that the next step was to wait for the governor to either approve or deny the board's recommendation. I knew this was a process and nothing would happen overnight; when I returned back to the prison I was excited. I was also hopeful, and I prayed that the governor would sign for my release. Several times over the next couple days I called the governor's office to check on the status, but a decision had not yet been made. I knew what they were thinking: it can be a political risk to sign and release a prisoner, because if that person re-offends, it reflects poorly on the governor.

While waiting for my release there was a new sense of hope within my life. I started seeing life differently. Makel came in with a short prison sentence, around six months, and he was housed in the building across from mine. He had a brand new pair of sneakers that he gave to me, and he also sent me a few snacks from commissary. It had been years since we had seen each other, and Makel informed me on how everyone was doing. He told me that my mother bought a nice house; I heard about the house from someone else, but I was proud of her accomplishment, since she had always lived in the projects. After working hard for many years, she had eventually gotten a job at one of the leading banks in the United States. I was glad to hear that things were going well for her.

My dad traveled to Delaware to attend several of my honor visits, which are when family or friends can bring food in for us. I used to refer to them as a "twenty second time out" from the realities of prison. The last honor visit that I received was with my dad and Jack Willie, when they drove up to visit me one last time before I was scheduled to be released. They brought all of the food that I requested, plus more than I could eat; we sat there and had a very good conversation, and I really enjoyed our time together. My dad informed me that the hustle game was over in Alabama; he wanted to make sure that I understood that he was clearly out of the game, and he reiterated it more than once. He also told me that I could work at his rim and tire shop once I got out. He knew what happened the last time I returned to Delaware, and he did not want to risk it again. Looking back, this visit played a very large part in my decision to not return to the hustle game.

Before I left prison, there was new group
of cadets who were escorted through the
compound so they could get a feel for the
prison. They split them up and sent a couple
to each housing unit. There was a young
female who came to the housing unit I was in;
she was with a seasoned officer and when she
came on the tier I spoke to her and she was
pretty friendly. She happened to be from
Wilmington and we asked one another a few
questions just to make small talk. I showed
her our rooms, and where we took showers,
and then went about my regular schedule of
physical exercise and going to my various
treatment programs. One morning shortly
after this, the officers informed me that I was
being transferred; finally, the process of my
release was in motion and after all of those
years, my time was finally coming! I was sent
to a treatment facility in order to work my
way back into society and after being there a
few days, I received a letter from an unknown
female. In the letter she explained that I may
not remember her but that she was "the one
who came through as a cadet." Yes, I did
remember her, and I was glad that she was in
a position to be able to keep track of the
prisoners who were being transferred. I
responded to her letter and we soon became

friends; we respected one another and actively communicated during my time at the treatment facility. I also contacted her once I was released, and let her know that I wished her the very best in her life. In response, she was supportive of my efforts to become successful. Her influence on my life at that time was significant, and I appreciate and respect her. The treatment facility was located near a road, and I remember noticing how much I had missed the sound of tires riding on the road; I had not heard that sound in years. I could also hear the loud music coming from those vehicles, and fresh air replaced the stale smell of prison.

From the treatment facility I had to go to a few programs and work release centers before being fully released into society. The first work release center was very structured and during groups and seminars the females sat on one side of the room while the males sat on the other. The same rules applied while eating chow. The director of this facility was rumored to be an ex-offender, and was subsequently well aware of the tendencies for relationship issues at work release centers. I received a job offer in Wilmington to transcribe braille at the Braille Materials

Center; this was a state job, offered by the same people who ran the braille program within the prison. My counselor assisted me in getting transferred to the new work release center and, once I arrived, I noticed that, unlike the last center, males and females were allowed to sit next to one another. Many of them were especially excited about this fact; me, I was just eager to start a new life and enjoy my freedom.

Chapter XIII
Life after Prison

It was now 2004, and at this point, I was very thankful that my life had not ended; how tragic it would have been to author a story of failure: "Young man goes in and out of prison, and then dies an early death!" or "Former drug dealer/drug addict dies after serving an extensive prison sentence!" Once I was released from prison, I believed in my heart that I was destined to do great things; I guess that this was my own way of thinking big. I knew I could not change the past, but I was determined to make something good out of the rest of my life, and I believed that I was destined to make my life more meaningful. Yes, this would take hard work, but I was ready for the task. After the life I had lived so far, no one thought that I would ever amount to much, or do anything meaningful, but God is merciful and can use anyone. True, I *was* a repeat offender, but God was leading me with a purpose. I had learned a lot of tough lessons while in prison, but I had grown into a man while I was there. I had taken a very good look at myself and identified my weaknesses and strengths. My experiences had taught me to deal with each person as an individual, and to try not to prejudge anyone. Now, I was full of positive insights and I wanted to share them with whoever would listen; I did not want to return to my previous lifestyle, so I decided to start giving back to the community by getting involved with troubled teenagers. I searched for local opportunities to speak to youth about the dangers associated with crime.

It was like I had been awaken from a very bad dream; finally, I had made it home, and I desperately wanted to get my life together. After being in lock-up for a long time, freedom was something that I needed to get used to again; no one was standing over me telling me what I could or could not do, and no longer were there officers watching me eat, sleep, or go to the bathroom. My adaptation to these restrictions and limitations had been both physical and mental, and my recovery from them would be the same. In jail, segmentation is foundational to everything; there was a wall, sometimes a glass, which separated visitors from inmates during visitation, and red tape on the floor represented a restricted area—I never wanted to find out what the consequences were if I stepped across that line. I needed to adjust to being free!

Once I made it to the work release center, I could taste my freedom. Uncle Mantol got a phone for me through his account and told me that I was responsible for paying the bill each month. He also advised me to follow the rules by not bringing my phone inside the work release center; that was obvious to me, but I respected his wishes because I knew that it was not worth it to get sent back to prison for something as mundane as having a cell phone—when I first got the phone, I did not even know how to turn it on! I had a very strong support network of family and friends and I knew they would all be hurt if I chose to do something foolish.

The very first thing that I did once I arrived at the work release center was go to my daughter's house. I was very excited to see her and be able to hug her and let her know that I loved her. At this time she lived with her mother and her mother's husband, who had both raised her. For a long time I had known that she was being raised by another man, and I respected him and appreciated everything that he had done for her. He treated her and loved her as his own. I asked my brother and Tomack to go with me; my brother knew the guy who was raising my daughter and I wanted him and Tomack to be there to help keep the peace. They could act as mediators in the event that there were any problems, and I also wanted the man who raised my daughter to feel comfortable; I just wanted to finally be there for my daughter, I wasn't trying to threaten him in any way. My daughter referred to him as "dad," and I did not want her to think I had any problems with that; I took full responsibility for making the decisions that caused me to miss most of her young life, but I hoped that she would allow me to participate now that I was able.

He opened the door when we arrived, and warmly welcomed us into his house; he was cool about the whole thing, and we spoke to one another respectfully. I told him that I appreciated all that he did, and that, if it could be arranged, I wanted to be a part of my daughter's life. He understood that I was trying to be a dad to her, and he and her mother asked my daughter whether she wanted to go with me. She said yes. We went to the Waterfront in downtown Wilmington and got ice cream, then walked the boardwalk together; she asked me a lot of questions and I answered every one of them as honestly as possible. It was a very special day for me, and my family was happy that I was able to be a dad to my daughter. During our visit, I told my daughter that I was planning to move to Alabama once I completed the work release program; I invited her to join me but she did not want to go with me because she felt that I was too strict. My daughter was accustomed to certain privileges at her mother's, and didn't want to give that up.

During my time at the work release center I learned about a sister name Tania that was doing a lot of positive things in the community. She had started a non-profit organization in remembrance of her brother and, knowing that I was on a mission to make a positive difference in the community, a mutual friend suggested I contact her. We set up a time to meet, and we had a good, long conversation about life and contributing to the good of society. Knowing that I had just served a long prison sentence, she wanted to know some of my goals; I shared a few of them with her and talked about how I wanted to give something back to the community, the ways in which I was focused on getting my life together, and being a positive role model to those around me, especially youth. Tania allowed me to attend a few of her community events, and as we spent more time together I eventually realized that we had grown up in the very same housing project. Tania did not remember me at the time, but I had been friends with her younger brother, Purcey; she had grown into a woman by that time and I did not recognize who she was until she told me this. After Purcey passed away, she started a non-profit organization which focused on reaching youth before the youth reached the streets. I had gotten the news about Purcey while I was in prison and I was deeply hurt; the word was that he was entering his house when he was senselessly shot. I also heard that something similar happened to my childhood friend Doelt. The news I received was that he had been doing well, which apparently caused someone he was previously affiliated with on the street to lash out in hatred and jealously; Doelt was found shot in the head in one of the buildings that he hustled in. Both Purcey and Doelt had served prison sentences for hustling, but they both remained associated to some extent with their former lifestyles and things ended badly. I heard of countless others I had known through the years that had been killed or received long prison sentences, and it bothered my soul because this is one of the end results of the drug game. Not everyone who enters the street life is guaranteed to come out alive. Meeting Purcey's sister Tania was an inspiration to me, and a comfort in the wake of my friends' tragedies.

My mother's family had a reunion at a public park in Delaware; it had been years since we had done this, and everyone was overjoyed to be there. When we were all gathered together, one of my sisters stood up to give a speech; she expressed how happy she was that I was home, and became so emotional that she shed a few tears. I had gotten permission from the work release center to attend this event, but I was only given a few hours. Everyone was conscientious of my time constraint, since they did not want me to get sent back to prison for missing my curfew, and every few minutes someone was asking me, "How much time before you have to be back at the center?" The reunion was just starting to get exciting by the time that I had to leave, although as I arrived back at the center I felt lucky to have been able to attend; I thoroughly enjoyed myself even though I had to leave early.

The work release center I stayed at while working at the Braille Materials Center was not strict, but simply structured. The usual routine after returning from work was to get searched, and given a breathalyzer; of course, my drug and alcohol tests were always negative but in an effort to be released from the center more quickly, I also went to several AA and NA meetings. After each meeting we were required to have our papers signed by the facilitators, and if we were given permission to go to other places, we had to get a signature from those places, as well. When we went job searching, we had to get our papers signed by the perspective employer. I did my best to stay on top of my game while I was there, and met all of the deadlines and time limits placed on me. Despite the restrictions, some people managed to find ways around them.

One day, I was called to the office and asked whether or not I had someone to host me out, or provide me with a house to stay in. I said, "Yes," and then called Tomack, who got to the center as quickly as possible. The center gave me an eight o'clock curfew, and told me that they would randomly be calling Tomack's house and checking up on me. They would ask questions to make sure they were speaking to the right person. One time when an officer called, he asked me to describe a picture that was on the wall in the chow hall; I had seen that picture plenty of times but I could not remember anything specific about it. Another time a different officer called and he asked me to name each of the guys who were in my room when I stayed back at the center. During my time there, I chose not to deal with anyone, so I did not know everyone's name.

One of my female cousins was scheduled to get married and desperately wanted me to attend; I decided not to get permission for this event because I did not want to deal with the time restrictions but my cousin really wanted me to and I felt bad disappointing her on her special day. I went to the wedding and it was a blast. Everyone appeared to be having a good time, but I had to leave early to meet my eight o'clock curfew. Prior to leaving the house, Tomack had showed me how to forward calls from the home phone to my cell phone in the event that the center called me before we returned home. On the drive home I received a phone call from one of the officers; quickly I motioned for everyone to roll the car windows up and to be quiet. We did not do it quickly enough, though, and the officer heard the wind blowing. He asked me, "What was that noise?" I told him that I did not know—all I knew at that point is that we needed to get to the house *quickly*—and that officer could send someone to the house to check on me if he did not believe I was there. Thankfully, I made it to the house and no one came to check on me.

Once leaving the work release center I got my probation transferred to the state of Alabama. My decision to leave Wilmington was based on my need for a fresh start. I was focused and determined not to return to prison and while I was confident that I could have been successful in Delaware, I wanted to start new somewhere else. There were also various challenges related to dealing with some of my old friends in Wilmington, such as having to adamantly say, "No" when I ran into a few people who offered to help me get back into the game while I was at the work release center. I had just served a long thirteen-year prison sentence and I wasn't planning on returning. Leaving town was the best option for me at the time.

I could now clearly see the value of freedom. There was a time when I did not value my life or my freedom at all. I did not know, love, or see value within myself, and my past was a direct reflection of that. Because I did not love myself, I took a number of unnecessary chances with my life and put my life on the line each day that I woke up. I was willing to die for a cause which, in truth, was no cause at all. I did not think about it like this, but in retrospect, my actions expressed those thoughts. I came to learn that freedom is something that is priceless, and should not be sold.

In prison, the consensus was that most prisoners wanted to get their freedom back, to eventually be released from prison. Some did not realize that freedom can also be mental and spiritual but, personally, I wanted to *fully* experience freedom. I remember a particular prisoner who felt that "today was the day" that he would obtain his freedom; he worked in the prison appliance shop, and was serving a life sentence. The appliance shop is where they fix and sell televisions and radios to the prison population. I had my television fixed at the appliance shop after I accidently spilled water in the back of it. The prices were high, but I had to pay for them if I wanted my television fixed, since this was the only shop in town. The appliance shop had a number of prisoners who worked there each day. One morning this particular prisoner decided that "today was the day" and he made his move. There was a trash truck which went out each day from the shop, and his master plan was to hide in the metal trash can that the trash truck picked up. I later found out that the trash trucks are required to crush the trash with the compressor before they can exit the prison gatehouse. Not until the prison count that night was it noticed that this prisoner was missing. They later found his body crushed in the trash truck. He must have died a horrible death, and I do not think this is what he had in mind when he planned his escape. I wanted and desired my freedom just as badly as he did but I had a different plan and I am glad I stuck to it.

After getting my probation transferred, I caught an airplane down to Alabama. When the plane initially took off, I started holding tightly on to the seat; the guy next to me looked over and jokingly said, "Boo." I just looked at him and smiled a little because I did not know that I was so obviously nervous on the flight. Needless to say, I am not a fan of flying on airplanes because of the turbulence, but it was the quickest way. I was grateful when I landed in Birmingham where my family picked me up, and I was excited to see all of them. My dad and I sat down and had a very good conversation; we discussed the necessary steps for my transition back into society and the importance of saving money and getting back on my feet. Everything was simple; I would go to work and then come home. My dad helped me draw up a plan on how I could save a few dollars; he offered to allow me to stay with him for free until I could afford my own place, and said that I could work at his wheel and tire shop. Things were going well for me, and I wanted to remain free and outside of prison; I was focused on avoiding negative situations. I did have probation to serve, but that's better than prison, and I was required to report once a month. I also had to pay the probation fee each month, and my fines. But as we used to say, "That's a small thing to a giant." While I wanted to respect my dad and his house, I think the fact that I had just served a long prison sentence concerned him; perhaps he expected me to get involved with women. I did meet a few females but I didn't dare bring anyone around my dad's house at that time, so mostly I spoke to them on the phone. My dad would say, "You would be a bad man if you could touch them through the phone."

One day my dad invited me to go to happy hour with him. I did not know what to expect, since I had never been before. When we got to the club, it was totally different than what I expected and I ordered some chicken wings and a soda. The DJ was playing music and a few people were dancing. Some people sat around the bar while others were at tables and there was a section on the second floor where people sat at more tables. I learned that the owner of the club was a friend of my dad and that when my dad came in his club, the owner would come out and visit for a while. At one point I was called into a separate room where I met the owner's son; I remember him from when I went to school in Alabama and we embraced one another, had a good conversation, and caught up on good times. He then gave me an invitation to get with him and hang out. I never got together with him, since I wasn't into the night life after being released from prison, but I did return to happy hour a few more times. Each time I order the same thing, chicken wings and a soda. Once I saw Cocoa, and he was dressed nice, as usual; he told the waitress to put my order on his tab and a couple of others who were dressed nicely did the same thing. There was a lot of love shown to me in the south when I came home, and I felt that my decision to leave Wilmington had been a good one.

I had a very strong desire to work with youth. I wanted to assist in the fight to prevent them from heading in prison, or facing some of the things that I faced. I believed that my experiences could assist others in understanding what not to do; most of my problems had stemmed from the fact that I had very low self-esteem and after seeing how a bad decision can mess up a person's life, I was now on a mission to help others. I refused to sit back and allow another life to turn out like my own. My first step in making my plan a reality was to seek out local opportunities to help teenagers; I visited several community centers and requested to speak to the children. The responses came more quickly than I expected, and I was given an opportunity to speak to a troubled teenager at one of the local Boys & Girls Clubs, as well as at a group home that housed male teenagers. I wanted to have a positive impact on the youth, and there were times when I got off work and went directly to a community center to volunteer. Sometimes after work I stopped by a community center that I saw near a local housing project; I felt that this was relevant because I grew up in a housing project myself and I really wanted to help keep some of the kids from going down the wrong path. Wherever I visited, I informed the people at the front desk that I wanted to assist in the efforts of helping youth; they would then ask me to fill out some paperwork and provide them with all of my personal information. Each place told me that I would eventually hear from them but as time went by I did not hear back. I called the various organizations on several different occasions but they said they had forwarded my information to the board, and would call whenever they heard back. This community looked similar to the one that I had grown up in as a teenager, and I really wanted to help. After several more fruitless phone calls, I eventually gave up.

Chapter XIV
Met Malinda

I was developing a deep sense of pride and satisfaction with my life; the only thing missing was *the* special person. I firmly believe that it is necessary for an individual to be complete outside of their mate, companion, or spouse; after that, they can then share their completeness with another. At this time I saw myself as being complete and I was just waiting for that special person to share my completeness with; I wanted that rib. Before leaving prison, I had several dreams of a young lady, the same woman in each dream, which was made for me, and while I never saw a face, I could only sense that our spirits were in agreement. I was eventually introduced to this very beautiful young lady through a mutual friend who informed me that said female was "all about me." After hearing this several times, I finally called her job; her name was Malinda and, since she was not able to talk for long, she gave me her personal phone number. When I later spoke to her on her cell phone we were able to enjoy a more relaxed conversation; we asked questions of one another and were both honest with the answers that we gave. Later that day, we met near my job; I asked her if she would be interested in cooking something for me, and she agreed. She cooked dinner one night and I found that she was a pretty good cook; the food was delicious. The more time we spent together the more personal our conversations became, and we both believed that there was a lot of potential for us to grow together.

Malinda was a very independent young lady. While in high school she played basketball pretty well, it was a career as a softball player that she sacrificed, along with other personal goals, in order to take care of her mother. She bought her first home at the age of twenty-one, and took her mother in. Before I met her, and while I was on my way to a long prison sentence, Malinda was on her way to a successful life. We were two very different people with very different backgrounds; Malinda was raised in the south and knew a lot about rural, country areas while I was raised in the northeast and was very familiar with urban areas. Even to this day, she still holds fast to some of the customs that she learned while growing up; southern hospitality is a real quality and something which is still practiced in Alabama. I spent my teenage years living the life of a street hustler in Delaware while she was making realistic plans for her future in Alabama. Opposites truly attract!

I was working at my dad's wheel and tire shop and she had a casual desk job. I lived in the city of Montgomery, Alabama, and she lived in Prattville, Alabama. We spent a lot of time commuting between the two locations and I eventually started spending more time at her house. I would show up at my townhouse once in a while, sometimes just quickly enough to get a few sets of clothes before heading to her house. The area where my townhouse was located was a good community, but one that was starting to decline due to increased drug activity. One day I arrived at my townhouse to find that it had been broken into, and I got so upset that I knocked on several of my neighbors' doors and asked if they knew anything about it. I wasn't blaming them, but I wanted answers. I then called my dad and informed him of the situation; he and a few of his friends came and spoke to some the people who hung out on the streets and I ended up getting everything back that was taken, except for some meat that was in the freezer. I think that they may have thought that my house was a stash house. My dad had told me on several different occasions that I needed to show up at my house more often and at random times since he knew that those on the street would notice that I wasn't there very much. For a short time longer, I continued to go back and forth from my condo to Malinda's, but eventually we decided that it would be better for us to stay in one place together and it helped us both financially.

Since I met Malinda, and most likely for all of her life, she had been a very motivated go-getter. When she wanted something she worked hard in order to get it. When I first met her she was working at a substance abuse company, but soon afterward she applied for another job. She prayed about the job, and on the morning of her interview she told me that she was going to get hired. I was somewhat hesitant, but she called me later and told me that the interview went well and a few days later she got a call with a job offer and accepted the position. This was a testament of her faith and an inspiration to me. I knew I wanted her to meet my family, and we decided it was time for a trip north.

My mother and Malinda had spoken over the phone several times but they had not met face to face, and I wanted her to meet my mother and other family members in Delaware. We caught a plane to Philadelphia, got a rental car, and drove the twenty-five minutes into the city of Wilmington. As we got off the interstate and drove into the city, Malinda noticed a lot of trash on the streets; I had not noticed it and realized, as I thought back to when I was younger, that this was normal. She also noticed that a lot of young children would walk in front of cars while crossing the streets, and that there were a lot of people hanging around on the street corners. I began to reminisce about when I was a kid on the streets, and how all of these things were part of life; I realized that I had never thought about it much while growing up because I thought that's just what people did. Despite all this, I enjoyed being back in my home town. We finally arrived at my mother's house and when my mother met Malinda, she really liked her. My mother was surprised by our impromptu visit, but was very happy to see me. Malinda got along well with everyone she met, my brother, sisters, aunts, cousins, my daughter, and a few friends. We planned on getting a hotel room but my mother insisted that we stay with her for that weekend.

I wanted to drive through the city and show Malinda some more of the area I grew up in. We rode through different sections of the city, and it felt kind of good to be back at home and to be looking at things from a different perspective. While riding through one area, I noticed a female who was out working the streets, and after taking a closer look, I realized that this was my cousin Shelly. I pulled over, lowered the passenger window, and leaned my head out as she started walking up. She suddenly stopped, and looked as if she had seen a ghost. I then said, "Girl, get in the car!" She started crying, and probably felt guilty for all the choices she had made, and was making, concerning her life. We drove around and spoke to her for nearly twenty minutes, and she said that she understood and appreciated my concern; she also told me that she was attending groups and programs and that she knew what she needed to do. She then asked if I could drop her off at the next corner because I was interfering with what she was doing. This particular cousin was struggling with a heroin addiction at the time; the very next day I spoke to her while she was sober and she shared her experiences of being taken advantage of on the streets, as well as some of the things she had done in the past. Today, she is still in recovery and appears to be doing well; I attribute this to the fact that she is real about her struggles with addiction and all that she has gone through. I respect her for doing this. We check up on one another often, and text encouraging words to each other. I am thankful that she is part of my family, and I know that recovery from drugs can be a lifelong battle, as can recovery from alcohol addiction.

I can't emphasize enough the value of having others around me who was also struggling to make their lives better. Even after we returned to Alabama, the incident with my cousin reiterated to me that I was not on this journey alone. I had also met, Marcus, a local hairstyle professional. We talked while he cut my hair, and I discovered that there were several parallels in our lives; he had recently been released from the federal prison system and had also served time in the state system. Marcus shared with me that he was in the process of getting his life together and making better choices; this man was a deep thinker and spoke with a lot of relevant wisdom, and over the years we grew into friends.

It wasn't long before Malinda and I fell in love, and I asked her to become my wife. We were engaged for a year before our official day, i.e. our wedding. I woke up excited the morning of our big day in 2005, and I knew it was going to be special from beginning to the end. My family from Delaware flew to Alabama to attend our wedding, and my mother, my daughter, my brother, my sisters, and a few friends all came to show their support of my union to the woman I had come to love. Malinda's family in Alabama was well represented, and my dad, his wife, my younger brother, my sisters, Cocoa, Marcus, our family friend Banks, and many others were there. Our wedding was very nice, albeit low budget and it was everything that we wanted it to be. The ceremony was held at a small church; my wife was the star of the day and wore a beautiful dress with a long train. My daughter was one of the bridesmaids and this added to the specialness of the day; this was Malinda's day and she deserved to be the focus of the event. The reception was held at the community hall and, while we chose not to provide any alcohol, everyone appeared to enjoy themselves. We had a DJ, and catered food, which looked and tasted delicious. We soon left the reception to begin our honeymoon; we had made reservations in Florida but our hotel had been damaged during hurricane Katrina, so we drove to Birmingham and made the best of our newlywed celebrations.

The following year, we were blessed with a big surprise; Malinda was excited to find that she was expecting our first child and this was a special moment in our lives. Our families and friends were also happy for us and, while we knew that being parents comes with great responsibility, we were up for the challenge. When my first child was born in 1992, I was serving my time in prison and unable to fulfil the component of being present in her life. This time was different; our daughter was born in 2006 and we gave her the name Mariah. I was determined to be there for my child and I felt that I was being given this opportunity to be a real father to her from start to finish. The pregnancy progressed without complication, as did the birth; when the doctor handed our daughter to me, I took pictures and tried to remember everything about her physical appearance. (I heard a few horror stories about babies being switched at birth and I did not want to take the chance of that happening to us.) I took her to the waiting area so that the rest of the family could see her. The doctors wanted Malinda to remain in the hospital for a few days, and I stayed there with her and the baby the entire time. Even though it wasn't comfortable, I slept in the chair each night.

We finally left the hospital with our newborn daughter and armfuls of cards, flowers, stuffed bears, and balloons. Malinda was able to take off from work since she had worked up until the day that she went into the hospital, and this time provided all of us with the opportunity to bond. I was the happiest man on earth at that time and though she was but a newborn, I could not stop thinking about all the things I wanted to teach her and do with her when she got older. One thing that I knew for sure is that I was going to set a very high standard for what she should expect from a man.

Our daughter was a few months old when Malinda and I celebrated our first anniversary and we took her along with us to Birmingham. We chose a short road trip because, with our young daughter, we wanted to stay fairly close to home. We stayed in a hotel and drove to different places within the city during the day, and though we had groceries in the room with us we tried a variety of different restaurants. On one particular day the weather was nice and it was a good day to be outdoors; we decided to go shopping at the mall and walk around together. Malinda purchased a few things but we were mostly window shopping. At one point she wandered off and I started checking out a display that was in the middle of the thoroughfare; suddenly, Malinda ran towards me muttering something so excitedly that I could not quite hear what she said. Someone was somewhere, but I did not know who or where! She grabbed my arm and hurried in the direction of where she had seen this person. Just then she pointed and said, "There she goes!" I responded with confusing and said, "There who goes?" "It's Gayle," she said, and I asked, "Gayle who?" Malinda looked at me and said, "Gayle, Oprah's best friend!" Suddenly, something possessed us to walk inside of the salon where Gayle was, and Malinda said, "Gayle!" Gayle King then replied, "Yes, that is me." Gayle walked with us out of the salon, along with two teenaged children who she introduced as her son and daughter. Gayle King was nice to us, and allowed us to take a picture with her even though her hairstylist was waiting; her children held our camera and took two pictures of us standing next to her. Gayle wanted to hold our daughter, then she gave both of us a hug before she said she needed to go. It is not every day that we come across a celebrity, especially not in Alabama, and we enjoyed this unique anniversary gift. Whenever the topic comes up, or others share their experiences of meeting a celebrity, we tell our Gayle King story. When our daughter got older, we told her that she was held by Gayle King when she was a baby, and she found this to be very exciting; sometimes she asked, "How did you get to meet Gayle?" or "What happened when we met her?" As she got older, sometimes we would bring up the story and she would just say, "I know." To this day, whenever we see Gayle on television, I usually point and say, "There goes Gayle!" The best thing about this story is that we have the pictures to prove it! We haven't shown them to many people, but a few family members have seen them.

Mark Baynard   246

While I appreciated the opportunity to work at my dad's wheel and tire shop, after a while I decided to start my own business. I wanted to open a small wheel, tire, and detail shop where I would wash and detail vehicles, sell tires and rims, and maybe a few four-wheelers. This was a big step for me, but also a huge accomplishment; I had to work hard but I was more than willing to do so, especially after having been in prison for so long. When I informed my dad that I wanted to start my own business, he warned me of the many challenges I would face, but gave me his full blessing. Several people were happy that I stepped out on my own and they were hopeful of my success given how hard I worked. My friend Marcus would come over to talk, play a few games of chess, or simply offer his support by sharing something inspirational. While I built my business—some days were good and some days were not so good—I continued to make myself available to volunteer with youth. I was invited by a guy named Mr. Felton to speak at a group home for boys; the young men gathered in the living area of the facility as I spoke to them about my life experiences. My dad's friend Frost also spoke that night, and my time there was a fulfilling success. A few weeks later, Mr. Felton asked me if I had ever considered working in such a place as the group home and I said, "No, I had not." He told me that, while they had never employed an ex-offender before, he would try to get me hired. I was invited back to speak a second time, and I was encouraged by the prospect of officially working there; I filled out the necessary application paper work, and was eventually hired as a youth care worker. On the forms, I was completely honest with them concerning my background and was grateful that they made an exception for me; I believed that my truthfulness to them assured them that I was serious about this job and that I was not going to let them down. Working at this group home for boys opened the door for me to professionally work with youth; for a long time, I had envisioned myself merely visiting different places and volunteering, but God obviously saw otherwise. I was still on probation when I got this job, but life was going well and I was excited to be free and to enjoy a life outside of prison. I was now a business owner and a full time employee. As with everything in life, however, I knew that challenges of some kind were not far away, and I soon faced a variety of frustrations.

There were a number of jobs that I did not get based solely on my criminal record, and I quickly learned that being an ex-convict comes with a number of complications. One job in particular stands out in my mind; I filled out and submitted the application, and soon received a phone call from the prospective employer. The excited voice on the other end offered me a job, and I accepted. I was so excited and I shared this information with Malinda, and other family members; Malinda even went out and bought me several new sets of clothes for my new job. I finally felt that I had overcome my past and was making strides towards a better future. The very next day, however, I received another phone call from the same person, but this time their tone was not one of excitement. She told me that, though she fully supported my efforts to get a decent job in spite of my felonies, she had to rescind the job offer. My heart dropped. After a slight pause, the woman explained that this decision had been passed down from a top administrator within the department. I asked why, but she would not give me any information and I even called the top administrator but was unable to get any further than his secretary. In the first call, I left a message with my contact information but I did not receive a phone call back; the second time I called, his secretary asked me if I was calling about the job and I said yes. She informed me that her boss was not required to give me a reason for the decision why the job was rescinded. I understood this, but I still wanted to know; finally she vaguely referenced my background, but when I asked what specifically about my background did her boss dislike, she reiterated the fact that he was not obligated to provide me with a justification and politely ended the call. I wished there had been a way for me to meet with him so that he could see *me* instead of merely my name and information on a piece of paper. This instance and others like it made me just want to give up and settle for much less than I had originally hoped for. After that I applied to entry level jobs only.

Chapter XV
Vicious Cycle Continues

Before going to work each morning, I had a habit of watching the news. One particular day, in 2006, there was a report that an officer in Montgomery had been shot. My initial thoughts were, "How could someone do such a thing?" I soon forgot about the news item, however, and headed to my shop. Work went well that day, and just before closing time, a county sheriff came inside my shop and inquired about one of the four-wheelers. He appeared satisfied with the prices I gave him, and he said that he would eventually return to buy one. I left the shop that evening excited about the potential sale. At home later that night, there was a knock on the front door. When Malinda opened it, there were several federal agents standing there; despite the fact that I knew I was not in trouble, I feared that I had somehow violated my probation and was going to be extradited back up north. I felt a surprising sense of peace at the prospect of being arrested, however, and stepped outside to speak with the agents. One of the officers

Mark Baynard   251

walked with me a short distance from the house, and the other agents soon joined us. One of them asked me, "Did you hear about the officer who got shot yesterday?" I answered, "Yes, I did." They then informed me that my younger brother was the prime suspect in the shooting, and wanted to know when I had last spoken to him. The rest of our conversation was somewhat of a blur, as I had absentmindedly walked out of the house without any shoes on and was being bitten multiple times by ants. After we had finished talking, the agents went through my cell phone, and came inside and looked around our bedroom.

The next day, the guys at the mechanic shop across from my wheel and details shop told me they had seen helicopters flying over my neighborhood the night before, and talk of the incident was on everyone's tongues. A short time later, a female friend stopped by and told me that my dad's shop was flooded with federal agents. I thanked her, and then called my dad several times but could not get an answer. Later I learned that the law had taken over my dad's work space, and told him it was their shop for the time being. They made my dad, his employees, and a few customers get on the ground and remain quiet; apparently, my brother was on the run, and they hoped that he would stop by, and they could make an arrest. I suddenly realized that the county sheriff who had visited my shop the evening before was not interested in buying a four-wheeler at all, but was simply conducting the investigation on my brother. While I in no way wish to minimize the severity of the other crimes and indiscretions committed by myself and others, the most serious case my family had to deal with was this accusation against my brother. We all knew that this charge was a capital murder offense, and that he could potentially face the death penalty.

After these events took place, I noticed a significant change in my business. Attempting to survive while trying to grow a new business had been difficult, but I was slowly establishing myself and picking up new customers on a daily basis. Most of the locals knew that I was the brother of the key suspect in the murder case; I began to lose a large portion of my customer base and subsequently my business started to suffer financially. Some of my customers either greatly decreased their visits to my shop or just stopped coming altogether. There were a few customers who came by the shop and asked me, "Was that your brother who shot the officer?" I cannot say absolutely that the decline of my business was directly related to the situation with my brother, but either way, I found another location to open my shop and was determined to be successful with my business. The world is a small place, however, and people will eventually find out who you are; work at the new location slowly began to pick back up, and I spent the next few years working hard to keep it above the ground. I realized, however, that my business was not growing as I had planned. I thought I had a good idea and believed that the business would eventually make it. I put forth a lot of hard work and effort, but ended up putting more into the business than I was getting of it; when all was said and done, I had invested around $40,000 into it, as well as several loans. Instead of living off the business, my business was living off me. I went through a number of financial problems in my attempt to hold on, and this became a burden on my family. I was putting all my money into the business instead of into the house, and I was ultimately unable to pay my bills or the property rent. I spoke to the owner of the property, but he would not let me out of the lease. Calls and letters from various financial institutions starting rolling in, and I became very frustrated with the whole situation.

Law officials finally found and arrested my brother, and I attended the court proceedings while he went to trial. The courtroom was full of law enforcement personnel and their families. During recess sessions, my family mingled in the lobby along with them. This was kind of awkward for me, but I was glad to be able to be there for my brother. This was a difficult time for everyone in my family, and it was especially difficult for the officer's family. The atmosphere in the court suggested a spirit of vengeance rather than justice, and my step-mother began to fear for her son's life. I understood that the officer was a victim and that his family deserved justice but I did not comprehend the logic of lashing out at the family of the perpetrator. The scientific laws of cause and effect directly correlate with the realities of our daily lives; just as gravity is a physical truth, so is the acceptance of the consequences of poor choices a psychological necessity. Hind sight is frequently 20/20, and standing beside my brother during his legal dealings emphasized this for me.

In 2009, one morning before work, I heard a knock at the front door. I asked who it was and a man said something—I could not fully hear him—about a letter; I asked him to please put the letter in the mailbox next to the door but he said I needed to sign it in his presence. When I opened the door, there was a man with a strange look on his face. I looked past him and noticed that there was a white car in front of the house; I thought that he must be from one of the financial institutions to which I owed money. The man wanted me to sign a document on the pad he held but I told him that I needed to see the letter first. He would not allow me to see it and, greatly flustered, I snatched the pad and signed my name. When he gave me the letter, I saw that it was indeed sent from one of the financial institutions.

A few hours later when I left for work, there were federal officers waiting for me in several parked cars at the end of my street. Through a loud speaker, one of them asked me if I had any weapons and, when I said, "No," he ordered me to step out of the vehicle. I complied, and he got out and met me in the street. He took my driver's license and asked me if I had hit the mailman who had come to my door earlier that morning. I said, "No." The mailman, who was apparently good at telling tall tales, was on the opposite side of the street with the other federal officers. The officer speaking with me called my probation officer, who requested that I go see him; when I went to see him, he asked me what had happened, and I assured him that I had not hit the mailman. He threatened to notify the officials in Delaware that I had violated my probation and have me sent back north; I begged him not to and, while he eventually allowed me to leave, he informed me that a warrant for my arrest would be issued. The next day, I reported to my probation officer and turned myself in; I was taken to the county jail, and made bail later that night. I searched hard to find a good attorney to represent me; the slightest violation of my probation would send me back to prison. My selection in an attorney turned out to be stellar, and he told me that the prosecution agreed to throw out the case as long as I paid the court cost, which of course I did.

It took me many years to realize just how badly my family had been affected by the prison system, and once I reached this knowledge, I did not want to sit quietly and not speak about it. Before leaving prison, I never officially made a commitment to myself to not be involved in the drug game ever again; I intentionally left the option open to myself in case things got bad and I needed to put my boots back on and head to the streets. This was far down on the list of my goals and priorities, but the idea was there, since I was still in the process of growing and needed more time, as well as a better understanding of life. Once released, however, I knew that I did not want to ever sell drugs hand to hand again, and that I wanted something better for myself than having to look over my shoulder at every turn. I came to see that my purpose in life does not include selling drugs or committing any crime, but rather strongly and positively impacting those around me by living a healthy and whole life.

Today, I can truly say that I have found my purpose in life. I know that sometimes "finding purpose" can sound cliché, but a thorough consideration of this concept assists in our understanding of both its importance and value. First, to find a purpose is like having a new level of understanding about something, such as "Why am I here on earth?" Secondly, finding a purpose is making the decision to act in a particular way, like choosing to do something positive. I found my purpose to be escaping and running away from the traps of drugs, street life, and prison, and positively touching those around me. Without first knowing my purpose, touching those around me was both an empty and meaningless gesture. For many years I lived a destructive life and made poor decisions; low self-esteem left me in a dark cloud of deception and faulty values, and my lack of self-love left a void in my life, heart, and soul. Selfish attitudes prompted me to desire things that were not good for me, and I lived many years thinking only of myself. Finding my purpose strengthened me against the many challenges in life and I came to the point where I could see the Most High working in my life through both the hard times and the easy times.

While I don't associate with a particular religion, I do have faith in who I refer to as the Most High God; he created the heavens and the earth as well as things that we have no knowledge of and he offers guidance to his children each day. I have learned a lot from reading different scriptures but have learned the most from listening directly to the Most High himself. I hear him speak to my spirit, and he always guides me in the right direction. I don't always follow the guidance that he sets for me, which is a testament of my imperfect humanity, and this always leaves me in a vulnerable situation; I have noticed that when I do not follow his guidance, the outcome is usually not good. In the past I wandered around as a blind man but I can see things more clearly now, and my goals are to simply continue growing into a better man as I live and learn. When I did negative things in the past, I did it with all of my heart, and now I put the same effort toward positive behavior.

As a young adult my journey as a street hustler was based on my belief that this was the only way that I could earn money. I thought that I was going to be a hustler for the rest of my life; if the streets offered educational degrees, I would have earned a PhD, and perhaps some would have even referred to me as Doctor. I do not accept any accolades for my past life, and there is no honor for anyone with O.G. status (old school gangster). These things can't be cashed in, and they don't assist in the care of ourselves or our families. Today I am on a journey to make something good out of the rest of my life based on my efforts to turn my negative experiences into positive things. I appreciate and enjoy my freedom and I willingly accept the responsibilities that come with that. Today, I embrace life, and understand the importance of family and being a good example to them; life has a lot to offer, and I will fight to protect the purpose I have found.

The focus of the motivation I have to work with troubled teenagers is to assist them in learning the process of making better decisions. I realize that I can't make the decision for anyone— you can lead a horse to the water but you can't make them drink it— but I can offer alternative options to some of the choices that I know are rolling around in their minds. Realizing my purpose has given me an enthusiasm about life that I never experienced before and I have learned that life is not about what you're given, but about what you make of it. I have learned that sometimes stumbling blocks and other things will hinder us in our goals, but my past has taught me that we do ourselves an injustice, and make matters worse, by making poor choices and getting felony convictions. Some people view the mark of a convicted felon as shameful, and will remind you of it for the rest of your life; my defense to this is to continue to work hard and purpose to not allow anything to hold me back. I know that God is real and that I wouldn't have made it to where I am today without him. There were many times when I did not think I was going to make it through, but the Most High God brought me out on the other side and gave me a purpose, namely that of ending the curse.

Chapter XVI
Ending the Curse

Ending the curse is an ongoing process. For my family, this required that we made positive changes within both our own, and collective, lives. On a more global note, this process requires the cooperation of individuals, families, and entire communities. Change in my family did not begin until I decided that enough was enough and until I was sick and tired of being sick and tired. Being fed up with my own situation was the catalyst for me to do what I needed to do to get more out of life than what I was getting. I want to set a good example for my two daughters, my younger brothers, sisters, nieces, and nephews; the changes in my contributions to my family subsequently inspired those around me to also seek change. While I am not proud of some of the mistakes I made, I am not ashamed of my past. I am always grateful for the opportunity to inform others of the mistakes that I've made; there are many people who did not live to tell their story. I chose the street, and I chose drugs; these choices led to numerous failed relationships, and a lot of jail time. The sentences I served contributed to the one hundred years my family cumulatively wasted within the prison system. I have learned a great deal through my mistakes and have become a better man as a result. I am thankful to be free and alive, and to have the opportunity to support my family.

Despite these changes, the curse continues. My younger brother and a few of my cousins are currently in prison, three of which have been serving time since the mid-1990s. The same is true for some of my nephews, and I am concerned about the future of my family, as well as that of other teenagers within our society. My hope is that by sharing my story, others will learn from my experiences and began to make better choices. I seek to encourage everyone to remain focused on their goals in life, and not allow difficult times to become a distraction or discouragement. No matter the problem at hand, crime is not the answer, nor is using drugs to get high because, aside from the damaging physical and psychological results, once the high wears off, the problems are still there. The only other option, then, is to work hard and never give up; while sometimes giving up seems to be the easiest way out of a situation, there is no growth in this, as strength is only developed by overcome adversity. On the other side of adversity lay character and courage. We have each been created by a great God who is able to guide us through difficult times; life is short and it is up to us to make the very best of it during our allotted amount of time here on earth.

Throughout my life many people offered information to me, and provided me with guidance and warnings about what would happen if I continued in the street life. I heard the words, but I had my mind made up to continue on the path of a hustler and I did not heed their counsel. The difficulty in reaching me at that time was the fact that the root of my problem was deep inside of me. We only take care of things that we value, and I did not love or value myself at that time. Today, I honestly love and value myself; I know this to be true because there are things that I wouldn't do today but would have done in the past. I am a cautious driver, for example, and often hesitate before crossing an intersection; in my previous lifestyle, however, I would have taken chances and attempt to beat the traffic.

I did not know it at the time, but during every moment of my previous lifestyle the Most High was looking out for me, and slowly began to get my attention. Eventually, as I started to listen, he guided me in learning to be accountable for my actions, and in making better decisions as a responsible man. While these transitions mostly happened inside the prison system, I do not attribute my transformation to prison; prison just happened to be the place where I experienced a lot of my growing up. Being in such an environment may have caused me to grow up faster, but a person doesn't have to be in prison in order to learn a lesson from the Most High.

The few college courses I took while I was in prison did not earn me a degree. The behavior treatment groups and parenting classes allowed me to honestly address some of my own personal issues, and this played a large role in my conversion into a man. My lack of formal education added to the challenges of successfully returning to society after serving a long prison sentence. The biggest thing that helped me during this frustrating time was the very strong support system of family, friends and others that assisted me when I came home. They encouraged me to make good decisions which would not put me in danger. I was very determined to do whatever I had to do in order to remain in free society, and I knew that attaining a legitimate job was vital to my success. I also knew that I had to tread lightly when dealing with others; my parole was hanging over my every move and offending others in any way was the last thing I wanted to do. In prison I learned that there are many different personalities, and I made sure to be cautious when dealing with others.

My friends and family continuously prodded me to return to school and, while I knew that school was a good and beneficial thing, a single thought about my high school failures made me wonder if perhaps academics were just for others. All my job applications had been denied due to my past, and this made me doubt that a college degree would benefit me in any way. As good as the rest of my life was at this time, I had settled for less with regard to employment; I believed my past limited my job qualifications and I simply learned to not expect more than that. Malinda had recently returned to school and was pursuing her degree; I watched as she worked her job, took college courses, and still found time to help our daughter study for her classes. When I still had my detail and wheels business, a guy came in one day too look at rims and, as we were making small talk, asked me whether or not I had ever thought about returning to school. I told him, "No" but he wouldn't take that for an answer. He came back later with a pamphlet from Troy University, and told me to look at it. I did, but did not pursue it at the time because I was struggling to get my business off the ground. Years later, his efforts to inspire me were a huge factor in my decision to eventually give serious consideration to the idea of returning to school.

I first attempted to gain admission at one particular university but I faced too many challenges, such as complications in getting my transcripts and the lack of certain necessary signatures. I realized that I should have better researched the admission process, but I moved on and applied at another. Finally, I was admitted to Ashford University; the advisors assisted me in gathering all of the necessary documentation, the admissions counselor helped me fill out the required paperwork, and my educations advisor guided me in choosing a major. I did not really know what major I wanted to pursue; I initially wanted a psychology degree in order to help others, but also considered a degree in education in order to become a teacher. The first two years were probably the hardest for me, since I had been out of school for a while and since this is when I took my Math, English, and Science courses. I started out with online classes, and benefitted greatly from this experience; I was proud and excited to improve my writing skills, which I managed to do after writing many six-, eight-, and ten-page research papers. At the end of my two years, I earned my associate's degree in Early Childhood Education from Ashford University.

My hard work resulted in a good GPA, and earning my first college degree greatly boosted my confidence; I felt a sense of accomplishment and was hungry to achieve more. I applied for admission to Faulkner University in Montgomery to pursue a bachelor's degree. One of the questions on the application form was, "Have you been convicted of a felony?" The last time that I had been convicted was twenty years prior to this, but I felt that I should answer the

Mark Baynard   269

questions honestly despite the fact that I knew this information may hurt me. Having earned an associate's degree at Ashford, however, I felt that I had a good chance, though I knew that the decision of being accepted could go either way, for me or against me. At this point in time, I had put together a list of a few long-term and short term goals; one of my main goals was to graduate from college so that I could get a good job, become more financially stable, and better support my family. Gaining acceptance into Faulkner University was a large portion of my long-term goal. Things were looking good and I was well on my way to a better life; I was a living testament to the fact that a person can get their life in order after making many bad mistakes. And that is exactly what I was doing: getting my life in order.

After sorting through the mail one day, I noticed a letter from Faulkner University. I excitedly opened the envelope and began scanning over the words on the paper; I saw the school's name and logo and visualized myself as a student there. I smiled as I started reading the letter, but my excitement quickly turned into disappointment when I read that I was *denied admissions*. The only thing that I could think was, "Here we go again," and I was overwhelmed with the feeling of not being able to measure up. I also felt guilty for my past wrongs; I felt unworthy, in a sense, and I started doubting my chances for a successful future. Suddenly, I snapped myself out of those negative thoughts and got my composure back. I would not allow this letter to deter me from reaching my goals; I took full responsibility for my past, and I understand that while society can sometimes be unforgiving, I wasn't going to allow myself to feel guilty any longer. I refused to take no for an answer; I wrote an appeal to the person who had notified me that I had been denied, and patiently waited for a response. A response never came, however, so I then wrote another letter of appeal and sent it to the director of the university. A couple of days later, I received a letter from him in which he personally informed me that I was *granted admissions*; he proceeded to extend a very warm welcome to me, and I felt a great sense of accomplishment. Overcoming the setbacks regarding my education reminded me that there were better days ahead, and I was able to see the big picture more clearly. I have learned that it is very important for us to appreciate the things that we have; once we appreciate and take care of the things we have we are able to receive more.

My first day at Faulkner University was memorable, and I was excited to be sitting in class on the main campus. The professor asked us to introduce ourselves and to share something with the rest of the students; my classmates spoke about their careers, professions, military and law enforcement experience. This made me nervous, and I decided that I wasn't going to share anything about myself, because I felt like I could not compare to my classmates. Then I realized my foolishness, and I told myself that I was not going to be concerned with how others may look at me because of my past. When it was my turn, I told them my name and I gave a brief background of having been in prison and of my goals to professionally working with troubled youth. After I finished speaking, my classmates immediately started clapping their hands. I had not expected this, and it caught me off guard, but I will say that it made me feel accepted. This experience increased my sense of purpose in returning to school for my bachelor's degree, and I felt empowered. I wanted to set a good example for my daughter and show her that, with hard work, all sorts of doors of opportunity are opened. In addition to this, I wanted to equip myself with the necessary tools and knowledge to be able to work with troubled youth. The more I thought about it, and the further along in school I got, the thought of expanding my original idea of working with youth to include adult offenders came to me. Perhaps I could start a program, or series of programs, and offer mentoring, re-entry programs, and support systems to address the challenges offenders face after being released. I believed that God was inspiring me with these ideas, and I applied myself to my academics with renewed fervency.

About a year later, the thought that I should reapply for the job I was denied nearly five years earlier popped into my head. After considering this idea, I had a strong feeling that it was important for me to act on it. Acting solely on faith, I submitted a new application. As far as I knew, all of the top executives responsible for making the decision to not hire me were still in position, but I was not concerned about this; my reapplication was not about *them* being in position, but about *me* being in position. My faith was a lot stronger now than when I had first applied for the job, and my life was at a much better place. When I turned in my application, I made a day of it; I took Malinda and our daughter out to eat at Red Lobster, and we enjoyed our meal together and had good conversation. I told Malinda that I believed I was going to get the job this time. After eating a good meal, we drove to the place where I had put in the job application and my wife and daughter dropped me off so I could attended the required two-hour tour of the facility. Afterward, we left to enjoy the rest of our day; I had claimed the job, and my heart was now at peace. One month later, I was selected to take the pre-employment test again, and I scored the highest in the entire state for the second time. I was officially offered the job—the same job in the same department at the same facility I'd applied to five years prior— and officially accepted it. Faith pays off!

Everything was coming together in my life. I continued going to school while working at my new job. My time at Faulkner University was truly stimulating and fulfilling and I eventually earned my bachelor's degree in Criminal Justice. I had a seemingly insatiable appetite, and was hungry to learn more. It was difficult for me to choose a graduate school and so I applied to, and received admissions letters from, Auburn University at Montgomery and Troy University. Both schools had great reputations and this decision was a difficult one to make. I finally chose Troy University because they offered classes for my degree program at a time that fit my career goals and schedule. I am currently pursuing a master's degree in Public Administration. So far I have had some great professors whom I have learned a great deal from. Graduate school challenges me on many levels, and I have learned to think more critically and logically.

Grabbing life by the horns is what living is all about, and it is the key component in the process of ending the curse. I have the ability to change only myself, and I have chosen to no longer allow the curse to live through me. This is my legacy. My hope is that my family, as well as the entire world, will wake up and put an end to this vicious cycle of prison and criminal behavior. It is my wish that the examples I have shared from my life can be a roadmap for anyone who is willing to follow; the steps do not have to be the same, but the foundational goal is to always be heading in a positive direction. My greatest desire is to leave behind accomplishments that my daughters can be proud of, and to set the best examples I can for my brothers, sisters, nieces, and nephews to follow. Maybe then the next one hundred years will be filled with accomplishments and redeeming stories.

The End

Epilogue

In the process of recognizing and ending the vicious cycle within his family, it was very important for Mark to take responsibility for his actions. He has been out of prison for over ten years now, and most of that time has been dedicated to working with troubled teenagers. His hope is that he can prevent others from experiencing some of the same troubles he has faced in his life. Though his dark past of the streets and drugs often seems a lifetime away, Mark still can feel the energy. He uses that energy, however, as motivation to continuously reach out and positively impact the lives of others. Many of the teenagers Mark works with are frequently caught up in the same cyclical process that he was caught up in at that age, and sometimes it is difficult for him to sit by and helplessly watch as they make the same mistakes he made. Mark never waited for God to make the changes in his life for him, and he actively seeks to inspire troubled youth to do the same, to take life by the horns and steer away from drugs and the streets. If he can prevent even a few of them from experiencing the pain, loneliness, anger and hurt of life on the streets, his own journey has been well worth it; he is humbled to be given the opportunity to be used by God in this way.

Mark credits his successes in life to a number of individuals who have intentionally or unintentionally helped him along this journey including his mother, father, wife, and a list of others too long to share. Although there are some people who may continue to look at him as a criminal, Mark chooses not to allow that to distract him; where he once was a menace to society he is now an asset, and he is motivated and determined to do great things in his life. Mark believes that these realities would be far less significant without his beautiful wife, Malinda, their eight-year-old daughter, and his twenty-two-year-old daughter; he is in this for the long haul and only the Most High God knows in which direction it will take him. What he does know, however, is that there is a lot of work still left to be done while here on earth, and Mark believes that the Most High will use the strength gained from his past to allow him to complete these tasks in the future. After all, with the guidance of the Most High God, all things are possible.

In the month of January of 2015, Mark got the news that his childhood friend Marlon was released after spending more than twenty-four years on death row. Marlon will now face the challenges of adjusting to life as a free man. Mark's hope is that Marlon will do well considering that he will be surrounded with positive support. The journey to end a vicious cycle continues!

References

(DHSS 2012) Delaware Health and Social Services, 2012 Delaware HIV/AIDS

Surveillance Report Retrieved from www.dhss.delaware.gov

(Jones, A. 2014) Jones, Abigail, Murder Town USA (aka Wilmington, Delaware,

Newsweek Dec. 9, 2014, Retrieved from www.newsweek.com

(Bible) The Holy Bible

Elena Poniato

Las mil y una...

LA HERIDA DE
PAULINA

Elena Poniatowska

Las mil y una...

LA HERIDA DE
PAULINA

Agradecimiento especial a Mariana Yampolsky

Edición: Magdalena González Gámez
Diseño de portada: Carlos Quezada
Foto de portada: Roberto Cordova Leyva
Digitalización de imágenes: Arte Digital y Gerardo Oynick

Primera edición: septiembre de 2000

ISBN: 968-11-0405-6

Diseño interior y formación
Jorge Aguilar, Ofelia Mercado, Elena Riefkohl

Impreso en México
Printed in Mexico

A mi abuela, Elena Yturbe de Amor, que nunca condenó a nadie.

Agradezco al filósofo Pablo Rodríguez el apoyo, las ciruelas, el aliviane y la compañía solidaria.

A Pilar Sánchez quien además de información, recogió el material gráfico en Mexicali.

A María del Consuelo Mejía, de Católicas por el Derecho a Decidir.

A los fotógrafos y periodistas de Mexicali, Roberto Cordova Leyva, Jesusa Gamboa, Sergio de Haro y Arturo Kasiyas que generosamente dieron su obra.

A Marta Lamas e Isabel Vericat, inspiradoras.

María Elena Jacinto Raúz, la madre, nunca pronuncia la palabra violación. Lo llama *eso.*

Yanet, hermana mayor, testigo, ya que en su casa se perpetró el atentado, tampoco lo nombra, al igual que su madre dice eso. Humberto Carrasco, el hijo mayor en quien María Elena se apoya, habla de *eso* o de la *grosería.*

María Elena, Paulina y Yanet.

Eso

—El sábado 31 de julio de 1999 a las tres y media de la mañana, nos acostamos mis dos hijos, de uno y seis años; aquí están, mírelos, ése es, el del pañal, el otro por allí anda, y mi hermana Paulina que se vino con nosotros porque hacía mucho calor y yo tengo un *cooler* muy ruidoso, pero de algo sirve —cuenta Yanet llorosa—. Dormíamos todos en la misma cama y desperté con el filo de una navaja en el cuello. "Levántense, hijas de su pinche madre". El ladrón tenía la cara tapada con una mascada azul. Buscaba qué robar dentro de la vivienda. A mí y a mis hijos nos amarró boca abajo en la cama, a Paulina de 13 años, con una patada la levantó y la estuvo picando con su navaja y diciéndole muchas groserías. Tomás mi hijo lo vio. "Voy a matar a los chamaquitos". A Paulina la violó en la misma cama donde estábamos amarrados. "¿Dónde tienes el dinero, hija de la chingada?", gritó. Le tuve que decir dónde guardaba el que me había mandado mi marido. Rompió la chapa del ropero, lo encontró, nos robó un celular Motorola y los mil pesos en efectivo. Y se fue.

"Pude soltarme y desamarrar a mis hijos. Aterrada, miré a Paulina, estaba como muerta, toda ensangrentada. Lloramos mucho".

Todavía hoy, Yanet llora y Paulina limpia las lágrimas que resbalan por sus mejillas redondas como una niña, con la palma de la mano.

Mamá, me violó ese hombre

—Apenas íbamos a hacer un año en Mexicali, faltaban nueve días —dice María Elena—, cuando le pasó esta desgracia a Paulina. Y ahora sí que a enfrentar todo lo que venía. Cuando vi cómo estaba mi hija, me desesperé y pensé que a ese hombre lo podría yo despedazar, hacerle lo peor. Encontré a Paulina con las piernas sucias de sangre: Mamá, me violó ese hombre. ¿Cómo?, le dije. Sí, me dijo.

"Ora sí que como es una niña, la desgració. Salí a la calle, busqué, corrí, pasó un taxi y le pedí auxilio: Oiga, usted trae radio, pida ayuda, le rogué, háblele a la policía. Sí, respondió. Vi que despegó el radio pero no sabría decir si llamó o no, pero ahí llevaba un pasaje y arrancó en seguida y ya no supe más.

"Por más que les grité a mis vecinos, nadie, nadie salió. Cuando llegó Humberto, él se encargó de todo, se fue a traer a las autoridades. A cada rato venían, tuvimos mucha ayuda de la policía porque cada que agarraban a un ladrón, nos avisaban y en el transcurso del mes, lo apañaron".

EL VIOLADOR HA ESTADO 40 VECES EN LA CÁRCEL

Las autoridades llamaron a las víctimas Paulina y Yanet para que identificaran al violador Julio César Cedeño Márquez, apodado El Cuervo. Su ficha policiaca data del 24 de abril de 1986 y cuenta con cuarenta encarcelamientos previos. Es de religión católica y adicto a la heroína. En enero de 1991 fue detenido tres veces, el 10 de enero por agresión, intoxicado con heroína, el 14 por asalto y golpes y el 25 por riña en el bar Azteca.

NOS CAMBIAMOS DE LA COLOSIO A LA LUCERNA

—A raíz de *eso*, nos cambiamos con mi hijo Humberto —explica María Elena—: Vénganse para acá, yo las cuido. Y no ha dejado de hacerlo. Mi esposo estaba con su barco en el mar.

FOTO: ROBERTO CÓRDOBA LEYVA

—Yo tenía mucho miedo y mucho frío. No quería dormir sola —dice Paulina—. Desde que me pasó *eso* siento que alguien me sigue y se va a meter a la casa. No se me quita la impresión, tanto que me pongo a temblar. No puedo comer. Antes no era llorona, ahora aunque no quiera, se me salen las lágrimas solitas.

"Nos pidieron a Yanet y a mí que fuéramos a reconocer al hombre. Él no nos vio. Lo tenían detrás de un cristal. El judicial le dijo: Tú mataste a no sé quien. No, yo no fui. Sí, tú fuiste. Era para que hablara y reconociéramos su voz. Todas las groserías que nos dijo las recordamos entonces y Yanet y yo nos soltamos llorando".

—¿Ya lo identificaron totalmente? —preguntó el judicial.

—Sí, ése es.

—Yanet fue la que lo miró más porque ya se había quitado el pañuelo de la cara —dice Paulina.

—¿Ése fue el hombre que entró a robar?

—Sí, ése fue.

10

—¿Y luego se aprovechó cuando vio a la niña dormida?

—Sí. Le preguntó que cuántos años tenía y ella respondió que diez: Pues no pareces de diez, le dijo, pareces de más. Le rogué: Agarra y llévate todo lo que quieras pero déjanos, y gritó: Cállate puta. Cállate porque te voy a matar delante de tus hijos. Mi niña se quedó quietecita quietecita pero escuchó todo. El hombre rompió una sábana y me amarró los pies, me puso boca abajo, me jaló los brazos por detrás, me los amarró y me tapó la boca.

"Ya le hizo *eso* a mi hermana, le hizo y empezó otra vez, se salía y entraba, se salía y entraba. Creí que él ya se había ido, pero no, volvía a entrar y nos amenazaba: No quiero que me hagan escándalo putas jijas de su mal dormir, porque van a ver, voy a venir y las mato. Volvió a gritar: Orita las voy a matar y nadie se va a dar cuenta hasta que ya apesten. Y se salió. Fue como a las tres de la mañana y dilató como la hora o más".

—Yo me enteré casi de inmediato —dice María Elena— porque nosotros tenemos que ir al baño a casa de Yanet.

FOTO: ROBERTO CÓRDOBA LEYVA

—Después Humberto y mi mamá buscaron al mal hombre y ya no se vio nada de él —apunta Yanet.

—Lleva a Paulina a ver a la doctora Sandra Montoya —aconsejó Humberto—. Esa doctora es buena, tiene un dispensario.

—A los quince días, el 19 de agosto de 1999, llevé a Paulina con la doctora porque no le bajó su menstruación —recuerda María Elena—. Su hija está embarazada —me dijo la doctora. A mí me dio rete harto coraje. Bueno, yo puedo hacer el legrado pero necesito la autorización del Ministerio Público, añadió. Inmediatamente nos movimos Humberto, Paulina y yo.

LA ORDEN DEL MINISTERIO PÚBLICO

El 3 de septiembre de 1999, la Agente del Ministerio Público acordó:

> Gírese oficio al Director del Hospital General de Mexicali a efecto de que sirva designar elementos a su digno cargo, a efecto de que le sea practicada prueba de embarazo a la menor Paulina del Carmen Ramírez Jacinto, en virtud de haber sido víctima de violación. Lo anterior con fundamento en lo dispuesto en los numerales 20 fracción segunda del código adjetivo a la materia 3 inciso A fracción IV y V de la Ley Orgánica de la Procuraduría General de Justicia... así lo acordó y firma la suscrita Agente del Ministerio Público Especializado en Delitos Sexuales y Violencia Intrafamiliar, licenciada Norma Alicia Velázquez Carmona, que actúa ante su Secretaría de Acuerdos que autoriza y da fe y razón en Mexicali, Baja California a los tres días del mes de septiembre de 1999, el personal que actúa, da razón que se dio debido cumplimiento al acuerdo que antecede.

El Ministerio Público le pasó el caso al Hospital General

de Mexicali. Y a partir de ese momento se inició el calvario de la familia.

¿POR QUÉ ESTAMOS EN MEXICALI?

—Desde Salina Cruz, Oaxaca, vine a ver a Yanet porque iba a tener su bebé, que hace poco cumplió un año. Humberto y Yanet, los dos mayores, llevan diez años en Mexicali. Yanet me dijo: Mamá, están sufriendo mucho allá, ¿por qué no se vienen para acá? Acá hay mucho trabajo, mis hermanos van a encontrar chamba. Es más, a mi papá, Mazatlán y Ensenada le quedan más cerca. Mi esposo trabaja en un barco camaronero. Le respondí a Yanet: Voy a hablar con él. Igual me insistió mi hijo Humberto. Al regreso, le conté a Tomás mi esposo: Fíjate que me platicaron los chamacos que allá hay trabajo, por qué no nos vamos. Se lo repetí hasta que se cansó: Bueno, vámonos para allá. Le dieron un préstamo y nos vinimos en camión en agosto, salimos el 5 y llegamos el 8. Vivimos primero con una tía, en la Luis Donaldo Colosio, que nos prestó un cachito. Como en Salina Cruz también hace

mucha calor, la de Mexicali no nos asustó, somos buenos para aguantarla.

La familia Ramírez Jacinto, compuesta de ocho miembros de marcados rasgos indígenas, vino de Oaxaca hace un año en busca de una vida mejor y se instaló en una de las múltiples colonias pobres de Mexicali: la Luis Donaldo Colosio. Antes habían emigrado Humberto y Yanet, los hermanos mayores, ambos casados. Humberto Carrasco es réferi y Yanet acude a una maquiladora, pero el suyo es un trabajo muy aleatorio, a veces hay chamba y a veces no. Ahora trabaja de lunes a viernes y le toca embobinar aritos, es decir, enredarles una tirita de metal para el tablero del sistema eléctrico de los aviones; la suya es una labor de ensamblado. Lupita también está en la maquila así como Tomás que enlata alimentos. Leonardo es pescador, igual que su papá. En las maquiladoras, los patrones prefieren al sexo femenino y la maquila engulle a las mujeres. Son más dóciles y más meticulosas. Nunca se quejan. En 1982,

FOTO: SEMANARIO *SIETE DÍAS*

por ejemplo, las obreras se pusieron felices porque les dieron un día más de descanso. Cuando regresaron a su trabajo el dueño estadounidense, el jefe de personal y el administrador se habían esfumado llevándose el equipo para maquilar piezas electrónicas. Setenta y cinco mujeres y ocho hombres se quedaron sin trabajo, sin indemnización y sin el salario correspondiente a una semana y cuatro días. En innumerables ocasiones, las maquiladoras desaparecen de la noche a la mañana, sobre todo cuando los trabajadores intentan organizarse. Yanet gana 300 pesos semanales porque sólo trabaja tres jornadas intensivas, que ahora llevan el nombre de "trabajo compacto". Su físico gastado por las maternidades, su llanto al hablar de su hermana, conmueven.

Como me lo hizo notar Socorro Maya, toda la familia compra chanclas. Se van turnando los buenos zapatos de acuerdo con quien tenga que salir, al fin que no importa que les queden grandes o apretados. A la escuela, Paulina lleva zapatos negros.

FOTO: MARIANA YAMPOLSKY

Los servicios de la colonia Luis Donaldo Colosio son muy caros, a pesar de que las calles no están pavimentadas. Paulina, fuerte y lozana (parece mayor que sus catorce años), iba bien en la escuela y se había adaptado a su nueva vida. En Salina Cruz bailaba en la escuela vestida de tehuana y comía chiles rellenos de picadillo. El padre de familia, Tomás, iba y venía porque ser marinero obliga a pasar largas temporadas fuera de casa.

16

Buscaban dólares,
encontraban rejas.

Arturo Bojórquez

¡MEXICALI, AY MEXICALI!

Si en 1969 Mexicali tenía 200 mil habitantes, ahora hay
un millón 500 mil, sin contar con el Valle de Mexicali y la
población flotante. Es fácil, por lo tanto, llegar a los dos
millones. Cuando Lázaro Cárdenas rescató las tierras y se
las entregó a los campesinos, el beneficio resultó enorme,
porque los mexicanos se encontraron con un valle muy fér-

til, un clima propicio para el algodón (todavía se habla del algodón de fibra larga), y se fueron para arriba hasta que los estadounidenses salinizaron el Valle de Mexicali con la sal del Río Colorado con lo cual el valle se vino para abajo. Las telas sintéticas también contribuyeron a que se redujera la demanda de algodón y ahora Mexicali ya no es la tierra fértil que atraía a los campesinos pobres de otras partes del país, sino un conglomerado de maquiladoras que emplean a mujeres jóvenes, a quienes se les exige habilidad y constancia y no una alta escolaridad.

En la revista *Ahí* de 1985, una fábrica puso el siguiente anuncio:

> COMPAÑÍA IMPORTANTE
> SOLICITA
> DIEZ MADRES SOLTERAS
> PARA SU DEPTO. DE PRODUCCIÓN
> Requisitos
> *Primaria o Secundaria
> *Buena presentación
> Interesadas acudir a Calle "G"
> No. 1897 Esq. Curtidora
> de 9 a 1 y de 4 a 7.
> Entrevistas con Sr. Valenzuela.

Se han hecho obras viales en beneficio de las maquiladoras para que las muchachas puedan llegar más pronto al llamado cordón industrial. De un lado están sus miserables viviendas, del otro, el Mexicali del siglo XXI, el pujante, el que se publicita en la televisión. Calexico (que para los estadounidenses es un pueblito mugriento), para los indocumentados es el cielo, aunque por lo pronto, en las ciudades fronterizas, miles de motores rujan calientes en espera de que les den el paso y supongo que desde arriba el espectáculo de estas perversas víboras de metal,

18

Antiguas oficinas de la Colorado River Land Mexicali, B.C.

arrastrándose una tras otra, dispuestas a todo con tal de entrar, debe causar una impresión menor a la del hallazgo de indocumentados asfixiados en un vagón de tren o deshidratados dentro de un camión tipo *torton* donde viajaban con otros cuarenta y siete en un espacio de cuatro metros cuadrados, cubiertos con una lona. Los que no mueren a mitad del Río Bravo, reciben un balazo en el pecho al llegar a Brownsville o se desangran en Texas cuando al ir a pedir agua, el ranchero Sam Blakewood les dispara dos veces a corta distancia con su .357 *Magnum,* como le sucedió a Eusebio de Haro, el miércoles 17 de mayo de 2000.

Sé que en todas las migraciones hay un elemento de catástrofe y que la mexicana es una prueba de la debilidad de nuestra economía. Los mexicanos emigran porque la patria, esa señora vestida de blanco que alzaba la bandera tricolor en los libros de texto, no puede ni sabe alimentarlos.

19

GET OUT, GO AWAY

FOTO: BEATRIZ LIMÓN

Aunque Tijuana se llama a sí misma la ciudad más visitada del mundo y tiene el más alto nivel de ingresos, de educación y de empleos del país (o uno de los más altos), y casi todos los tijuanenses llegan a conducir su propio automóvil, prefiero Mexicali, su desierto y su cordialidad. Además no cuenta con un galgódromo, ni con Carlos Hank Rhon, lo cual es un alivio y tampoco se ve a la patrulla fronteriza amenazar a todas horas a los indocumentados que esperan tirados en el suelo a que caiga la noche sobre el Cañón Zapata, para jugarse la vida, porque la Border Patrol arresta a más de medio millón de hombres y mujeres cada año a lo largo de la frontera más extensa del mundo entre dos países: del Océano Pacífico al Golfo de México, 3 mil 234 kilómetros de línea fronteriza. Al año emigran a Estados Unidos siete millones de jornaleros, dejando atrás sus pueblos fantasmas. En California y en Texas se ha triplicado la población de *hispanics*. La frontera es una cicatriz que no cierra, como lo dijo alguna vez Carlos Fuentes. Cada año crece en 150 mil el número de mexicanos en Estados Unidos. Angélica Enciso y Guadalupe Ríos, de *La Jornada*, afirman que tan sólo en el tramo correspondiente a Tamaulipas, de 1993 a junio de 2000 han muerto 872 personas. Helicópteros artillados y lentes infrarrojos ayudan a la Border Patrol a detectar migrantes por el calor de sus cuerpos.

FOTO: BEATRIZ LIMÓN

FOTO: BEATRIZ LIMÓN

Si el gobierno de México invirtiera en generar empleos y fomentara mejores condiciones en el campo, arraigaría a los campesinos en sus lugares de origen. Claro, muchos regresan y muchos pueblos se vacían sólo seis meses al año. En 1996, Julio César Castillo Godínez, de 19 años, se internó con cinco compañeros, que se veían por primera vez, en el desierto de Arizona: "Contábamos con comida y litro y medio de agua cada uno. Hacía un calor horrible. Cuando el agua se nos terminó, nos bebimos nuestros propios orines y cinco compañeros se dejaron caer en la arena del desierto, los animé a continuar. Respondieron: No podemos... vamos a morir... lo único que te pedimos es que avises".

Ya en la caseta de retención, Castillo Godínez, el único sobreviviente, envió un mensaje a los indocumentados: "No crucen, no lo hagan por favor". En el camino encontró cadáveres mutilados por los coyotes.

Otro mexicano, Ricardo Javier Mercado Martínez, de 30

años, cuenta que el cansancio y la falta de agua y alimento le hicieron perder la cabeza después de caminar dos días y medio: "Yo no sabía si regresaba o avanzaba". A él lo salvó un helicóptero de la *migra* que descendió a recogerlo y lo condujo a un centro de retención en el que fue empujado e insultado. Luego de registrarlo, lo subieron a un autobús para llevarlo a la frontera de Calexico con Mexicali, donde lo deportaron.

AGUANTAN TODO CON TAL DE QUEDARSE

Tragedias como éstas abundan en la frontera. ¡Qué mal trato recibirán en México que están dispuestos a aguantar todos los abusos: *polleros*, *pateros* y *coyotes*, todas las humillaciones, las vejaciones físicas y morales, todo el racismo, el fascismo, el fanatismo segregacionista, el antimexicanismo oficial en Estados Unidos y afrontan hasta el peligro de muerte con tal de cambiar de vida!

Jorge Bustamante, del Colegio de la Frontera Norte, ha señalado ante comisiones de derechos humanos que a los *wet backs* que sí la hacen, los gringos e incluso los mexicanos les arrojan basura, los atropellan, destruyen sus campamentos, roban sus sueldos y los atacan físicamente.

SORRY, TENGO QUE CORRERTE

Dóciles, de trato fácil, delgados, ágiles, pequeños, tanto que hasta parecen adolescentes, los trabajadores mexicanos son fácilmente desechables, según la antropóloga Margarita Nolasco. Mano de obra barata, hacen lo que no quieren hacer los gringos y su propio desinterés permite deportarlos cuando se les ha exprimido. A pesar de que viven mal, estas condiciones adversas les son favorables porque los bajos sueldos estadounidenses representan altos ingresos para los mexicanos.

Rolando Cordera escribió en *La Jornada*, el 18 de junio de 2000: "Sabemos también, como lo saben allá, que la migración ha implicado cambios formidables en la democracia y sociología de Estados Unidos y que su economía, hoy tan pujante y victoriosa, tiene en el trabajo mexicano (y latinoamericano), una fuente importante de dinamismo, por las destrezas que aporta y por los bajos salarios que en general acompañan a los migrantes de hoy".

MIS AMIGOS CACHANILLAS

Siempre me encantó Mexicali por nuevo, por pionero, por su gente luchona y, aunque no lo crean, por su calor, la temperatura ha llegado a 125° Farenheit. A diferencia de lo que me habían vaticinado, jamás lo vi como un pueblo plano del oeste. Me emocionó ser testigo en la Universidad de Mexicali del amor de los estudiantes por

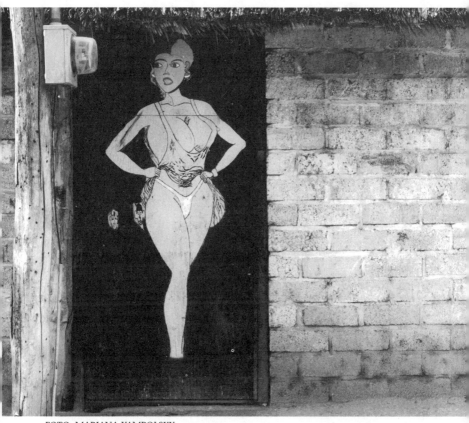

FOTO: MARIANA YAMPOLSKY

México. Nunca, en ningún estado de la República, he presenciado una defensa tan ardiente de México como la que hacen los jóvenes en las vilipendiadas ciudades fronterizas. La *Suave Patria* de López Velarde se queda corta al lado del fervor de Mexicali (que tiene su contraparte en Calexico), Tijuana (San Diego), Ciudad Juárez (El Paso, Texas), Nogales (Tucson), Agua Prieta (Douglas, Arizona), Ciudad Acuña (Del Río, Texas), Ojinaga (Presidio, Texas), Piedras Negras (Eagle Pass, Texas), Nuevo Laredo, (Laredo, Texas), Camargo (Río Grande City, donde por primera vez

25

se publicó *Los de abajo* que Mariano Azuela vendió en 50 dólares), Reynosa (Mc Allen, Texas), Matamoros (Brownsville) y así, hasta cubrir los 3 mil 234 kilómetros de frontera.

La lluvia casi nunca se detiene sobre la extensa arena de Mexicali. Mis amigos *cachanillas*, así llamados porque al igual que un arbusto cachanilla se agarran a la tierra norteña y no los vence ni el calor, ni el gran valle arenoso, son gente directa y valiente, sin pelos en la lengua y de una lealtad a toda prueba.

Soy feliz en Mexicali, quizá por la presencia de algunos buenos amigos: Guadalupe y Luis López Moctezuma, Rebeca Vizcarra y Hugo Abel Castro Bojórquez; Leticia Maldonado, Maricarmen Rioseco, Blanca Villaseñor, además de la formidable religiosa Noelle Monteil, a quien todos le decimos "madre" y Nicole Marie Diesbach, autora de varios estudios sobre Mexicali. Los estudiantes universitarios, el paisaje, la cordialidad de la gente, el desierto, que conocí al lado de Guillermo Haro (quien buscando un sitio ideal para

Catedral de Nuestra Señora de Guadalupe. Mexicali, B.C.

su nuevo observatorio, nos hizo subir a Mane y a mí hasta el Pico del Diablo, desde donde se ve el Pacífico y el Golfo de Cortés), la chimichanga cachanilla, los dragones en los excelentes restaurantes chinos, todo me pareció mágico y atrayente. Ir a Mexicali resultó siempre un estímulo y una ilusión. Lo único que lamento es que el ingeniero Luis López Moctezuma, que conocí como rector de la Universidad de Mexicali, no sea gobernador del estado, porque además del amor por su tierra, defiende los derechos humanos.

LOS CHINOS, FUNDADORES DE MEXICALI

A los chinos nunca les ha ido muy bien en nuestro país, no así en Mexicali. Atraídos por el auge de California, intentaron llegar a Estados Unidos y como fueron expulsados, cruzaron la frontera por Sonora y Baja California, aunque también en México se daría un clima antichino debido a la envidia de su disciplina laboral, su cultivo del arroz y su pericia en la elaboración de calzado. En 1910 había en México 13 203 chinos. En Torreón, 303 fueron brutalmente asesinados en 1911, pero a pesar de nuestras actitudes racistas y xenofóbicas siguieron llegando.

Lo más típico de Mexicali es el barrio chino llamado La Chinesca, que al principio era un simple callejón (como el de Dolores en la ciudad de México). Para los mexicanos resultó peligroso andar por los fumaderos de opio, las vecindades "sólo para chinos" y los comercios tambien "sólo para chinos".

Quizá los más antiguos pobladores de Mexicali sean los chinos, quienes fueron los primeros en creer en la fertilidad de la llanura, que pertenecía a la Colorado Riverland Company. Originarios de Fujian, una provincia de la costa, colonizaron el valle y construyeron una ciudad que en 1919 tenía 15 mil chinos y 2 mil mexicanos. Sólo los

(...)
*al norte del río
grande,
al sur del río
bravo,
que vuelen las
palabras
sobre México,
sobre Estados
Unidos,
tan lejos de
Dios
tan cerca el uno
del otro.*

La frontera de
cristal
Carlos Fuentes

28

Nadie del otro lado debe ver

campesinos de China soportaban el intenso calor del desierto sin insolarse. Los chino-mexicanos se convirtieron en una clase profesional y comercial que todavía hoy es dueña de más de 100 restaurantes. La conexión cultural estimuló la inversión asiática.

Otra conexión menos celebrada, descubierta por los investigadores de Estados Unidos y México, según Sebastián Rotella, es que los chino-mexicanos en Baja California actuaban como agentes entre los contrabandistas chinos y los mexicanos.

Los chinos siguen desembarcando en los puertos de Baja California, mucho menos vigilados que los estadounidenses. Todavía en 1993, los mexicanos se conmovieron con los 306 chinitos hambrientos y deshidratados encontrados en Ensenada; les llevaron comida y cobijas, y se dispusieron a protegerlos.

En las ciudades fronterizas se escucha desde el "cuac cuac" del pato Donald hasta el tableteo de las armas de alto poder. De los automóviles apantalladores descienden las *Barbies* aún más deslumbrantes porque acaban de teñirse el pelo y, los cholos, tras su trinchera de desperdicios se dan de codazos: "Oye carnal ¿tú ya te echaste a una gringa?"

En las ciudades fronterizas como

Mexicali, se confrontan lo peor y lo mejor de los hombres, lo peor y lo mejor de varias culturas. Un flujo de energía y de dólares es lo que las hace tan atractivas para los inmigrantes que las convierten en sus puertos de esperanza, sus tierras de promisión. Aquellos que aguantan el clima extremoso, los rigores del frío en invierno y el sol cegador en verano, están dispuestos a pagar el precio del triunfo. Aquellos que no logran pasar del otro lado permanecen en el borde mexicano y resisten azorados y temerosos las secuelas de los misterios de Lomas Taurinas, en ese aciago año de 1994, que según nuestro iluminado Carlos Monsiváis marcó el año en que fue imposible aburrirse en México. Carlos Fuentes declaró también que no era necesario escribir ficción, bastaba con describir primero el asesinato del arzobispo de Guadalajara, luego el de Colosio, el de José Francisco Ruiz Massieu, el imperio de Carlos Salinas y el enriquecimiento desorbitado de Raúl Salinas de Gortari, hermano de Salinas, para hacer una novela cuya truculencia haría palidecer las tragedias shakesperianas.

Todos estos fenómenos forman parte de la vida del norte del país y a pesar de su cercanía con Tijuana, Mexicali conserva un aire curiosamente provinciano. En cierta forma, se ha mantenido al margen, quizá porque es menos cosmopolita, más recatada. Si el pato Donald y el ratón Miguelito se pasean en todas las camisetas, también la virgen de Guadalupe protege el dorso de los *espaldas mojadas*, si los *braceros* después de cruzar el Río Bravo siguen braceando en el aire, los gringos bailan al ritmo de Selena, si se fríen hamburguesas y se hierven perros calientes, también los tacos, las enfrijoladas y el tequila han sido entronizados, si las *rockolas* avientan a la calle a los Bukis y a los Tucanes de Tijuana, *Amorcito corazón* se compadece por aquellos que después de cruzar el río les urge un trabajo y son recibidos por los dueños de billares y canti-

Nadie se mete al agua, está contaminada

Abogada María del Socorro Maya Quevedo

nas y barras de espejos que les anuncian cerveza Bud Light: "Órale, no mamen, si apenas se están secando los pies".

En el año 2000, Mexicali sigue siendo un faro para los mexicanos más desamparados de la República, entre ellos la familia Ramírez Jacinto, que buscó trabajo en el corredor industrial de la frontera.

MARÍA DEL SOCORRO MAYA QUEVEDO, LA ABOGADA DE PAULINA

El Grupo de Información en Reproducción Elegida (GIRE) encabezado por la feminista Marta Lamas, se enteró del caso de Paulina por el grupo Alaíde Foppa de Mexicali y la decidida actuación de su presidenta, Silvia Reséndiz

34

Flores, así como la de Rebeca Maltos Garza de DIVERSA, una agrupación política de 17 mil mujeres dirigida por Patricia Mercado.

Isabel Vericat, licenciada que trabaja con GIRE en la ciudad de México, y su segura servilleta, viajamos a Mexicali el miércoles 29 de marzo de 2000. En el aeropuerto nos esperaban la abogada de Paulina, Socorro Maya Quevedo, quien ha llevado el caso espléndidamente, y Liliana Plumeda, joven pasante.

María del Socorro Maya Quevedo es muy joven; su rostro redondo, bonito, alberga una voz delgadita como de niña. Siempre la vimos acompañada de Liliana Plumeda, quien manejaba el automóvil, creo que de su madre, comprado en el otro lado, con placas amarillas, permitidas en Mexicali. Socorro va y viene muy acelerada y se mueve por el mundo con facilidad. El último día que nos vimos se cambió tres veces de ropa, primero unos *bluejeans*,

Silvia Reséndiz Flores

35

luego un vestido, después una camiseta con estoperoles. A su amiga Liliana, risueña y cálida, no se le va nada de lo que sucede a su alrededor. Inseparables, Liliana y Socorro completan frases una de otra. Socorro sabe lo que hace y lo hace con inteligencia. Obviamente, Liliana admira a la abogada Socorro y se coordinan muy bien para sacar adelante su trabajo.

María del Socorro pertenece a una de las familias pioneras de Mexicali: "Cuando llegaron mis padres no había casas, puras parcelas". Oriundo de Toluca, su padre trajo a su novia a Mexicali porque su futuro suegro y dueño de la panadería se oponía al casamiento de su hija con un empleado. Empleado sí, yerno no. Como Romeo y Julieta, tuvieron que huir para poder amarse, pero como no tomaron ningún veneno, dieron a luz a diez hijos, y su padre, trabajador como pocos, se hizo de su propia

Paulina con su abogada Socorro Maya y sus amigas

36

panadería, su propia casa, su propio automóvil, su propia cuenta bancaria y fundó con otros amigos, del Distrito Federal, la Cámara de la Industria de la Panificación.

Socorro, al igual que Paulina, proviene de una familia numerosa, seis hombres y cuatro mujeres. Sus padres nunca imaginaron que existía el control de la natalidad y en el momento del alumbramiento del séptimo hijo, la madre solicitó a su cónyuge que la llevara a la clínica:

—Espérate que ahorita voy a entregar todo ese pan —respondió el panadero.

La madre no pudo esperar y nació el retoño.

¿Cómo me llamo? María del Socorro Maya Quevedo, un nombre bien largo, que primero se muere uno y luego me alcanzan a gritar ¡Socorro! Nací en 1972. Ya perdí la cuenta de cuántos años tengo litigando pero son más de cinco. Mi familia es de las pioneras de Mexicali y esto me enorgullece.

¿Cómo llegué al caso Paulina? Silvia Reséndiz, María del Carmen Rioseco y Rebeca Maltos habían presentado la denuncia en contra de médicos y autoridades. Entonces conocí al grupo Alaíde Foppa, fundado el 7 de mayo de 1993, asociación civil feminista de carácter no lucrativo. Antes de esta asociación la ausencia de apoyo a la mujer era notoria. El Alaíde Foppa creó centros de atención integral, grupo y refugios para mujeres víctimas de la violencia. Asimismo, promovió talleres y conferencias en los municipios de Baja California para hablar contra la violencia. Participé en actos públicos que me entusiasmaban.

"Entre tanto, me enteré por el periódico del caso de Paulina: 'El caso de la niña está atorado, no encontramos abogado, nadie quiere llevarlo ¿quieres tomarlo tú?', me preguntó Silvia. Pues yo sí, encantada, le respondí.

"Y así fue como me convertí en la abogada de Paulina."

Javier Mejía dio la noticia

En *La Voz de la Frontera* apareció la noticia que dio Javier Mejía sobre la detención del director del Hospital General, que yo llamaría una "detencioncita". A Ávila Íñiguez lo detuvieron cuatro horas en sus oficinas, nunca lo trasladaron a los separos.

Primera visión del Hospital General de Mexicali

El Hospital General de Mexicali, enorme y feo, cuya monumentalidad como la de otros edificios de gobierno, cumple con creces la sentencia de Jorge Ibargüengoitia, quien afirmaba que los mexicanos confundimos lo grandioso con lo grandote. El hospital se traga a la gente, es una auténtica romería, como si la salud fuera una rueda de la fortuna. Aquí van los hígados en sillas voladoras, allá los corazones se infartan en carritos chocones, el martillo es un surtidero de *electroshock*. Más allá bailan peronés y metacarpios en la danza frenética de El látigo. Sólo los caballitos de feria son inofensivos. Niños, mujeres y ancianos atiborran los pasillos y afuera, como en todos los hospitales de México, esperan los vendedores ambulantes junto a sus puestos de tortas, jugos y refrescos.

Durante siete días me tuvieron en ayunas y no me dieron ni agua: Paulina

—En estos siete días me trataron mal porque me tenían en ayunas y no me daban ni agua. Me metieron donde ponen a todas las mujeres que van a dar a luz. Esperaban subirme "a piso" para darme de comer.

"A las demás sí les daban de comer. Afuera esperaban mi mamá y mi hermano y nunca los dejaron pasar alimentos.

Hospital General de Mexicali

¿Ya le hicieron *eso* a mi hija? ¿Cómo está?, preguntaba mi mamá".

—¿Cómo se llama su hija?, inquirían a su vez. Y así a diario. Yo me sentía mal, como si no fuera gente.

"Ella es una niña, no una mujer de edad, y a mí me preguntaban constantemente por qué estaba allí y yo decía: Por *eso*. Y me respondían: No, no le han hecho nada, allí está.

"Allí me dormía yo, me llevé mi cobija, me tiré en el piso los siete días, en un pedacito en la sala. No me despegué para nada. Cada tres o cuatro horas preguntaba con mucha discreción por mi hija a las enfermeras, a las recepcionistas. Me respondían a gritos: A ver, ¿qué tiene? ¿Por qué está aquí?

"Yo buscaba el modo de decirles, ¿verdad?, porque había mucha gente y me daba pena. Y ya metía yo la cabeza en la ventanilla y decía muy bajito: Pues mi hija está aquí porque le van a hacer un legrado.

39

"Nunca me daban razón y nunca le hicieron nada. En el segundo turno, otra vez lo mismo. Preguntaban quién era yo y por qué estaba allí: ¿Qué quiere?

"Y yo otra vez con lo mismo. Nos humillaban.

"¿Quién es Paulina del Carmen Ramírez Jacinto?, preguntaba a gritos una enfermera.

"¡Habiendo tanta gente y la enfermera gritando! Humberto y yo sentíamos bien feo. ¿Qué podíamos hacer? ¿Para qué, pues, gritarlo en esa forma?"

GASTAMOS 6,000 PESOS

—Nos daban largas, me pidieron un medicamento de 400 pesos para dilatarle la matriz, una inyección que nunca le pusieron. Tampoco se le hizo el ultrasonido. ¿Saben qué? No sirve el aparato. Tienen que hacerse los análisis por fuera. Nosotros no tenemos el equipo. Total, gastamos 6,000 pesos. De hecho uno de los médicos de allí, uno ya mayor, el doctor Conrado Calderón, ofreció hacer el legrado alegando que si a él le hubiera pasado lo mismo con su hija, la habría atendido, y me pidió otro medicamento. Lo compré y el doctor se esfumó. Pasó el viernes, el sábado, el domingo, el lunes. Todo el día preguntaba por él, que tiene una operación, está en una junta, anda muy ocupado, no ha salido del quirófano, ya se retiró. Entraba a las seis de la mañana y salía a las dos. Entre tantas negativas decidí madrugar y atajarlo a las seis en el lugar donde checan tarjeta los médicos. Pues fíjese, doctor, que ya tengo una semana, ya compré el medicamento. Y me dijo: Sí, es cierto, mira, la verdad, no lo voy a hacer. Le respondí: Me lo hubiera dicho desde un principio para no gastar lo que he gastado y tampoco mi hermana hubiera estado tanto tiempo aquí. Pasó un doctor junto a él y Calderón me dijo: Permíteme un momento. Y se fue y me

40

dejó con la palabra en la boca. Le valió. Me enojé, fui al Ministerio Público. Si en ese momento me dicen aquí está la orden (o la autorización) y con esto la doctora de ustedes puede hacerles el legrado, en ese momento nos vamos con la doctora, pero como nunca me informaron nada, tuve que atenerme al Hospital General. En cambio, a mi hermana la dieron de alta, sólo para que volviera a entrar el día martes. Resulta que tampoco le hicieron nada. El director del Hospital General, Ismael Ávila Íñiguez, nos llamó a la dirección: Miren, estos son los riesgos y son muchos. Luego pasó sola mi mamá y salió muy agitada. Nos trataron muy mal y a mí nunca se me va a olvidar.

EL DIRECTOR DEL HOSPITAL GENERAL DE MEXICALI, ISMAEL ÁVILA ÍÑIGUEZ

El doctor Ávila Íñiguez nos hace pasar a su despacho a Isabel Vericat, a Silvia Reséndiz Flores y a mí. De inmediato Isabel lleva la batuta de la entrevista. Lúcida y convincente, Isabel Vericat se crece mientras Ávila Íñiguez, que de entrada no me pareció antipático porque le encontré un ligero parecido con Manuel Peimbert, se fue desinflando. Joven, nada prepotente (a diferencia del doctor Carlos Alberto Astorga Othón, director de Isesalud), el doctor Ávila Íñiguez respondió a todas nuestras preguntas y sin capote enfrentó a Isabel, que lo embistió como toro de Miura.

—Paulina llega aquí con una autorización del Ministerio Público para una interrupción del embarazo por violación. Entonces, como director del Hospital General, mi función consiste así, entre comillas, en dar una orden para que uno de los ginecólogos del hospital la cumpla.

"Aquí nosotros íbamos saliendo de un problema laboral muy serio. Tomé la dirección de este hospital en septiembre, luego de un paro de diez o quince días. El jefe de ginecobstetricia me dijo: Consulté a los médicos de servicio y ellos no están dispuestos a realizar el procedimiento".

—¿Qué razón adujeron?

—Dijeron que son médicos para preservar la vida, no para quitarla. Fue una decisión muy propia del servicio de ginecobstetricia.

—Un objetor de conciencia es todo lo respetable que se merece, pero a nivel institucional siempre tiene que haber médicos dispuestos a cumplir, porque el aborto por violación es legal según el Artículo 136 del Código Penal de Baja California. ¿Usted se declaró objetor de conciencia?

—No, en absoluto. Cuando nos pusimos a buscar un poquito de antecedentes vimos que era la primera vez que había un caso semejante y enfrenté el primer bloqueo de los médicos. Al día siguiente, yo tenía una especie de motín aquí de los ginecólogos. Dijeron que se iban a amparar porque ninguna autoridad los obligaba a realizar algo con lo cual no estaban de acuerdo y para lo cual no habían sido formados. Una respuesta que me exigían los médicos era: ¿Por qué el Hospital General de Mexicali es el que tiene que resolverle estos casos al Ministerio Público? El Ministerio Público tiene presupuesto para atender a sus judiciales en hospitales particulares.

—Pero el derecho de Paulina era totalmente legal.

—Los médicos alegaron: Si es una situación legal, que lo haga el Ministerio Público. No tiene por qué involucrar al hospital.

—Oiga doctor pero es una operación muy fácil ¿no?

—Aquí en el hospital no tenemos el método de aspiración, lo que hacemos son legrados. El problema es que en este asunto entramos al terreno de las convicciones y lo más difícil es obligar a la gente a hacer algo contra su voluntad. No, ¿sabes qué? yo no estoy dispuesto. Los médicos sabían que Paulina era menor de edad y que era un aborto por violación. Uno de ellos me dijo: Ninguno de nosotros vamos a realizar el procedimiento. Es más, si tú me presionas, yo renuncio, y el doctor Leonardo Garza, jefe de ginecobstetricia, renunció. Esto sucedió durante el primer internamiento de Paulina, el de los ocho días. Ante esta situación, yo le pedí tiempo a la familia: ¿Saben qué? Tengo un problema laboral.

La niña ya había estado una semana entre los "ahorita y al rato" de los médicos.

—¿Y por qué la tenían en ayuno? ¿Por qué no podía comer?

—La situación del ayuno era para que uno de los médicos que aceptara hacer el procedimiento lo hiciera en cualquier momento. Llamé al doctor Astorga Othón para decirle que los médicos se negaban al legrado: ¿Sabes qué?, me respondió Astorga Othón, yo voy a hablar con el Ministerio Público porque soy la autoridad de salud en el estado y por mí debió haber llegado esa orden.

VIOLACIÓN DE LA INTIMIDAD DE PAULINA EN EL HOSPITAL

—Una anomalía muy fuerte, doctor, que rompe con los derechos humanos, es cómo se violó la intimidad de esta niña. Eso verdaderamente desborda toda previsión. A Paulina la vinieron a visitar, con consentimiento del hospital, dos mujeres de Provida* a decirle que... —interrumpe el doctor.

FOTO: ARTURO KASIYAS

Provida es parte de Human Life International. Nació en México en 1978 como respuesta a una iniciativa de ley para legalizar el aborto.

Socorro Maya atrás de Paulina.

—¿Con consentimiento de la dirección? No, en ningún momento. Desgraciadamente nuestro servicio de seguridad no ejerce control absoluto, sobre todo en el turno vespertino. La verdad es que yo ignoro cómo entraron estas personas.

—Dos mujeres entraron con una pequeña cámara de televisión para enseñarle un video de Provida contra el aborto: *El grito silencioso*. Las imágenes no corresponden a las fechas legales de interrupción de la vida; es decir, el feto es mucho mayor, casi un recién nacido, tasajeado y ensangrentado, lo cual lo hace muy impresionante.

Marta Lamas conoce bien estos videos y los considera amarillistas y científicamente equivocados. Muestran abortos realizados cuando el feto tiene ya más de tres meses de vida. Como lo afirma Marta, son videos trucados: *Eclipse de la razón, El grito silencioso, Una ventana al seno materno o Los primeros días de vida*.

Además de estos horrores de videos, las dos integrantes de Provida, que obviamente son fundamentalistas, sometieron a Paulina a pruebas verdaderamente primitivas e inhumanas. Le mostraron una hoja blanca en la que se pueden adivinar los rasgos estereotipados de Cristo, una suerte de negativo donde las partes negras aparecen blancas y el contorno también.

MIRA, ESTAS SON SUS MANITAS, ESTOS SON SUS PIECITOS

—Dos señoras, una güera y otra de pelo negro como de 45 años, peinadas de salón, entraron hasta donde yo estaba —cuenta Paulina—. No me preguntaron ni cómo me sentía, ni si había comido o algo, sólo sacaron su camarita, la prendieron, pusieron el video y me dijeron: Tú, como tienes tres meses, si abortas, mira cómo va a quedar el

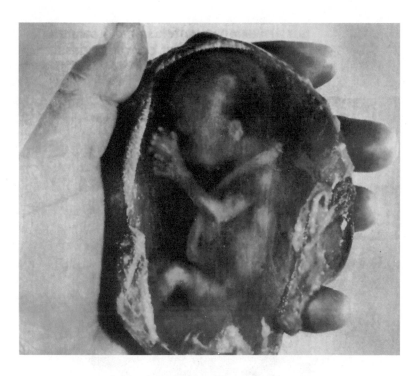

bebé. Me enseñaron un bebé despedazado. Mira, estas son sus manitas, estos son sus piecitos. Y decían puras cosas muy feas y yo nomás me les quedaba viendo. Primero me dieron un broche donde venía la virgen María. Y después una hoja blanca de papel en el que vi unas manchas negras: Fíjate muy bien en los cuatro puntos en el medio del cuadro, concéntrate hasta que se te queden grabados. Cierra tus ojos, manténlos así diez segundos y echa la cabeza para atrás. Vas a ver un círculo de luz. No dejes de ver el círculo porque se te va a aparecer Nuestro Señor y te va a hablar.

"Lo hice y sí era cierto. Esas manchas negras formaban a Cristo con sus pelos largos: Mira, te vamos a ayudar a la hora del parto con alimentos, medicina y si lo quieres dar

CONCENTRATE ON THE FOUR DOTS IN THE MIDDLE
OF THE PICTURE FOR ABOUT 30 SECONDS,

THEN CLOSE YOUR EYES AND TILT YOUR HEAD BACK.

KEEP THEM CLOSED. . YOU WILL SEE A CIRCLE OF LIGHT.
CONTINUE LOOKING AT THE CIRCLE...

WHAT DO YOU SEE?

en adopción, conocemos personas que quieren al bebé. Hay muchas parejas que no pueden engendrar hijos y vamos a buscar a unos con una posición económica buena para que al bebé no le falte nada.

"—No, no es eso lo que yo quiero. Yo lo que no quiero es estar embarazada.

"—Si así lo deseas te podemos mandar a Tijuana para que no te vean en ese estado.

"—No, yo no quiero ir a Tijuana. Yo quiero ser como antes.

"—Bueno, pues vamos a regresar a hablar a solas contigo.

"Me preguntaron si yo no amaba a mi hijo y les dije que no era eso, que lo que yo no quería era estar así, con eso adentro. Entonces me dijeron que tenía que conformarme porque era cosa de Dios.

"Cuando vino mi mamá le pedí: Mamá, dígale al doctor que no deje pasar a nadie." ¿Por qué?, me preguntó. Porque vinieron unas señoras a enseñarme cosas muy feas y me siento mal."

—¡Ah no! —le dijo María Elena— los del hospital no tienen por qué dejar pasar a nadie. Ellos no son quien pa meterse en la vida de uno.

La *Voz de la Frontera* dio la noticia

—¿Cómo supieron las señoras que estabas allí, Paulina?

—Porque se lo dijeron los médicos o a lo mejor el director.

—Pero ¿alguna vez les contaste que tu embarazo fue producto de una violación?

"—Pues no, ellas ya iban con toda la información. Además se publicó en *La Voz de la Frontera*. Nosotros nunca hablamos con ningún periodista, es más, no tenemos acceso a ningún periódico, por eso a nosotros nos sorprendió.

—Mientras, en el mismo hospital —continúa Paulina—, nos volvimos como payasos de circo. Los médicos decían que aunque los corrieran, ellos preferían mil veces renunciar que practicar el legrado. Las enfermeras, las recepcionistas nos hacían el feo. Fue entonces cuando el director pasó a mi mamá a su privado y le habló de todos los riesgos que según los médicos yo corría. Entonces dijimos que ya no. Mi mamá firmó un papel y nos fuimos para no regresar jamás, porque nunca vamos a volver a ese hospital.

¿Cómo puede decírsele a una madre que su hija va a morir si aborta?

—La madre de la niña contó que usted, doctor Ávila Íñiguez, la puso delante de un pizarrón y le explicó que la niña podía morir o quedar estéril ¿Eso le dijo usted, verdad, doctor?

—Sí, pero creo que esa situación está un poquito manipulada. De hecho, jamás se le mencionó la palabra muerte, sino las complicaciones de una interrupción del embarazo.

El doctor Ismael Ávila Íñiguez utiliza muchísimo, casi para todo, la palabra "situación".

—¿Pero usted cree de veras, que en esta etapa tan temprana de embarazo podría haber riesgos?

—No son tan altos los riesgos, yo creo que están exagerando un poquito. A la madre se le mencionaron los riesgos tal cual existen. Están escritos.

—¿La infertilidad, la perforación de la matriz, la hemorragia, el desangrarse?

—Si ustedes revisan la situación de riesgos en una interrupción de embarazo, esos son. Esta es una situación en la que se tienen que poner los puntos sobre las íes. A la madre también le dije que si existía una perforación se le podía resolver, que si existía un sangrado teníamos un banco de sangre, pero que sin embargo, las complicaciones podían

48

existir, que si era una en diez mil o una en cien mil, bueno, pero que ella tenía que autorizarlo finalmente.

—Usted le dijo que si moría la hija, ella sería la culpable.

—No, eso no es cierto.

—Eso no se le dice a una madre, doctor —se violenta Isabel.

—Nunca se le dijo eso, la situación...

—Eso no se le dice a una madre —repite Isabel.

—Yo no se lo dije.

—María Elena, que defendió el derecho de su hija al aborto hasta con los dientes, sólo retrocedió ante la posibilidad de que su hija muriera.

—La madre creía que la operación podía realizarse sin ningún problema y a la media hora irse a su casa. Yo creo que ni en Estados Unidos, donde las reglas están mucho mejor escritas, permiten una intervención de esta índole sin que la paciente dé su consentimiento por escrito. En México, también los pacientes tienen que darlo y aceptar los riesgos, si bien es cierto que éstos son mínimos.

—¿Por qué entonces se le dice a la madre que existe la posibilidad de que su hija muera?

—Yo no se lo dije.

—Pero doctor, esta madre y esta hija se mantuvieron firmes durante un mes y veinte días, (del 1 al 7 de octubre y luego del 13 al 15), después del horror de una violación, y vinieron decididas a que el producto de aquel horror no naciera. En realidad, ellas conocen sus derechos humanos desde las entrañas. Y así los ejercen. Nos dan una lección formidable. Fueron valientes, sólo retrocedieron ante la afirmación de

María Elena Raúz

49

que su hija podía morir y que ella (la madre) sería la culpable.

El ameu (Aspiración Manual Endouterina)

—Verdaderamente el riesgo que corría la niña era nulo —prosigue Isabel Vericat—. Yo he estado presente en procedimientos de interrupción de embarazos con ameu y la mujer llega, se le da una pastillita, se acuesta, se le absorbe, descansa un rato y a la media hora está fuera y no le pasó nada. Y se hace con pleno consentimiento de la persona, explicándole todo lo que va a suceder en su interior y se le da ayuda sicológica. No me diga que este procedimiento tiene comparación con el embarazo y la cesárea a la que va a ser sometida Paulina a los 14 años de edad. Usted, como médico, sabe muy bien que el riesgo es mayor.

—Si vamos de las complicaciones de una cesárea a las de un legrado, a lo mejor van parejo.

—¿Parejo, doctor? Yo tengo testimonios donde les dicen a médicos y pacientes que la proporción es de veinte a uno.

—Lo que pasa es que es diferente leerlo en una revista y trasladar la experiencia de un sistema médico de Francia al sistema médico de México.

—El ameu es lo más seguro que hay en Francia, en Suiza, donde sea. No hay otro procedimiento más higiénico y de bajo costo, doctor. Los días que pasaron desde que Paulina entró por primera vez, hasta que tuvieron que desistir porque las aterrorizaron con argumentos falsos, fueron un mes y veinte días. Allí hubo todo un trabajo de amedrentamiento ¿sí? Es obvio que ellas estaban decididas, si no ¿qué hacían aquí, doctor, si no querían interrumpir el embarazo? Doctor, la escena del pizarrón no está grabada, pero la madre la vivió con usted. Yo no veo por qué usted lo tiene que negar.

—Yo no estoy negando nada, ni la escena del pizarrón. Usted puede manejar la información que le conviene y veo que así lo está haciendo la mamá. En el pizarrón le expliqué exclusivamente a la señora el procedimiento del legrado y punto. Esto se hace regularmente con todos los pacientes. En nuestro hospital existe la norma de que si el paciente va a ser intervenido, se le explica todo. ¿Por qué? porque finalmente son casos legales. Este es un hospital de 140 camas.

—¿Y usted, aquí recibe casos de complicaciones de abortos clandestinos?

—No.

—O sea, si una mujer se viene desangrando ¿usted no la recibe?

—Ah no, eso sí, pero no determinamos si es un aborto clandestino.

—Bueno, pero ¿ustedes reciben mujeres con hemorragias provocadas por un aborto inducido?

—Aquí se hacen bastantes legrados mensualmente.

—¿No se denuncian?

—A la persona que viene en una situación de este tipo, se le hace el interrogatorio para ver si fue encaminada la situación por un aborto clandestino.

—¿Y la mujer les cuenta la historia que quiera contarles?

—Así es, básicamente.

—Sin embargo, con Paulina y su mamá no hicieron lo mismo porque a ustedes les tocaba hacer la interrupción. Por eso, a ellas las aterrorizan, lo cual hace que la madre diga: Ojalá y esto nunca les pase a ustedes. Si querían meterme miedo ya me lo metieron. Usted le dijo que su hija podía morir y ella sería la culpable de su muerte.

—¿La posibilidad de morirse? Jamás mencioné esa palabra. La familia desistió.

—¡Vaya manera de solucionar la historia tienen ustedes!

Centro de Gobierno Mexicali, B.C.

O sea, toda la lucha de la familia no existió. Se la pusieron muy difícil, pasar un mes y veinte días para una interrupción de embarazo que normalmente es cosa de 20 minutos.

ESTAMOS EN UN ESTADO LAICO ¿O ME EQUIVOQUÉ DE PAÍS?

—Asimismo, el procurador del estado, Juan Manuel Salazar Pimentel, se encargó de llevar a Paulina y a su madre con un cura. Oiga doctor, ¿en qué Estado estamos?, ¿estamos en un Estado laico o me equivoqué de país? —insiste Isabel.

—No, no se equivocó de país.

Entre el doctor Ismael Ávila Íñiguez, Isabel Vericat, Silvia Reséndiz Flores y yo la discusión es candente. En un momento dado, trato de que baje la tensión y digo:

—Pero doctor, ¿cuál es la gran diferencia entre las mujeres que llegan al hospital en mal estado por las consecuencias de un aborto, y ustedes les hacen un legrado, y

52

una niña de 13 años que ha sido violada y trae una orden del Ministerio Público para que se le practique?

—Para mí no existe ninguna, pero me gustaría que pudiera preguntárselo a uno de los ginecólogos del hospital cuando dice: Yo no estoy aquí para matar a nadie, yo estoy aquí para tratar de preservar la vida, no para acabarla. Como le digo, ésa es su situación particular, ni siquiera es la mía. Mi papel es decir: Tengo una orden de la autoridad que debe cumplirse. Si el médico se ampara al día siguiente porque sus creencias le impiden practicar la intervención, tengo que buscar a otro. Hasta ahora, en este penoso asunto, mi problema ha sido laboral.

—Doctor ¿y su especialidad cuál es?

—Soy cirujano general.

—Incluso usted hubiera podido hacerlo.

—Desgraciadamente hice cirugía general y si hay ginecobstetras aquí, ellos son los especialistas. Yo hice legrados hace 15 años, ya no tengo la experiencia y no me atrevería.

—¿Cómo es posible que usted se atreviera a imponerle una maternidad que ella no buscó a una niña de 13 que dijo muy claramente que su deseo era abortar tras ser violada?

—No me impuse, desistieron.

—Pero doctor, ¿no fue Paulina víctima de una doble violación, la física que le provocó su embarazo y la violación de su intimidad? ¿Por qué le impidieron librarse de tamaño trauma que va a cargar durante el resto de su vida? En 31 estados del país existe la legalidad del aborto en caso de violación.

—Fui respetuoso con los médicos ginecólogos y finalmente lo fui con la decisión de María Elena, la madre de Paulina, y de la propia Paulina.

—Es que a mí, doctor, lo que no me cabe en la cabeza es que una niña llegue con un problema semejante —la monstruosidad de una violación— y nadie se ponga en su lugar, nadie la apoye, nadie le diga: No te preocupes, esto te lo vamos a resolver. ¿Cómo es posible? ¿Dónde está el rechazo a una acción indignante? ¿Dónde la compasión?

—Puedo asegurarle que en este hospital todos somos humanistas.

No es legítimo dejar a un paciente tirado

Isabel vuelve a la carga diciéndole que es perfectamente respetable que un médico se declare "objetor de conciencia", pero es indispensable que en todos los hospitales públicos haya un grupo de médicos dispuestos a acatar la ley y hacer un legrado cuando es necesario, y él, Ismael Ávila Íñiguez, como director del Hospital General de Mexicali, no garantizó que hubiera un médico dispuesto. Isabel insiste en la urgencia de encontrar mecanismos mucho más eficientes y expeditos que cumplan la ley. La ley no basta. El caso Paulina lo demostró. Mientras Provida y la Iglesia católica o cualquiera que argumente en defensa de la vida le deje la responsabilidad de la manutención del bebé a Paulina y a su familia, la defensa de la vida es puro cuento, es *bluff*, hipocresía.

A la mayoría de los médicos no les gusta que una mujer les diga: Quiero hacerme un aborto. No sólo es un problema de conciencia, es fácil personalizarlo: Bueno ¿mi mamá

nunca pensó en abortarme? ¿Fui una hija o un hijo deseado? A lo mejor en mi inconsciente pienso que nunca lo fui.

MI HIJA ES UNA NIÑA, SEÑOR PROCURADOR

Según el relato de María Elena Jacinto Raúz, el procurador Juan Manuel Salazar Pimentel tenía que dar su visto bueno, y Paulina y ella fueron a verlo.

—Nos preguntó si estábamos de acuerdo en hacer lo que íbamos a hacer y le dije: Yo soy su madre y estoy de acuerdo porque mi hija es una niña. Ella lo que está sufriendo no es porque ella se lo *haiga* buscado o por su gusto, le tocó una desgracia y yo quiero que se le haga el aborto.

—Pero señora, esto es un crimen porque ya es una criatura —dijo el procurador.

—Yo sé que todavía esto no es una criatura, claro que ya empieza a ganar vida pero si esto se interrumpe ahora, se va a terminar pronto. Usted va a dar una firma para que se lo interrumpan y espero que así sea.

—Pero señora, ¿por qué no lo piensa usted mejor?

—Ya está decidido y no tengo nada que pensar. Quiero que se lleve a cabo.

—Señora, ¿no es usted católica?

—Sí, soy católica y creo en Dios, pero porque soy católica y creo en Dios, voy a hacer esto. Si Dios ha perdonado a tanta gente, ¿por qué a mí no? Yo no estoy haciendo una injusticia, estoy haciendo un bien para mi hija porque Paulina todavía no tiene edad para tener una criatura.

—Piénselo mucho señora, esto es un crimen.

—No, yo ya lo pensé.

—Mire, ¿qué le parece? La voy a llevar con un sacerdote para que le haga ver las cosas. A lo mejor cambia de opinión.

—Ya está decidido, y no tengo por qué cambiar, pero si usted quiere, vamos...

"Nos llevaron con un sacerdote en el automóvil que manejaba su chofer y un guardaespaldas. Nos acompañó la secretaria de acuerdos del Ministerio Público. El procurador Juan Manuel Salazar Pimentel habló largo rato con el sacerdote cuyo nombre nunca supe. Quién sabe qué hablaron los dos, yo no le puedo decir, y luego me indicaron: Pase".

—A ver, platíqueme, ¿qué es lo que piensa hacer? —preguntó el sacerdote.

—Pues mire, a mi hija la violaron y no quiero que ese producto nazca. Si fuera algo que ella hubiera buscado, está bien m'hijita, ténlo, pero ella no se lo buscó. Fue una desgracia. Yo quiero que me dé la autorización para que mi hija se haga un legrado. Soy católica, pero no porque sea católica no puedo hacer lo que tantas católicas han hecho ¿Por qué yo no, por qué? ¿No tenemos derecho porque somos pobres? A ver, dígame usted ¿en qué forma no tenemos derecho?

—Es un crimen, piénselo mucho señora, porque esto es un crimen.

Resulta muy grave que funcionarios públicos confundan sus convicciones personales con la ley y no ejerzan su función médica.

En el caso de Paulina, violada a los 13 años y madre a los 14, los ginecólogos del

María Elena

57

Hospital General de Mexicali se negaron a hacerle el aborto, olvidando que a diario reciben en el hospital a muchísimas mujeres a consecuencia de un aborto mal practicado y hacen entonces un legrado sin juzgar a la mujer ni darse por enterados.

En este tipo de abortos, una comadrona inserta una sonda o un catéter que sólo inicia el aborto y le advierte a la mujer que tan pronto empiece a sangrar vaya al hospital. En algunos casos desesperados, las mujeres llegan a introducirse ganchos de *crochet*, agujas de tejer, alambre, cucharas, ganchos de ropa, lápices, varillas de paraguas y sombrillas u otros objetos filosos, y corren el riesgo de perforarse, no sólo la matriz, sino los intestinos. Los tés abortivos son otro recurso, así como los laxantes, el cloro inyectado, sustancias cáusticas y hasta colorantes. En su angustia, algunas mujeres llegan a darse golpes en el vientre o a pedir que alguna otra persona se los dé, se tiran de una escalera o de un árbol y los hospitales se llenan de caídas intencionales. La quinina, el ergotrate y el pitocin son otras técnicas farmacéuticas que en algunos casos han dado resultado. De lo que nadie tiene la menor duda es del trauma espantoso que vive una mujer quien frente a un embarazo no deseado cae en el fondo del pozo de la angustia.

Según The Alan Guttmacher Institute (AGI), cada año los hospitales públicos de América Latina reciben a más de ocho millones de mujeres que sufren complicaciones por abortos inducidos.

Vivimos en un estado laico, y aunque Baja California votó por el PAN, el partido político mexicano que más cercanía tiene con la Iglesia católica, la orden del Ministerio Público era muy clara: interrumpir el embarazo. En un estado laico donde se respetan las distintas iglesias, ningún funcionario puede imponer sus creencias religiosas por encima de la ley. Sin embargo, contra Paulina

FOTO: MARIANA YAMPOLSKY

se ensañaron todos los fundamentalismos, a tal grado que obligaron a la niña a proseguir con su embarazo (aunque, según los médicos, a los 13 años es más riesgoso llevar a cabo un embarazo que interrumpirlo).

EN 87 POR CIENTO DE LOS PAÍSES DEL MUNDO EL ABORTO ES LEGAL

En 87 por ciento de los países del mundo el aborto es legal si se hace antes de los tres meses. Si el Estado mexicano dijera, como en Brasil, que los niños producto de una violación gozarán de un salario mínimo hasta los 21 años, sería magnífico, no sería necesaria la petición de legalizar

59

el aborto, pero como esto no ha sucedido, para miles de niños la vida es un mal sueño. Indefensos, maltratados, la situación de angustia y temor en la que viven afecta su desarrollo personal. Dentro de ese marco ¿qué futuro le espera a un niño engendrado por estupro?

Cuando Valéry Giscard D'Estaing fue presidente de Francia, en 1982 se legalizó el aborto. Siendo católico, fue interrogado por las razones que lo habían llevado a tomar esa decisión. En *El poder y la vida*, su libro de memorias, Giscard D'Estaing escribió su respuesta:

> Yo soy católico, pero también soy presidente de una República cuyo Estado es laico. No tengo por qué imponer mis convicciones personales a mis conciudadanos, sino que debo procurar que la ley responda al estado real de la sociedad francesa para que sea respetada y pueda ser aplicada. Comprendo perfectamente el punto de vista de la Iglesia católica, y como cristano lo comparto. Juzgo legítimo que la Iglesia pida a los que practican su fe que respeten ciertas prohibiciones. Pero no corresponde a la ley civil imponerlas con sanciones penales al conjunto del cuerpo social.

La posición de Giscard D'Estaing es clara: un Estado laico no puede regirse por una prohibición religiosa.

Resulta difícil cerrar los ojos a una dura realidad: las mujeres decididas a interrumpir un embarazo no deseado, lo harán por encima de cualquier prohibición legal o religiosa. La penalización no las disuade, sólo dificulta su acceso a buenos servicios médicos, con las graves secuelas que ya conocemos.

Marco Tulio Ruiz Cruz, en el excelente borrador de su autopropuesta para la defensa del caso, relata que:

> Con motivo de la Primera Guerra Mundial (1914-1918), surgió un problema que antes sólo se había conocido en

mínima escala, muchas mujeres de países ocupados fueron víctimas de violencia por parte de los soldados enemigos; de esa violencia resultaron embarazos y las mujeres procuraron y ejecutaron maniobras abortivas para deshacerse del producto de una infamia. Esto hizo que Marañón expresara: "La función sexual es en el hombre breve y pasajera, de unos minutos o de menos de uno. Pero en la mujer esos minutos no son sino el comienzo de la larga serie de fenómenos complicados y molestos, en cuyos largos meses de transcurso, todo el organismo materno, hasta la última de sus células, se modifica profundamente para culminar en el trance doloroso del alumbramiento y seguir en el periodo dilatado de la lactancia. Un soldado ebrio viola, a su paso por la ciudad conquistada, a una mujer desmayada de horror y sigue su camino, sin conservar tal vez, ni el recuerdo de la pobre hembra pasiva a la que la naturaleza ordena, sin embargo, la misma esclavitud al ciclo sexual que la madre fecundada en una hora de amor consciente y entrañable". Aquí queda planteado en su profunda esencia natural y humana, el problema de la mujer embarazada mediante la violencia. Siendo la maternidad el más alto de los atributos femeninos, ¿puede y debe imponérsele ese maravilloso sacrificio de su ser y de su sangre a quien no ha consentido, ni presuntamente, en la posible procreación?

La respuesta de las legislaciones a partir de la postguerra de 1914-1918, empezó a ser en sentido negativo y este criterio se plasmó en nuestra legislación en el año de 1931, conforme a lo que dice el artículo 333.

UNA VIOLACIÓN ES LA PEOR MANERA DE VENIR AL MUNDO

—Doctor, nosotras no somos abortistas —continúa Isabel—. Aquí nadie quiere el aborto, doctor, nadie lo está promoviendo. Lo que buscamos es que no nazcan niños no deseados para que no haya más vidas desdichadas. Eso es todo. Una violación es la peor manera de venir al mundo. Además, algo debe andar muy mal en el mundo porque se realizan millones de abortos todos los días. En este país ni se diga, según el CONAPO, (Consejo Nacional de Población), en cifras de 1993 a 1995, se hicieron 200 mil abortos anuales, entre inducidos y espontáneos. Su costo moral y humano es altísimo. Y no se diga el de las violaciones que la mayoría de las mujeres se abstienen de denunciar porque al ir a la delegación caen en el infierno del primitivismo, del machismo y del "tú te lo buscaste", que curiosamente coincide con la declaración de Jesús Marcos Giacomán de *Vértebra*, Nuevo León: "Las violaciones suceden porque la mujer está provocando o anda en lugares muy aislados, por donde no debe caminar, ya que es más fácil tomar un taxi. Si es violada y no quiere tener al bebé, puede darlo en adopción; incluso en Estados Unidos están dando hasta 20 mil dólares por un niño. Entonces sí conviene que las mujeres violadas tengan su hijo".

YESSICA YADIRA SE SUICIDÓ A LOS 16 AÑOS

En 1997, en Durango, Yessica Yadira Díaz Cázares de 16 años fue violada por tres tipos, en el camino de su casa a la escuela. Los denunció y no sólo no se le hizo justicia sino que los agentes del Ministerio Público se burlaron de ella, la maltrataron, la insultaron; cayó en una profunda depresión hasta que se suicidó. Recientemente, el 3 de febrero de 2000, una mujer de 22 años se tiró desde una ventana a siete metros de altura en Ciudad Juárez, Chihuahua, no sólo porque la habían violado sino porque en el Ministerio Público se burlaron de ella: "Tú te lo buscaste. Además de qué te quejas, para eso están ustedes, pinches viejas."

El recuento de horrores es tan atroz como las cifras

negras de la violación. El 4 de abril de 1995, con 13 años de edad y tres meses de embarazo, según Eduardo Monteverde, Teresita N. recorrió varios hospitales sin ser atendida de un embarazo resultado de una violación. Pasó por el Seguro Social, el Instituto Nacional de Perinatología y el Hospital de la Mujer, donde se negaron a interrumpírselo.

—A nosotros que no nos llamen espantacigüeñas —dijeron los médicos.

Devolvieron a la niña al Centro de Terapia de Apoyo a Víctimas de Delitos Sexuales, cubierta sólo por una bata de quirófano.

¿El violador? Francisco Contreras Albarrán, de 24 años, tío de Teresita; la golpeaba en ausencia de la madre. El malhechor, siempre vestido de uniforme azul porque era policía auxiliar o preventivo, anda prófugo, y seguirá

FOTO: MARIANA YAMPOLSKY

estándolo según la experiencia del Centro de Terapia de Apoyo a Víctimas de Delitos Sexuales de la Procuraduría.

La niña, que apenas entraba a la pubertad, fue llevada al Hospital Gea González, de la Secretaría de Salud, donde los médicos la atendieron de inmediato.

El Centro de Terapia informó que de 3 306 víctimas que acudieron de enero a diciembre de 1994 por delitos sexuales, 47.8 por ciento corresponden a violación, 26.8 por ciento a abuso sexual. Sólo dos victimarios son detenidos de cada 100 víctimas que denuncian el delito. El 67 por ciento de los agresores son conocidos de la víctima, y más de la mitad son familiares, padres o padrastros.

Según María del Socorro Maya Quevedo y Liliana Plumeda, el número de violaciones en Mexicali es de 700 al año. "Y en vez de disminuir va en aumento —dice María del Socorro— porque no estoy contando a todas las que pasan al otro lado y pagan 300 dólares por un aborto. Abortar en los estados norteños, tan cerca los Estados Unidos, nunca ha sido un problema".

Hay miles de Paulinas

No sólo es Mexicali, México está lleno de Paulinas. Ramón Esteban Jiménez, director de la Clínica para la Atención y Prevención de la Violencia de la UNAM, declaró que el 90 por ciento de las víctimas de violencia intrafamiliar son mujeres. Generalmente es el padre quien agrede a la mujer y a los hijos. Ruth González Serratos, directora del Programa de Atención Integral a Víctimas y Sobrevivientes de Agresión Sexual de la Facultad de Psicología de la UNAM, declaró: "Es una prerrogativa de todos los hombres utilizar a las mujeres para su servicio, para su complaciencia. Es un sistema de roles perfectamente armado en las leyes, la escuela, la religión, los medios de comunicación, es decir, siempre hay una situación de poder sobre la mujer, de conquista, donde se espera de la mujer la sumisión y el servicio en todos los sentidos".

El grupo Alaíde Foppa

Quien atrajo la atención del subprocurador de Derechos Humanos de Mexicali, Federico García Estrada, al caso

FOTO: MARIANA YAMPOLSKY

de Paulina fue la singular asociación de mujeres Alaíde Foppa, dirigida por Silvia Reséndiz Flores. Maricarmen Rioseco Gallegos redacta desplegados, cartas y protestas, Socorro Maya es la defensora, Lourdes Sánchez, Sara Silva Reyes, Cristina Peralta, Conny Guzmán, Liliana Sánchez y Silvia Medel son activistas. También han participado activamente en el caso de Paulina integrantes de DIVERSA, con Rebeca Maltos Garza a la cabeza. Ninguna de las dos dirigentes tiene pelos en la lengua. ¿Conociste a Alaíde?, le pregunto a Silvia, y me dice que no. ¿Qué diría Alaíde de toda esta lucha que lleva su nombre? Seguramente pensaría que no vivió en vano y se sentiría orgullosa de darle su sello a una batalla semejante, y ver su rostro multiplicado en carteles como el que ilumina con una luz azul el despacho de Federico García Estrada.

QUÉ BUENO QUE HAYA MUJERES PARA DEFENDER A OTRAS

Resulta lógica la existencia de este grupo de apoyo a mujeres en Mexicali, donde la agresión que sufre la mujer es cotidiana: malos salarios en las maquiladoras, falta de prestaciones sociales, un gobierno que se empeña en impulsar los corredores industriales pero no las escuelas ni las guarderías, viviendas y servicios públicos que dejan mucho que desear, sobre todo en las colonias como Mayos, Cachanilla, Azteca, De los Santorales, Virreyes, Nacionalista, Lucerna y Luis Donaldo Colosio, con sus baldíos desolados y mal alumbrados, sus casas de cartón donde viven otras paulinas y en las que hubo 700 violaciones el año pasado, cifra desmesurada en una ciudad de un millón 500 mil habitantes. Como dice Rosa María Méndez Fierros en el semanario *Siete Días*, se trata de zonas de miseria donde la mano de Dios no ha pasado y mucho menos la de las autoridades panistas o priístas.

Al Alaíde Foppa de Mexicali lo integran mujeres de diversas ideologías que Silvia Reséndiz Flores hace coincidir: Silvia Beltrán del PRD, Aurora Godoy, Leticia Maldonado del PRI, María Santos de La casa de la tía Juana,

50
Aniversario
de la Declaración
de los
Derechos Humanos

Bastaría quizás
Una palabra
Para abrir de par en par
Una ventana.
Una palabra clave,
Una llave
Que penetre el silencio.
Y si no la encuentro,
Seguiré viviendo
Encarcelada.

In Memoriam
Alaíde Foppa

una ONG, Nancy Soto y otras que brindan todo tipo de ayuda a las mujeres víctimas de la violencia, cuando "ayudarlas legalmente no es suficiente", como bien dice Socorro Maya.:

—Uno de los logros más importantes del grupo ha sido la declaración del 14 de noviembre de 1999, a propósito del caso de Paulina, en el que privaron los intereses de un grupo de la Constitución estatal y nacional: ...*Es obligación del estado de Baja California garantizar a las ciudadanas que acudan a las instituciones de salud a solicitar un aborto legal, que reciban atención médica, expedita y confidencial.* Por desgracia, ésta se violó en el caso de Paulina.

LA MAGNÍFICA RECOMENDACIÓN DE FEDERICO GARCÍA ESTRADA

Si Socorro Maya, la abogada de la familia, llama a Paulina "la personita", el subprocurador de Derechos Humanos de Mexicali, Federico García Estrada, la llama "la menor de edad". Moreno, de pelo blanco, sus recomendaciones han causado la admiración de las integrantes de GIRE y aunque es Socorro Maya Quevedo quien lleva el caso legalmente, la aportación de Federico García Estrada resulta esencial.

EL HOSPITAL RECURRIÓ A LA DILACIÓN Y AL TORTUGUISMO PARA CANSAR A LA FAMILIA

—La violación fue el 31 de julio de 1999 —dice Federico García Estrada—. El 20 de agosto Paulina y su madre consultan a una doctora y les confirma: La niña está embarazada. La misma ginecóloga les dice que consigan la autorización del Ministerio Público y que ella practicará el legrado inmediatamente. El 3 de septiembre la señora María Elena obtiene la autorización. A partir de ese momento campean la dilación, el tortuguismo y el burocratismo con el propósito de cansar a la familia. A pesar de todo María Elena, Paulina y Humberto se mantienen incólumes: No queremos que el embarazo prosiga. Un sacerdote les dice que su familia va a ser excomulgada y se mantienen firmes. Intervienen las enviadas de Provida, violando la intimidad de la paciente, el procurador de justicia, el sacerdote, la absoluta indecisión del director del hospital y la familia sigue adelante. Nada ni nadie la hace cambiar de opinión: Somos gente que *no conocemos* ni hemos estudiado pero sabemos lo

que queremos. Estamos seguros. Ejercen sus derechos: Este embarazo no es producto de un descuido en una relación de noviazgo, es el resultado de una violación. Tienen derecho al aborto. Paulina además va muy bien en la secundaria y es la única de los ocho hijos que ha llegado hasta allá.

ADIÓS MIS 15 AÑOS

—La niña, porque así le decimos, además de tener que dejar la escuela (es la única de mis hijos a punto de terminar la secundaria y teníamos la ilusión de que saliera adelante) estaba esperando su fiesta de

Federico García Estrada

15 años, con su misa, su baile, su vestido rosa largo, sus padrinos, sus damas, sus chambelanes, su pastel, su primer vals del brazo de su padre. ¿Ahora con qué cara se la hacemos? Es la última de mis ocho hijos. Teníamos ya una alcancía. Desde que llegamos de Salina Cruz no hemos sino ahorrado para su baile de quince años. Ella ya había enlistado a sus compañeros de escuela. ¿Cómo vamos a festejarla ahora con un niño?

LA VOLUNTAD INQUEBRANTABLE

"El recurso de la muerte fatal fue lo que doblegó a la familia Ramírez Jacinto, pero los que diariamente con-

Paulina embarazada

ducen a la esterilidad y a la muerte a muchas mujeres en el mundo son los abortos clandestinos mal practicados. El doctor Ávila Íñiguez tan logró su cometido que la respuesta de la mamá de Paulina es memorable: Ojalá nunca les pase *eso* a ustedes, pero si lo que querían era intimidarnos, ya lo lograron.

"Sólo entonces doña María Elena firmó el documento en que la familia desistió.

"Por lo tanto nosotros estamos profundamente convencidos de que las autoridades del Ministerio Público, del Hospital General de Mexicali y la Procuraduría de Justicia son responsables de negarle su derecho. No sólo no respetaron su decisión sino que hicieron todo para nulificar su voluntad. Ella tenía un derecho que no podía inhibírsele absolutamente bajo ningún concepto. Jamás se le dio una información científica fidedigna y respetuosa a la familia, por ejemplo: Ustedes pueden ir al Hospital General que es del sector salud donde no les van a cobrar, o pueden ir con un particular a que les practiquen la interrupción. Paulina y su familia se acogieron a la ley y la ley se rió de ellos.

"En su caso, hay una violación al derecho a la información, una intimidación fatalista y una coerción. Para tener validez, la autonomía de la voluntad debe darse sin ninguna presión. Su desistimiento por lo tanto no tiene validez. Lo tendría, de haberse hecho sin violentarlas, pero alego que Paulina y su familia vivieron un mes y veintinueve días en un estado de permanente violencia psíquica y física —un calvario—. Resulta absurdo que las autoridades produzcan un documento alegando: Desistieron. Es igual a si les hubieran puesto una pistola en la cabeza.

"Otro de los derechos fundamentales que se violaron es la intimidad de la paciente que en relación con la autoridad estaba en plano de desigualdad. Tiene que darse el llamado 'consentimiento informado', pero en este caso la desigualdad entre el médico y la paciente es notoria".

Indemnización para Paulina

El procurador de Derechos Humanos, Antonio García Sánchez, acaba de emitir una recomendación dirigida al gobernador del estado, Alejandro González Alcocer, en la que pide la destitución del director del Hospital General y la creación de un fideicomiso para reparar el daño material y moral causado a la futura madre, para cubrir los gastos realizados hasta ahora, la educación y atención médica de la madre y la criatura hasta la mayoría de edad.

FOTO: LUZ SERRANO. SEMANARIO *SIETE DÍAS*

Diálogo entre el director de Isesalud en Baja california, Carlos Astorga Othón y el gobernador Alejandro González Alcocer, durante la inauguración del Centro de Salud Valle Verde, en Tijuana.
Alcocer a Astorga: "¿Ya declaraste algo sobre Paulina?"
La respuesta: "Ya dije que no comentaría nada sobre el caso".

Ninguna mujer tiene garantías para ejercer su derecho al aborto

—¿Ha aceptado el gobernador González Alcocer la recomendación?

—No. Al contrario. A raíz del caso, el PAN vuelve a presentar una iniciativa de ley al Congreso para reformar la Constitución Federal y defender el "derecho a la vida" desde la concepción —termina García Estrada.

Me quedo petrificada. Si yo misma, ya vivita y coleando, nunca he sabido cuándo comenzó mi vida a ser mi vida, si hice verdaderamente lo que quise hacer ¿cómo voy a saber cuándo comienza la vida de un embrión? Si ni siquiera sé qué es *alma* y la confundo con *espíritu, cerebro, conciencia y sique* (los indios no tenían alma, según el dictamen de la Universidad de Salamanca; no éramos gente de razón, según los conquistadores), ¿qué voy a hacer ante semejante disyuntiva? Marta Lamas, mi entrañable amiga feminista, me dijo alguna vez que el embrión no tiene desarrollo neurológico en el primer trimestre. Éste sólo ocurre a partir del cuarto mes. Así, un aborto practicado en los primeros tres meses significa quitar un tejido que no siente ni sufre. ¿Existe la vida desde la concepción? Luis Villoro asevera: "No hay un criterio seguro, con bases científicas, para determinar cuando comienza a existir una persona humana". ¿Cuándo comienza la vida? Y me hago otras preguntas. ¿Es la niña Paulina sólo un aparato reproductor? ¿No tiene Paulina derecho al placer, sólo lo tiene a la violencia? ¿Cuál puede ser el proyecto de vida de una mujer violada?

Según el artículo 329 del Código Penal del Distrito Federal, el aborto es la muerte del producto de la concepción en cualquier momento de la preñez.

Según la ciencia médica no es lo mismo la muerte de un

cigoto, de un embrión, de un feto viable o de uno no viable. A continuación se desglosan los conceptos médicos:

Cigoto: fruto de la fecundación, resultado de la unión de un espermatozoide y un óvulo. Se desarrolla hasta llegar a implantarse en el útero, siete o quince días después de la fecundación.

Embrión: el producto recibe este nombre a partir de su implantación en el útero y hasta los tres meses de embarazo.

Feto: existe desde los tres meses hasta el momento del nacimiento. En esta etapa comienza el proceso de adquisición de las características reconocibles como humanas.

Viabilidad: un feto es viable cuando está lo suficientemente desarrollado para sobrevivir fuera del útero materno. Ha terminado el proceso de desarrollo del cerebro, los pulmones y los riñones. La viabilidad se establece a partir el séptimo mes.

El cristianismo apoya la idea de que la vida comienza desde el momento de la fecundación. Cuando el espermatozoide y el óvulo se unen, un grupo de células vivas pero no concientes conforman al ser humano.

De acuerdo con el argumento que prohíbe el aborto porque implica el asesinato de células, cortar nuestro cabello, nuestras uñas o podar el césped, también sería cometer un crimen, para no hablar de la matanza de otras especies para alimentarnos.

Aunque no hay un único criterio que defina cuándo comienza la vida humana, el punto de vista de la ciencia contemporánea coincide en señalar que esto ocurre en el séptimo mes de embarazo, cuando se desarrolla el sistema cerebral cortical y con ello la conciencia. Hasta ese momento el feto comienza a desarrollar las funciones específicas del ser humano. Es también hasta entonces que el feto puede vivir en el mundo exterior.

FOTO: MARIANA YAMPOLSKY

El pensamiento de santo Tomás de Aquino, que dominó a la Iglesia católica hasta fines del siglo XIX, concebía la relación entre alma y cuerpo de una manera análoga a la relación que establece la ciencia entre vida y conciencia. Para la filosofía tomista, el embrión masculino no recibía el alma sino hasta los 40 días y el embrión femenino hasta el octagésimo día de su concepción, recuerda Gabriela Rodríguez en su artículo para *La Jornada* del 17 de abril de 2000, "Joven sacrificada por el PAN". Dada esta creencia, era lícito y moral practicar el aborto en un feto inanimado, es decir, antes de los 80 días. Hoy en día, en cambio, la Iglesia se opone frontalmente al aborto en cualquier caso, aun en el de una violación. Prefieren sugerir a la madre entregar en adopción al niño, lo cual no siempre ocurre, siendo la madre quien sufre las consecuencias.

—Lo común en los casos de las doctrinas panistas y católicas —continúa Rodríguez—, es que no les preocupan los efectos psicológicos, económicos, ni el futuro de la mujer preñada, que la suerte del futuro ser siempre tiene preferencia sobre la madre que ya existe, que la decisión debe estar en manos de los médicos y teólogos y en ningún caso de las madres. Ellas deben ser sacrificadas para salvar a un ser potencial a quien poder bautizar y librar del pecado original (...) Mientras no mejoremos las condiciones de vida y la balanza del poder entre hombres/mujeres, ricos/pobres, funcionarios/pacientes y ministros/feligreses, muchas mujeres como Paulina seguirán siendo injustamente presas del pánico ante la violencia.

Esto completa la idea ya presentada por Gabriela también en *La Jornada* del 30 de enero del 2000, "El miedo a la Iglesia", donde afirma, frente a la evidente preferencia de Norberto Rivera por el partido oficial, que: "El peligro es real y más que miedo debería generar pánico, no sólo entre políticos, sino, sobre todo, a los ciudadanos creyentes de los valores democráticos ¿Cómo defenderse al mismo tiempo de un nuevo PRI y de una nueva evangelización?"

El aborto se permite por cinco causas:

1. Violación
2. Peligro de muerte de la madre
3. Malformaciones del producto (en algunos Estados)
4. Grave daño a la salud (si una mujer prediabética se puede volver diabética)
5. Pobreza (Yucatán)

Y no se castiga por imprudencia o por inseminación artificial no consentida.

Legalizar el aborto no es volverlo obligatorio, sino regularlo, reglamentarlo. La discusión es si la maternidad debe ser voluntaria o no. Una vida hasta que no sale del cuerpo de la mujer no va a tener autonomía.

CATÓLICAS POR EL DERECHO A DECIDIR

Católicas por el Derecho a Decidir, Catholics for a Free Choice, forma parte de una red internacional que surgió en Washington en 1973 y en América Latina en 1987, a raíz del interés de

Pilar Sánchez y María del Consuelo Mejía

79

una sexóloga uruguaya, Silvia Marcos, en México. Conocidas internacionalmente como las Pro Choice en contra de las Pro Life o sea Provida, luchan contra el anquilosamiento de la Iglesia y como lo dice Pilar Sánchez, para darle "el total apoyo hacia los más jodidos, los más olvidados, los más vulnerables, los que antes fueron los leprosos y hoy son los portadores de VIH. Si Jesús estuviera aquí estaría con ellos y no se apoltronaría en los bienes materiales". Hoy su dirigente en México es María del Consuelo Mejía, que no considera infalibles las enseñanzas sobre anticoncepción, sexualidad y aborto de la Iglesia católica:

—Santo Tomás decía que no se podía hablar de una persona con alma por lo menos cuarenta días después de la concepción en el caso de los hombres, y ochenta días después en el de las mujeres. San Agustín decía que no se podía pensar que el alma llegara a una forma tan primitiva como el óvulo fecundado, tenía que haber un tiempo de desarrollo para merecer el ingreso del alma. Estas posiciones datan del siglo II. En la *Biblia* no hay referencias al aborto, salvo en una disputa sobre si la mujer pierde el embarazo, debe penar en monedas, pero no por la vida del feto sino por su propia salud. Dentro de la misma doctrina católica hay enseñanzas morales que nos hablan de la libertad de conciencia, la capacidad de tomar decisiones y la de disentir de las enseñanzas que no son dogma. Los teólogos desarrollaron el principio de probabilismo a finales del siglo XIX, que nos dice que cuando hay duda hay libertad, sobre todo en un tema que tiene que ver con moral, porque la conciencia está por encima de las enseñanzas de la Iglesia. La conciencia está concebida, valga la redundancia, como el recinto más íntimo de nuestra relación con Dios. Las decisiones que tomamos a conciencia con nosotras mismas, son las decisiones válidas moralmente. Cuando actuamos en contra de nuestra conciencia es cuando pecamos. ¿Cómo es posible que el creador nos construya de una manera para luego cercenar nuestras posibilidades?, pregunta una teóloga feminista estadounidense que si Dios no hubiera querido que las mujeres sintieran placer, no nos hubiera dejado con clítoris, porque el clítoris no tiene más función que la del placer.

"Jesucristo rompió con la normatividad de su época con respecto a las mujeres que fueron esenciales en su vida. María Magdalena, la samaritana, la mujer menstruando a quien tocó, la prostituta a la que rescató, es un mensaje olvidado o silenciado por la Iglesia. La palabra divina no es la palabra de los jerarcas, la Iglesia somos todas, y todos y tenemos derecho a participar, expresar nuestras necesidades y deseos y considerar que nuestra conciencia también es una conciencia moral.

"La Iglesia católica acostumbra decirle no a las evidencias científicas. Hasta 1997 aceptó la teoría evolucionista de Darwin como cierta. Descendemos de los primates, no de Adán y Eva. La Iglesia tardó más de siglo y medio en aceptarlo. Ahora la Iglesia alega que el alma entra al óvulo en el momento mismo de la concepción. ¿Qué hará cuando la ciencia demuestre que esto es imposible? Si la Iglesia tardó siglo y medio en aceptar el evolucionismo, ahora sigue con el mito del alma al igual que el de la pareja mítica: Adán y Eva.

"¿No es de una gran arrogancia seguir diciendo que no a la evidencia científica cuando la mayoría de las sociedades democráticas y avanzadas del mundo tienen legalizado el aborto justamente por ella? ¿Qué defiende la Iglesia católica hoy en el mundo? Antes su batalla era contra el comunismo, hoy pretende ejercer un control absoluto sobre la pareja, la familia, la sociedad".

¿El alma?

—¿Qué entendemos por alma? De la misma manera que la Iglesia usó la metáfora de Adán y Eva para explicar el origen del género humano, se inventa una entelequia a la que llama *alma* para hablar de lo que nos caracteriza como seres humanos: la conciencia.

La ciencia argumenta que del tercer mes hacia atrás, no hay la menor respuesta neurológica. Provida alega que la respuesta son los reflejos musculares. Sin embargo, un embrión abortado a los tres meses no puede sentir dolor porque no tiene conexiones neurológicas.

We Are Church. Somos Iglesia

—En 1996 surgió en Estados Unidos un movimiento muy interesante: Somos Iglesia, We are Church, para pedirle al Vaticano cambiar sus enseñanzas sobre anticoncepción, el respeto a los homosexuales y lesbianas en la Iglesia, el celibato como opción y no como obligación para los sacerdotes, y el ministerio para que las mujeres puedan ser sacerdotisas. Se hizo un plebiscito y se reunieron millones de firmas que se llevaron al Vaticano. Posteriormente, el movimiento se desarrolló en Austria, Francia, España, Italia, en Bolivia, Brasil, Uruguay, Colombia, Argentina, México y otros países.

Sólo Dios puede dar o quitar la vida

—La Iglesia católica parte de la idea de que Dios es el único que da o quita la vida, los seres humanos no tenemos derecho sobre ella, por lo tanto no podemos usar anticonceptivos y los que se suicidan son condenados.

La Iglesia se ha entrampado

—En 1963 —continúa María del Consuelo Mejía, de Católicas por el Derecho a Decidir— Juan XXIII convocó a la Comisión Papal del Control de la Natalidad, formada por cuarenta médicos, abogados (pocas mujeres), que sesionaron durante tres años para estudiar si podían cambiar el uso de métodos anticonceptivos en el interior de la Iglesia. Como había mucha resistencia, cuando terminaron de sesionar, Juan XXIII había muerto. Su sucesor, Pablo VI, convencido por un cardenal de que se minaría la autoridad de la Iglesia católica, emitió la *Enciclica Humana Vitae* que prohíbe el uso de los anticonceptivos. Hoy, muchos católicos modernos alegan que la Iglesia no debería opinar en materia de sexualidad y reproducción porque va a ser totalmente rebasada por los descubrimientos científicos.

María del Consuelo Mejía

Todos somos Iglesia

—Estamos acostumbrados a no nombrar, porque nos han obligado a invisibilizar —dice Pilar Sánchez de Católicas por el Derecho a Decidir—. El que la mujer planifique su familia o evite tener un nuevo producto, por su situación económica, familiar o por violación, resulta inaceptable para la Iglesia.

"Hay una contradicción en torno a esta vida que se quiere preservar. ¿Por qué se da a escoger a los creyentes entre la vida del feto y la de la madre? ¿Por qué se elige la vida del feto?

"Las mujeres no importamos. El que vale es el que todavía no está formado, el que no es persona. Lo que más cuestiona e increpa a la jerarquía es que la mujer decida, piense, tenga voz, imponga su voluntad. No está bien visto en la vida religiosa (yo fui religiosa durante 12 años), en la vida matrimonial, en la familiar y en la laboral."

¿Qué justifica que Paulina cargue durante el resto de su vida con un hijo que no deseaba? ¿Por qué? ¿Porque es pobre? ¿Porque su familia no ha tenido el privilegio de la educación? En lugar de volver los ojos a los países europeos, donde el aborto dejó de ser un problema para pasar a ser un derecho y una decisión que TODA mujer, —cualquiera que sea su estatus económico y su rol social— puede tomar, México se empantana y olvida el inalineable derecho que una mujer tiene sobre su cuerpo.

El *bunker* de isesalud

Un monumental edificio de piedra que parece un *bunker,* en una plaza que responde al nombre de Centro Cívico y Comercial de Mexicali y abarca otras dependencias gubernamentales como los tres poderes locales, legislativo, ejecutivo y judicial (ya que también allí se encuentra la Procuraduría General de Justicia del Estado) impresiona a los visitantes. En el asta ondea la bandera de México grande y hermosa y la magnitud de la plaza y de los edificios nos comprueba que estamos en lo alto de la pirámide. Aquí están los mandamases. Me gustaría que las construcciones inspiraran menos reverencia y que su color estuviera más acorde a los rosas, los ocres y a los amarillos del desierto, y no ostentaran

Monumento a los pioneros

la negrura del basalto, pero supongo que el poder debe imponer y atemorizar. El Centro Cívico también alberga un monumento que me conmueve porque se trata de un homenaje a los pioneros, y es fácil imaginar a los tres que llegan como Jesús, María y José a pedir posada. No viajan en burro sino a caballo, el padre de familia lleva su pico y su guaje, y la madre exhausta y lánguida esconde al hijo en el regazo.

Doctor Carlos Alberto Astorga Othón, director de ISESALUD

El director de ISESALUD (que corresponde a nuestra Secretaría de Salubridad y Asistencia), nos recibe de inmediato. De hecho, todos los funcionarios a quienes acudimos nos recibieron sin hacernos esperar y nos trataron con exquisita cortesía. Pasamos a un salón de actos con una mesa larguísima, la bandera nacional y una extensa hilera de fotografías de quienes antes fueron directores (busco a alguno con cara simpática al menos para mí y encuentro a varios), y nos ofrecen café, refrescos, galletas, chocolates, lo que queramos. Un secretario del secretario nos pregunta cuál es el motivo de nuestra visita, qué tema vamos a tratar para avisárselo al señor secretario. Yo digo tímidamente que el de la niña Paulina, a la que se le negó un aborto hace meses y ahora va a dar a luz. El secretario del secretario sale y entra Karla Gómez, fotógrafa que trabaja en el departamento de comunicación de ISESALUD. Karla nos retratará insistentemente a lo largo de la entrevista e incluso al día siguiente en el Hospital General de Mexicali, cosa que irrita a Isabel: ¿Para qué es esto?, pregunta.

—Es un trámite que hacemos con todos nuestros visitantes: los

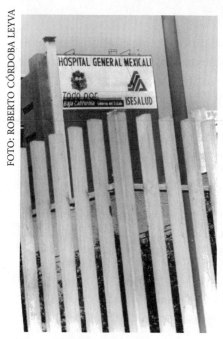

fotografiamos para llevar un registro—, responde Karla.

El director y médico Carlos Alberto Astorga Othón es joven, lleva una camisa azul y un aire de gran seguridad, como la mayoría de los jóvenes que llegan antes de tiempo a un puesto de mando. Colgado del cinturón de su delgada cintura, un *biper*. Asimismo, coloca un celular sobre la mesa. Lo acompañan todos los atributos de la tecnología más avanzada. Isabel, de inmediato, emprende la batalla y Astorga Othón se

86

pone a la defensiva. Tras él entra un secretario y el doctor Óscar del Real, que Astorga Othón nos presenta:

—El doctor Óscar del Real es el director de Servicios de Salud y responsable del sistema hospitalario del estado.

De camisa a cuadros, Óscar del Real se sienta al lado de Isabel y no pronuncia una sola palabra. Me cae bien por instinto y porque su actitud no es nada prepotente. De inmediato un secretario pone una grabadora sobre la mesa y Karla Gómez nos retrata. Clic, clic, clic, clic. Vehemente, Isabel le dice al director que considera que la actuación de Paulina y María Elena su madre es un ejemplo ciudadano:

—A Elena y a mí nos interesa saber por qué Paulina no pudo ejercer su derecho y qué pasó. ¿Qué pasó?

—Pues simplemente sus papás renunciaron a que se le practicara el aborto —responde el doctor Carlos Alberto Astorga Othón, parapetado tras su camisa azul y sus múltiples aditamentos, que no dejan de fascinarme porque fascinarían a mis nietos quienes de inmediato le preguntarían: ¿No me lo prestas tantito?

—Desistieron al final de mes y medio, cuando la niña ya tenía tres meses de embarazo.

YO DI LA ORDEN DE QUE SE BUSCARAN MÉDICOS QUE QUISIERAN HACER EL ABORTO

—No, todavía había tiempo. Incluso la noche en que los padres se desistieron, yo había indicado que se preparara un equipo técnico para que se efectuara.

—Usted dice que estaba dispuesto a hacerlo —vuelve a la carga Isabel— pero ya había pasado más de un mes, la niña había sido internada ocho días, la primera vez, tres días, la segunda. ¿Por qué fue tan difícil?

Astorga tiene una expresión muy seria y tengo la leve sospecha de que está comenzando a enchilarse.

—Doctor, se trata de un aborto por violación y del respeto al consentimiento informado de la paciente. ¿Por qué es tan difícil que las mujeres ejerzan su derecho? ¿Cuenta más la ideología de la gente que maneja los servicios? Eso es ilegal. Usted dice que la niña y su madre se desistieron luego de un mes y veinte días de acoso y de estarlas llevando y trayendo sin sentido dentro de los servicios públicos de salud.

—No le lleva a nada arrinconarme a mí —se enoja Astorga Othón—. Como autoridad, cumplimos con la autorización para que se practicara el aborto. El retraso provoca que el Ministerio Público ordene la intervención del director del Hospital General, quien, cuando acude, es detenido. Esto molesta enormemente al gremio médico del hospital. En ese *inter*, al día siguiente se buscan médicos, pero no hay un médico que quiera practicar el aborto y, como usted sabe, un derecho que no puede tampoco desaparecer, es aquel de no arriesgar la vida del paciente. Los médicos ejercieron su derecho. Nosotros recomendamos e instruimos al hospital para que se hiciera el aborto, no hubo quien lo quisiera hacer. En ese transcurso los papás y la niña se desistieron y ahí terminó el caso para nosotros. Si hubo o no una visión ideológica, eso ya no me toca a mí juzgarlo y ésa es la función de las ONG, que la sociedad dirima esas diferencias, para que llegue a puntos concretos que luego se utilicen en la ley, ¿cierto?

—Sí, por eso estamos aquí. No se sienta acorralado.

—Ya la Comisión de Derechos Humanos emitió una recomendación con la cual ni nosotros ni el gobernador estamos de acuerdo, porque pide que se sancione penalmente a los funcionarios que han participado en ese desistimiento cuando no hubo coerción para que se diera el mismo.

—¿No está usted de acuerdo con la magnífica recomendación del subprocurador de Derechos Humanos, Federico García Estrada?

—Al contrario, estoy en desacuerdo.

Más tarde, en otras declaraciones periodísticas, Carlos Alberto Astorga Othón habría de decir: "El caso Paulina es una infamia y perversidad del subprocurador Federico García Estrada y en eso coincidimos totalmente el gobernador Alejandro González Alcocer y yo... Por puro protagonismo desató una campaña, sólo para posicionarse, y todo lo hizo porque quería la Procuraduría de Derechos Humanos y esto lo considero infame, perverso y atroz", publicó *La Crónica* el 2 de mayo de 2000.

—Pero ¿está usted en desacuerdo con un fideicomiso?

—Si después, moralmente, debe crearse un fideicomiso para atender a la niña y al producto de su embarazo, estoy de acuerdo. Hay que buscar mecanismos con los que la sociedad proteja a estas personas lastimadas.

—¿Usted sugiere algún mecanismo?

—Grupos de ayuda vinieron a ofrecer su apoyo a la niña, grupos que no coinciden con ustedes y están en medio de una pugna ideológica. Yo me limito a lo que en la legalidad me es permitido.

—Concretamente, cuando llega la autorización del Ministerio Público al hospital y usted le turna a la autoridad competente, ¿no cree que en un hospital de servicios públicos debe haber alguien dispuesto a practicar la interrupción del embarazo si hay una ley que así lo dice?

—Ésa es una interpretación suya.

—No. A mí me parece que hay un vacío, una falla en la reglamentación, una falta de mecanismos.

—Ésa es su opinión.

—Usted acaba de decirnos que no había nadie dispuesto a hacerlo. A mí me parece que esto viola los derechos ciudadanos.

—Yo no dije que no había nadie sino que los ánimos estaban molestos y no se localizaba quién practicara el aborto. Tan es así que el mismo día que se desistieron los padres se formó un equipo para practicar el aborto. Insisto en la palabra "autorización", porque no es una orden.

—Pero entonces, ¿por qué no se practicó?

—Porque hubo un desistimiento de la familia.

—Eso no es cierto. ¿Está de acuerdo en que pasó un mes y veinte días desde la primera entrada hasta el desistimiento?

—Como le comenté, el sábado en que se desistieron se le iba a practicar la interrupción.

—¡Qué casualidad! Un mes y veinte días y tenía que ser ese mero día.

—No, no fueron tantos días.

—Lo tenemos en actas con fechas y todo —contesta Isabel.

—Según mi expediente, del sábado que autorizan a la formación del equipo para practicarle el aborto, apenas pasa una semana.

—Bueno y usted, ¿por qué cree que se violó la intimidad de la paciente? ¿Por qué no se respetaron los derechos humanos de Paulina? El asunto no es sólo el desistimiento, doctor Astorga Othón, también es el de la información a la prensa. Usted puede decir lo que quiera, usted es el director de Salud, pero usted también es responsable ante la opinión pública de cómo funcionó el sistema que usted encabeza.

—Y créame que lo hago y lo voy a hacer. No soy quien debe estar ventilando en la prensa asuntos que debo corregir adentro. Tampoco soy responsable de que un periodista ande en los pasillos hurgando por todos lados. Se enteró de que el director del hospital estaba detenido y lo sacó a ocho columnas al día siguiente.

—El periodista Javier Mejía tuvo razón, póngase en nuestro lugar, doctor. Yo como ciudadana me entero a través de la prensa de la calidad de los servicios públicos.

Astorga Othón está que trina y nos pulveriza con la

mirada. El aire puede cortarse con cuchillo. El cenicero frente a Isabel, retacado de colillas, humea.

—Yo creo que usted no debe sentirse acorralado —digo conciliadora—. Sabemos que usted es de formación católica y todos aquí estamos en la misma situación; nos educaron dentro del catolicismo. Estudié en un convento de monjas. Lo que da dolor y mueve a compasión es que se trata —otra vez— de gente muy pobre que en vez de ir con una comadrona, cosa que fácilmente pudieron elegir, busca la defensa legal a la que tiene derecho y una solución que le garantiza la Constitución. A su actitud de confianza y de respeto por sí mismos y por la ley que va a pro-

Paulina embarazada

tegerlos no tiene respuesta, sólo indiferencia. Después de ser violada, Paulina recurrió a las autoridades y buscó apoyo como lo haría con sus mayores. Nuestro primer impulso, el de Isabel y mío y el de miles de mujeres mexicanas igual a nosotras, habría sido ayudarla. ¿Cómo? Liberándola de un embarazo por violación. Finalmente, la niña salió igual, sólo que aterrada y más sola aún. ¿Cómo puede remediarse eso? Supongo que usted tiene hijos. ¿Qué pasaría si su hija es violada?

—No me lo puedo ni siquiera imaginar, no lo toleraría.

—¿No quisiera usted matar al tipo?

—No lo sé, no me quiero poner en ese escenario. Ni que nadie en el mundo lo estuviera. Causa mucho coraje que esto le ocurra no sólo a personas de escasos recursos sino a cualquier mujer. Para ello, hay mecanismos y agencias especializadas de ayuda.

—¿Cuáles? ¿Dónde están? ¿Por qué fallaron entonces?

—Lo desconozco. Hicieron bien o mal, no lo sé. Lo que sí sé es que hay agencias y grupos especializados de ayuda, tanto de los que están a favor como de quienes están en contra del aborto, y ambos se acercaron a ofrecer su ayuda a la niña.

"Frente a este tema, hay una polarización que ustedes conocen. Nosotros nos ajustamos al proceder de la ley y si alguien de nuestro equipo ha cometido alguna barbaridad habrá que reclamarle, pero nunca dejó de conmovernos el caso, como no nos dejaría de conmover cualquier otro suceso que violentara la seguridad personal".

—Pero esa misma lentitud, ese darle largas, impidió que Paulina saliera del hospital con su problema resuelto. Al día siguiente hubiera ido a la escuela en vez del embarazo prolongado que la fue marginando de sus compañeras y de su vida de antes. La vida de Paulina no volverá a ser igual. No tenía por qué convertirse en una tragedia que nos atañe a todos. El aborto es una experiencia atroz que ninguna mujer toma a la ligera porque interrumpe la vida. Y si en el momento mismo lo toma a la ligera, las repercusiones vendrán más tarde. Siempre las hay. Nadie se salva de ese tipo de reflexiones. Uno se pregunta cada día, ¿por qué estoy aquí? ¿Para qué sirvo? ¿A quién puedo servirle? Por el caso patético e injusto de una sola niña, Paulina, pensamos en el problema en el que se ven muchísimas mujeres, hermanas, hijas y los hijos y las hijas de todo el mundo que son también nuestros hijos.

"El aborto también ha deshecho parejas. Deberíamos vivir, ¿o no, doctor?, pensando que a todos nos puede suceder lo mismo. Además de temor e indiferencia, creo que hubo dureza por parte de las autoridades".

—Yo creo que no hubo dureza. Tal vez fue lenta la orden de autorización, más no la jurisdicción por parte del hospital. Se lo digo porque yo seguí el proceso. Si ustedes revisan el procedimiento de la procuraduría, verán que fue puro trámite legal. Yo desconozco si así es siempre o fue específicamente lento en este caso. No lo sé.

Después de su último "no lo sé", el director de ISESALUD se despide, enojado. Su secretario sale tras él. En cambio la fotógrafa sigue sentada y vigila la grabadora así como la cámara vigila nuestros rostros. Isabel y yo permanecemos ancladas frente a la mesa, ella al lado del médico Óscar del Real, que al menos tiene una actitud más abierta que la de Astorga Othón, y yo frente a él, a quien, por lo tanto, también puedo ver de frente. Definitivamente, le tengo mucha más confianza que a Astorga Othón. Es otra gente y otro modo de ser, gracias a Dios y a la virgen de Guadalupe.

El doctor Óscar del Real habla de la intimidad del paciente hospitalizado.

—Hay gafetes para manejar el acceso del público a los

servicios, pero, déjenme decirles, que yo fui director del Hospital General de Mexicali durante cinco años y director del Hospital de Ensenada, y en varias ocasiones recuerdo haber solicitado la autorización del Ministerio Público para llevar a cabo interrupciones del embarazo.

Desde luego este doctor se ve muchísimo más accesible y mucho menos violento que el doctor Carlos Alberto Astorga Othón. Está dispuesto a dialogar y no nos echa miradas asesinas, sobre todo a Isabel.

—Por lo menos en tres ocasiones yo le solicité al Ministerio Público autorización para llevar a cabo interrupciones del embarazo en mujeres que teniendo una enfermedad ponían en peligro su vida: leucemia, cáncer, cáncer de linfoma, etcétera, pero siempre fue un problema obtener la autorización.

"Primero, no estamos muy acostumbrados a la aplicación de este tipo de leyes y segundo, aunque yo tenía confianza en los jefes de servicios, en el anestesiólogo, en los ginecobstetras, una parte importante de los médicos no aceptan la interrupción del embarazo. Hay otros que sí. De cualquier manera, siempre ha sido difícil reglamentar lo que sucede ante la comisión de un delito, por ejemplo, la violación. La autorización por parte del Ministerio Público para la interrupción del embarazo y finalmente su ejecución en los servicios de salud son pasos lentos y no están bien reglamentados. ¿Quién, cómo, dónde y cuándo?

"El caso que nos ocupa, tuvo tres etapas: la primera, la orden directa del Ministerio Público al director del Hospital General para llevar a cabo la interrupción del embarazo; la segunda, la presentación del director ante los separos de la policía judicial del estado al no llevarse a cabo con la prontitud solicitada; y la tercera, aunque la policía libera al director del hospital, los médicos se sintieron humillados, agredidos, cerraron filas y dijeron: No podemos trabajar con el Ministerio Público.

—Aunque es respetable la creencia o la conciencia de cada quien, tiene que haber un servicio seguro para el paciente. Alguno o alguna tiene que estar dispuesta a hacerlo, esté de acuerdo o no.

—Así es. La vinculación entre la parte procuradora de justicia y los servicios de salud es difícil, no de ahora sino de siempre. En los hospitales recibimos heridos que presumiblemente fueron objeto de agresiones o cometieron un delito; fueron heridos por la policía o por ellos mismos y sobre ellos tenemos que informar al agente del Ministerio Público, que en muchas ocasiones entra al hospital como Pedro por su casa, sube a los pisos, entra a Terapia Intensiva, en plena violación de las normas de atención a los enfermos. Interroga a los heridos o a los presuntos responsables, exige certificados médicos en el acto y cuando eso no sucede, gira una orden de presentación al médico interno, becario o residente.

—Supongo que esto genera grandes fricciones.

—En mi época de director promoví una reunión entre el procurador del estado, los agentes del Ministerio Público y los jefes de servicio del hospital, y nuestras relaciones mejoraron considerablemente.

Hace falta reglamentación

—Hace falta reglamentar lo que sucede a partir de que se autoriza la interrupción del embarazo, quién lo va a interrumpir, en qué servicio. ¿Por qué en la Secretaría de Salud y no en los servicios médicos municipales?¿Por qué no en la Cruz Roja o en el Seguro Social? Lo que sucede en el caso de Paulina, es que se da una lucha de poder para ver quién prevalece sobre quién.

—Es una cuestión interna, doctor del Real, pero es también una cuestión de ética médica. Si los médicos

Grabado de Alberto Beltrán

públicos siguen funcionando así, estamos perdidos porque va a prevalecer su creencia o su ideología sobre la ciencia médica.

AÚN ES UN ESTIGMA SER UN ENFERMO DE SIDA

—Mire, lo mismo sucede con los enfermos de Sida. Luchamos todos los días por atenderlos de manera digna, humana, pero desafortunadamente hay resistencia en ciertos grupos de servidores del Seguro Social. Estos pacientes tienen el estigma de ser contagiosos y

pertenecer a grupos minoritarios que no merecen la consideración del resto de la sociedad. Si un director de hospital le ordena a un médico hacer una interrupción de embarazo, responde que no tiene por qué hacerla, porque dentro de su capacidad deliberativa como profesionales de la salud está decidir si lo hacen o no.

"Volviendo al caso de esta niña, hubo una sobrerreacción de parte del Ministerio Público y del personal médico involucrado. De tener la decisión, lo que yo hubiera hecho es sacar a la niña fuera de ese contexto e interrumpirle el embarazo bajo otras circunstancias, quizá a nivel privado."

—El meollo de la cuestión —dice Isabel— es que los médicos violaron el consentimiento informado, que es uno de los parámetros de la ética médica en los sistemas públicos de salud en México.

—Tenemos hojas de consentimiento informado para intervenciones quirúrgicas de todo tipo que alertan al paciente acerca de los riesgos que corre. No hay que perder de vista que el hospital de Mexicali realiza entre 300 y 400 abortos anuales.

—¿Ah sí? ¿Legales?

—Legales, es decir, las pacientes llegan no por órdenes del Ministerio Público, sino con abortos inducidos...

—¿A consecuencia de un aborto clandestino?

—Que no nos interesa investigar. La atención de la salud a la enferma se da no por los aspectos punitivos o de presunta ilegalidad. Lo digo porque he estado 20 años en el hospital, y siempre ha sido así. Nunca verán ustedes que de la institución surja una denuncia o un señalamiento a las autoridades para que sea perseguida como delito la práctica del aborto clandestino.

La salud no tiene colores

—En el hospital atendemos específicamente el caso de salud —continúa el doctor Óscar del Real—, lo mismo ocurre cuando un presunto delincuente llega herido. También recibimos a las mujeres que se presentan con un aborto en evolución. Tampoco crean ustedes que hay una tendencia ideológica diseminada dentro de nuestros servicios contra de la interrupción del embarazo. No hay un conservadurismo despiadado en el gremio médico. El aborto es una cuestión controversial en todos lados, como las pláticas de sobremesa que pueden llegar a ser tan irritantes sobre si existe Dios o no. Por otro lado, en los servicios de salud, no hay colores, la salud no tiene colores. Pensamos más en términos científicos y de salud que en términos ideológicos y le voy a poner de ejemplo el programa de salud reproductiva, que tiene varias vertientes, ayuda a la mujer en salud perinatal, salud clínica, salud familiar. En el estado de Baja California tenemos la cobertura más alta de todo el país de mujeres en edad fértil con métodos de planificación familiar: el 79 por ciento. Tenemos la tasa global de fertilidad más baja de todo el país: el promedio es de 2.4 hijos por mujer a nivel nacional y aquí es de 2.05.

"Por un lado, el 100 por ciento de la población tiene acceso a los servicios de salud, ya sea de la seguridad social o de la población abierta, a través de la medicina privada. Hay un impulso fuerte de las políticas gubernamentales y estatales para hacer disponibles métodos anticonceptivos, información, consejería, etcétera. Estos programas nos permitieron de un año a otro duplicar el examen Papanicolau. Este año echaremos a andar el programa de cáncer de mama".

La salud de la mujer, un derecho fundamental

—En su proyecto de planificación familiar ¿hay anticoncepción de emergencia?

—Todavía es una cuestión muy polémica. Ya contamos con las prefectas para iniciar la capacitación, pero no nos han dado la orden de echarlo a andar. Es un tema muy controversial, precisamente por las fuerzas antiabortistas.

—¿La Iglesia católica?

—Sí, porque la anticoncepción de emergencia inhibe la implantación del huevo.

—¿Y aquí los hombres se hacen la vasectomía?

—No son muchos, pero sí hacemos con cierta frecuencia jornadas de vasectomía sin bisturí, que son gratuitas, y realizamos algo así como 300 intervenciones al año.

—Volviendo a los médicos, doctor ¿nunca ha sucedido que un médico se ponga a decirle a una paciente, mira tú, pecadora, tú te lo buscaste, y le eche una filípica?

—Jamás. Al contrario, hay solidaridad con las mujeres.

—¡Sin embargo viene una niña pidiendo un aborto al que tiene derecho y todos ponen el grito en el cielo, doctor! Cuando usted fue director, ¿tuvo algún caso en que peligrara la vida de la mujer y tuviera que decidir hacerle un aborto?

—Sí, tres o cuatro casos.

—¿Y no recurrió al Ministerio Público?

—No, porque eran casos de daño en el corazón que hacían que la paciente no soportara su embarazo, o cáncer y leucemia, y el bebé habría tenido malformaciones por la quimioterapia.

—Aquí, en Mexicali, ¿los médicos que hacen abortos han sido perseguidos?

—Pienso que no, por lo menos no recuerdo denuncias expresas en los periódicos. Probablemente sólo uno ha

sido señalado a lo largo de diez o quince años.

Nos despedimos sonrientes del doctor Óscar del Real. Obviamente se trata de un hombre bueno, comprensivo y dispuesto a escuchar; todo lo opuesto al joven Astorga Othón. La prepotencia de muchos funcionarios jóvenes que creen que "ya la hicieron" es apabullante.

Salgo reconfortada por esta entrevista con un hombre conciliador e inteligente: del Real.

Nos disponemos a ir a la procuraduría de Justicia del Estado a entrevistar al procurador Juan Manuel Salazar Pimentel. Esperamos un rato en la antesala, Liliana Plumeda, Socorro Maya, Silvia Reséndiz Flores, Isabel y yo. Nos ofrecen refrescos. Finalmente advierten con cautela y amabilidad que el procurador no está en Mexicali y por lo tanto no podrá recibirnos. ¿Queremos ver a alguien más? ¿Pueden servirnos en algún otro trámite? ¿Otro cafecito? ¿Tenemos transporte para ir al aeropuerto? Una secretaria nos cuenta aquí en confianza que el procurador no tiene hijos y sí llevó personalmente a Paulina y a su madre a hablar con un sacerdote, quizá se deba a una razón íntima y familiar además de religiosa, claro está. Pero si la religión católica lo permite y el penalista Ruiz Cruz afirman que aun el derecho canónico consiente el aborto (en caso de riesgo para la vida de la madre o por violación), el celo del procurador Juan Manuel Salazar Pimentel resulta totalmente fuera de lugar.

Salimos de la Procuraduría y nos despedimos con ligereza a pesar de tanta amable galleta, amables refrescos y cafecitos endulzados. A quien sí abrazamos con tristeza porque han sido intensos estos tres días de camaradería es a Socorro, Silvia y Lilia desde ahora nuestras amigas.

Paulina y María Elena son pioneras

En México, la gran mayoría de las mujeres se tragan el trauma de la violación, no lo denuncian porque saben que en el juzgado serán vituperadas, es decir, doblemente violadas y asumen de por vida el estigma de tal violencia. Por lo tanto, María Elena Jacinto Raúz y su hija Paulina son unas pioneras y su lucha es admirable porque sus derechos humanos corren al natural, alimentan su sangre.

El tema del aborto es angustioso y complejo y nos afecta a todas las mujeres. Los fundamentalistas hablan siempre a favor de la vida que "ya está allí palpitando" en el vientre de la madre y no de los derechos de los miles de niños estigmatizados por el rechazo de sus padres. ¿No habría que pensar que el abandono "está allí palpitando"? Rechazados, los niños de la calle viven en las alcantarillas y los *niños bien* se la pasan abandonados afectivamente aunque los cuiden nanas y choferes.

Denise Dresser escribe el 23 de abril de 2000 en *Proceso*:

El tema del aborto es difícil para cualquier persona que piensa, reflexiona, siente. Es difícil pensar que cualquiera que haya tenido un aborto lo haya hecho en forma casual. Aquellas mujeres que han abortado seguramente piensan en lo que pudo haber sido; en la niñez con zapatos de charol, en el niño con la camiseta del América. Un aborto desgarra y desanima y hiere y humilla. Pero el derecho a abortar —un derecho que tienen las mujeres en la mayor parte de las democracias occidentales— no fue una propuesta de sobremesa de feministas que lo sugirieron una tarde compartiendo café, especulando cómo irritar a los hombres, planeando cómo conquistar al mundo. El derecho a abortar forma parte de esas largas luchas que han movido las ruedas de la historia milenio tras milenio.

En México se intenta desacreditar el tema de la legalización del aborto argumentando que pertenece al coto feminista, al mundo de las mujeres gritonas y guerrilleras. Pero no se necesita ser feminista para creer en los derechos de la mujer: derechos universales, humanos, esenciales. la Corte

Suprema de los Estados Unidos ha dicho que el derecho de una mujer a optar por un aborto es algo central a su vida, a su dignidad (...) y cuando un gobierno controla esa decisión, le está negando la posibilidad de ser tratada como un ser adulto entero, responsable de sus propias decisiones. Los gobiernos que penalizan el aborto siguen percibiendo a las mujeres como madres, amantes, esposas, concubinas, secretarias, subalternas. Quieren mantenerlas en su lugar, en el infantilismo invariable, en el sótano del segundo sexo.

CRÍTICA AL HOSPITAL GENERAL DE MEXICALI

Según *Novedades*, el 14 de marzo, Socorro Díaz tildó como desacato la actuación de las autoridades de Baja California. Declaró que se violentaron los derechos humanos de Paulina al ser víctima de un ultraje sexual y después mediante el desacato de las autoridades de Baja California, que se negaron a practicarle el aborto. Se olvidan de una regla fundamental: que la moral es personal y a cada uno obliga, y que la ley es general y a todos obliga. Eso no lo digo yo, lo dice santo Tomás de Aquino.

Así como Católicas por el Derecho a Decidir, asociación a la que me gustaría pertenecer, otros reconocen a la mujer su igualdad ante la ley. Don José María Hernández, digno obispo de la diócesis de Nezahualcóyotl, sostiene en *El sol de México* del 2 de marzo de 2000:

Hoy, cuando la mujer es concebida más que nunca como objeto de placer y no como sujeto de amor; cuando la sociedad de consumo pretende encontrarla en un exhibidor como una mercancía de moda, cuando parece alcanzar un estatus laboral que nunca acaba de llegar, cuando se pregona su igualdad frente al hombre pero se sobrestiman otras definiciones sexuales, es necesario dar testimonio del auténtico valor de ser mujer.

Los migrantes abandonan a sus hijos en la Casa Pepito

Denise Dresser se pregunta por los miles de niños abandonados en México y la vida potencial de los miles de bebés botados en la basura. En la frontera todo se agudiza y el tema de la violación se vuelve abismal. Provida debería pensar en una noticia de *Novedades* del viernes 27 de abril de 2000. En Agua Prieta, Sonora, una casa hogar, Casa Pepito, se ha convertido en un orfanato para niños mexicanos abandonados por sus padres en su éxodo ilegal hacia el norte, aunque su directora, Rosa Isela Acosta, prefiere considerarlo un "hogar temporal" y se pregunta: ¿Por qué las madres no vienen a buscarlos?

La mayoría de los niños que han pasado por sus dormitorios en los últimos dos años fueron dejados por sus padres antes de cruzar la frontera con Estados Unidos o se perdieron en el intento de cruce. Otros niños trataron de atravesar solos y fracasaron.

Rosa Isela Acosta comprende las necesidades económicas de las familias que se van al norte, pero no entiende cómo un padre o una madre abandonan a sus hijos en aras de lograr una vida mejor para ellos: "Creo que es mejor comer juntos tortillas y frijoles".

El cruce fronterizo entre Agua Prieta y Douglas, Arizona, es el de mayor tránsito de indocumentados a Estados Unidos. Docenas de hoteles y casas de huéspedes se han levantado para albergarlos. La delincuencia aumenta y los servicios sociales apenas si se dan abasto. La Casa Pepito, inaugurada en 1998, se encuentra junto a una carretera de grava oculta tras un muro de seis metros de altura, a cinco kilómetros del cruce fronterizo. Un guardia vigila la reja de entrada y cinco empleados, entre ellos un cocinero y una recamarera, se turnan para atender el hogar día y noche. El asilo alberga a 30 niños que oscilan entre las tres semanas de nacidos y los 15 años. 28 niños han sido adoptados. Las paredes están decoradas con fotos de niños de Casa Pepito acompañadas de sus nombres y datos. Entre ellos figuran Mario de 3 y Christian de 5 años, hijos de una *coyota*, que llegaron en enero de 1999. Un vecino los encontró abandonados en una casucha de Agua Prieta. Al cabo de un tiempo, su madre fue localizada en la cárcel, acusada de

FOTO: MARIANA YAMPOLSKY

F.C. de Tecate

tráfico de inmigrantes. Otro niño, Agustín, fue llevado a la Casa Pepito a las dos semanas de nacido; Estefani, al mes. El primero lleva allí siete meses y la segunda, año y medio. Según Rosa Isela Acosta, familiares de ambos niños trataron de venderlos y fracasaron. Con el tiempo, algunos de los niños son adoptados por estadounidenses o mexicanos.

¿Son niños felices y que aman la vida? Habría que preguntárselo a Provida.

No hay escapatoria

—El de Paulina —dice Federico García Estrada—, es un caso de violación obvia e inobjetable de derechos humanos... No hay escapatoria (...), en los derechos humanos hay casos difíciles y casos trágicos. Éste es trágico.

La joven Liliana Plumeda califica como "retroceso histórico" la violación a los derechos humanos de la que fue víctima Paulina. Que un criminal viole es un problema serio que cuestiona la estructura social desde sus bases, pero que las instituciones no reconozcan los derechos del individuo resulta aún más escandaloso. Paulina y su familia confiaron en las autoridades demandando el aborto. Tanto en el Código Federal de Baja California como en el de cada uno de los 32 estados del país, el aborto por violación es legal. Se toparon con engaños, mentiras y chantajes.

—Este relativismo moral atenta y no respeta la autonomía de los seres humanos —dice Liliana Plumeda—. Si deciden practicarse un aborto, las mujeres ricas lo hacen con facilidad y más en ciudades fronterizas, mientras que las pobres deben recurrir a abortos clandestinos que ponen su salud en peligro y sólo benefician a quienes los practican, ya que el aborto clandestino genera una fructífera economía subterránea.

Pueblo Amigo

El aborto es decisión de la mujer: Marta Lamas

Jorge Alberto Cornejo, en *La Jornada* del 25 de abril de 2000, dice que el obispo de Tijuana, Rafael Romo Muñoz, pidió que sea reformado el marco legal vigente en Baja California para prohibir bajo cualquier circunstancia el aborto y que el gobierno del estado establezca el compromiso legal de velar por la seguridad y la educación de los niños que pudieran nacer producto de una violación.

Si es así, al rato ya no cabrán más cabrones en México. El obispo de Tijuana coincide plenamente con el cura involucrado, en que el procurador Juan Manuel Salazar Pimentel buscó a Paulina para convencerla de renunciar al aborto. El párroco les comunicó que era pecado matar a un ser que ya vivía y que si se practicaba el aborto, la Iglesia las excomulgaría.

La feminista Marta Lamas afirma que el aborto es un problema de la mujer y no de gobierno, iglesia o partidos.

—Cambiar la ley, hacerla más flexible y expedita no significa estar promoviendo el aborto.

"¿Quién decide sobre el cuerpo de la mujer? ¿El gobierno? ¿La Iglesia? ¿Los diputados? ¿Los médicos? ¿El sacerdote? La tendencia mundial es que cada mujer, en la intimidad, tome su decisión. Dentro de pocos años, las mujeres podrán abortar en su casa tomándose una pastilla.

"Para allá vamos, a pesar de la resistencia de la Iglesia católica". Confirma Marta Lamas.

Curiosamente, un diputado panista, Rubén Fernández Aceves, coincide con Marta Lamas en el semanario *Mayor*, el 24 de mayo de 2000: "Dos pastillitas con un vaso de agua, en medio de la declaración de la mujer violada, son suficientes para evitar la posibilidad de que exista un embarazo no deseado. Para evitarlo, no para interrumpirlo. Y al evitarse el embarazo no deseado, producto de una violación, se evita el aborto y el debate sobre el tema, que igual salpica al gobernador que a los médicos del Hospital General de Mexicali o a la flamante agencia *changarro* especializada en delitos sexuales."

LA DEFENSA DEL ESTADO LAICO, LA ÚNICA OPCIÓN

En México, la única opción que tenemos es la defensa del Estado laico. México es un país plural en el que coexisten varias religiones, y el número de laicos es cada vez más numeroso. Nuestro Estado garantiza la existencia de todas las creencias religiosas. ¿Puede la jerarquía católica conferirse la representatividad absoluta de la sociedad mexicana? El respeto a la libertad de creencias consagrado en la Constitución se extiende a la sexualidad y la reproducción incluyendo el aborto. La decisión de tener todos los hijos que se desee de manera libre e informada está garantizada por el artículo 4o constitucional.

¿De qué democracia estamos hablando, si las mexicanas según su clase social y el estado en el que viven tienen distinto acceso a la salud pública?

EL NIVEL DE INJUSTICIA SOCIAL ES ENORME

El grado de injusticia social contra las mujeres más pobres de nuestra sociedad es enorme. Son ellas las que tienen menos información y arriesgan sus vidas. Dice Marta

Marta Lamas

Lamas que a una "chava clasemedia" no le hubiera pasado lo que a Paulina, porque la habrían llevado a San
Diego y aborta en media hora.

GIRE, Católicas por el Derecho a Decidir y otras organizaciones feministas han defendido siempre la idea de
aumentar los servicios de salud reproductiva y difundir
la información sobre derechos y salud sexuales y repro-
ductivos. Católicas por el Derecho a Decidir ha tenido
una actuación admirable. En 1987, en el Cuarto Encuentro
Feminista Latinoamericano y del Caribe, en Taxco,
Guerrero, fue fundamental su apoyo cuando acordó continuar la lucha por la despenalización del aborto y desmi-

tificar la culpa, que por haberse practicado alguno, supuestamente debían sentir millones de mujeres cristianas.

LAS REGLAS DE LA VIDA Y JOHN IRVING

Según el escritor norteamericano John Irving, crítico del fanatismo del movimiento Provida, cuya novela *Los príncipes de Maine* se transformó en la película *The Cider House Rules (Las normas de la casa de la sidra)*, que él mismo convirtió en guión de película sobre el aborto y en México se lanzó como *Las reglas de la vida*, ha causado una honda impresión. La película enseña que el aborto, puede practicarse sin mayores consecuencias. John Irving hizo un reconocimiento público de la ayuda que recibió de la Planned Parenthood Federation of America y de la National Abortion and Reproductive Rights Action League, dos de las organizaciones que protegen el aborto en Estados Unidos y en el resto del mundo. "Lo que subyace en el mensaje del derecho a la vida forma parte del puritanismo sexual básico de Estados Unidos", dice John Irving. Sus partidarios creen que lo que ellos perciben como promiscuidad debería recibir un castigo. Las chicas que quedan embarazadas deberían pagar el pato.

Esta manera de pensar es más invasora que muchas otras maneras de invasión de la intimidad. ¿Hay algo que requiera mayor intimidad que la decisión de tener o no tener un hijo? ¿No debe primar el sentido común en semejante decisión? (Si no apruebas el aborto, no te sometas a él: si no quieres tener un hijo, aborta).

Según John Irving, en Estados Unidos, aunque el procedimiento OB GYN (aborto médico) es muy fácil, tanto que hasta podría hacerlo un chimpancé, éste no se enseña en las escuelas de medicina. Hay más de cuatro mil jóvenes estudiantes y residentes de medicina denominados Estudiantes de Medicina en Favor de la Elección. Si sólo la cuarta parte lo practicara, salvaría la situación.

A una señora de Provida que le reclamó a John Irving porque interpretaba mal a Provida, el escritor le contestó como su personaje, el doctor Large, de la novela *Los príncipes de Maine*: "Si espera usted que la gente sea responsable de sus hijos, tiene que concederles el derecho a decidir si quieren tener hijos o no."

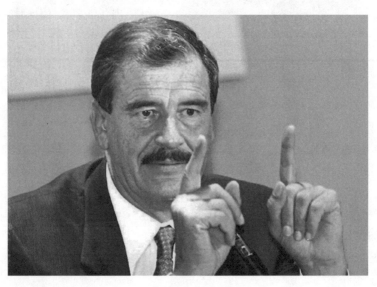

Paulina, doble víctima, tiene ahora dos vidas: la suya y la de su maternidad no deseada.

¿Cómo la auxiliarán ahora los defensores de la vida? Sólo me quedo con una certeza, la de que las verdades absolutas no existen y de que lo primero que hay que hacer cuando se acerca un fundamentalista es echarse a correr.

VICENTE FOX NO CONOCE EL CASO, PERO OPINA

En los días siguientes a la difusión de "El caso Paulina", la prensa, la radio y la televisión del Distrito Federal, se volcaron en opiniones, una de ellas, la de Vicente Fox. En el noticiero *Séptimo día,* que conducen Ciro Gómez Leyva y Denise Maerker en el Canal 40, Fox respondió: "A la mera hora esa chica está enamorada de su hijo. Así es, me consta. Yo soy padre de cuatro hijos adoptivos y conozco miles de casos, porque soy presidente de una casa cuna, donde muchas mujeres que en principio decidían abortar y después de tratar el caso con especialistas, reflexionan y quedan enamoradas de sus hijos. Pero, además, salvamos una vida, una vida que está en el vientre de una madre. Yo creo en la vida desde el momento de su concepción".

A la pregunta: ¿Hicieron bien las autoridades de Mexicali?, la respuesta de Fox, siempre contradictorio, es de una irresponsabilidad absoluta: "No conozco el caso, pero te puedo hablar también de los *table dance,* las minifaldas y los desnudos; serán como el pozole, como los bailes folklóricos y los trajes regionales en el sexenio de Luis Echeverría, en el que todos nos sentamos en equipales a sorber nuestra agua de jamaica. No voy a intervenir en las conciencias de nadie".

115

¿Qué tienen que ver los *table dance* y las minifaldas con la tragedia de Paulina? Eso sólo Fox lo sabe. Como lo dice bien Denise Dresser: el liberalismo panista condena la violencia en las calles, pero hace poco por condenar la violencia en las camas.

Niñas violadas, ¡a dar a luz en Los Pinos!

En la revista *Proceso* del 30 de abril de 2000, Carlos Monsiváis, escribe: "Si mi tía tuviera ruedas, convertiría a Los Pinos en un gran establo donde todas las niñas violadas darían a luz al mismo tiempo".

Carlos Monsiváis vuelve a indignarse en "Por mi madre bohemios" de *La Jornada* del 24 de abril de 2000:

> Para ser el Almacén General del Depósito del Voto Útil, Fox es levemente olvidadizo. Para empezar, Paulina y su madre exigieron la operación en atención a las leyes vigentes en Baja California, muy específicas en lo tocante a violación. No fue nada clandestino. Luego, la protesta en torno al caso no va en contra de los sentimientos maternales de Paulina, sino de la violación descarada de la ley de unos médicos y unos funcionarios panistas. En tercer lugar, algo muy concreto, Fox, el Tesorero del Voto Útil (para los clubes de fans de las contradicciones), ha declarado, no una, sino varias veces (con portada en *Proceso*, por ejemplo) que está de acuerdo con la práctica del aborto autorizada por la ley en caso de violación. Pero claro, nadie discute su derecho a contradecirse, porque nadie cree en la memoria.

FOTO: PROCESO

Julia Preston

El 10 de abril de 2000, en *The New York Times*, Julia Preston publicó: "La violación de una adolescente mexicana revive la discusión sobre el aborto":

La conducción del caso de Paulina estuvo dominada por las preferencias éticas de los funcionarios involucrados —dijo Antonio García Sánchez de derechos humanos, quien exigió al estado que creara un fondo a largo plazo para cuidar de Paulina y del niño.

El gobernador panista, Alejandro González Alcocer, rechazó el dictamen de una corte sobre la base de que la familia nunca había presentado una denuncia formal. Funcionarios estatales han ofrecido ayuda a Paulina sólo si entrega al bebé para su adopción, algo que su familia se muestra renuente a hacer.

Según las leyes de Baja California, Paulina, como víctima de violación, podía haberse sometido legalmente a un aborto en el curso del primer trimestre de su embarazo. En 1998, los grupos opuestos al aborto, con el apoyo del PAN, realizaron una campaña para prohibir todos los abortos y especificar que la vida comienza con la concepción. La legislatura estatal, sin embargo, no aprobó la medida.

Como lo dice Jaime Sánchez Susarrey en *Reforma*, el 5 de abril de 2000:

En el caso del PAN lo sucedido en Baja California es particularmente preocupante porque en los hechos equivale a operar como si el derecho a la vida hubiese sido elevado a rango constitucional. Pero como todo mundo sabe o debería saber, la confusión de los espacios de la moral pública con la privada es un rasgo propio de una mentalidad conservadora y premoderna. Quien quiere imponer una moral particular al resto de la población atenta contra uno de los principios esenciales del Estado laico y contra uno de los derechos humanos elementales, que establece la libertad de profesar la fe (y los principios) que a cada ciudadano convengan. De ahí que los actos reiterados de cerrar tables dances o de oponerse a los programas de educación sexual en las escuelas resulten no sólo absurdos, sino además contraproducentes porque les quitan, a los panistas, la simpatía de los ciudadanos que no ven con buenos ojos la intromisión de la autoridad en ámbitos que no son de su competencia.

Santiago Creel y José Luis Luege Tamargo, honrosas excepciones

A nombre de su moral y su muy particular visión del mundo, el PAN, con su gobernador Alejandro González Alcocer a la cabeza, tiene en su haber, primero, en Mexicali, el caso de una niña de 13 años, Paulina, a quien finalmente se le negó un aborto legal en 1999 y, segundo, en Ciudad Juárez, una gran parte de los asesinatos de mujeres, cometidos de 1993 hasta la fecha, años del PAN.

Vicente Fox propone, como lo vimos

en el Canal 40, que todas las niñas violadas den a luz, ya que él, presidente de una casa cuna, se responsabilizará tanto de madres-niñas como de hijos de la violación, puesto que él es padre de cuatro hijos adoptivos.

Bueno, también dentro del PAN hay honrosas excepciones. Tanto el panista Santiago Creel como el dirigente del PAN capitalino, José Luis Luege Tamargo, dijeron estar en desacuerdo con la presión sicológica y el fanatismo religioso que ejerció Provida contra la menor Paulina del Carmen Ramírez Jacinto.

Santiago Creel afirmó que Provida debe evitar presiones sicológicas: "El decidir abortar, en este caso, es responsabilidad de la niña y de los padres, la ley es suficientemente clara. En casos como ése, las personas pueden hacer uso de los derechos que les consagra la Constitución a todos los mexicanos, y el gobierno debe dar la garantía de que esos derechos se ejerciten... Se trata de un caso verdaderamente lamentable y muy triste pues estamos hablando de un acto de violación en una menor, que va a tener consecuencias para muchos años en la vida de la niña. Tenemos que ser prudentes si así lo establece la legislación. Las personas afectadas están en condición de ejercitar sus derechos. Ellos son quienes deben decidir".

Tamargo declaró: "Nosotros hemos reiterado que el aborto por violación está permitido por la ley, y consideramos que así como está debe quedarse; es decir, una mujer violada está en su derecho de practicarse un aborto".

Por otro lado, Tere Vale se pronunció abiertamente por la legalización y reglamentación del aborto en una conferencia impartida en el Tecnológico de Monterrey,

Tere Vale

campus ciudad de México, porque, según ella, el aborto es una realidad que se vive en la capital y no se puede seguir ocultando ni haciendo en la clandestinidad.

En el debate entre los candidatos a la presidencia del martes 25 de abril de 1999, Gilberto Rincón Gallardo, dijo muy bien: "Rechazamos la intolerancia que ha crecido en México con el beneplácito de partidos como el PRI y el PAN. No podemos aceptar que queden impunes asesinatos de homosexuales como los ocurridos en Chiapas, la violación y asesinato de mujeres en Ciudad Juárez y la perversidad del encarcelamiento de campesinos que defienden su bosque en Guerrero, no podemos aceptar un país en donde el gobierno de Baja California obliga, por encima de la ley, a una niña de 13 años a continuar un embarazo producto de una violación. No podemos aceptar que un solo grupo, utilizando la fuerza del gobierno, imponga su moral y su visión del mundo a todos los ciudadanos".

120

La libertad individual y la responsabilidad social

Luis Villoro se sorprende de que algunos quieran imponerle su criterio a otros, porque él no podría infligirle a nadie su juicio personal: una postura ética implica respetar la autonomía de cada ciudadano para decidir sobre su vida.

Dice María Teresa Priego en "Se llama Paulina y ya había elegido", en la revista *Milenio*

Gilberto Rincón Gallardo

el 31 de marzo de 2000: "¿En qué creencias se sostiene esa vida desde la concepción que, en el caso de Paulina, se traduce en crónica del abuso insoportable? Las connotaciones de la palabra *vida desde la concepción,* en este caso, no pueden separarse de un discurso que persigue y condena el ejercicio de la sexualidad y es incapaz de concebir el erotismo como deseo humano independiente de la reproducción. Defender a ultranza el derecho del óvulo fecundado a la continuación del proceso que lo convertiría en un preembrión —ignorando el deseo y las circunstan-

Luis Villoro

121

cias de la mujer implicada—, después en embrión, más tarde en feto y posteriormente en bebé, no es de ninguna manera defender el absoluto de la vida, sino los valores, creencias e intereses de la actual jerarquía católica".

Aún reconociendo que el aborto es un hecho sangriento y doloroso, como lo dice Luis Villoro, la ausencia de un criterio único que determine el origen de la vida nos obliga a dejarle esa decisión a cada quien: despenalizar el aborto no implica justificarlo, menos fomentarlo. Implica sólo respetar la autonomía de cada ciudadano para decidir sobre su vida, respetar tanto a quien juzga que el aborto es un crimen como a quien juzga lo contrario.

Enrique Maza

La niña estaba en todo su derecho de abortar: Enrique Maza

En "Las lecciones del caso Paulina", en el semanario *Zeta* de Tijuana, Baja California, del 28 de abril al 4 de mayo, Enrique Maza escribe:

> Con respecto al aborto sólo hay un asunto que se debe discutir, si es o no el asesinato de un ser humano: si es asesinato, el aborto es inmoral. Si no es asesinato, el aborto es legítimo.
>
> Para que se dictamine un asesinato, es necesario que haya y que conste un cadáver humano. En consecuencia, el asunto que debe discutirse es si el conjunto de células que se extraen o se arrojan en un aborto, o el contenido del proceso biológico que se interrumpe, es o no es un ser humano, y en qué momento y por qué el feto se convierte en persona; es decir, cuál es el constitutivo esencial de la persona humana, qué hace que un feto se vuelva persona, en qué consiste ser persona, qué hace que un ser humano sea un ser humano.
>
> Este es el punto clave. Si esto no se dilucida, no hay manera de saber si el aborto es asesinato.
>
> Pero no hay manera de dilucidarlo. Nadie tiene la respuesta y todos la tienen, es decir, hay muchas teorías al respecto, pero no hay una certeza. La respuesta depende de cada escuela o teoría filosófica, de cada escuela sicológica, antropológica, sociológica, teológica, bíblica, hermenéutica.
>
> A mi juicio hay dos respuestas fundamentales: la primera concibe al ser humano como cuerpo y alma, dos componentes distintos y separables: uno corporal y efímero, concebido y gestado por varón y mujer. Otro espiritual e inmortal, llamado alma, creado directamente por Dios e infundido en el óvulo en el momento mismo de la concepción.
>
> La segunda concibe al ser humano a partir de sus facultades superiores, inteligencia y amor, que se unen y traducen en su capacidad de relación (relaciones intelectuales, humanas y amorosas). Ésta parece ser, a juicio de hermenéuticas

importantes, la concepción bíblica del hombre. El componente específico que constituye al ser humano es la relación. Según esta interpretación, la Biblia no sólo no conoce el alma, sino que no acepta la constitución del hombre en dos partes separables (...) En este caso, dado que no hay alma, la relación depende del cuerpo. Por tanto, no puede haber capacidad de relación mientras no se formen y se establezcan en el feto las relaciones de las células cerebrales... Estas relaciones se forman entre el quinto y el sexto mes del embarazo... Hasta entonces puede hablarse de un ser humano, de que ya hay en el vientre materno una vida específicamente humana. Antes, sólo hay un proceso celular o biológico.

Si las dos teorías son válidas —no conozco ninguna prueba apodíctica en contrario— hay que sacar algunas consecuencias:

El Estado, al legalizar determinadas causales legítimas de aborto, desecha la primera teoría. Si el aborto es un asesinato, no puede haber causales legítimas de asesinato. Si las hay, el aborto no es asesinato. El Estado mexicano ha tomado partido: el aborto no es asesinato de un ser humano y es permisible en determinadas circunstancias. Uno se pregunta: ¿por qué no es permisible mientras no conste que el feto ya es un ser humano, es decir, hasta el quinto o sexto mes? Ahí hay una incongruencia o un compromiso político, posiblemente para no ofender al Papa, a los obispos y a la mayoría católica.

Es necesaria y moralmente obligatoria la tolerancia de quienes piensan distinto que uno. Tanto de los que aceptan el aborto, para con aquellos que no lo aceptan, como de los que no lo aceptan para con aquellos que sí lo aceptan.

Son necesarias la madurez, la apertura y la humildad, para no querer imponer la propia conciencia a los demás en ninguna de las dos direcciones.

En el caso de Paulina, la niña violada en Mexicali, estaba en todo su derecho de abortar al producto de una violación.

El director del hospital y los médicos tenían la obligación legal de practicar el aborto. Violaron la ley, violaron el derecho legal de una persona y causaron a la niña un daño de magnitud y de por vida.

El gobierno del estado, sin importar sus creencias particulares, no debe asignar a los hospitales públicos a personas que no están dispuestas a cumplir la ley, al margen de sus conciencias individuales. Nadie puede imponer su conciencia a los demás. El gobierno no gobierna solamente para los católicos, y no puede imponer una ley católica a la conciencia de todos sus *súbditos*.

En una nación plural, como la nuestra, en la que coexisten tantas religiones, creencias, culturas, etnias, lenguas, tipos de educación y normas de vida, el único terreno común de armonía social y de subsistencia ordenada es la ley, y eso fue lo que se violó y se rompió en este caso.

En Francia y en Italia, países de tradición católica, muchos hospitales realizan abortos. Con esto, como dice Enrique Maza, la sociedad consigue representar legalmente a todos los individuos y no sólo a algunos.

La frontera

Barda de los muertos

Epílogo

El día que salió de la clínica

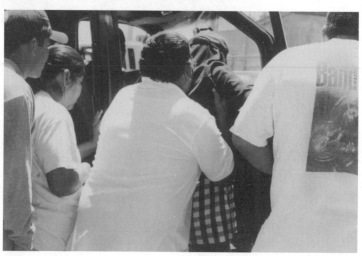

La salida de la clínica Independencia con su papá Tomás

El advenimiento de Isaac

El viernes 13 de abril, en Mexicali, en la Clínica Independencia Paulina dio a luz, por cesárea, a Isaac, a las 21:37 horas.

Provida pagó el parto y los honorarios del ginecobstetra César Hernández Elenes: 8 000 pesos.

Las fotos confirman el estado de ánimo de Paulina y su familia. Provida debería examinarlas con cuidado.

La dirigente de Provida en Mexicali, no es bienvenida en casa de Paulina

La dirigente de Provida en Mexicali, Marcela Vaquera, sintió rechazo de parte de la familia de Paulina. María Elena creyó que Provida quería ayudar de buena fe y recibió los 8 000 pesos, pero Provida publicó un desplegado diciendo que le habían dado 100,000 pesos. "¿Por qué mienten? Si yo ahora acepto su ayuda quién sabe que irán a decir mañana".

En la entrevista en el semanario *Mayor*, de Mexicali, Paulina culpa a Provida y afirma que se dio cuenta que todo lo que hacían era para forzarla a tener un bebé que no era su obligación traer al mundo. "Mienten quienes dicen que desistí de abortar, lo aceptamos sólo cuando los médicos nos asustaron, cuando me dijeron que me iba a morir por una hemorragia: Me eché para atrás porque ellos nos metieron miedo".

Unas cuantas latas de leche

Aunque Provida se comprometió a la manutención de Isaac, hasta la fecha Paulina ha recibido (además del pago del parto) unas cuantas latas de leche y el ofrecimiento de una beca para estudiar Relaciones Internacionales en una universidad católica.

Del gobierno, nada

El 18 de mayo, Paulina y su abogada Socorro Maya se presentaron en el Congreso del estado para exigir el fideicomiso y la diputada Olivia Villalaz Becerra sugirió al pleno que cada uno diera mil pesos para entregárselos a la menor. Los legisladores no aceptaron y propusieron buscar recursos especiales para formar el fideicomiso.

Asimismo, Olivia hizo un llamado a "salir a las calles a hacer sentir la fuerza de las ideas progresistas y libertarias que han prevalecido a lo largo de la historia del país".

—El rechazo al fideicomiso "porque al rato van a querer que el gobierno mantenga a todos los hijos de las violaciones", como dijo Cervantes Govea, es una postura ruin y mezquina que refleja una visión caciquil del gobierno panista —señaló Olivia a *La Voz de la Frontera*, el 1 de mayo de 2000—. Demuestra que los panistas están gobernando la entidad como si fuéramos un estado conservador y retrógrado. No es posible que se agravie así a la Constitución.

Socorro Maya declaró que evitará que se congele el caso y demandará al procurador de Tijuana, Juan Manuel Salazar Pimentel, quien llevó a Paulina en su auto con un sacerdote para persuadirla de que no abortara. En las autoridades recae la culpabilidad de este atropello a las garantías de Paulina.

Germán Dehesa, en su columna "La Gaceta del Ángel" de *Reforma*, el 12 de Abril de 2000, expresa su desconcierto ante la imagen del gobernador González Alcocer en el televisor: "con Cara de perfecta inocencia y enjuagándose la boca con algo que llamó ética personal, que le sirvió para otorgarse la absolución inmediata y para hacerla extensiva a todos aquellos que fueron parte de un atropello que no sólo incluye a una mujer, sino a eso que llamamos Estado de derecho. A mi juicio, Paulina ha sido

Germán Dehesa

víctima de múltiples violaciones. Enumero algunas: la física, la moral, la sicológica, la emocional, la legal. La primera corrió a cargo de un miserable; de las demás son responsables unos cómodos fanáticos que lucran con los prejuicios y que todavía no se enteran en qué año y bajo qué Constitución están viviendo; unos cuantos funcionarios médicos y funcionarios políticos que dan por no recibido el mensaje legal y fundamentado que reciben y una sociedad que prefiere no meterse en problemas (hasta que los problemas la alcancen a ella). Me imagino (espero) que el conflicto no termine aquí. Por lo pronto, en Nuevo León los panistas se aprestan a echarle más lumbre al fuego con su legislación sobre el derecho a la vida. Me queda una pregunta: ¿qué opinarán sobre esto las cada vez más lúcidas mujeres (y un buen número de hombres) de este país?"

Silvia Reséndiz Flores,
sus mantas y sus pancartas

La presidenta del grupo feminista Alaíde Foppa, Silvia Reséndiz Flores, informó que interpuso una denuncia por los delitos de abuso de autoridad, infidelidad de custodia de documentos, coalición de servidores públicos y tortura, en representación de la familia.

135

Paulina

Silvia y otros miembros del Alaíde Foppa y Diversa pusieron al gobernador en aprietos al llevar mantas y pancartas al desfile del 1 de mayo exigiendo la renuncia del procurador: "El gobierno se ensañó con Paulina por ser pobre y mujer". "La farsa sigue, más pobres los pobres y más ricos los ricos". Otra de las mantas clamaba: "Apoyo a la recomendación 2/2000 de la Procuraduría de Derechos Humanos, la de la ayuda económica para Paulina y su hijo". (...) Cientos de personas demandaron justicia para Paulina; llovieron las protestas y los funcionarios tuvieron que aguantar los reclamos.

—Las corrientes ultraconservadoras del PAN se portan en forma enfermiza, quisieran tener a la mujer relegada en un torreón medieval—, volvió a decir Olivia Villalaz.

TODAVÍA NO ES BUENO SER MUJER EN ESTE MUNDO

En México, entre 850 mil y un millón de mexicanas abortan voluntariamente cada año de manera ilegal. Ninguna va a la cárcel, como lo estipula la ley. ¿De qué sirve una ley que no se cumple y que, al mismo tiempo, impide una reglamentación humanitaria?

Hay abortos porque hay embarazos no planeados, resultado de varias causas:

—Errores humanos (olvidos, irresponsabilidades)

—Fallas del método anticonceptivo

—Violencia (violación dentro y fuera del matrimonio)

—Ignorancia

Cuando una mujer se da cuenta que está embarazada sin haberlo planeado, tiene tres caminos:

1. Reconciliarse con la idea de tener un hijo y llevar a término su embarazo.

2. No desear tener un hijo, pero ser incapaz de abortar (por razones religiosas, de salud o de tiempo del

embarazo) y llevar a término ese embarazo para darlo en adopción.

3. Interrumpir el embarazo lo más pronto posible.

Si las mujeres contaran con el apoyo material del Estado y la sociedad para enfrentar un embarazo no deseado, probablemente muchas optarían por continuar el embarazo, pero esa decisión implica un ajuste personal y familiar brutal, con graves consecuencias económicas y sicológicas, que no todas las mujeres ni todas las familias pueden asumir. ¿Qué hacer ante la ausencia de un Estado y de una sociedad que garanticen la atención indispensable y amorosa de los hijos no deseados?

El derecho inalienable de la mujer sobre su cuerpo

¿Cómo legislar en un asunto crucial como el aborto, donde existen posturas irreconciliables? ¿Por qué los países más adelantados en derechos humanos, la mayoría de las democracias occidentales, tienen legalizado el aborto? ¿Por qué Italia, España y Francia, católicos como

el nuestro, han modernizado las leyes del aborto, y lo permiten por voluntad de la mujer, por razones sicológicas y económicas? En esos países es la mujer la que toma la decisión de un aborto.

Una moral distinta para ricos y pobres: Arnoldo Kraus

"La moral es un gran invento humano, plagado de

espinas", dice Arnoldo Kraus, y tiene razón porque todos queremos elevar nuestras creencias a principios universales y de allí vienen la intolerancia, las guerras, el fracaso de las relaciones humanas:

1. Mujer.
2. Menor de edad.
3. Oaxaqueña.
4. La pobreza como destino manifiesto (Arnoldo Kraus *dixit*).
5. Perteneciente al grupo de los sin voz.
6. Paulina, antes anónima ahora noticia.
7. Niña y ahora, después de la violación, señora.
8. Embarazada, condenada, manipulada.
9. Sujeta a las presiones de Provida.
10. Alaíde Foppa, GIRE y DIVERSA, Católicas por el Derecho a Decidir, Red de Mujeres de Baja California (grupos feministas de Tijuana, Ensenada, Mexicali y Tecate) la otra cara de la moneda.

Según el doctor Arnoldo Kraus: "Desde la violación hasta la cesárea, el periplo de Paulina es ejemplo de que la moral se aplica en forma distinta para ricos y pobres. Es imposible encontrar un caso en el cual la indicación para provocar un aborto humano sea más clara que en el de esta joven. Salvo que se hubierse demostrado la transmisión del Sida al producto o a la madre durante la transgresión, es difícil pensar en un escenario más dramático. Incluso, en circunstancias como la descrita, el Código Penal avala el legrado en el artículo 126, fracción II que establece que el aborto no es punible cuando el embarazo sea resultado de violación".

En La *Crónica* de Mexicali, el 9 de abril de 2000, el pedagogo Alfonso Lizárraga Bernal exige:

1. Pago del daño moral.

2. Castigo a los funcionarios del hospital aliados cómplices del grupo Provida.

3. Crear un fideicomiso para garantizar la sobrevivencia del niño por nacer y ofrecerle una vida digna. (Salud, educación y vivienda).

4. Pago de los gastos realizados por la familia durante el embarazo.

5. Cursos de ética médica, derechos humanos y valores, dirigidos al personal del hospital.

El PAN en el ejercicio del poder actúa con una intolerancia similar a la del Opus Dei, pasa por encima de la ley, transgrede los derechos ciudadanos, impone su ideología y remata su actuar con una negativa advirtiéndose su hipocresía valoral. Al menos tendría que reparar el daño de por vida provocado a Paulina concediendo los cinco puntos.

¿PELIGRA EL CARÁCTER LAICO DEL ESTADO?

María Consuelo Mejía, dirigente de Católicas por el Derecho a Decidir, declaró a *La Jornada* el 20 de marzo de 2000 que lo sucedido en Mexicali debe llamar a la reflexión, porque es un indicio de que en nuestro país es necesario reafirmar el carácter laico del Estado, para evitar que grupos conservadores en el poder modifiquen las políticas públicas atendiendo a sus intereses personales.

IMPEDIR EL ABORTO AÚN EN LOS CASOS DE VIOLACIÓN

El cardenal Norberto Rivera Carrera, en una homilía en la Catedral el 4 de mayo, dijo que ningún producto de una violación merece la muerte: "Un niño en el seno de la madre no se puede defender, ni siquiera su grito se oye". Hizo un alegato en favor de la familia: "La Iglesia está convencida de que en la familia se fragua el futuro de la humanidad y es donde se pueden concretar los verdaderos valores evangélicos".

¿Sabrá el cardenal que el aborto inducido representa la cuarta causa de muerte materna en nuestro país? Por fin qué ¿la vida o la muerte?

Católicas por el Derecho a Decidir opinó que los ataques al sexo seguro, esgrimidos por Rivera Carrera, constituyen una actitud inhumana y de falta de respeto a las personas que responsablemente ejercen su sexualidad, pero que además son creyentes de la fe católica. María Consuelo Mejía, recordó que el sexo seguro (condón) protege de enfermedades de transmisión sexual, de embarazos no deseados e incluso de abortos.

LA IGLESIA SE OPONE A LA "CULTURA DE LA MUERTE"

El presidente de la Conferencia del Episcopado Mexicano Luis Morales Reyes, según el corresponsal de *La Jornada* en Monterrey, David Carrizales, informó que el clero católico entregará al Congreso de la Unión miles de firmas en los templos de todo el país, para que eleve a rango constitucional el derecho a la vida desde la concepción hasta la fase terminal:

"Considero, como obispo, que el respeto a la vida debe darse irrestrictamente. La Iglesia vota por la vida, la Iglesia veta la cultura de la muerte, defiende la vida desde su concepción hasta la fase terminal, y no es porque así lo haya decidido sino porque es un derecho natural".

En el caso del hijo de Paulina, a quien las autoridades de Baja California le impideron abortar, dijo que "si el niño es fruto de una violación, ¿por qué asesinarlo? ¿por qué matarlo? ¿Por qué no pedir mejor la pena de muerte para el violador, en lugar de pedirla para el producto de la violación?"

Morales Reyes agregó: "Estamos aquí en la línea de Juan Pablo II: no por violación ni fruto de una violación realmente del esposo hacia la esposa?. Ahí sí, aunque la Iglesia sea muy criticada, pero la vida es la vida inmediatamente después que es fecundado el óvulo femenino". Morales sostiene que desde ese momento hay un ser humano independiente de la madre.

FOTO: MARIANA YAMPOLSKY

Ofrenda en el Borde

José Isidro Guerrero Macías, Obispo de la Diócesis de Mexicali

"Si nadie quiere al niño que me lo entreguen a mí..."

El obispo de la diócesis de Tijuana, Rafael Romo Muñoz, afirmó que si nadie quería al niño se lo entregaran a él.

Habla Socorro Maya de los cambios de Paulina

—Una de las gratificaciones más importantes de la abogacía es ver cómo la gente reacciona. He sido testigo de los cambios de Paulina y de su familia, y me enorgullecen. Ahora Paulina, antes callada y sumisa, se ha afirmado y quiere combatir. Cuando nació el bebé, no hablaba más que para decir: Tengo frío. Si le preguntábamos algo movía la cabeza negativamente, o respondía con monosílabos, como bloqueada, paralizada. En realidad, así se mantuvo durante el embarazo: embotada. No era para menos. No amamantó al bebé, en realidad ni ella ni María Elena lo quisieron. ¿Cómo vas a ir a la escuela con la leche escurriendo?, le dijo su madre. Tampoco ha vuelto a la escuela.

"Por lo pronto ambas están preocupadas porque malformación ni por otro motivo puede quitársele la vida a un ser inocente, el más débil y el más indefenso".

Por lo pronto ambas están preocupadas porque no le queda su uniforme de secundaria. El *zipper* se le atora a la mitad de la espalda. La mamá le da tés de hierbas que se acostumbran en Oaxaca para adelgazar.

No nacemos madres, nos hacemos madres

Al saberse embarazada, Paulina, metida en sí misma, veía su sufrimiento materializarse en ese cuerpo que se inflaba. Para todas las mujeres, la maternidad es una deformación y para muchas una tortura.

Isabel Vericat alega: "Inevitablemente pienso en *El grito* de Edvard Münch, que para todos simboliza la angustia. ¿Qué más angustia que la de un embarazo no deseado e impuesto? Sostengo: las mujeres no nacemos madres: nos hacemos madres. Si el Estado no hace nada por apoyarnos, a pesar de una tragedia como la de Paulina, las mujeres tenemos la capacidad de superarnos, evolucionar y proyectarnos a algo más elevado".

Tener un hijo del enemigo

El instinto materno no es un absoluto. Miles de mujeres

rechazan a sus hijos, los golpean, los queman, los odian. Un hijo a la fuerza crea conflictos. Quizá los de Paulina surjan dentro de algunos años, pero aunque Paulina quiera a su hijo no olvidará que fue producto de una violación.

DE NUEVO, LA INDIGNACIÓN

Con la maternidad, la Iglesia fomenta el mito de que somos el instrumento y el vehículo para que una vida venga al mundo, como la virgen María fue un instrumento de Dios para traer a Jesús a la tierra. Esa idea de que el cuerpo de la mujer es un recipiente, una ánfora por donde pasa la vida, hizo que la Iglesia le dijera a Paulina: "Tú no cuentas".

En Proceso No. 1224 del 16 de abril de 2000, Álvaro Delgado dice: "La vida de Paulina cambió radicalmente. El daño es irreparable. Hoy su caso es un pleito político, una lucha partidista".

VOY A PELEAR, DICE PAULINA

—Después de que nació Isaac —continúa Socorro Maya— Paulina volvió a pelear con sus hermanos. Ahora habla mucho. En el periódico *El Mayor* sentencia: No quiero que esto les suceda a otras, por eso voy a pelear.

Paulina empieza a sacar todo el coraje que tiene. Se ve a sí misma como era antes del embarazo, como si dijera:

"Ahora que ya se me salió ese chamaco sí soy yo".

Hoy ve a su hijo con ternura, pero al principio veía con desprecio a esa cosa que le había salido de adentro.

UNA NUEVA DIGNIDAD

Socorro Maya se emociona: "El drama de Paulina les ha

dado a los Ramírez Jacinto una nueva dignidad. Cuando Silvia y yo tomamos el caso creían que su única salida era resignarse. Su humillación era profunda. Ahora luchan con fortaleza. A la carta de un médico que la felicitaba, Paulina contestó: Me da mucho gusto saber que gente que ni me conoce se preocupa por mí. La firmó con su nombre y el de Isaac, su hijo".

LA FIRMEZA DE LA FAMILIA EN EXIGIR SU DERECHO LOS SALVA

—La firmeza de la familia en pedir el aborto al que tenían derecho fue lo que ayudó. Su aplomo fue definitivo. Exigir justicia, la dignificó. Por todo lo que le ha pasado, Paulina quiere estudiar derecho penal—, refiere Socorro.

"A lo mejor es pretencioso de mi parte, pero siento que la lucha de Silvia Reséndiz y la mía han influido en ella. Silvia también ha sido una inspiración para mí: me enseñó a ser feminista".

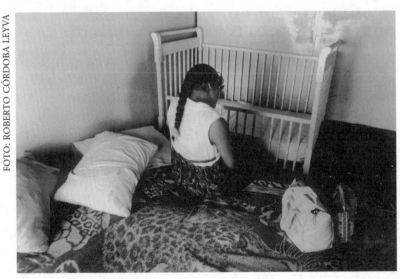

Paulina en espera

147

Nadie es insensible a la tragedia de Paulina

—De cada diez cartas que llegan sólo una o dos son en contra de Paulina. La gente no es insensible. Yo no soy quien para juzgar. En lugar de condenarla, los corresponsales opinan que a Paulina debieron dejarla elegir libremente y respetar su individualidad.

"Es maravilloso saber que no estás sola, el problema de mujeres que sufren violencia doméstica es que se lo callan; primero, porque les da vergüenza, segundo por la familia y tercero porque el Estado no las defiende. Sin embargo, las mujeres tenemos la capacidad de superarnos después de una tragedia, de evolucionar y crecer.

"En Mexicali, hay una violencia muy elegante; esposos que atormentan a su mujer sin siquiera tocarla. Todo se lo guardan hasta que un día estallan, quieren divorciarse y entonces buscan el apoyo de grupos como el Alaíde Foppa".

Silvia Reséndiz Flores, excomulgada

A Silvia Reséndiz Flores su excomunión la preocupa no sólo por el mensaje amenazante de la Iglesia católica sino porque a cualquiera le atemorizaría una condena semejante. María del Consuelo Mejía dice: "La excomunión no es una decisión de un vicario de Mexicali sino un decreto al que se llega con un estudio serio por razones serias, porque el código del derecho canónigo es serio", y coincide con Silvia Reséndiz al decir que sólo sirve "para que las mujeres sigamos siendo sumisas".

—El obispo de Mexicali, Isidro Guerrero Macías —continúa Silvia Reséndiz—, me pidió que lo fuera a ver (no sé para qué), y me voy a quedar con la duda porque no tengo ningún interés en ir. El vicario de la diócesis, Raúl

Enriquez Ramírez, fue quien afirmó que no podía yo ser la madrina de Isaac, el hijo de Paulina.

A pesar de su valentía, para Silvia (de formación católica como todas nosotras), no debe ser agradable saberse acusada desde el púlpito a la hora de la misa en varias iglesias, y sus amigas, ofendidas y agredidas, se han dolido al escuchar a los sacerdotes. También su familia se siente lesionada.

La Iglesia le echó encima a Silvia toda su artillería y la sentó en el banquillo de los acusados. Desde que inició su lucha por Paulina, la hostilidad de la Iglesia contra ella no ha cejado. Silvia se mantiene firme: "El ámbito de la salud pública —le dijo a Jesusa Gamboa, subdirectora de *Mayor*— es científico y cuando nos apartamos de la ciencia estamos perdidos porque el aborto es un problema de salud pública que no va a resolverse en el ámbito de la fe. Hago responsables de la muerte de todas las mujeres por abortos mal practicados a esas personas que anteponen su fe religiosa a la ciencia".

María del Consuelo Mejía con Doña Jesusa

EL CASO DE PAULINA: UN RETO PARA LOS GRUPOS FEMINISTAS DE MEXICALI

Al igual que Silvia Reséndiz, Maricarmen Rioseco trabaja desde 1976 por los derechos humanos de la mujer, inspirada en la revista *Fem*. En 1991, ya casada y con hijos, ingresó al grupo Alaíde Foppa: "Nos propusimos, en el caso de Paulina, que ninguna mujer volviera a pasar por lo mismo.

José Isidro Guerrero Macías

Queremos que prevalezca el Estado laico.

"Vemos con grave preocupación que en Baja California estamos retrocediendo históricamente a esa primera mitad del siglo XIX, con una Iglesia beligerante, con una gran influencia en el poder político, que les abre espacios en lo civil a una violación de la ley y un atropello a la laicidad. Por ejemplo, un procurador de justicia que lleva ante un sacerdote a una niña y a su madre para que desistan de su derecho al aborto legal, o unos médicos que se niegan a cumplir la ley, o un obispo católico que da lecciones de valores y moral religiosa al personal de la Procuraduría General de Justicia del Estado, o un poder religioso que desde el oscurantismo de la Santa Inquisición excomulga a quienes se atreven a enfrentar al Estado en defensa del derecho vigente. En un Estado laico se tiene una actitud positiva de respeto y tolencia a todos los credos y maneras de pensar, claramente señalados en el artículo 24 constitucional, que garantiza la libertad de creencias y fomenta la convivencia social.

"Intentamos mover la conciencia de mujeres y hombres contra el riesgo de conservadurismo que avanza en Mexicali.

"Con el apoyo de la Red de Mujeres de la Península de Baja California y de *Milenio Feminista*, logramos abrir la discusión acerca del avance de la ultraderecha en Mexicali, que se debe a la relación entre la jerarquía católica, el gobierno estatal y municipal y la influencia de un periódico muy conservador, filial de *El Imparcial* de Sonora, llamado *La Crónica*, de Mexicali.

"Dar la batalla contra la ultraderecha no es fácil y estos meses han sido de mucha tensión. Personalmente me encargo de las relaciones públicas. Por ejemplo, invité a María Aurora Mota de *Milenio Feminista*, ya que acordamos organizar visitas a Mexicali de representantes de asociaciones como GEM, SIPAM, GIRE, y Católicas por el Derecho a Decidir, y la llevé a la televisora local.

"Durante el noticiero, el obispo felicitó a Paulina por su hijo y anunció que El Vaticano había nombrado a la catedral de Mexicali *La catedral de la vida*. Al saber que María Aurora era feminista y pertenecía a Católicas, no le dio la mano. *La Crónica* le dio primera plana a la misa que celebró el obispo en la calle frente a catedral y a María Aurora la sacó en interiores. En Mexicali se rompe diariamente el Estado laico ya que el obispo da clases de ética a los agentes judiciales, bendice patrullas y edificios públicos, inaugura escuelas y preside la toma de protesta de la

Asociación de Padres de Familia, acompañando al presidente municipal y al secretario de Educación Pública del estado".

La eliminación de Federico García Estrada

—Por ser feministas, nos tienen satanizadas. Fui rechazada para continuar siendo Consejera Ciudadana del Instituto Estatal Electoral, lo mismo que Federico García Estrada fue descartado en la terna para procurador de Derechos Humanos. El caso de Paulina fue la gota que derramó el vaso porque trascendió a nivel nacional e internacional. Fuimos a protestar con pancartas que decían: "El pueblo observa, el pueblo demandará si ensucian el proceso de Federico para procurador". "Diputados, escuchen la voz del pueblo, Federico procurador". "Apoyo a Federico García Estrada para procurador de los Derechos Humanos".

Un entierro de almas

Carlos Monsiváis escribe en *La Jornada*, el 2 de mayo de 2000:

> *La Jornada* del 29 de abril de 2000 nos informa de un entierro de almas. El vicario de la diócesis de Mexicali, Raúl Enríquez Ramírez, exigió la excomunión de los activistas que apoyaron a la menor Paulina, de 14 años de edad, en su deseo de abortar el producto de una violación. El vicario consideró que su actitud atentó contra los principios fundamentales de la Iglesia católica. Este es el caso, dijo, de la activista Silvia Reséndíz Flores, representante de la organización Alaíde Foppa, que apoyó con asesoramiento legal a la menor y su familia. Por su parte, el gobernador panista Alejandro González Alcocer declaró: Poco ayudan a Paulina y su hijo las campañas orquestadas alrededor de las actividades de proselitismo político."

¿Qué sucede si las activistas no son católicas? ¿Por qué se canjea entonces la excomunión? Si, como sucedió, las activistas actuaron en apego a la ley, ¿se puede excomulgar a la Constitución de Baja California? Y en cuanto a González Alcocer, ¿no será ya tiempo de que enfrente las acciones ilegales a su cargo y se diese cuenta de que no es catequista, sino gobernador?

LA CERTEZA DE QUE EN MEXICALI LA LEY NOS HA DADO LA PAZ

—Para mí ha sido muy gratificante el reconocimiento de que la ley nos ha dado la paz por que en Mexicali cohabitamos muy bien las diferentes religiones y corrientes, y nos respetamos.

"Tenemos un marco para vivir en paz y esto lo valoro mucho.

"Paulina tuvo un careo con el violador, lo enfrentó y la sicológa la valoró y la felicitó por valiente.

"Al grupo Alaíde Foppa se nos han acercado mujeres y organizaciones interesadas en dar su apoyo".

LAS MENTIRAS DE PROVIDA

En *La Jornada* del 15 de abril de 2000, Mireya Cuéllar escribe la crónica de un plantón de Provida frente a la Secretaría de Gobernación en protesta por la entrega del premio de población de las Naciones Unidas a la Fundación Mexicana para la Planificación Familiar (MEXFAM):

"¡Son unos sádicos, son unos sádicos! ¡Hicieron la *malobra*!, y después se fueron y hasta que los denunciaron fueron a ofrecer su ayuda," un hombre de mediana edad encaró a Jorge Serrano Limón, dirigente de Provida. La gente que pasaba por

Gobernación les gritaba: "¡Están locos! ¡Es el colmo! Se salvó una vida pero perdieron otra... y así se han perdido muchas gracias a sus mentiras", le reclamaba airadamente a Serrano Limón otro transeúnte. Una mujer que había participado en el acto que se dio dentro de Gobernación le gritó: "Al limón hay que exprimirlo, por eso está tan agrio".

Los mirones que se acercaban a Serrano Limón también lo interrogaban sobre sus deseos de prohibirlo todo. "No, se excusaba, nosotros estamos por la sexualidad plena, maravillosa, una ordenación sexual hacia el matrimonio, el uso responsable del sexo".

—¿Por qué quieren que todos vivan como ustedes? ¿Por qué no dejan a la gente que viva según su conciencia? ¿Qué piensa del fascismo?

—No voy a responder cuestiones personales.

No más paulinas

¿Por qué impactó tanto el caso Paulina a la sociedad mexicana? Primero, porque muestra la vulnerabilidad de una jovencita a la que un tipo viola mientras duerme en su cama. Segundo porque pone en evidencia la fragilidad de nuestro sistema jurídico, la ley no se cumplió y Paulina acabó pariendo al hijo. Su vida podría haber sido otra; podría haber elegido el padre del niño, tenerlo después de haber estudiado o trabajado; la violación por un heroinómano seguido por un embarazo no deseado la volvió madre niña en contra de su voluntad y la de su familia.

FOTO: MARIANA YAM

Escribí *Las mil y una... (La herida de Paulina)*, no sólo porque me lo pidieron Marta Lamas e Isabel Vericat, sino porque es indignante que en un estado donde el aborto por violación es legal, éste le haya sido negado a una niña de 13 años. Médicos y asociaciones religiosas se salieron con la suya en aras de una abstracción.

¿Cómo se atreven grupos religiosos a intervenir en la vida de los demás? ¿Cómo pueden juzgar qué es lo mejor para Paulina? ¿No debería la niña estar en la escuela, platicar con sus amigos, comerse un helado, pensar en el futuro? La Iglesia católica que está detrás de Provida considera que tiene la verdad revelada. "Esta es la palabra de Dios". A propósito de una campaña en Francia defendiendo la vida ante todo, la sicoanalista francesa católica Françoise Dolto declaró que para que tuviera validez, "el Estado tiene que responsabilizarse de la manutención de los hijos no deseados".

Al igual que muchas feministas, no estoy a favor del aborto. Al igual que muchas Católicas por el Derecho a Decidir, también fui una niña de convento de monjas que durante siete años comulgó diariamente. La Iglesia tiene dogmas de fe y los acepté sin chistar. Fui hija de María y creí a pie juntillas que por haber ganado la medalla, la Virgen vendría por mí a la hora final para llevarme al cielo colgada de su efigie. Al regreso del convento del Sagrado Corazón en Estados Unidos enseñé catecismo (ligada siempre a la parroquia francesa), fui jefa *scout*, hice campamentos en Soria, cerca de Atlixco, en Tlamacas y en Cuernavaca. La noche en torno al fuego fue el preludio de otras exaltaciones, canté a la alegría en una ronda de inocentes (e incautos), busqué el tesoro y leí a los grandes católicos: Bernanos, Maritain,

Psichari, Mauriac, Claudel, Gabriel Marcel, Péguy y naturalmente St. Exupéry, que habría de desaparecer en su avión en 1944. Aunque el catolicismo es una parte entrañable de mi cultura, a los 19 años descubrí que también dentro de la Iglesia puede haber disidencia y el contacto con los sacerdotes obreros el abate Pierre, los misioneros, el órgano del doctor Schweitzer en África, me hicieron ver que la infabilidad no era tal y que hablar ex cátedra no sólo en un acto de soberbia sino, en muchos casos, de ignorancia.

En los cincuenta, ni mi hermana ni yo tuvimos información acerca de esa cosa llamada cuerpo. Alguna vez le pregunté a mamá por mi nacimiento y me dijo que se había ido de cacería. Por lo tanto nunca he podido hacerme una carta astral: no tengo hora, sólo día. Desde Acapulco, en su noche de bodas, Kitzia, mi hermana, llamó para preguntar si ya estaba embarazada. El doctor Kinsey habría celebrado nuestra erudición sexual.

Si me hice periodista es porque sólo he tenido preguntas, nunca certezas. De lo que sí estoy segura es de mis intenciones. Siempre me han atemorizado los juicios devastadores, los que descalifican, los que condenan, los irascibles, los defensores de verdades absolutas o los que se atreven a ir en contra de la integridad de los demás. Muy pronto descubrí a las minorías y me identifiqué con ellas. Son mi legión. Los que creí más cerca, los que para mí eran el reflejo del amor de Dios, me sentenciaron y de haberlo podido habrían vulnerado mi tímido proyecto de vida.

A través de los años me di cuenta de que aunque el Papa prohibe los anticonceptivos, las católicas los usan. Acuden al confesionario y vuelven a usarlos. Las más conscientes se atormentan y supongo que viven con el alma dividida. Seguramente en la intimidad de muchas mujeres, allá en lo oscuro, en lo más hondo, allí donde los pensamientos duelen mucho, hay un aborto. Dentro de mí lo hay.

La interrupción del embarazo es parte de la libre decisión de las mujeres. Mi evolución ha sido lentísima y podría decir como los campesinos de Rulfo que soy de chispa retardada. Viví el pecado, la zozobra, la confusión (ésa todavía me acompaña). La culpabilidad es la mejor arma de tortura, dijo Rosario Castellanos. Recuerdo que en los cincuenta, al cruzar la avenida Baja California con Martha Bórquez, quien me instaba a ir a un Congreso de la Paz en Viena, le pregunté:

—Pero, ¿tú eres comunista?

Ante la confirmación, me eché a temblar. ¿Qué estaba yo haciendo? Ahora sí, caminaba al borde el abismo. ¡Ojalá y nos machucaran a las dos en ese mismo instante! Naturalmente fui al Congreso de la Paz en Viena y comprobé que sus promotoras eran más rojas que los geranios de la calle de La Morena y algo peor, se proclamaban ateas.

Al lado de Guillermo Haro descubrí que la ciencia no tiene las certezas de la Iglesia, es más humilde y parte de verdades mucho más fragmentarias. Como nunca tuve una verdad total que me diera la explicación del universo, me resultó más difícil entender la posición de poder de la Iglesia. ¿Cómo se puede vivir con principios éticos sin tener princios religiosos? La ética laica de Guillermo Haro me dio una respuesta.

Reconocí a lo largo del tiempo que son muchos caminos y no hay una sola verdad, mucho menos dogmas de fe. Claro que resultó arduo comprobarlo. La alianza con los hijos, la fe en los libros, la naturaleza, fueron mis refugios. Hoy veo a Dios en la pantalla de la computadora, en el café con leche matutino, en la capacidad de entrega de Mane, en los ojos de mis nietos, en los de mi madre, en las críticas de mis amigas y en mis amigas las críticas, y en Gazpacho, mi gato pedorro.

Paulina entró a mis días sin pedirlo ella, ni quererlo yo. Me asombró su capacidad de denuncia y su fuerza de niña de 14 años. Me hizo pensar en lo inútil de esta falla endémica que padecemos las mujeres al no protestar. Es nuestra ira la que nos salva y sin embargo nos resulta casi imposible sacarla y darle coherencia.

La joven poetisa de veinticinco años, Marlene Gómez, "con su cuerpo de fusil y caña", espera que este libro despierte la conciencia de hombres y mujeres, y se atrevan como Paulina a cambiar una sociedad patriarcal que las menosprecia y decide por ellas. Marlene dice: "Son los tiempos de tirano". Sin embargo, las tiranías persisten mientras la indignación se calla. He aquí la indignación de Paulina hecha papel. He aquí el apoyo de mujeres y hombres y agrupaciones sociales contra el ultraje a la hermanita menor.

Junio 2000